Echo of Another Time

Without fear now, she waited.

'I am to go back to my regiment soon, Celie.'

'Yes.'

There was a long moment in which the whole woodland seemed to hold its breath in a fluttering silence, then, 'How lovely you are.' His voice was no more than a soft whisper.

She did not answer, merely regarded him gravely in the deep shadows beneath the trees and when he reached for her other hand she stood quietly. Taking both of hers in his he raised them to his lips, rubbing his mouth across the backs of them. His lips were warm and she shivered in delight, a strange delight, but sweet as this afternoon had been sweet.

About the author

Audrey Howard was born in Liverpool in 1929 and it is from that great seaport that many of the ideas for her books come. Before she began to write she had a variety of jobs, among them hairdresser, model, shop assistant, cleaner and civil servant. In 1981, out of work and living in Australia, she wrote the first of her eleven published novels. She was fifty-two. Her fourth novel, *The Juniper Bush*, won the Boots Romantic Novel of the Year Award in 1988. She now lives in her childhood home, St Anne's on Sea, Lancashire.

Echo of
Another Time

Audrey Howard

CORONET BOOKS
Hodder and Stoughton

First published in Great Britain in 1994 by Hodder and
Stoughton. A division of Hodder Headline PLC.
First published in paperback in 1995 by Hodder and
Stoughton. A Coronet Paperback.

10 9 8 7 6 5 4 3

British Library CIP
Howard, Audrey
Echo of Another Time
I. Title
823.914 [F]

ISBN 0 340 62875 8

Typeset by Hewer Text Composition Services, Edinburgh
Printed and bound in Great Britain by Cox & Wyman Ltd,
Reading, Berkshire

Hodder and Stoughton
A division of Hodder Headline PLC
338 Euston Road
London NW1 3BH

For my grandson
Daniel Russell Pitt

The best things in
life are worth
waiting for

Author's Note

I have taken some liberties with the dates and the movements of the 1st and 2nd Battalions of the King's Regiment (Liverpool) though one or other of the Battalions did serve in the places mentioned.

Chapter One

Celie was at the spuds when the boy was brought in and at once her somewhat preoccupied expression changed to one of sharp interest. The smoky-grey eyes which had been hazed with the tediousness of the task she had been put to became as clear as crystal and her rosy mouth popped open. She held her breath for a moment, her eyes and her mouth widening in anticipation, for surely here was something to put a bit of sparkle in her day and even, if she was lucky, get her away from the everlasting spuds.

She was always at the spuds, was Celie. Apart from the time she spent at Prince Albert Road Board School where she had been a pupil for the last five years it seemed to her she occupied her every waking minute at the sink in the scullery and all on account of Mr Latimer having such a big family. Thirteen of them, with Mr and Mrs Latimer, and thirteen people, plus the servants, added up to an awful lot of spud peeling and it meant that Celie was up to her elbows in the potato water until the skin of her hands wrinkled like an old prune.

Of course Kate was supposed to be working alongside her but Kate was of an indolent nature and when Cook's eye was not immediately upon her she was inclined to slow down, her hands idle, her brain the same, in Celie's scornful opinion. And when the pair of them, her and Kate, had finished the spuds there were the Brussels sprouts, the swedes, the turnips, the spring cabbage to be stripped and washed, peas to shell and carrots to scrub. Not that Celie minded really, even with Kate dawdling along beside her, because you had to make a start somewhere, didn't you? Particularly when you meant to get on as Celie Marlow did. She had her eye on Cook's job when Cook had finished with it, though naturally she'd said nothing to Cook. Well, she couldn't, not yet, could she? Celie was ten years old.

The boy was older than she was, she decided, with that keen interest she took in everything that went on about her and which was inclined to get her into trouble. He was tall, thin and wild-looking with a thatch of uncut, uncombed hair which fell about his ears and over the collar of his shirt. Celie especially noticed his hair because it was such an unusual colour. Like honey it was, with streaks of gold in it, just as though it was laced with sunlight and his eyes were the loveliest blue, the colour of hyacinths or a cornflower, and as bright as the crystals of dew which caught in a spider's web on an autumn morning. They flashed all about the kitchen and Celie was reminded of that horse Mr Latimer had brought home a while back, a thoroughbred it was said to be, but which Mrs Latimer had declared far too wild for Master Richard to ride.

'Take it back, Mr Latimer,' she had commanded her husband, standing well away from the animal's lethal skittish hooves, its frenzied rolling eyes. 'It will not do,' Celie had heard her say in that high-nosed way Mrs Latimer had, for at the time Celie and Alfie Ash had been deep in the rhododendron shrubbery at the front of the house, dared by Alfie's brother, Bertie, to get as near to the front steps as they could without being seen. Alfie, even at the age of five or so, was not one to refuse a dare.

Of course Mr Latimer had obeyed at once for it was Mrs Latimer who was the mistress *and* master in this house, and if she saw the unwashed and ragged state of the creature who had just been led into her immaculate kitchen, there was no doubt in Celie's mind she would say exactly the same thing about him as she had about the horse. The boy stood quite still, pulled as taut as the wire which her Pa had stretched about his own vegetable patch. Mr Ash's hand was clamped tightly on his shoulder, just in case he took it into his head to do a bunk.

'And who, may I ask, is this, Mr Ash?' Cook asked the handyman tartly, her small, blackcurrant eyes travelling in horrified scrutiny from the boy's riotous tangle of curls in which there was bound to be something nasty lurking, to the soles of his battered boots, which were bound to have brought something equally nasty onto her well-scrubbed kitchen floor.

'The master found him.'

'*Found* him?' Cook's voice was incredulous. If Mrs Latimer ruled this house and all who lived in it, then Cook ruled this kitchen and all who worked in it and though Mr Ash was *outside* and strictly speaking, did not come under her jurisdiction, it was all the same to her.

'Aye,' Mr Ash answered patiently, well used to Cook's ways, as they all were, and taking no offence. 'Down by t'docks, he were, only tryin' ter gerron board the *City of Richmond* which was to sail within the hour.'

'Never!'

'Aye, an' wi'out a ticket an' all. He were about ter be hauled off to Inman's offices in Water Street, it bein' their vessel, when Mr Latimer come across him an' if it hadn't been fer him, they'd have charged lad as a stowaway for sure. They give him over in ter Mr Latimer's custody, the master being well known an' he brought 'im back 'ere. "See if yer can do summat with him, Ash," he says, "or maybe Marlow could find him a job. He's a bit young fer gaol," he says, so here he is, Cook, an' so far he hasn't had a word ter say fer hisself.'

Celie stood on tiptoe, making herself as tall as possible, her nose no more than an inch from the window of the partition which separated the scullery from the kitchen. The sink had been sited to accommodate a grown woman and not a ten-year-old child and Celie was forced to stand on a box in order to reach it. The sink was shallow and wide and next to it was the draining board on which an enormous bowl of unpeeled potatoes stood. To the back of her and between her and Kate, was a bucket of cold water in which each finished potato was flung. Years of practice had made their aim accurate and the bucket was half-filled with neat white ovals, the water in it preventing them from turning brown.

The box on which Celie stood tilted dangerously but Celie righted it with a deftness born of long practice, balancing precariously on its edge in her effort not to miss a moment of the drama beyond the window. The door to the front house opened and through it came Dorcas and Fanny, the parlourmaids who had just served luncheon to Mrs Latimer and her daughters and for several moments the sound of their laughing voices and the clatter of the trays which they put on the table drowned out Cook's words. Without thought for the consequences, so deep was her curiosity, Celie stepped down from her box, wiping her hands on the large square of sacking which served her for an apron, and crept to the doorway leading into the kitchen.

'You'll cop it if Cook sees you.' Kate's voice was hopeful since she liked nothing better than to see Celie Marlow in Cook's bad books.

'She won't,' Celie answered absently and seeing that Cook's attention was completely absorbed by the strange boy, she edged a little further into the kitchen. Her eyes glowed. It was not often something came to brighten the drabness of Celie Marlow's day and she did not mean to miss any of it.

'Is that so,' Cook was declaring ominously, folding her plump bare arms beneath the ample jut of her bosom in a way all the kitchen staff recognised. The maids about her pressed forward eagerly, ready to enjoy it since her displeasure was not directed at them. 'Well, we'll see about that. Now then, my lad, first of all we'll have your name.'

They waited with bated breath, Dorcas and Fanny whispering to Patsy, longing to know what was up. Patsy was the kitchen maid, Cook's assistant. There was Mary and Lily who did the heavy cleaning and Kate, still at her post in the scullery, but none showed more fascination than Celie Marlow who as yet had no particular function in the kitchen and so was at everyone's beck and call.

The boy's eyes darted from one to the other and he took a deep ragged breath but still he did not speak. His shirt was wet about the collar for it was a dank and raw November day and he was shivering. His threadbare jacket did not quite button at the front and the sleeves were far too short, revealing the bony slenderness of his wrists. His big-knuckled boy's hands, which indicated the size of the man he would one day be, clenched nervously and as though he was suddenly aware of them, he shoved them deep in the pockets of his trousers. The stance he took up gave him a jaunty air of defiance and Cook took exception to it.

'And we'll have none of that, young man,' she thundered. 'Take your hands out of your pockets when you speak to me,' though as yet he had said nothing, 'and stand up straight, an' all. We'll have a bit of respect here, if you don't mind.'

The boy gave her his full attention until she had finished speaking, then when she did, he turned to gaze about the spacious kitchen eyeing the enormous table which stood in its centre. Cook had knocked up a few scones for the servants' tea and those that had just come out of the oven were cooling on a wire tray. The boy's eyes dwelled on them for several seconds and Celie could feel the hunger in him just as though she suffered it herself but his wandering gaze moved on, studying the shelves lining the whitewashed walls where dozens of copper pans of every shape and size were stacked, each one burnished until Cook could see her face in it. For all the concern the boy showed, Cook's heated remarks might have been directed at one of the others and Celie drew in her breath apprehensively. *Nobody* defied Cook, not if they wanted to avoid her displeasure, which was short, but sharp. Celie had felt it a time or two about her own ears. This was Cook's domain and she ruled it with a rod of iron. She did not care for what she called "dumb insolence", which meant anything from a sullen look to downright rebellion, though the latter had never yet happened in Celie's time.

'P'raps he's deaf, Cook,' Patsy giggled unwisely, turning to the other maids for recognition of her own wit.

'Try not to be more stupid than you really are, Patsy,' Cook told her with acid in her voice.

'Sorry, Cook.' Patsy's smile died away.

'And get back to them strawberries, if you please. They won't hull themselves, will they?'

'No, Cook.'

'Well then, what're you waiting for? This is not a side show.'

'No, Cook.'

The kitchen maid scuttled back to her post at the table where a glowing bowl of strawberries, brought in from the greenhouse half an hour since by Cec Marlow, were awaiting her attention. Celie, safe, as she thought, in the knowledge that Cook's attention was elsewhere, crept a little closer to the excitement which had come to brighten her long and extremely hard-working Saturday.

'You'd best not let Cook see you, Celie Marlow,' Kate hissed from the scullery doorway, picking on the one person in the hierarchy of servants who was beneath *her* and could therefore be safely intimidated. She said it just loud enough for Cook to hear, but Cook was intent on some intimidation of her own and the words did not reach her.

'Now listen here, young feller-me-lad. Mr Latimer has sent you here out of the goodness of his heart.' Her hazardous gaze was no more than six inches from the boy's face. They all knew what a good heart Mr Latimer had, and if this boy didn't, then he'd soon learn. A kinder-hearted, more generous man didn't walk this earth and she did not care to see his benevolence treated in the rude and indifferent manner this guttersnipe had assumed. Standing there like a young cock-o'-the-north, his hands in his pockets taking absolutely no notice of what she was saying to him and if it was the last thing she did she'd wipe that disdainful look off his face.

'You should count your blessings that Mr Latimer got hold of you, my lad. In the Borough gaol you'd be by now if he hadn't, and there's no doubt you'd meet some queer customers in there, I can tell you, any one of them ready to . . . well . . . we'll say no more about that but I hope you realise how lucky you are, boy? Now then, stop gawping around my kitchen, tell us your name and how you came to be stowing away on the *City of Richmond* and then I'll see if there's any of that mutton stew left we had for our dinner. You look as though a good feed wouldn't do you any harm.'

Cook was not unkind at heart. Strict, yes, but as she said

a dozen times a day, mostly to herself, you had to be with six great girls ready to idle about the place the moment your back was turned. She didn't include Celie Marlow in her accounting, for the child only worked Saturdays and an hour or two each weekday, and that because her father was gardener to Mr Latimer and her mother was dead. Cook had taken on Celie as a favour to Cec, keeping her out of mischief, her having no mother. The rest of them, well, give 'em an inch an' they took a mile, lolling about the place as though they'd nothing better to do than stand and gossip. They weren't what they used to be, maidservants, she was ready to tell anyone. Not as they had been in *her* day, and she blamed it on the schooling every Tom, Dick and Harry, and their female counterparts, had been granted sixteen years ago by the Education Act of 1870. Every child could go to school, the Act said, no matter what their circumstances, and really what good did it do them? She herself could read, naturally, since she came from a good home and was an upper servant. She wrote a fair copperplate in the neatly bound and enormously thick recipe book which she meant to pass on one day to a girl she thought worthy of it. A girl with her own superb talent and imagination at the kitchen range. She'd not met such a paragon yet and not likely to, not with this ham-fisted lot she often thought sadly.

'I'm waiting for an answer, young man.' Cook's face was a bright, enraged pink, becoming duskier with every moment the boy's insolence continued, and Celie strained forward, her own young face rosy with the effort to drag a word from this foolhardy boy. Oh please, boy . . . speak . . . speak . . . tell Cook your name, she begged him, inside her head, of course. She didn't know what Cook meant by "queer customers" in the Borough gaol but she certainly agreed with her about the boy's good fortune in falling into Mr Latimer's hands. He was the best master anyone could have, Celie's Pa said so often. It didn't matter who came to the back kitchen door – that's if they got past Pa or Mr Ash – Mr Latimer had given orders that they were to be fed and, if they were in need of it, provided with some cast-off clothing which Mrs Latimer was to put aside for the purpose. And if Cook wasn't so strict with the house servants Celie knew they would have lounged about all day long, stuffing their faces with the good food the Master insisted on providing. Did one of them complain of a headache or a cold and news of it got to Mr Latimer, he'd have the sufferer in their bed with a hot-water bottle and the doctor sent for at once. He was soft with everyone. His own children, had it not been for Mrs Latimer, would have run wild, doing exactly as they pleased, he was so fond of them and so indulgent of their every whim, she had heard Mr Ash tell Pa. Of course, Mrs Latimer watched him like a hawk, curbing the worst of his over-enthusiastic knight errantry, or he would have been in queer street long ago, so she had heard Cook say, the way he flung his money about. Open-handed and big-hearted and forever bringing home waifs and strays for whom he found employment of one sort or another, as he seemed intent on doing with *this* boy.

Celie did her best to make herself into the smallest possible target for Cook's eagle eye, for it would be just her luck to be sent back to the scullery with Kate when she did so want to see what happened to this boy. If he didn't answer Cook's questions, continuing to defy her as he was doing, there was no doubt Cook would tell Mr Ash to haul him away and lock him in the shed. If he hadn't the sense to recognise his own luck in finding a place in this benevolent household, then he'd best get back to the Borough gaol or at least be given some kind of work away from Briar Lodge, Cook would argue. There were factories and warehouses, labouring jobs on the docks or railways and with Mr Latimer's influence, he'd have no trouble being placed. Cook wanted no sullen, ungrateful faces around *her* table and the sooner the boy was made aware of it the better.

'Come on, young man, speak up,' Cook continued ominously. 'Cat got your tongue, has it? Tell us what you were doing tryin' to get on that boat to New York.'

Celie distinctly saw the boy's face change. The cool expression of indifference, of inattention and another expression which seemed to her to be a sort of . . . of . . . heavy *sadness*, fled away and his face was lit up from the inside, the light beaming out of his lovely blue eyes like beacons. They shone suddenly with a bright awareness which fell warmly on all those about them.

'I think you hit a nerve there, Cook.' Mr Ash's tone was laconic. The boy turned at once to look at him, then back to Cook, and he smiled. Oh, how he smiled! A great grin which revealed even, white teeth; which lifted the corners of his well-shaped mouth and narrowed his long eyes; which re-arranged the muscles beneath his smooth young skin into a shape of such joyful understanding, everyone was quite electrified. Celie could see it in all their faces. A response which brought smiles to their lips and eyes, a kind of flowing towards him, a feeling of fellowship which was quite amazing. Even Cook's face softened and a look of wonderment clouded her eyes.

'New York.' The two words tumbled from between his lips exultantly and they all smiled and nodded, pressing closer to this quite startling boy who, with two words, had completely defused the hostile tension in the kitchen.

'New York,' he said again, his eyes sweeping the circle of their rapt faces, evidently waiting for them to answer. They looked at him expectantly. What would he say next? their eager expressions asked, urging him to open himself up to them for they were very willing to listen.

'Yes? New York?' Cook repeated encouragingly and Celie wanted to laugh, really she did for she had never seen Cook with such a *soft* look on her face. Not soft like the fur on the kittens which the kitchen tabby produced with tedious and awkward regularity but soft as in *daft, half-witted, loony*! And they all looked the same, even Mr Ash, watching the boy as though he was one of the entertaining acts she had heard tell of at the Music Hall in Liverpool. As though he was going to break into a song and dance for their amusement. All he'd said were two words, for goodness sake: *New York*, and what was so damned clever about that, and yet they were all studying him as though he'd repeated from beginning to end that lovely poem Miss Entwistle had told them about the other day at school. "A host of golden daffodils", it was called, and Celie had thought it was quite breathtaking.

'Yes?' Cook nodded her head smilingly at the boy. 'Yes . . .

New York? Did you want to get there, is that it? Is that why you were trying to get on the boat?'

'New York,' the boy said again looking appealingly from one face to the other, his eyes bright and warm and lovely, at least Celie thought so. He held out his hands which were exceedingly dirty, palm upwards, and lifted his shoulders in a gesture which clearly asked something of them and without realising she was doing it, and certainly without thought or care for the consequences, Celie moved round the table, and across the scrubbed flags until she stood directly in front of him. Even Cook felt compelled to move aside at the strangeness of it and Mr Ash's hand fell from the boy's shoulder. It was as though they were all in a trance, from Mr Ash and Cook, right down through the ranks of the servants to this lowliest of them all. The little kitchen skivvy who was the daughter of the gardener.

They waited for her to speak but it was several moments before she did. She came barely to the boy's chin, a comical figure in her old working boots, her wrinkled stockings which had once belonged to Miss Prudence who was a year older than Celie, her short skirt and drab cotton top and the enormous sacking apron which enfolded her in its coarse embrace from neck to ankle. On her head and resting in its enormity on her small neat ears – otherwise it would have slipped over her face – was a cap of balloon-like proportions lolling slightly to one side.

They studied one another. The lanky boy and the comical child. Bright blue eyes looked steadily into soft, velvet grey, the expression in them one of curiosity. The silence was deep and unusual as though even these servants about them, everyday, ordinary, no-nonsense kind of servants, sensed something that was unique. The boy's face was soft, still with a slight smile about his mouth and on it was a questioning expression which said he knew she was going to speak and he was waiting, for what she had to say would be important.

Celie was very serious. Squaring her shoulders she placed her hand firmly on her flat chest. She patted it a couple of times and the boy watched, fascinated. They all did. They were all fascinated.

'Me Celie Marlow,' then she pointed at the boy. 'You . . . ?' He knew at once what she meant and his bewitched smile flew at her like a homing bird. Placing his hand on his own chest he spoke two words, first to Celie, then repeated them round the circle of his spellbound audience.

'*Anders Sigbjörn*,' he enunciated carefully.

'What did he say?' Cook asked doubtfully.

'Beats me.' Mr Ash was clearly disappointed.

'It's his name, Cook,' Celie ventured and the occasion was so extraordinary Cook had nothing to say on the matter of Celie's behaviour.

'It doesn't sound like any name I know.'

'Perhaps he's a foreigner,' Dorcas offered. 'There's a lot of 'em hanging about the docks waiting for the immigration ships.'

'You could be right, Dorcas. *Are . . . you . . . a . . . foreigner?*' Cook mouthed loudly, under the impression, as most people like her were, that if you spoke loudly enough and slowly enough, the person to whom you addressed your question would be bound to understand. At the glass partition Kate had her nose pressed to the window, unwilling to miss a word spoken or a gesture made by this mysterious boy who, it seemed, was a foreigner. The kitchen was filled with the delicious smell of baking, for Cook's second batch of scones, put in the oven before the disturbance began, was evidently ready to come out.

'Lord, me scones,' she said, suddenly remembering, the fragrant aroma triggering off that instinct which told her, without looking at the clock or counting the minutes, that what she had put in the oven was ready to come out. 'See, Dorcas, fetch those scones out of the oven or they'll be burned to a crisp, whilst I see to this lad. Fanny, make the tea, there's a good lass, and then fetch the butter and a pot of my strawberry jam from the pantry. And get from under my feet, Celie Marlow. I can't imagine what you think you're doing out here where you've no right to be. Those potatoes will be needed in five minutes if they're to go in with the roast. Now then, Mr Ash, while you're here you won't say no to a nice hot buttered scone, will you, and you . . . what's a name

. . .' turning to the boy, 'go and wash your hands and face
before you sit down at *my* table. No, don't just stand there
. . . *Go . . . and . . . wash . . . your . . . hands*, oh, lands
sakes, Mr Ash, take him to the washhouse, will you, and
show him what to do. See, Patsy, warm up that mutton
stew for the lad'll need more than scones inside him if he's
to give Mr Marlow a hand. Fancy, a foreigner in my kitchen.
Who'd have thought it. *What* did he say his name was, Mr
Ash? Sounded like *Dan* something or other to me.'

For several minutes there was pandemonium in the kitchen
and a casual observer might have been forgiven for thinking
a banquet was about to be prepared instead of a simple cup
of tea and a scone or two. There was much brisk stirring
and beating, the crashing of pans as Cook set about some
task of her own, the noisy placing of plates and mugs and
cutlery on the table for the servants' tea and with a great sigh
Celie dragged herself back to her box at the scullery sink and
thrust her hands into the water in which the potato peelings
drifted. She found the discarded knife and, picking another
potato from the basket beside her, began her neat removal
of its skin. Whilst she was at it, she kept an eye on the back
kitchen door for the return of the boy. Anders . . . that was
his name, though what had come after had sounded just like
a sneeze to her. And it was *her* who had discovered it, not
Cook, or Mr Ash, who had both been ready to chuck him out
for his insolence. Her, Celie Marlow! She was the one who
had realised that he was not insolent or deaf or half-witted
but a foreigner in a foreign land who could not understand a
word that was said to him. And how was he to manage all by
himself if he couldn't speak the language, and how had he got
to Liverpool? She deftly cut the potato into pieces exactly the
size Cook liked for her "roast" as she pondered on the plight
of this strange addition to the Latimer household.

They came back, him and Mr Ash. The boy's face was all
bright and shining, his wet hair slicked back and Celie's hands,
beginning to pucker again at the finger ends, became still, and
her crystal grey eyes narrowed in sharp concentration. She
didn't want to miss what Cook might say to him and, more
importantly, what he might say to Cook.

'If you ask me he should go back where he come from,' Kate said peevishly, chucking a potato in the bucket with such force the water slopped over the rim onto the floor.

'. . . comin' over here an' taking jobs from English lads. My cousin Frank'd give his eye teeth for job as gardener's lad here. A crying shame it is . . .'

'Ssh!' Celie hissed, terrified Kate's whining voice might prevent her from hearing what was being said beyond the glass partition.

'Don't you shush me, Celie Marlow . . .'

'Oh, be quiet.'

'*Well*! wait till I tell Cook you cheeked me, you little . . .'

Kate was bridling up to Celie who, standing on her box, was exactly the same height as Kate. She'd have no lip from a kitchen skivvy, Kate's truculent expression said, especially one who was only ten years old, two years younger than she was. Kate might only be a scullery maid but she was far above this impudent kid and for two pins, when Cook wasn't looking, of course, she'd box her ears until they rang.

'Celie.' The voice was hesitant.

It was perhaps the absolute silence in the kitchen behind her which warned Kate that something was happening. There was no clatter of cup against saucer, no murmur of voices nor sounds of chairs being moved and for some reason the hairs at the back of her neck prickled.

When she turned she did so slowly, recoiling away from the tall thin figure who stood in the doorway.

He was smiling, but not at her. He was holding out his hand, but not to her. His eyes were warm, but not for her.

'Celie,' he said again, quite distinctly but in it was a strange twist of his tongue almost as though the "C" was not "C" but "SH". He gestured towards the table in the kitchen, then beneath the open-mouthed gaze of those who watched he bowed to the astonished child, just a small bending of his neck before taking her hand. He helped her down from her box as though she was royalty descending from her carriage, led her through the scullery door to the table and with a smile of such sweet charm she could not possibly resist, bowed again to Cook before seating Celie in the chair next to his. A heaped plate of mutton stew steamed where he had been sitting.

'Well,' Cook gasped, 'he's got nice manners whoever he is but, my Lord, has he got a lot to learn before he fits into this household. Now then, girl, see if you can get it out of him where he comes from, where he was going, and why!'

Chapter Two

The servants were staggered by the way the new boy and young Celie Marlow seemed able to communicate with one another. At first he spoke not a scrap of English except the words "New York", "Celie", "yes" and "no", and the kid spoke not a word of whatever language *he* gabbled and yet by means of some sort of comical pantomime, a gesture of the hand, a wag of the head, a smile, a string of words from him, some from her, a charade which fascinated those who watched, they could understand one another. They each seemed able to determine exactly what the other meant by these mimes and garbled dialogue and there was none of the impatience and exasperation between them which the other servants could not help but feel in their dealings with him.

'Will you have one egg or two, boy, and how about a piece of fried bread?' Cook would ask him, as she had asked the others, from her stand by the range, throwing the question over her harassed shoulder since this was a busy part of her day. There was the master and the older children who ate together to see to, nursery breakfasts to be got ready and which the nursery maid collected, the mistress's tray of hot tea, lemon and wafer-thin unbuttered toast to be sent up to her room, not to mention half a dozen servants waiting and it was no hot tea, lemon and unbuttered toast for them but fried eggs, crisp bacon, fried mushrooms and kidney, sausages, fried tomatoes and fried bread, for those who worked manually, as *her* lot did, liked to do it on a full stomach. The boy, who sat at the kitchen table, always had his knife and fork at the ready, which she supposed

was only natural since he had been half-starved when Mr
Ash brought him in.

'Yes,' he would answer, ready to smile engagingly at
anyone who looked in his direction, since "yes" was one
of the words he knew and if it was to do with food, he never
answered in the negative.

'Yes, what? one or two? Come on boy, I've not got all
day. Is it one or two eggs?', though why she asked she
really didn't know since it was usually two and more often
than not, three!

The boy would nod, his eyes on the frying pan.

'Yes . . .' This time hesitantly.

'Do . . . you . . . want . . . one . . . egg . . . or . . . two?'
The boy, realising that something important was being asked
of him about his breakfast and that the provider of it was
becoming irritated, would turn anxiously to Celie, as Cook
did. Celie would put her hand on his arm and with a signal
which involved her fingers, her eyebrows and her most
serious expression, she would convey the question to him,
at the same time speaking the words in a slow, careful tone.
She would point to the egg, the frying pan, at Cook, the plate
and at him, holding up first one finger, then two, mouthing the
names of each object, watching his lips intently as he watched
hers, making him say the words over and over again until she
was satisfied.

Cook would become even more irritated. 'Lands sakes,
girl, there's no need for speechifying. Can't you just ask him
without all that fuss? I've others to cook for besides him, you
know,' one hand holding the pan, the other waiting impatiently
with the egg which she could crack neatly and cleanly – with
that one hand – into the hot fat with the dexterity of a
magician.

'I'm teaching him to speak English, Cook. He'll never learn
else. He's doing right well, an' all. I say the words and he says
them after me . . .'

'Yes, yes, I realise that, girl, but this bacon fat's going to
catch fire if I don't get the eggs in . . . oh, and don't forget
to ask him about the fried bread.'

Eat! She'd never seen anyone – and she'd served a few

good eaters in her time – put it away like young Dan Smith, as it appeared the boy was to be called, and you could certainly see the difference in him as the weeks went by, Cook told herself with great satisfaction, since there was no doubt in her mind that his improved appearance was down to her, a kind of supple, healthy glowing, like that of a young puppy thriving on its mother's milk, a filling out of the hollows, an added brightness to his eyes, a straightening of his youthful back and shoulders, an elastic spring to his step. First at the table was the new lad, and last to leave, stoking himself at every meal as though he hadn't eaten for days, giving serious consideration, and bringing a good deal of enjoyment to every dish Cook put in front of him and when it was finished catching her attention and when he had it, smiling and rubbing his stomach to let her know how good it had been. You couldn't help warming to him, really you couldn't, but it was so dratted inconvenient having to wait for young Celie to come home from school to find out what the dickens he was getting at, at times.

There was the question of his clothes, for instance. Though they were far too small for him and none too clean, would he be parted from them? Not he! Cook had instructed George Ellis to take him into the washhouse before Madge Evans, the daily laundry maid, turned up. 'Strip him off,' she told George. 'Fill the bath,' referring to the one which hung on the wall and was used by the "outside" men, 'tip him in it and get him to give himself a damn good scrub,' and then, when he was as clean as Cook liked things to be clean he was to be put in the underdrawers, the long-sleeved woollen vest, the good woollen shirt, cord breeches and the tweed jacket Mr Latimer had provided for him. There were long, serviceable woollen socks and a stout pair of ankle boots and even a jaunty cap, but when the time came the boy took fright, running off towards the bit of wood at the back of the house and only Cec Marlow's intervention had stopped him from jumping the six foot high wall which surrounded the property, and hot-footing it for town.

''Tis only for your own good, boy,' Cook said to him firmly when he was brought before her. 'Look at the state of you. Lands sakes, those trousers are half-way up your legs and your elbows are coming out of the jacket. You're not decent, lad. You're getting too big to be . . . well . . . squashed into those pants and if anyone outside the gates was to see you, they'd wonder what Mr Latimer was thinking of, letting one of his servants go about like you do. It's not right. And will you look at them boots,' pointing to his feet, which he did, following her finger. 'You can't wear them for much longer, not with the soles flapping like that. See, won't you go and have a good hot bath and then put on these clothes Mr Latimer left for you.' She smiled encouragingly. 'They're good and warm and you can't expect to stay in them things for ever, can you?' again pointing to the offending garments. The boy looked down at them and from his action Cook took it that he understood, but of course he didn't, he was merely following her finger and when, satisfied, she told George to return him to the washhouse and to look lively because Madge would be here shortly, the whole rigmarole was repeated.

Celie knew at once what was up with him, though God knows how, Cook said distractedly. She'd not let that ragamuffin back in her kitchen, she had threatened him, telling him to be off from her back door but when he huddled on the doorstep in the chill November morning she had relented, thrusting a thick bacon sandwich at him with one hand, at the same time and for good measure, boxing his ears with the other.

'He doesn't want to part with them, Cook,' Celie explained importantly when she came home from school, gazing up with complete understanding into the boy's face, reaching for his hand and holding it comfortingly between her own.

'*Doesn't want to part with them*! Lands sakes, whatever next? They're not fit for dusters. What's the matter with the boy, for goodness sake. There's a perfectly good, *decent* set of clothes here for him to wear and he refuses to put them on. Doesn't he want to be warm and dry? I never heard anything like it in my life . . .'

'His Ma put him in them, Cook,' Celie cut in and Cook was silenced immediately. In Celie's smoky grey eyes was a deep and sorrowful understanding since she too had lost her Ma and she knew exactly how she would feel if she were to be forcibly parted from anything her Ma had given her. Not that her Ma ever had but she thought she knew what it would be like and this boy, whose Ma was, apparently, no longer with him, would want to cling to something, no matter how dirty and tattered, that had his Ma's hand on them.

'Aah . . .' Cook touched his shoulder hesitantly, apologetically, regretting the boxed ears, '. . . I wonder where she is, his Ma?' Then, as though to say she'd no time to be dithering about here, she squared her shoulders and raised an imperious head '. . . nevertheless, he's got to get into them duds, Celie, and he's to have a bath first, tell him . . . tell him Madge Evans'll wash what he's got on and he can hang on to them, if he wants to.'

They called him Dan. Celie kept insisting that his name was Anders. She'd even written it down for Cook on a bit of paper but the servants couldn't shape with such a foreign, *awkward* thing on their tongues, they said, or at least Cook did, and naturally, what Cook decreed was law in the kitchen.

'Oh, Dan's nice and easy, girl, and it sounds near enough to whatever it says on that there bit of paper. If he's to settle in here, he'd be better off with a good plain English name, stands to reason,' and Celie could not help but agree with her. 'Tell him, will you, girl,' just as though Celie could speak the language, whatever it was, that tripped off the boy's tongue.

'Get him to say something, Celie,' the servants would beg her when they all sat round the table during the servants' tea-time, just as though he was one of those performing, scarlet-jacketed monkeys perched on the shoulder of the organ grinders who plied their trade in Canning Place. Mr and Mrs Latimer dined at seven. Mr Latimer, who was a partner in the export and import firm of Noble Shippers in Water Street, did not return home until six o'clock. He liked to spend half an hour in the nursery with the younger children, getting them so giddy with excitement, Nanny Ella could do nothing with them, she complained to Cook, who was the only servant whose standing Nanny Ella thought approached her own amongst those who were employed at Briar Lodge. The younger children had nursery tea at five o'clock and the three older ones, Master Richard, Miss Anne and Master Alfred, seventeen, fifteen and thirteen years of age respectively, were allowed, when the boys were home from school, to dine with their Mama and Papa. So it was often after nine, or later if there were guests for dinner, before the servants had what Cook described as a bit of something substantial inside them. To keep them going until then, just as though they might fade away to nothing whilst they waited, they usually had "tea" at five. Sandwiches of whatever cold meat was left over from the previous night's meal, or the children and Mrs Latimer's luncheon, cheese, pickles, put up by Cook of course. No *bought* stuff for *her*, fresh crusty bread with lashings of *best* butter, hot scones and jam, again made by Cook. A couple of fruit pies, perhaps, and a fruit cake since they needed to keep their strength up.

The Latimer children came down to inspect him when news of the "foreigner" reached the nursery, ready to be fascinated by this strange species which had ended up in their Mama's kitchen. The older boys would not bother of course, even if they had been at home, which they weren't, for now that they went away to school they considered they had been out in the world and were well acquainted with persons from other countries. Master Richard was in his last year at his father's old public school, Master Alfred was in his third year and Master Robert his first. They mixed with boys, not only from many parts of England but from many parts of the empire, India and such places, with boys who spoke with strange accents and whose skin was not the same colour as theirs, so young Dan would not be the curiosity to them that he was to the young Latimers.

'Now then, Miss Prudence, don't you go getting flour on that there pretty dress of yours or Nanny Ella will have something to say about it, and see, Master James, put that rolling pin down before you crack open Miss Katherine's skull. Now then, Miss Margaret, get from under my feet. Why don't the four of you sit down round the table and you shall have one of my almond squares, or a shortbread perhaps. Look, Patsy's just iced some biscuits, now what would you like, Miss

Prudence, one with a flower on it . . . no, don't squabble, there's plenty to go round . . .'

'We've come to see the new boy, Cook,' Prudence, who was eleven, said politely, her small tongue delicately licking the pale pink icing flower from its chocolate background and Celie, from her position at the scullery sink, watched her enviously through the dividing window for she would dearly have loved to sit at her ease and eat Cook's iced biscuits dressed as Miss Prudence was. Miss Prudence had a self-assurance, a self-esteem, the haughty self-confidence of her class together with a pale prettiness which Celie, having no conception of her own fledgeling beauty, wished could be hers. Miss Prudence wore what every little girl of her age and social standing wore. Attitudes towards children's clothing were changing as the century drew towards its last decade and the fashion of dressing little girls in smaller but exact replicas of what their Mamas wore was becoming rare. Mrs Latimer's three young daughters had on ankle-length dresses of lawn with wide sashes. They were smocked across the bodice, high-necked with long sleeves which had a faint whisper of the "leg o' mutton" about them. Their hair, all exactly the same colour, was tied back in enormous satin bows. None had the curls necessary for the ringlets which were fashionable and so each night they slept in the "curling papers" Nanny Ella rolled laboriously in their soft brown hair. The two smallest boys, who at twelve months and two years were considered too young to leave the nursery, had not yet been "breeched" of course, and were still encumbered by dresses abounding in frills and flounces, lace, ribbons and fine embroidery. Mrs Latimer approved strongly of white, especially next to the skin since white had the advantage of showing dirt and was therefore hygienic, and the four children around the table were dressed in that colour, even Master James in his "Jack Tar Demi Suit" which consisted of jersey knickerbockers and a blouse, loose and comfortable, and allowing free movement, which was a mistake in Cook's opinion as she watched the child clamber over the bench, the table, the *back* of *her* chair, like some playful kitten.

'Well, he's not here, Miss Prudence,' she replied in answer

to the child's statement. 'He has a job to do, you know, just like your Papa.'

'I know, we saw him with Marlow when we were walking with Nanny Ella but she wouldn't let us stop to talk to him.'

I bet she wouldn't, Cook thought, imagining Nanny hurrying her charges past the foreigner as though he was some dreadful bit of flotsam the tide had brought in and deposited in their path. By now, of course, young Dan was tricked out in the good, second-hand garments, probably once belonging to Master Richard, that Mr Latimer kept for those whose need was great, and would have been perfectly presentable, but he would be far beneath Nanny Ella's and therefore the children's notice.

'Marlow said they would be in for a brew directly so we came down as soon as we could,' Prudence continued, daintily licking the chocolate from her fingers whilst Cook shuddered at what Nanny would say if she heard her charge use the word "brew". The child was completely unconcerned by the antics of her younger brother since it was not *her* responsibility to curb him. That was the job of the servants whom her father employed and Cook sighed as she heaved young Master James from the imminent danger of the open range where it seemed he was intent on "peeping" into the oven beside it for some more of Cook's shortbreads.

'See, Dorcas, take this young imp and strap him to the bench will you? How am I expected to cook luncheon with this lot under my feet, tell me that? Now put those almond squares down, Miss Margaret. You've already had three. Do as you're told now or it's out you go, the lot of you. Patsy, where are you, girl? I need that saddle of lamb basted and there's the mint sauce to be made. Oh, lands sakes, Master James, will you put that knife down. D'you want to cut your sister's throat . . . ?'

It seemed Cook was about to land Master James one, Celie was sure, and didn't he deserve it but just at that moment, the back door opened and bringing with them the damp smell of leaves, a whiff of woodsmoke from the fire on which they had been burning them, and the raw chill which is peculiar only to the end of the year, Dan and her Pa came into the kitchen. Pa smiled at her before seating himself at the table, as far away from the Latimer children as possible since, though he had her, he was not easy in a child's company. Dan moved to the table with him, seating himself quite naturally between Master James and Miss Margaret, who was only four.

The children, for some reason, became as still as little mice, staring up at him with wide eyes, their rosebud mouths slightly open. Perhaps it was the way he sat between them, a good-humoured and unselfconscious action to which they were not accustomed. Their mother treated them with reserve, their father with too much exuberance, or so both Mrs Latimer and Nanny Ella thought. The servants, to whom they were usually a nuisance as they worked about the "front" house, the kitchen and the gardens, were often impatient with them but Dan grinned, putting an arm round Master James's neck in the kind of grip older brothers sometimes use on a younger, but gently. He said something, reaching for one of Cook's shortbreads, then breaking it in two, offered half to the boy, popping the other half in his own mouth.

'Now then, lad, he's had enough,' Cook admonished, but half-heartedly. Margaret leaned confidingly against him staring at his mouth as she did her best to decipher the words which came from it and she and Katherine, who was almost five, jostled to get near him. His own face was soft and pleased as he lifted Margaret on to his knee.

'Well, you've certainly got a knack with little 'uns.' Cec sipped the almost black tea Cook had put before him and reached for a shortbread. Though they had both thoroughly washed their hands beneath the washhouse tap before they came in, his hands had the ground-in earth of the garden engraved in every crease and beneath his fingernails.

Dan turned to him as he spoke and said two words which everyone in the kitchen recognised as names. One was *Birgit*, the other *Margareta*, the rest was gibberish as far as they were concerned. He took the second little girl on his other knee, holding them both close with gentle arms and they made no objection, resting comfortably against him and again he looked at Cec. He said something else unintelligible, shaking his head with a sadness which moved Cook's heart painfully in her breast and caused Cec to swallow uncomfortably. Those names he had spoken meant something to him, obviously, and in a way that was to do with the children, and he was trying to tell them what it was but it was beyond any of them.

They did not see a lot of Dan for he spent most of his time with Mr Marlow working at the gardener's command which somehow he made the boy understand. Show him something and he soon got the hang of it, even if they couldn't *tell* him how to go about it, and he was a hard worker, too, Mr Ash, who often "borrowed" Dan from the gardener, confided to Cook, and strong. No one knew where he'd come from or how he came to be alone in Liverpool, but he settled in and was no trouble and when Mr Latimer put his first month's wages in his hand, he seemed quite bewildered.

'Tell him it's his to do with as he likes, Celie,' Cook said when with the rest of the servants, he returned to the kitchen, the seven shillings Mr Latimer had given him resting on the palm of his big square hand. 'He seems fair flummoxed. Don't they get any wages where he comes from? *Don't . . . they . . . get . . . wages . . . where . . . you come . . . from, Dan?*' she mouthed loudly. The lad looked from the money and then round the circle of interested faces.

'New York,' he said.

'What is he on about now?'

'I don't know, Cook.' Dorcas was preoccupied with counting her own wage and her reply was absent-minded. Besides, they were getting used to Dan by now and those two words he would keep repeating had begun to get on *her* nerves as they did on everyone else's but Celie's. He could say the servants' names and understand one or two simple commands like "sit down" and "come here" which young Celie had taught him but when you can't hold a proper two-way conversation with someone it gets a bit wearing after a time, those in the kitchen agreed.

It was Celie who answered.

'He wants to go there, Cook.'

'Well, I can't think why,' Cook grumbled. 'What more could a lad want than a grand job with Mr Latimer? And would you look at the way he eats. He'd not get that in New York.'

'Why not, Cook?'

'Why not? Because he wouldn't, that's all.'

'Don't they feed their servants there, Cook?'

'Don't you cheek me, Celie Marlow, or I'll box your ears for you.'

'I was only wondering, Cook.'

'Well, don't wonder. Just get stuck into them veg and hold your tongue. It's none of your business.'

Celie Marlow, Cook had observed more than once, had a bright and inquisitive mind, an almost obsessive interest in everything that went on about her, even if it was nothing to do with her. She would fix her intense and earnest concentration on you and ask you the most awkward questions, as innocent as you please, and watch while you did your best to find an answer. Cook had found the best course to take was simply to tell her to mind her own job and let others mind theirs, though it didn't always work. A little slip of a thing whose bright spirit, no matter what you said or did, just would not be stifled. Not that Cook tried to break it, for truth to tell she couldn't help having a soft spot for the girl who had grown up with no mother's care, which probably accounted for it. She was as dainty and fragile as a scrap of lace with her clear, translucent grey eyes, the fine cream and rose of her skin and the tumble of dark, feathered curls about her head. A bit of delicate gossamer to be blown about by a thread of wind, which was exactly what she was *not*. Strong and enduring she was, interested in everything was Celie Marlow, and ready to get into trouble because of it before Cook took her in hand, with her poor Pa at his wits' end when he had been forced to leave her in the none too capable hands of Mrs Ash. Mrs Ash, though a somewhat careless mother, had been none too pleased when five-year-old Celie Marlow, whose imagination was fertile, set *her* lads, who had as much imagination as the cauliflowers in Cec's vegetable garden, to wondering how the world would look from the branches of the tallest oak tree in the wood. Boys climbed trees of course, everyone expected that, but not to the topmost branches where they, and Celie, had been trapped for three hours. And what about the time when they had dammed the fast-flowing stream which ran at the back of the cottages? Only a couple of inches deep until Celie Marlow put her vivid mind to work when, with a clutter of mud, stones and a small log across it, it became three feet deep and only George Ellis's sharp hearing had saved the drowning two-year-old Ethel Ash from coming to a watery end. Thank God Celie was about to go to school, Mrs Ash was heard to say, and when she got home, was to be put in Cook's firm guardianship.

Celie got no wages because she was too young to be in full employment. Peeling the spuds and cleaning the veg was not considered *real work* and as her Pa lived free in an estate cottage and had the use of a bit of ground behind it to grow his own vegetables, it seemed fair enough. When she left school in four years' time, she'd work a full day in the kitchens, it was generally agreed, and until then she "helped out". It suited her Pa who really had no idea what to do with, or make of, the girl child his wife had left him, and it suited Cook because Celie did well at the spuds. She was, as Cook had expected her to be, inordinately interested in everything that went on about her. She had a quite astonishing fascination with and an affinity for whatever Cook was doing and was already beginning to cause trouble in the kitchen, even at ten years of age. Cook had been forced to reprimand her more than once for hanging about the centre table where Cook did all her preparation. Patsy was kitchen maid and Cook's right hand, and it was Patsy who was being trained up to be a cook herself one day. Not that Cook had much hope for her. Patsy was clean and tidy and followed Cook's instructions to the letter but there was no *heart* in her, no *flair*, no imagination which to Cook, was the very sum and substance of what made up a *proper* cook. There were thousands of competent women who could produce a decent meal or a fancy cake, but they did not quite reach that pinnacle of creativity which made a superb cook out of a good one.

Cook often deplored the fact that she had not been born a man for there was no doubt in her mind that had she been, she would have climbed up there to the top beside the greats, César Ritz or the magnificence of Escoffier himself and Cook sometimes wondered, when she saw Celie Marlow with her little uptilted nose stuck in some dish or other which was none of her business, whether Celie might be the same as herself. She seemed to Cook, despite being no more than ten years old, to have that keen sense of curiosity – that was pretty obvious of course – not just in what ingredients should be put together to make the mixture into a . . . well, what in Cook's case, always turned out to be a miracle of perfection, but in *how* the miracle happened. She quite enjoyed the child's wide-eyed fascination with what *made* the chocolate soufflé rise. *How* the whisking of egg whites and sugar achieved the wonder known as meringue, *why* was aerated bread different from wheatened bread and a hundred and one questions which Patsy never thought to ask nor even considered there was anything to be asked *about*. Accepted everything Cook told her without a scrap of curiosity as to how it came about. Patsy would make some household a good plain cook one of these days and none in it any the worse for it, she supposed, but what was to become of Cec Marlow's little lass was anybody's guess.

Chapter Three

Dan Smith, once Anders Sigbjörn, had at the age of twelve come from Gothenburg in Sweden on a steamer bound for Hull accompanied by his parents and two young sisters. They were to sail for New York where, they hoped, believed that, along with the millions of others who had gone before them they would find a better life than the one they had known in the old country. Only just above destitution level they had been there and it had taken Anders' father a long, wearying time to put together the money needed for the tickets – and a little bit besides – for the five of them.

They had finally reached Liverpool where much of the immigrant traffic of Europe to the "new worlds" began but being of simple peasant stock, trusting and unwary, they were soon parted from their tickets by an "official", who told them, in pantomime, that it would take no longer than five minutes to have them "checked out" and that they and their luggage must wait just by the Pier Head until he returned.

They waited for five hours and even then, unable to speak or understand a word of English, Anders' father could not make the porter he accosted comprehend what had happened to them.

'Nowt ter do wi' me, lad. See the immigration people,' the porter bellowed before throwing off the frantic hand of the jabbering foreigner.

They had watched in total disbelief, Anders and his family, as the ship on which they were to sail, the berths for which they had paid presumably filled by now by the passengers to whom the "official" had sold them, cast off and edged its way out into the wide river Mersey.

His father had just enough spare cash, meant to support them for a week or two in New York whilst he and Anders found work, to purchase a bit of deck space for himself, his wife and his two small daughters on a filthy old steamer taking salt to New York. They had sold everything, even the family's change of clothing, leaving them nothing but what they stood up in and certainly nothing on which they might exist until his father found work when they got there. Despairing, distraught, his mother collapsing and carried aboard the ship, his sisters wailing their terror, young Anders Sigbjörn had been left behind to fend for himself.

'I'll find work and follow when I've got a ticket,' he promised his father desperately. 'With only myself I'll soon have another berth. You must go, take Mother and the girls and it won't be long before I'll be with you. Leave your name and address at the Customs Office in New York. Go, you must go. I'm strong. I'll find work . . .'

It had taken many months for the full story of young Anders Sigbjörn to emerge, many months before he had enough command of the English language to tell Celie and Cook, who in turn told Mr Latimer, why he had been doing his best to stow away on the *City of Richmond* bound for New York. When he did, giving the names of his parents, the name of the ship they had sailed on, Mr Latimer had gone at once to the authorities to ascertain the whereabouts of the Sigbjörn family.

Oh yes, they said, the owners of the filthy old steamer, it had docked in New York, as far as they could tell, at about that time but Mr Latimer must be aware that almost a year had gone by and how, even so, were they supposed to keep track of every passenger they took on board? Once they arrived at Ellis Island, which was the entry point for all immigrants, they were no longer the shipping line's responsibility.

Mr Latimer knew a great many people in the world of ships and shipping, Cook said as she comforted young Dan in those first anxious months, and who better than he to find his family? If they'd left their name and address . . . yes, yes, she knew they wouldn't *have* an address when they arrived, but Dan's Pa would go back to the Customs Officials as soon as they were settled, wouldn't he? and leave a forwarding address.

None of them, least of all Cook, had the faintest notion of the chaos and confusion which reigned as thousands upon thousands of men, women and children, not one speaking a word of English, poured into the limitless enormity of the United States of America from every country in Europe and Scandinavia. Many had names which the harassed officials – concerned only with the health of the newcomers – could not pronounce so they were given new ones, simple ones, ones that *they* could get their tongue round and as they were passed through they just vanished, the great continent swallowing them like so many drops of water going into an ocean.

'When I save money I go,' Dan said stubbornly again and again. 'I find. I look in New York.'

'It's a big place, lad,' Mr Latimer said in his kindly way. 'Big as Liverpool, and where would you start?'

'I start at dock.'

'I've already done that, Dan. The agent we employ in New York has questioned all the customs officials and even given them a description of your family, the one you gave me, and not one remembers them, nor has anyone left a message for you. Yes, I spelt your name just as you told me . . . no . . . I'll keep on trying, my agent will call at the Custom House on Ellis Island whenever he is in the vicinity, he promised me, and if your father leaves a message, it will be relayed at once to me. If it is . . . *when* it is, you shall go immediately. I will pay for your berth, but until then, stay here with us, Dan. Don't go off again on your own until . . .'

Gradually as he settled and saw the sense of what Mr Latimer said, and when no such word came, Anders Sigbjörn, Dan Smith as he allowed himself to be called since it made life much simpler, came to realise that the family who had been forced to leave him behind, were lost to him. If he grieved for them, no one saw it. He had become part of the Latimer servants' household, doing, as Celie did with Cook, many of the jobs which slowly got beyond Cec Marlow, lifting and heaving weights which were nothing

to his strong young muscles, helping Cec and Mr Ash,
cleaning and sharpening the family cutlery, polishing boots
and windows, mending bellows and hand-mills, attending to
the whitewashing of outside buildings, stables and privies. He
did all the heavy digging ready for spring planting and, as the
evenings lengthened, waited for Celie, walking with her to the
cottage she shared with her father. He gave George a hand
with the mucking out of the stables, rubbed down the carriage
horses and learned from those about him how to speak fluent
English but with a strange mixture of his own Swedish accent
and the faint nasal sound of the Liverpool "scouser".

Though he could not, in the accepted sense of the word,
be called handsome, his face was pleasant, open, his mouth
wide and inclined to humour and though he had known nothing
but hardship from being a child, his engaging expression said
he was well used to overcoming it. Those he worked with
discovered that he was naturally easy-going, even-tempered,
cheerful, uncomplicated and eager to please. Not in a sub-
servient way but because he genuinely liked his fellow man,
despite what had been done to him, and wanted only peace.
He was still growing into young manhood, all long legs, big
and awkward hands and sharp shoulders, clumsy at times but
endearingly so, and one day he would be a fine-looking man.

He had retained the spun gold curls with which he had
been born but he kept them cut short, so short Cook swore
he took a razor to his head, but no matter what he did to
them, even to greasing them with pomade in an attempt
to make them lie flat to his head as was the fashion, they
continued to spring up abundantly with a life and colour of
their own. He could not, of course, afford the expensive,
scented pomade used by gentlemen of wealth and the lard,
beef or mutton suet with which the cheaper ones were made
soon became rancid. The unpleasant smell, unconcealed as it
was by the expensive mixture of musk, oil of cloves, cassia
or verbena, had the kitchen staff turning away from him with
cries of horror.

'Go and put your head under the yard pump, Dan Smith,'
Cook would shriek, 'and use that there carbolic soap to get
that muck out of your hair. You stink like a pole-cat,' never

having seen or even smelled one, 'and I'll not have you in my clean kitchen in that state. You'll taint the food.'

His eyes were the clear and incredible blue of the sky but not the sky which stretches above the roof-tops of Liverpool. They were the rich blue which is seen arching over the high mountain regions of Scandinavia, over the great lakes and forests, the many rivers and the sweeping plains of his own native land, the deep blue which lifts across the Norwegian Sea to the North Pole. When he looked at you, you would swear he could see right through you, Kate said, shivering dramatically, her own sea-green eyes narrowing admiringly in her smooth and colourless face. His skin was amber tinted from the days he spent out of doors alongside Cec, as were his strong, well-muscled forearms, his throat where it dipped into the open neck of his shirt and on the back of his neck where when it grew, his golden hair curled crisply above his collar.

He played football every Saturday afternoon for a local team got up by the young working men of Wavertree and that, with the training he did one night a week – with Mr Latimer's permission, of course – plus Cook's good food, was hardening his lean boy's body to that of an athlete. A personable lad and well liked, not only by the other servants both men and women, but by Mr Latimer who was pleased with the progress of the youngster who had had such sad beginnings.

He and Celie were inseparable. She did not remember her Ma, well she wouldn't, would she? since her Ma had died when Celie was born, but Pa often spoke of her and when he did a funny look came over his face and Celie could tell, young as she was, that he had loved her and missed her still.

'Tell me about Ma,' she would say to him when she was old enough to understand and Pa would sit her in her own chair before the fire, though she would dearly have loved him to gather her onto his lap, his pipe between his teeth, and open his mind to let Celie look at the lovely memories he had of Mary Marlow, who had been her mother.

It seemed they had lived in a little terraced house in Sydney Place, off Graham Street, he and Ma, moving there when they were first married. Pa had been twenty-two then, gardening lad at Briar Lodge where he had started as a boy of twelve, well thought of by old Mr Latimer, who had been master then, with a grand and secure future ahead of him. Ma had been laundry maid, only eighteen, and as pretty as a wild hedge-rose, that's how Pa described her, with that funny, sad look on his face. And for twenty odd years they had lived together in the house in Sydney Place, Pa making steady progress in his chosen profession, reliable, straightforward and held in high esteem, first by old Mr Latimer and then by his son Mr Richard Latimer who was the present owner of Briar Lodge. When old Mr Knowles had died, Cec had become head gardener and he and Ma had been as happy as any two people could be but for one thing and that was their lack of children.

'She wanted a nipper, did your Ma, Celie, and only the Good Lord himself knows why he didn't send us any until your Ma and me were well past such . . . well, we'd given up even thinking about it, settled down to believing there was to be only her an' me an' then, right out of the blue she finds out she was to have a baby.'

That was *her*, Celie knew.

'How, Pa? How did she know?' Celie used to ask at first, when she was perhaps three or four years old, breathless with wondering excitement, never tiring of it, no matter how many times she heard it. 'How did she know, Pa?' but Pa would look away and begin to fill his pipe, or reach for the poker and give the fire a stir, clearing his throat and shifting in his chair.

'She just did, child. You'll understand when you're older.'

'But Pa . . .'

'Now then, our Celie, am I telling this, or are you?'

It was not until she began to work in the kitchen of the "Big House" as the servants called Briar Lodge and Kate had described to her in graphic detail what men and women did to one another when they got married, which she thought sounded pretty ridiculous anyway, and the results of it that she understood Pa's reticence. It was not something you would like anyone else to know about, would you?

Mary Marlow was in her forties when Celie was born, not the right age to be having a first child, the doctor had confessed privately to her husband, and he was to take great care of her and not let her do too much or lift anything heavy. Which was all well and good, as far as it went, but Cecil Marlow was out of the house by seven every morning on his two-mile walk to Briar Lodge along the full length of Picton Road, through Wavertree Village and on to Briar Lodge. He did not get home, sometimes, until seven of an evening, especially in the summer, which it was then, so Mary Marlow was alone for the best part of twelve hours each day.

'There's a cottage empty in the row by the spinney, Marlow, if you're interested,' good, kindly Mr Latimer said, having heard of his gardener's dilemma. 'You wouldn't have so far to walk and could keep your eye on your good lady at the same time. I'm aware how worrying these things are,' and of course, who would be in a better position to know than he, his own wife having just been delivered of her sixth. Not that it was *quite* the same, Cec privately thought, since Mrs Latimer had the attentions of half a dozen servants to call on and that was only *indoors* with no need to lift a hand or put a foot to the floor during the whole nine months of *her* pregnancy. Still it was very good of Mr Latimer to offer and Cec was only too glad to accept.

But it was all to no avail, as far as Mary Marlow was concerned, for the doctor was proved right. Forty-one had turned out to be a dangerous age for Celie's mother to give birth to her first, and she slipped quietly away in a pool of her own blood, too weak to fight after thirty-six hours of hard labour, leaving Cecil, Cec as he was known to his friends, to bring up young Celie as best he could.

In that respect, the cottage had proved to be a godsend for it meant that Cec had the help of the women, the wives of George Ellis and Reuben Ash, who were employed in the stables and gardens of Briar Lodge and who were only too happy to shove the infant amongst their own for a few pence a week. Maidservants too, who could slip away for an hour, amongst them the laundry maid Madge Evans, who was more than willing to look after Celie for nothing and on a permanent basis, given the chance, for Cec Marlow, though well over forty himself was an amiable sort of a chap with a steady income and a cosy cottage.

But it seemed that the capacity to love which Mary Marlow had lit in her husband's heart so many years ago had been extinguished when she died and Cec kept himself pretty much to himself, fond of the pretty little thing who was his daughter for she was the "dead spit" of his Mary. She was content to settle with Mrs Ash or sometimes Mrs Ellis, whose husband worked in the stable and doubled up as coachman when Mrs Latimer needed him, thriving like some bright flower planted among the stolid and wholesome weeds of the Ash and Ellis children. Independent she learned to be, even as a baby, letting nothing get the better of her, gritting her teeth and straining her young muscles until her face was crimson, performing tasks which were often beyond the strength of a child twice her age.

She had her Ma's startling grey velvet eyes, set in a fringe of thick black lashes and a mass of dark, lustrous curls which, as they grew, fell in a riot down her small back, defying the hairbrush which Cec's clumsy, masculine hands had the greatest difficulty in employing. Try as he might he just could not get the hang of it and as for the female fashion of plaiting, or worse still, tying the ribbons which went on the *end* of the plait, well, it was just beyond him. He did his best, dragging the brush through the tangle until he brought tears to Celie's eyes, though she did not complain.

'Couldn't we cut it, Pa?' she asked helpfully, her face flushed from his endeavours. 'It would be easier to brush.'

'Nay, our Celie, females don't have short hair,' remembering perhaps the lovely feel of his Mary's waist-length hair and his own young man's hands in it.

'Please Pa, I could do it myself then.'

'Well . . .' Cec was very tempted for really this twice-daily battle with the hairbrush and ribbons was getting beyond a joke.

'Go on, Pa, I'll get the scissors.'

Well, Mrs Ash shrieked as though Cec had cut off his daughter's head along with her hair, clasping her hands to her breast in the most dramatic fashion, but then really, could you expect anything else when the child was, for the most part, more lad than lass anyway. Always up to some mischief, leading her own and Jeannie Ellis's three into all kind of scrapes, her imagination so vivid and her wayward nature so overpowering, so unafraid she could talk the others into doing the most dangerous things. She should have been called *Cecil*, not Cécilie, as her Pa had christened her, the name given to her, in Nelly Ash's opinion, because Cec Marlow, deep in his grief, couldn't think what else to call her.

Mind you, after the first shock and though she was loth to admit it, Mrs Ash was forced to agree that the short cap of layered curls suited young Celie, the very "boyishness" of it enhancing her already quite incredible childish loveliness with her flushed cheeks of rose and those enormous and strangely piercing grey eyes set in lashes so long they swept her cheek. She was a bonny little thing, everyone agreed. Before she went to school and when it was convenient for him to do so, Cec would take her about the grounds with him, giving Nelly Ash and Jeannie Ellis a "breather" as he put it, knowing his own daughter's tendency towards mischief by now. She helped him to put in his seedlings or lead the mowing pony, to gather leaves and burn them on the fire at the back of the vegetable garden.

But it all came to a head just before her fifth birthday and Cec only wondered that it had not done so sooner. She was found, not knowing any better since her Pa had not thought to warn her about it, taking Master James and Miss Katherine on an "adventure" in the spinney which stood between the big house and her Pa's cottage.

What a commotion *that* had caused. Master James and Miss Katherine, younger than Celie, had been missing for two hours. Nanny Ella, helped by the maidservants, shrieking hysterically all over the house and Mrs Latimer ready to send for the Constable, Mr Latimer brought home from the office and the whole place in such a turmoil that Cook had declared – only to herself, of course – that nothing short of a tot of whisky would set her right again.

They were found, the three of them, their feet bare and their legs exposed to the tops of their thighs, "paddling" in the stream, Master James, who had fallen in, soaked to the skin. Nanny had screamed and Mrs Latimer had swooned – or pretended to since she was not one for such a weak female pastime – when Master James had objected most strenuously to being brought home, saying he didn't give a damn about nursery tea, and who else but Marlow's child could have taught him such an obscenity and, to cap it all, he and Miss Katherine begged to be allowed to play with their new friend the very next day.

Nanny Ella had been mortified, from then on acting as though the gardener's daughter was some guttersnipe who had strayed from the stews of Liverpool, invading the grounds and the house, and *her* clean children with all manner of nasty things and from that day to this Cec Marlow had been inclined towards coolness whenever he and Nanny Ella had met on one of her sedate walks with the perambulator about the formal gardens and down to the small lake where her charges were accustomed to feeding the ducks.

'I am afraid I will have to ask you to . . . er . . . watch Celie a little more closely, Marlow,' Mr Latimer had said somewhat apologetically to his gardener, later that evening. 'You see, Nanny Ella has this strict routine which she likes the children to follow and it caused quite a disruption when Master James and Miss Katherine took it into their heads to . . . well . . . I'm not awfully sure of how it happened and I'm certain Celie did not mean any harm. They are only children, after all . . .'

'It won't happen again, sir, you can rely on it.'

'I'm sure I can, Marlow,' and it was then, when Celie was five years old and just starting school, that she was told to report to the kitchen the moment she got back home where Cook would find her some "light" duties. To give Cook her due, she was against it. Five years old was, in her opinion, far too young for a child to be put to work, even on "light" duties, whatever they might be, but orders were orders, come directly from Mrs Latimer herself and therefore not to be ignored.

'Now then, girl,' she had said on that first day when Celie presented herself at the back door on the dot of quarter past four. She always called Celie "girl". It had been "little girl" when Celie was a toddling child who had come into Cook's kitchen with her Pa, given a gingerbread man or a lemon biscuit. But this was different. This was not a social visit and Celie must be made to see the difference. 'Now then, girl, the first thing you can do is run home and change into something more suitable for kitchen work.' Celie was dressed in an ankle-length blue dress, a white pinafore, the wide frills of which ran over her shoulders and were tied at the back in a huge bow, and a pair of highly polished black boots. What she put on, in fact, to attend school each day. Neat and clean and respectable, but not at all the outfit for peeling spuds.

From that day onwards, she had worked after school for a couple of hours in Cook's kitchen dressed in any old cast-off which the Latimer girls had outgrown, protected by the sacking apron and the over-large hat. There she would remain until her Pa came to fetch her when his own day was done. In the winter, of course, it was earlier than the summer, though very often, when the short winter day was ended, the light gone sometimes by four o'clock, Cec Marlow would be found in the company of Reuben Ash. Mr Ash had fitted out one of the tack rooms in the stables, making it into a neat workshop where, besides cleaning the family's boots and shoes, he repaired anything from chairs with an unreliable leg, a clock which had for some reason stopped and refused to be wound, a child's toy, a worn wicker seat, an apple-corer from the kitchen, a bench, the glass in a firescreen, the handle on the coal box. A man clever with his hands was Mr Ash, who could turn either of them to anything, and the two men, both somewhat taciturn and therefore easy in one another's company, their pipes gripped between their teeth, the smoke from them wreathed about their heads, would work together in amiable silence.

'I'd best be off then, Reuben,' Cec would say as the stable clock struck six.

'Aye, that lass of yours'll be waitin' on you.'

'Night then, Reuben.'

'Night, Cec.'

Cec and Celie would walk home across the rolling lawn

which it was Cec's task to mow, with the help of the
mowing pony, during the summer months. Through the
dark-shadowed area of the vegetable gardens, ready and
waiting for the planting of his "veg". Beyond the looming
edifice of "his" hothouses, along which, in neat rows, were
his "hot beds" covered with frames to protect his young
seedlings, taking the narrow path through the spinney where,
several years ago, Celie had led Master James and Miss
Katherine so sadly astray.

The fire in the kitchen range which stood in the fireplace
recess illuminated the cosy room. Coals kept to glowing
embers whilst Celie and Cec were out would be replenished
and the flames would leap merrily, yellow and green and
blue. The kettle would soon be singing on the central fire
and a pan of stew or a casserole, tucked into the oven
first thing to slow cook, would signal to the hungry man
and child that their bellies would not be empty this night.
The ginger tabby would rise to greet them, purring for her
supper and father and daughter would soon be at the table
tucking into the good heartening meal Cook made sure they
ate. What the servants in the kitchen put inside them, so
did Cec and Celie Marlow. There would be fresh bread,
brought over from the "big house", an apple cobbler, or
a chunk of Cook's plum cake, rich with brandy and solid
with fruit.

Above the length of the fireplace was a wooden mantelpiece
and arranged on this were an assortment of Cec and Mary
Marlow's treasures, made the more precious by her untimely
death. A wooden clock, an ornamental brass kettle, a toby jug,
candlesticks, a souvenir mug with Her Majesty's face painted
on it, a china lady with a parasol and a blue-and-white plate in
a willow pattern.

The table was covered by a chenille cloth when the meal
was finished and on it Celie would spread her pencils and
exercise books and do her homework. Cec would pick
up the *Liverpool Echo*, three days old and read in turn
by Mr Latimer, Reuben Ash and himself. When he had
done with it, it would be passed to George Ellis in the
stables.

And Celie had grown and thrived in the measured affection which was all her Pa could give her, unaware that there was any other sort between father and child, or even between man and woman.

Chapter Four

Over the next few years they grew like weeds, Cook was fond of saying, Dan and Celie, and not only them, but the children in the "front" house. Young Master Thomas and Master James had gone off to board at the preparatory school to which all the Latimer boys were sent, leaving only the "babies" in the nursery and the girls in the schoolroom under the supervision of Miss Gibson who was employed by Mrs Latimer as their governess. Miss Anne had put up her hair and had been deemed mature enough to finish with her education. She was occupied with her mother in the endless trivial pursuits ladies of their class followed. Their day was punctuated by regular changes of costume, for the gown a lady put on for breakfast could not be worn for luncheon, nor would the clothes she wore for luncheon be suitable for tea and the tea-gown, worn only for a few hours, would be unacceptable at dinner! They spent their time reading, doing fine needlework, writing letters, playing the piano or a genteel game of croquet on the lawn if the weather was fine. They took "carriage exercise", paid and received calls and did charitable work for the poor and needy of Liverpool, of whom there were a great many. They went shopping, of course, which took up a lot of their time.

Mr Latimer was the head of the household, at least in theory, and it was his natural right – again in theory – to be obeyed, not only by his wife, but by his children. The Latimers took a great pride in their family name which was old and honourable and they lived the busy, community life of a large upper middle-class family, as did their friends. A close eye was kept on their young unmarried daughters and elaborate steps were taken by Mr and Mrs Latimer to see that Miss Anne, ready now for the marriage market, met only male friends who were socially acceptable. Under proper supervision, naturally. They spent a great deal of their time at family tea parties, dinners and dances, outings, picnics and other social occasions and should their daughter have shown signs of forming an undesirable attachment, which might have been thought to be impossible, so closely was she guarded, she would have been taken severely to task, if not by Mr Latimer who was known to be lax, then by her mother, who was not.

In most households, at least those that Cook knew of and had worked in, the concept of family life was almost sacred and there was no song more popular than "Home, sweet home", the words of which both Miss Prudence and Miss Katherine were stitching into their samplers, and which, when finished, would be hung on the nursery wall beside those done by Miss Anne. It was customary to expect from all children the strictest submission to a parent's will, obedience to one's father – in the Latimers' case, to one's mother – being held as essential. So what had gone wrong in this family? Cook was heard to say several times a week when her kitchen was invaded, not only by the four older children but by Mr Latimer's two younger sons, now that they were breeched and could escape Nanny Ella. The trouble was, of course, that Nanny Ella was getting "past it"! Cook confided to Celie who was, at almost fourteen, working full time in the kitchen now.

'I was half expecting them to offer you nursery maid,' Cook added, standing back to admire the fine intricacy of spun sugar icing she had just put on a cake for Miss Margaret's birthday which was the next day.

Celie looked up from the biscuits on which she was piping the prancing figure of a clown. It was delicate work needing a steady eye and a steadier hand. The biscuits had been iced in pink, yellow, brown and white and each surface was decorated with the clown in two contrasting colours. White and yellow on brown, brown and yellow on white, pink and brown on yellow.

She was so absorbed with her own artistry she had even piped in a tiny smiling mouth, dots for eyes and a flower growing out of each clown's hat. She was not, strictly speaking, on duty at that moment for it was her day off but Cook had allowed her to bake and decorate the biscuits for Miss Margaret's birthday since Cook had to admit the girl really was coming on a treat and should be encouraged in her chosen profession.

She had grown twelve inches in the last four years, standing just over five feet two which it seemed was to be her full height. She was still a child in many ways, slender and budding into girlish maturity, inclined to seek Cook's company rather than that of her contemporaries. To be, as the other servants called it, "stand-offish", which was really no more than a natural reserve, a shyness which had come upon her as she entered adolescence.

'Me?' she said in amazement. 'Why me? I don't want to be a nursemaid,' for didn't they all know what Celie Marlow wanted, and it had nothing to do with the nursery. She was only really completely happy when she was in the kitchen with Cook, being allowed to "try her hand" at the simpler jobs Cook put her way, and the idea of being shut up at the top of the house with Nanny Ella and those two "holy terrors" was something she could hardly bear to contemplate. A *cook* she meant to be, just like Cook, only better, she thought privately, creating her own recipes and becoming famous for them. Oh, no, she'd not end up playing "slavey" to Nanny Ella and those lads who came to cause mayhem in the kitchen. She'd hand in her notice first, really she would.

The biscuits finished, Celie stood deferentially beside Jess Harper with a look of rapt attention on her young face. Cook, the cake put to one side, whilst the icing set, had begun to put together a steak and kidney pie for the servants' dinner and in Cook's opinion, many of the what she called "ordinary" dishes, the plain dishes which did not come under the title of *gourmet* food, took the most talent to produce and the homely steak and kidney pie was one of them.

'Watch this, girl,' for she never missed an opportunity to pass on to Celie a word of counsel on her own particular vocation. 'The pastry must be short enough to fall apart when the knife cuts it and yet not too short so that it sticks to the rolling pin on the board. Too much flour will make it heavy, see, and never, never put anything but shin of beef and lamb's kidney beneath that crust.'

'But won't the shin be tough, Cook?'

That's what Cook liked about the girl. She put her finger right on the nub of the matter, seeing things at once that Patsy took for granted. Shin of beef *was* tough unless it was put in a slow oven to cook in its own delicious juices for at least five hours. Shin of beef was the tastiest, the most nourishing part of the beast and cheap too, though that did not concern Cook. It made the best steak and kidney pie which, served with a heaped pile of fluffy mashed potatoes and savoy cabbage, boiled for exactly the right length of time, which Cook of course had down to a fine art, chopped with butter and pepper, was a meal which the Prince of Wales, known to be a lover of good food, would not be too proud to sit down to.

'And there's something else, girl.' Cook's voice lowered almost to a whisper and she looked about the kitchen to where the others, well used to Celie's ways by now, were bustling about in the intense activity which preceded the serving of every meal in the Latimer household, no matter how many were to sit down to it. Patsy lifted the lid and inspected the contents of each pan simmering on top of the oven, and Dorcas was chopping parsley and in the scullery Kate was bossing the new girl whose name was Isabel, but called Belle by them all.

Celie crouched at Cook's shoulder, watching with the fascination of an acolyte being initiated into some religious order, as Cook took a half a teaspoon of something from a small canister and put it in with the cooked steak and kidney.

'You put that in all your meat pies, girl, and you'll have them clamouring for more every time,' Cook whispered, then to Celie's delighted amazement, she winked, drawing Celie into a cosy conspiracy.

'But it's . . .'

'Ssh, ssh, girl! It's something I learned from a great cook

when I was a girl and I've kept it a secret until now. There's many a person I've given my recipes for steak and kidney to, but I never tell them about . . . you know what. They're always mystified when theirs don't turn out like mine.' She nudged Celie and winked again. 'You only need a level teaspoon or it's too salty, so mind.'

'Yes, Cook.'

'Now just slip into the dining room and see if everything's in place on the table'

'But Dorcas . . .'

'Never you mind Dorcas. Go on, do as you're told. It's time you had a look at the "other" side. The family's not in yet. They've all gone to church and they'll not be back for another hour at least, so have a good look round. Go on, you'll meet no one.'

Celie had never been into the "front" house before and she stepped with cautious hesitation through the green baize door which separated it from the back. The hallway was dim and hushed, wide, lit only by the fanlight over the front door and two long narrow windows on either side of it. There was a deep porch beyond and Celie could just see the four slender columns which supported it. They were a familiar sight to her from the garden where she had once helped her father to prick in his seedlings but they looked strange from *this* side.

She gazed about her with growing pleasure. She had come into the hall from beneath the curving centre staircase and on either side of the hall, leading to the front door, were other doors, all of them standing open, revealing, as she peeped into them, the drawing room, the library, the dining room, Mr Latimer's study and Mrs Latimer's small parlour.

You could tell at once which rooms were used by Mr Latimer and which by Mrs Latimer, Celie decided. The drawing room was emphatically for ladies, fitted and furnished in a most feminine way. It was here that Mrs Latimer received her carriage call ladies and where they took tea together. There was a piano with a lovely peacock shawl draped across it, which Celie had heard Mrs Latimer played for the entertainment of her guests in the evening at what she called her "musicales". There were chairs of spindly

legged gilt, dainty rosewood tables of all shapes and sizes
on which a hundred years of polishing had put a mirror-like
shine. There was silk and delicate chintzes, for parts of Briar
Lodge had been furnished before the coming of their present
Queen and the taste for the solid, overwhelming, ornamental
grandeur which had developed during her reign. Only in Mrs
Latimer's parlour were displayed the opulence and deep rich
colours which were so fashionable nowadays. The library was
a marvel of hushed reverence to the occupation of reading
and the young girl who had never in her life seen more than
two or three books together at one time, was overwhelmed.
On every wall except the one that bore the long, elegant
Georgian windows and through which she could see the wide
sweep of the lawn rolling down to the small lake, known as
the "pond", were deep shelves and every shelf was crammed
with books, hundreds, thousands of them, Celie supposed,
wondering why Mary and Lily the two "dailies" who had the
cleaning of this room, as well as the rest of the house, had
not told them about it. She would if it was her. She wouldn't
be able to stop herself talking about it if it was her! Dorcas,
who was often summoned to fetch coffee to Mr Latimer in
the library, had never mentioned it either. There were work
tables and writing desks on which journals were scattered,
of what sort Celie could not imagine. Glass-fronted cabinets
contained besides books, a miscellany of objects, carved and
intricate, some of them, with grimacing faces, smiling faces,
little dogs and flasks and openwork balls with other smaller
balls inside them and Celie wondered how such a thing could
be achieved. They looked foreign to her and she was not to
know that they came from Japan.

In the fireplace which was enormous with a stone surround,
a cheerful fire blossomed though it did little to warm the area
more than a few feet away from the hearth. There were
deep leather armchairs, in which she could just imagine
herself curling up with one of these handsome books, and
rugs scattered all over the dark-stained wooden floors. A
large central chandelier hung from an acanthus leaf-strewn
central rosette, magnificent with twelve candle-laden arms to
light the room.

It was the same wherever she peeped. Elegance and comfort, crackling fires, deep carpets, clocks ticking, harmony and peace. The large table in the dining room was set for the family's luncheon, gleaming with cutlery and crystal and white damask napkins. The walls were papered with what looked like silk and from the three sash windows which lined one wall, she could see the terrace. On it were tastefully arranged ornamental tubs of different sizes planted with rounded shrubs. Wide steps led down to the garden of pathways and ornamental beds which Dan and her Pa kept in meticulous symmetry and order, with lawns on either side. There were trees beyond the lawns and the delicate outline of a folly.

On the floor of the dining room and surrounded by highly polished wood was a rich Turkey carpet. Celie wanted to stroke the soft drape of the curtains which were in some lovely rich material in a shade of deep plum but she did not dare. She stood rooted to the spot just inside the door of each room, breathing in the splendour, the bright colours, the fragrance of the bowls of flowers, grown by her own father, the dazzle of silver and intricately engraved crystal, the gloss and glory and wonder in which the Latimer family lived.

She was at the staircase which led gracefully up to the first floor, just about to put one hesitant foot on the bottom step, when the front door opened with an enthusiastic clatter and with the instinct of a young animal caught by a predator, she froze. Just where she was. One foot on the black-and-white tiled hall floor, the other on the deep pile of the dark blue carpet which went up the staircase. Her heart lurched sickeningly in her breast then began to knock itself inside its cage like some frantic bird doing its best to get out and she simply did not know what to do. She had wandered in a spellbound daze round the perimeter of the large, square hallway, studying the majestically ticking grandfather clock, trailing a reverent finger across the polished surface of a round silkwood table with delicately turned legs. She had stood before the marble fireplace in which yet another fire glowed, gazed at the moulded arches, painted white, the hanging glass lamps, bemused, bewitched, unaware of how much time had passed and now, in the trance the beauty of the house had cast about her she was discovered in her innocent but surely forbidden entry into the world of the Latimer family.

'Hello,' a young and cheerful voice called, and the front door closed just as enthusiastically as it had opened. 'Hello . . . Mama . . . Papa . . .,' a cultured voice, a male voice and though she had never actually spoken to him since he had gone away to school when she was barely more than a toddler, she knew it was Richard Latimer. Young Master Richard who was probably twenty-two years old and who, when he left school, had become an officer in the 2nd Battalion, the King's Regiment (Liverpool) and was now Second Lieutenant Richard Latimer. He wore the smart undress uniform of an infantry officer. He was a gentleman and they, of course, made the best officers in the world, or so had said the Duke of Wellington, for they needed no other qualification or training than the upbringing which made them natural leaders, and providing an officer showed courage in battle, nothing else really mattered. Twenty-two years old, Second Lieutenant Richard Latimer had not yet been tested.

Celie turned very slowly and as she moved, her white dress drifted in a misted haze against the dark blue of the stair carpet and the young soldier saw her.

'Hello . . . ?' he said again, this time with a questioning note in his voice. Celie had on her "best dress", her Sunday dress, made for her by Mrs Ash who was clever with a needle. It was in two pieces, a separate bodice and skirt, a style which was becoming increasingly popular, made of a dressed cotton muslin known as "batiste". It was simple with tight-fitting sleeves and a round neck framed by a small frill. Around the waist was a sash of blue jaconet taken from a dress of Miss Anne's which she had outgrown years ago and which had been handed over to Mrs Ash to be cut up for one of her own girls since Mrs Latimer did not "pass on" to her younger daughters what had been worn by her eldest.

Celie's hair was still cut short, a cap of dark glossy curls which swirled about her head and fell over her ears and forehead in soft feathers, revealing the white, satin texture of her neck. Though she was only just fourteen, her body was already maturing. Her tiny breasts pressed against the fabric of her bodice and the sweet girlish curve of her shoulders was proudly set. But she was still awkward, only just across the threshold between childhood and young girlhood and it showed in the way she moved as she took another faltering step in the gloom. Despite this and because of the way she was dressed, he took her for a friend of his sisters and he smiled engagingly.

'Good morning and who are you?' he asked her, 'and what are you doing all alone in the dark? Where's Anne . . . ?' Or was she one of Prudence's intimates since she looked to be more or less of the same age?

'She's out.' It was all she could manage to stutter from between lips which were stiff with alarm. Her mouth was dry and her heart would just not settle down. He was so . . . so . . . *magnificent*. So handsome . . . and tall . . . his head almost brushing the glass of the hanging lamp . . . and his smile . . . his dashing smile . . .

Richard Latimer, Second Lieutenant Richard Latimer was the embodiment of what all young girls, as they lie in their virginal beds at night, dream of. He was a beautiful young man, the darling of his mother's heart not just because he was her first born but because from birth he had drawn admiring murmurs from everyone who had been invited to view him. And yet the beauty of him was not of the fairy prince variety, it was completely and absolutely male with even a touch of earthiness in it though his mother would not have admitted it, even to herself. He was tall, long-boned, hard-muscled and his shoulder had broadened from the day he had begun to row for his school at the age of fourteen. He had a narrow waist and the tight trousers he wore clung to his hips and strong thighs, clearly revealing the delightful shape of his slim buttocks. His legs were long and shapely and were in exact proportion to his body. He had deep brown eyes, glowing with health and contentment and his strong uncompromising young mouth had an endearing curl at each corner as though to announce that he could not be more pleased with himself and the world in which he lived. The skin of his face was smooth and well shaven, the colour amber-tinted, again almost swarthy and his dark hair curled crisply in the nape of his neck. He was pliable with youth and bounteous energy and an added challenging toughness and durability seven years at public school and four years in the army had given him. As he moved towards Celie, he did so with a tensile spring to his step, light and buoyant, his movement as graceful as a cat. He was put together with the measured symmetry, the balance and composition of a thoroughbred and his wit and charm matched his supreme looks.

He wore the undress uniform of the Regiment in which he was an officer. A medium grey frock coat, double-breasted and reaching to just twelve inches above the ground. Removing it he let it fall carelessly to a convenient chair, revealing beneath it a scarlet tunic with a high stiff collar and a crimson silk net sash over his left shoulder. Round his waist was a sword belt of white enamelled leather. His trousers were dark blue, narrow, with a red welt down the outside of each leg and on his head was a straight-sided forage-cap with a band of black oak-leaf pattern around it. As he spoke to her he whipped it courteously from his head. He was only a second lieutenant and so as yet, bore no badge of rank.

'Where are the others?' he asked almost in a whisper as he moved to stand before her. It was as though he had interrupted a game of hide and seek, his eyes twinkling with good humour and an admiration he could not quite conceal, for she was an amazingly lovely girl. He had never seen her before since he was sure he would have remembered those incredibly wide smoky grey eyes if he had. They were set in lashes so thick and black they almost touched her eyebrows and spread a dark fan nearly to her cheekbone. Her skin was without blemish, smooth and fine and so white the full coral pink of her mouth was startling against it. At her cheekbone was a flush of rose, and her hair! Cut short and close to her head, yet thick and curling, dark as his own but where the light struck it, streaked with rich chestnut. It fell across her brow, a strand catching in her eyelashes and she blinked. Without thought, he lifted a hand and gently pushed it back from her forehead. Her lips parted in a soundless "oh" and in the eerie hush which wrapped about them, he bent his head.

He would have kissed her, he knew he would, and afterwards he felt a deep flood of shame since she was no more than a child, but though he had not heard the carriage, nor indeed anything but the deep, slow tick of the clock, the front door burst open and James came through it at a gallop. Behind him was his mother and behind her his father and the rest of his brothers and sisters.

Even then Celie did not waken from the spell he had cast about her. Though she heard them and was aware of the presence of someone other than this tall stranger, she could not seem to care about them, nor tear herself away from the glow of his eyes and the smiling curve of his mouth. It was not a sensual feeling which had crept into Celie Marlow's heart since she was too young and inexperienced for that. It had none of the carnal element which stirs between a man and a woman but at the same time she had known with some female instinct, not yet awakened fully, that he had been about to kiss her and that she had wanted it.

Richard Latimer was a man who was not unfamiliar with matters of the flesh, for young as he was he had had his share of sexual adventures. Women liked him and who could blame them? He was at this moment involved with a young married woman whose husband, an officer in the 1st Battalion King's (Liverpool) Regiment, was away quelling the riots in Belfast but no member of the opposite sex had moved him like this young girl had done. Nevertheless he was a soldier. He had been taught to make quick decisions, to use not only his sword and revolver, but his wits; to "muddying" the waters of a situation so that no one, including the enemy quite knew what he was about. He was the first to recover of them all, even young James.

'Mama . . . Papa . . . how well you both look . . .' managing to turn and stand so that the bewitched child, whoever she was, was behind him, giving her a chance to pull her own wits about her. 'I've just this moment come though the door . . .' strolling across to kiss his mama and take his father's hand, all the while shielding the girl from the shrewd and piercing gaze of his mother who was the one to be reckoned with. 'I've left my stuff on the porch. It's a wonder you didn't fall over it . . .'

'Yes, darling, we saw it.'

'Run through to the kitchen, young James, and fetch the lad to bring it in, there's a good fellow . . .'

'There is a bell at your elbow, Richard. There is no need to send James.' Phyllis Latimer's eyes rested fondly on the erect and soldierly figure of her son, distracted as he knew she would be from the "girl". By now his quick brain had realised that she could not possibly be a friend of any of his sisters since they were all here, milling about him, and the only other young females in the house were servants. God Almighty, she was a servant! Not only a child still probably in the schoolroom, but a servant and he had been caught almost in the act of kissing her.

Celie stood where he had left her and gradually the mist of confused enchantment parted and fell away and she was herself again. Celie Marlow, the gardener's lass, soon – hopefully – to be kitchen maid to this family who were swarming about the hallway and the tall soldier who had taken his mother's arm, doing his best to lead her into the drawing room, was the son of the house and nothing to do with her.

But Phyllis Latimer, though charmed at the unexpected arrival of her son, was still alert to the strangeness of finding her gardener's daughter standing in her hall. Of course, never in her wildest dreams would she have believed what she had thought she *saw*, as she entered her own house, but nevertheless, Celie Marlow had no right to be here. Phyllis Latimer had never forgotten that day when this very girl had taken her own gently reared children and subjected them to God alone knew what tomfoolery, and now here she was gawking in the hallway as though she had as much right here as Dorcas or Fanny.

'Just a moment, darling,' she said to her son, turning back to where Celie stood. Richard turned with her and again, as his eyes met Celie's, he felt the impact of her fresh, fragile loveliness and had to look away in case what had almost happened should be revealed, not by him, but by her who was so young.

'What are you doing here, Celie?' Mrs Latimer asked in her autocratic manner.

Celie! Good God, not that wisp of a child who had clung to the gardener's hand . . . his daughter . . . yes, her name had been Celie . . . but his mother was speaking.

'And who gave you permission to come into the front house?' Mrs Latimer continued, ready to be cutting.

'Cook, madam. She asked me to check on the dining table.'

'Why should she do that, it is Dorcas's job?'

'Yes, madam, but Cook wanted me to see how it should be done.' Her chin lifted in a way which had defiance written in its firm line and Richard groaned inwardly.

'I see, well, you'd best get back to the kitchen. Let Cook know we will eat in half an hour.' Mrs Latimer turned away. 'Now then darling, tell us what you are doing home so unexpectedly. Come along, Mr Latimer,' to her husband, 'Let's all have a sherry before luncheon. Anne, ring the bell for Dorcas, will you, dear. Do you know, I really think we should have a butler, my dear,' Celie heard her say to Mr Latimer, 'or at least a footman . . .'

'Well?' Cook said when Celie returned to the kitchen. 'What did you think?'

'What about, Cook?' Celie answered casually, drifting over to the table. She was back in familiar surroundings now and therefore safe and she slowly let out her breath on a long sigh of bright-eyed bemusement. What had happened? What had it all been *about*? She had seen Master Richard a dozen times in the past years since he had gone away to school, in the garden and stable yard and had thought him quite unremarkable and no different from his brothers. The younger ones she knew better, of course, because they had been in and out of the kitchen when she was younger. She had seen them all in the gardens and woods, climbing trees when Nanny Ella was not dancing attendance, then they had gone away to school and it was only during the holidays that she had caught glimpses of them about the place. Master Richard had been almost a man then, far above her, remote as a star as he came and went with his dashing school friends and when he had gone into the army, he had not been home a great deal and when he had, his life certainly did not touch hers. Dorcas talked of him, of course, for she and Fanny served at meal times, saying how handsome he looked in his uniform and how the young ladies hung on his every word. The apple of his mama's eye, Dorcas said, and a son any man would be proud of.

'What about? *What about*!' Cook was incensed. 'Lands sakes girl, where have you been? Down to the pierhead to see the boats? The house, of course. What did you reckon to the drawing room?'

'Lovely, Cook,' Celie answered dreamily, picking an apple from the bowl on the table and sinking her teeth into it.

'Is that all you've got to say about it, girl? What about all those books in the library?' Cook was occupied with the greengage pudding and vanilla cream she intended to give the family for dessert. Hare soup to start with, made from the meat of a freshly killed hare delivered to her kitchen door only that morning, and in it would be lean gravy beef, ham and plenty of vegetables, good stuff for growing children since she had been told by Mrs Latimer that they were to luncheon *en famille* today. There were roast ribs of beef ready to come out of the oven and in a moment she would mix up the batter for the Yorkshire pudding to go with it. Horseradish sauce, french beans and roast potatoes. A simple meal but suitable for a family gathering.

Celie was beginning to come out of the dream-like state into which the encounter with Master Richard had spun her and it was beginning to assume its proper proportions. She smiled at her own foolishness, for what had there been about it to make her so woolly-headed? He was only Master Richard, after all, and nothing to do with her. It had been like a dream really, one of those which are so nice you don't want to wake up from them. A dream or a very simple occurrence which she herself had *dreamed* into something more than it was. Master Richard had merely greeted her, asked her who she was . . . hadn't he? Been polite and smiled . . . but he had . . . and the memory tripped her pulse a little . . . brushed back her hair

. . . what of it? She was a little girl to him . . . like one of his sisters . . . but had he not . . . ? don't be foolish, nothing had happened which she could not tell Cook about and as though to prove it to herself she heard her own voice say,

'Master Richard's home, Cook, and Mrs Latimer says to have luncheon in half an hour.'

'Lands sakes, girl, you didn't meet the family!' Cook turned, the flour in one hand, a spoon in the other, ready to begin the delicate task of making Yorkshire pudding which was, again, a simple, homely dish but one which needed care to produce.

'I was in the hall when they came in.' The statement included Master Richard in it, just as though he had entered at the same time as his family and it was almost as though he had, and that the dream-like quality of what had happened between them had not taken place at all.

'And what did Madam say?' Cook was aghast. Celie Marlow was the lowest of the low in the ranks of the servants and certainly had no right in the front house and who would be blamed but her if Mrs Latimer took exception to it.

'Nothing. She didn't seem to mind . . .' because she was under the sweet enchanting spell her eldest son knew how to weave, but of course Celie's young mind did not think in those exact terms.

'Thank God for that. Now put your apron on and reach me those eggs will you, girl, and get the butter from the pantry, and it's no good sitting there with your knife and fork in your hand, Dan Smith, because there's no steak and kidney pie for you until the family's been served.'

Celie smiled at Dan who winked at her, then, tying the apron strings about her waist, she moved on light feet towards the pantry.

Chapter Five

When Celie had left school at the age of fourteen, she didn't know whether to be pleased or sorry about it because in a way she'd enjoyed learning and Miss Entwistle had told her it was a shame she couldn't have continued since she'd got a good brain. Some girls, Miss Entwistle said, went on until they were sixteen or seventeen and a few, really clever ones, really *lucky* ones, even went to college, just like gentlemen did, but of course, not girls in Celie's situation and though she had not voiced this last, Celie knew what she meant.

For a year after that she continued with her work as scullery maid, skivvy really, at everyone's beck and call, even Kate's who, now that Celie Marlow was a "proper" servant just like her, felt she was entitled to fling an order or two at her, especially as, when Patsy left, Kate expected to be put up to kitchen maid. It was not just the relatively light jobs such as peeling spuds that Celie must now share but the scrubbing. The scrubbing of the kitchen floor, the scullery, the pantry, the still room, the laundry, the kitchen tables and chopping boards, the scouring of the mountains of saucepans, steamers, frying pans, baking tins, roasting pans and all the utensils Cook used in her preparation of three hearty meals a day.

She cleaned windows and washed down walls, blackleaded the cast-iron kitchen range and brought in the coal which heated it. The enormous machine was the bane of Kate's life and she was only too glad to pass the job onto Celie, as Patsy had passed it on to *her* when she was a newcomer. The fire in it, which burned all day, was left to go out at night and every morning at precisely six o'clock, which was when her day started, Celie had the task of cleaning it, sifting the ashes, then re-laying and lighting the fire before she began her other duties. The cast iron must be cleaned with blacklead which was rubbed in, then brushed and buffed with a felt pad, the brass fender round the range had to be polished and all these tasks must be accomplished before Cook came into the kitchen to start *her* day's labours. There was the mincer which clamped on to the kitchen table, to be cleaned, choppers, slicers, corers and all the gadgets Cook used during the day; the heavy stockpot which was always kept simmering on the range to ensure a constant supply of soups and broths and which was emptied into a crockery container last thing at night, to be returned to the scoured pan the next day to heat up again.

The kitchen was a constant hive of industry from six thirty in the morning when the rest of the servants began their day until the last pan was cleaned and stacked neatly away as Cook liked it at about nine thirty in the evening. Of course, they were not at it for the whole day since Cook allowed them half an hour here and there when the pace slackened and now that Celie was a full-time servant and spent much of her time in the kitchen, she ate with the other servants and the meal times were another rest period in their arduous day.

'Your Pa had better do the same, Celie, tell him, eat with us, I mean. That's if he would like to,' for Cec was something of a solitary man and sure enough Cec declined, saying he would either knock a bit of something up for himself or, if Cook would be so kind, take a dish of "tatie hot-pot," or mutton stew, or scouse, whatever the servants were having, and warm it up in his own oven.

In April Patsy was to take up employment as cook in the household of a young doctor and his family in Rodney Street and though far from the standard of Cook herself, she was considered to be competent enough to manage the job. She had been Cook's right-hand woman for six years, ever since she had been made up in her turn from scullery maid at the age of fourteen. The young doctor couldn't afford much, to be honest, Cook had confided to Cec, when the question of

Celie's future was discussed, but Patsy would do well enough. Of course it would be a bit ticklish on how best to break it to Kate that she was being passed over, for the young scullery maid fully expected Patsy's job to be hers.

Jess Harper had gradually been made aware of Celie's particular talent in the culinary arts. Indeed she had watched her for years, *chided* her for years for getting under her and Patsy's feet and seeing which way the wind blew, she wasn't going to pass up the chance to train such a promising young lass as Celie, just to avoid ructions in the kitchen, she said to Celie's father. Another skivvy would be taken on to fill Celie's place. Fanny and Dorcas would continue as housemaids, working for the most part in the "front" house, and Mary and Lil at the heavy cleaning.

There *were* ructions and for several minutes it was touch and go whether Kate, whose temper was quick and hot, would strike either Cook or the flushed and delighted Celie. Kate had been strutting round the kitchen for weeks, especially during the last one, confidently begging Patsy to pass on any tips she might have, tossing her head and letting Celie Marlow know that when she, Kate Mossop, was kitchen maid and Celie still, despite her elevation to Kate's old job, *her* minion, she would have her hopping from morning till night. The new skivvy, Belle, two years younger than Celie, was inclined still, missing her family in Wavertree from whom she had never before been separated, to lean over the scullery sink and drip desolate tears into the spud water. She looked up to Celie, who was kind to her, as though she was as high in the echelon of servants as Cook herself, which Celie quite enjoyed since she had been the lowest of them all for so long. When Cook called them all together on Patsy's last day, Belle huddled close to Celie's shoulder as the only steady thing in this new world of shifting quicksand which was the Briar Lodge kitchen. She really had no idea who was who – except Celie – and Cook's words passed over her homesick head like the clouds in the sky.

'Now we all know Patsy is to start her brand new job on Monday and right well she's done so we all wish her every happiness,' Cook began. 'The mistress would like a word later, Patsy,' turning to the beaming kitchen maid, 'but now there is the question of who is to take Patsy's place. I have discussed this with Mrs Latimer . . .' noticing out of the corner of her eye the way Kate's bosom rose in gratification and the complacent manner in which her head turned to look about her at the other servants, 'and we have decided that the job is to go to Celie Marlow. I know she is young but after watching her over many years, I have formed an opinion that she has an aptitude for . . .'

'*What?*' Kate's face had turned the colour of the tomatoes which were waiting to be sliced on the table. She whirled about in disbelief, looking first at Patsy and Dorcas, then at Fanny all of whom cast their eyes down, unable to meet hers. She couldn't believe her ears, her expression said, and for confirmation that she'd not heard correctly, she turned back to Cook.

'What . . . ?' she said again, her usual eloquence on anything she thought was detrimental to *her* and her rightful place in the order of things swept away by her amazement.

'I think you heard me, Kate. The mistress and I have . . .'

'But what about me? I've been skivvy, then scullery maid since I was twelve and Patsy's job was mine . . .'

'No, it was not, Kate. A job has to be earned . . .'

'An' she's earned it, has she? Bloody favouritism, that's all it is, an' it's not fair.' She turned ferociously on Celie, her face white now with her venomous rage. Kate Mossop was sixteen, not an especially pretty girl, but one with unusual looks which, in certain circumstances, could turn to real beauty. Her hair was so pale and silvery it was almost white. When she removed the pins from it at night, it hung in a straight and heavy curtain down to her buttocks, defying her every attempt with curling tongs and papers. She wore it in an enormous plait under her scullery maid's cap, dragged back from her face in which extraordinary eyes gleamed. They were a pale, cat-like green, long and narrow and surrounded by pale brown lashes. When she had on her scullery maid's outfit, she was nondescript, insipid almost and exciting no glances from any man. What she did on her day off, no one knew, since she made friends with none of the girls in the kitchen. She was uneducated, barely able to read or write since attendance at school was not yet compulsory, just available, but she was sharp, shrewd and self-seeking and she was incensed at being passed over in favour of fourteen-year-old Celie Marlow. She'd noticed, as who had not, Celie's interest in anything to do with the cooking side of the kitchen work but never in her wildest dreams or nightmares, had she considered that Cook would put the kid in the place that was undeniably Kate Mossop's. She had heard Cook tell Celie off for hanging about the kitchen table and the range, saying that it was Patsy's domain and not Celie Marlow's, and now the little bitch was to be given *her*, Kate Mossop's, job. So what was to become of Kate Mossop? Was she to stay bloody scullery maid for the rest of her life, stuck in that bloody scullery, wearing her bloody sacking apron, whilst Celie Marlow queened it over her, and her two years younger than herself? It wasn't to be borne.

She said so. She pushed out a truculent jaw and said so.

'It's not bloody fair an' if you think I'm going to take orders from some bum-sucking kid, then . . .'

Celie's eyes began to narrow dangerously, surprisingly, for she was not a girl for quarrelling, and her small jaw tightened. She was made up with the idea of being kitchen maid and learning to cook properly. She had always been intrigued by the creation of a perfect dish, or sauce, or the result of the care and talent Cook herself used in the preparing and cooking of a meal. She knew Cook *had* favoured her somewhat above the others but then that was because Celie had shown her interest, but she had never imagined – hoped perhaps – that she would be given what had been taken for granted as Kate's job. And if Kate Mossop thought she could insult Celie Marlow and get away with it, then she was badly mistaken.

'Don't you call me names, Kate Mossop. Look to your own ability before you go abusing mine. Perhaps I shape better than you with a mixing spoon, have you thought of that?'

'I'm as good as you, any day of the week, so there's no need to go using them big words and anyone here will . . .'

'Is that so, well Cook doesn't think so and neither does Mrs Latimer.'

'You crawling little bitch. You smarmy, crawling . . .'

'If you call working hard . . .'

'*Hard*! You don't know what hard work is . . .'

'And you *do*! Times I've stood beside you and watched you idling the hours away while I'm going hell for leather . . .'

'You're nothing but a . . .'

'*Kate, Celie,*' Cook said warningly, understanding how Kate felt. Kate was, despite her tendency to create arguments and strife amongst the servants, a good worker and because of it, Cook did her best to keep her own temper in check. 'That's enough, both of you. I have decided to . . .'

'That was *my* job, Cook, and you know it.'

The trouble was, Cook *did*, but she was not about to let a scullery maid, despite her own slight feelings of guilt, dictate to her, and in front of the other servants too. If it had not been for the awkwardness of the situation there was no doubt that she would have sacked Kate on the spot and reprimanded Celie severely for their rudeness, their offensive language; but Jess Harper was a fair woman and in the circumstances she decided to overlook it.

'That's enough, Kate. I have told you the situation and that is the end of it. I have no need to explain my actions to you or anyone else in this house except the mistress. Belle is to work under you as Celie did, but I have this to add. If one of the housemaids, either Fanny or Dorcas, should . . . well, if there is ever a place in the "front" house, *and* you shape yourself and show me that you are capable of earning such a place, then you will be the first to be considered for it. And that is all I have to say on the matter. Now, back to your work. Enough time has been wasted as it is. Patsy, start mixing the batter will you, and Celie . . .' evidently feeling Celie's job might as well begin now '. . . fetch the damsons, the plums and redcurrants from the pantry to be washed. We'll have a baked batter pudding for dinner. Don't forget to sift the flour, Patsy . . .' giving the maid instructions, as she had done a thousand times before, just as though Patsy was not off next week to be Cook in her own kitchen.

Celie was allowed to wear the neat, ankle-length grey cotton dress of the kitchen maid on the following Monday.

The full, waisted apron covered her to her boots and the little frilled cap to which her new position entitled her bobbed merrily as she took her place beside Cook as her assistant. The dress had a high neck from which it was buttoned in a long, graceful row down across her neat breasts to her waist. It had gathered sleeves which could be turned back to the elbow if necessary. There was pretty tucking on the bodice, for Mrs Latimer did not care to have her servants in inferior uniforms, not unless it was a "dirty" job when the enormous sacking apron was, of course, a necessity.

Celie could not help throwing a triumphant look at Kate who, crashing about in the scullery beside the terrified Belle, gave the appearance of a wild animal barely restrained by the bars of its cage and which, when they were opened, would fly at her victim's throat with the greatest of pleasure.

Celie loved her new job and it appeared to love Celie, for almost overnight she began to develop her own style and imagination in the dishes she produced and it brought out in her a quiet confidence which was in direct contrast to the child who had been at everyone's beck and call for so long. She was still at Cook's of course, but even Dorcas and Fanny, who were both almost twenty, knew that Celie Marlow was destined to be, if Cook had anything to say about it, as good as herself, and though she was young yet, they treated her as an equal. She had her work to do, as they did, and was no longer the "kid" who had run here and there at their bidding.

She thrived on it, becoming as bright and rosy as one of her Pa's polished russet apples, her snowy white apron gleaming about her young hips in a graceful fall as she bustled to Cook's orders, many of which, as the months went by, she forestalled, performing them before Cook had time to speak. Her jaunty little cap clung precariously to her bouncing curls and her step was light and swift as she moved dexterously from one job to the next, learning, always learning, soaking up Cook's own knowledge like a dry sponge and yet always able to absorb more, it seemed.

She went with Cook into town when the larder needed restocking, moving into another world where Cook, as a member of staff of a prominent and wealthy household, was

treated with deference, seated in style at the counter of
the grand grocer's shop in Bold Street, whilst the aproned
shop assistants ran to fetch the commodities she ordered.
Not that Cook carried them back to Briar Lodge with her,
of course, but she did like to *see* the sago, the rice, the
split peas, the tea, the giant 14 pound loaves of sugar
she was about to purchase, before they were delivered
to her kitchen door. Many of the cooks and kitchenmaids
from other households who frequented the grocer's shop,
smaller households, naturally, carried away their purchases
in paper bags or cornets, but Cook, with over two dozen
mouths to feed each day – less when the older boys were
away – and requiring a delivery at least once a week was a
valued customer and treated as such.

'Always have a good look at everything you buy, Celie,
before you do so, and when it is delivered, check that the
quality is the same as what you inspected at the shop. Not
that Irwin's would send shoddy goods but it pays to let those
you buy from know that you are alert.'

They visited the food markets, purchasing, or at least
ordering, poultry and game, looking out for those which were
well fattened and tender.

'A young chicken is the most delicate and easy to digest
of all animal food, Celie, but it must also be tasty. At a year
old a cock is fit for nothing other than soup so you must
learn to recognise a bird's age. Now a capon, well fed and
well dressed, does not dry up as it gets older. Indeed, like
wine, it will mellow with age.'

Her sound advice poured from her in a never-ending flow
and she found an avid and receptive listener in Celie.

'See that duck there,' pointing to one among the dozens
which hung above their heads. The stall in the market was
crowded with everything from the homely rabbit and hare to
the plump goose, the more exotic lark and pigeon, grouse,
in season, partridge, pheasant and quail. Celie said she did.
'Now that looks right rank and oily to me and I wouldn't touch
it with a ten-foot barge-pole. You'll learn how to tell which is
a savoury one in time, and that goose, d'you see it,' whilst
the stallholder put his hands on his hips, his face reddening,

taking umbrage at what he thought was undeserved criticism
of his splendid birds, but Cook went on, undeterred by his
belligerence. 'Now that's what I call of the highest perfection.
It's in its full growth but it's not yet begun to harden.'

The stallholder, mollified, would be pleased to deliver a
brace to Briar Lodge, he said, and perhaps one of his fine
hares, Cook added, since she did love a dish of jugged hare.
It was the same at the fish market.

'Look and make sure there are plenty of scales on the fish,
girl, because if there's not, it's a sign that it's not fresh. A
good, fresh fish is always covered with scales. Now that
turbot there on the slab, that's a good size, it being what I
call "middling". No . . . no thank you . . .' waving away the
hovering stallholder who knew her for a good customer . . .
'I'm showing the girl here and I'm not yet ready to make a
purchase. Now see . . .' turning to Celie again '. . . if it's
too large, the meat will be tough and thready. Now when it's
soaked in salt and water it'll take off all the slime . . .' While
the man winked at Celie appreciatively, looking forward to the
day when *she* would be here in the place of the forbidding Mrs
Harper.

Celie's culinary education continued to widen, and not only
in the matter of purchasing and preparing the ingredients for
the meals served at the table of the Latimer family – and their
servants – but in that of the household budget. A good cook
who is in charge of the ordering must also be in control of
the accounts and Celie could soon add a column of figures
in her head as quickly as Cook. She wrote a neat, compact
hand and was not only polite in her dealings with tradesmen,
she was shrewd. She grew sleek and contented like a young,
well-tended cat, bright-eyed and lively, shining with good
health, for though she worked long, hard hours, she loved
what she did, which made those hours no hardship to her at
all. Her skin took on a fresh glowing, her hair, always glossy,
was burnished to the hue and shine of a dark horse-chestnut
and her slender figure ripened into womanhood. She might
have been born to it, Cook told Cec privately, so well did
she take to her new place in life, mixing on equal footing
with Dorcas and Fanny, and treating Belle, Mary and Lily,

who were now her subordinates, with a calm, diplomatic but firm resolve which offended no one.

She and Kate, however, kept a well-balanced distance between them like two young female animals of like strength who know that should they confront the challenge which sometimes crackled the air as they exchanged glances, it would not be Celie who would suffer. Kate kept well out of Celie's way and when Celie wanted something fetching or cleaning she asked Belle who was not only willing to be Celie's friend but her slave. Celie, though high above Belle in rank, at least in Belle's eyes, was approachable, ready even for a bit of a laugh when they had a moment to spare and Belle would have done anything for her. Kate ran about after Cook right willingly, the promise of becoming parlourmaid, should the chance arise, a shining star leading her on the path of cheerful, eager obedience.

Cook left matters as they were for now, keeping her eye on them both, watching which way the wind blew, ready to intervene if Kate caused trouble, but the weeks and months passed and the tension eased. A wise girl, Kate Mossop, Cook told herself, for jobs in a house such as Briar Lodge were hard to come by and the girl had been sensible enough to realise it.

Kate Mossop kept her thoughts, her plans, her dangerous venom to herself, even her eyes hooded and unreadable when they passed over Celie Marlow.

'I'm not having our Celie Marlow walking home by herself after dark,' Cec had said to Cook on Celie's first full day in the kitchen.

The light was gone from the sky by four thirty in the afternoon, it being the depth of winter and the path behind the house, across the wide lawns, through the vegetable gardens and spinney to the Marlow cottage was pitch black and isolated. Nearly a ten-minute walk and that was in broad daylight and who knew what might be lurking in the undergrowth, Cec added. One heard of such tales these days of young girls being molested, though Cook thought privately it was hardly likely in the security of the Latimer grounds and Celie knew every inch of the way, after all, having walked it since babyhood.

Certainly unescorted females moving about the streets of the city after dark put themselves in great danger, Cook was well aware, but not out here surely? Still she was Cec's girl and if he insisted that Celie must wait until he came across to fetch her then Cook must bow to his wishes. After all, he was her father, but it might prove awkward for if Celie was kept over, as sometimes happened, there was Cec sitting waiting for her, getting under everybody's feet, yawning and ready for his bed, looking pointedly at his watch time and again. Celie tried to hurry but there were often last-minute arrangements to be discussed between herself and Cook and Cook found herself longing for the light nights when Celie could walk home alone.

'I'll walk Celie home, Mr Marlow,' Dan said, after a particularly awkward moment when Cec, who should have known better, asked his daughter for the third time if she was to be much longer.

'About another half-hour, I should say, Pa.' Celie was irritated. 'Cook and I just want to go over these invoices from Irwin's.' It was ridiculous, in Celie's youthful opinion, for her Pa to have taken this protective attitude. Dear Lord, she'd been in those woods after dark a hundred times, though her Pa didn't know it, of course, and knew them like the back of her hand. She *liked* the woods and she liked to walk there and there was nothing in there to frighten the most nervous of women – a dormouse or two, rabbits and owls and such – and besides, her Pa worked a long day and at his age was ready for his chair by the fire. But no, he'd taken it into his head that she must be *escorted* home as if she wasn't at home wherever she happened to be on the Latimer property.

'Can they not be done in the morning, our Celie?' Cec's voice was quite sharp and Cook turned to look at him for he was usually the most even-tempered of men. 'Only I'm that tired,' and it was then that Dan made his offer.

Dan often stayed behind after the servants' evening meal, curling himself in the chimney corner with some book or other, preferring the bustle and companionship of the kitchen to the lonely quiet of his room over the coachhouse. He seemed to have the knack of turning himself off, so to speak, so that nothing disturbed his deep concentration of whatever he was reading. That is unless Celie Marlow's name was mentioned and then it was as though some connection, which he had severed as he opened the book, was joined together again, putting him once more in touch with the swirling activity about him.

Cec turned to look at him. They had been working together now for just over four years and Cec, especially these last few months, did not know how he would have managed without the boy. He was sixteen now, strong, willing and, once he had settled in and accepted the loss of his family, cheerful. He'd made good progress and seemed to have a feel for the things which he planted, tended and watched grow from seed or seedling to full flower, fruit or vegetable. He knew he himself was past his best at the age of fifty-five, or was he fifty-six, it didn't seem to matter, and Dan was indispensable to him. At first the lad had been appropriated now and again by Reuben Ash and even as helper to the handyman, he had shaped well, but he had proved as time went on to have an aptitude for the earth and what grew in it. A patient lad, happy to wait for the fruit of his labours to appear in six months' time or perhaps even longer, and one day when Cec retired he'd have no hesitation in recommending him to Mr Latimer to take his own place.

Aye, a steady lad and one to be trusted not only with Cecil Marlow's gardens and hothouses, but with Cecil Marlow's daughter as well. He was still a boy, slender and rangy with the awkwardness of boyhood which he had not yet outgrown and though he ate enough for two men, Cook could testify to that, he put on no weight. He was always ready for laughter, youthful and artless, and you could tell just by watching where his eyes went, and the expression in them, that he thought the world of his Celie. No, Cec had nothing to fear from Dan Smith.

'Well . . .' he began slowly, since that was his way, deliberating on the question or so it seemed, though he knew very well what he was going to say. The thought of traipsing over here every night for the next few months was not a happy one. Once he got settled by his own fire with the

Echo in his hand, his feet to the crackling coals, it was hard to put his boots and muffler on again and tramp through the night to the big house. There was a sharp frost tonight, the air so cold it had cut right to his chest as he dragged it into his lungs. The moon had hung, so close and clear just beyond the skeleton silhouettes of the great old trees he felt he could have reached up and touched it. The ground was like iron, thick and coated to the depth of two inches with hoar frost so that his boots crackled in it. Even the cat had raised its head from the hearthrug and looked at him as if he'd lost his mind as he stepped through his own front door and he thought so himself but what else could he do? Their Celie must be protected, but now it seemed, the answer was here, smiling engagingly from the chimney corner.

'I'll have to think on that, lad,' he said ponderously.

'Cec Marlow, what on earth is there to think on?' Cook's voice was testy. 'The lad's to go back to his own place before long and it'd take him no more than five minutes to see the girl home and be back at the coachhouse. See, have a cup of hot chocolate and then get yourself to your bed. The girl'll be no longer than half an hour behind you.'

'Well . . .'

'Eeh, Cec, give over. Drink this and then be off with you.'

It *was* no more than half an hour later when Dan and Celie stepped out of the lovely fragrant heat of the kitchen and into the breathtaking, numbing cold of the night. The moon had risen since Cec had set off, resting on the top of the stable roofs and lighting the yard to almost that of the day, but it was an unearthly light, a pale silvery blue light which laid long soft shadows across the cobbled yard.

Celie shivered and Dan took her bare hand in his.

'Where are your mittens?' rubbing her hands between his own.

'I don't know. I must have left them in the kitchen. Where are yours?' for Cook's endless knitting was a source of amusement between them.

'I don't know,' smiling. He shoved both their hands into the depth of his jacket pocket. With his other hand he gave his muffler another twist about his neck, then turned to her, pulling her coat collar up about her neck and adjusting *her* muffler about her chin as though she was a small girl. They smiled at one another, their teeth shining white in the lovely moonlight, then began to stride across the yard towards the gate which led out to the gardens at the back of the house. They stepped through dappled shadows and into the fierce silvered light, their feet crunching sharply into the frost. They did not speak. Their breath wreathed from between their parted lips and hung about their heads in the absolute stillness where they left it as they strode on. They were completely at ease with one another for in the four years since Dan had come to Briar Lodge they had formed an attachment, a bond which had seemed natural somehow to the girl whose father constantly looked back over his shoulder to his beloved dead wife and to the boy who had lost his family in circumstances so sad they could scarcely be imagined. They were drawn and held together by a need in both, he in the absence of the family to protect, to cherish, to sustain in the way of a male, she by the lack of true warmth from the kindly but reserved man who was her father. They each filled a gap which had been left in the other's life by life itself, and their affection for one another had begun on that day when Celie had told him her name and discovered his.

Sometimes, though, she was exasperated by his casual lack of concern about what she called 'getting on' as she meant to do. He was vital and merry-faced, infectiously good-humoured with an enthusiastic capacity for hard work, laughing, giving that laughter to others, her included. He was strong but gentle, steady, patient, young as he was, but his easy-going, "come-day, go-day, any day will do day" acceptance of what life had brought him and which he expected to continue just as it was, infuriated her.

'Don't you want to *be* somebody?' she would ask him.

'I am somebody, Celie.'

'No, I mean, make something of yourself.'

'*Make* something? I make plants grow.'

'You could be more than gardener to Mr Latimer, Dan.'

'What for?' He honestly could not see why they should

strive for anything more since they were both doing what they wanted to do, and were *happy* doing it.

The lawn was crisp as they stepped off the path and when, half-way across it, Dan pulled her to a stop and looked back, there were the clear imprints of their booted feet side by side in the silvered whiteness. They stood for a moment or two in the enchanted stillness which occurs only in the moonshine of a frosty night, scarcely breathing in the perfection of it. Dan pulled his hand from his pocket, leaving hers snug inside and putting his arm about her shoulder hugged her closer to him. He was tall, almost at his full man's height and her head rested easily against his shoulder. He smiled down into her upturned face, then spoke some words in his own language.

'Min liten älskling.' His voice was soft. 'Kara du kärlek.'

'What?' she smiled back, her face a pure white, her lips losing their colour in the light of the moon 'What did you say?'

'I'll tell you one day.'

'Oh, you're always doing that, Dan Smith, saying something in your own language and then not letting on what it means.'

'I said I'd tell you one day.'

'And when will that be?'

'When you're grown up.'

'Anybody would think *you* were. You're only two years older than me.'

'Two years is a long time in a person's life.'

'You talk in riddles, Dan Smith.'

'Riddles?'

'Yes, making a . . . a mystery out of everything.'

'No, no mystery, min liten älskling.'

'There you go again.' She whirled away from him and began to run towards the dense yew hedge which separated the lawns from the vegetable gardens. There was a gap in the hedge and she ran in its direction, her soft laughter like a muted bell in the silent night. He followed, his long legs easily overtaking hers and when he caught her, he whirled her about on the stiff frozen grass, their faces young and joyous in their shared merriment. From a window on the ground floor a slice of light suddenly fell across the garden as a curtain was pulled aside and the figure of a man in uniform looked out, the cigar between his lips glowing behind the polished glass.

'What is it, darling?' Mrs Latimer said from her chair by the fire.

'Nothing. I thought I heard someone laugh, that's all.'

'And is there someone there?'

'No.'

Chapter Six

Dan Smith knew exactly when the maids in the kitchen became aware of him, not as Dan, the lad who helped in the yard or the garden, but as a male, a person of masculine gender in their female world towards whom they immediately became coquettish, lifting their pert young breasts beneath their snow-white apron bibs, and tossing their cap ribbons in his direction. They would smile and dimple, brushing against his shoulder where he sat before the fire, putting a hand on his knee to steady themselves as they lifted a pan from the oven, displaying themselves like preening birds for his inspection. He liked it, of course.

He would stamp into the kitchen after first removing every vestige of "muck" from his boots since there was nothing Cook detested more than "muck" on her clean kitchen floor, scrubbed sometimes twice a day, if necessary, by Belle. Cook would be at the centre of the intense activity which preceded any meal served in the Latimer household, keeping a critical eye on the saucepans which simmered on the top of the oven or whatever was roasting inside it. She was a firm believer in leaving nothing to the less able ministrations of underlings, supervising the preparing of the meal every step of the way, her handmaidens at her elbow ready to leap into action at her slightest gesture or sharp command. Each would be at her allotted task, chopping, whisking, stirring, basting, mixing.

'Put a bit of elbow grease into them pans, girl,' he would hear her say to Belle, for Cook was a lover of "elbow grease", 'and leave the greasiest pans to the last. Method, girl . . . method. What have I told you . . . ?'

'Method, Cook.'

'That's it. Now then, where's my omelette pan, I can't make Mr Latimer's omelette without my omelette pan.'

'Here, Cook.'

'Mr Latimer is particularly fond of my omelettes, especially with some of those fresh mushrooms that came this morning. Now then, Belle, where are those mushrooms, are they not cleaned yet?'

'Well, I . . .'

'Will you never learn? What have I told you?'

Dan could see Belle's not over-active brain desperately searching around in its depths for the particular bit of information Cook referred to among the dozens she had poured into it since she had come to work in the scullery of Briar Lodge. Her young face went quite blank.

'Er . . .'

'Ask the Cook what ingredients she'll need and have them ready for her. That's what I've taught you and it's the same with pans and if you want to amount to anything then you'd better learn.'

'Yes, Cook.'

'Right then, fetch the mushrooms and clean them ready for the omelette.'

'Yes, Cook.'

Dan caught Belle's eye and winked, though not when Cook was looking, of course, and at once he saw Belle relax, ready to giggle. Oh, yes, he knew the girls liked him and he also knew that had he had a fancy for it, he could have found one willing to share a kiss and a cuddle with him in the cosy room he had made for himself above the coachhouse. He had a comfortable bed, a chest of drawers, an old desk with a chair, a faded, sagging armchair from some long-ago age before the present generation of Latimers, a couple of oil lamps and an oil heater, several rugs and even a picture or two on the wall.

Dan could speak good English by now, of course, with a slight but lilting accent which he knew fascinated the opposite sex. There were books sitting in a long row on top of the chest of drawers. Books from the William Brown Library in Liverpool, mostly about gardens and gardening, or animal husbandry and farming methods or indeed anything to do with the land. He would go anywhere to find out more about what interested him most.

'There's an exhibition of farm machinery on next week at the Mechanics Institute, so I think I might go on my afternoon off,' he told those in the kitchen, though nobody took much notice. Who was interested in farming machinery, for goodness sake, and only one name came to mind? So those who were in the kitchen were not surprised the next week when he came in from the yard to say goodbye to Cook, to see Celie Marlow by his side. Of course they all knew, they told one another, for when did anyone else get a look in with Dan Smith when she was around, forgetting as they spoke that Celie was only fourteen and a half and the tall lad beside her only two years older. Cook of course, could see the way the wind would one day be ready to blow between Dan Smith and Celie Marlow. Had done from the first and in her opinion – when they were older, of course – a match between them would be eminently suitable. A cook, as Celie would be and a gardener would not find it hard to get employment together since both, if they had anything about them, were hard to find. They would do well together, Dan and Celie and she would not have allowed them to spend their free time in one another's company had she not trusted Dan as completely as she did. A good head on his shoulders he had, despite his liking for a bit of fun, and there had been a bond between the two of them ever since Celie had made him "speak".

'Now then girl, you be back by six and see here, lad, I'll not have you keeping this child out after dark. You're lucky to both get your afternoon off together and how you manage it, I'll never know . . .' which was slightly ridiculous and far from true for did not Jess Harper have the final say in the comings and goings of all her staff?

Celie earned ten shillings a week now which to her was riches. She had, for the first time in her life, money to spend on whatever she wanted, within reason, of course, for her father could see no sense, he said, in taking money for her board. She ate in the kitchen of the big house or if not, then the food she cooked in their own cottage kitchen was brought over from the kitchen, for both his and Celie's wages included food and board. Celie spent most of her wages on clothes and it showed in the simple but fashionable skirt and jacket she had on on this soft autumn day. It was what was called a "walking-out" costume in a fine tweed, the material for which she had bought as an "end of roll" from a stall at St John's Market. It was a pale dove-grey flecked with white and cream. A perfect foil for her own clear silvery eyes, though at the time she had not consciously thought of it in that way, only knowing instinctively that it would suit her colouring. The skirt was quite full, almost touching the arch of her black buttoned boots, but without a bustle. The coat bodice was tight to her neat breast, with a short basque cut into her waist, almost in a military style with similar braiding across the front to that on Second Lieutenant Richard Latimer's uniform frock coat. Again she had not purposely copied the style but the memory of that afternoon was still curiously alive in the fathomless depth of her young girl's memory and it showed in the high, tight neck of the bodice and pert "jockey-cap" she wore tilted over her forehead. Mrs Ash was only too pleased to earn a few bob and she and young Celie pored over copies of *The Tailor and Cutter* which Mrs Latimer had discarded. Mrs Ash, in Celie's opinion, could have made a living at dressmaking if she'd had the space to do it in, and if Mrs Latimer had allowed such a thing, but the Ash cottage was filled with children of all ages and sizes and when they were in bed of a night Reuben could not abide having his kitchen cluttered up with "women's things" he said, wanting his hearth to himself after a hard day's work. He liked to take his boots off and undo the top button of his trousers and he couldn't do that with young Celie Marlow hanging about, could he? Their Alfie, who was a clever young lad and intent on getting his Master's Ticket in the Merchant Navy, studied at night in the parlour. So Mrs Ash "made up" for Celie when she was needed, in the parlour of Celie's Pa's cottage.

Celie had a full, elbow-length cloak for when it was colder, with a high Medici collar made of good quality wool, again from St John's Market where many a bargain, if one was prepared to search, might be found. It was a lovely rich plum colour lined in pale grey satin, making her skin seem even whiter. She had a dress of saxony, again of a simple design, buttoning from her throat to below her waist at the front, but all in one piece with a high frilled neck and long tight sleeves frilled at the wrist. She chose a rich cream, though Mrs Ash thought it highly unsuitable on a girl so young and it would show every mark she said, but Celie had her way and with a tiny "shell bonnet" in cream straw, a structure shaped like a scallopshell, pinned to her curls and bought for a shilling in the market, she looked a real picture, Mrs Ash told Reuben, quite tearfully, for she could remember the poor motherless little thing when her father had hacked off her hair years ago. Celie's tormenting presence amongst her own children and her determination to lead them into the devil's mischief was quite forgotten.

The exhibition was as boring as Celie knew it would be, and though she did her best to share Dan's enthusiasm it was a bit hard when you were only fourteen and dressed in a new outfit which she knew was drawing appreciative glances from the numerous gentlemen who had come to see the machinery which so fascinated Dan.

Celie Marlow was growing up and, knowing full well her own attractions by now for had she not seen the reflection of it, not only in the mirror and in Dan's eyes, but in those of Richard Latimer, she was quite ready to be admired. She idled along at his back, twitching her skirt and lifting her head on which the grey velvet jockey cap perched, trying not to return the smile directed at her by a presentable young man in a smart pair of narrow "shepherd's" check trousers, a check waistcoat to match and a plain lounge jacket. He carried a fashionable "bowler" hat much favoured by sporting gentlemen. His hair was smoothly brushed and his eyes were a bright and mischievous blue. She turned away, not trying very hard – she was the first to admit it – to curb her own young and carefree inclination to smile back but he had seen it and to her horror, thinking she was alone and ready for a dalliance, came strolling across the crowded hall towards her.

'Are you as bored as I am?' he said in the smiling, drawling tones of a gentleman. 'You certainly look it, so why don't you and I get out of here and go where there is a bit more fun? I know of a charming tea room in Bold Street and I would be honoured if you would allow me to buy you afternoon tea. Then perhaps we could stroll along the Marine Parade and watch the ships. It's such a lovely afternoon and I believe the *Teutonic* is berthed at Alexandra Dock which . . .'

He got no further. Celie was looking up at him with the appalled expression of someone who has reached out a hand to stroke a kitten only to find it is a full-grown tiger. Her eyes were wide with shock but there was, unfortunately, still a remnant of the smile she had done her best to stifle about her soft, coral pink mouth and it was this which Dan saw first as he turned to speak to her. That and the young man who was also smiling down into her face.

The words he spoke were unintelligible for in his hot and jealous anger he at once fell back into the language which came more easily to his tongue. But if his words were not understood, his actions were, for the male's possessive guarding of what is his cannot be misinterpreted, at least by another male. He took hold of Celie's arm and dragged her backwards, putting her behind him and holding her there as though convinced the young man was going to make off with her. His eyes had become almost black, so thick was the blue depth of them, and his hard young jawline clenched tight so that he could barely speak.

The young man looked quite bewildered. He held up his hands in a show of defensive apology and his eyes widened so that the blue of them was completely surrounded by the white.

'I say, I do apologise. I meant no offence, really. I thought the young lady was alone so . . . well . . .'

'Is no reason to speak to her,' Dan said through clenched teeth, overwhelmed with his need to smash his fist into the apologetically smiling face. 'She not . . . she is not . . .'

'I know, I know and I'm sorry, but I could not help but admire . . .'

'She not for admiring.'

'No, I do apologise but you must admit she is very pretty,'

doing his best to win Dan's reluctant truce with his own engaging smile, but Dan squared his shoulders, taking up that stance of prickling umbrage Celie had seen in a dog insulted by another. His candid young face was truculent, but he was doing his best to control himself.

Celie could feel the irritation well up in her and she turned away, ready to stamp her feet in temper. About her the serious decently dressed young men who were mostly of the working classes, and like Dan, had an interest in other things besides "footy, fags and a bevvy", had begun to turn and stare at the small commotion which was taking place. Two attendants, having been alerted that there was a fracas taking place in the Machinery Section were hurrying towards them.

'Now then, young sirs, we cannot allow this kind of behaviour here. If you want to fight, kindly do it outside.'

'I don't want to fight,' the young gentleman spluttered.

Celie was trembling and when Dan put his hand to her elbow to lead her down the wide steps and into Mount Street she twitched it away. She was ready to cry, really she was, and if she could have found a place less public she would have done so since she had never felt so embarrassed in her life. She almost ran down the steps, holding up her long skirt to reveal the high, black polish on her boots and a tantalising glimpse of the white lace on the petticoat she herself had sewn during the long summer evenings. When she reached the bottom of the steps, she lifted her jaunty capped head, squared her shoulders and crossed Mount Street into Rodney Street then round the corner and on to the steep incline of Knight Street. She could hear Dan's footsteps behind her and though he called her name, asking her to wait, she continued on until she turned into the busy clatter of Bold Street.

Bold Street was a wide and pleasant thoroughfare, described in the old days as a "promenade" for the fair and gay, lined on both sides with smart shops to which those with wealth gave their patronage. The buildings were tall, several storeys high, grand and richly ornamented. The arched shop windows were large and elegant, sparkling like crystal in the afternoon sunshine, and above the shop windows were rows of others, each one sporting a tiny, wrought iron balcony. Shop windows in which costly sable and chinchilla were carelessly draped and beside them ermine muffs, sable capes, shawls, boas, everything that the fashionable lady might require to keep her warm in the coming winter months. A Tailors and Drapers discreetly advertised "suitable" mourning dresses and "outfits for India" whilst its windows contained all the lovely regalia the autumn or winter bride would be charmed to wear.

There were furniture stores presenting exceedingly costly and quite exquisite gilt-framed mirrors and sparkling chandeliers, carved mahogany, gleaming silkwood and the satin finish of rosewood on tables and chiffoniers. Vases of Sèvres and Meissen, crystal lamps and porcelain figurines so dainty and fine they were almost transparent. A silversmith's and jeweller's, cheek by jowl with a grocer's and tea merchant's; an importer of foreign fruit, parmesan and Gruyère cheese, macaroni and vermicelli; a wine merchant's dealing only in the finest wines and a photographer's where a full-length portrait might be taken and which could be adapted to be contained in a locket or a brooch. A large pair of spectacles hung on a sign jutting out over the heads of the pedestrians indicating an "Ophthalmic Optician". Many of the shops carried an awning above their windows to keep the bright sun from their expensively displayed goods. The sound of a piano could be heard coming from the open doorway of a music shop. It was hesitant as though the player was not sure of the tune, presumably trying out one of the new songs for which the shop sold the sheet music. A fragrance like that of a rose came from a shop which declared itself to be a "haircutter's, perfumer's and patent wig maker" but which also provided for its gentlemen customers a stock of collars, braces and a special line in dressing cases.

There were ladies in pairs, each one carrying a parasol, "browsing" along the pavement, studying the window displays, well-dressed and fashionable in their promenade dresses, the skirts draped over enormous bustles. These were in the form of a straw-filled cushion sewn into the back of the skirt below which were half-loops of steel bands which were fixed horizontally into the lining, causing the back of the skirt to project away from the body almost a foot, whilst the front was flat. Hats were tall, the crowns rising abruptly into flower-pot shapes and decorated with feathers, flowers, ribbons, even a mausoleum of dead birds and insects!

Carriages open and closed moved at a steady pace up and down the street, keeping well away from the tram lines down its centre and along which the horse-drawn trams crawled from stop to stop. There were wagons and drays pulled by the patient, plodding magnificence of Clydesdales, bending their heads into the weight of their loads. Cyclists swooped and horses whinnied nervously since they had not yet become accustomed to the frail swiftness of the new-fangled machines. It was a teeming multitude of men in top hats, ladies in no hurry, vehicles and animals which did not seem to care who they were in danger of sweeping aside as each moved purposefully on its business.

Celie glanced neither to her right nor her left as she hurried in the direction of Lord Street. In other circumstances she would have been delighted to have the chance to dawdle before each shop window, studying their contents, none of which she could afford. To watch the smart ladies who could, and to take in the warm sunshine which must surely be the last before winter began. She had no idea of where she meant to go, she only knew it must be as far away as possible from the scene which had just taken place in the Mechanics Institute. She had walked, almost run, the length of Lord Street, past St George's Hall and on down James Street to Strand Street when she felt his hand on her arm.

'Hold on, Celie, there's no need to run. Where d' you think you're going all by yourself?'

'I'm not by myself. I'm *never* by myself. There's always someone either by my side or behind me and don't pull at me like that, Dan Smith. I was doing no harm. I *am* allowed to speak to other people, you know.'

She had dragged herself away from him again and on the corner, just where the bridge led across the water from George's Dock to Canning Dock, two sailors pushed themselves away from the wall, their eyes narrowing suspiciously as they watched the tall boy struggle to keep a hold on the lovely young girl whose arm he held.

'Be still, Celie, and will you let me speak?'

'No I won't, I don't care to hear what you have to say, so just leave me alone.'

'No, I want you . . .'

'Now then, you, take your 'ands off that young lady. It seems she don't want to go with you, so just let go of . . .'

Dan's equable nature had been sorely tried this day. He really didn't understand why the sight of Celie Marlow smiling at another man should have made him feel as he did and when the violence had fallen about him, no one could have been more surprised than himself. All he had wanted was to hustle Celie away from . . . from whatever it was that had tensed in him, and have it eased. It was spiky and hurtful and he didn't care for it and the only way to stop it seemed to be to attack the one who had caused it by smiling and talking to Celie. Now, just as he was about to explain, as best he could, there were two more interfering in what was none of their business and without even thinking of the consequences or even caring, since what sensible lad will take on not one, but two tough sailors, he swung round blindly and just as blindly aimed his fist at whoever it was who had spoken.

When they came in Cook dropped a pan of carrots and turnips which she had been just about to place on the top of the oven, and the contents went not only over the rag rug before the fire, but splashed on her feet and up her clean white apron. A good job the pan had been going *on* the stove and not coming off, she snapped later, or there would have been a nasty accident, but the sight of Dan with his eyes half-closed and swollen, his lip cut and bloody, his collar stud lost and his collar sticking every which way was enough to startle anyone.

'Two sailors attacked him,' Celie sobbed as she clung to his arm, *helping* him over the doorstep, though Cook was of the opinion it was really the other way round, Celie was so upset. She'd blood on her lovely dove-grey outfit, which proved to be Dan's, thank the Lord, since, for one awful moment Cook thought *she'd* been at it as well. A fight, if you please, down by the docks and she was only thankful Mrs Latimer hadn't seen the pair of them coming up the drive or the sparks *would* have flown then. What was it about? she'd asked them as she dabbed iodine ruthlessly on Dan's cuts and bruises, for two sailors would hardly have set on one lone boy for no reason at all, would they? But neither seemed inclined to tell her, though by the way Celie clung to him, begging him to let her know if there was anything, *anything* he needed, he'd only to say and she'd run for it, Cook made up her mind it had been over *her*. She'd have to keep her eye on these two. Not allow them quite so much freedom to go about together in the future. They were both of an awkward age, too young for the kind of decent "courting" which led to marriage and too old for the innocent and youthful outings on which they'd gone in the past. Dan was more mature, of course. She'd seen the maids about him and she was only too well aware, not being daft, that he would soon be ready for the . . . well the *sexual* carryings on young men got up to, but Celie certainly wasn't. She was growing up but not that fast!

No, she'd best keep an eye on them, Jess Harper told herself, though she made no mention of it to Cec when he came to collect Celie later. Well, men have no sense about such things, have they?

Dan was turning over the soil vigorously to Mr Marlow's instructions and the fine muscles in his back rippled beneath his thin shirt. Though Richard Latimer's property and the land that surrounded it were not grand by some standards, the house was large and handsome, built in the early part of the century of a stone somewhere between the colour of oatmeal and honey. It was square and spacious with long, elegant, narrow windows across its façade in the middle of which was a large pillared porch. There was a bay on the left-hand side of the house in which the drawing-room windows were set and above the drawing room, those of the bedroom Mr Latimer shared with his wife. To the right of the house was a long two-storeyed extension in the shape of an "L", the bottom stroke being the stables and coachhouse and forming the yard which backed onto the kitchen quarters. All very secluded and well away from the family's fragrant gaze.

The gardens and rough ground which encircled the house were extensive, covering about ten acres. To the front and at each side were wide lawns rolling down from the terrace in a gentle incline to a small lake, called for some reason the "pond", on which ducks glided and fought one another for the bread the children threw at them. Though Phyllis Latimer would dearly have loved a couple of swans to glide beside them since swans were so *elegant*, she had to admit that the "pond" was just not *patrician* enough for such graceful birds. There were trees, older than the house, for the Latimer who had built it had set it in what had once been woodland. Oak existed serenely beside yew and birch, chestnut and larch and sycamore amongst which tawny owls swooped silently at night; rabbits and dormice hid by day, and when they could, the Latimer boys swung from the low branches of the trees and kicked their heels in the carpet of fallen autumn leaves.

Closer to the house, where Mrs Latimer might enjoy them from her window, were gravel paths lined with flower beds, rose gardens and rockeries covered with alpine plants, lupin beds, a small maze of yew hedges, tall conifers, peonies, Michaelmas daisies, dahlias and mopheaded acacias to give height and contrast, all under the tender loving care of Cec Marlow and now, Dan Smith.

Mr Latimer watched them both from the breakfast-room window whilst he drank a last cup of coffee before calling for the carriage to take him to his office and he noted that it was Dan who did most of the work. Marlow had his hand in the small of his back in the classic pose of a man who is doing his best to ease an ache there, whilst he leaned heavily on his spade. Richard Latimer studied the two men, then let his gaze go beyond them to the long sweep of the lawns, the overgrown vegetation about the lake, the trees, the paths, the shrubs, the beds waiting to be tended, and he was struck by the magnitude of the work Marlow must have done, almost single-handedly, for the past forty years. There was far too much for one man, even a young one, to manage on his own, he realised, and yet, until the boy came, he had done so.

Mrs Latimer had already made her wishes known, for her husband had heard her on the matter of planting flowers: she liked to see a rich floral display as she sat in her window, from the blossoming of the first snowdrop until the planting of the geraniums. There was no reason in her opinion why a garden should not yield as much beauty and enjoyment during the early months of the year as in the summer and autumn, and of course, when she had said so to Marlow, he could only agree. From January when the snowdrops and winter aconites timidly offered their simple charm for Mrs Latimer's pleasure; through May when the ranunculus and anemone would appear and on until the summer bedding would begin, Marlow had never complained nor failed to produce anything but perfection to delight his mistress's senses. But perhaps the time had come to employ not one, but two boys to do his bidding, to manage the labouring, for really, the elderly man looked very frail. He wondered why he had not noticed it before.

He said so to Mrs Latimer as she drifted from the breakfast table to stand beside him at the window. The sight of the boy digging so furiously with none of the slow care Marlow took with *her* soil was strangely irritating to her.

'Have you noticed, my dear,' her husband asked, 'how Marlow seems to have slowed down recently?'

'He is just methodical, Richard. Careful with the plants.'

'I know that, dearest, but he is getting no younger and perhaps . . .'

'Oh, I appreciate that,' his wife interrupted him, 'but really should that boy be quite so . . . energetic?'

'Well the soil does have to be prepared, I believe, and Marlow impressed on me only the other day the need to dig deep and make sure Ellis puts by all the manure from the stables to . . .'

'Really Richard, is there any need to mention such things whilst we are at breakfast?'

'I'm sorry, my dear, I meant no offence.' Richard Latimer's voice was mild, a tone he used not only with his wife but everyone with whom he came in contact. 'I merely mentioned . . .'

'Yes, yes, I know, Richard, but you were speaking of Marlow. Do you really think he is getting too old for the work he does?'

Phyllis Latimer sounded quite resentful as though the idea that her gardener, who had been at Briar Lodge since she came as a bride and who was surely immortal, might not last her lifetime and it seriously displeased her.

'Oh, I wouldn't say that . . .'

'So you don't mean to replace him?'

'No, not at all, but that boy has learned a lot from him and perhaps he could be moved up and, with another boy under Marlow's supervision, at least for a while, it might make it easier on the old chap.'

'How old is the boy, Richard?'

'I believe he is approaching his seventeenth birthday. He's been with us for over four years.'

'Really, as long as that?'

'Indeed.'

'And has nothing been heard of his family?'

'Nothing, I'm sorry to say.'

'Do you really think he is capable of doing Marlow's job? He is awfully young.'

'Oh, yes, on the understanding that Marlow kept an eye on him, yes. He is a conscientious worker, Marlow has told me a dozen times, and appears to have an aptitude for it.'

The room was soft with the hazed sunshine of the autumn day, its pale lemon rays touching and burnishing the lovely satin finish of the oval table, the matching sideboards, and resting in neat symmetrical oblongs on the velvet carpet as it fell through the windows. Still at the table were Anne and Prudence Latimer, the latter at fifteen, considered by Mrs Latimer to be old enough and sensible enough to breakfast with her parents. The two young girls were reflected in the table's mirror surface, their smooth, unruffled faces; the shining, pale brown wings of hair on the eldest, the long, tidy plait of the youngest which fell across her immature breast ending in an enormous blue bow. They were both in white, virginal as young, unmarried girls were intended to be, docile and patient as doves, as *ladies* were meant to be as they waited for their mother to finish breakfast and discuss the duties of the day with them. There would first be the interview with Cook which took place each morning after breakfast on the subject of menus, accounting and any other matter which either Cook or their mother might wish to bring to the other's attention. Mrs Latimer was a firm believer in training her daughters to the position in life which they would naturally obtain in due course, which was that of wife, mother and mistress of a large household such as this one and only by doing as *she* did in these, their formative years, could such expertise be gained.

At the back of the room, in the shadows where the sun did not reach, stationed one on either side of the sideboard in readiness to serve the family, stood Dorcas and Fanny, pretty and neat in their pale, lilac-striped cotton morning dresses, crisp muslin aprons and caps, the latter frilled with wide starched ribbons which fell down their erect backs. They both wore expressionless faces though their bright eyes revealed they had missed nothing of what had been said during the past fifteen minutes.

As though suddenly aware of this, Mrs Latimer waved an imperious hand in their direction.

'You may go now,' she commanded. 'I will ring when I need you.'

'Yes, Madam.' Both maids bobbed a curtsey before leaving the room, closing the door quietly behind them.

Cook was sitting with her feet to the fire for though it was not cold in the kitchen she was of the opinion that the warmth of the leaping flames and glowing embers soothed her feet and ankles which were already swollen. It was barely two hours since she had put them to the floor at the side of her bed and though she complained to no one, not even the girl of whom she had grown increasingly fond over the years, she could feel them throb just like a toothache. And her veins were playing her up, which didn't help, thick and ropy, writhing down each leg from the back of her knee and knotting about her calves so that she felt she could scream with the pain from the dratted things. These afflictions were the resulting scourge of all women who spent their lives standing for twelve or fourteen hours a day at one job or another and she accepted it, at the same time thanking God for sending her Celie Marlow. It was quite justified for Cook to sit down, still in charge, of course, whilst she directed the girl in this or that task, under the pretence – which was no pretence at all, really – of allowing her to try her hand at the many dishes Cook devised for the family's meals.

'You'll not learn if you don't *do*, girl!' she said a dozen times a day, particularly when her legs, ankles and feet felt as though she was standing in the very coals of the fire, but though she had been Cook's assistant for such a short time, really Celie Marlow was fast approaching Cook's own standard in the art of cuisine. She had a way with her, some knack, an instinctive talent which had nothing to do with recipes, with the heat of the oven, the lightness or strength of her own touch, the utensils she used, the quality of the ingredients she used, though these, naturally, were of the best. Her sauces whispered over the tongue, her tipsy cake melted in the mouth, her preserves and jams were a delight to the palate, and seemed to retain the essence of the sunshine which had ripened the fruit. Her herbed partridge was a feast, her ragout of lamb a banquet. Her apple snow was the prettiest thing you ever set eyes on, garnished with bilberries and whipped cream and her chocolate soufflé fit to be fed to the angels up in Heaven, and as for her soufflé omelette, Mr Latimer, begging Cook not to take offence, would have one at every meal, she said. She was a natural, Cook admitted to herself, though not to Celie since she didn't want the girl to get above herself, and if she could cook as she did now, at her age, what heights might she obtain as she matured?

And she was clever too. She begged Dorcas and Fanny to save all the national newspapers Mr Latimer had finished with, scorning the *Liverpool Echo* which even so, went to her Pa, studying what went on in the world in what was described as the *Age of Promise*. She was aware, long before the rest of the servants, of the influenza epidemic which was sweeping the country, taking with it not only the common man in his thousands, but Her Majesty's grandson, the young prince, the Duke of Clarence, who was shortly to have been married to his cousin, the Princess Victoria Mary of Teck.

She parted with a precious shilling for a publication called *Complete Etiquette for Ladies and Gentlemen* since you never knew in what circumstance you might find yourself, she said, and it was as well to know how to behave as one should, whatever that behaviour might be. She had requested, bravely Cook was inclined to think, admiring her for it, of Mr Latimer, the right to borrow "a book or two" from his library, shrewdly waiting until he was alone to do so, and promising earnestly to take good care of them, overjoyed when he permitted it. When she was not working she could be found in the chimney corner, or when the weather was mild and dry, curled in a tree root at the foot of the gigantic oak at the back of the house.

She had begun lightly with *Little Women* by Louisa May Alcott and had been entranced and then, because she liked the title, *The Moonstone* by Wilkie Collins. Having enjoyed it she took its partner by the same author *The Woman in White*, moving on to *The Mill on the Floss* and *Alice's Adventures in Wonderland. Twenty Thousand Leagues under the Sea, King Solomon's Mines*. Encouraged by the enchanting tales of romance and adventure, she had attempted *Far from the Madding Crowd* by Thomas Hardy, admiring Bathsheba immensely for her courage and beauty, going on to *Dr Jekyll and Mr Hyde* which was not quite so much to her taste.

The other girls, at first disparaging of what seemed to them her resolution to show herself better than they were, became used to her engrossed and silent figure curled up on the hearth rug in front of the fire, so much so that Mary had told Lily, whilst they were both scouring the flags and out of earshot of Cook, the intimate details of her Alf's attempts to get "it" up and in her the night before, with much coarse hilarity, before they realised they were scrubbing round the feet of the absorbed young girl. But her passion for the written word, which went on to encompass poetry, gardening journals, Mrs Beeton's *Book of Household Management*, articles by leading politicians and journalists, indeed anything which her bright and enquiring mind thought looked "interesting", became commonplace as the servants grew accustomed to it.

Dorcas and Fanny exploded into the kitchen, the bursting excitement they could scarcely contain ready to spill out of both of them at the same time. Celie was engrossed with the rapt, delicate task of laying a lattice-work of spun sugar icing on a cake for her Pa. It was his birthday at the end of the week and with Cook's permission she had made a rich pound cake in which butter, flour, sugar, currants, eggs, candied peel, sweet almonds and citron had been beaten for twenty minutes before being baked for two hours.

'Put a glass of wine in it,' Cook had whispered from her chair by the fire, and Celie had done so and it smelled quite delicious. It had cost nearly four shillings for the ingredients, which was expensive but it would be well worth it to see her Pa's face when he was presented with it. She'd got him some tobacco and a brand new pipe, an elaborately carved Meerschaum, which meant "sea foam" in Germany where it had come from, the tobacconist had told her, which she thought was lovely. Dan had bought him a tobacco box, designed to be carried round in his pocket with a steel, tight-fitting lid and a stopper, so that, wherever he was, he could get the best out of his pipe by having fresh tobacco which would, the same tobacconist told him, be well compacted by the stopper for a cooler, longer smoke. Cook had knitted him a new muffler for he seemed to find the need of one all the year round now, she had noticed. Getting old, like herself, she mused as her fingers grappled with the knitting needles and the lovely scarlet wool she had picked for him.

'You'll never guess,' Fanny was the first to speak and Dorcas gave her an aggrieved look for *she* was the head parlourmaid and should have been the one to tell them.

They all turned as one, even Celie lifting her dedicated gaze from her Pa's cake. Kate and Belle in the scullery and even Madge Evans, who was about to make her way to the laundry where a mountain of the Latimers' soiled clothing awaited her, paused by the kitchen door and at the table, Mary and Lily who were sipping a welcome cup of tea before departing, the heavy cleaning done, placed their cups carefully on the table.

'What is it, Fanny?' Cook asked warningly, since they were all aware that she did not care for gossip about the family.

'Oh, it's not the Latimers, Cook, it's one of the servants.'

Everyone in the room drew in a breath and held it warily. The sack for some unfortunate, was the question written on every face except Belle's who was not awfully sure what was up.

'Well?' Cook's voice was sharp and her legs were savage in their painful throbbing. She knew she shouldn't have said it as soon as it was out of her mouth but she couldn't help it. Had Mrs Latimer noticed her increasing dependency on Celie Marlow? . . . Oh dear Lord, not that . . . but then her face cleared for the mistress would hardly have discussed it with *these* two, would she? even if she had.

None of them noticed Cec Marlow as he opened the back kitchen door, not even Madge who was as worried about her job as Cook, nor did they see him step inside to the welcome warmth of the kitchen. He was not expected, for if he had been, Celie would have hidden his birthday cake. He stood there, ready to smile, for it was evident the women were indulging in the female love of gossip which Fanny was about to impart.

She did.

'Cec Marlow's to get the sack and Dan's to be put in his place.'

The red, pulsing blood drained away from Cec Marlow's heart and flooded his head and even before his body hit the floor, he was dead.

Chapter Seven

'You know you can't stay here on your own, girl. Your Pa wouldn't have liked it and Mrs Latimer certainly won't allow it. It wouldn't be right. Besides which, Mr Latimer might be giving this cottage to the new gardener when he comes. Nothing's been said about Dan having . . . well, taking over from your Pa, and they'll need a full-time man to do what your Pa did. If he's a family or even if he hasn't, he's bound to be put in here, you know that, don't you?'

Celie sighed sadly. Yes, she knew that. Cook was right and the sooner she accepted it the better and she *would* have accepted it but for the awful realisation that she might have to share a room in the big house with Kate Mossop. Kate Mossop, of all people, who had good reason to feel animosity towards Celie dating back to the time when Cook had chosen Celie to be kitchen maid instead of Kate. Not that Kate did anything that Cook could take exception to, or even Celie herself, for Cook would stand for no bickering amongst her staff, nor would she put up with what she called an "atmosphere". No, Kate had been mim as a mouse, doing her work conscientiously, and her application to it was to have its reward for next week she was to start as parlourmaid in the front house.

It was always the way, Cook said ominously, let one catastrophe happen and another followed on its heels, looking about her fearfully to see who would be next, for these things happened in threes. Who would have thought it, first poor old Cec and now poor Fanny.

Fanny, who was the eldest daughter in a family which grew

yearly had been called home by the death of her mother in
childbirth. Her father couldn't manage on his own, he had
told Mr Latimer, apologetically, when he came to break the
news, twisting his cap round and round in his rough labourer's
hands, not with ten children under the age of twelve. The
boys, closer in years to Fanny, had already left home, but
the eldest girl was barely eight years old and ten children
wanted some seeing to and Mr Latimer must realise that
he had no option but to fetch his lass home to see to them.
Nobody thought to consider the "lass" in question since it
was assumed she knew where her duty lay. Fanny had cried
sharply, not for her mother who had, in Fanny's opinion, made
a muddle of her life, but for herself who had made such a good
start with her own.

It was an ill-wind, Cook said, shaking her head, sorry to see
neat, hard-working Fanny go, but she had made a promise
to Kate Mossop and the girl had done nothing since to which
Cook could take exception. She had shown great patience
and fortitude, losing that tendency to be resentful and cause
trouble amongst the others with her sly innuendos. She had
trained up young Belle a treat. Belle who was herself now
ready to be called scullery maid and in her turn have a skivvy
under her. Cook's only dilemma had been when it was realised
that Mrs Latimer expected Celie Marlow to share a bedroom
with Kate Mossop. On the face of it an excellent idea. Dorcas
was now head parlourmaid and would rightfully expect to have
a room of her own and young Belle would naturally share with
the new skivvy called Maudie, so where else would Celie go
but in with Kate?

'I know what you're thinking, girl, but Kate's changed since
. . . well, you know what I mean. She was inclined to cause
trouble once but now she's been made up to housemaid she'll
be fine. She only needed a bit of encouragement.'

Cook was snatching the opportunity to take the weight off
her feet as she folded the clothing that had once been Cec
Marlow's, not much since he had been buried in his best suit,
but as Mr Latimer said, and if Celie didn't mind, which was
kind of him to ask, Cook thought, some poor soul would be
glad of them. There was bedding to be packed and stored

ready for the next occupant, though certain items, like the beautiful hand-worked patchwork quilt done by Mary Marlow for her "bottom drawer", belonged to Celie. All to be put away for the day when Celie would herself be married and, in Cook's private opinion, to someone not a million miles away from this cottage.

'I suppose so.' Celie picked up the ornamental brass kettle her Pa had told her he and her Ma had bought on a day trip to New Brighton when they were first married. She studied her own distorted reflection in its brightly polished surface, then wrapped it carefully in newspaper before placing it in a box which stood on the table. She did the same with the wooden clock, wiping its face with a duster before it was put away. The toby jug, the candlesticks, the souvenir mug, the china lady with the parasol and the blue-and-white willow-pattern plate went the same way, reverently placed amongst all she had left of her Ma and Pa. The life she had lived with her Pa and which had ended when he had died two weeks ago on Cook's kitchen flags.

She could cry now at the thought of it, as she had then, as they all had, particularly Fanny who was convinced it was her thoughtless words which had brought about Cec Marlow's death. Mr Latimer had had to bring the doctor, not only to attend to Cec but to the hysterical girl, and Cook had been only thankful their master had not set out for his office when it had happened. He had come at once, called to the kitchen by the excited Kate, the only one who was, it seemed, to the distracted Cook, to be still in control of herself. Celie crouching over her father's body like some whipped animal, shaking him and begging him to speak to her, not prepared to move an inch until young Dan had led her away somewhere whilst his body was removed. Dorcas had done her best to contain the hysteria of Fanny, while Mary and Lily and Madge stood about like great, avid lumps, mouths open, and Belle, who, Cook was becoming more and more convinced, was a bit simple, scouring pans as though nothing untoward was happening in the kitchen.

He had been a rock to them all, had Dan, just as though the pain and fear and loss he himself had suffered had given him the sympathy and compassion to calm it in others, to give them comfort and support, and none had needed it more than Celie.

'I'm an orphan now, Dan.' she'd said to him broken-heartedly.

'You have family, min liten älskling,' he had answered tenderly, reverting to the language of his childhood as he did at times of great stress. Celie would never forget those strange, intimate moments they had shared whilst Mr Latimer and Doctor Maynard had dealt with her Pa's body.

'Come, älskling,' he had said, leading her from the kitchen and out into the pale lemon sunshine of the yard, his arm about her, her head pressed into his shoulder. Instinctively he had taken her beyond the garden gate and down by the side of the house to the spinney, leading her amongst the wide trunks of the trees.

He turned her towards him, cupping her white, shocked face in his hands, brushing away with his thumbs the tears which slid across her cheeks, bending his head to look into her eyes. They were deep and grey like the lake at the front of the house on a winter's day, the surface of them dappled with silver as the lake was when the wind crossed it. Without thought, his love sheltering her for a moment from the ache which would come, he laid his young man's lips first on one wet eye and then on the other, then drew her shuddering frame against his lean, long-boned body. He bent his head, resting his cheek on her hair and she pressed her face beneath the curve of his chin, straining close to him in her grief. His arms held her tightly to him, folded across her upper back, letting her know she would not fall, not whilst he was there, that she would *never* fall whilst Dan Smith was there to support her.

'You have no Mama, no Papa, now Celie, but you're not alone and never will be. We love you, Cook and me and . . .' who else loved her, he thought for a desperate moment? then his brow cleared, '. . . and Belle,' and it was true. Belle admired and looked up to young Celie even though there was scarcely any difference in their age. Celie had been kind to her in those first homesick days away from her Mam and Dad. She had shown her how to do things in the minefield of the kitchen where many of the marvellous things about it had never before been seen by Belle. She had taken her home to her Pa's cottage for Sunday tea now and again when Cook allowed it and told her about things which were happening in the newspapers. She talked to Belle, though the inarticulate girl had nothing to say in reply, reading to her from her books, begging her to 'listen to this, Belle' and Belle did, though it was not certain the skivvy understood.

'We all love you, Celie. We are your family. You will never be alone, I promise you. Cry, älskling, it is good to cry,' and she had, she remembered, in a great torrent against his comforting chest beneath the sheltering branches of the venerable oak trees. Cried until it was all gone and she was calm enough to go back to the kitchen, her hand in his, to talk to kind Mr Latimer about the funeral and listen to his assurances of her own firm place in his household.

Now she and Cook, in this quiet Sunday afternoon hour whilst their services were not needed, had walked across to Cec Marlow's cottage to pick up his and Celie's few belongings. They were to be stored in Dan's room above the coachhouse until the day came, in a couple of years if Cook's private hopes were realised, when they would be got out again to make the start of Celie and Dan's . . . well, she mustn't get ahead of herself, Cook thought, as she watched Celie drift aimlessly to the window and stare out onto the little strip of flower garden which her Pa had created.

'Couldn't I stay in the room I've been sleeping in for the past fortnight, Cook? It's only small, I know, hardly bigger than a cupboard, but I'd sooner sleep there than . . .'

'No, you can't,' Cook interrupted. 'Mrs Latimer wants you in with Kate and that's that. Maids share, Celie, you should know that and that there room you've been in is a lumber room. I know it's got a truckle bed in it but it will be folded away so that the . . .'

'I don't mind sleeping amongst the lumber, Cook, honestly I don't. You know how it is with me and Kate Mossop. Oh, I know we've kept our distance but . . . well, she can't abide me, Cook, and if her and me were made to share a room,

God only knows what it'll come to. Blows, for sure. She's never forgiven me for pinching *her* job.'

Celie turned imploringly to the woman in the chair, her eyes gaining a brilliant silvery shine in her eagerness. They looked enormous in her pale face, accentuated by its complete lack of colour except for the soft coral pink of her mouth. She looked so fragile, Cook had often thought, as though the hot air which came from the oven when the door was opened would knock her for six and yet she could work, cheerfully and uncomplainingly, for sixteen hours out of twenty-four. She was no weakling, physically or emotionally, this past two weeks had proved that, tackling the burden of the work she did, despite her youth, with a sure confidence which said she was well aware of her own worth. She moved about the kitchen which was her own absolute element, knowing it to be the place where she most wanted to be and where she intended, when her time came, to make her mark. She aspired to be the best cook in Liverpool, in the country, she had revealed in her youthful simplicity to Jess Harper, Cook to the Queen herself and she had it in her to do it, Cook thought, if her sweet and female loveliness and the men who would one day desire it, did not stop her. She was fully grown now, slender with small, swelling breasts, but not tall. She was not pretty in the way it was meant by today's fashions, but there was something indefinable and unique about her which Cook knew would capture the attention of not a few men. Her face was a perfect oval, as smooth as silk and creamy as the buttermilk in the pantry. Her top lip was long and the bottom one, full, delicately curved, seeming to draw all the colour from her flesh to itself. It was soft and vulnerable. Though her parents had been of common stock, at least as far as Cook knew, there was an air of fineness about her like the thoroughbred horses Cook herself had seen at the racecourse at Aintree, many years ago. She had a still quality about her and a . . . well you could only call it a . . . refinement, and how she was to get on in the same room as Kate Mossop who was as plain and earthy as a farmyard animal, Cook did not know, but she would damn well have to try!

'Listen to me, girl, you've got to make your mind up that

things have changed now with the death of your Pa.' She hated to see the wretched look on Celie's face but she had to be told and there was no one else to do it but Jess Harper. It was for her own good, wasn't it? 'You've had a . . . special place here in this house because of your Pa. He was always there at the back of you and I suppose if you'd not taken to it you could have come home to this cottage and kept house for him. You were . . . independent, in a way, tripping over here every night, getting away from the other servants to your own place, which none of them could do. Now I'm not saying you've had it easy, far from it, for you've been a bright little . . . well . . .' Cook cleared her throat, realising she was about to break her own strict rule which was never to let those who worked under her see her softer feelings. Favouritism was something she abhorred and she'd shown it to none, but this lovely child had, over the years, got under Cook's tough skin like no one had before and if she wasn't careful she'd be getting silly about her.

If Jess Harper had been told it was too late by several years she would not have believed it.

'Well . . .' she continued, her mind wandering from its first intention which was firmly to let Celie Marlow know that she was no different from the rest of the maidservants. She had a good "place", better than most domestic servants, where it was not uncommon for them to start the day on no more than a bowl of bread and milk. In some houses the maidservants slept in a kind of dormitory, six or eight of them in a row with no privacy, not even a bit of curtain to hang between the beds and with only a little box at the end in which to put their bits of things. When Jess Harper, at the age of ten, had started as maid-of-all-work in a gentleman's country residence near Leeds, she had begun her day at five thirty, a solitary day in which it had seemed to her her work would never be done. Rough treatment she had received, not only from the other girls who had started as she had done and were looking for someone on whom to vent their spite, as it had been vented on them, but from her mistress and master. She had cleaned the kitchen range, lit the fire in the kitchen, the breakfast room and many others, swept and shaken mats, scrubbed the doorsteps and passages, cleaned boots and all this before she had taken even a sip of tea. She had come up the hard way, had Jess Harper, and Celie Marlow must be made to realise that she could not have the choosing of her own life from now on, nor where she laid her head at night. She had her own way to make like Cook had done, but it was . . . well, she was such an endearing *likeable* child, and could you help but . . .

Cook shook herself, making an effort to get back on the subject which she was addressing, unaware of the fond expression in her small, blackcurrant eyes.

'. . . you've done right well, girl, and Mrs Latimer is pleased with you but you've got to understand that what she tells us to do, we do. She said you'd to move with Kate into the room Dorcas and Fanny shared and that's where you're to go, no argument.' Her face became even softer without her being aware of it.

'It's a nice little room, lass, and you and Kate will rub along together all right, see if you don't. Now look, here's Dan come to fetch the boxes up to the coachhouse so take that woebegone look off your face and give him a smile.'

But to Celie's enormous relief, she and Kate Mossop had no need to rub along together, for it seemed by some stroke of good fortune, Cook had caught her mistress in the middle of some small family crisis to do with Mrs Latimer's sister's daughter who had formed an attachment for a completely unsuitable young man. Mrs Latimer, in full sympathy with her sister, since had she not daughters of her own, had no time to concern herself with the question of where her kitchen maids were to sleep, telling Cook she would leave it all in her capable hands. Who shared with whom, providing it was decent, naturally, was trivial indeed compared to her poor sister's dilemma.

Kate, put in with Maudie, found she could queen it over the girl with whom Cook proposed she *should* share, taking the best of everything in the bedroom herself and as much space in the chest of drawers as she cared to since Maudie, though by no means as timid as Belle, was only twelve and in awe of the new parlourmaid. So it all worked out for the best and Cook was pleased about it. She'd promised Kate the job of parlourmaid and she'd kept her promise. Kate seemed grateful for it, telling Cook she'd not regret it. Kate Mossop was changed beyond recognition and Cook could only put it down to her new position but whatever it was, she was not about to find fault with it and it certainly made life easier for everyone.

It was a week later. Mr Latimer rang the study bell and when Dorcas answered it, asked her to get a message to Dan Smith to come to the house at once, as he wanted a word with him.

They were all on pins for over half an hour, each one of them, whilst Dan was in with Mr Latimer, even Belle and Maudie, who was as sharp as a tack and one day would be over Belle, Cook was certain, watching the door anxiously for Dan's return.

'What can it be, Cook, d'you think?' asked Celie.

'Nay, don't ask me, girl.'

'D'you thing he's . . . well, you know, what Fanny said on the day Pa . . . when she and Dorcas . . .'

'Aye, I remember child, but that was three weeks ago.'

'Yes, but nothing's been said about a *new* gardener, Cook.'

'Well, let's wait and see, shall we? Now get on with that batter for it'll not beat itself.'

They could tell without asking. His face was split from ear to ear with the size of his grin, a vivid gleam of white in his brown face. His expression glowed with triumph and as he moved across the kitchen floor he raised both arms in the air, clicking his fingers and performing some intricate little step with his booted feet which Cook noticed still had mud adhering to them. Grabbing Dorcas round the waist, he began to spin her about in a whirl of joy, then did the same with Cook, though gently.

'Put me down, you fool,' she screeched, the ladle which she had just dipped in a pan of soup on the range, spattering the liquid all over her scrubbed floor.

'I'm to be head gardener, Cook. Another boy to be got, two if I need . . .' and away he'd gone, jabbering in his own "lingo" and no one, not even Celie, noticed he had not put his arms around *her*.

There was further great rejoicing later on that year when *Captain* Richard Latimer, God bless him, came home from what had been known as the Third Burmese war. The Queen's army in Burma had fought long and bitterly against the rebellious "dacoits", as they were known to the British soldiers, for the past eight years. The Burmese had ignored their treaty obligations with Britain, persecuting and insulting British traders and officials. A British ultimatum had been followed by a strong Field Force, including the 2nd Battalion of the King's Regiment (Liverpool), the objective being to take Mandalay and capture the anti-British King, Thebaw. The British troops had suffered severely from the heat and humidity, from malaria and dysentery but nevertheless they had won the battle and King Thebaw had been deported to India. Upper Burma had been annexed but the dacoits had continued to resist and the Field Force had become no more than an army of occupation, sending columns to pursue the guerrillas and their leaders. They had finally been disbanded but not before Captain Latimer, leading one of these columns, had been slightly wounded by a Burmese arrow in the upper arm. He had been returned with his Battalion to India where it was stationed but the wound had proved troublesome, refusing to heal, and Captain Richard Latimer had come home to recuperate.

You would have thought the whole of his regiment was to dine the day he returned to Briar Lodge, so intense were the preparations in the kitchen. The family only on that first evening, no more, his Mama had insisted, since though he and his wound were well on the way to recovery, he had told her in a letter, she did not want him to overdo it. Now what did Cook suggest? Something light and tasty, enough to tempt perhaps an invalid's jaded palate, but nourishing enough to put strength in him. At the same time it must not seem to be *invalid* food since she did not want her son to feel *fussed*, if Cook knew what she meant.

Cook could tell Mrs Latimer was nearly bursting with

nervous excitement, she confided later to Celie, her mind on the return of her boy whom she had not seen for over a year and could you blame her for being jittery, not at all like her usual self, constantly jumping up to peer from the window, demanding to know if Cook could hear the carriage. He was to come by train from London where he had stayed overnight with a brother officer and Mrs Latimer had declared in Cook's hearing that she was going to have one of these new-fangled things, what did you call them? Celie must know what she meant. You put it to your ear and like magic you could hear someone's voice who was miles and miles away, yes, that was it, a telephone. It would have done away with all this uncertainty, Mrs Latimer had said to Miss Anne, for Master Richard, *Captain* Richard now, could have telephoned his Mama and let her know exactly when he would arrive. Could anyone imagine it, talking to someone who wasn't even in the same house, let alone the same room, because she couldn't, and who would speak into the dratted thing because *she* wouldn't, not for a gold clock! A bell rang, she had been told, and a servant must answer it, just as though it was the front door.

'Dear Lord, it won't be me, will it, Cook?' Dorcas put a shaking hand to her mouth, looking fearfully over her shoulder towards the door which separated the kitchen quarters from the front house.' I couldn't bring myself to pick it up. I don't even know what makes it work. Is it this *electric* stuff, d'you think? Maisie Donaldson, who works for the Hemmingways, says that they've got it in the house and it can give you a shock of some sort. Oh, please, Cook, tell Mrs Latimer I'd rather not touch it,' just as though the instrument was already standing on a table in the hallway and was ringing its head off.

'I'll speak to it, Cook,' Kate said airily, tossing her head. 'It doesn't frighten me.' She winked at Maudie, who began to laugh. She and Kate were becoming thick as thieves, Cook had noticed, and needed to be watched. Maudie was only young and easily influenced. Kate was lively, yet not in the way she had once been. It was as though the flaunting vulgarity of her nature had been turned down like a lamp until, though it is still bright, it is softer and less abrasive, giving out a glow which makes you relax. She just loved her new job, she told everyone who would listen. She was a person of some importance now, she believed. She had her own housemaid's box containing a banister brush, a staircase brush, a cornice brush, a dusting brush, floor cloths and dusting cloths, which it was her duty to keep spotlessly clean. There were different polishes, one for marble, another to brighten gilt frames, and one that contained linseed oil for the buffing of furniture. Under Dorcas's eagle eye, she had learned how to polish the furniture, the likes of which her dazzled eyes had never before seen, clean windows and carefully dust all the exquisite vases, ornaments, glass and chinaware, the Wedgwood and Sèvres and Coalport, the clocks and pot-pourri bowls and all, if you please, which she liked better than anything, to be done in fine white cotton gloves. It gave her poor ruined hands a chance to heal, especially with that fragrant cream Dorcas had lent her to rub into them. They had to be nice, you see, she explained to one and all because when you served tea in the drawing room and waited on at the table, which she was to do, you couldn't have great red chapped hands like hers handing out the cucumber sandwiches, could you? It was this slightly irreverent humour which the other maids found appealing, a rather unkind inclination to poke a bit of fun at things, making those about her laugh, and Cook didn't want young Maudie tainted with it.

Dorcas was exacting, brisk and quite accustomed to the grandeur of the front house, with no time to stand and stare as Kate had wanted to do, for the "light" cleaning which was separate from the "heavy" work Mary and Lily performed, must be done and finished before the family came downstairs for breakfast and if Kate came across any of them during that work period, she was to bob her curtsey and fade into the wallpaper, Dorcas told her. Could you imagine it, Kate giggled, *her* fading into the wallpaper, looking down at her own splendid breast and curving hips, doing her best to draw Dan Smith's eyes to their magnificent proportions. But on this day, the day the young master was to come home, the matter of the telephone and who was to answer it was swept away by the absorbing question of what should be prepared for Master Richard's homecoming dinner which Cook and Celie discussed at length.

'Well, Mrs Latimer was in such a taking,' Cook divulged confidentially to her handmaiden, 'I said to her why don't you leave it to me, Madam, I know what Master Richard's favourites are . . .'

'What are they, Cook?' Dan begged to know from the door which led into the yard and through which he had just come, his own face split in a wide grin. 'Go on, go on, let me guess. A chip butty, a wet nelly and a tatie pie followed by a pint of stout . . .'

'You cheeky young devil. A wet nelly indeed, I don't know where you pick these things up, I really don't. At that there football club, I shouldn't wonder. Just a minute, you're not telling me you've . . . you have, haven't you, I can see it in your eyes, you limb of the devil. You've been in that pub, what's it called . . .'

'The Swan, Cook,' Kate said, winking at Maudie before turning her gleaming green cat's eyes on Dan.

'That's it, the Swan. Have you been having a bevvy on the night you go training, Dan Smith, because if you have I'll . . .'

'I *am* eighteen, Cook,' Dan said mildly moving up behind her, doing his best to untie the ribbons of her apron, then dancing away again on his light, footballer's feet. His eyes had been drawn momentarily to Kate for he was a man and a man would look at any woman who displays herself, but they returned as they always did to Celie's rapt face.

'Will you get out of my way, Dan Smith,' Cook said tartly, 'Celie and I have this meal to see to and it's hard enough to concentrate without you playing the fool. What d'you want anyway, we've no time to be making tea, if that's what you're after.' Cook pretended exasperation.

'No, me and Jim were passing through the yard with the pony and wondered if there was a chance of a glass of that lemonade you were making last night. It's thirsty work rolling those lawns, isn't it, Jim?'

The boy who had been employed to help the new "head

gardener" ducked his head shyly, his face a bright and shining crimson beneath the concentrated gaze of six females. He twisted his cap in his hands, staring furiously at the floor, wishing it would swallow him up, Celie could see, and she smiled, taking pity on him.

'Sit down a minute, Jim. See, Maudie, fetch that lemonade from the pantry and two glasses and there's fresh ice on the marble slab. The ice man's just been so you can put a lump in the glasses while you're at it.'

Celie sounded so like her as Maudie ran to do her bidding that Cook turned away and, catching Dan's eye and recognising that he had had the same thought, she nodded her head at him. Celie was nearly a woman now.

She was sixteen next birthday and in a year or two would be ready for marriage and who was more suitable than Dan Smith, with his fine new job for which he was now paid a man's wage, and could support a family, plus all the food he could eat and the snuggest little cottage you could find anywhere. What had once been Celie's Pa's was now Dan Smith's and you could tell he was made up with it. A grand lad with a grand future ahead of him, secure and bright, and how right it would be for him to take Celie back to her old home.

It did not occur to Cook that beneath Celie Marlow's bright, young innocence, her warm, affectionate trust, her shining belief in life which had never been seriously tested, was a strong spirit, an untapped reserve of strength which would, when the time came, resist all efforts to lead her where she did not care to go. That as she matured, her own will would be unbreakable, resilient, needing support from no one.

They were sitting sprawled about the kitchen table, Dorcas and Celie on one side, Kate on the other, sipping a mug of Cook's hot, sweet cocoa before they made their weary way to their beds. Cook was in her own chair, her feet up, the tabby purring its fat, contented song on her lap to the rhythm of her stroking hand. The round mahogany-framed kitchen clock hanging on the wall to the side of the dresser, the one which Cook wound every night before going to bed, chimed musically, sounding ten o'clock, and four pairs of eyes turned to look at it. Belle and Maudie, the "pots done" and every pan and dish scoured to Cook's satisfaction, the scullery as clean and neat as a new pin, again as Cook liked it, had been sent to their beds, and it wouldn't be long before they all went up the "dancers", as Cook put it. A long day, it had been, but a happy one, with the return of the eldest son of the house, safe and sound and looking, both Dorcas and Kate had reported, fine and handsome in his lovely uniform. They'd carried his bags up to his room, unpacking them, and run here and there after him, drawing his bath, twinkling and dimpling at the things he said to them, their young faces rosy, their eyes bright, quite taken out of themselves at having a man in the house again. Well, you couldn't count *Mr* Latimer could you, him being . . . so elderly, and the boys were just . . . *boys*, but Captain Richard had a joke and a smile and a certain look in his eye which had them all aflutter. And he'd enjoyed the meal immensely, he told them after they had finished serving and when his Mama had gone into the drawing room.

When the kitchen door opened and he walked in, Cook said afterwards you could have knocked her down with a feather. Her, with her boots off on account of her swollen feet, a thing she'd only taken to doing just recently for she'd certain standards to keep up if she was to set an example to the other servants. But her poor ankles were like balloons and her feet like puddings, or was it the other way about? Whatever it was, they were giving her gyp. And not only that, she'd her skirts half-way up her calves just like any gin-swilling "Mary-Ellen" in a Liverpool gutter.

They leapt to their feet, even Cook, her skirts falling about her swollen legs and bootless feet, the cat thrown in an indignant heap on the hearth rug, mugs clattering and slopping cocoa on the white scrubbed kitchen table, as the four maids bobbed their curtseys.

'No, for God's sake, don't get up, any of you. Lord, I wouldn't have come if I'd thought . . . well, to tell you the truth Cook, I didn't think and I'm sorry. You work so hard I forget . . . now listen to me rattling on and all I wanted to do was to thank you for that splendid meal. How you remember, I'll never know, but you always do. Please do sit down, all of you . . .' which they did reluctantly except Cook '. . . but that lamb was superb and as for the apple snow, you surpassed yourself. I think it's the best one you've ever made, Cook.'

'Not me, Master Richard, t'was Celie here who made the apple snow,' watching as his gaze moved to her handmaiden and remained there. Credit where credit was due Cook's expression said, for Jess Harper believed in truth and fairness even if it did take some of the credit from herself. 'But I'm glad you enjoyed the meal, sir. And it wasn't hard to remember your liking for lamb. Every Sunday from you being a boy I can still hear you whispering "Is it lamb for lunch, Cook?", when your Mama wasn't listening, "lamb and mint sauce." And may I say how glad we are to see you back home in one piece, Master Richard. A worrying time for your poor Mama and your Papa, of course . . .' she added hastily, since she did not wish to imply that Mr Latimer was uncaring '. . . and relieved they were to know your wound is not serious.'

She smiled respectfully at the side of his head since his gaze was still on Celie, gritting her teeth at the agony which surged up her legs, longing to sit down as the maids had done. Well, all except Celie who, though she had returned to her seat on the bench which lay at the side of the table when commanded to by Master Richard, had inexplicably stood up again. She had the most peculiar expression on her face, an expression which Cook found to be strangely familiar. It reminded her of . . . yes . . . Celie Marlow looked just like a sleep-walker . . . that was it, it was coming back to her now. Cook had once shared a room with a girl who had been one. A sleep-walker. She used to scare the living daylights out of her, trailing about in her long white nightgown and her face all pale and staring, eyes wide open but kind of . . . blank, dark and misted as though a veil hung over them. What was the word . . . *opaque*! that was it. What on earth was the matter with the child? Was she so overawed at coming face to face with the Master's son she had become as dim-witted and speechless as Belle? Really, what would Master Richard think of her, the silly child? She'd have to learn how to speak to her betters if she was, one day, to go into service in the kitchen of a decent household.

Cook turned back apologetically to Master Richard, ready to ease the awkwardness, and was quite astounded to find that on his face was exactly the same "daft" expression as that on Celie Marlow's.

Chapter Eight

Celie was considerably startled several days later when he rose from what seemed to be the very ground on which she walked, appearing before her as he had in her every waking thought, every dream she had dreamed at night since he had come home. She was still in that state of shock and of something else she was at a loss to recognise which he had induced in her in the kitchen and the memory was so vivid, it was as though it had only just happened. She had carried it about with her, held it close to her, hidden it from sight, terrified someone would see it and call her bad, wicked, but unable to cast it off. When she was alone she took it out and studied it distractedly, having no idea what to do with it, nor wanting it, for such curious emotions were not for the likes of Celie Marlow, at least not about *him*. She had wandered across the grass at the back of the house to the bit of woodland where, if the day was warm and she could snatch a moment from her busy day, she came to read, to dream, to be alone when she needed solitude, and here he was, just as though her soul-searching had conjured him up.

She flinched away from him as he put out a hand to her, and her eyes widened in nervous alarm. Seeing it, he put his hand in his pocket, then the other one as well so that she could clearly see he meant her no harm, but his eyes had the greatest difficulty in retaining the casual, *friendly* expression he knew he must do his best to assume with her. He had no idea what to say to her now that he had come. Good afternoon, lovely day isn't it? That was so . . . so formal. The sort of thing his father would throw at a maidservant,

courteously, of course, as he passed her on the stairs. Hello,
I just came to . . . *what*? What could he be doing here in the
middle of the spinney, the spinney in which, driven by some
instinct and force over which he had no control, he had waited
for her for the past week. Celie, how nice to see you. What a
surprise. Do you come here a lot . . . Oh, Jesus . . . she was
so afraid of him. Like a fawn which has stepped, unsuspecting,
into an empty sunlit clearing, only to find that what she thought
was safe had in it a ravening wolf. She stood in that quivering
attitude a wary animal assumes when it is not sure whether
to stand still or run like hell, her great silvery-grey eyes . . .
God in Heaven, he'd never seen eyes quite like them before
. . . they were enormous, the pupils black as sable, shaded
with long, fine lashes, like a child's. He thought she was the
loveliest thing he'd ever seen. As he had that last time in the
hallway, his heart remembered . . . and in all this time it had
not allowed him to forget. He had not thought about her *all*
the time, of course not. Days would go by, *weeks*, whilst he
had been away, first in Burma then in India, weeks in which he
had spent his days and nights in the duties of his profession,
a perfectly normal soldier's life, a young man's life in which
other women had played a part. But now and again, perhaps
on patrol as he and his men sought out the guerrillas who
harassed the Field Force, or in the dead of a sleepless night,
her face had unexpectedly imprinted itself upon his closed
eyelids, surprising him in its clarity. The white drift of her
dress, the dark, glowing cap of her hair, the depthless smoky
grey of her eyes, the soft, parted coral of her mouth and that
sweet, defenceless air of a child caught in some naughty deed
which had made him want to smile . . . and kiss her . . . *as
he did now*.

He turned away from her whilst he did his best to get
his confounded senses under control, staring blindly at the
mossy trunk of the tree against which he had been leaning.
The grass at its roots was crushed, bearing the imprint of his
body, for he had been sitting here for more than an hour, and
not just today. His eyes followed a drip of honeydew moving
slowly across a broad leaf, watching the aphids from which
the sweet liquid had exuded. He found himself noting in every

detail the pattern of furrows across the tree trunk, radiating from a central furrow which was the work of a bark beetle.

The bark of the tree was rough, scraped off here and there to reveal the smoothness beneath, and he studied it with the intensity of a naturalist though in reality he saw none of it, only those wide, frightened eyes which he knew were at his back. He shouldn't have come, not yet.

Not yet! What did that mean? Did it imply that one day, when she was older, more mature perhaps, that there could be something . . . *would* be something . . . oh, Jesus, what in Hell was wrong with him? She was a child, dammit, and he must leave, make some excuse and sidle off like some . . .

He pushed his hand through his thick, tumbled hair, forgetting the half-healed wound in his upper arm, wincing as the movement reminded him of its presence. Making a decent effort to appear at ease, casual, just as though there was nothing untoward in the son of the house standing in a woodland clearing, staring like a bloody idiot at the trunk of a tree, he turned and did his best to smile naturally.

'I'm sorry if I startled you . . . Celie, isn't it?'

She nodded and the feathers of her dark hair which fell over her forehead and almost into her eyes moved in a way which enchanted him and again he felt that strange and powerful temptation to reach out a hand and brush them away from her creamy skin.

'I was . . .' What the deuce was he doing here? It had better be believable for he had the feeling she was getting ready to make a bolt for it. He really could not understand *why* this child . . . this young woman should be so afraid of him. After all he was an officer and presumably a gentleman, the son of the house, with every right to wander where he pleased, and she must be aware that in his *mother's* house there would be none of the diversions some sons of the gentry got up to with their mother's maidservants.

'I was . . . the doctor told me I must . . .' yes that was it, a perfectly logical reason . . . '. . . exercise and as yet I cannot ride so here I am, walking through the woods and about to take a turn around the pond.' It seemed so natural, so right to speak to her as though she was a friend of his sisters, perhaps, or a guest of the house. It was strange that even though she now wore the uniform of a servant and was obviously *not* a friend of his sisters, there was a sense of intimacy, as though he had known her always, a sense so strong that for a horrified moment he almost asked her to accompany him on his walk. He tried to imagine his mother's face on looking from her drawing-room window to see her son strolling down the lawn with her kitchen maid beside him. The thought made him smile, a soft and whimsical smile and quite visibly he could see the tension seep out of her and a tiny twitch of her lips rewarded him, just as though she had read his mind.

'Your arm is . . . improving?' Her voice was low and he was amazed at his own delight, not only that she had answered, speaking to him for the first time, but that the tone of it was muted and with barely a trace of the adenoidal dialect of Liverpool in it. Her eyebrows rose delicately as she asked the question and he watched them, and the shaping of her soft mouth as she spoke, with a fascination which astounded him.

'Oh yes, thank you. It's a bit stiff at times.' He put a hand to it, rolling the shoulder joint to let her see there was nothing serious to worry about, and again he was confused by his own response to her. Her eyes were filled with concern and yet there seemed to be relief in them as though his well-being was of great importance to her.

'I'm so glad. It must have been . . . very frightening.'

'What?' His eyes focused on the movement of her lips. She shrugged gracefully.

'To be shot at by . . . whoever they were.' She had moved fractionally closer to him, her initial alarm almost gone. 'Cook had it from your . . . from Mr Latimer that they fire arrows . . . the enemy soldiers and that . . . it was one of those which . . .'

Celie contemplated the rich, soft brown of his eyes and saw them darken. He blinked, a long, slow drooping of his thick lashes. About his eyes were faint lines, a small fanning out from the corners, pale in the deeply sunburned skin of his face, burned by a sun far more compelling than that which shone in English skies. He wore a soft white shirt, open at the neck, with long full sleeves which he had turned back at the wrist. His slender, long-fingered hands and strong forearms were the same rich amber as his face and from his knuckles, moving up his arms, were fine golden brown hairs, catching the sun as they must have done in that far-off Eastern land from which he had just returned. His pale buff riding breeches were of doeskin, fitting smoothly to his lean hips, his neat buttocks and strong, muscled thighs, tucked into knee-length, well-polished brown boots. He was watching her intently, noticing where her eyes strayed, seeing the sudden rosy flags at her high cheekbones, and he knew it was up to him to put her completely at her ease. She had not the faintest conception of how to handle a situation like this, one in which he had found himself many times, but none so fraught with pitfalls, he thought wonderingly. But he was a man, for God's sake, with several years of experience in the delights of the flesh, of flirtations and dalliance, though none of these words described the way he felt *now*, he thought sadly – and surely he should be able to take charge.

'Is this a favourite spot of yours, Celie?' he asked her gently and was again rewarded by her quivering smile and the way in which her breath ebbed from her in a sigh.

'Yes, yes, it is. I often bring a book here to read. It's not easy sometimes to find somewhere quiet. The kitchen is always . . . well . . .'

'I know,' he went on for her, his face betraying none of his feelings now. 'I have the same problems in the mess. What do you like to read? What are you reading now?' praying it would not be some trashy novelette he had heard housemaids favoured.

She bobbed her head, wondering feverishly what a 'mess' might be. 'It is by an American gentleman called Henry James. Perhaps you've heard of him?'

'Indeed I have but I must confess I'm not a great reader. What is it called?'

'*The Bostonians.*'

'Really. And what is it about?'

'Well . . .'

'Please, I'm fascinated,' and he was, smiling down into her face for they had imperceptibly drawn closer to one another.

'It's about the . . . the struggle of . . . women to be . . . well . . . themselves, I suppose, though . . .' again the bewitching bob of the head '. . . well, I can only tell you how I . . . see it.'

'That is the only way,' he said gravely. 'And, if I may ask, where do you get these books you read?'

'The library, sir.' The "sir" jarred at him and he frowned. At once her face lost its look of shining trust and she became uncertain.

'Mr Latimer gave me permission. He said I was to help myself whenever your mother . . . whenever . . . I was to make sure I disturbed no one . . .' She had begun to flounder since she could hardly tell this smiling, *beautiful* man that if his mother found out it would be the end of Celie Marlow's journeying into the joy of reading. That this was a secret between herself and Mr Latimer.

'Celie . . . please. I was not . . .' He could not explain to her that her forays into the library at Briar Lodge amazed and delighted him and that it was the sudden reminder of their disparate place in the house with her use of "sir", that had jarred him and his joy in her. He could only get by it in one way.

'I had no idea there were new books in there,' he continued hastily. 'Whenever I peeped in all I saw were enormous tomes on subjects far too clever for me to handle.'

'Oh, no. There's lots I know you'd enjoy. I've read Dickens and Jane Austen, Thomas Hardy and Rudyard Kipling. Haven't you tried them?' She could scarcely credit that someone with access to such a splendid library had not read the lot.

'I can't say I have,' ruefully. 'Your classical education far exceeds mine, Celie.' Again the shy bob of the head.

'Oh, I can't believe *that*. You've been to university, sir.' There it was again. He gritted his teeth and at once she noticed it. Her face closed like a flower deprived of sunlight and once again he was sorry for it.

She was quite incredible, this young girl who was something

in his mother's kitchen, not only was she as well read, more so, probably than many girls in his own class, but she was bewilderingly sensitive to the slightest change in his own attitudes towards her. She knew at once that he was displeased though not why, and he longed to hold her hand and explain to her. To sit her down on the grass beneath the trees and tell her that she was not to address him as "sir". His name was Richard and just to hear it on her lips would be an honour, if she would only . . .

Jesus, what was he to say to her? What *was* there to say? The gulf between them was unbridgeable and this strange enchantment she cast about him must be torn away for it was trapping him, making him helpless. He was Captain Richard Latimer of the King's Liverpool Regiment with a fine future ahead of him. The son of a foremost Liverpool family. The heir. He might, if she was willing and discreet, make free with his mother's kitchen maid and be thought none the worse for it but how could any man take advantage of this child who was looking at him with such a clear and steady gaze? A gaze which unmanned him with its wary innocence. And yet there was something else in her that as yet he knew she was not aware of. Though her expression was innocent, it was also bewildered as if deep down she recognised that something was happening between them which she could not understand.

Of its own volition, his hand rose, reaching out to tuck a springing curl behind her ear and he saw her eyes widen but she did not draw back. The tip of his finger moved to her cheek. She looked up at him, waiting, not knowing, he was fully aware, what she was waiting for, and it was he who moved back, conscious that this was all he could allow himself. He drew in a long breath, watching the dark depths of her pupils become even darker. Everything seemed to have slowed. The world had stopped turning and they stood together in the timelessness it had brought about.

'Oh, sweet Christ,' he muttered, 'this wasn't supposed to happen.'

He saw her lips form the word 'What?' but he turned away for a moment or two, knowing he should send her back to the kitchen at once, *at once*. When he turned back to her the words he spoke came from his heart, his mind denied a voice.

'Sit down and talk to me, Celie,' he heard himself say and his ironic mind whispered "so much for gentlemanly ethics". 'Unless I'm keeping you from . . . something?' he added hastily. He was loth to say "your work".

'No, it's my afternoon off.'

'And where do you usually go on your . . . afternoon off?'

'I come here, or if Dan, he's the gardener, is off too, we go into Liverpool.' Jesus Christ, the gardener . . . *the bloody gardener* had access to this lovely child, access that was denied *him*. It seemed like an obscenity, even to imagine the . . . fineness, the delicate rarity of this . . . girl, being paired with the coarse and earthy rustic which females of her class would dally with. It could not bear thinking about. She was well read. She had . . . dignity, an innocent dignity which was touching . . .

'Dan likes the exhibitions,' she continued, 'but I'd rather go to . . .'

'Yes? Where?' His voice was brusque and he did his best to soften it.

'To look at the shops in Bold Street, to Sefton Park, or the Marine Parade to see the ships.'

'You like the ships, Celie?'

'Yes, sir.'

'Don't . . . don't . . .'

She shied away from the vehemence in his voice and from something else she knew lay behind it. Celie Marlow was no simpleton and her mirror, and men's eyes when she was out with Dan, told her she was not unattractive. She had seen the way they looked at her, that certain narrowing, speculative gleam in their eyes that all females recognise from the age of twelve. She had watched, her gaze narrowing, when Kate tossed her head at Dan in that bold way she had, smiling at him from the corner of her eye, arching her back for him. She had seen Dan's confusion but she had also seen that same admiring look, perhaps reluctant, but there nevertheless in Dan's eyes that was now in Richard Latimer's. She had been stunned when she had come across him in this place, *her* place, the instinctive alarm felt by a solitary female in the company of an unknown and therefore unpredictable man. She knew him, naturally, for he was the son of the house. She had last met him in the hallway of the house and even then she had felt the strange pull of his masculinity drawing her towards him. She did not, of course, describe it to herself in that way for she was an untried, half-educated girl with no knowledge of the male sex. It was her instinct, deep, primeval, female, which whispered to her of this thing between them, this soft and lovely drowning in the honeyed sweetness of his eyes, of his voice, and of the betraying gentleness in both.

'Sit . . . for a minute,' he begged her, putting out a hand to help her as he would any lady, then withdrawing it hastily, knowing any further physical contact between them would be disaster.

The shade under the trees would soon be gone, for already the leaves were shaking themselves free from the twining branches to which they had clung all summer. The grassy path on which they stood was barely used and it was wild and thick with summer growth. Small plants, seedlings, pushed their way fiercely up towards the sunlight, determined on their bit of space, and around each tree trunk, growing in the wide-spread roots were earth-carpeting mosses like velvet cushions. They covered fallen logs and even the stumps of trees cut by Cec Marlow in his care of the land. There were toadstools in attractive shapes and colours adding to the profusion, ivy and traveller's joy, honeysuckle and fern, woodsorrel still bursting forth their delicate white flowers. The sun shone through what was left of the almost transparent leaves, high on the branches, turning them to a soft pale green, darker the lower down the tree they grew, but already many were turning to gold, amber, russet and terracotta as they took on autumn's hues. The soft, throaty whir of a wood pigeon made a rhythmic melody high above them and Celie looked up. It was as though the gentle familiar call of the birds soothed her anxieties and she sank down to the soft cushion of moss at the foot of the tree.

They sat for an hour, whilst he slowly drew out of her

details of her life at Briar Lodge. She told him about her
mother and father, of her mother's death when Celie was
born, and of her father's earlier in the year. She was reluctant
at first, overwhelmed by the presence of him, believing that
a man such as he could find nothing of interest in a girl such
as herself. He had to prompt her time and time again. He
sat well away from her, his knees drawn up, his arms about
them, watching her intently as she spoke, and gradually her
diffidence left her. He made no attempt to touch her. She
was encouraged by his interest in what she read, what she
thought, what she did on her day off which came once a month
– he did not dare to ask when it was – even her opinions on
the politics of Mr Gladstone who had been returned to power
that year, which, astonishingly she seemed to have knowledge
of, since she read the newspapers his father discarded, she
told him.

'And what will you do now?' he asked her, beginning to
believe that this remarkable girl could do anything she pleased
and certainly would not be content to stay as assistant to his
mother's cook. She was sixteen, she told him, and had been
in the position for well over two years, learning from Cook,
who was the best in Liverpool, she had added ingenuously.
Now his question startled her and she frowned, narrowing
her gleaming silver eyes in concentration.

'I'm not sure I know what you mean,' she said hesitantly,
leaning towards him.

'I mean you won't stay here for ever, will you? At Briar
Lodge.'

'Well . . . ?'

'Have you no ambitions to become . . . oh, chef at the
Adelphi, or even the Ritz in London?' He was smiling, ready
to tease her a little for she was such a serious little thing. He
wanted to see her smile, grin, laugh out loud but it seemed he
had offended her and he was instantly contrite. His expression
said so.

'You're laughing at me,' she said accusingly, and her eyes
darkened. He watched them, spellbound. 'I'm a good cook,
sir, ask anybody, well not Kate, 'cos she'd give you an
argument.' Her eyes were vivid for a moment, 'And if I

made up my mind to it, and I might, I could be cook to
. . . to . . . the Lord Mayor of Liverpool.'

'Of course you could. I'm only teasing you, but not . . . I
don't mean to hurt you, Celie. I'm sure you can do whatever
you set out to do. I only wondered if you knew what that
is. I have wanted to be a soldier ever since I was a small
boy but my father didn't think it suitable for me.' His eyes
left hers for the first time, narrowing as he studied some
memory which was not pleasing to him. 'He wanted me to
go into the firm, the shipping business, as his family have
done for generations. Noble Shippers have been importers
and exporters for more than a hundred years and every
eldest Latimer son has carried on the tradition. I went to
university because that's what Latimers do, then they go into
the business, but I told Father that he had six more sons to
take my place, though he would have to wait for the three
youngest . . .' smiling into her bemused face '. . . and that if
he wouldn't allow me to become a "King's man" I would run
away and become a drummer boy. Also I think it helped to
win my case that twenty years ago army reforms brought
about the ending of the system of purchase of commissions
by officers. They could be damned expensive, even for a lowly
subaltern. Well, you know Father . . .' smiling affectionately.
Celie nodded breathlessly, for didn't they all, '. . . he was all
for letting me have my own way but . . . well, Mother was
harder to convince.'

Oh, yes, Celie could just imagine it. Mrs Latimer would
not want her eldest boy, her favourite, they all knew that in
the servants quarters, going off to unknown parts where *she*
could not keep her eye on him, and a tight rein too, as she
did on them all. A place in the firm, a well-bred girl to marry,
a girl Mrs Latimer could mould into a replica of herself until it
was time for her son's wife to take *her* place – though not for
a long, long time – and for her son to become senior partner
in the firm of Noble Shippers. She would not like it at all to
have that son remove himself, not only from the house and
from Liverpool but from the country, which he had done and
would continue to do in his career as one of Her Majesty's
Officers.

'But you did it.' Her breath sighed from between her lips at the marvel of him and the expression in her eyes, though she was not aware of it, was one of glowing admiration.

'Oh, yes, I did it, which brings me back to you.'

'Me?' The colour flooded her face and she looked down at her hands. Her eyelashes formed a fan on her rose-tinted cheeks and he leaned towards her.

'Yes. Will you . . . become a . . . ?' He found he could not go on. The picture of this delicate-looking girl with her ethereal beauty, her slender body, her narrow shoulders, her fragile wrists and hands which looked as though they should be burdened with nothing more challenging than a posy of flowers, borne down with the work of a servant in another woman's kitchen, was something he could not bear to contemplate. She should be waited on herself, petted and protected, treated with gentle kindness, allowed to do no more than sit with her feet on a dainty stool, a bit of fine embroidery in her hands, fussed over, comforted, loved . . . oh Jesus Christ . . . yes . . . loved.

'I'll be the best cook in Liverpool,' she said simply. Her young dreams, not yet taking her beyond her own environment, shattered into a million appalling pieces the lovely image he had had of her and which, for a moment, he had allowed himself to dwell on. Not in any precise way, for it was a bright dream created in his young man's fanciful heart and not the practical detachment of his brisk soldier's mind. There was no depth or truth to it, only the imaginings, blurred, soft, glowing, of his emotions which had been painfully stirred this day.

'The best cook in Liverpool.' His voice was flat but this time she did not hear the change in it. As his had done, her eyes wandered away into the slow, faltering fall of the dusky evening which neither had noticed.

'Yes, the very best cook in . . .'

'I thought our cook was that.' He did not mean it to be but his voice was sharp. He was coming out of his bright daydreams and the return to reality was painful.

'Oh, yes . . . she is *now*,' Celie lifted her head, 'but . . . one day . . .'

'Yes?'

'I will have my own place with . . .'

'With Dan, I suppose.'

She looked astonished, then, just as he had imagined it, she began to laugh. She put her head back, the lovely slender line of her throat white and pure in the deepening shadows. Her eyes narrowed, the lashes meshing, and her mouth moved in a wide curve over her good white teeth. She had a tiny indent at the corner of her mouth which he had never seen before and he felt the gladness, the delight, the sweetness of it surge inside him like a bird longing to escape.

He opened his heart and allowed it to go free and, seeing the change in him, she let the laughter die away for there was something about him which did not call for it. She could see it in his eyes, an expression, a knowledge of something unusual which had suddenly happened to him and which she shared. She shared it without being entirely sure what it was. In his eyes was an expression which was telling her something, something beyond the admiration a man feels for a pretty girl. It came softly stealing, an unbelievable and breathless awareness which, in a moment, she would be able to grasp. Her heart was thudding so strangely, so *painfully* and she could only stare into his eyes, waiting, waiting for him to . . . tell her . . . what . . . ?

He stood up suddenly, straightening his tall frame to its full height, wincing a little as the wound in his arm, which had stiffened, dragged at him like barbed wire in his flesh.

'Come, little Celie, it will be dark soon,' he said lightly, his voice perfectly normal, revealing none of the turmoil; none of the sudden terrifying acceptance of what had happened to him. He held out his good hand and she put hers in it as he drew her to her feet and without consciously thinking about it, allowed it to remain there. He turned towards the edge of the spinney. They walked slowly, not speaking now. The autumn sun was setting, just about to touch the tops of the trees, and the shadows lengthened about them. Their steps were as silent as the coming night, and neither spoke, for it seemed they were wrapped about in some enchantment, which though she felt it, Celie did not understand. In the west the sky was turning to the palest lemon and above it the lemon merged into green as the sun descended. Outlining the dark trees it was fast turning to brown, then orange and, at the edge of the trees where they stood, hidden still from all eyes except the wood pigeons, the couple watched in silence as an arch of pure rose-pink spread above the yellow, the orange, the orange-red.

'Wait a moment,' Richard said softly, his voice almost a whisper, and she obeyed for she was held in the breathless trance of her hand in his, his voice in her ears and the beauty about them both.

'Look.'

The sky became violet, then plum purple, spreading a clear twilight glow across the heavens, and as they watched a star was revealed, pricking the deepness with a brilliance which was eternal.

They stood for perhaps five minutes watching the sky as it darkened further and across it began to drift the night birds and the soft rush of bats' wings. He turned towards her, his teeth white in the dark oval of his face and without fear now, she waited.

'I am to go back to my regiment soon, Celie.'

'Yes.'

There was a long moment in which the whole woodland seemed to hold its breath in a fluttering silence, then, 'How lovely you are.' His voice was no more than a soft whisper.

She did not answer, merely regarded him gravely in the deep shadows beneath the trees and when he reached for her other hand she stood quietly. Taking both of hers in his he raised them to his lips, rubbing his mouth across the backs of them. His lips were warm and she shivered in delight, a strange delight, but sweet as this afternoon had been sweet.

'God damn it to hell,' he whispered so softly she could barely hear him.

Slowly she released her hands. She lifted her head which had been inclined achingly to his, straightened her young back with a curious dignity and stepped away from him.

'I must go now, sir. Cook will be looking for me. I hope your shoulder will soon mend and . . . goodbye, sir.'

Chapter Nine

By some error or perhaps a memory lapse on the part of the reverend gentlemen who had baptised Cecil and Mary Marlow's infant daughter, the name on her baptismal certificate was given as Cécilie instead of the more usual Cecily. Though this caused considerable confusion at Prince Albert Road Board School where the principal declared he had never *heard* of it and was it *French*, Cec Marlow would not allow it to be changed. The baby girl whose wide eyes were the exact colour of those of his dead Mary, herself buried no more than a few weeks before the baptism of her child, and who was certainly up in Heaven, must surely have been *meant* to be called by the name of Cécilie. In the over-emotional state to which his grief had flung him, it had seemed to Cec that Mary, on the right hand of God, so to speak, must have put it *directly* into the parson's mind to call her child by the somewhat outlandish and foreign-sounding name and who was Cec to alter that? So, Cécilie Marlow she had remained, though it was soon *Celie* for the offspring of Reuben Ash and Mrs Ash; of George Ellis and his wife with whom Celie spent the first five years of her life, and who were distinguished with names such as Fred, Alfie, Tom, Bertie, Jack, Ethel, Sal, Florence and similar plain, no-nonsense labels, were not inclined to struggle with the awkwardness of *Cécilie*.

Though Celie, from a young age, had worked hard, labouring all day at the Board School and for an hour or so after that at the scullery sink, she had in a way been as gently reared as the four daughters of Phyllis and Richard Latimer. She had not, of course, in the true sense of the word, been raised as they were, to be a lady. One of those who were moulded for the sole purpose of becoming the wife of a gentleman and the mother of his children. They were protected, sheltered, their innocent lives untouched by any disagreeable or harmful contact with the world outside the high and sturdy walls which surrounded Briar Lodge. Just as Celie Marlow was. She had gone to school but it was a village school where the pupils were not of the sort one found in the city. They were children brought up as she was, in a decent environment with careful, industrious parents, innocent and ignorant for the most part of the "goings on" which affected the world even as near to them as Liverpool. When she returned to Briar Lodge at the end of the day she was at once set amongst the hard-working, clean-living servants, all under the auspices of the ever watchful Jess Harper, and but for that one incident in which Kate Mossop had whispered details to Celie about how she had been created – which she didn't understand nor believe really, it was so *silly* – she was as safeguarded, inexperienced and unworldly as the children in the "front" house.

At sixteen her character had not yet fully formed. She was still a combination of all the circumstances, events and emotions with which her young life had been made up. In some respects she retained many of the characteristics of her childhood, the sheltered childhood which because of its nature, gave her no reason to mistrust those about her. Her naivety and need for approval was still with her for in many ways she had not completely left girlhood nor had she yet become a woman. The servants at Briar Lodge were her family. She was fond of most of them, starting with Mrs Ash who had carelessly but cheerfully, from Celie's babyhood, planted her among her own brood and given to the motherless child what she gave to Fred and Albert and Ethel and Florence, which was a heedless but protective affection. Though Celie had loved her father, because he *was* her father, there had been no warm demonstrations of family fondness between them. She had received patience and kindness and resigned good humour from every worker in the house and garden, from Madge Evans in the laundry, from

Mary and Lily who often brought her a few "dolly mixtures" in a screw of paper, from Mr Latimer who would, when Mrs Latimer was not about, squat on his haunches to talk to the bright and lovely child. She admired Cook, holding her in the greatest respect and latterly, as they worked together, with a growing and surprising affection. Dan was her older brother, and as such her love for him was incontestable. She did not *think* about it. It just *was*. For the past six years he had been there, whenever she needed him, a part of her, though again she did not dwell on it. It just *was*! He felt as she did, she knew it, for she had seen it in his eyes, the loving concern if he thought she was troubled, the goodness of him, the merry humour which, though it made him tease the other girls quite mercilessly at times, always softened with her. He was sweet-tempered and easy-going, content with what he had, "made up" as he called it, using one of the Liverpool expressions he had learned over the years, with the job of work he did. She was happy at Briar Lodge if she thought about it, though she was well aware that there would come a time when she must move on. Even Cook admitted – only to *her*, naturally – that Celie Marlow was almost as good at her job as Jess Harper and that there was little more she could teach her.

'I've got something for you, girl,' she had said abruptly to her one quiet spring Saturday afternoon when they were alone. Dorcas and Kate, since the family was out for the day, had been told to clean Mr Latimer's decanters, a job they hated. They were in the still room, the decanters carefully arranged – for they were a beautiful cut crystal and must be treated with respect – on the table. Small pieces of blotting paper were rolled up and soaked in soapy water. They were pushed into the decanter which would be half-filled with warm water, and after a vigorous shaking they would be rinsed with cold water. Wiped with a clean dry cloth and left to drain they would sparkle like the stars in the skies. A "fiddly" job Dorcas called it, but one which must be done, for not only Cook but Mrs Latimer had the eyes of an eagle about such things.

The two scullery maids were on their knees in the laundry making ready for Monday's "big wash" and would be a good hour, for they were well aware that if Cook was not completely satisfied it would all have to be done again. Dan had gone off after their midday meal to play football. An "away" game with a team from West Derby, he told them as he slung his cap to the back of his short golden curls, 'and we're going to murder the blighters,' he grinned. 'At least four two, in our favour, of course, so don't expect me home early, Cook.'

'By that I take it you'll be out celebrating your win.' Though Cook's voice was sharp the soft, almost fond look in her eye belied her tone for really could you argue with the lad? Well, lad no longer, for at nearly nineteen, Dan Smith had attained his full growth, all six feet two of him though he hadn't an ounce of fat on his well-muscled body. Big shoulders on account of the digging and manual labour he and that Jim got up to. Three of them now with Reuben Ash's Albert, known as Bertie. Dan was *head* gardener, which was a credit to him at his age, and Jim liked to call himself under-gardener, with young Bertie in the position Dan had once held.

'Just a pint . . . well, perhaps two, Cook.' Dan grinned endearingly and began to whistle as he moved towards the kitchen door.

'Haven't you forgotten something, my lad?' Cook peered at him over the top of the spectacles she had taken to wearing, her double chin pressing painfully into her stiff, immaculate collar.

'Oh, sorry, Cook, I'd forget me head if it wasn't fastened to me neck.' Indolently he sauntered across the space between them then, with a theatrical flourish, kneeled down before her astonished figure and pressed a swift kiss on her crimson cheek.

'You silly beggar, get off me. Get off your knees, you daft happorth . . .' flapping at him with her hands, turning away from him in pretended outrage but laughing just the same, her blackcurrant eyes buried in the increasing flesh of her round face.

'I mean your muffler, Dan Smith. It's a cold day out there and I didn't spend half the winter knitting a muffler for you, along with socks and waistcoats and gloves and Heaven knows what else to see my work wasted.'

'It'll be underdrawers next, Cook.'

'DAN SMITH!' Horrified, Cook turned to peer about the kitchen as though Mr and Mrs Latimer might be lurking there. 'You just watch your language in front of this child,' indicating Celie who was curled up in the chair opposite with a book on her lap, oblivious to Dan's antics or Cook's response to them for they were not uncommon. Thought the world of Dan, Cook did, though she would have denied it strenuously, but you could see at once she was secretly pleased when he acted the fool with her as he was doing now, and no one took a great deal of notice.

'Anyway, you put your muffler on. And *keep* it on . . .'

'What, while I'm on the field?'

'Oh, go on with you or you'll have the game over before you even get there. And mind that bicycle of yours. There's a fair amount of traffic on that Wavertree Road.'

'Yes, I heard a brewer's dray went through yesterday . . .'

'Cheeky young beggar!'

Dan laughed and blew her a kiss as he banged the door behind him and Cook clicked her tongue irritably as the crockery on the dresser danced.

'That boy, will he never learn!'

'No, Cook.' Celie did not raise her head from her book. She was reading Robert Louis Stevenson's *Treasure Island* and had completely missed the exchange between Dan and Cook. This was really her afternoon off and Dan had begged her to go with him to see the match but she did not care for football and besides she was longing to get on with the adventure story and find out what became of young Jim.

There was a deep and contented silence, broken only by the tick of the clock on the wall, the hissing of the glowing embers in the fire, the droning of the cat and the click of Cook's knitting needles, and even these stopped as Cook spoke again.

'I've got something for you, girl.'

For a moment Celie went on reading then the serious-ness in Cook's voice brought her back from the thrillingly fearful apparition of Long John Silver and she lifted her head.

'Did you speak, Cook? . . .'

'I said I had something for you and I think this is the right time to give it to you. I often thought it would go with me to my grave, the girls I've had under me. Well, I despaired, really I did. I've had bad lasses and good lasses but for the most part it was only with the pots and pans, the scrubbing and all the rough work that's to be done in the scullery and kitchen, all finger and thumbs when faced with a bit of baking, fluttering and clumsy when what you need is *sureness*; dropping spoons and forgetting what I've told them the minute the words are out of my mouth, and I'd not have allowed *any* of them dipping into my . . . Well, I'll get to that in a minute. Yes . . .' Her gaze drifted above Celie's head as her mind was filled with pictures of her past and those who had peopled it, of which there were a great many. 'Aye, talk about slapdash, some of them. Put a spoon in their hands and ask them to make the simplest baked apple pudding would be like asking young Master Edward to take apart and put together again that there grandfather's clock Mr Ash's just repaired. D'you know what I mean, lass?'

'I . . . think so, Cook,' though she didn't at all.

'Now you I can rely on. You do as I *tell* you precisely in the way I tell you, but at the same time you've . . . an instinct for it. How to stir a sauce, the measuring of seasoning in a soup, the timing of a soufflé or a meringue. You've been *me*, in a way, *my* hands and so . . . well . . .' She shook her head as though irritated with her own meanderings. 'Go and fetch the recipe book from the drawer. Go on, girl,' as Celie continued to stare at her in a mystified way.

Celie closed her book, marking her place with the leather marker Dan had bought her for her last birthday, and stood up.

'*Your* recipe book, Cook?' she asked hesitantly, wondering why at this precise moment, Cook needed to study the enormous leather-bound volume in which every dish, cake, pudding and sauce that Cook had ever produced was preserved within its pages.

'What other recipe book is there, girl?' Cook demanded to know tartly.

'Well . . . none, Cook.'

'For goodness sake, child, fetch me book over here and look sharp.'

When it was in her hand she turned it over a time or two, then opened it at a page, smiling fondly at some memory the writing there evidently brought back to her.

'Apple hedgehog,' she murmured sighing, 'I remember the first time I made this. I was under Mrs Grimshaw then, at Fanshawe Hall in Scarborough, a right martinet she was an' all, and when she said *hedgehog* and I pulled a face, she nearly landed me one. Well, I didn't know what it was then, but when it was made and I tasted it, it was one of my favourites from then on. I remember there was a young footman, tall he was and good-looking. Well, he loved my apple hedgehog, he did. Jess, he used to say, I'm right fond of almonds . . .'

Cook's eyes, which had become somewhat glazed as she looked back to what had evidently been some precious moment in her young life, focused again on Celie, and she shook her head at her own foolishness whilst Celie watched in bemused fascination. It was hard to imagine this strict, uncompromising but dependable woman being any other than what she was now, and the idea that she might have had warm feelings towards a member of the opposite sex, which her words implied, was quite incredible. Celie waited for more revelations.

'And this, fricaneau of veal, what a job I had to satisfy Mrs Grimshaw that the surface was completely even. Well, it has to be, as you well know, and why is that, girl?' unwilling to resist a chance to test her pupil.

'The glaze won't sit right, Cook.'

'That's it, girl. Well, I got it as she liked it and there it is in me book, alongside all the recipes she gave me and hundreds of me own and . . . well, Celie Marlow, I reckon that you've earned this book with what you've become under my supervision. I'm not saying that it's done with yet because I'm expecting you to add to it, like I did, but though I never thought I'd say this to any lass, there's not a lot more I can teach you, so . . . here . . .' thrusting the book into Celie's hands.

There was a deep, tense silence, then with a gesture which was completely spontaneous, the book held in trembling hands, Celie sank to the floor in front of the elderly woman, placed her head in her lap and began to weep as though her heart was broken.

'Nay, give over, love.' Jess Harper felt the tears, tears she herself had not shed for years, come to her own eyes and her plump hands hovered over Celie's head. 'What's to do? There's nothing to cry over, girl. It's only a recipe book . . .' Which, of course, it wasn't. It was a symbol, a giving of something precious from Jess Harper to this child whom she had come to . . . yes, she admitted it now, this child who had become so dear to her in the past ten years or so, ever since she had stepped up on the box in the scullery and bravely tackled the enormous pile of pans Cook herself had used in the preparation of the family's dinner. Aye, a good lass, a clever lass and she'd climb to great heights with her talents, especially now she had Jess Harper's recipe book.

'Now then, lovey . . .', for Cook was never to call Celie "girl" again, 'dry your eyes,' her hand, for the first time in years seeking loving contact with another human being, smoothing back Celie's hair, 'and blow your nose before them lot come back and wonder what's up. You know what they're like. No . . . I want no thanks, Celie, so say nothing. Just look after me book . . . *your* book, and go on as you're doing and one day, who knows . . .' smiling down into Celie's tear-dewed face '. . . you'll be cooking for royalty.'

It was a few months later when His Highness the Duke of Connaught, the Queen's third son, visited Liverpool. It was a warm July day, and to the servants' delight, Mr Latimer gave those who wished to do so permission to take the horse-drawn tramcar down London Road to the city to watch the procession. His Highness had already unveiled a tablet to the memory of the late Mr James Beazley before being driven to the Royal Southern Hospital where he was presented with an address by the President, Mr William Anderson, and where he had opened a superb new operating theatre.

But the real purpose of His Highness's visit, and by far the most important, at least to the people of Liverpool, was St George's Hall where he was to inaugurate the Vyrnwy Water Supply, a process which would bring fresh water by vast pipe-lines from Lake Vyrnwy in Wales to pour in a sweet, *clean* flow from every tap in every house in every street in the city. Thousands of spectators were expected to cram the area about the hall, for His Highness was to press an *electrical* button, setting in motion two magnificent fountains supplied by Vyrnwy water and which were to be illuminated when night fell.

'Whatever next?' Cook declared, settling herself down in her own special chair before the fire, her dreadfully swollen feet and ankles propped up on the stool Celie set before her, a cup of strong, sweet tea, just as she liked it and just as Celie knew how to make it, in her hand.

'All that way through those miles of pipes,' she mused as she sipped her tea 'and what I can't help wondering is what it will pick up on its journey? I mean to say, it's a long way isn't it, under all those mountains and then the River Mersey which is none too clean at the best of times, so what will it be like when it comes out of that tap? I've never tasted *Welsh* water, that I know of, so will it be any different to English water, tell me that, Celie Marlow?'

'I couldn't say, Cook. I only know that I heard Mr Latimer and Master Alfred discussing it the other day when Master Alfred was home and Mr Latimer said it was the best thing to happen to Liverpool since the Corporation purchased the Harrington water works in 1848. Unclean water's the worst killer there is, he said to Master Alfred and if everyone had proper water supplied to their home it would eradicate, that's the word he used, Cook, many of today's illnesses.'

'Fancy that now,' Cook said comfortably.

'So it sounds as though it's going to be a good thing, doesn't it, Cook?'

Celie replaced the teapot on the table close to Cook's hand where she could easily reach it, then looked about her with that air of efficiency and conscientious application to the work in hand which was second nature to her now, before moving towards the kitchen door.

'I'll be off then, Cook,' she said, for Dan and Kate were waiting for her in the yard, 'if that's all right with you. Everything's done ready for the evening meal. I've cleaned the salmon trout and put it on the cold slab in the pantry and Dan's sent in the parsley for the sauce. There's new potatoes and spinach and the veal's all ready to go into the oven. I've hulled the gooseberries and when I . . .'

'Celie, for the Lord's sake, get you gone. I can see to what's not done though I suspect I'll not find anything.'

'I was going to do the custards . . .'

'Never mind the custards, now go or it'll all be over before you get there. Dorcas, Belle and Maudie left half an hour since. Not that you can expect anything else from that Maudie. Cute as a cart load of monkeys, she is. If I hadn't eyes in the back of my head she'd have left that stack of pans from luncheon. Now *go*!' She waved her hand, indicating that Celie was to be off, but not before she had run her eyes approvingly up and down Celie's neat figure, looking for faults but finding none. There was no grime under her fingernails, her boater was tipped saucily over her shining, clean face, her boots were spotless and Jess Harper could not help the flood of warmth to her heart, a fond and proprietary glow which was almost maternal. The girl was neat, immaculate and quite without fault in Cook's eyes. There was a flush of carnation beneath her creamy skin, high at the cheekbones, no doubt put there by her excited anticipation of the day's outing and her smoky grey eyes snapped joyfully.

She was a bonny little thing, Cook thought affectionately, with her glossy good health and her trimly rounded figure. Aye, not so little now, and it was no wonder that Dan Smith's eyes, though he was not consciously aware of it, followed her about the kitchen.

As though conjured up by Cook's own thoughts of him, the kitchen door which led out into the yard opened with a flourish and Dan entered. He came to an abrupt halt when he saw Celie, his boots scraping on the flagstones. He sighed in exasperation, the cap in his hand beginning to beat a tattoo against his leg. Kate Mossop's bold face peered round him and her voice, as she spoke, showed her irritation.

'Aren't you ready yet, Celie Marlow?' she said. 'We'll have the thing over if you don't look sharp.'

'Now then, Kate Mossop. You watch your tongue or you'll not go,' Cook remonstrated. 'Celie's coming now. See, leave the milk and sugar handy, there's a good lass. Now be off with you and give my regards to His Highness.'

'Let's walk it, shall we?' Celie said as she stepped out beside Dan. On his other side, Kate did the same, her pretty pale straw bonnet with its dashing red feather perched on the shining pale gold of her smoothly brushed hair. Her walking-out costume was a pale apple-green cotton, matching her eyes, and her white skin gleamed like fine bone china in the sunshine.

'What! Walk, all the way to St George's Hall?' she asked in consternation. 'I can't walk that far in these heels,' taking Dan's arm as though to demonstrate her frail state, though she was almost as tall as he was.

'Well, you shouldn't have put the things on then, should you?'

'Oh, come on, Kate,' Celie coaxed, 'it's a lovely day for a walk.'

'We'll not get there at all at this rate, never mind seeing the thing turned on,' Dan snorted.

'Of course we will if we step out.'

'You try stepping out in these boots, I doubt I'll get through the day in them. I want to stay and see the fireworks and by then . . .'

'Fireworks! Cook'll skin us if we stay out after dark,' but for once Celie agreed with Kate and the words had been no more than a token protest.

'I don't care. I want to do something wicked,' and Kate's eyes gleamed like a cat's in the dark as she looked up at Dan and he flushed.

They turned the corner from Knowles Lane and into Picton Road where the playing-fields stood. It was here on a Saturday afternoon in winter that Dan played centre-half for the Wavertree Wanderers, a local club got up by enthusiastic young men who fancied themselves for Everton or Liverpool, but until the scout they were convinced would one day take a trip up here to watch them play, kicked and headed the ball about the field with more vigour than talent. There was a cricket pitch where, on this warm summer afternoon, a match was in progress between regulars of The Swan, the pub which stood in the centre of Wavertree village, and its rival, The Bull and Bush, in West Derby. They were working men and youths with no money to fling about on extravagances but they all sported white flannels and shirts and a club cap, proudly displaying the club's emblem.

Dan paused to watch a run and the two girls were forced to stand with him, though their faces clearly showed their impatience with this "daft" game grown men liked to play. There was a hush as the bowler, poised and graceful, began his run, his young legs a blur of white against the trim green of the pitch. His arm flashed and the ball moved in an arc which the eye could scarcely follow. It met the bat of the batsman who lifted it cleanly into the air and barely before it had gone away, so had he, yelling to the man at the other end to 'run, Fred, run'. They flew past one another, the fielder chasing the blurred ball, and from those seated about the ground in their striped deckchairs and on scattered rugs, or perched in a row on the benches, a small cheer rose, accompanied by clamorous clapping. Some men lolled on the grass in the shade of the full-canopied trees which surrounded the ground, whilst others, waiting to bat, raised their foaming beer glasses in appreciation.

'Good run, that.' Dan would have waited to watch another but Kate pulled at his hand. She had noticed the envious glances of many of the men going into the ground, no doubt pondering on the good luck of the chap with not *one* young lady on his arm but two, and she smiled under the shadow of her long silkily pale lashes.

Dan too noticed their smiles, their knowing winks and the way they nudged one another as the three of them sauntered by and he wished Kate would let go of his arm. He knew exactly what they were thinking, these unsubtle, working-class lads he played football with, and he wanted to walk over to them where they stood with their Woodbines stuck to their bottom lips and their jaunty caps thrown to the backs of their heads and tell them it was not like that between him and Kate. She was no more than a fellow servant who thought of him as a friend, then he relaxed, smiling down into Celie's excited face. Now *she* was the loveliest thing he had ever seen. She wore a long-sleeved dress of some soft material, he didn't know what it was but the pale colour suited her. A rich cream, sprigged with tiny pink rosebuds, and about her slender waist was a sash the colour of strawberries. On her head, flat but tipped forward slightly over her brow, was a cream straw boater, the crown tied about with strawberry pink ribbons which fell down her straight and graceful back between her shoulder-blades. She wore cream cotton gloves and high black boots. Kate looked just what she was, a pretty housemaid on her day off, but Celie could have been that housemaid's young mistress in her simple but elegant outfit. And yet she was like a child, delighted with everything she saw.

'Look, oh look at the flowers in that field,' she was saying. 'They're like a carpet of gold shining in the sun.'

'They're only buttercups,' Kate said loftily, tossing her head, and Celie sighed. There was not much changed between her and Kate Mossop.

They walked on, Celie on one side, Kate clinging to Dan's other arm, past the park and the fields of Wavertree, past the tall and elegant houses of the middle-class Liverpool merchants who had, when prosperity came, moved their families out to this still rural area of the city's limits. As they moved further away from Wavertree, walking along the sunlit length of Edge Lane and into West Derby Street, the houses became small, drawing close together into long, symmetrical chains, marching along side by side, street after street exactly the same, even to the women on their knees, scrubbing not only their own doorsteps but the flagged pavement in front of it. Just a doorway and one window wide, the houses were, flat and faceless but spotlessly clean, unlike the endless, squalid back-to-back tenements in the city with their scores of over-crowded, overrun courts in which thousands lived and died in complete ignorance of anything better. A city of contrasts was Liverpool, where the untold riches of its merchants flourished beside the drunkenness, depravity and crime of its indigent poor. Where work was largely casual and ill-paid, where the "butty", the "wet nelly", bread and "taties" were the staple diet. Where there was one gin shop to every forty persons. Where disorderly men and black-shawled, bedraggled women fought drunkenly or sprawled brazenly in gutters.

It was forty years since Britain had been the richest country in the world with no rivals in commerce or in industry. Since then there had been a Great World Depression lasting from 1873 to the present day, but those who remained in employment were not adversely affected by it, and Dan and Celie, cosseted by the household of Richard Latimer, saw none of this as they moved in their smiling youthfulness through the bustling traffic of London Road, the horse-drawn cabs and trams, the bicycles which were becoming so popular, the carriages and drays, towards St George's Hall.

They had seen the water come gushing out of the fountain and been spellbound at the magic of it. They had sauntered with the rest of the crowds down William Brown Street and the length of Dale Street, after the ceremony, moving towards the Pier Head, waiting for darkness to fall and the fireworks to begin. People, Liverpool people, who liked nothing better than a "good time", pressed all about them so that they were in distinct danger of being pushed into the river and Celie was to take his arm, Dan insisted, holding it out to her. Kate still clung to his other.

The firework display began the moment dusk fell, the excited "oohs" and "aahs" of the spectators chorused between the explosions and long whizzing shrieks of the rockets which streaked across the skies. Celie's back was pressed against the railings of the Marine Parade, her neck arched, her boater almost falling from her head as she tipped it back to stare into the darkening sky. They had become wedged, the three of them, in a shadowed corner formed by the landing stage and the railings, and as Celie clung to her boater which was about to fall into the river, she felt Dan's shoulder which had been pressed against hers move away. A great shower of brilliant light streaked across the sky, a million stars chasing one another in a silver and golden stream, and she turned in delight to Dan and Kate but they weren't there. For a moment alarm caught at her then she saw Dan's bare golden head bending to something and she called to him to 'look, look Dan, isn't it lovely', but Dan did not hear her for his young mouth was firmly gripped by Kate Mossop's and the explosion in the sky was nothing to the explosion which was taking place in his eager, masculine body.

Chapter Ten

The sound of weeping was not loud but it was persistent, and Celie, who had hoped to find half an hour of seclusion in her favourite spot beneath the wide branches of the oak tree in the spinney, hesitated, reluctant to intrude on such grief. She had in her hand a copy of *Northanger Abbey* by Jane Austen which she was about to read for the third, or was it the fourth time, and for a moment she felt a surge of irritation at the intrusion of the unknown woman whose soft keening had quietened the usual sounds of birds and the small animals whose habitat this was. She didn't get a great deal of time these days to be by herself and indulge in her passion for the written word. Cook had become almost chairbound in the past few months, though so far she had managed to keep her growing dependency on Celie Marlow from her mistress. Each morning she walked, straight-backed as always, head up, steady as a rock, to consult with Mrs Latimer in her parlour on the day's menu and the accounts, only to collapse in her chair by the fire, her face a strange, muddied colour, the moment she got back to the kitchen. She relied on Celie to keep the other servants too busy to notice her own increasing incapacity, neither of them discussing it, even with one another, and in the often frantic hum and bustle about her, directed by Celie who was growing into a quiet maturity brought about by the greater responsibility she now had, Cook would recover and take over again.

'See, Dorcas, fetch me those peas. I might as well shell them while I'm sitting here. I don't like idle hands, even my own.'

'Now then, Kate Mossop, straighten that cap of yours and go and answer the bell. It'll be the master wanting fresh coffee, I'll be bound. Make another pot, will you Celie?'

'Belle, Maudie, what's all that giggling about? Oh, yes, I can see you from here. Show me that pan, Maudie, that's right, fetch it here and if I can't see my face in it, there'll be trouble.'

'Celie, attend to that fishmonger, will you? Tell him I wasn't a bit pleased with that salmon he brought me last week.'

Everywhere at once her eyes were, if not her feet, and in the general fuss which she created, had always created, in the management of her kitchen, none of them seemed to notice that most of it took place from her chair by the kitchen fire. At this moment between luncheon and the start of the preparation for dinner, she was having a five-minute doze, though the five minutes invariably stretched to an hour. Celie had made a batch of scones, a few coconut biscuits and a dozen light buns for the servants' afternoon tea, and whilst they cooled she had taken it into her head to have a moment alone, away from the bird-twittering of the other four maids. She hoped she wouldn't come across Dan. It was not that she didn't want to see him, or that the kiss he had exchanged with Kate Mossop had in any way changed her own feelings for him. It hadn't, but it had shocked her, for in her affection for him she would have liked to see him with almost any other young woman than Kate. She and Kate got on well enough together now but Kate was . . . well, she didn't like to use the word she had heard Dorcas use for people who were . . . well, Kate was vulgar, brash and cheeky and not at all what Celie would have chosen for Dan, if it had been up to her, which of course, it wasn't. She was not even sure what *was* going on between Kate and Dan, if there was *anything*, but she felt slightly uneasy in Dan's presence now if they happened to be alone together, so she avoided him if she could.

But she couldn't stand here dithering on the edge of the wood, could she? She must either go on or go back. Somebody was obviously in deep trouble and though she had no idea who it could be, the sound was so heart-breaking she couldn't just walk away without seeing if she might help.

It was the beginning of October, a warm, bright day, one of those which sometimes comes as winter approaches, as though to tell us that summer was reluctant to leave and would not give way without a struggle. There was an enormous bramble bush creeping steadily as each year passed across a fallen tree trunk, and on it there was a rich harvest of berries waiting to be picked. Celie saw them with the part of her mind not concerned with the sorrow of the woman and made mental note to ask Bertie to pick some for her. It would be grand to have a blackberry and apple crumble for tonight's meal. The leaves above her head were vivid with their autumn colours, the foliage at their tops crimson and scarlet, further down a deep orange, but there was still a fading splash of green amongst them. Acorns had settled in the vegetation underfoot which was beginning already to rot down, and among it was a scatter of crimson toadstools splashed with white spots.

The woman sat with her back to Celie in a small grove of lovely birch trees. The tiny leaves on the branches looked like a shower of gold moving in a delightful dance in the soft breeze. Though it was quiet where the woman sat weeping, further away on the far side of the small stand of trees, as though to mock her grief, a woodpecker laughed. A rabbit, startled, darted across the path on which Celie moved. It stopped for a moment, sitting up to look at her, its whiskers comically wobbling, then it flashed under a dogwood bush, its small scut white against the dark wood.

The woman did not hear her and when Celie, not knowing what else to do, cleared her throat, she froze as though in the greatest terror, then, her back still to Celie, she reached into the pocket of her soft, blue serge skirt, produced a handkerchief, scrubbed at her face with it and then turned.

It was Prudence Latimer. Not a woman, or not quite, for she was no more than a year older than Celie. She was a girl one could call neither pretty nor plain. Soft brown hair and eyes, a clear skin and a mouth which had a strange vulnerability about it. Quite unremarkable, really, with none of her brother's engaging good looks, Celie had time to think, wondering how the odd thought had crept into her mind at this particular moment. Perhaps it was because it was here in these woods that she had last seen him.

It was almost a year since she had spent that strange and enchanted hour with Richard Latimer and in that time she had not seen him once. But then neither had his family, a fact which Mrs Latimer bemoaned frequently, or so Dorcas and Kate told them when they came back to the kitchen after serving at table. It seemed Mrs Latimer never ceased to regret the day her handsome, charming eldest son had joined that "dreadful" regiment and though she brooded on it constantly, the resentment flared up each time a letter came from him. He had been in Burma when he had received his wound but it was to a place called Dinaport, where his regiment was then stationed, that he had returned when his wound was completely healed. It was in India, Kate said airily, as though she had been there quite recently and had found it pleasant enough. His battalion had since moved again, to Aden, and Kate kept quiet about that since she was not awfully sure where Aden might be and she did not wish to show her ignorance. And when would he be home to see his worried Mama, his Mama begged his Papa to tell her, and of course, not being privy to the army's secrets, his Papa could not answer.

The afternoon Celie had spent with Richard Latimer had become unfocused, insubstantial like some half-remembered dream which remains for a while and then is lost. The sharpness, which had lasted in Celie's mind for several months, had slowly faded, becoming vague so that she had to deliberately force her memory to bring it back. And yet she still retained an impression of sweetness, of something matchless and perfect, a remembrance of trust and something she tried hard to explain to herself but could not. Sometimes she would awake in the night, Belle's light breathing rustling about their shared attic bedroom, and in the dark, just before the dream she had been in faded away, she would see a pair of golden brown eyes, fringed with long dark lashes, laughing eyes softening to a warmth she found strangely comforting, strangely disturbing since what did Richard Latimer's eyes, or any message which they might have in them, have to do with Celie Marlow?

Now, looking like a pale carbon copy of him, just as though he, being the first child, had taken all the depth, the colour, the warmth and humour, the *beauty* to himself, leaving only remnants to be shared amongst his brothers and sisters, here was one of those sisters and in the deepest distress.

'Miss Prudence?' Celie's voice had a question in it as if she was not quite sure that this *was* the daughter of her mistress and master, for she certainly did not expect to find one weeping broken-heartedly in the bit of woodland at the back of the house.

'Oh, Celie, you startled me.' Prudence Latimer, reared to be steady, calm, authoritative in the presence of servants, and never, *never* to show emotion, to *anybody*, did her best to be what she was, the well-bred, well-brought-up young daughter of her parents, but slowly from her eyes two more tears leaked, running silently down her pale cheeks, hanging for a moment at her chin before spilling on the pristine crispness of her white lawn bodice. The bodice was yoked, with a turn-down collar. The "leg o'mutton" sleeves were full to her elbow where the material gathered and became fitted to her wrist. The blouse was tucked into an "umbrella skirt" which was of blue serge, cut on the cross with as few gores as possible, fitting snugly to her narrow hips by means of darts. She wore a broad leather belt about her tiny waist and at her side, thrown carelessly to the log where she sat, was the cream straw boater, without which no young lady, if she *was* a lady, would dream of leaving the house.

'Are you not well, Miss Prudence?' Celie knew the diffident question was foolish for if Miss Prudence or indeed anyone in the family should be ill, *everyone* would know of it. Maids running up and down the stairs with trays and hot-water bottles, Dr Maynard at the front door and the patient would certainly not be crouched on a log in this bit of woodland which Celie had come to think of as her own private property. Only *she* came here, and . . . once . . . him! Naturally, Dan or Jim cleared the undergrowth out now and then but she always knew when it was to happen and stayed away.

'No, oh no, Celie. I'm quite well, thank you.' But two more tears slipped silently to follow the others and Prudence bent her head in an attitude which said she was far from being 'quite well, thank you.'

Celie moved across the little beech grove, then, not knowing what else to do she sat down on the fallen log next to her mistress's daughter. She shouldn't really, she knew that. A servant never sat in the presence of the family, unless invited to, but Miss Prudence seemed quite dazed, drowned in some depthless grief which, though it had stopped for a moment at the sight of herself, had begun to flow again into a torrent of desolation.

Celie said nothing for several minutes, nor did she touch Miss Prudence but sat quietly, letting the distraught girl know that, should it be needed, comfort, or help, whatever Miss Prudence asked for was near at hand.

After a while the storm seemed to be passing and, accepting Celie's silently offered handkerchief, her own soaked and useless, Prudence Latimer lifted her head and turned to the concerned gaze of her mother's assistant cook, or what was her *true* title, kitchen maid.

'I feel better now,' she said, a rueful smile twitching her lips.

'That's good.' Celie returned the smile encouragingly.

'You'll wonder what it was all about, I suppose. Why I should be howling like a baby and making such a ninny of myself.'

'Well, only if you want to tell me, Miss Prudence. Cook always says a problem shared is a problem halved,' nodding her head sagely.

'Does she?'

'Mmm, but it doesn't always work.' Celie smiled candidly as though many of Cook's maxims, which were well meant, could be taken with a grain of salt.

'You mean some . . . sadness should be kept . . . private.' It was said so hopelessly, Celie's expression turned to one of surprise, for what sadness, what total absence of hope would the sheltered and truly blessed daughter of Mr and Mrs Richard Latimer possibly know? She had led, within its boundaries, a privileged upbringing in which, Celie would have sworn, nothing could touch her, but here she was, weeping alone as though her heart was broken.

'My Ma died when I was born and my Pa last year,' she found herself saying. 'My Pa loved my Ma a lot. I never knew her, of course, and my Pa . . . well, he was . . . not close to anyone but her. Funny, I never realised it until now. He was always kind to me and patient, but not what you'd call . . . loving. I didn't understand it at the time and . . . well, it was a sorrow to me, but I suppose he gave it all to her, my Ma, and when she went there wasn't much left for me.'

'I know what you mean, though I believe that love should be, how can I describe it . . . immeasurable. No matter how much you give or receive from someone you care about and who cares for you, there should be always more. More to give to other people besides the man you . . .' Her voice trailed away to nothing and Celie turned to look at her. A careful look which had a glimmer of understanding in it.

'Yes,' she said after a moment. 'I know exactly what you mean.'

'Do you, Celie? Are you in love then?' Prudence asked, though the question was absent-minded and the speaker was gazing off somewhere into a memory or thought which totally absorbed her.

Celie was about to laugh but even as her mouth curled into the shape of it, a man's face imprinted itself on her mind, a face of humour and sensitivity, a young man's face with a well-cut mobile mouth and a hard jawline. Brown eyes, those brown eyes again, like the ones in the face of the girl who sat next to her, but as warm and glowing as a topaz with deep golden flecks hidden in their depths. Where this girl's were a pale brown, like the coffee Mr Latimer drank, *his* were dark and rich, as rich as the chocolate on Cook's favourite cake. The same shape but . . . but different. Again she felt confused since it seemed she did not care to answer Miss Prudence's question, though she really could not have said why.

'Oh, no,' she heard herself say in a determined way.

'Have you a young man, perhaps?'

'Oh, no,' and this time she answered truthfully.

'I sometimes wish . . .'

'What do you wish, Miss Prudence?' for surely this girl had everything *any* girl could want. Loving parents, a large, happy family, money, lovely dresses, parties and dances which the Latimers frequently went to, and in time, she supposed, a husband to continue the privileged life she had always known.

'Freedom, Celie. That is what I wish for. Freedom to . . . well . . .'

'*Freedom*! But surely you can do what you like . . .'

'I can do *nothing* I like, *nothing*, Celie. I am hedged about from morning until night by . . . people and when I ask permission to . . . oh, God, what's the use. I've tried reasoning with her, after all it's not as though there was something *dreadfully* wrong with . . . him but . . . well, of course, she says . . .'

Her voice, which had begun to rise in hysteria, stopped abruptly as though Miss Prudence Latimer, for she must remember that was who she was, had realised what she was saying and to whom. Her face became blank, polite, and she stood up, brushing bits of bark from her skirt. At once Celie did the same.

'I must get back or I shall be missed,' her mistress's daughter said. 'I have been gone an hour.'

'Of course, miss.' Celie's tone was as polite as the girl's before her.

For the first time Prudence Latimer looked completely at Celie, giving her her full attention and her pleasant but quite ordinary face relaxed into a small smile.

'You have been very kind, Celie.'

'Oh, no, miss.'

'Indeed you have, listening to my tale of woe . . .' though she had said nothing that Celie could understand.

'If it helped . . . with anything . . .' Celie smiled back and for several moments they were just two young girls trembling on the brink of what, in different circumstances, might have been friendship.

'I was just being silly and you were patient to put up with it.'

Celie's smile deepened for it was hardly likely that a *servant* in the house would show impatience with the *daughter* of the house, telling her to pull herself together perhaps, or even walk away without concern. Miss Prudence was talking as though Celie had a choice in the matter. She would not have ignored Miss Prudence, of course, nor been anything but sympathetic, but the idea that she had any option, or that this girl thought she had, was ironic.

'No, Miss Prudence. I'm sure you would have done the same in my place,' and astonishingly she knew it was true.

'Thank you, Celie.' Prudence put her slim white hand on Celie's arm, her gaze intent, and Celie noticed that her eyes were really quite lovely. Pale, yes, but steady and kind. They dropped to the book in Celie's hand and she smiled.

'Aah, *Northanger Abbey*. How I love that story.'

'Do you?' Celie looked down at it eagerly, as though ready to open the pages and dip into it.

'I must have read it half a dozen times.'

'So have I. Well, perhaps not half a dozen, but three or four.'

'You like reading then?'

'I love it.'

'Tell me your favourites.'

Somehow they were sitting on the log again, earnestly discussing the books they had read, the merits of their favourite authors. A play, *Cymbeline*, that Miss Prudence had seen at the Prince of Wales theatre the previous week, in which Ellen Terry had played the part of Imogen. And had Celie read Shakespeare? Oh, then indeed she must try it. Her father had all his plays in the library and she was sure he would not mind . . . oh, *Northanger Abbey* was from the library and her father had . . . well then, of course, if Papa had told her to . . . They talked of music and art, at least Miss Prudence did, for Celie knew nothing of such things, though her rapt attention, the lovely gleaming interest in her eyes said that she would dearly love to.

'I go to the Art Gallery quite often. They have such good exhibitions there. In fact I am to go next week. Have you heard of a painter called Turner? No, then do go and see his works which are to be shown there. I would so like to have your opinion on *The Evening of the Deluge* which is my particular favourite. In fact, why do we not go together?'

Celie was astonished. Surely this girl was not so naive as to imagine that she and her Mama's servant might spend an afternoon in one another's company, a *social* afternoon, just as though Celie was a friend of the family. Surely she did not really believe her Mama would *allow* it. Or perhaps she had no intention of telling her. But then . . . Dear Lord . . .

'I'm sure you would enjoy it, Celie,' Miss Prudence was saying, 'then we could take tea at the Adelphi, that is if Mama . . . well . . . just recently she has been . . .'

From a quite lovely enthusiasm which had lit her eyes and put a flush of pink beneath her skin, Prudence Latimer seemed to fold in on herself and slowly her erect shoulders sagged and her head bowed. She seemed to Celie to be like a doll Ethel Ash had once owned, though Heaven only knew how she had come by it, and which her brother had flung about the garden until the material of its body had burst, allowing all the stuffing to flow out. Prudence Latimer's manner changed from an eager dedication to the arts and what was obviously a great love of hers, to the lifeless and yes, the *hopeless* misery in which Celie had found her.

She could not help it. She put a gentle hand on Prudence's arm, bending her own head to look into her face.

'What is it, Miss Prudence? What is making you so . . . sad?' Dear Lord, she hardly knew the girl. She had been a part of Celie's life for as long as she could remember. A beautifully dressed little girl walking sedately by the side of Nanny Ella, well away from the sometimes rowdy comradeship of the Ash and Ellis children who played at the back of their own cottages. They and Celie had peeped over the wall to watch the quiet procession of Latimer children, Miss Anne and Master Alfred before he went to school, forced to walk hand in hand, Miss Prudence and Master Robert, and in the baby carriage, Master James. Sometimes Miss Anne or Miss Prudence would catch a glimpse of her, and Fred or Alfred Ash, being boys, could not resist a bit of "derring-do" when Nanny Ella wasn't looking, pulled the most hideous faces and the "young misses" had turned their pert noses up and walked haughtily on. Miss Prudence had come into the kitchen, she and her brothers eating Cook's almond slices, talking in her cultured voice of where they were to go with Nanny Ella, to the zoo or the botanical gardens or in the carriage to the Marine Parade to see the boats. Children from another world to Celie's. Children from another planet, for all that they and she had in common.

Later there had been games of croquet, picnic lunches, afternoon tea on the lawn where Mr and Mrs Latimer's young daughters were put on show for the appraisal of suitable young gentlemen and their Mamas, and where, from a distance, of course, Celie had caught sight of this girl taking tea, playing croquet, chatting politely to her Mama's guests and where, she supposed, Miss Anne, who was to be married next year, had been found a fitting husband.

And here they were, Miss Prudence Latimer and her mother's kitchen maid, Celie Marlow, together in the most intimate of circumstances just as though the pair of them were from the same class and had been friends for years. But somehow it didn't seem to matter. Miss Prudence had no, well . . . what Cook would call "side" to her. She had been open, frank, friendly, making nothing of the gulf between them. And she was so evidently a woman in the deepest trouble and how could Celie, another woman, ignore it?

Prudence sighed, her eyes closed and her young face, though it was still smooth and taut with youth, looked suddenly old.

'You made me forget for a while,' she said simply, 'now it is returned and I cannot bear it. You see, I . . .'

'Yes . . . ?' Celie said gently. How could she convey to this girl who was only a little older than herself that, though she had no wish to pry into her secret, whatever it was, if she wanted to unburden herself she would find no more willing or discreet a listener than Celie Marlow. She had no friends of her own, only Dan and that was not the same, especially now, and though she had become quite fond of Belle since they had shared a room, for Belle listened to her as though everything Celie said was from God himself, she had exchanged confidences with no one. She kept herself to herself, anyone in the kitchen would tell you that. She was friendly, she hoped, and agreeable to her fellow servants, but she did not hang about gossiping, as Kate would do if Cook was absent.

'If you would . . . it might . . . perhaps help you if . . .' my lips are sealed, was what she wanted to say, but really, it was very difficult.

'You are trying to say you would tell no one, are you not? Even Mama,' Prudence said.

Well, she would not have put it quite like that, the last two words at least, but that was the gist of it and besides, when would Celie Marlow exchange chit-chat with "Mama"!

She nodded sympathetically. Prudence lifted her head and stared sightlessly along the path which led out of the wood.

'My sister and I were never . . . are not close, Celie. She likes to do things . . . Mama approves of her. She is exactly how she should be. You understand?'

Celie nodded, her hand still on Prudence's arm.

'Anne is content to live this life we have been brought up in. She is to marry a man my Mama approves of though I suspect she does not love him . . .'

Aah, there it was again, that reference to *love*.

'. . . but it won't matter because she will have what she wants. And then it will be my turn.'

She sighed deeply again and her hand came to rest on Celie's as she lifted her head to look into Celie's eyes.

'Which I would welcome if I could marry a man of my own choosing.' Her gaze was steady and in it was the answer to Celie's wondering, an answer Prudence allowed her to see.

'I have met him, you see,' and into her eyes came a blaze of such joy, such unconcealed and absolute joy, Celie felt a need to look away for it did not seem right to examine too deeply an emotion which was so obviously precious.

'And your . . . Mama does not . . . approve?' she said softly, for what else could have flung this girl into such despairing depths.

Prudence let out her rapturous breath in a long-drawn-out

shudder and the light left her, leaving her extinguished, plain, lifeless.

'He is, they tell me, very rich but his money is newly acquired, you see. He comes from . . . Yorkshire and his accent is not . . . like ours. My father had some business with him, I was not told what it was since, being a woman without a sensible thought in her head, I was not able to comprehend it, you see! *He* knows, of course, that I can. That I am, or would be if I had been educated as my brothers were, clever.' It was said simply without meaning to boast. 'He came for dinner, my father being obliged to invite him, though Mama was mortified. Oh, he was dressed as all the gentlemen were, in fact I'm sure his evening clothes were better cut and probably cost more than any gentleman there, which to my mother proved his ill-breeding. He was . . . large . . .' she smiled fondly and her gaze turned inward – looking to some memory she found to her liking '. . . and . . . well, I thought . . . handsome. Older than I am by fifteen years, my Mama told me later when she saw how . . . well, he *talked* to me, Celie. Asked my opinion and *listened* to it and for the first time I felt I was . . . a real person.'

She dreamed on, her eyes unfocused, her hand amazingly held in that of her mother's kitchen maid to whom, to her knowledge, she had never before spoken. It seemed so natural, so ordinary, just as though they were truly friends and neither wondered at it until, with a shiver, both of them realised that the shortening autumn day was almost at its end. That it had become chilly and that both of them must go or they would be missed.

They stood up, neither feeling the slightest embarrassment, not even Celie, to whom nothing like this had ever happened. At least . . . her mind whispered for a moment, remembering the deep brown eyes and merry face of this girl's brother, not with another woman.

'I feel better, Celie. To have told someone about him. My Mama will not have his name mentioned but I cannot just . . .' Her voice became urgent as though, having found an ear, a sympathetic ear, she could not bear to part with it.

'May we meet again, Celie? Can we talk again? I have so

much to tell you . . .' for what man or woman can resist the
need to talk endlessly on the subject of the beloved.

'Well, if I can get away . . .' Celie's voice was doubtful.

'When is your day off?'

'Next Sunday, I could manage the afternoon . . .'

'Here?'

'Yes . . .'

'We could perhaps . . . slip out somewhere, go and see
the Turner exhibition.'

'Well, I don't know about that.'

'Please say yes, Celie . . . please.'

She did.

Chapter Eleven

In November of that same year, the 2nd Battalion of the King's Liverpool Regiment disembarked at Portsmouth and proceeded by train to Manchester, where most of its officers and men were given leave to go home to their families. The battalion had been on duty in India and Burma since September 26th 1877.

The house was an incessant hive of activity for days before the expected arrival of Captain Richard Latimer. He had not been home since the summer of last year when he had been recovering from the wound he had sustained in Burma, and the excitement was intense. There were to be dinner parties in his honour, at Briar Lodge and at the homes of many of Mr and Mrs Latimer's friends, informal buffet parties, family gatherings, even a small dance in the large drawing room, which was to be cleared for the occasion and of course, as Captain Latimer was to be home over the Christmas festivities, the entertaining and the invitations of friends where *he* would be entertained would be doubly extended.

They were flat out in the kitchen, so much so the frequent cry of 'I've only got one pair of hands, Cook' nearly got Kate Mossop into serious trouble and, had it not been for Celie's soothing intervention of herself between Kate and Jess Harper and the rest of the staff, the lot of them would have been sacked on the spot. There was no doubt Cook was growing increasingly irritable. The trouble was it had become just too much for her excruciatingly painful legs to withstand, even though she sat at the table on the special stool Reuben Ash had made for her – just the right height it was, with a back rest to support her – to do most of the tasks she performed there. By now, of course, the servants had become aware of the pain she suffered though, thankfully, none knew of the true state of affairs which was that, apart from her teeth-gritting duty in Mrs Latimer's parlour each morning, she could barely stand. She had developed ulcers on the shins of both legs and try as she might, she just could not get them to heal and though Celie begged her, as she bathed and bandaged them for her in the privacy of Cook's own room before she got into her bed at night, she would not allow the doctor to be called, nor Mrs Latimer to be informed.

'Slip into the kitchen when the girls have gone to bed and mix up those coltsfoot leaves Dan gathered this morning. Crush them with a little honey and when it forms a firm poultice, spread it on this clean cloth and then put it on my legs. My mother used to do that for my Pa when he cut himself with the scythe and the wound wouldn't heal. A good old country remedy that is, old-fashioned but good just the same. Now don't let anybody see you, my lass.'

Though it was not spoken in so many words, it was perfectly understood between the elderly woman and the young girl that this must be kept from Mrs Latimer, particularly now, for though Jess Harper was the best cook Mrs Latimer had ever had or was *likely* to have, she would not hesitate to let her go if she thought Cook was not capable of doing her job. Cook wondered despairingly as she lay in her bed at night, her legs like tree trunks on fire, how much longer she would be able to get up the hallway to the parlour for her daily orders, only blessing the gods who had given her Celie Marlow, for how would she have managed without her? She even dwelled on the possibility of sending Celie in her place, for there was absolutely no doubt in her mind that Celie would cope with it, *and* impress her mistress with her neat and immaculate appearance, her instant understanding of a problem or query and her efficiency in immediately solving it, her quiet and dignified manners and her ability to discuss articulately with Mrs Latimer what her mistress's requirements for the day might be. Perhaps Cook could make the pretence that it was all part of Celie's training, without arousing her mistress's suspicions, but the truth was Celie wasn't employed to be *trained*, she was a kitchen maid, pure and simple, there to *help* Cook, not to *become* her, and so the torment went on, Cook biting the inside of her mouth to hold in her own groans at times and counting the days to when Christmas would be over and Master Richard back with his regiment. She could manage the ordinary, day-to-day routine of the household, and the occasional dinner party but she and Celie knew the next few weeks would be difficult to say the least.

He came to the kitchen, as he had done the last time, and Celie had the distinct feeling that had she not been leaning over the table, both hands flat on its surface as she studied Cook's, *her* recipe book, she would have fallen. He had arrived home only that day in a great flurry of boxes and trunks, of packages and equipment, leaping from the hansom cab which had brought him from the station and dragged quite shamelessly into his ecstatic Mama's arms, Kate and Dorcas reported. Passed from one female embrace to the other as his sisters clamoured to be allowed to greet him and ''er not best pleased about it, neither,' Kate added cheekily, 'wanted 'im all to 'erself and could you blame her, him being so handsome in that lovely uniform. I'd 'ang on to him an' all,' Kate added, 'given the chance.'

'Now then, Kate Mossop, don't let me hear you speak of your betters like that again.' Cook's voice was savage and she looked ready to aim the rolling pin with which she was rolling out pastry at Kate's mischievous grin. 'Now get those apples and start peeling them . . .'

'*Me*, Cook? What's up with Belle or Maudie . . . ?'

'Never you mind Belle and Maudie. I'm telling *you* to do them.'

'But I'm parlourmaid, Cook, and the table's still not finished.'

'I don't care *what* you are . . . oh, very well. Maudie, see to those apples, will you. And you, Kate Mossop, get yourself out from under my feet or I'll not be answerable for the consequences.'

He was already in full dress uniform, for tonight was his welcome home dinner. He was simply magnificent and as he looked at her over the misted passage of time since their last strange meeting and the one before that in the hallway of this house, it was in his eyes how it still was with him.

The splendid uniform he wore was, strictly speaking, for State occasions, Balls, Royal Escort Duty or Guards of Honour but his Mama had begged him to wear it, proud now of this dashing, strangely hardened man who was her soldier son. His jacket of scarlet had a high collar cut square in front and hooked close beneath his proudly lifted chin. There was gold braid on it and on the blue facing at his cuffs. He wore a gold lace sash over his left shoulder with two crimson silk stripes running through it, the fringe at its end on a level with the bottom of his tunic. His trousers were blue with a one-and-a-half-inch-wide gold lace stripe down each outside leg seam, the centre of which was faced with a red silk stripe. A red morocco leather belt faced with more gold lace was strapped about his waist. His buttons gleamed, his eyes smiled, his teeth shone white in his brown face and his bemused gaze captured and held on to Celie's and would not let her go.

Celie could distinctly feel her mouth dry up and if anyone had spoken to her she could not have answered. Her legs seemed to have had the bones taken from them and she felt that if she did not sit down immediately she would fall. He looked so incredibly *beautiful*.

For several seconds she was frantically preoccupied with that female dilemma which asks despairingly, 'What must I look like?' She had been up since six thirty, helping in the preparation of a dinner party for thirty people, absorbed in the complexities of pheasant soup, turbot in oyster sauce, fried whiting and herbed trout; of fillets of grouse and sauce piquante, curried lobster and sweetbreads; of Beef à la Jardinière and game pie, of Apricot Tourte and Tipsy Cake, of champagne jelly and iced pudding, and in that time she had not looked once in her mirror. She had been as immaculate as she always was when she had started, but that was thirteen hours ago and she had not sat down since. Her hair would be in a tangle about her crimson, sweaty face, she was convinced, and was her apron stained? Did she look what she was, a tired kitchen maid, Cook's assistant, a girl who was in the service of this splendid young man's family? She was not to know that to Richard Latimer she looked quite bewilderingly lovely. Her hair *was* in disordered wisps about her face, curling tendrils which fell from her white frilled cap onto her forehead, to the back of her neck and about her ears. Her cheeks were stained with rose, for the kitchen was hot, but she was tired and beneath her enormous, startled, velvet grey eyes were deep smudges, like those of a child at the end of the day. Her mouth, full and pink as coral, drooped with fatigue and on one cheek was a dab of flour.

They both felt the shock at the same moment, a moment so short it went unnoticed by the rest of the staff. Something softened inside them both, slowed, then moved on again in quiet pleasure. His darkened eyes remained on hers for perhaps ten seconds and then went to where Cook was struggling to get to her feet.

'No, please don't get up, Cook. I only came to pay my respects. I know how hard you have all worked . . .' smiling round at the gaping, open-mouthed admiring girls. Even Mary and Lily were there, pressed into service in the kitchen, for Dorcas and Kate, with Fanny, who had deserted her family for the evening to help out, would be busy serving at table.

'Eeh, Master Richard, it's good to see you, sir, back from those foreign parts, an' you'll be glad to have a bite of decent food inside you after all this time, but you'll be disappointed for there's no lamb on the menu.' Cook was all smiles, her round face softened, her eyes ready to become moist for he was the only one of all the "lads" who took the trouble to come down to see her. Oh aye, when they were children they had always been under her feet, begging for biscuits and gingerbread men but this one held a warm spot in her heart. *He* had a good heart, bless him, which was more than could be said for the rest of them. Of them all, he was the one most like his Papa, though by the set of his strong jaw and firm mouth – which was smiling now – he'd not be put upon by a woman, as his Papa was.

'Cook, I've thought of nothing else but your apple snow

and tipsy cake whilst I've been in India. I used to make the other officers drool when I described them. So what is it to be tonight, then, if not lamb? No, don't tell me, let me be surprised and I'll forgive the absence of lamb if you've made me a tipsy cake.'

'Not me, sir.' Cook smirked in the direction of Celie and again he turned to look at her. 'Celie made it and it's as good as mine, well, nearly,' she added hastily.

'I'm sure none could be as good as yours, Cook, but if you've taught Celie . . .' unknowingly his voice caressed her name and Cook looked at him sharply '. . . then it can't be far behind.'

He could scarcely bear to look at her now and yet at the same time it was all he could do to keep his eyes from straying constantly to her tired face. She was so frail-looking, slender and drooping over the table and though she had straightened up at the sight of him, he wanted to move round to her, take her arm, lead her to a chair and tell her she must stop this nonsense since it was obvious that she was not up to it. She was not meant to be a kitchen maid, not with her frail and slender loveliness, that weary droop to her soft, vulnerable mouth. Her eyes were heavy like those of a sleepy child and surely . . .

He dragged his gaze away from her, smiling automatically at whatever Cook was saying, nodding pleasantly at the other maids who were rosy-cheeked, sturdy-shouldered, country girls, strongly built for the tasks they performed, not like . . . Jesus, what the devil was the matter with him! He was appalled at his own disjointed thoughts which were, after so long away, and only two minutes back in her company, galloping off like some wild untethered horse at the sight of her. She was his mother's kitchen maid, doing what she was paid to do – *and* was *well able* to do. This was only the third time that he had seen her, *really* seen her and each time she had had this strange effect on him and he did not care for it, nor that soft and dreaming look in her smoky-grey eyes. It was so damnably *silly* to allow a maidservant, no matter how pretty and appealing, to do to him what this one did with one slow drooping of her long eyelashes. He wouldn't look at her again, dammit, in fact he wouldn't come to the bloody kitchen again.

With a murmured farewell he turned about and . . . well, he could only describe it as . . . *stumbled* from the kitchen, cursing himself for his own crass foolishness. His Mama had told him there were to be several attractive young ladies at the dinner party and he would give all his attention to the best-looking one amongst them and forget those gossamer soft, smoky soft eyes, which he knew were following his back to the kitchen door. And if no one at the dinner party captured his interest then he was sure he could find distraction in the arms of one of the lovely and willing young women whose services might be bought in places he knew of in Liverpool. Goddammit, he'd never felt so gauche, so . . . fatuous in his life, even when he was a boy, and the sooner he stopped this . . . whatever it was he felt each time he saw her, the better.

Celie watched him go and when the door shut behind him, she let out the breath she had been holding in a long, shuddering sigh. Though all about her the other girls had resumed the tasks they had been at when Master Richard had come in, she could not seem to get back to hers, whatever it had been. She could still see him in his glorious uniform, standing on the other side of the kitchen table. Still see his long, brown hand, the fingers of which had beat some urgent, unnoticed tattoo on its surface. She could see the just shaved texture of his cheeks and chin and smell the sharp, clean fragrance of the lemon soap he used. His eyebrows which, curiously, had dipped in what appeared to be a scowl, had been dark, thick and silken and below them his eyes, a deep tobacco brown, had shone with some light which had allowed her to see her own face reflected in them. He had blinked in that long, curving arc, she remembered, then turned away, the gleaming accoutrement of his uniform dazzling her already dazzled mind. She wanted nothing more than to leave this place and find a secluded corner where she might sigh and dream over what had just taken place, for something had. She was not sure what it was but inside her was a stretching, languorous feeling which enchanted her and which she was afraid that in the long and burdened hours ahead of her, she might lose. That spellbinding emotion which sang inside her each time they met was something she must take out and study, marvel over since it was so . . . so overwhelming and yet . . .

'Celie, what's the matter with you, lass? I'm still waiting for you to tell me how long . . .'

'Sorry, Cook.' She felt as though she was being physically pulled from the warmth and comfort and enthralment of a dream, one of those from which, as morning comes, you are reluctant to let go. As though someone had forcibly thrown back the soft eiderdown and told her to wake up, to get up and look lively, for the *real* world was waiting.

Her friendship with Prudence Latimer had grown so quickly and so strongly over the last few weeks, she could hardly keep up with it, nor believe it was actually happening. It was incredible to her that a young woman from the class in which Prudence had been born, and with the cultural interests with which Prudence concerned herself, could find anything of merit in a girl like herself, and yet it seemed she did. On the Sunday following the day she had found her weeping in the spinney, she had put on her bonnet, draped her shawl about her shoulders and told Cook she was going to visit Mrs Ash since she had a fancy for a new winter dress and the clever fingers of Reuben's wife would be glad to fashion one for her.

'I may stay to tea, Cook, so don't expect me back early,' she had said, finding it surprisingly easy to be airy about it and bar telling her to be in before dark fell, Cook seemed to find nothing strange about it, nor need to argue.

Within five minutes of her arrival in the birch grove, Miss Prudence was beside her, having crept stealthily across the lawn, or rather round its boundaries beneath the shelter of the yew hedge, looking about her like a convict escaping from a prison cell.

For some reason they both began to laugh, the natural laughter two young people can share which is really about nothing, just a joyous reaction to being young and free from restraint. They held on to one another, each begging the other to "ssh, someone will hear," "oh, do stop, Celie" . . . "what is the matter with us" . . . "I thought I would never get away, Mama was . . ."

'Yes, I know, Cook kept asking for . . .'

'. . . and then Papa wanted to know . . .'

'. . . I'm supposed to be with Mrs Ash . . .'

'. . . and I'm sketching . . .'

'. . . but you haven't any sketching pads or . . .'

'. . . oh Lord, I forgot them . . .'

There was more soft laughter, the excited murmur of two young females who are suddenly free, at least for an hour or two, to do exactly as they please and entranced with the thoughts of how they were to spend it.

In the end they did not go to the exhibition.

'Well, you never know who might be there, Celie, someone who knows me and will tell Mama and then I would be in trouble. I'm sorry, Celie. I know you were eager to see it, as I was, but perhaps we can arrange something before it ends. Do you mind if we just walk instead?'

Celie didn't care *where* they went. The novelty of this excursion with Prudence Latimer was enough for her at the moment, and all she wanted to do was enjoy it, *anywhere*, to watch Miss Prudence and her lovely, ladylike ways, to listen to her speak in that grand way she had, to glory in the amazing fact that this girl found her, one of the servants in her parents' house, amusing, good company, wanting to be with her above all others. The feelings she herself had were not servile. It wasn't as though she expected, or even wanted to gain anything from Miss Prudence, she just . . . she just *liked* her. It was as simple as that. She . . . she warmed to her, something she had done with no other girl of her own age.

'Where'll we walk then, Miss Prudence? We'd be round the garden in half an hour, besides which Dan's about and though he'd say nothing, if I told him not to, Jim might, or Bertie.'

'Are they the gardener's boys?'

'Well, Dan's head gardener,' Celie said, and in her tone and expression was the pride she felt for the way Dan, who had been no more than a gawky immigrant boy without a word of English until she took him in hand, had got on.

'And is he your beau?' smiling wickedly in a way which caught Celie's breath for it was so like that of her brother.

'Beau,' she managed to say, 'what's that?'

'Your . . . young man.'

'Oh, no, oh Glory be, no.' She grinned at the very idea. 'He's . . . well . . . he's like a brother, but before I tell you about him,' since she had a feeling she and Miss Prudence would be exchanging one or two confidences this day, 'shall we decide where we're going. It's too cold to sit and . . .'

'I believe there's a way out of the garden at the back of the cottages, did you know that? It's in the garden wall, just beyond the spinney. When we were children my brothers and I often wanted to explore what lay beyond it, but of course, Nanny Ella would have been horrified. In fact she had no idea it was there. It was just one day when Richard and I . . .' not seeing her companion's sudden gleaming interest, '. . . escaped for half an hour and we found it. We could slip through there and out into the lane. Perhaps have a walk up . . . well, no not towards Wavertree, but in the fields where no one would see us. If anybody did I should be in deep trouble and would never be allowed to go out again.'

Celie glanced hopefully at Prudence for her words seemed to imply a continuation of this delightful friendship, a promise or what *seemed* to be a promise, of further outings and it gave Celie a great deal of satisfaction. 'Yes, I seem to remember that gate from when I used to play in there with Bertie and Fred and the rest.' She could see Prudence's eagerness to know more about Bertie and Fred and the rest and about the lives and worlds of those outside her own but Celie took her hand quite naturally, hurrying her on.

'It might be blocked up though, on the other hand I don't think Dan would let it get overgrown. It's bound to be bolted on this side but we could let ourselves out. Where would you like to go, Miss Prudence?'

'Well, first of all, what I *would* like, indeed *demand* is that you should stop calling me *Miss* Prudence. If we are to be friends then I want it fully understood we are *equals*."

'Well, Prudence then,' ready to duck her head shyly.

'And we'll dispense with the curtseying and such nonsense, d'you hear?'

Celie smiled and said she did.

'Right then, let's go. And I don't mind where it is as long as it's outside these walls.'

With a great deal of pushing and pulling, of breathless laughter and skirts caught on brambles, they fought their way through the tangle of undergrowth which lay beyond the spinney, finding the small gate just where they remembered it to be. It *was* bolted on this side, and rusted too, but to the detriment of Prudence's white kid gloves, without which, like her hat, no young lady would venture outdoors, they managed to heave on the bolt and force it open with a great shriek of unoiled hinges.

Still laughing, somewhat hysterically by now, they found themselves out beyond the six-foot-high walls which surrounded Briar Lodge though they were still on Richard Latimer's land as they stepped into the overgrown, sun-dappled lane outside the gate. There was a quickthorn hedge on the far side of the lane rioting with what remained of summer's campanula and beneath it a grass verge edging the lane. Foxgloves grew and dozens of wild flowers, going over now as autumn drew towards its closing. Along each border of the lane were trees in every shade from pale cinnamon to rich tobacco, from faded gold to chocolate brown, magenta and rusty pink. The fallen, dried-out leaves crunched delightfully under their booted feet and they stamped on them like two children just escaped from the schoolroom. As though the wall had resisted its efforts to get inside, a merry wind pounced on them the moment they escaped, tugging at their shawls and bonnets, loosening their neat hair and putting roses in their cheeks. Further on there was a stile which led to a field rustling with deep grasses and dandelions and a herd of soft-eyed cows which began to wander with the curiosity of their kind, in the girls' direction. The lane, apparently leading to one of the farms which lay at the rear of the property, was deserted.

'Oh, Lord, which way shall we go now?' Celie demanded to know.

'Well, if we go left we'll be on the road to Wavertree so why don't we turn to the right and do a bit of exploring? Mercy, did you hear me say that! *Exploring*! Did I ever think I would be engaged in such a wondrous activity? Oh, Celie, this really is fun.'

'Oh, Miss . . . I mean, Prudence, you make me feel . . .'

'What, Celie?'

'Just . . . light-hearted.'

'Me, too,' and Prudence put her arm through Celie's.

They walked for half an hour, across what Prudence declared was a ploughed field and would Celie look at her boots and if Mama could see her now she'd faint right away – though she didn't seem to care. The field was, in actual fact, a rough pasture belonging to Cobbs Head Farm, which was leased by the farmer from Richard Latimer.

They came to another lane at right angles to the first, narrower but dry, leading from the pasture, spilling over with wild flowers, field pansies, creamy and spotted with yellow and violet. They would bloom right through the winter if the weather was mild, Celie told Prudence, for once the purveyor of knowledge, for had she not been brought up the daughter of a gardener? The remains of cranesbill, strong-smelling and suffused with a vivid red but fading now as October gave way to November. The hedges on either side were thick with buckshorne plantain, its long flower heads and veined leaves beckoning them on in this "lark" as Prudence joyfully called it.

They turned onto a broader lane which led away to the west, obviously in the direction of Liverpool, so instead they went to the right, wandering along in the autumn sunshine, the words spilling out of them, two young girls who, through circumstances beyond their control, had never indulged in this joyful exchange of ideas and thoughts, plans and hopes, and which neither had confided to another before this. It was heady, this sudden awareness and freedom and pleasure they found in one another's company, and they were quite drunk on it.

Prudence spoke at length, and lyrically on the subject of Jethro Garside, the wealthy, the large, the handsome but completely unacceptable man she loved. Celie talked of Dan, of her dead father, and of Cook and when they found a clump of coltsfoot, Prudence helped her to gather some for the poultices which eased Cook's ulcers, having no conception of what they were, only too willing to help to ease them, and Celie was not at all surprised by her own absolute trust in this girl who, with one incautious word to her mother, could ruin Cook's life.

In the four weeks before Richard Latimer's return from India, she and Prudence had managed three of these meetings and of the two of them it was herself who found it the most difficult to compose some reason why, on her afternoon off, she simply disappeared. She could no longer claim she was going to the woods to read her book, since it was too cold for that as winter approached. The fitting for her new dress, which she was compelled to attend, sufficed for the moment, but these must come to an end soon. She simply could not bear to think that this new-found and very satisfying companionship she had formed with Prudence Latimer might be brought to an end. Why could they not be friends, Prudence reiterated time and time again? What was *wrong* with it, as though it was Celie who found fault with it, though of course she knew. They were doing no harm to anyone, were they? turning passionately to Celie and Celie could find no answer.

'If only we could find some plausible reason, both of us, to go about together, into Liverpool, I mean, to go to the gallery, to the exhibitions, to the theatre, to concerts. If we could go about openly as young men are allowed to do, I would go as far as to say our excursion would be more innocent than any of theirs, for what *we* did, would be completely harmless.'

'It's not me you have to convince, Prudence, but your Ma, and Cook would have something to say, as well, if she knew. You're not the only one who's . . .'

'What?'

'I was going to say "stepping out of her station in life".'

'Celie, how ridiculous. As though that matters.'

'Oh, it does, believe me. And you know it.'

'I . . . suppose you're right, but it's still ridiculous and so . . . confining, for both of us. Oh, I'm well aware you have to earn a living, I'm not a fool, Celie,' squeezing her new friend's arm, 'but you're the first girl I've met with more than a grain of sense in her head and I can think of no one with whom I would rather go about, if only it were allowed. There's a concert next week which I would dearly love to attend. The Liverpool Philharmonic, an afternoon concert, and it could be your introduction to the music of Mozart and Beethoven, but what's the use? Mama, if I asked, would only believe it was some ruse to see Jethro.'

'Oh Jethro, Jethro, Jethro,' she would say, her heart shining from her soft brown eyes, 'when shall I ever see him again, Celie?' And again, Celie had no answer.

And now, as Celie flung herself about the kitchen at Cook's bidding in a hectic flurry of activity to produce the homecoming dinner to welcome the soldier son of the house back from active duty in India, she despaired, as Prudence despaired, for now there was another complication in this secret she and Prudence shared, for not only did she long to continue the exhilarating and fulfilling friendship she had formed with Prudence Latimer, she longed to be with, to talk to, to share and be admired by, the rich brown glance of Prudence Latimer's brother.

Chapter Twelve

The note was in her apron pocket and she was sure someone would see the astonished expression on her face when her hand closed over it, since she had no idea how it had come to be there. She almost drew it out, ready to say aloud the words which were on her tongue. "What on earth is this, and how did it get here?" but she managed to bite them back for it came to her then, and she had to bow her head to her mixing bowl to hide her crimson face, smiling.

'I have a fancy for one of your lemon biscuits, Cook,' and when Cook, startled, looked up from the peas she was shelling, she had nearly dropped the lot, basin and all, when she saw Miss Prudence standing there, as though she was seven years old instead of nearly nineteen. A lemon biscuit if you please, she said afterwards to Celie, just as though the things were hanging about waiting for her to come and sample after all these years and then, the moment a substitute, one of Celie's ratafias had been found for her, off she'd gone with herself. And all that fuss over that jug of cream she'd knocked over as well, with everyone running around mopping it up and her just standing there with a daft look on her face. These remarks were for Celie's ears only, of course, for to no one else would Cook say a word against *any* member of the Latimer family.

The note was short and to the point.

'Meet me at the corner of Picton Road and Knowles Lane tomorrow, two o'clock. Don't be late.'

It was not signed, but since it was evident Prudence had put it in her pocket under the cover of the commotion caused

by the spilled cream, who else could it be but her? Celie felt
her heart which she was sure had stopped when she read the
words, surge again on a tide of excitement and dread which
made her feel quite sick, but of the two the excitement was
stronger. She glanced furtively over her shoulder to make
sure no one had seen her read it, pushed it back in her pocket,
then closed the recipe book she was pretending to study.

'I'll do the Veal à la Bourgeoise, I think, Cook. Fetch me
that stewpan, Belle, and then you and Maudie start on the
veg. I'll want a dozen carrots, green onions, new potatoes
and fresh peas. Has Dan brought them . . . ? Good, and
when you've done the veg, run and ask him for a bunch of
fresh savoury herbs, will you Maudie?'

Cook nodded approvingly from her chair, taking a last sip
of the tea Maudie had put in her hand five minutes ago then
heaved herself to her feet. 'Well, whilst you're doing that I'll
have a look in the larder and see what needs ordering.'

'The flour's low, Cook.' Maudie's bright face peeped from
beyond the scullery window where she was about to start on
the veg and her voice rose above the crash of pans Belle was
attacking in the sink. Both girls were good, honest workers,
striving to please, not only Cook who ruled them, indeed
owned them to all intents and purposes, but Celie, whom they
saw as Cook's right hand and therefore almost as important.
The approval of Cook and Celie was eagerly sought and in
their different ways they did their best to win it. Maudie was
like a little sparrow, plain but cheerful, quick to see what
was needed and quick to do it. She was irrepressible in her
hopeful acceptance of her lowly place in life, in the kitchen and
the room beneath the eaves which she shared with another
"higher being" in the ranks of the servants, Kate Mossop.
Kate Mossop bossed her about, but she did not complain.
Kate's things took up most of the space in the drawers but
she did not complain. Kate was first with the hot water, had
the softest bed, the warmest quilt, and even the bit of matting
put there for both maids was beneath Kate's feet when they
touched the floor. But Maudie did not complain. And if Kate
was missing sometimes during the night hours it was not up
to Maudie to enquire where she was, nor who with, was it?

No, she kept her trap shut, did Maudie, and did not complain. Neither did Belle, but then, besides sharing a room with Celie who, she and Maudie were both agreed, was not as high and mighty as Kate, Belle never opened her mouth except to put food in it, only speaking when asked a direct question. Maudie did all the talking, keeping up a breathless flow of words, a ceaseless monologue, a constant blithe volubility to which Belle listened, answering with a nod or a shake of her head, a stare, a smile, a gasp, whatever the situation demanded so that Maudie knew no lack and indeed felt that she and Belle had some right interesting conversations. It was not that Belle was eleven pence halfpenny in the shilling or anything like that. She had the calm, contented face of one of the animals on the farm from which Maudie came and eyes that lit up in appreciation of a bit of fun. She just had nothing to say, no one in the kitchen knew why, not bothered really for one girl was enough always at the jabber. Belle was a demon with the pans, the scrubbing brush and anything which needed elbow grease, the brawn of the twosome while Maudie was the brain.

'Yes, I noticed that, girl,' Cook bristled, turning her suspicious gaze on the girl who spoke. 'But what were you doing in the flour bin? The flour bin's nothing to do with scullery maids, except to scrub out when it's needed.'

'I told her to fetch me a cupful, Cook, when I was making that batter this morning. She mentioned it then. I thought at the time that . . .'

It came to her then, as clear and perfect as the dew which hangs like diamond drops on a leaf. From the time of the note being read, not more than five minutes since, she had found a faultless excuse to get out tomorrow afternoon. She had hardly had time to digest the contents, the intoxication of the words Prudence had written, when Cook and Maudie had presented her with an excuse to leave the house and she didn't know why she hadn't thought of it before. Of course, it didn't happen more than once every week or ten days and even so, though she could go into town quite legitimately, it didn't mean that Prudence could, but apparently some opportunity had presented itself and Prudence had snatched at it.

It was months now since Cook had attempted the longish
walk to the tram-stop at the corner of Picton Road and the
bone-jerking clatter of the tramcar's dash down to St John's
Market. Her legs just would not stand it, not any more,
she confided to Celie and so Celie had taken to going,
not on her own, since Cook would not countenance a girl
as young and sheltered as Celie moving about the town
by herself, but in the company of Belle. Belle was, in
Cook's opinion, slow thinking, but she was big and strong,
dependable and obedient. The perfect companion for Celie
on her trips to the market and to Ingram's to order the
provisions for the Latimer household. The markets were held
on Wednesdays – which was tomorrow – and Saturdays and on
these days immense quantities of produce of all descriptions
were brought into Liverpool from Lancashire and Cheshire,
especially vegetables of the best quality. Not that these were
needed in the kitchens of Briar Lodge where Dan's hard work
and genius produced all the fruit and vegetables *they* were
ever likely to need. Produce came from Ireland, from Wales
and Scotland to the market stalls meant for the rich man's
table, at the same time providing at low prices for that of
the man of humble means. There were several markets in
Liverpool. The Pedlars' Market in Diane Street where stalls
sold what used to be called *pedlars*' ware, the sort which
had been hawked from door to door on a donkey cart by
travelling men. Baskets and earthenware, glassware and toys
and bonnets. St James Market was at the top of Great George
Street and there were fish stalls, fruit stands, poultry stalls,
provision shops, butchers' shops, egg and cheese stalls and
all providing fresh produce which had, apart from the cheese
and provisions, still been on the trees or in the ground only
the day before. St Martin's Market on Scotland Road catered
to the working man in that area. Gill Street Market, Cleveland
Square Market, Pownall Square Market, all providing for
the needs of the Liverpool housewife. The fish market had
recently been rebuilt, and it was packed with shops and stalls,
all fitted up with slabs of white marble, and underneath it
was a positive labyrinth of vast cellars to provide space for
the enormous quantities of fish of every kind which flooded

from the fishing boats onto the docks on market day. But of them all, St John's Market was the most popular. It was an enormous building covering an area of almost two acres, with no particular pretensions to architectural beauty. There were a dozen entrances, 136 windows to provide light and air, and around each wall and in the centre were 312 shops and stalls allowing the careful housewife to make her prudent choice from any one of them, the standard was so high. Elegantly dressed ladies and persons of the highest quality thronged the well-kept, well-scrubbed areas about the stalls during the morning; the butchers' stalls, the provisions dealers, game and poultry dealers, bakers, pork stalls, fruit stands, green stalls, egg boxes and the 350 yards of tabling erected to provide extra space should it be needed.

In fact, an environment in which it would be very easy to get lost, or to lose a companion!

Cook made no objection to Celie's sudden decision to slip down to Ingram's for provisions tomorrow since it seemed that, like the almost empty flour bin, the larder did need replenishing; nor did she object to her added rejoinder that whilst she was at it she might visit the market and order the poultry for the week, a sirloin of beef, some shin and a piece of rump steak.

'Best order a shoulder of lamb and two legs for Sunday while you're at it, Celie. You know how Master Richard do like lamb.'

Why did her heart lurch when Cook mentioned his name? she asked herself, as she wrote the order down on the notepad she kept in her apron pocket. She could feel her cheeks flame and her fingers tremble and she had to turn away, thankful of the cover of the usual hurly-burly which went on in the kitchen. Dan was at the table with Jim and Bertie, one on either side of him, tucking into a steaming bowl of her own vegetable broth, smacking their lips appreciatively and telling each other how good it was. Dan raised an enquiring eyebrow, his spoon half-way to his mouth, and she fanned her face smiling foolishly, she was sure, and blowing out her breath.

'Phew, it's hot in here,' she said before turning away

from his quizzical gaze. 'Now is there anything else, Cook? What about some sweetbreads? We could do some with asparagus.'

'Good idea, and I think a leg of pork, about eight pounds, I'd say, and a loin about the same. Oh, and two dozen cutlets. I do like a nice pork cutlet . . .' taking for granted the way in which the open-handed Mr Latimer fed his servants.

'And fish?'

'I quite fancy a bit of turbot, Cook.' Dorcas looked up from the dainty tea tray she was setting for the ladies in Mrs Latimer's drawing room. 'With that lovely sauce of yours.'

'Right, a turbot for Friday, tell the fishmonger, middling size then it'll do us all. Oh, and some lobster spawn for the sauce.'

'Is that it, Cook?'

'Mmm, I think so.'

'Only when I've finished the ordering I'd like to see if there's any fabric going cheap at Miss Hawkins'. Something for a winter dress.'

'Mrs Ash has only just finished you one.' Cook turned in amazement to Celie. 'Are you made of money, lass? Two dresses in a month?'

Celie felt the greatest urge to tell Cook to mind her own business. That if she wanted two dresses in one month and could afford the few bob it cost to buy the material and pay Mrs Ash to make them up for her, then she would do. She was eighteen in January and yet Cook at times treated her as though she was the child who had begun work here twelve years ago. She was, she knew, still only Cook's assistant, despite her own worth in the kitchen, but she was surely permitted to spend her own money as she thought fit. She had a few pounds put by – her Pa had left almost twenty guineas which he must have saved over the years, found in a box under his summer shirts when he died – and she was well able to afford a few pretty things for herself. She had her cream sprigged muslin which would not be warm enough for this time of the year and her cream and grey tweed, worn for three winters now, and far too tight across the chest. The new dress, well, it was a two-piece, was lovely. Mrs

Ash had made it, somewhat piecemeal since Celie never had the time to do more than "pop in" and immediately out again for a fitting, Mrs Ash grumbled. A rich cherry-red merino purchased this time from Miss Hawkins of Bold Street, a milliner's and dressmaker's which she had passed many times on her way to Ingram's. Celie had been on her own on this particular day and had noticed that Miss Hawkins had a discreet sign in her window informing her customers that she had on hand an assortment of "best corsets", "best sateen" and "Paris wove corsets" and also at a reduced cost, several dozen yards of "shop-soiled" fabrics. The cherry-red merino had been among them.

The two-piece outfit which Mrs Ash had made for her was quite severe in its design, the jacket fitting neatly to her softly swelling breast and tiny waist, with a high buttoned neck piped in a pale silver grey velvet. The "puffed" sleeve was full to the elbow where it gathered into a long cuff to the wrist which was also edged in pale grey velvet. The gored skirt was remarkable in that the goring was carried up to the waist without any gathering except in the fashionable fullness at the back.

Just as Celie had been about to leave, Miss Hawkins, who turned out to be a comfortable little woman with a broad Lancashire accent and not the elegant and lofty personage Celie had expected, had diffidently enquired of her whether she would be interested in a bonnet which exactly matched the cherry red of the fabric.

'Not enormously expensive, miss,' she had added, but very respectfully, just as though seventeen-year-old Celie Marlow was one of her most esteemed customers. It had turned out to be a delightful little thing in the shape of a boater with a small brim which tipped over her eyes, decorated with a bit of veiling and a silver-grey velvet rosebud. She had not yet shown it to the others, it was so *very* elegant.

She would wear it tomorrow! But Cook was still waiting for an answer and would not be satisfied until she had one. Celie shrugged as though it was of no importance.

'My sprigged muslin is far too tight across my . . .' Again it was as though some angel, or was it an imp of hell, put the idea in her head. She lifted her young breasts and the mouths of the three young men on the bench at the table fell open as they eyed them in awe. At once Cook became flustered, ready to do, or say, anything that would draw their attention away from Celie Marlow's very evident and very inappropriately displayed charms. The minx! It was not like her to make a show of herself, Cook thought, innocent as it had been – or so she *hoped*. Now if it had been that Kate Mossop!

'. . . so I'm going to see if Miss Hawkins has any more shop-soiled fabric,' Celie was saying. 'That merino was hardly marked and when Mrs Ash had cut it the stain was inside. I thought I might have a gown . . . !'

'A gown, is it?' Kate chortled, 'a gown . . .'

'You be quiet, Kate Mossop.' Celie turned on her fiercely. 'You know nothing about fashion . . .'

'I know as much as you . . .'

'What! That green thing you wear on a . . .'

'That's enough, the pair of you. See, Kate, help Dorcas with that tray and you'd better get on with the veal, Celie, or it'll not be done in time.'

Kate flounced towards the tray. 'Well, I thought . . .' she began. Cook turned on her. 'Well, you know what thought did, don't you? It followed the muck cart and thought it was a wedding.'

Celie and Belle stepped out of the kitchen the following day at just gone one o'clock. Her "two-piece" had been admired by her fellow maidservants though not with a great deal of enthusiasm, since it was far too plain for their taste. Even the hat which she had hesitantly put on had evoked little interest. A bird on it would be nice, Dorcas had said, considering it somewhat disparagingly, or some fruit and feathers, which was fashionable. Bows is what you need, and on the dress, Lily had offered, having bought her own hat on the second-hand stall at Paddy's Market which dealt in such things, testifying to her own lack of discernment where fashion was concerned.

Belle was dressed neatly, plainly, drably, greyly in a ground-length woollen skirt made over from one Mrs Latimer had discarded years ago. Mrs Latimer had worn it during her last pregnancy and because of its fullness it had been just the thing for Belle, Cook had said, eyeing it triumphantly. A bit of a tuck here and there, put in by Mrs Ash, a decent blouse and an ill-fitting dark grey jacket from God alone knew where, but did it matter, and Belle was fitted up "for best". Her hat was the only jaunty thing about her. A straw boater of Miss Anne's with a pale yellow ribbon round its crown. She was tall and in the years she had been at Briar Lodge, had filled out and at fifteen looked older than Celie. She had ample breasts and hips and yet she was not fat and her round, impassive face was rosy with health. In her eyes, as she looked at the slender, fragile loveliness of the girl who swayed at her side as they walked down the drive towards Knowles Lane, was no envy, only the devotion and admiration which Celie's careless attention to her had planted in her heart.

'Now then, Belle,' Celie began briskly, doing her best to give the impression that what she was about to say was nothing out of the ordinary. 'I want you to listen to me. Are you listening?'

'Yes.' Belle nodded ponderously.

'What would you say if I was to give you . . . two hours off this afternoon? To do just as you like. Go where you please. How would you like that?' She peered eagerly into Belle's face, a light-footed, gracefully sleek thoroughbred horse moving beside the lumbering bulk of the Clydesdale which pulled the coal cart. They had reached the gate by now and had turned into Knowles Lane. It was tree-lined, the trees in their stark November nakedness, hedges bordering the few, select, upper-class residences which sat along its length beyond the walls of Briar Lodge. There was no one about as the two girls, one looking for all the world like the mistress of the other, walked briskly towards the corner where the lane met Picton Road.

'Well . . . I . . . I dunno . . .' Clearly Belle could make neither head nor tail of the question and had no idea of the answer expected of her. Was it a joke, or . . . what? Her thought processes got no further than that when the rapier-like mind of Celie Marlow overtook them. It had, during the hours of darkness, whilst Belle dreamed heavily in the next bed, pondered on how to go about solving this stimulating problem. She must find a way to spend an hour or two with Prudence . . . Oh, Lord . . . where were they to go? . . . the Concert Hall, perhaps, which Prudence had gone on about at great length. Some symphony, was that the word, Prudence wished her to hear, or was it the Art Gallery to study . . . now what was the man's name? . . . Turner . . . yes, that was it, which was all well and good but what on earth were she and Prudence to do with Belle whilst they did these exciting things? The plan had come at last, clear and perfect in its symmetry, as the other one had, but she had not dared reveal it to Belle before they left in case Belle, in her simplicity, let the cat out of the bag and blurted it to Maudie, or worse still to Cook. She might still do so when they got back, but by then Celie would have had her outing with Prudence and what could Cook do about *that* without getting Prudence into trouble, she had asked herself triumphantly?

It did not occur to Celie that Cook would get every member of the household, aye, and right willingly, into trouble with the exception perhaps of Celie herself, to save her own job. With her legs and without Celie, where would she get another? would be Jess Harper's reaction!

'I have somewhere to go, you see . . . with . . . with a friend . . .' which was true, her excited heart whispered '. . . so you could go and . . . I know . . . where does your family live? . . .'

'My family . . . ?'

'Yes . . .' getting somewhat exasperated for really it was a very simple question, but it was not the matter of her family's whereabouts which was confusing Belle but the extraordinary nature of Celie's behaviour. Belle had put her simple mind to the normal and familiar trip on the tramcar which she did most weeks with Celie. She was, she clearly understood, a kind of guardian, a protector of Celie's delicate person, a trust put in her by Cook, which was only right and proper, for in Belle's humble opinion there was no one more in need of protection than the fragile and incredibly beautiful Celie Marlow. And *who* better to be her . . . what had Cook called it? . . . her *chaperone* . . . than Belle who, as the eldest of six brothers and sisters and being what her Ma called *sturdy*, had stood up for them all of her young life. Now Celie was telling her she was to leave her. Belle was to go off somewhere on her own because Celie was going to meet a friend, and all Belle understood was that Cook would make mincemeat of both of them if she found out.

All this cogitating took a great deal of time to wend its way through Belle's slow mind and Celie gave her a little shake.

'Come on, Belle, I haven't got all day. I'm meeting my friend at two o'clock and I can't just leave you here. Don't your Ma and Pa live somewhere round Wavertree?'

'Salisbury Terrace.'

'Where's that?'

'Salisbury Terrace.'

'Yes, I heard you, but whereabouts is it? Is it in Wavertree?'

'Pa works at St Mary's Church. He's the grave-digger.'

'Is he? I didn't know that.' For a foolish moment Celie's attention was captured by the macabre nature of Belle's Pa's occupation, then her irritation made her shake her head. 'Is it in Wavertree?' she asked again.

'Aye, oh aye, by the . . .'

'And can you find your way there?'

'O'course I can. I live there.' Belle was slightly insulted, you could see that, but Celie had no time to stand about arguing with her.

'Right then, you go off and see your Ma and when I come back I'll . . .' She bit her lip anxiously and her smooth young brow was furrowed at the alarming complexities of the expedition. The thing was she couldn't stay *too* long or Cook would become worried and in her anxiety might raise the alarm with Mrs Latimer. Mrs Latimer would then want to know what the kitchen maid and the scullery maid were doing out alone and the answer that the kitchen maid was being entrusted with the ordering of provisions, was indeed allowed to handle the finances of the household, would not please the mistress. Not only would Celie be in the direst of trouble, which was bad enough, but Cook might get the sack.

If only she knew what Prudence had planned for this afternoon Celie could make her own plans and give Belle her orders. "Be at the corner of Picton Road and Knowles Road at four sharp," she would say, but what if she was late? Belle hanging around on the road to Briar Lodge might, if seen, cause some comment and the girl herself would be uneasy with no one to direct her. "Tell me where your Ma lives and I'll pick you up in two hours' time" perhaps, but that was not much better for no doubt Belle's mother, unless she was as unthinking as her daughter, would question the kitchen maid at Briar Lodge "calling" for the scullery maid, who should not be there in the first place. And what had compelled Prudence to arrange such a haphazard scheme? She must have known that a girl such as Celie could not just slip out at such short notice, or indeed at *any* time without the permission of *someone* and it was only by the merest chance that Celie had managed to get away. What had seemed so perfect and so *easy* as she lay in her bed last night was becoming more and more entangled the nearer they got to the corner of Picton Road.

Anyway, it did no good churning her brain into a muddle over it. She must place Belle somewhere safe before she set off on this exhilarating adventure with Prudence Latimer.

Her heart was beating like a hammer on an anvil but her steps were jaunty, her eyes bright as crystal, her back straight and her head high, for not in a million years would she have missed this great expedition. She had, of course, been on outings with Dan, more than a few times, but this was different. Dan was grand, but Prudence had opened up something inside her, awakened some quality, made her aware of how . . . how fine it was to have another female for a friend. Dan was fun, but he had not the tendency to *giggle* in the ridiculous way she and Prudence seemed inclined to do, to share that foolish – she was aware of it, but what did it matter – chatter which one woman can engage in with another. She had not even known it existed, the closeness of friendship which can develop between females, but now she did and she found it delightful. It was not that Prudence, or even herself, were particularly prone to giddiness, for their upbringing, though different, had not allowed it, but nevertheless when they were together, the inhibiting shackles of convention fell away.

There was a two-wheel hansom cab standing at the corner of Picton Road and Knowles Lane. The driver on the seat at the back appeared to be dozing. The horse which pulled it stood patiently, its head down, its left back leg slightly bent, its hoof resting lightly on the surface of the lane, as though it too was glad of a bit of a respite.

Celie's pounding heart gave another great leap of excitement. She straightened her smart hat, though the gesture was not needed, smoothed down the wool of her skirt and began to smile.

'There's my friend now, Belle,' all thoughts of what to do with the scullery maid speeding like summer swallows from her young mind. Belle must do as she thought best, just as long as she was at the gates of Briar Lodge when Celie returned.

'It's not a . . . ?' Belle was clearly labouring under considerable embarrassment.

'What?' Celie strained away from the surprising hand Belle had put on her arm.

'Well, yer not going wi' . . .'

'What, for God's sake?'

'It's not a . . . a . . . chap, is it, Celie?' Belle's face was like a beetroot when Celie turned to her in amazement.

'A chap!' She began to laugh then. 'Oh, Belle, of course it's not a chap. Whatever gave you that idea?'

'Well . . .' What else was Belle to think, Belle's concerned expression asked.

'Belle, for goodness sake. Where would I meet a man, you great daft thing . . .' then she was sorry for that was exactly what Belle was and the remark was cruel.

'Look, Belle, you slip home to your Ma's. Tell her . . . tell her you've got an unexpected afternoon off, which is true and . . . oh, Lord . . . be back at this corner by four thirty sharp. No later because it'll be getting dark. D'you understand?'

'An unexpected afternoon off,' Belle repeated woodenly, the long words sounding strange coming from her lips which barely uttered even the most ordinary.

'Yes, now off you go.'

'Bye, Celie,' still not sure.

'Bye, Belle,' shooing her across the road smilingly before turning to the hansom cab, the half door of which had just opened.

'Get in, Celie,' Prudence's voice demanded urgently. 'Oh, do hurry up,' and she began to laugh, sharing, it seemed, Celie's almost hysterical excitement.

Chapter Thirteen

His laughing face was the first one she saw as she stepped up into the cab and again, as on that night a week ago when he had come into the kitchen, she felt the blood rush from her brain, leaving her breathless and light-headed!

'It's all right, Celie, really it is,' she heard Prudence say. 'Richard insisted on coming. Well, that's not quite how it was, is it, Richard? Had he not spoken to Mama, I wouldn't be here myself and neither would you. "Prudence and I want to go and view the Egyptian Antiquities at the museum, Mama," he said, and of course, being the brave and handsome soldier he is, the hero of the King's Regiment and all that and the light of his Mama's life, how could she refuse him? Yes, you've guessed it, Celie, I've told him everything. There was a . . . a . . . drama . . . yes, it concerned Jethro and . . . well, here we are. But the best, the very best . . . oh, Celie, you'll never guess . . . oh, dear, dear Celie, I am to see Jethro. Yes, Richard has arranged it all and if Mama knew she'd throw a fit. Jethro sent me a note you see, not knowing that Mama opens my letters and of course when she did at the breakfast table . . . it's a wonder you did not hear of it from the maids . . .'

Celie, even in her spellbound consternation wondered too . . .

'. . . the enormous furore which went on and then . . .'

Suddenly Prudence put both hands to her face, which in her exquisite happiness was almost beautiful. Her eyes widened, her mouth closed, then opened again as though her own bad manners quite appalled her.

'Oh, do forgive me, here I am rattling on and I have not introduced my brother to you. Of course you know each other . . . well . . . you have . . . met . . . but . . .' The sudden and embarrassing realisation of *where* they had met, and the circumstances of their relationship to one another overcame her for a moment since, as far as she knew, there were no rules of etiquette governing the introduction of servant to master. And all the while she talked, Richard Latimer and Celie Marlow sat locked in the perfect stillness this meeting had brought about, the stillness and silence from which, though they were aware of her and could hear her voice, Prudence Latimer was excluded. It was soft, dreaming, familiar, a melting of the spirit, two spirits, so that they merged and became one.

So it is still the same, his asked gently of hers?

Oh, yes . . . hers answered his, though Celie, in her innocence, had no conception of what was happening to her.

'How do you do, Celie, or shall it be Miss Marlow?' His voice was whimsical and his eyes narrowed in smiling recognition.

'Master Richard,' she lowered her eyes shyly, staring with absorbed attention at her own gloved hands.

'Richard, please.'

She looked up, startled, knowing she could never call him by his Christian name, never, but his eyes were kind and his face so . . . so warm and . . . what was it . . . something·so lovely . . . the confusion in her deepened.

'Richard, please,' he repeated. He nodded encouragingly, but when she did not answer he pressed her no further.

'And now that is done with, I think explanations are in order, don't you, Richard, and do please beg that man to hurry. Jethro told you two thirty and it is almost that now. We are to meet at the corner of William Brown Street and then go into the large salon in the art gallery where it will be . . . quiet. Richard arranged it . . . oh, Richard, you tell her because I swear the excitement is too much for me.'

Richard Latimer sighed, tearing his gaze from the still face of the girl who, as yet, had not leaned back in the cab, but sat upright beside him in a daze of wonder. He knew what it was he saw in her since it was the same with him. Her eyes were filled with what he was reluctant to call stars but they shone in the dimness of the cab and in them was the depth of her emotion. She made no attempt to hide it and indeed he thought she was probably too young, too inexperienced and innocent to do so, and he knew that very soon his sister would see it, and be puzzled. But then, perhaps in her own state of delirious happiness Prudence would not notice it in another, just as she had shown no surprise when he had suggested that Celie Marlow should come with them on this outing. After all, he had told her, if Celie was to accompany her on further outings, which it seemed she was, for it would not do for Prudence to go out alone, then this might as well be the first, besides which, she would be company for him and he for her whilst Prudence talked to Jethro. It was logical, wasn't it? and in her ecstasy Prudence could only agree.

They had been idling about on the other side of the pond when she had blurted out her love for Jethro Garside. Richard was to rejoin his regiment in Manchester soon, he had been telling her, and from the way he said it, he knew she could not fail to recognise that it could not come soon enough, for the cloying atmosphere of his mother's proud and proprietary love was, after only a week at home, beginning to stifle him. He had lived for years in the company of other soldiers, officers and gentlemen like himself, and before that had been at school and university and he found it hard to do nothing but idle about as he did at home. His Mama longed to show him off, parading him before her friends – and their very suitable young daughters – at dances and dinner parties and all manner of entertainment and social functions where he was, though he had done nothing to merit it, he said, the hero of the hour. The ladies fussed him and the gentlemen asked his opinion about everything under the sun, just as though his soldiering in India had conferred on him the wisdom of Solomon.

He had been saying as much to Prudence who, of all his brothers and sisters, was the one he found the easiest to talk to, though when he had left home to become an officer in the King's Liverpool Regiment, she had been little more than a child. She was almost nineteen now but despite her

unworldliness, she had, it seemed to him, a practical mind
which kept her in touch with the ordinary people who moved
about in her world. Those who were not family. The poorer
members of the community, the sick and needy whom she,
her sister and her Mama visited, as did many ladies of the
parish. She believed in God because she had been taught
to do so but kept her beliefs to herself, inflicting them on
no one. She had a genuinely kind heart and would make a
splendid wife and mother since she was unselfish and always
willing to help those in trouble. She was a quiet girl with a
good brain and sensible, but at the same time he found her
to have a slightly irreverent sense of fun which he thought
most appealing.

When, as they strolled in a sudden silence, turning at the
top of the small lake in the direction of the house, she began
to weep quite desolately, he had been so amazed that for
a moment he could do no more than stand and watch her
helplessly.

'Pru . . . Good Lord, Pru, what on earth's the matter?' he
exclaimed, at a loss as to what to do next for though he was
a kind man and could not bear to see a woman in distress,
he had not the slightest notion of what to do about it. 'Are
you . . . unwell?' he had asked her, just as Celie had done
in exactly the same situation.

It had all come out then, her frustration and longing to be
something other than an extension of her Mama, her boredom
with and contempt for the trivial round of calls, of evening
soirées and afternoon teas, of parties and dances where she
met only the most *asinine* of gentlemen. That was all she did
except for what she jokingly called her "good works". She was
bored with doing no more than embroider and play the piano,
not even allowed to visit the William Brown Library to choose
her own library books, nor go to the Walker Art Gallery to
view the pictures which pleased *her*. She and her older sister
Anne had nothing in common since Anne was preparing for
her wedding next June and was interested in nothing unless it
concerned orange blossom, veiling, or the agonising decision
of whether to have deep plum or sage green velvet curtains at
her own drawing room windows. And then, of course, there

was Jethro, Jethro Garside, who was the only man she had ever met who had made her laugh out loud, much to Mama's annoyance; who shared her taste in art and literature and music. Who liked walking, reading, *arguing* about everything which interested them both, though he was polite enough to describe what they did so easily together as *discussion*. He was kind, gentle, courteous to her Mama. He was wealthy, though from what she did not know since it would have been ill-bred to ask on the three occasions they had met. He had a large detached house on Croxteth Drive opposite Stanley Park. He had shown his interest in her quite without reserve and she loved him but he was not, unfortunately, a gentleman.

'And he's the one who wrote you the note that Mama opened?'

'Yes,' she wailed.

'What was in it?'

'How should I know? Mama did not *show* it to me, merely hauled me off to her room when she had recovered from what she described as her appalled sense of shock at my behaviour, and told me that I was to cut off all communications with . . . with Jethro and when I told her this was the first time he had . . . oh, Richard, what am I to do?'

'Does anyone besides Mama know?'

Only Celie, she had told him, weeping, but no one else, inconsolable, failing to see his own astonishment at the mention of the girl who worked as kitchen maid in his Mama's kitchen.

'Celie?'

'Yes, we have become friends,' just as though there was nothing at all amiss with that.

'Friends?' he had asked carefully.

'Yes, I am doing my best to think of something to allow us to . . . go about together, perhaps a concert or . . .'

'You and Celie?'

'Mmmm . . .'

'And . . . perhaps Jethro?'

'Oh Richard, don't . . . twinkle at me like that. I am not making use of Celie, if that's what you're thinking. I like her immensely. She is clever, really clever, and so incredibly . . .'

'Lovely . . .'

'You've noticed?'

'Yes, I've noticed . . .' then went on hastily, '. . . and you were planning to meet her somewhere and when you did it might be possible to . . . include Jethro?'

'Oh, Richard, do you think it could be managed?' meaning could *he* manage it. He knew he could. He had to. He did.

'. . . so you see, Miss Marlow,' his engaging smile lingering about her absorbed, enchanted face as it glowed at a distance of no more than six inches from his own. There was not a great deal of room in the two-wheeled hansom cab. 'My sister persuaded me that if I did not seek out a certain gentleman . . .'

'Richard, I'm warning you. This is no laughing matter.' From his other side Prudence struck his arm in mock outrage, in reality too bewitched to care *what* he said, or to whom. She would have her hour or two with Jethro whilst Richard walked on the Marine Parade with Celie, and if it had occurred to her to wonder why Celie should have come on this outing at all, it was shrouded in the marvel of being alone for the first time with Jethro. She went no further than the next two hours, nor did she dwell on why Jethro had written to her. It was enough that he had. It was enough that she was to see him. That he wished to see her.

He was standing on the corner of William Brown Street, a well-built, quite ordinary gentleman in his mid-thirties, impeccably dressed. He wore a dark-coloured double-breasted overcoat with a half-collar of velvet, a top hat which he whipped smartly from his head as he handed Prudence down from the cab, and carried a pair of cream kid gloves.

'Miss Latimer.' He had a pair of merry blue eyes which managed to twinkle and at the same time gaze seriously down from his great height into Prudence's rapturous face.

'Mr Garside,' she breathed, allowing her hand to remain in his for longer than was necessary, or even well-mannered, and her brother was forced to clear this throat several times before either of them came from their absorbed contemplation of one another and turned their attention back to him and Celie. Richard had helped Celie down from the cab, giving her his gloved hand. She too wore gloves but through the thickness of the material she could feel the warmth of him wrap around her fingers, his grip firm, inclined to linger, reluctant to end that first contact, it seemed. His expression was serious, almost grim now, his eyebrows dipping in what she thought might be a frown, and she faltered for had she offended him in some way? She hastily withdrew her hand from his and Prudence did the same with Mr Garside.

'Latimer.' Jethro Garside greeted Richard Latimer curtly in that way gentlemen had, but nodding pleasantly at the same time. 'It was good of you to . . . to arrange this. I had . . . I wanted to . . . that is, with your permission, of course, since I mean no dishonour to . . . well, the thing is . . .'

Poor Mr Garside, Celie thought, but at the same time knowing exactly how he felt for he seemed to be in the same overwrought state as herself. You could see at once that he had a high regard for Prudence. Well, that was a daft thing to say. The man was in love with her and she with him, you could tell at a glance. They could hardly keep their hands from lifting, wanting to touch and cling, their eyes constantly turning towards one another, smiling, mouths ready to lift and curl in soft, delighted laughter. Prudence had that tendency to sway towards him in the way of a woman in love, whilst he obviously longed to support, to cherish, to protect in the way of a man in love. They had done no more, if Prudence was to be believed, than talk at the dinner table. First at the Latimer home, and on a couple of occasions when they had met at a dinner party given by mutual friends, and yet the strong force of their attraction was very evident. Celie had time to think to herself that it was no wonder Mrs Latimer had been alarmed by it, when Richard drew her forward with the courteous attention a gentleman affords a lady.

'Say not another word, my dear fellow, I was only too pleased to be of help. Now then, Celie, may I present Mr Garside . . . a friend of . . . Prudence's,' with barely a falter in the introduction.

'Garside, this is Miss Marlow . . . a . . . friend also of

Prudence's,' smiling down at her, as though she was the most precious thing in the world to him now. Again confusion overwhelmed her.

'Miss Marlow.' She almost bobbed a curtsey to Mr Garside! Dear God . . . she had almost bobbed a curtsey, for after all she *was* a servant, so what was she doing here with these splendid people, this group of well-bred, superior beings in whose kitchen, not so very long ago, she had scoured pans and scrubbed floors? Was she in danger of getting above her station, as her Pa would have said, and if so, she had no right to accept the friendship of a girl like Prudence Latimer. As Prudence Latimer had absolutely no right to make a friend of her mother's kitchen maid. It was like expecting oil and water to mix. Both essential liquids and necessary to the lives of the people who used them, but neither one with the ability to merge with the other. How blithely she had run out to the woods to hold long and absorbing conversations with the daughter of the house. How easy it had seemed to engage in the joyful laughter, to walk beside Prudence Latimer in the autumn lanes and fields, to listen to Prudence Latimer tell her, to believe her when she did, that they would go to concerts together, to the Art Gallery and exhibitions which interested them both. It had seemed a natural progression of their growing liking for one another, their curiosity to know what the other thought, believed in, had hopes for, opinions on everything from the defeat of Lord Salisbury in last year's summer elections and the new ministry formed by Mr Gladstone, to the shocking but – to the two young girls – exciting apparel called knickerbockers which were being worn by a few, a very few, daring lady cyclists. *Then*, she had seen nothing strange in the way she and Prudence had seemed to share the same views, but now with Richard Latimer introducing her to a gentleman of his acquaintance just as if *she* was a lady of *his*, it suddenly brought it home to her as though she had fallen unwittingly into a lake of ice cold water. A deluge of ice cold water that brought her shivering to the surface, weighed down with it so that she almost sank but striking out, nevertheless, to the safety of the shore.

Had she but known it, her appearance *was* that of a

lady, a member of the class which had bred Prudence and Richard Latimer and it was only in her tremulous face that her nervousness showed. She was unsteady, ready to shy away as Mr Garside took her hand to bow over, as she knew gentlemen did, smiling, nodding to her with a kindness which said there was nothing wrong with being young and shy. She could feel the strong presence of Richard Latimer close to her side and somehow she got through it.

They chatted for several minutes, none of them really knowing what about. Prudence and Richard were accustomed to the light conversational small talk which they had been brought up to practise in the company of their Mama's friends. Celie Marlow, now that she had recovered a little, had the instinctive good manners and the sense to nod in the appropriate places, to bob her head and smile in the most enchanting way and to keep silent since she had nothing to say. She was not to know that both gentlemen found her shyness and modesty quite delightful.

Jethro Garside was a self-made, self-taught, businessman, and accustomed in his dealings with other businessmen to engage them and their wives, when he was a guest in their homes, in polite conversation. Not as easily as those born to it, but well enough to be at ease. He was a man come, like Celie, from humble beginnings, but with an in-born flair for knowing how to go about making money. He had few academic qualifications. He could really do no more than read and write, but it was in his head, his keen mind which could calculate to a farthing what profit might be gained in the "deals" he made, that his talents lay. He dealt with *anything* in the world of buying and selling, whatever the commodity which would most benefit his bank balance, and in the great sea port of Liverpool, to where he had come as a boy of fifteen, there were many such opportunities. He had offices in Water Street amongst those of the shipping men and from where he purchased merchandise which was low in price. Anything from a cargo of timber, of raw sugar, to a piece of land no one seemed to want, waiting until the price was right, and which he of course knew to a nicety, then selling to his own advantage. In twenty years he had made himself a millionaire, though he was careful not to boast about it, since that was not his way. He had, from that day when he had arrived in Liverpool, almost without boots to his feet, quietly gone about the business of getting everything he had ever wanted from life. Now, though he could not have said why, he wanted Prudence Latimer. She was neither beautiful nor a great heiress but there was a lovely and genuine light about her. A sincerity, a *womanly* softness which had woken some shimmering thing within himself he had not even known he possessed. He meant to marry her, and soon.

'Well . . .' Prudence said, her longing to be off on the stalwart arm of Mr Garside so evident Celie felt a small smile tug at her lips and she bent her head to hide it. When she lifted it again, she found Richard's eyes on her, one whimsical eyebrow raised as he shared with her that moment of amusement. Not unkindly, since he was fond of his sister and thought she would do very well with the estimable Mr Garside.

He had not arranged this meeting lightly. He had made very extensive enquiries discreetly, of course, amongst the wide circle of his own and his father's acquaintances, business and personal, about the man his sister loved, finding that, though he tended, as all gentlemen did, to visit a certain very discreet house in the city now and again, there were no entanglements, no rumours or scandal of any sort attached to his name. He was well respected, and though one or two might mutter of his "sharp" business sense, implying it was *too* sharp, they were men who had, through their own fault, lost money to him. He liked a small gamble at the race course and at the gaming club in Duke Street but he was prudent and not a heavy drinker. Had Richard found the slightest hint of impropriety this meeting would not have taken place. He meant to do no more than allow Jethro Garside this one chance and after that it was up to the man who loved his sister to fight for her, as any man of character, of daring and determination would fight for the woman he loved, his eyes straying of their own accord to the quiet girl beside him. He would leave Jethro Garside the hard task – and it would be hard – of persuading his Mama to allow Prudence to marry him. But first, the poor chap must be given the chance to ask *Prudence*.

'Well, now, I have a fancy to take a walk,' he smiled, 'along the Marine Parade, I think. Get some of that fresh sea air into my lungs.' He put his hand to his chest, smiling quizzically down at Celie, drawing her into the innocent charade they were acting out for the sake of his sister and her would-be lover. He was not dressed in his uniform today but had on a knee-length Chesterfield overcoat with side vents in a fine tweed wool and narrow trousers. The collar at his neck was high with the points slightly turned down, and his neck tie was tied in a very small knot. He wore the very latest thing in hats, a soft felt trilby, casual but suitable with his less formal attire. His strong body was arresting and vigorous, his physique superb, and the richness of his brown eyes in his sun-darkened face drew sidelong and admiring glances from more than one passing lady. 'I have been told,' he continued, 'that there are two or three splendid passenger liners at berth which are worth having a look at. Her Majesty's Battleship *Royal Oak* was recently floated from the building yard and is said to be a fine sight. She's the largest vessel ever built on the Mersey, did you know that, Celie?' Celie said she didn't. 'Perhaps you would like to have a look at her. We could walk down to the Pier Head and then, if you would care to, take a hansom back to the Adelphi for afternoon tea. Would you like that?'

Would she like it? *Would she like it*! She could think of nothing more enchanting than to put her hand in the arm Richard was gallantly offering her, and walk with him in the crisp December sunshine down the length of Dale Street and Water Street, beyond the imposing edifice of the Town Hall to the Pier Head. Her expression told him so, and even in the midst of their own rapture, the faces of Prudence Latimer and Jethro Garside registered their dawning and startled recognition of what lay between Richard Latimer and Celie Marlow.

The docks and vast quays of Liverpool, cut in the grey granite blocks of Lancashire, stretched for six and a half miles along the shore of the River Mersey, their rich maritime history evident in every cobbled stone, in every landing stage, in every ship tied up there, both steam and sail. In its Custom House, its Dock Offices, its frantic industry. There still remained a surprising forest of masts, those of the sailing ships, crowding Brocklebank Dock, their denuded rigging a frail lacework against the pale blue of the sky. The wind sang a haunting melody through swinging spars, and winches creaked as bales swung free from hold to shore accompanied by the harsh cries of the gulls. Liverpool's heritage was built into every weighted keel that threaded its way out to the open sea and into the great four-funnelled Cunarder as she bore slowly to her mooring after her race across the Atlantic. The ocean passenger liner *Arcadia* of the P & O Line was just about to berth, coming alongside Princes landing stage, her movements orderly, leisurely, graceful. Gangways were lowered, and on the dock the cheerful banter of the men who were involved with the berthing of the ship intermingled with the strident whistling of the dockers waiting on the contents of the *Arcadia*'s hold. The porters' shouts as they vied with one another in the carrying of the luggage which would soon be unloaded, and the excited cries of those who had come to meet the travellers who had just crossed the Atlantic. Richard had been ready to tell her of the luxury of the solid marble baths of which the liner boasted; of the hot and cold sea-water showers and the marvel of the patent spring mattresses in each first-class cabin, but he stood without words since they seemed paltry between them, not worthy of being uttered.

They had barely spoken since they had left Prudence and Jethro, walking at a good pace, for the day was cold and even now it seemed they were content just to stand in silence, letting the hullabaloo whirl about them. Orders were bellowed and obeyed. Those lining the rails of the ships called out to friends recognised on the shore. Sailors moved briskly about the decks, each one intent on some important business known only to himself. Lines were thrown and deftly caught. There was a smell peculiar only to dockland: a mixture of tobacco smoke, for most of the men labouring there had a short, stubby pipe gripped between their teeth; there was the pungency of the sea, of tar and timber and coffee beans and any of a dozen commodities being loaded and unloaded along the docks in their immediate vicinity. Victoria and Trafalgar and Salisbury Docks on their right, Canning, Albert, Salthouse and Wapping to their left, where a scene in reverse was being enacted.

Since 1860 and the real start of the emigration trade, of the fourteen or so million people who had sailed to other worlds, almost five million of them had gone from Liverpool. Competition between the shipping lines had been fierce and in this year of 1893, a mere £5 would carry a would-be new American to his goal, providing he did not require a private cabin, in which case the rate would be doubled. The low prices naturally made it imperative to increase the number of passengers carried, and even now, a traveller, presumably the man paying £5 to go steerage, had to supply his own bedding and eating utensils.

The Cunard liner *Lucania* was preparing to steam to the "New World" and George's landing stage, from where she was to leave, was a mass of seething activity, hundreds of people doing their best to get aboard, whilst those who had come to see them off did their best to prevent it, grief-stricken at the impending parting. Officers were shouting commands and seamen and dockers were preparing to juggle with ropes and cables. Smoke poured from the funnel which carried the Cunard emblem, and the deep roar of the ship's siren momentarily silenced the ever increasing shrillness of the people packed on the dock. Mothers were sobbing broken-heartedly as they pressed departing, excited young sons to their bosom for the last time and men cleared their throats.

'Don't forget to write, son,' and son promised he would, longing to be away to this bright adventure, but saddened, sorry to be saddened, irritated by his sadness, as he hugged his mother before dashing up the gangway.

A strange quality of hush had fallen on the crowd which minutes before had been frenzied. The vessel cast off. The gap between shore and ship widened and the inevitability and sorrow of the partings silenced all those who had been parted.

'Shall we walk?' Richard asked Celie, conscious of her own pitying silence and, still holding his arm, her hand covered by his where it rested in the crook of his elbow, they turned and began to saunter up the floating roadway towards the parade which ran beside the river. There was a small flock of sheep coming from the dock gates, heading for the hold of some cargo ship, and several ewes broke away. Without thought, Richard took off his hat and waved it in front of them and at once they turned and scampered to rejoin the flock.

'Thanks, lar,' their amiable shepherd said, tipping his jaunty cap in Richard's direction, but it was to the bright loveliness of Celie that his admiring glance was directed. They moved round the Princes Dock basin, crossing the arched bridges which connected one dock to the next, still not speaking. It was as though they were in a dream world, contained in a bubble, or under one of those smooth domed glasses Richard's mother had in her drawing room. They could see and be seen but inside their world was silence, fragrant and complete. They had no need of words, only the occasional smile, a slight lifting of Celie's head to meet Richard's gaze, a sharing as soft grey eyes met the impact of deep glowing brown.

They moved slowly along the parade, its cobbled setts worn and hollowed by the hundreds of thousands of feet which had trodden its surface, a waist-high chain to their left erected there to prevent the unwary from falling into the river and on which small boys swung to the despair of their Mamas. There were bollards to which the ships were securely fastened and the high walls of the ships themselves created a protection from the sharp wind coming up the river. To their right were Waterloo Dock, Victoria Dock, Trafalgar Dock and when, beyond the busy loading and unloading of the cargo which came from every corner of the world, they came to the end of the parade, they both stopped. Celie found herself leaning her shoulder against Richard's but when, suddenly aware of her own boldness, she moved away, he bent his head to smile, drawing her back and it seemed quite natural.

They watched the busy shipping lanes, the ships great and small cutting through the silvered grey waters of the wide river, the sun making little dashing ripples which fetched up against the dock wall. The squat tower of the Hornby Lighthouse, known as the Bootle Bull because of its deep foghorn, sat placidly in the river, not needed on this bright and lovely day, and on the far side of the water was the sky-snipping elegance of New Brighton Tower, etched like an imperial crown with its centre edifice tapering over 600 feet to a point in the sky.

Lights were beginning to come on, on both sides of the river, their golden glow reflecting in the shadowed water, and at his side Richard felt the long sigh flow in deep contentment from Celie Marlow. He did the same, the peace so perfect, the unspoken awareness of one another so deeply felt that when he turned her to him, holding her upper arms in his gloved hands she stood quietly, trusting him completely. The short December day, the lovely crisp December afternoon was nearly gone but they studied one another gravely, the past, this morning, the future, this evening and what awaited them at Briar Lodge, forgotten in the beauty of the moment.

He took off his hat, holding it by the brim, then put the hand which held it to the back of her head. Bending his, he placed his lips softly on hers, his mouth closed, as hers was, for it was her first kiss. He lifted his head, searching her face with anxious eyes for he had no wish to alarm her, but she was smiling. Her lips parted and, still smiling, both of them, they exchanged a second kiss, then a third, their mouths warm and sweet and soft, eager now and slightly moist. The parade had become deserted in the last quarter of an hour, for winter darkness falls quickly, and when he put his arms about her and drew her willing body to his, there was no one to see as they stood for several minutes in a long embrace, her face pressed into the hollow beneath his chin.

'Celie . . . Dear Lord, but you're beautiful . . . Celie . . .'

She did not answer, but, more sure of herself now, pressed her young mouth to the bare flesh of his jaw and throat just above his collar. He felt his body stir in response and knew he must get her home.

'Celie . . . I must . . . we must go . . .'

'Richard . . .'

'Aah . . . you can say my name now . . .' smiling down into her shy face.

'I must go or Cook will . . .'

'Indeed, and Prudence and Jethro will be waiting . . .'

'And Belle . . .' Belle . . . Dear God . . . *Belle* . . .! The girl with whom she had set off from the kitchen . . . when was it . . . hours . . . *days* ago and whom she was to meet in ". . . no more than two hours . . ." she had said, and here it was almost dark and her standing in the joyous dream of Richard Latimer's arms as though she . . . *they* . . . had all the time in the world and were at liberty to do as they pleased in it. She must be off her head, which of course she was, trapped in the loveliness which had drawn her into its web, binding her in a spell in which not only Prudence and Mr Garside had been cast carelessly to the four winds, but Belle as well. Belle who would surely, by now, be dithering on the corner of Knowles Lane and Picton Road, close to tears if she was not already *in* them, waiting on Celie's return. And what about the ordering of the pork and the veal and the fish, and *Ingram's* . . . Oh, Lord . . . Cook would tear her limb from limb, and then there was the fabric she was supposed to be buying, not that that would matter for she had only to say there was none suitable, but Cook had expressly told her to be back before dark and here it was dusk gone, and she had *miles* to cover before . . . oh, God . . . !

'What is it? Who's Belle?' Richard was looking down into her face which he could barely see by now, his hands again gripping her upper arms. 'What's the matter, Celie?' which in the circumstances exasperated her for surely he knew servants were not allowed to go about wherever and whenever they pleased.

'She's the girl I came out with, that's who, and if I'm not back on the corner of Knowles Lane within fifteen minutes, she'll run crying to Cook and the fat *will* be in the fire.' She had begun to jabber in her terror, doing her best to shake off his hands, to tear herself away from him, bewitchment gone as reality returned. 'I'll have to get to St John's Market and Ingram's and oh, sweet Jesus . . .' forgetting herself in her desperate need to be off '. . . and just hope to God Belle stays where . . .'

He shook her then and her dainty little hat wobbled dangerously.

'Calm down, now stop it . . . *Stop it*! Tell me all about it and leave it to me. There is nothing to be afraid of . . .'

'*Leave it to you! Nothing to be afraid of . . .*'

'*No, there is not!* Explain it to me and I will put it right . . .'

'Oh, please . . . sir.'

'*Tell me.*'

She told him, almost dragging him by the sleeve of his Chesterfield along the length of the parade, but he steadied her, remaining perfectly calm himself, taking charge as an officer in Her Majesty's Army does under stress. All the way to the Pier Head where the driver of the hansom cab was told there was a guinea for him if he covered the three miles to Wavertree in less than half an hour.

'Prudence . . . ?'

'Will be perfectly safe with Mr Garside. She is *with* me, you know,' smiling, 'at least Mama thinks so and will not concern herself.'

'The shopping. I was to order . . .'

'Is it to be delivered to the house?'

'Oh, yes, every day the . . .'

'Is there a list?' he interrupted.

'A list?'

'For the ordering of the provisions?'

'Yes, I have it here in my . . .'

'Give it to me.'

'I can't . . .'

'Give it to me, Celie, and *trust* me. You know you can, don't you?'

'Oh, yes, sir.'

'And *don't* call me *sir*.'

Chapter Fourteen

The provisions came in the usual way the following morning, though Cook was not particularly impressed with Celie's choice of turbot, she said disapprovingly, and that leg of pork was far too big. 'I said about eight pounds, Celie, and the butchers sent at least twelve. Who d'you think we're serving, the Liverpool Regiment? Nay, there's no need to hang your head like that, lass, I can use it up for something but it's not like you to make such a mistake. I suppose you were hurrying to get to that there fabric shop and could think of nothing else. It's a pity she'd nothing to suit you after traipsing there special. Never mind, there'll be other days but you really must take more care, my girl. The restocking of the larder and the correct choice of fresh meat and fish is a very important part of a cook's job. You know that, don't you?'

'Yes, Cook.'

'You should do, I've told you enough times. Now go and fetch that roasting tin and we'll get the pork in the oven. And you, Belle what's-a-name, what are you standing there for like a wax dummy? I don't know what's got into you this morning, gawping about the place without a sensible thought in your head. You were bad enough last night when you and Celie got back and I've a good mind to make you pay for that plate you broke. Lands sakes, girl, there's no need to blubber. It was only a . . .'

'I'll pay for the plate, Cook.'

Cook turned to Celie in amazement, her elderly chin sagging, her eyes round as saucers.

'*You'll* pay for it? Why should you pay for it? It was this great daft lummox here who broke it, though God only knows why. Jumped out of her skin, she did, and me only wanting her to hurry with the veg . . .'

'I know, Cook, but it wasn't her fault . . .'

'*Not her fault*! Then whose was it, tell me that? The thing was in her hands and *she* let go of it . . . Oh, for goodness sake, Belle, get back to the scullery and dry your eyes. I can't make rhyme nor reason out of either of you today. I can see I'm going to have to think again about letting the pair of you go to the markets by yourselves if this is what it does to you . . .' but Celie knew she wouldn't, not with her legs in the state they were.

But it had been close, so close it made her shiver at the thought of it. Not that the closeness of the shave they had had was the only thing that was making her shiver today.

The thrill of quivering excitement ran through her in spasms, beginning at her heart, or at least in the middle of her chest where she thought her heart to be, trailing delightfully through the whole of her body and right down to her knees which trembled in the strangest way. She found she had to clutch at the table, or the back of a chair or her hands would have hovered quite foolishly about her cooking utensils, and no matter how hard she tried, she found she just could not concentrate on what Cook was saying, or even what she was supposed to be doing. What *was* she doing? her day-dreaming mind asked, pictures of yesterday still printed on it where she knew they would remain for ever. Oh, yes, the roasting tin . . . Dear God, where was it kept . . . ? The trouble was his face kept coming between her and what she did. A face which even in her ignorance of men, she recognised as complex for in it she had seen love struggling with bewilderment, presumably at feeling it. Vulnerability for he was not at all sure how to deal with it. Gravity since to be in love was serious, all mixed with the joy which comes to lovers, since to love and be loved in return is the most joyful gift of all. How did she know? She did not *know* how she knew. Though she was but a girl moving towards womanhood, she sensed that Richard was a man of many layers, the outward layer that of smiling charm, of vitality and confidence in himself and what he did, of arrogance, for he had been brought up to privilege and the belief that that privilege carried a certain responsibility which he was well able to carry out. But beneath that pleasing exterior were many others. One of sensitivity, another of kindness which would extend to small children and animals. A susceptibility to those weaker than himself, an inclination to give the other fellow a second chance, or even a third. A brave fighter who, when he had wounded his opponent, would hold out his hand to help him to his feet. She loved him. His kisses had bemused her, dazzled her, taken her sense, but not her senses since she had never felt so alive, so glowing, so vigorous. She had dreamed of him last night, first in the cold dark of the bedroom she shared with Belle, her face pressed into her pillow, her body warm and vital beneath the covers, then in her sleeping dreams where he had kissed her again until she had awakened with her flesh on fire for something she could not name. Even Belle's tears, her fearful, dreading worry that Cook would find out, that she herself might let it out, had not concerned her.

'Just say nothing, Belle, *nothing*. Nobody's going to ask you what you did, you daft thing, because they all think they know what you did. *I'll* do all the talking that's necessary, d'you understand?'

Belle said she did, still snivelling, so woeful she did not even think to ask Celie where she had been or with whom.

She found the note from Prudence under her pillow the following night, left there some time during the day and she shivered at the risk Prudence had taken, for if anyone had seen her on the narrow staircase which led up to the maids' bedrooms, it would have invited awkward questions.

"Can you come to the wood tomorrow afternoon," it said. "I must see you urgently." It was, like the first one, not signed.

Celie had seen neither Prudence nor Richard since *the* day, though the talk was that Captain Latimer was to report back to his regiment within the week. Her heart sank woefully at the thought, then lightened again for she knew he would find a moment for her before he went, even if it was only to say goodbye. He would say goodbye to her, wouldn't he? Surely, after what they had shared together on Wednesday. He wouldn't just take himself off without a word, would he? And her trusting heart smiled a little at the very idea.

'I heard him tell his Mama at luncheon that it'd be only for a few days, though, then he'd be home again,' so even if he went he'd soon be home again.

'I should hope so,' Mrs Latimer had said to him, Kate told them, 'seeing as how you've been back from that there India no more than a fortnight, she ses. And it is Christmas soon.'

'Don't worry, Mama, I'll be home for Christmas, ses he, and you'll never guess . . .'

'What?' Mary and Lil and Maudie hung on Kate's every word.

'Now then, Kate Mossop,' Cook began, for she couldn't abide what she called "table gossip".

'No, let her speak, Cook,' Celie pleaded, since there was nothing on earth she wanted to hear more than what Richard Latimer might have said to *anyone*, even Kate Mossop.

Cook turned to her in surprise and Celie could tell by her expression that the thought which was uppermost in Cook's mind was "What on earth is the matter with Celie Marlow?" for she herself had never been overly concerned with the doings of the family.

'That's not like you, Celie, listening to gossip.'

'Well . . .' she shrugged, not quite knowing what to say but the chance of hearing what Richard had done or said was just too much for her.

'Go on, Kate, tell us.'

'Well, when he said it, *he winked!*'

'*Winked!*'

'Yes,' Kate preened. 'I think he's taken a shine to me.'

'Don't be so bloody ridiculous.'

She knew she'd made a mistake the moment the words were out of her mouth. They all turned to stare at her, even Belle who was, as usual, deep in the soapy water of scouring and scrubbing and mopping which occupied her time. Celie never swore for a start. None of them did for it was another thing which Cook could not abide. And it was so unlike her to become involved in what the rest of them called "Kate's antics". She was a real card was Kate, at times, and you couldn't help but laugh at her. She had a wicked turn of speech when Cook wasn't about, not offensive but verging on the coarse, and this was really only one of her jokes, so what on earth was Celie Marlow so worked up about? She could see the question on each of their faces.

'Sorry, Cook,' she mumbled, turning to continue the mincing of yesterday's beef which she had been busy with when Kate and Dorcas returned from the luncheon table. 'I only meant that . . .'

'I don't care *what* you meant, Celie Marlow. I'll have no bad language in my kitchen. Really, I don't know what's come over you this last day or two, I really don't. Now then, Kate, don't stand there gossiping, get those trays into the scullery and then you can begin the afternoon tea trays. Celie, you start on the lemon biscuits, they'll be a change for . . .'

'I feel sick, Cook.'

'*Sick!*' Really, whatever next! You could see it in Cook's face, but it was all Celie could think of to get herself out of the kitchen and into the little wood at the back of the house. Prudence should have known better, she had said to herself hopelessly a dozen times since last night, for how could a servant, with no excuse at all, simply drop everything and declare she was off out. Perhaps in a lull in the kitchen activity, in the summer, or on a fine day, she might be allowed to slip away for a breather, and *had*, but it all depended not only on the work to be done, but on Cook's mood. She was, she knew, more favoured than the others, though she was conscious that Cook did her best not to let it show, but this afternoon she was already under Cook's suspicious eye because of the strangeness of her behaviour.

'Yes, in fact I think I'm going to be sick right now,' and with a dramatic gesture which involved clapping her hands to her mouth and a sound with made Dorcas turn away in horror, lest it go on her, Celie dashed into the scullery and, pushing Belle aside, leaned over the sink, gasping for breath.

'Say nothing, Belle, or I'll strangle you,' she muttered to the astonished scullery maid. 'I'm being sick, d'you understand?' since of course Belle could see she was being nothing of the sort!

'Oh, I'm so sorry, Cook.' She managed to stagger a little as she came from the scullery. 'I don't know what it was . . .'

'Well, it's nothing you've eaten in *this* house, Celie Marlow, that I can say. But you do look pale and see, your face is all sweated. P'raps you'd best lie down for half an hour.'

Celie felt a pang of shame for Cook was so concerned, laying her hand on Celie's forehead, fussing about her, beseeching Dorcas to get the child a chair, whilst in the scullery Belle stared incomprehendingly first at Celie, then at her clean sink which she had just wiped round and in which there was no trace of Celie's "sickness".

'I think just a breath of air, Cook . . .' Celie said faintly.

'Open that back door, Kate, it is hot in here.'

Celie began to heave again and everyone stood hastily back.

'Oh dear . . .' she gasped, 'perhaps I'll just walk to the yard gate.'

'Good idea. Kate, you go with her . . .'

'Oh no, Cook, really, I'll just borrow your shawl if I may, I don't need anyone with me, and a walk to the gate and back . . .'

'I'll come with you, Celie.' Kate was only too eager to get away from the routine of work and any pretext would do, but Celie wouldn't hear of it, she said, desperation in her eyes which she did her best to conceal for Kate Mossop was sharp.

'Well, if you think . . .'

'I do, really, Cook, I'll not be long.'

'I could go with her, Cook . . .'

'No, it's only to the gate . . .'

'Well . . .'

Whisking Cook's old shawl, the one she put about her stiff shoulders – going the same way as her legs, Jess Harper wondered sometimes – and which kept the draught off her, Celie, remembering to be frail, opened the door, flung the shawl about her head and made her way as slowly as she could towards the gate. Dear God, please dear God, please don't let Dan be about or Mr Ash, or indeed any of the men who worked outside, and it seemed the Lord heard her prayer. The moment she had got beyond the yard gate, she began to run frantically, skirting the wide area of the rolling lawn, through the vegetable garden where Dan's winter vegetables lay in neat and well-tended rows, beyond the dark shapes and greenhouses, and his "hot beds" and the cottage where once she and her Pa had lived and which was now Dan's.

At the back was the wide stand of trees. There had been a frost the night before and though the sun had shone that morning, it had no warmth in it. The grasses snapped beneath her feet. There were pools of water on which a thin layer of ice had formed and beyond the stark, denuded lattice-work of the tree branches, the sky was a pale fused lilac. A mist hazed their trunks, ethereal and drifting, and from it Prudence Latimer stepped, a warm and luxurious bottle-green cloak about her. It had a hood and about the hood and edging the hem was a pale grey fur and her hands were tucked into a grey fur muff. She was very pale, her face unsmiling and yet in her eyes was a serene and luminous light which told Celie exactly what she was to do.

'I've come to say goodbye, Celie. I couldn't go without seeing you. We have been friends such a short time but it has meant so much to me. There has been no one . . . another woman who . . . I was wondering, can I write to you?' Her lovely clear smile beamed for a moment as joy enveloped her, then she became serious again. 'I have no wish to get you into any trouble, but I could send a message to the kitchen door. I would so like to let you know how I am. Of course I know how I shall be . . . oh Celie . . .'

'Mr Garside?' Celie put out her hand and taking one of hers from the muff, Prudence clasped it affectionately.

'Oh, yes.'

'Does your Mama . . . ?' which was silly, she knew.

'Oh, no! I . . . mentioned him when Richard and I got home. I told her that we, Richard and I, had met him, quite by accident, naturally. I lied to her, which did not matter, though I hated it because of Papa. But . . . well . . . she said I was not to . . . mention him again. The matter is closed, she said. I knew it would be, but Jethro wanted me to . . . try once more. He wished to call formally on Papa. He wanted to do the honourable thing, you see. A proper wedding, as Anne is to have but . . .' Again her smile broke out just as though the happiness which was inside her could not be contained, '. . . I don't care, Celie. I would go with him, even if we were not married. I told him so but he was shocked and so . . . we are to . . . elope, Celie. Can you believe it? We will marry . . . Oh, Lord, I don't care where, but I shall not wait. Tonight I shall be Mrs Jethro Garside. You understand what I mean, Celie?'

'Yes,' and so closely attuned to one another had they become, neither girl was embarrassed.

'Jethro is waiting in a carriage beyond the gate. You remember the gate, Celie, and the walks . . . of course you do, so . . . dear Celie, will you visit me, will you? You shall be my first caller.'

'Well . . .' Celie clung to Prudence's hand.

'Please, Celie, I shall need friends and you are my dearest . . .'

'Oh, Prudence, I'll miss you . . .'

'I *shall* get word to you somehow, Celie. Look, I have written Jethro's address out for you. Promise me you'll come . . . promise.'

'Perhaps when I go to market . . .' diffidently . . . 'we could meet . . .'

'Of course. Why didn't we think of it before. You could come for tea and then the carriage could take you home.'

'Well, I'm not sure about that . . .'

'Oh, Celie, say you will, please.' Prudence's voice became rueful. 'I have a feeling you might be my only friend. So say you will come.'

'I'll come.'

'Promise?'

'I promise.'

'Then . . .'

For a moment the two young girls, so sharply diverse,

one in her lovely, fur-trimmed cloak, the other in the old shawl worn by the "Mary Ellens" of Liverpool, stood with their arms about one another, then they parted and without looking back Prudence slipped through the trees to the open gate where the large caped figure of Jethro Garside stood. The gate closed. There was the sound of horses' hooves on the hard, rutted ground, the creak of a carriage, then it was silent.

Celie didn't know who was more pleased, Kate or Maudie, at the chaos that overtook Briar Lodge that evening. Dinner was to be served as usual at seven. Just the family. Captain Richard and Miss Prudence, Miss Anne, Master Alfred home from university, Masters Robert, Thomas and James home from school, Miss Katherine and Miss Margaret, the two youngest girls to dine with their parents, only the two little boys excluded.

'And where, may I ask, is your sister?' Mrs Latimer enquired, looking round the table until her stern gaze came to rest on her eldest daughter. 'She knows we dine at seven when we are *en famille* and I am ashamed at her lack of manners. The soup will be cold if it is not served immediately. Dorcas . . .' beckoning to the hovering maid who had been about to put the ladle into the tureen of Cook's steaming artichoke soup which was a particular favourite of Mr Latimer's and which his palate was already relishing.

'Go and fetch Miss Prudence if you please, Dorcas. She is to come at once, tell her.'

'Yes, madam,' dropping a graceful curtsey.

'We will wait, James, so don't scowl at me like that.'

'Yes, Mama, I'm sorry, Mama.'

'I should think so.'

For several minutes Mr Latimer exchanged casual remarks with his soldier son who seemed, he thought, somewhat distracted himself. Mrs Latimer gazed complacently about the table at her family, two young gentlemen and two young ladies on one side and when Prudence arrived, three young gentlemen and two young ladies on the other. The glowing mahogany of the long table pleased her, its mirror-like surface reflecting her handsome sons, her well-bred daughters and

the splendid branches of the two candelabra which lit their
faces. Her husband had been begging to be allowed to
install the new electric light along with the telephone but
she did think the candle light was so flattering to the ladies,
particularly those over a certain age like herself. Of course
they had gas lighting, which was lit on occasions, but she
supposed one must keep up with the times. She drummed
her fingers on the table, then tutted irritably. Richard, who
was on her left, sighed deeply for some reason, then:

'Mama, I think . . .' he began, his face somewhat strained.
Whatever it was he was about to say was cut short for at that
moment Dorcas returned and at once everyone in the room
was aware that she was barely in control of a high-pitched
excitement. The deferential respect with which a servant
approaches her mistress was missing entirely as she burst
noisily into the room.

'Dorcas! What on earth is the matter with you?' Mrs
Latimer demanded to be told but even as she spoke it was
evident that the rebuke was purely automatic.

'She's gone, madam.' Dorcas had her hand to her bosom
in the most dramatic fashion, but her eyes shone and her
cheeks were flushed. Even her pretty housemaid's cap was
quite rakishly tilted as though she had flung herself about
quite feverishly in her search for Miss Prudence.

'Gone! Do you mean Miss Prudence? Gone where?' All
around the table young faces stared wide-eyed and open-
mouthed as their mother asked the question. Indeed where
could Prudence have gone at this time of night? Or at any
time without the express permission of her Mama? It was
quite ridiculous, you could see it in every face, except one,
and he was looking not at Dorcas but down at his own hand
which was toying with a spoon, turning it over and over
beside his soup plate. Mr Latimer stood up, ready to smile
because surely the silly girl, meaning Dorcas, was making a
fuss about nothing, and it would take but a moment to sort
this nonsense out.

'I don't know, madam,' Dorcas answered, her eyes wide
and bright, moving from Mr Latimer and back to her mistress.
'She's not in her room so I ran to the nursery to see if she was

with the children but Nanny said they hadn't seen anyone since you . . .'

'Yes, yes, Dorcas, thank you, and please get a grip on yourself. There is absolutely no need for all this drama. Now take Kate with you and go and look . . . well . . . in the library . . .'

'I've looked there, madam. That's why I was such a long time.'

'The conservatory . . . ?'

'Yes, madam,' with what seemed suspiciously like satisfaction. 'And in the drawing room too.'

'Well . . .' Mrs Latimer, for once at a loss for words, turned helplessly to her husband. 'Well, she must be . . . *somewhere*. Mr Latimer . . . ?'

'Of course she is, my dear, and will soon be found, don't you worry.' As her husband spoke, Mrs Latimer, her momentary and quite astonishing weakness over and done with, stood up resolutely, her back straight, her usual expression which said she would not be made a fool of by a silly girl, returning to her calm face.

'Go and look all over the house, Dorcas and Kate, search in every room, including the servants' quarters, and you help them, girls,' she said speaking to her daughters. 'All the bedrooms and bathrooms, and try the kitchens, if you please. She has a silly tendency to go there, I believe. Alfred, question the kitchen staff, would you, dear, and Richard . . .' turning to her son and smiling to show him she was not at all worried about her wilful daughter, though in her eyes were chips of ice which told everyone that Prudence would be sorry she had caused this *brouhaha*. She had a leaning towards rebellion, had her second daughter, and if it was the last thing she did, Phyllis Latimer would nip it in the bud. To disrupt the family's dinner like this was not only the height of bad manners, but a waste of perfectly good food. The soup would be cold and the duck ruined.

'Darling, would you take the boys . . . there are some lanterns somewhere, I believe . . . and look about the gardens, though what the foolish girl could be up to in the gardens, I cannot imagine.'

It was not until an hour later that it was discovered that along with Miss Prudence, her new bottle-green cloak with the expensive fur trimmings, her pale, dove-grey woollen dress, and several other items of clothing were missing, plus a small leather overnight bag. The note was delivered to the front door by hand at the same time. No, the cabbie who brought it said, he didn't know 'oo the lady was what give it to 'im. When? Well, it'd be about three o'clock this afternoon, as far as he could recollect, or perhaps a bit later 'cos he'd been down by Lime Street station . . . what? . . . beg yer pardon, lady . . . 'e were only trying to 'elp, weren't 'e? Well, the young lady said not ter bring it up 'ere until eight o'clock at the earliest . . . What? . . . no, sir, at t'station . . . well, 'e didn't know if the lady was alone or not, 'e didn't question . . . no, she'd said to deliver this 'ere note at eight o'clock and given 'im . . . well, if that was all, he'd be off.

The note was short, curt even.

'Dear Mama and Papa, I am to be married to Mr Jethro Garside within a day or so. Do not look for me. It will be too late. I'm sorry, Papa. I would have liked the parish church and all the family, and so would you, I know.'

In the commotion caused by the discovery that the clothing and the bag were missing, and by the unexpected arrival of the hansom cab, Mr and Mrs Latimer quite forgot the presence of the housemaid who had brought the cabbie and the note to their attention and so Kate was able to convey a description of the whole explosive drama back to the kitchen. It seemed Mrs Latimer remembered that Miss Prudence had met Mr Garside during the last few days, Kate reported gleefully, when it seemed she had accompanied Captain Richard to town, and the long and the short of it was that Captain Richard was now being accused by his incensed Mama of complicity, whatever that might mean, in the matter and they were going hammer and tongs in the drawing room, with Miss Anne and her two younger sisters in tears. Mr Latimer was doing his best to come between the protagonists, and the boys were standing about like dummies in Lewis's window. Everyone knew how Mrs Latimer doted on her eldest son and there she was calling him names like Judas and the Captain telling his Mama she was heartless. Unfortunately, at this juncture Kate's hovering figure had been noticed and she had been sent off with a flea in her ear, just as though the whole thing was *her* fault, she said resentfully.

The house positively seethed with it, not that Miss Prudence had run off with Mr Garside, though that was bad enough, but that Mrs Latimer, when she had got over her shock, had refused, absolutely refused, to allow Mr Latimer to do anything about it. Of course the poor young lady's reputation was irretrievably damaged whatever the outcome, they all knew that, even though, they all supposed, *hoped*, she would soon be Mrs Jethro Garside, but you would have thought Mrs Latimer would have made *some* effort to ascertain the whereabouts of her own daughter, wouldn't you? Cook declared, deeply shocked. None of them in the kitchen knew much about Mr Garside, of course, except that he was supposed to be very wealthy and had a splendid house in Croxteth Drive. A nice enough gentleman, Dorcas said, she and Kate having seen him when he had dined with the Latimers. Cook was so upset she could not even seem to arouse her usual condemnation of gossip, nor quell the turmoil in which the servants ran riot, and nobody noticed Celie Marlow's unusual quietness. Dinner, of course, was completely ruined, not that that mattered in the face of this crisis. Speculation was rife, caps bobbing together in the kitchen, cups of tea being drunk, one after the other. Would the police be called, since Miss Prudence was only nineteen, and perhaps Mr Garside did not intend to marry her, they speculated amongst themselves, but it seemed Mrs Latimer neither knew nor cared and had told her family who were gathered in the drawing room, that the name of Prudence Latimer was never to be mentioned in the house again, or so Kate said. She had been told to leave the room when she had served the coffee Mrs Latimer had ordered, but she had remained for several minutes with her ear to the keyhole and heard it all, though she did not mention the keyhole to Cook.

'Poor Miss Prudence, poor little girl,' Cook said sadly, but Celie, remembering the expression of tremulous joy which had glowed in Prudence Latimer's eyes, knew that whatever else she might be feeling Prudence would certainly not be in need of pity.

'Well, he's gone,' Kate said cheerfully as she bustled into the kitchen the next morning, bearing the laden tray on which the family's breakfast things were loaded and dumping it in front of Belle.

'Who has?' Cook asked, turning to look in Kate's direction. Despite her rule about tittle-tattle, the events of the night before had been so earth-shattering she could not help her own sympathetic interest and concern for Miss Prudence's welfare. Only through Dorcas and Kate who had contact with the family and who, more often than not, were seemingly invisible as they served at table therefore hearing more than they were meant to, did the servants get to know what was happening in the front house. Though Cook consulted with Mrs Latimer on the day's menus and the general running of the household, Mrs Latimer was not about to discuss family matters with her cook, was she?

'The Captain. Packed his own bags, if you please, and sent Bertie to fetch a cab from the corner of Picton Road. I just seen it going down the drive.'

'No!'

'Yes, and Madam still in her room. She'd like a tray please, Cook, and then she doesn't want to be disturbed.'

'Was the rest of the family at breakfast?'

'Oh, yes, and a sorry lot they are, an' all. Even Mr Latimer looked as though he'd been having a good cry.'

'That's enough, Kate. Don't speak of the master like that.'

'No, Cook, but he did,' Kate answered irrepressibly.

'Has he gone to the office?'

'No, he's in with Mrs Latimer.'

'Lands sakes, what a to-do-ment.'

'Yes, Cook, and if you want my opinion . . .'

'Well, we don't. Just get a tray and set it for Mrs Latimer. Where's Dorcas?'

'Clearing the table, Cook, but . . .'

'But me no buts, Kate Mossop. Just get on with your work,

and see, Celie, don't stand there with your mouth open. What on earth's the matter with you, girl? You look as though you've seen a ghost. Now go and get your hat and coat on and get down to Ingram's. I've made a complete list of things we need for Christmas so I'll just go over it with you and see if you can think of anything I've missed. The menus have been done for the Christmas period. Thank the Lord me an' Mrs Latimer did them the other day for there's no doubt about it she'll not be feeling like bothering with them now, poor soul. Eeh, I wonder if the captain'll be back for Christmas? What a time to have this happen. I don't know, it seems worse when it's at this time of the year, the season of good will towards all men, though any time's bad enough to lose a daughter. I wonder if they'll make it up. Lord, I do hope so. Families shouldn't be split up, and what about the captain, him being such a favourite of Madam's. He must've been . . . well, I suppose if it was him that helped to arrange it . . .'

Suddenly realising that her staff were standing about the kitchen listening to her musings in various poses of avid interest, her mouth shut like a trap and her eyes flayed them so that without another word they jumped to attention and ran to their posts.

No one noticed Celie Marlow's slow, almost dragging footsteps as she fumbled her way into her hat and coat, nor the transparent whiteness of her face, and if they had they would no doubt have put it down to her strange indisposition of the day before. She answered when spoken to, making sense as she did so, taking the list from Cook's hand and tucking it into her jacket pocket.

'Don't take Belle, Celie. There's no need, really. You're old enough and sensible enough to go on your own now, I think. Besides I need her here in the kitchen.'

Cook began to laugh then and everyone turned to see what at, joining in when it was discovered that Celie was about to go out of the kitchen door still with her apron on under her coat.

Chapter Fifteen

The lawn at Briar Lodge, freshly mown that morning by Dan Smith guiding the lawn-mower which was pulled by the pony, still had the faint mark of the animal's hoof-prints in it. It should not really be cut whilst the dew was still on it, he had grumbled to Celie as he tucked into the bacon and eggs she had just put before him, but Mrs Latimer, after walking across it, the evening before, a last-minute inspection, she had said to her husband, had told Dan she would like it gone over one more time. To his mind, and after all, *he* was the expert since he had been gardener at Briar Lodge for over six years now, it would do the grass no good, and besides it was like a billiard table, as it was, but no, Mrs Latimer wanted it doing and that, as far as *she* was concerned, was that.

'Well, she does want everything to be perfect, Dan. You know what she's like, and Miss Anne's marrying into a very good family, Cook says. The Osbornes and Hemmingways are two of the oldest shipping families in Liverpool and Henry Osborne, though he is only a second cousin or something, is well-placed in the family business. There'll be all the best people in Liverpool here today, the cream of society, Cook says, and everything must be just right.'

'Well, you'll not find a better display than my dahlias, Celie, an' me an' Jim and Bertie went over every damn rosebush dead-heading last night.'

'I know, Dan, it's a picture, really it is.' Celie's tone was pacifying. She knew Dan and his lads had been stretched to the limit by Mrs Latimer's constant supervision of their work during the last few weeks, bringing the extensive gardens of

Briar Lodge up to the pinnacle of perfection she required.
Not that they were not always immaculate, with the gravel
paths raked every day, the beds weeded, the lawns cut and
fed, the pond cleaned and the trees and bushes pruned to the
magnificence Cec Marlow had demanded and which Dan kept
up. The flower-beds were at the peak of their summer beauty.
Trailing and climbing plants had been gone over to make them
neat and secure, for the mighty Osborne family would be
sure to notice if they were not, Mrs Latimer fretted. Smith
must examine the hollyhocks, the hydrangeas, the petunias,
verbenas, the heliotropes, the salvia and lobelia, and had she
noticed a gap in the stretch of geraniums which bordered the
drive as she went by in the carriage yesterday? Dan's and
Jim's and Bertie's, and even Mr Ash's services had been
commandeered to bring into the house the dozens of flowering
plants which Dan had potted and nurtured in preparation for
this great day. They were to stand everywhere, in every
corner, on every stair up to the first floor, bowers of them in
the dining room and drawing room where the reception was to
take place, and as for the enormous winter garden which was
attached to the back of the house, it was a credit to Dan, it
really was, Cook had whispered to Celie last night when they
had peeped in at midnight on their weary way to their beds.
They had seen it before, of course, for the conservatory had
been there for years and Mrs Latimer often consulted Cook
whilst sitting in the warm sunshine which streamed through its
glass walls and roof. It had been "refurbished", Mrs Latimer's
word, for the occasion of her eldest daughter's marriage to
young Henry Osborne, the polished wooden floor buffed with
beeswax-impregnated cloths by Mary and Lily until the two
cleaning maids had been red-faced and perspiring. The high
domed ceiling glass had required Dan's services to reach it,
inside and out, and the white-painted wrought-iron tables and
wicker chairs had spent weeks in Mr Ash's workshop having
coat after coat of fresh paint applied to them.

But it was the flowers which were breathtaking, hanging
baskets of them in a vividly colourful display with delicate
trailing ivy, in all shades of green, terracotta pots erupting
with geraniums of every hue from the palest pink to a startling

red, set about with white mock orange blossom, just like that which was to crown Miss Anne's brown hair this day. Even the cages in which singing birds poured out their sad and tiny hearts had been decorated with camellias and glossy green leaves.

They could not manage a buffet luncheon of such vast proportions with just the two of them, her and Celie, naturally, even Cook had admitted that, but it had all been planned, prepared and cooked in the Latimer kitchens, with Cook, Celie at her elbow, in control of every last pinch of salt. Two extra cooks and an army of maids and footmen had been hired for the occasion and the excitement was a palpable thing as Celie entered the kitchen that morning dead on the stroke of six. She and Cook were, naturally, first there since Cook was in charge and Celie was her right hand and if the strangeness of a girl of seventeen carrying such a weight of responsibility on her young shoulders had occurred to Jess Harper, she certainly did not show it.

'Right, Cook.' Celie's voice was steady and her eyes clear and unafraid. 'Where do we start?' I'm here, her manner said, and you can trust me to do whatever is necessary. I won't let you down on this most important day so tell me what to do.

She was dressed in what she called her "working clothes", those she put on when some particularly arduous, perhaps mucky work was to be performed in the kitchen. Later, when it was all ready for the bridal party, when what she and Cook, and those who helped them, had put together was set out in the dining room, the drawing room and the winter garden, then she would change to her "best" uniform, the grey striped cotton dress, the frilled and starched white muslin apron and saucy cap, and help to serve the splendid meal they had prepared. They were to go to the wedding service, of course, to see Miss Anne joined in matrimony at the tiny country church of St Luke's in Wavertree, but after that, after the photographer had finished with the bride and bridegroom and their families in the garden – please God, don't let it rain, Cook droned at intervals – it would be back to their duties in the kitchen and dining room.

The weather was perfection itself, everyone agreed. The

sunshine fell in endless benison from the clear sky, washing the back of the house and the magnificently ordered garden with a gold-edged brilliance. The lawn over which at dawn Dan and the pony had laboured, was clustered with elegant, fashionably dressed ladies and gentlemen drinking champagne. The grass was a vivid green, thankfully dried out after the heavy dew and round its edge the geraniums and fuchsia were brilliant against the dark green of the yew hedge which surrounded it. There was wisteria in a dense blue curtain growing up the wall of the house, carefully clipped by Dan around the windows, and below, in great banks, were lupins and stocks. The french windows which led from the morning room to the garden were open and on each side of them hanging baskets showered a cascade of sweet-scented verbena.

The buffet luncheon had been superb, Mr Latimer, God bless him, had whispered to Cook, and later he and Mrs Latimer would personally thank all the servants for their hard work. Hard work it had certainly been and Cook's massively swollen feet and ankles testified to the hours and hours without remission she had stood on them during the last few weeks. Eighty persons to be fed was not a task she would care to undertake every day of the week, she told Celie privately, though that roast sucking pig had looked a treat and well worth every moment she and Celie had worked on it. There had been mayonnaise of fowl, a ham garnished, fowl with béchamel sauce, ornamental tongue, chicken and pheasant, galantine of veal, lobster and lobster patties, lobster salad, all the colours and flavours of the various dishes contrasting most handsomely. She and Celie had personally supervised the setting and decorating of the buffet tables, using the abundance of fresh cut flowers and fruit from what had once been Cec Marlow's greenhouse, the cold meats garnished with cut vegetables. The eye, in fact, as Cook insisted it always should, as much gratified as the palate.

To follow there were ornamental trifles, custards in glasses, swiss creams, fruited jellies and blancmange, charlotte russe and whipped cream, cream and water ices of every flavour and colour, a Tipsy cake in which there was so much wine, sherry and brandy, it was possible to become inebriated without touching a drop of the vintage champagne Mr Latimer had put down for this particular event, on the day his daughter was born. Or so Cook said on the day she made the cake, and *no*, Dan could *not* clean the mixing bowl. She didn't care to be blamed for getting him drunk on duty! And the bride's cake was a marvel of Cook's ingenuity and talent, rich and fruity containing *pounds* of best butter, currants, loaf sugar, dozens of eggs, sweet almonds, candied citron, orange and lemon peel, wine and brandy. Celie had been allowed to help in the delicate heart-wrenching precision of icing the three tiers, almost weeping at the intricate beauty of lovers knots, hearts and fragile rosebuds, all in the palest pink which Cook fashioned.

Mr and Mrs Latimer, their well-brought-up children about them, greeted each guest with the courtesy they themselves had been tutored in and which such grand folk deserved. Captain Richard Latimer was twenty-four years old and simply superb in his full dress uniform. Master Alfred stood beside his older brother. He was just twenty and was to join his Papa in the business, a somewhat frivolous-minded young man, who would need watching. His Mama did not care for the "set" in which he now moved and if Mr Latimer did not speak to him, she would. Master Robert, eighteen and about to leave the fine English public school to which all the Latimer sons had gone, studious, reserved and shy but doing his duty as a son should on this day, and his brother Thomas who was sixteen. Miss Katherine, twelve and pretty as a picture in the rich cream organdie her sister had chosen for her, Miss Margaret and Master James who had carried a basket of rose petals apiece, scattering them for the bride and groom to walk on. The younger boys, Masters Edward and Charles, were too young and too boisterous for an occasion such as this, their Mama had declared and were to remain in the nursery with Nanny Ella, where cake and trifle would be sent up to them. Prudence Latimer, now Mrs Jethro Garside, was not present.

The bride herself, Miss Anne Latimer who, at twenty-two, might have been considered to be almost on the shelf, had been shyly pretty, as most brides are on their wedding day, for if you can't manage it with all that misted gauze and orange blossom about you, then you never will, Reuben Ash remarked dourly to young Dan later as they watched from the shelter of the shrubbery the confusion and chaos of the wedding photographs being taken.

'Now, Celie'd look bonny wi' a bit of old sackin' draped about her,' he added.

Dan nodded his head, more concerned at that moment with the state of his lawn and the effect all those shuffling feet would have on it. Some of those chaps didn't seem to care *where* they put their boots and already the geraniums in the borders looked somewhat the worse for wear. Master Alfred and that crowd he was with were engaging in some foolish horseplay and if Mrs Latimer spotted him, he'd be for it. The family and the bridegroom's family were smiling fondly at the happy couple who were being posed against the wisteria, and had not yet noticed the silly state Master Alfred and his friends were fast approaching.

'Don't you think so, lad?' Reuben was saying.

'What?'

'That our Celie knocks spots off them grand ladies.'

'She does, Mr Ash, that she does.' He could see her now, moving among the guests with a tray of something in her hand which she offered to those who were watching the bride and groom being photographed. She bobbed a curtsey to Master Alfred who looked very smart in a formal grey frock coat and pale grey waistcoat. He smiled and said something into her ear, holding her by the arm whilst he did so.

At once she pulled back and the smiling, respectful expression on her face slipped away. Alfred still held her arm but her sharp reaction unbalanced the tray she was holding and it was only her own adroitness that prevented it from tipping and its six fluted glasses of champagne from crashing to the grass. Alfred grinned, and turning to the group of young men with whom he was chatting, made some remark which had them roaring with laughter and brought a vivid splash of poppy to Celie's cheeks. Several heads, including that of Alfred's Mama, turned in their direction.

From the doorway which led into the conservatory where he had been lounging, Richard Latimer saw the exchange and quite slowly he straightened, placing the glass of champagne he had been sipping on the window ledge. It seemed he was about to move across the grass, his face tight and expressionless when a young lady, her smile simpering, but determined, her gown fashionable and expensive, her bonnet no more than a froth of rosebuds, laid her hand lightly on his arm, saying something to him which he evidently did not quite hear. Though his expression was momentarily murderous, he had no choice but to stop and listen for she was a guest in his parents' house.

Behind Reuben Ash, Dan Smith, who had also noticed the exchange and without appearing to move, shifted to the edge of the lawn though he was still out of sight of the guests.

'Now then, lad.' Reuben put a warning hand on his shoulder. 'Where are you off to?' His voice was placid for though he too had seen the offence given to Celie, Dan's reaction had been too quick for his liking. 'Leave it alone, Dan, you know what these young sprigs of the gentry are. See, it's all over now,' and indeed Celie had moved away from the group of young men, offering her tray to several other guests before disappearing through the french windows into the dining room.

The photographs were done with, the meal, the speeches and the cutting of the bride's cake, finished. The bride and groom, changed now into their travelling clothes, were gathered with the wedding party on the wide front steps of Briar Lodge for the "send-off". The carriage which was to take them to Lime Street station from where they were to proceed on their honeymoon was drawn up with George Ellis at the reins and Dan at the horses' heads for they were restive in the midst of so much merriment and boisterous good wishes. This was the age of Victoria's high moral standards and her own view of what constituted good taste, but the ruling classes of the country did not always follow what their Queen considered to be correct. Not that they were in any way vulgar or offensive but it could not be ignored, at least by the men, and many of the women, though for different reasons, that this young and innocent bride would undergo tonight something she could not imagine in her wildest dreams. "It will be . . . over quickly, darling," her Mama would have told her "and will not damage you in any way. Men like it you see and if you wish to have children, and I know you do, then you will . . . not mind." It was said to all young brides, conjuring up horrific pictures, but the gentlemen had different images in their minds as they watched young Mrs Osborne being handed into the carriage.

Celie stood at the back of the laughing crowd of guests with Kate and Dorcas one on either side of her. Cook had gone to sit down, her overburdened feet and ankles giving way at last, she said privately to Celie, and no, she'd not watch Miss Anne, Mrs Osborne now, bless her, go off with her new husband. A cup of tea, she thought and a slice of her own Tipsy cake, but Celie was to go and watch the "send-off" with the other girls. Never mind the clearing up, the thought of which made Cook blanch, Belle and Maudie would see to that; in fact, Mary and Lil had already started on it.

The hand on Celie's arm made her jump and when it pulled her sharply backwards, Kate and Dorcas were so busy with their "oohs" and "aahs" and exclamations over Miss Anne's beautiful going away outfit, they did not notice, but Richard Latimer, whose sombre gaze had been filled with her lovely laughing face did, *and* the flushed and lascivious one which belonged to his own brother and which had appeared behind her.

'There you are, my little dove,' a drunken voice babbled, though not loud enough for anyone but Celie to hear, and a pair of wet lips fumbled at her ear. 'Come and have a little glash of champagne. A pretty girl like you shouldn't have to mish out on all the fun.'

Celie turned, outraged and revolted, and her velvet grey eyes hardened to the clear-cut brilliance of diamonds. Celie Marlow had grown up since last Christmas when Richard Latimer had played fast and loose with her girlish emotions, and she was not about to go through the same nonsense with his brother.

'Get your hands off me, Master Alfred,' she hissed, doing

her best to keep her own voice down. 'D'you want your Ma and Pa to see you? Your sister and her new husband are just leaving. You should be out there . . .'

'Don't be shilly, Shelie, I'm only offering you a glash of champers.'

'That's not what you offered me in the garden, sir. I don't know what sort of a girl you think I am but if you don't leave off I'll box your ears. Now take your hand off my arm and stop dragging me about as though I was a damned horse.'

The hallway was completely deserted, every single member of the household, apart from Nanny and the boys in the nursery and Cook in the back reaches of the kitchen, out on the sun-dazzled gravel driveway cheering off the happy couple. Confetti was being chucked about and how in hell's name he was to brush it up when this lot had gone, Dan couldn't bear to think, and would you look at them great feet trampling all over his rose beds, for God's sake. In his horror at what was being done to his garden, Dan Smith did not miss the rosy smiling face of Celie Marlow.

Richard Latimer did, though, and without a moment's hesitation he let go of his sister's arm, which he had been holding, and plunged madly through the crowd of well-wishers who thronged the steps, thrusting into the shadowed hallway as Celie, her heels desperately trying for purchase on the tiled floor, was being pulled into the confines of the large cloakroom beside the front door.

Celie didn't know what Richard Latimer said to his brother in that hoarse and snarling voice he had suddenly acquired, for he spoke in some men's language she and the rest of the guests who witnessed the scene, had never heard. Before she could stop him, before she could even guess his intention, he had dragged his brother from the cloakroom by the lapels of his splendid grey frock coat and in a manner which would have appalled his Commanding Officer since *gentlemen* did not engage in fisticuffs, hit him squarely on the nose with his clenched fist, dropping him where he stood.

'Bloody hell, Ritchie,' Alfred whined, the blood exploding from his burst nose onto his pale grey waistcoat, 'what in hell's name was that for?' then made the mistake of struggling to his feet, whereupon Richard knocked him down again, the savage joy in his eyes again not one his Commanding Officer would have cared for.

'Stand up and fight, you bastard,' he snarled, ready to lash out with his feet as well as his fist, his normally cool brain boiling in the outrage of his male jealousy.

'Sir, for God's sake, Master Richard, leave him, oh please, it was nothing, really . . .' Celie heard herself shrieking, 'he meant no harm . . .' Her voice, high and piercing in her fear, not for herself but for Richard who would surely hang if he killed his brother, as he seemed intent on doing, reached the bewildered ears of not only those who were turning in appalled horror towards the hallway, but Dan Smith and without a moment's hesitation, since he recognised it, he let go of the horses' heads and pushed his way through the confused crowd and into the hallway in much the same manner as Richard Latimer had done thirty seconds before. It was dim after the brilliant sunshine in the garden and in the dimness he saw Celie struggling in the arms of his master's son, his vivid scarlet jacket stark against her pale grey and white uniform.

The horses, unattended, reared up quite frighteningly and had it not been for the quick thinking of Mr Latimer himself, who immediately grabbed at them, they might have lunged into the crowd. As it was, the new Mrs Osborne was flung back quite dangerously in the carriage, her brand new hat coming to rest in a very rakish fashion over her eyes.

'What on earth . . .' Mrs Latimer shrieked, holding her hand to her palpitating breast, her gaze following the tall, menacing figure of her gardener as he disappeared into the shadowed dimness of her hallway.

Again, those who watched were stunned, for the young man – was he the stable-boy – roared like a wounded stag, and again it was in some incomprehensible language none of them recognised as Swedish and before anyone could stop him, even Celie, who had at last managed to bring Richard to his shuddering senses, he had dragged Richard Latimer from her and given him a sharp "Liverpool kiss", a movement

with the head known to every street fighter from one end of
dockland to the other.

Mrs Latimer screamed. Celie stood as though turned to
stone and in the kitchen Cook dropped the fine bone china
cup from which she was appreciatively sipping her tea. It
smashed into a dozen pieces on the flagged floor. One of
Mrs Latimer's best it was, too.

Master Alfred and Captain Richard Latimer lay on their
backs, dazed, their eyes glassy, and in the middle of each
face a crimson flower bloomed. Celie was backed up to the
hallstand in absolute horror, and, his fists clenching and
unclenching, the expression on his face letting everyone know
he was longing for either of his master's sons to get up so that
he might knock them down again, Dan Smith crouched, his
own eyes a brilliant icy blue.

'Dear God in Heaven . . .' Mrs Latimer began to wail and
at her back her splendid guests, many still clutching their
champagne glasses, gaped at the man who, it seemed, had
just knocked the two sons of the house senseless. He was
at least six feet tall and splendidly built as he circled the
two prone figures and from his stretched lips several words
were spat though none of the assembly could have said what
they were.

Slowly, for he was still somewhat dazed by the attack from
a quarter he had not expected, Richard got to his feet. His
face had lost the rich amber colour the sunshine of India had
painted there, turning to a hue which reminded Celie of tallow
but high on each cheekbone was a feverish circle of red. His
eyes had narrowed to gleaming slits of venomous rage and
his lips curled back on his fine white teeth in the manner of
an enraged leopard. The blood which poured from his nose
went unheeded as he lifted his clenched fist.

'So that's the way of it, is it? You want her too, do you?'
he snarled at his mother's gardener.

'You put your hands on her again and you'll regret it,' Dan's
mouth was just as viciously curled.

They moved together, two wild young animals and when
their strong, muscled bodies met, the impact of it could be
heard in the kitchen and out beyond the front door where Mr

Latimer still struggled with the horses. Alfred groaned feebly doing his best to roll out of the way of the lethal boots of the two mindless men.

Celie let out her breath on a long shuddering sigh and her shoulders, which she had been holding rigidly up to her ears, sagged in despair. Putting one foot gently in front of the other, as one does when one is about to walk across a stretch of ice the thickness of which is unknown, she edged towards the two brawling men. Mrs Latimer had sunk into a deeply shocked state, though Heaven help them all when she came out of it, and from the open front door which had become jammed with silent guests, Celie could hear Mr Latimer beseeching them to let him through.

'Dan,' Celie's mouth was dry and the word came out in a faint chirrup. She tried again.

'Dan,' and this time she clutched at his arm. He whirled in her direction and she recoiled sharply for in his madness he didn't seem to recognise her. He was ready to flick her away without thought for the consequences, irritated by her interference as he did his level best to maim Richard Latimer in any way he could. He was unreachable, she could see it in his eyes, in his wild need to inflict more damage on the man he thought had set his hands on her.

'Dan . . . come away, Dan . . . please, it wasn't Master Richard.' Her hands tried to get a grip on his sleeve, her face straining into his, beginning to screech his name for somehow she must get him away from here, away from Richard, who seemed intent on not only beating Dan, but her. She must get him away from this hallway . . . these staring, incredulous people . . . Mrs Latimer . . . Oh, God . . . Oh, Jesus God . . . damn Alfred Latimer . . . damn Richard Latimer . . .

The thoughts, wild and disjointed, crashed about her aching head which felt as though those wild punches Richard was throwing in her and Dan's direction had actually landed. Richard's eyes were shot with blood but even so she could see the appalling expression in them. It was a look of such absolute contempt she knew he was telling her this whole thing was her fault, and perhaps it was. But she had done nothing . . . it was he . . . he and Master Alfred who had . . . oh, Richard, Richard . . .

'What is it? What is happening?' she heard Mr Latimer say and the crowd parted to let him through.

'Stop it . . . oh stop it . . .' Mrs Latimer was moaning. Her fine satinwood table splintered as Dan's heavy body hit it and the mirror above it was dislodged, shattering into dozens of pieces, the shards dangerous as they slithered about the tiled floor where the two young men were still fighting.

Celie had backed away now, praying that Dan would come with her but he and Richard were snarling at one another like two dogs. Her skin was the colour of putty. Her hands were at her mouth and her eyes were deep, shocked, pewter-grey pits in her face. She kept backing away from the horror and the shame for surely this *must* all be her fault, until she touched the door which led to the passage into the kitchen and when it opened and two strong arms grasped her she turned, burying her face against Cook's shoulder.

'I can't stop him, Cook. It was nothing . . . I would have slapped his face . . . a kiss he said . . . champers . . . and I would . . . but Richard hit him, it would have been nothing . . . and then Dan . . .'

'Hush, hush now, come away . . .'

'But they'll hurt one another . . .'

'Nay, they'll not . . .'

'Oh, Cook, it was my fault . . .'

'Hush now, come away into the kitchen . . .'

'I can't just leave him,' and Cook was not awfully sure which *him* she meant.

'Yes, you can. This is no place for you, girl. Mr Latimer will attend to it. See, come with me and I'll put the kettle on . . .' and gradually, firmly, Cook coaxed her out of the maelstrom of the hallway and down the passage to the kitchen. They could still hear shouts and crashes and Mr Latimer's voice doing its best to make itself heard but the kitchen was relatively peaceful. Belle and Maudie, with Mary and Lil, after a sharp word from Cook, resumed their endless task of washing the china, the glassware, the cutlery, which eighty guests had accumulated.

Celie began to tremble. Her teeth chattered and she was inclined to cling in the arms which held her, familiar arms and therefore soothing, safe. She wanted to have a good cry, really she did, to shout her outrage and fear and pain, outrage at the nasty things Master Alfred had said which had involved more than just *kissing* her. Fear for Dan who would certainly be arrested and put in gaol and the awful pain the flat brown expression in Richard's eyes had threaded into her heart. Certainly he had done no more than kiss her on that day before Christmas but those kisses and what they had seemed to imply had been sweet, so sweet and loving she had trusted him, believed in him, been absolutely convinced that it was not just a case of the master's son toying with the maidservant. She had been wrong. She was not awfully sure in her dazed confusion why he was fighting, first with his own brother, then with Dan and why he had seemed to blame her but whatever the reason, Mrs Latimer would certainly not let the matter rest. Celie had seen the horror, and yes, *hatred* in her Mistress's eyes. This had been Mrs Latimer's day, not Miss Anne's, not the bride's, but the bride's mother's, for it had been a social triumph for the Latimer family. This day had been one of splendour, the culmination of the uniting of the best families in Liverpool. They had been guests in *her* home, had been gathered together to see *her* family joined with one of Liverpool's oldest and best. The Osbornes and the Hemmingways, all *their* friends and hers, and she had been degraded in front of them by the spectacle of a common fist fight in her own home. Servants, a kitchen maid, her *own* kitchen maid and gardener, her two sons who had been knocked almost senseless by the man's vicious attack.

That was how Mrs Latimer would interpret it, so that was how it would *be*, and the blame, because of it, would be laid, *had* been laid already, Celie had seen it in Mrs Latimer's eyes, well and truly on Celie Marlow and Dan Smith's shoulders.

'I must go and explain, Cook,' she muttered, throwing off Cook's patting hand and placing the tea cup, from which she had been about to take a sip of the hot, sweet tea Cook thought appropriate at times like these, on the table. 'I can't just sit here while they . . .' She stopped and her face crumpled '. . . oh Cook, what will they do to him?'

'Nay, girl, it beats me, but whatever it is you'd better stay here with me until we find out. D'you want to tell me what happened . . . ?' though she could guess, of course. A bonny girl like Celie, a kitchen maid in his mother's home would be fair game to a young gentleman like Master Alfred, or Captain Richard even, and if Dan Smith got a whiff of it, which he apparently had, there'd be no holding him. She'd seen it coming. Oh, not with Master Alfred, but with some bright spark who would take a fancy to anything Celie might allow and her so naive and inexperienced. Celie'd not seen what was in Dan Smith, not yet, but Cook had, and now it was out but who'd have thought it would have been today, of all days? Gawd, Madam would be livid. Someone would have to pay for what had happened in her hallway and, Cook thought sadly, it didn't need second sight to know who it would be.

Chapter Sixteen

'They must *both* be dismissed.'

The elder Richard Latimer stopped his restless pacing of his wife's small parlour and turned to her, appalled. His agitation was so great he almost dislodged a Staffordshire figurine of Florence Nightingale who had been a particular heroine of his wife's.

'My dear, please, you can't mean that. It was all a misunderstanding.'

'Richard, I know exactly what it was and I have never been so humiliated in my life. Our daughter's wedding day. Our house full of important guests and both our sons attacked by a servant. That's what it was and I cannot countenance it. A ferocious madman loose in our home . . .'

'Oh come now, my dear, Dan is not a madman . . .'

'Then why did he fall on a defenceless boy and break his nose? And when Richard rushed to defend him, turn on him as well?'

'It was not quite like that, dearest. Richard . . .'

Mrs Latimer continued as though her husband had not spoken.

'My son has been disfigured, my daughter's wedding day ruined, my friends insulted, my home wrecked, and you are defending . . .'

'No Phyllis, I am not defending . . .'

'Then what are you doing, Richard?'

Richard Latimer twisted about in distressed anguish, throwing out his arms as though begging for her understanding but Phyllis Latimer watched him in calm detachment. She was not to be moved, her demeanour said, no matter how her husband pleaded.

She was seated in her favourite chair which she prized for its comfort but which also allowed her to sit in the straight and regal fashion which, in her opinion, was the mark of the true lady. A lady did not slouch or loll, or even lean back to read the newspaper as a gentleman did, but had at all times a graceful carriage – even when sitting – and an erectly held head.

She replaced her cup and saucer carefully on the octagonal tripod table at her side, then turned back to her afflicted husband. An expression of sorrowing regret lit her smooth face.

'You surely can understand my position, Richard? Those of our guests who witnessed the . . . incident, and from what I can remember it must have been everyone, will be concerned with what has been done with . . . the culprits, and personally, as you well know, I think they should be behind bars . . .'

'Really, my dear . . .'

'No, let me finish, Richard, behind bars, but as you refused to send for the police . . .'

'It was our daughter's wedding day, Phyllis . . .'

'Precisely, Richard, and I would be obliged if you would not keep interrupting me.'

'I'm sorry.'

'You would not have the police, as I was saying, and . . . being somewhat incapacitated, I did not insist, but I insist on this. Yes, yes, I know the . . . young man will go but surely the girl who is, after all, the *real* cause of the trouble . . .'

'Our son was trying to interfere with her, Phyllis, against her will . . .'

'So *she* says but these girls are known for their loose ways, and besides, I am not at all convinced Alfred would involve himself in such a sordid . . . well . . . I know young men must sow their wild oats, and they must sow them with *someone* and who but the lower orders would oblige them but . . .'

'*My dear*! I am appalled, Celie is only seventeen and a *good* girl. We have known her all her life. Her father was our gardener and a most respectable man. Celie has never caused a moment's . . .'

'May I remind you of the day when she took our children to the woods and Nanny and I were out of our minds . . .'

'She was a child . . .'

'Are you defending her actions *again*, Richard? Then, and now, because if you are, I can only feel deeply offended by it. I am well aware that Celie Marlow was born here, has lived and worked here all her life but I cannot help but feel that there is, as they say, no smoke without fire. I shall have her in here shortly and will certainly see if she has anything further to say on the matter but really the evidence of my own eyes cannot be denied. It seems to me that she and . . . the gardener were . . . they had a relationship of some kind. I do not know exactly what Alfred and Richard were doing in the hallway at the time, though I imagine they were trying to separate the girl and her . . . her paramour and he turned nasty . . .'

'But he was outside when it began, Phyllis . . .'

'There you go again! Really, Richard, *however* it happened, *someone* is to blame and I am certain it was not *my* sons, but whatever it was it seems Smith took exception to it, and that he became violent because of it. I cannot have it, Richard. I *will* not have it.'

'Phyllis, please . . .'

'No, Richard, no. Ring the bell, if you please, and send for her.'

She knew why she had been summoned, naturally. She had been waiting for it for hours, ever since the last of the shocked guests had been driven away in their carriage. Dan had already been told to pack his things and be ready to leave the premises first thing in the morning but what else did Mrs Latimer need to ask of *her*?

She had not a word to say in her own defence, standing quietly before her master and mistress with a young dignity which, though it left Mrs Latimer completely unmoved, touched a sad chord in her husband. Mrs Latimer spoke at length, her bitterness irreconcilable, her enmity obvious, her gaze baleful, and though the words she uttered asked for an explanation, both her husband and her kitchen maid were left in no doubt that she had no real interest in one.

'Have you nothing further to say?' She could not even bring herself to speak Celie's name.

'No, madam. I've told you what happened, Master Alfred . . .'

'Yes,' Mrs Latimer cut her short and her face spasmed in distaste.' There is no need to go into that again. My son has denied having any part in what you described and naturally, I can only believe his word before that of a servant.'

'Phyllis, my dear, can you not . . . ?'

'Thank you, Mr Latimer.' Mrs Latimer shot her husband a venomous look from beneath hooded eyelids, warning him that she did not care to hear her Christian name on his lips before servants.

'But my dear . . .'

'That is all that is needed to be said, I think,' turning back to Celie, her contempt for her husband and his opinion a cruel and heartless thing. 'There just remains the question of what is to be done with you and in the circumstances I feel I have no choice but to give you notice. You will leave in the morning with . . . with your . . . with . . .' She shuddered delicately. 'You will receive a week's wages in lieu. That will be all.'

Celie moved heavily along the passage and into the kitchen and every face there turned in her direction. Her heart felt as though it was bruised inside her chest, hurting so badly she knew a distinct need to put her hand to it and press it soothingly. She could barely think straight and when Cook took a step towards her, her suddenly old face twisted with worry, she had a great deal of difficulty dragging herself back from the deep shock she had fallen into at Mrs Latimer's sharp and vicious words.

'Well?' Cook said.

'I got the sack.'

Dorcas stopped mincing the remains of the cold meat which Cook intended to make into a curry for tomorrow and said 'Never!' Belle dropped the china tea cup she had been washing and had carried from the scullery, her wet hands dripping all over the floor, and Cook had time to consider distractedly that that was two of Mrs Latimer's best tea cups smashed to smithereens in one day.

'What for?' Belle asked, and Maudie put a red, wet hand

to her mouth in horror. Celie played an important part in this busy kitchen, and in Maudie's busy life, and it was hard to imagine her no longer being there. She certainly could not be replaced in Maudie's opinion and like Belle, whose comprehension of the story was hazy, she was at a loss to understand why she was to go. She was not the only one. The servants were agog with it. The master's son and Dan had been fighting in the hall, God alone knew why, and on the day of Miss Anne's wedding, which was dreadful in itself, but what had Celie to do with it, they all wanted to know? There was more here than met the eye, the sharp minds, not only of Maudie but of Kate and Dorcas told them. Whatever it was, Mrs Latimer condemned it, and Dan, who had been involved in the fisticuffs, *and* Celie who had been implicated at some other level, were both to go.

'What's been going on?' Kate asked unguardedly and was amazed when Cook turned on her.

'It's got nothing to do with you, Kate Mossop, so get back to the china. That lot's all to be put away before anyone gets to their bed. See Dorcas, leave that mince and clear up those pieces of china before someone steps on them and you two, back to the scullery. Celie, you come here and tell me what happened.'

'Nothing happened, Cook.' Celie was still deep in shock and was unguarded of her tongue 'She didn't believe me when I said Master Alfred tried to pull me into the cloakroom . . .'

'Tch . . . tch.' Cook did her best to shut Celie up since Mrs Latimer would not like it if gossip got round about one of her precious sons, but it was too late.

'So *that's* it, is it?' Kate pounced on the words triumphantly, and in a moment they were all at it again, jabbering amongst themselves, telling one another that they had never trusted that there Master Alfred who had shifty eyes and was always ready to leer at a girl, speaking as though they were constantly in his company and subject to his coarse demands. They became excited and out of hand again and it was perhaps this, and her own sudden exhausted reluctance to make the effort which was needed to get them all back to their places, which made up Jess Harper's mind. A shaft of pain raced up her swollen legs and into the small of her back and she winced before she spoke savagely.

'Yes, *that's* what it was all about, Kate Mossop, and I for one have had enough of it.' A habit of a lifetime slipped away. The pain in her and the worry unchained the usual tight rein she kept on her tongue and she let it say what *she* thought, what she had been compelled to keep to herself by the nature of her employment ever since she had begun it nearly fifty years ago. 'All my life, ever since I was ten years old I've been at the beck and call of women like her, and ever since I was fourteen, doing my best to avoid men like her son.' She tossed her grey head in the general direction of the front house. 'Oh, aye, I was once pretty like Celie and fair game for the masters and their sons, though I can see you don't believe me, Kate, nor you, Dorcas.' She smiled sourly, then sat down heavily in the chair before the fire. 'All these years I've dreamed of getting away from it and having something of my own and there's no need to look at me like that, Celie Marlow. I've not gone off my head, in fact, I'll be honest with you, I'm not sorry it's happened because it's made up my mind for me. I've been putting it off, wanting to see you settled first, with . . . well, enough said about that for now. So we'll get our bags packed, you and me and Dan, and first thing tomorrow we'll be off. You may well look astonished, Kate Mossop, but I mean it, so now there's a chance for you, Dorcas,' turning to the parlourmaid, 'if you've a mind to take my place, though you'd not fill my shoes, not in a hundred years.' She beamed in great good will at Dorcas, 'but you're welcome to try and I'd shut my mouth if I was you, girl, or that fly'll be in there, quick smart.'

'Cook . . .' Celie found she had no voice and indeed no legs and she sat down heavily in the chair opposite Cook.

'I mean it, lass, I've had enough. You know what my legs are like,' not caring who heard her now. 'Besides, I can't manage here without you,' not caring who heard her say that either because it was the truth.

'Cook . . .'

'Nay, not another word. We'll clear up here and leave it as I would like to find it myself and then we'll get ourselves to our beds. Oh, before we do, run to the cottage, Maudie, and fetch Dan, we'll need to speak to him before we set off.'

'Is . . . is he to come too, Cook?' Celie whispered, not at all sure she wasn't going mad, or was in the throes of some wild dream, one of those which made no sense, but from which, soon, she'd awaken and it was not noticed that Kate was hanging on to every astounding word. The others were still floundering in the consternation of this kitchen without Cook in it, without Celie in it, and what was to become of them all with no one at the helm; what would Mrs Latimer say; who would cook the breakfast, tell them what veg to peel, what floor to scrub? But Kate had the whole situation clear in her mind and knew exactly where she intended to fit into it.

'I'll fetch Dan,' she said, elbowing Maudie aside, and Cook, who did not like her orders to be countermanded, made nothing of Kate's overturning of them. What did she care now? the elderly woman taking her ease for the last time by the fireside thought. These were no longer her staff and this kitchen which had been hers for over twenty years, was no longer hers to rule. She would see Mrs Latimer in the morning. *No*, heaving herself spryly to her feet, she'd damn well see her now and if the mistress told her to go now, go now she would.

Dan was standing in the middle of the small cottage kitchen when Kate pushed open the door. He was doing nothing in particular. His hands were in his pockets and his eyes were unfocused as though he was looking back to something he was desolate to leave, or perhaps looking forward to something he was afraid to contemplate. When Kate touched his shoulder, it took him several moments to blink and bring himself back to the present which he did not seem to care for either.

'Dan,' Kate said softly, moving to stand before him. She smiled sadly, lifting her hands and putting one on each of his shoulders. She reached up and placed a moist kiss on his lips. There was no response, merely a long shuddering sigh which told of his complete misery. Moving slightly, she pressed the soft swell of her breast against his chest over which he wore no more than a shirt. On the way to the cottage she had undone the three top buttons of her bodice and the white flesh revealed gleamed in the dim light from the small window. She kissed him again lingeringly and with great satisfaction felt his body move against hers.

'I'm so sorry, Dan,' she said at last, her voice husky and as his arms went round her involuntarily, glad of the comfort it seemed, her eyes gleamed over his shoulder. 'What will you do?'

'God knows,' again the long dejected sigh.

'I can't bear to think of it, really I can't.'

'It's not your fault, Kate,' kissing her again, deeper this time and with what was evidently a familiarity to which she did not object.

'Dan . . . oh, Dan . . .' Her throat arched and his lips travelled down to where the top of her bodice gaped open. His hand moved to it, slipping inside to cup her full naked breast. Pushing the fabric aside, he freed the white globe, bringing it out to fasten his mouth on her distended nipple. He began to groan then, to shake his head as though it had suddenly occurred to him that this was neither the time nor the place, but with a swift movement Kate pulled her bodice and the chemise beneath it off her shoulders, and the high, proud jut of her full-nippled breasts broke free, a magnificence which Dan Smith could not resist.

'It will have to be quick, Danny,' she moaned, lifting her full skirt about her waist, 'for I've to be off to pack.'

'What . . . ?' His mouth was at her breast, her hands at the buckle of his trousers, his own pulling down her white frilly drawers.

'I can't stay here without Cook, Danny, can I?' Her voice was plaintive as he lifted her to sit on the kitchen table where Celie Marlow had once done her homework.

'What . . .' he said again, as his penis thrust vigorously between her thighs.

'I can't stay here without Cook, Danny,' she said again. She began to moan, arching her back and widening her legs the better to accommodate him. 'Not with Mr Alfred the way he is. And they're both going . . . oh Danny . . . Danny . . . that's lovely . . .'

'Who . . . ?'

'Cook an' Celie, they're both leaving an' Cook says you're to come right over.'

'Bloody hell . . .' Kate was nettled when Dan's ardent manhood disappeared as quickly as it had come.

Two hours later Jess Harper, Dan Smith, Celie Marlow and Kate Mossop, their bags heaped around their feet, stood outside the gates of Briar Lodge whilst in her own small drawing room, Phyllis Latimer, though not allowing it to show, faced the appalling prospect of having lost not only two good maids and a splendid gardener, but the best cook the Latimer family had ever known.

Of the four of those who stood that evening in the lane, only Jess Harper seemed to be in good spirits for of the four of them, only Jess Harper knew what they were to do and Kate didn't really care. This was excitement of the highest order and she loved excitement, did Kate Mossop. The tale she had told Cook had been true up to a point but when she lied and told her of Master Alfred's attempts to drag *her* into any convenient doorway and even, she said, hanging her head, of trying to put his hands on her, well . . . on her . . . bosom . . . it had been as easy as falling off a log. Kate had no intention of being separated from Dan Smith, even if he was, like herself, temporarily jobless, for she'd plans for her and Dan, had Kate. She had for some reason, a feeling that she'd do well if she stuck to him, besides which, Dan had been in Kate's bloomers for a while now, though no one knew of it, of course, and she couldn't continue with that if he was in Liverpool, or wherever, and she was at Briar Lodge, could she? And then, of course, there was the matter of Celie Marlow who had once taken the job Kate Mossop had had her eye on! Kate had not forgotten that, if Celie Marlow had.

Cook had been decidedly put out, and showed it when Kate swore she couldn't stay here on her own, since Dan and Celie had been the only ones included in Cook's plans but she supposed that if Dan agreed to it, which it seemed he did, there was nothing she could do about it though it was the first she'd heard about Master Alfred trying to take liberties with Kate's person and why hadn't she been told before, she demanded to know? Kate couldn't, or wouldn't say, clinging to Dan's arm in a way Cook did not like, but still, she was a good worker and they might need someone to do the heavy work in what she proposed.

'Run and fetch a cab from Wavertree corner, there's a good lad. It'll be dark soon,' Cook told Dan now, gazing across the fields which lay on the other side of the lane, thanking the fates that today was the longest day of the year and that despite being gone nine o'clock, it was still light. The low evening sun hung like a great ball in the perfect sky. Along the far horizon was a wide band of pink and below it the earth was turning slowly to darkness. It was beautiful, peaceful, absolute stillness, except for the sound of birds settling for the night. She felt the tranquillity fall about her, entering her soul, making her want to sigh with that deep contentment which comes so rarely but which, when it does, is so perfect. It was as though nothing mattered, really, except this unhurried moment in time which had about it the feeling that all was right with Jess Harper's world. She had not the slightest doubt that what she had done had been the right thing and there would be nothing but times like these for ever more. By heck, she felt grand, wondering why that was when you thought back to what had happened this day.

No one had seen Captain Richard Latimer since the tearful bride and her groom had been driven to the station and the last guests had gone, but it was said he himself had called for a cab and gone dashing off to some destination known to no one. There had been a few sparks flying in the Latimer household lately, Cook thought, and it seemed every one had involved him. In Cook's opinion he was the only one with the guts to stand up to his Ma. Well, that was all over, she told herself comfortably, over and done with now.

'Where are we going, Cook?' Celie asked as Dan strode off towards the village, not much caring, really, since she was still in a state of appalled shock. She clutched her reticule to her, her last link it seemed with the life she had known and the people she had known in it and who had all cried when they came, disbelieving, to the back door, to say goodbye.

Mrs Ash, as upset as if it had been one of her own, she said; Mr Ash, quite distraught at "their Celie" going, Jim and Bertie Ash, Ethel Ash and Sal Ellis. Dorcas had clutched at her, and then at Cook, terrified at being left in charge, and then there was Belle, begging to come with her and Maudie. They'd be like the tribes of Israel soon, Cook had protested but if things worked out, she added mysteriously, perhaps they'd send for Dorcas who was in the meanwhile to pull herself together. She was an experienced housemaid and would soon have someone to tell her what to do, Cook said sternly, for even Dorcas knew she could never take Cook's place.

'We'll find somewhere to stay for a few days until we get our bearings,' she answered Celie now. 'I know of a good, clean lodging house in Cable Street, just off Castle Street. A friend of mine from when we worked together in Yorkshire. She's clean and keeps a good table,' which told Celie all she needed to know about Cook's friend.

If Mrs Petty, as she was called, was surprised to see the cab draw up at her front door and her old friend from their Yorkshire days get out of it, she did not show it. It was a tough, mean neighbourhood, most of the streets stretching away from the docks, lived in by dockers' families who survived on next to nothing. Dock labouring was casual work and the majority of those who occupied the narrow houses were frequently without work, existing on "outdoor" relief and managing, just, to survive on it. They had many other small jobs, husbands, wives and even children, working in sweat shops, or making matchboxes at home, or the piece work of any kind which was available in the clothing trade.

But Ivy Petty, the widow of a seaman killed in an accident at sea had, by dint of sheer bloody hard work and a tiny insurance her Stanley had left her, managed to keep her place in the order of things by taking in lodgers, seamen who came and went, sleeping in her bare, well-scrubbed rooms, eating her plain, nourishing and plentiful food. Decent men who did not come back drunk of a night when they were in port, or if they did, were polite about it. They were clean and avoided fights, as many sailors seemed incapable of doing.

'Jess,' she remarked, 'don't stand there ont' step, come in,'

just as though she and Jess had met no more than a week
ago. She eyed the two pretty girls and the good-looking chap
who huddled at Jess's shoulder with all the lively interest of
the Liverpudlian but being a woman who, in her own words,
poked her nose into no one's business, and allowed no one
to poke theirs into hers, she merely opened the door wider
and indicated with a toss of her iron-grey head that they were
to step over her immaculate doorstep and into her narrow,
immaculate, linoleum lined passage.

'Come through, Jess,' she said, 'kettle's on.'

The kitchen where Ivy Petty led them was tiny. There
was an enormous black leaded range on one wall and an
equally enormous Welsh dresser on the other, crammed
on every shelf with serviceable crockery and in between a
round table, covered with a fringed red chenille tablecloth. A
couple of worn but comfortable armchairs were drawn up to
the range, which was lit, and between them on a home-made
rag rug was a stout ginger tom cat. It stood up angrily as its
peace and comfort were disturbed, then, after turning a time
or two, settled itself into a ball, its tail curled neatly about its
body. There was a small window looking out onto a barren
back yard and beside the window a door led into a long thin
scullery containing a shallow stone sink and draining board.

'Well, I were about to say sit down but I've only the two
chairs.'

'I'll sit, thanks Ivy, me legs're givin' me gyp.'

'Aye, so do mine, chuck. Comes with being on yer feet. A
cook's heritage sure enough but . . .'

'Oh, they're young an' can stand,' tossing a weary hand
in the direction of Dan, Celie and Kate, who leaned against
the fourth wall, being careful not to disturb Mrs Petty's
numerous framed pictures which were hung there. One
depicted a Grecian lady gathering shells on the seashore.
There was a portrait of an elderly lady and gentleman in the
fashion of three decades ago, and the rest were images of
sailing ships battling in heavy seas beneath lowering skies.
In pride of place and apart from the others was a likeness
of a grim-faced, bearded gentleman with a stiff wing collar
holding his head up in a fearsomely unnatural posture.

'Well, Jess,' Ivy prompted when they all had a cup of tea in their hands, 'what's brought you down 'ere? You 'ad a grand job up Wavertree way, if I remember,' taking a deep and appreciative sip of her own strong, almost black tea, which was the way she liked it and so the way her guests must drink it.

'We've . . . had a bit of a set-to, Ivy.'

'Oh, aye.'

'Aye . . . well, it's a long story which I'll get round to later but the long and short of it is we want rooms for a week or two.'

'How many?'

'Well, three if you can manage.'

'I only take gentlemen boarders, Jess, you know that.'

'Aye, but I thought . . . well, you know me, Ivy, if I say we'd be no trouble, then we won't . . . I'll cook for us if I can have the loan of your stove so you've no need to have any extra work. Keep our own rooms clean an' all. My girls know how to scrub, lass.'

'They would if you trained them, Jess.' They both smiled grimly at some shared memory.

'So, can you help us out then, Ivy? It would get me over a right bad spot whilst we look around. Dan here'll do any jobs that need doing, won't you, Dan? And these two'll keep out of the way of your gentlemen. They're good girls and will do as they're told.'

'Well, I've only one room free. It's three beds in it though, if that'd suit, an' I could put the lad 'ere on a camp bed in the attic.'

'Champion, that'd be gradely,' and the three young people leaning tiredly against the wall looked at one another in astonishment for the further away from Briar Lodge they had come and the longer the period of time since leaving it had elapsed, the stronger Cook's accent became. It had broadened, its vowels flat and long drawn out. They were not to know that Jessica Harper had been born in a small mining village the other side of Huddersfield and that, on her way up the servants' ladder, she had made a determined effort to lose the broad Yorkshire dialect she had grown up with. Now, it

seemed, just as though it no longer mattered since she was
beholden to no one and therefore could please herself, she
had, in the space of three hours, relaxed into what she was
comfortable with.

The room they were put in, Celie, Cook and Kate, was achingly clean, the inevitable linoleum on the floor so thoroughly
scrubbed the pattern on it was long gone. There was a narrow
wardrobe, a chest of drawers, a chair, a washstand and three
narrow beds, the spotless sheets tucked under the mattress
so tightly that Celie had a great deal of trouble sliding between
them. The counterpane was as smooth and unwrinkled as the
tablecloth on the table at Briar Lodge, and folded neatly at
the bottom of each bed was a blue eiderdown.

There was slight confusion caused by Cook's stern command that both girls were to "avert tha' eyes, if tha' don't
mind" whilst she struggled her way out of her clothes, had
a bit of a wash and put on her nightgown, but as Kate was
already asleep, her mouth slightly open, the operation was
completed successfully and the candle blown out.

'Good night, lass,' Cook's voice was low and comforting.
'Sleep tight.'

'Good night, Cook.'

The blackness closed in about Celie, as heavy and hopeless
as the lump which seemed to have settled itself in the vicinity
of her heart. For several seconds, though her eyes were
wide open and, despite her exhaustion, refused to close,
she could see nothing. Then, as they became accustomed
to the darkness, the faint glow coming through the curtains
from the street light picked out the shape of the furniture,
the chest of drawers on which the candle stood and the chair
where Cook had neatly folded her corsets, her bloomers and
the intricate and mystifying undergarments she wore.

The silence was broken by a sudden gurgling snore as Cook
fell into instant sleep and from outside the window came the
quick "tip tap" of feet as they hurried past the house. From
somewhere beyond the walls of the bedroom, next door,
perhaps, a baby began to grizzle, then stopped as though
some patient mother soothed it.

Her weariness was absolute and yet she could not seem

to unwind the tension which had her in its grip. It was unbelievable that she had risen from her bed beside Belle this morning with no inkling that she was never to get back into it again. That she would, at the end of the same day, lie down to rest in another, in another house, in another world, her own turned upside down in the most frightening way. So few hours . . . was it only this morning? . . . It seemed days, weeks, months and . . . oh, how her heart ached . . . the pain of it unbearable . . . his eyes . . . staring . . . staring at her bleakly as they had done today . . . gone the soft expression they had shown in the past . . . last Christmas . . . so long and no word . . . Richard . . . why? . . . That day on the Marine Parade . . . so perfect, its loveliness must be guarded in order that, when she needed it, she could take it out and dream over it . . . why? . . . Richard . . . Richard . . .

Her exhausted body slowly succumbed to its desperate need of rest, drugging her mind at last to sleep.

Chapter Seventeen

It was several weeks before Celie Marlow was released from the strange, dream-like state she had fallen into after the appalling incident on Miss Anne's wedding day, and during that time she drifted, ghost-like, beside the surprisingly brisk figure of Jess Harper, scarcely noticing what Cook was up to. She heard snatches of her conversation with Mrs Petty but though the words entered her ears they did not infiltrate her stunned mind and wisely, knowing that her former kitchen maid was still deep in shock, Cook left her alone to come out of it in her own time.

The front parlour at number five Cable Street was Mrs Petty's pride and joy, everything in it gathered and arranged there by Ivy and her Stanley during their twenty-five years of marriage. It was crammed with black horsehair sofas and chairs, mahogany "what-nots", a chenille-covered table and even a piano. A potted aspidistra stood on a stand beside the fall of snow-white net curtains which shrouded the window, and every flat surface except the floor was covered with bric-à-brac. It was here, when they had finished their tea in the back kitchen, that Mrs Petty's "gentlemen" sat, if they were so inclined, though most, Cook noticed, probably overcome by the stiff and desperate cleanliness of it all, went to the corner pub for a "bevvy" and a game of either darts or dominoes. Not to get "legless" mind, for if they did they would be asked to vacate their room at once, for Mrs Petty could not abide drunkenness.

Mrs Petty's four new boarders kept out of the way of her gentlemen at meal times, sitting patiently on their beds until the back kitchen was clear then, when Mrs Petty said they may, coming down to crowd the already crowded room. It was a bit of a squash and when Kate, never backward in coming forward, asked Cook's permission for them to take a walk, it was readily given. Cook was glad of a chance to chat to Ivy whom she'd not seen for more than ten years, besides which with only two chairs it was cumbersome to have the three youngsters leaning restively against Ivy's wall.

No one could have been more delighted than Kate when Celie, in that hesitant way she seemed to have adopted, said she would rather stay with . . . stay here with . . . her eyes on Cook, just as though she did not care to be separated from the only stable fixture in her unstable world.

'I don't feel like a walk just now, Cook.'

'That's all right, Celie, me an' Dan'll just go an' look at boats, won't we, Dan? We'll not be long, Cook,' cheerfully dashing up the stairs to fetch her hat.

'Come with us, Celie,' Dan pleaded, taking her hands between his own, his eyes concerned since it seemed to him she was not at all herself. Not that you could blame her, the speed with which their lives had been changed around. He was somewhat overcome himself since he had been perfectly satisfied with the way things had been at Briar Lodge. He had thoroughly enjoyed his job and had been good at it, he knew, following faithfully all that Cec Marlow had taught him. He liked the outdoor work and had been deeply satisfied at some basic level of himself in watching what he planted grow and mature, his flowers and shrubs giving pleasure to the eye, his vegetables giving sustenance to the belly. He had been proud of what he did, of the responsibility placed trustingly on his shoulders by Mr Latimer and the guidance and training he was giving to young Jim and Bertie. He had taken to sitting of an evening with Reuben Ash who had shown him how to use a hammer and a saw and a plane and all the other tools which were part of Reuben's trade, and the feel of a bit of wood in his hands had given him deep pleasure. He was as uncomplicated and wholesome as the ground in which he sowed his seeds and his heart and mind, which had recovered slowly from the tragedy of losing his family, had received a severe blow

when he had been dismissed. He fretted over what was to
become of it all, for Jim and Bertie, though "coming on" nicely
under his tutelage, were far from capable of carrying on in
Cec Marlow's and *his* footsteps. What about his flower-beds?
Those pansies and anemones should be out by now and would
those lads remember to check the stakes on the standard
roses? The asparagus must be constantly watered and the
last of the beans sown and next week he had meant to put
in the leeks . . . until even Ivy, who was the most patient of
women, threw him a look of sheer exasperation and asked
him if he'd nowt else to think on but damned vegetables.

But despite what had happened, he was aware, even
knowing the outcome, that he would have acted again just
as he had when his placid, easy-going nature had been
inflamed to madness at the sight of Celie struggling in the
brutal arms of Richard Latimer. He would never forget the
image of her slight figure against the splendid scarlet jacket
of his master's son and even now his heart jumped erratically
when the memory came to plague him.

She meant more to him than anyone in the world, did Celie,
and he would give his life for her, never mind his job. He had
been devastated when, after he and Kate had . . . well, pulled
themselves together, he had finally assimilated the news that
not only was he to leave Briar Lodge, but Celie and Cook were
to go as well, though Cook's departure was her own decision.
He had wanted to march right into the Latimer drawing room
and tell Mr and Mrs Latimer exactly what he thought of
them, though he had suspected that the fault lay mainly at
Mrs Latimer's door. It was only Cook's sharp rejoinder that
stopped him and the knowledge, since he was of a sensible
turn of mind, that it would do no good. They would still sack
Celie and Cook would still leave because of it. If he could
have got his hands on that bastard, *both* those bastard Latimer
sons, he'd break every bone in their arrogant contemptuous
bodies. Look what they'd done to her, his lovely girl, turning
her bright-eyed confidence and contentment into a hesitant
vulnerability which tore at his heart.

His eyes were warm and infinitely loving as they looked
down into Celie's, his feelings for her there for her to see

but Celie Marlow was blinded by her own despair and she did not notice.

Cook did, though, and she sighed with satisfaction. She caught Ivy Petty's eye and saw there her own understanding and they both nodded in agreement, needing no words.

'Leave her be, Dan, there's a good lad. Tha' go and take Kate down to't docks. She be a restless lass, that there Kate and wi' nowt ter do she's a damn nuisance. Do me a favour, will tha', an' keep her out the house for an hour. See, Celie . . .' Celie turned in relief to the familiar words with which Cook started many of her sentences, '. . . fetch that tuffet I saw in't parlour . . .' turning for a polite moment to Ivy for her permission and when she had it, continuing '. . . and come an' sit here by us while I talk to Mrs Petty.'

Their days formed a kind of pattern. They washed and dressed and remained in their rooms until Mrs Petty's last "gentleman" had banged the front door behind him and clattered off up the street towards the docks. The "boarders" changed as those who were employed on the merchant ships, or even the great passenger liners which docked daily, sailed off to some foreign part, and others came to take their place. A few nights at most and then they were off again, but it was rare for Mrs Petty to have an empty bed and she was glad of Jess Harper's help and of her two girls, in the scrubbing of the linoleum, the changing of the beds, the washing, mangling and ironing of the bed linen, the cleaning of windows and paint-work which took place each day.

When this was completed, the four of them set off in what seemed to Dan and Kate, to be an endless, *aimless*, wandering of the streets that ran like the spokes of a wheel from the central hub which was the main shopping area of Liverpool. Lord Street, Church Street, Bold Street, Paradise Street, Whitechapel, Colquitt Street, Upper Duke Street, Princes Road moving through a labyrinth which threaded away in all directions. Going north, the further they got from the fashionably thronged thoroughfares where the great stores and smart shops were, the more down-at-heel the area became. Factories and warehouses and steel foundries, all jumbled up with small, poverty-stricken, back-to-back houses, their walls blackened by factory smoke and years of industrial grime, and each time Cook would cluck her tongue irritably and turn back.

'What are we looking for, Cook?' Dan asked, staring about him at the dark, mean-looking buildings which seemed to press against one another as though the working classes who lived in them needed the comfort of one another's closeness.

'I'll know when I see it, lad,' was the enigmatic reply.

'Well, if we knew, perhaps we could help,' Kate said pertly, her irrepressible good spirits not at all diminished by the upheaval in their lives. With Celie apparently content to cling to Cook's arm, even now walking beside her ahead of Dan and herself, Kate felt as though she was on her holidays – not that she had ever had one – especially on the short excursions she and Dan were allowed by Cook. Yesterday evening, which had still retained the heat of the day, after what, in Ivy Petty's opinion, had been "a real corker", the two of them had taken a turn round Sefton Park, where they had strolled about the perimeter of the lake and across the deer park towards the bandstand. In the balmy evening air, hundreds of people lounged in deck chairs or were sprawled about the sun-warmed grass to listen to the band. She had clung to Dan's arm, for with the instinctive knowledge which is born in women like her, she had soon come to realise that there was a part of Dan's nature which liked to protect. Perhaps it was in most men, Kate didn't know, or care, but Dan responded most satisfactorily if she pretended to be frail, vulnerable and in need of his strong right arm to get her by almost anything from a barking dog to the firing of the one o'clock gun on the river.

The band had been lovely. They had tapped their feet and smiled at one another and though Kate was perfectly well aware that Dan would sooner have Celie Marlow at his side than herself, despite their physical relationship which was satisfying to them both, even that didn't matter. She had, she knew, "seduced" Dan Smith, gradually leading him on until one warm July night last year, she had got into his bed at midnight and taken his virginity, though he had not taken hers since she was no longer in possession of it. He had been very willing. Was he not a man with a man's needs? and though at times she was perfectly well aware that he was trying half-heartedly to resist her, she had only to rub against him, let down her cape of silver hair, give him a glimpse of a white thigh or a pink nipple, and he was lost. She didn't love Dan Smith. She didn't love anybody, never had. She knew what she *wanted*, though, and while Celie moped about like the spineless creature she was, she, Kate Mossop would, in due course, get what she had set out to get. In the park she had bewitched him into kissing her at the back of the pavilion, enticing him there in the ways she knew so well.

'Not afraid of the dark, are you, Dan Smith?' she had laughed up at him, and he could not help but laugh back at her. She recognised the narrowed unconscious speculative gleam in his eyes telling her it might be more than a kiss if it didn't take too long.

She was having the best time of her life, was Kate Mossop, she told herself, and though she had no idea what the old lady was up to, she didn't care what it was, or how long it took. It could go on for ever as far as she was concerned.

She and Dan almost bumped into Celie and Cook as they walked behind them that day, well, into Cook, for though Celie had gone on, her head in the clouds, thought Kate scornfully, Cook had stopped and turned to stare at the building to her left which stood on a corner, a crossroads really, on which five or six other streets converged.

They had set out that morning in the opposite direction to the one they had taken on previous mornings, moving on a south-easterly course, up Duke Street, past St James Cemetery, turning from Upper Parliament Street into a broad tree-lined avenue down the centre of which was a neatly mown strip of grass about ten feet wide. The Boulevard, it was called, which sounded very grand, foreign somehow and different, Kate thought as she looked about her approvingly. There were neat, semi-detached villas on either side, newly built, it seemed, and well kept. As they walked along it they caught glimpses of the bigger, detached houses that lined the crescents leading off the Boulevard, elegant houses, again newly built, but which were evidently the homes of the wealthy.

'This looks promising,' Cook muttered, turning to stare across the street to where, beyond a row of detached houses, the green of a park could be seen.

'That's Princes Park, if I'm not mistaken,' she continued, talking, they were all aware now, not to them, but to herself, 'and beyond that, Sefton Park, not too far out and this . . .'

She shifted her sharply focused gaze back to the buildings on their left, a small crescent of three shops, the centre one of which was very evidently empty.

'What is it, Cook?' Kate asked carelessly, admiring her own reflection in the blacked-out, filthy window of the building. She had on her "walking-out" dress of apple-green gingham, the colour several shades deeper than her cat-like eyes. Her silver-pale hair was drawn back from her face and gathered into an enormous coil at the nape of her neck and above it was perched a tiny jockey-cap of black velvet. The peak was tilted over her eyes and beneath it they gleamed and narrowed, her long eyelashes meshing together. She studied her own image in the shop window. Her white skin was fine, translucent, like the white china cups of Mrs Latimer's tea set, the ones Cook and Belle had smashed on the day of the wedding. She arched her back and thrust forward the quite magnificent swell of her young breasts, hoping Dan would notice, but both he and Celie had gathered at Cook's side and were looking in bewilderment, first at Cook and then at the dirty window.

'This could be it.' Cook pulled on her lip and behind her Kate cast her eyes to Heaven. What was the old biddy on about now? Dragging them all over bloody Liverpool, day after day, nearly two weeks now, up one street and down another and none of them having the faintest idea what she was up to.

'Could be what, Cook?' Celie asked tentatively, showing for the first time a faint spark of interest in what was happening about her. She could feel it inside her, a kind of awakening, a registering of where she was. Well, perhaps not *where* she was, for she had no idea of the name of the street, but of being beside Cook and Dan *in* a street,

staring without comprehension at whatever Cook was so
interested in.

'I'm not sure yet, Celie, but this is a good spot for . . .'

'For what?'

'A nice area an' all.' Cook looked about her like a bright
sparrow, cocking her head and probing the doorway of the
rather seedy-looking building with her beady eyes.

'What for?'

'And it won't have passing trade, so not too expensive,
I'd say.'

'What d'you mean, Cook?'

'There's room for carriages here, wouldn't tha' say, Dan?'
and again her eyes scanned up and down the road, the brightness in them promising something which Celie suddenly found
concerned her as nothing had done since Richard Latimer had
turned his hard, contemptuous gaze upon her.

'*A carriage*! Are we to have a carriage then?'

'Don't be daft, Celie Marlow. Now then, tek a look at that
sign int' window an' tell me what it ses.'

'It says "To Let". Apply to Mr William Pembroke, 10 South
Castle Street, for particulars.'

'Eeeh, that's right handy, South Castle Street. It's near
Cable Street. Come on then, there's no time like present as
my old mam used to say.'

This was the first any of them had ever heard of Cook's
mam, imagining, as young people did of the old, that they had
come into the world just as they were now, wrinkled, grey,
inclined to stoutness and with "bad legs".

Cook's bad legs did not appear to bother her now as she led
the way back up the Boulevard and left into Upper Parliament
Street, just like a majestic liner followed by three mystified tug
boats. Along the length of Bold Street which was heaving with
fashionably dressed ladies, parasols raised to protect them
from the midday sun, cyclists, hansom cabs and horse-drawn
tramcars clattering down its centre. Outside the public house
on St George's Crescent where Lord Street ran into Castle
Street, men stood outside the pub, pint pots of ale in their
hands, for Cook and her followers were back in the working
man's district now, no more than a few hundred yards from

the docks. There were other men, clerks and office workers, smart in their bowlers, carrying walking sticks, following the dictates of fashion, since none of them were old or infirm.

William Pembroke turned out to be a small firm of Solicitors, not the sort Richard Latimer senior would use, nor indeed any of his acquaintances, but Mr Pembroke had an open, honest face, and a pleasant manner which seemed to satisfy Cook.

'You wait here,' she said to Dan and Kate who each wore the expression of someone who finds himself in a world in which, somehow, he has been deposited whilst his attention was temporarily elsewhere. They looked in consternation around Mr Pembroke's small outer office and at his elderly, world-weary clerk, then back at Cook, even Kate for once at a loss for words.

'See, both of thi', sit thi' down.' She turned to the clerk, 'they *can* sit down, can't they?'

'Of course . . . madam.'

'Right then, Celie, tha' come wi' me.'

It was to be a shop, not just your ordinary bakery where only bread, scones, fruit and meat pies would be sold, she said, but what Cook called grandly, a "speciality" shop, one which would, in time, attract carriage trade. She knew what the gentry liked, see, and what's more, she knew how to provide it, and with Celie beside her that's exactly what she meant to do. Gourmet food, like the French knew how to cook, but at the same time good, old-fashioned "stand-bys" that the ordinary housewife would be glad to purchase. They knew what she meant, didn't they? she asked the three open-mouthed faces briskly, four if you include Ivy Petty's as they sat round the table that night. Home-made foodstuffs of every sort, those that she could conjure up with one hand tied behind her back, so to speak, seeing as how she'd had a good many years' experience of it. She'd not say how many, winking at Ivy Petty, once again amazing the three young people who, for all their working life, had known Cook for a strict disciplinarian, a hard taskmaster, a perfectionist who demanded their best and got it, the ultimate authority who had ruled their lives, even their thoughts, and never, not once, had shared a joke with them. Her very presence had scattered them like rabbits at a poacher's gun, and now, here she was, smiling and *winking* in a way, two weeks ago, they would not have thought possible.

'I'll have the key, if you please, Mr Pembroke,' she had declared haughtily to the solicitor. 'I and my staff would like to see the size of the premises and the suitability of them for the purpose I have in mind.' She had resumed her Briar Lodge accent for Mr Pembroke.

'And what is that, Mrs Harper?' Mr Pembroke asked. Of course Dan and Kate were not privy to this conversation but Celie, who accompanied them on their next "outing", was, and having recovered her senses or so it seemed, annoyingly to Kate, and become Celie Marlow again, had repeated it to them.

'I intend to cater to the carriage trade,' Cook answered Mr Pembroke grandly.

'Indeed, and what experience have you had of the retailing trade, Mrs Harper?'

Cook looked affronted, considering this to be none of Mr Pembroke's business.

'I have been a cook for thirty years, Mr Pembroke, and if that's not enough experience for you then I don't know what is.'

'And I'm sure you are a splendid cook, Mrs Harper, but that is not quite the same as *selling* what you make, is it? I presume that it is what you intend to do . . .'

'Indeed it is . . .'

'. . . but what I must determine is whether you will be able to pay my client's rent.'

Cook's face became an alarming shade of crimson, Celie reported later to Dan and Kate, and she could see Cook would have liked nothing better than to box Mr Pembroke's ears.

'I am willing to pay six months' rent in advance, Mr Pembroke and if, at the end of those six months I have not succeeded, then I deserve to lose it. I have two willing and hard-working girls and a clever handyman. I am the best cook in Liverpool and I'm sure if you were to approach Mr Latimer of Noble Shipping, he will vouch for me, not only as a cook, but as a woman who has run his household and household accounts for more than twenty years. I am honest and . . .'

'Why did you leave Mr Latimer's employ?' Mr Pembroke's voice was quiet.

Cook was not at all rattled. 'I resigned, Mr Pembroke. I wished to be self-employed, but if you do not care to rent your shop . . . your *client's* shop to me, then I'm sure there are others just as suitable. Come, Celie,' rising royally to her feet and gathering herself to leave.

Mr Pembroke sprang to *his* feet.

'Now then, Mrs Harper, don't let us be hasty. I will ask my clerk to call a cab and I will personally take you and your staff to look over the premises. The rent, by the way, is half a guinea a week. Is that . . . ?'

'We'll see, Mr Pembroke, but first let us look at the premises.'

The premises were quite appalling. There was a double-fronted bay window, its paint peeling, with a door between which almost fell inwards when Mr Pembroke pushed it open. The shriek of its unoiled hinges grated on Dan's nerves and you could see he longed to be about them with his oil can. The air inside the shop which even on this warm day was dank and chill, spoke of damp cement and bricks, rotting timbers and what Cook for one, recognised as the stink of rodents.

'Bloody hell,' Kate muttered, picking up the skirt of her apple-green gingham as she moved hesitantly across the threshold.

'That will do, Kate,' Cook said sharply.

'Sorry, Cook,' Kate's response was automatic but her eyes continued to show her horror as they slid from one rotting pile of rubbish to another. There was a counter across the width of the large shop area and a door behind the counter leading, Kate was sure, into some other equally ghastly quarters and on either side of the door, the wall was lined from floor to ceiling with shelves. Filth into which their boots literally sank lay evenly across the floor as though no feet had disturbed it for many years. Cobwebs were draped like lace from floor to ceiling and from one end of the room to the other, clinging

in heart-stopping dreadfulness about their heads, and Kate
shrieked shrilly, declaring she couldn't stand it, really she
couldn't, and she was off right now.

'Very well, Kate Mossop,' ignoring Mr Pembroke who
seemed to agree with the silly girl, 'off you go but remember
if you leave my employ now I shall not take you back.'

Cook hoped Kate would take her at her word and hop
it for though Kate Mossop was a good worker, Cook had
a feeling she might be trouble and besides, hard workers
were two a penny in this part of the country and Kate would
be easy to replace. Even now, she was still not certain she
believed what Kate had said about Master Alfred interfering
with her since, when questioned, none of the other girls had
been troubled. She didn't like the way Kate hung about Dan
either, but she couldn't just turn the girl off, could she, not
without a legitimate reason.

Kate had not been aware she was *in* Cook's employ and
was about to say so for she had received no *wages* in the two
weeks she had been at Mrs Petty's, when her attention was
caught by the sight of Dan and Celie moving slowly through
the far doorway and into whatever was beyond it, with every
evidence of a great, and *shared* interest.

'Kitchens, Cook,' she heard Celie say, 'and in need of a
damn good scrubbing.'

'That will do, Celie.'

'Sorry, Cook, and look, there are stairs going up . . . come
on, Dan, let's go and have a look . . .' Celie's voice trailed
away as she evidently moved up the staircase with Dan
following her, Kate presumed sourly, and with Celie beginning
to be more her old self, God alone knew what the pair of
them might get up to. Nothing *bad*, of course, not with the
old woman about, but a firming up of the relationship they
had shared for so long and from which she, Kate Mossop,
meant to keep them.

There were big cast-iron ranges across the wall of the back
room with several flat hotplates over what would be the fires
and beside them the ovens. There were cupboards and two
enormous tables and everywhere the stinking, rotting rubbish
left by the previous occupants.

'Before it was a shop, it was a house,' Mr Pembroke explained to Cook's back as she bent to study what might have been a dead rat on the hotplate, by her expression, 'made over as many others were as the shopping area expanded. This would have been the kitchen and scullery beyond,' indicating another door, 'and the front was the dining room and parlour knocked into one.'

'Yes, I can see that, young man,' Cook's voice was discouraging and Kate began to take hope. She was about to follow Dan and Celie whom she could hear clattering about upstairs when Dan's voice, filled with some strange excitement, came floating down to them.

'Four big bedrooms on the first floor, Cook, and three more above that and . . . oh, Lord, will you look at that. Celie, for Christ's sake come . . . come quick.'

'What is it, Dan?' Cook called anxiously, not at all sure she wanted to trust her legs which suddenly she was aware were throbbing in agony, on the stairs. Kate was eager to go up, though, longing to push Cook aside but Cook would not be budged.

'Open the back door, Cook,' Celie's voice beseeched her, light, animated, buoyant with something Kate did not care for.

'The back door! I don't even know where it is.'

'Allow me to show you.' Mr Pembroke bustled forward, keys at the ready. He bowed Cook and Kate through the kitchen with the air of a man producing a rabbit out of a hat and into the scullery which Kate scuttled through with her face averted from what lay in the double sinks. They came to another door which evidently led out of the back of the house.

'Now then, which of these keys . . .'

'Have you seen it yet, Cook?' Dan's voice yelled from above their heads.

'Give us a minute, lad.'

At last the right key was found, the door was opened and the late afternoon sunshine fell across the two women and the man, bathing them in a warm and golden shaft and illuminating the dust and filth behind them which they had disturbed. It lay across the long garden dozing at the bottom of the four steep steps, across the tangled magic of wild, cultivated foliage which had been left untended for years, like the shop, stretching away into the warm distance. It was hazy, somnolent, humming with the sound of pollen-laden bees, soft and dreaming all by itself in shades of green from the palest of birch to the deepest dappled forest green of an oak tree which stood, ancient and wise, defending its far end. There were bushes over which ivy had climbed. Hollyhocks stood like soldiers with the blue and white of delphinium, struggling through the undergrowth with the tenacity of weeds. Apple trees and plum trees, so old and untended their branches had become woven together in what, when spring came, could be a trellis-work of blossom. There was a mossy, red brick wall about it and beyond the wall, far enough away to allow solitude, other tall narrow houses across whose backs *their* garden ran.

Yes, *their* garden. They knew it at once, two of the women at least, even before Dan almost jumped the stairs in his eagerness to get down to it. To *his* place in the natural order of their new life, whatever it was to be. He was jabbering in that sing-song language of his own which he fell into at times of great sorrow or joy, and this, it was very evident, was the latter. A garden, his vivid blue eyes seemed to shout. His *own* garden where he could be what he was. A grower, a nurturer of the land as his forefathers had been in the fertile south of far-away Sweden. A creator of the fine fruits, the vegetables and the glory of the flowers he had sown, tended, cherished and brought forth with such pride at Briar Lodge.

'Look at it, Cook,' he yelled in words they could all understand now, flinging himself down the steep steps and into the waist-high, gently moving, weed-infested grasses. He opened his arms wide and spun round in dizzying circles before looking up to the first floor window where Celie's face peeped through the grime.

'Look at it, Celie. Come down, Celie and have a look at it.'

'Eeeh, Dan, it's grand.' Kate, not at all sure she cared for the way in which he had included Celie and not her, and unable to understand what all the bloody excitement was about anyway, wobbled down the steps, venturing gingerly into the weeds, the deep undergrowth that lay directly at the bottom. 'What'll you do with it?'

'*Do with it*? You stupid girl, what I've always done with the earth. Grow things in it, of course.'

'Now then, Dan Smith, who you calling stupid?' Her cat's eyes gleamed malevolently as though she would take offence, then she smiled her sweetest smile as Celie ran down to where Dan stood. She brushed by Kate as though she was no more than a bit of statuary left lying there by the previous tenant, but Kate kept the smile fixed in position. It was not time yet.

Celie took Dan's arm. 'It's beautiful, Dan,' she breathed. About the pair was a mist of hazed sunshine in which midges danced and as they turned to look about them, tasting the soft, warm air, a cloud of butterflies lifted from an overgrown Buddleia bush, performing a joyful, colourful dance before settling once more on the drooping blue of the blossom. 'It's all so beautiful, and so . . . right.'

Jess Harper turned to Mr Pembroke, a satisfied expression on her rubicund face.

'This will do very nicely, Mr Pembroke,' she told him.

Chapter Eighteen

The two young women stopped to glance into the window of the smart dress shop, and one said something to the other which made her laugh. They stood for several moments, studying what claimed to be the latest fashions from London. Smart, "tailor-mades" meant for women who led a more active outdoor life in this last decade of the nineteenth century and there was no doubt that such women, especially those known as the "new women", were increasingly determined to wear them. Blouses and plain skirts which could now be bought ready made, suiting today's women who, the fashion writers declared, "had a fine physical development and a vigorous contempt for all forms of softness". It was the fashion to look tall and healthy, with a nineteen-inch waist and a splendid bosom and God help those who, having neither, aspired to style.

'Lord, will you look at that "shooting" costume,' one said to the other. 'The skirt is at least six inches from the ground.'

'But how comfortable for striding out.'

'Mmm, though I doubt my husband would care to have his wife's ankles on display for any gentleman to ogle.'

'Oh, come now, you know he would allow you to shave your head if you had a fancy for it. And still think you divine.'

Prudence Garside smiled wickedly and tucking her hand through Celie Marlow's arm, drew her away from the shop window.

'I know, isn't it absolute Heaven? I can do nothing wrong in his eyes, which, though I find it very congenial, can be a great responsibility. It is so easy to *hurt* him, you see, without meaning to, knowing I am the centre of his universe, but then he is mine so that balances it out nicely.' She leaned forward a little to peer anxiously under the brim of Celie's boater. Prudence was taller than Celie by about six inches and in order to see her face, she had to bend her head, which she did. 'I'm not being too bold, am I, Celie, speaking in such a manner, one I know Mama would despise?'

Celie stopped, causing several ladies who were following her and Prudence along Bold Street to tut irritably as they almost cannoned into them.

'How can you say that, Prudence Garside? You know very well I think you and Jethro are perfect for each other and I never tire of hearing you tell me so. To see you so happy together makes *me* happy and I only wish . . .' She stopped suddenly, aware that perhaps she was treading on delicate ground for no matter how welcome she was made in Prudence's house in Croxteth Drive, and no matter how kind Prudence and Mr Garside, or Jethro as he insisted she must call him, were to her, she could not quite forget that not so very long ago, she had been maid in this woman's Mama's kitchen.

Not so very long ago. Those words were so easy to say, and they were true and yet it seemed a lifetime since that day when she and Dan, Kate and Cook, had stood on the back step of the shop and squinted into the sunshine and shade of the garden. What heady intoxication that moment had inspired, the moment when Cook had told Mr Pembroke that "this will do nicely", and though none of them had known, not properly, not concisely, what was in Cook's mind, they were made aware that with those words, this was the beginning of it.

Even Mrs Petty had become involved, persuaded by Cook, or perhaps needing no persuasion, to give a hand in the great undertaking which had started the moment Cook had placed the first six months' rent of ten and sixpence a week into Mr Pembroke's hand.

It was a mammoth task. The boiler which Dan found in the subterranean bowels of the cellar, was taken to pieces, lying about the freshly brushed floor while, in the candlelight – which was all they had at first because, as Dan said, he only had one pair of hands and would get round to the gas lamps as soon as *this thing* was working – he cleaned and scraped and oiled and then put it all back together again as neat as you please. Hot water was what they needed more than anything and by God, Jess Harper wheezed to Ivy Petty, they needed *gallons* of it if they were to get this place as *she* liked it. Ivy knew exactly what Jess meant. The two elderly women were on their knees, side by side, scrubbing out the back scullery, something neither of them had done since they were skivvies many years ago, smiling wryly together at the irony which had brought them back to it.

'Thought I'd seen the last of a scrubbing brush, Jess Harper,' Ivy said, pushing back her wispy grey hair with her red wet hand.

'Me too, Ivy, an' my old back don't like it one bit.'

Weeks it had taken the four women, whilst Dan restored the boiler and the cracked lanterns on the gas brackets which illuminated each room; replaced rotting door frames, shelves, floorboards; put new glass in cabinets, painted miles of skirting board, peeled off layers of old wallpaper and applied acres of fresh white paint to the walls. He had some help, of course, from the two men Ivy found for him, men who were on "outdoor relief" and glad of anything to earn a few bob. Windows were cleaned and polished with vinegar, Kate and Celie working together harmoniously until the glass gleamed in the sunshine which seemed to fall about them in smiling gladness that summer as though in approval of their efforts. It shone on the large square of cardboard which Celie had placed in the sparklingly polished window.

OPENING SHORTLY, it read

'HARPER'S ON THE BOULEVARD'

HOME-BAKED AND SPECIALITY FOODS

'We need to advertise, Cook,' she had said earnestly, taking her first step on the road to retailing.

'Nay, what for? They've only to get a whiff o' my fruit cake or thy apple snow an' they'll be queuin' outside t'door.'

'But they won't *know* about your fruit cake *or* my apple snow if we don't tell them, Cook.'

Cook was quite amazed at the child's shrewdness, she

confessed to Ivy as they sat, their feet up, in Ivy's back kitchen that day. Ivy had to get home for her gentlemen's tea, she had explained, leaving Jess and her staff to follow, for until the bedrooms were furnished, the four of them were to remain in Cable Street. They had gone to their beds, the two girls and Dan, obedient to Cook's command, the habit of a lifetime of servitude hard to break.

'She's got a right good head on her 'as that lass,' she went on, her eyes on the enormously puffed sausages which were her ankles and feet. Well, she hadn't any ankles really. Her plump calves simply continued in a swollen line down into her boots which she had just eased from her feet, wincing as she did so. 'Advertise, she says. Does tha' know what she wants me to do?' she asked Ivy, her eyes wide with her own admiring amazement.

'No, what?'

'Put an advertisement in the newspaper.'

'Get away! In the *Echo*?'

'Aye, and not just in the *Echo*, but in a *decent* newspaper like the gentry read.' She nodded sagely, a look of awe crossing her face. 'She's got her head screwed on has our Celie and work! She's a demon for it, an' so's that there lad.' She nodded again, taking a deep satisfied sip of Ivy's black tea, and again Ivy was left in no doubt about Jess's plans for Celie Marlow and Dan Smith.

There was some mind-searching over what to call the shop, with scatter-brained flights of foolish fancy from Kate Mossop which was all you could expect from a daft 'apporth like her, Cook said scathingly. What was wrong with her own surname? she wanted to know, and since it was *her* savings which were financing the whole thing and from which she was already paying Celie and Kate ten shillings each a week, and Dan fifteen shillings as handyman, gardener and delivery man – which he would be, when they began delivering – plus board, no one felt the need to argue. Which Celie wouldn't anyway, since she thought HARPER'S ON THE BOULEVARD done in gold lettering on a dark green background with SPECIALITY FOODS beneath, was in very good taste. The colour scheme of dark green, gold and pristine white would be repeated inside and outside the shop and in its two double windows where samples of their trade, fresh each day, would be displayed. Dark green stands at different levels and of different shapes, round, oblong and square, on which a lone iced tipsy cake might repose in solitary perfection, perhaps a carefully balanced and planned arrangement of fancy biscuits, a tasteful grouping of jars of chutney, jams, perhaps pickles and how about cheeses she said eagerly, arranged into a display with fresh fruit? Pies of different fillings, artistically decorated in the way she and Cook had done for the Latimer table, and placed on white, gold-edged doyleys, and then there was . . .

'Whoa, slow down, my girl.' Cook put a fond hand on Celie's arm, tickled pink with all her grand ideas, but thinking she must learn to walk before she raced off into the ambitious schemes it seemed had sprung, almost overnight, into Celie's intoxicated head. 'Us've to get this place ship-shape with a bed each to sleep in before . . .'

'But I still think we ought to set ourselves a date, Cook, and advertise in the newspaper. A grand opening . . . yes, that's it, with tea and cakes, just like Mrs Latimer used to have, free, of course, you'd know what to do there, Kate,' bestowing a shimmering look of approval on Kate who, having felt sourly that Celie Marlow was taking over the whole bloody enterprise lock, stock and barrel and that Cook appeared to be letting her, preened, glancing about her at Ivy and Dan, for indeed she did. She'd been serving tea to Mrs Latimer's callers for several years now and had it down to a fine art, neat and dainty, unobtrusive and efficient, and she'd show them a thing or two when the time came. She quite fancied herself behind the newly scrubbed, waxed and polished counter of Harper's which now smelt as sweet and clean as the house at Briar Lodge, waiting on the "carriage trade" ladies, or their housekeepers, selling the "speciality food" Cook and Celie were to produce in the back reaches of the kitchen. A nice little cap and apron, snowy white muslin, she thought, over a well-made bright green dress since Celie seemed bent on the colour, but she didn't mind because green suited her, Dan had said so, matching her long, cat's eyes. There was to be a stool at the back of the counter next to the enclosed coal-burning fire, for Cook meant to create an atmosphere of pleasant warmth and comfort during the winter months in *her* shop, and on the customer's side, several chairs upholstered in a dark green, hard-wearing fabric so that the ladies who came to make their purchases or place their orders, might do so in comfort.

Kate was to be sadly disappointed since Cook had no intention of encouraging the erstwhile housemaid to remain in her employ, let alone queen it over the others in the shop where first impressions were so important, and if she could have found a decent excuse she had intended to give Kate the sack. It would be a bit awkward at the moment, seeing that Kate had left the Latimers on their account. So the only way to get rid of Kate was to set her to the most menial of tasks, the scrubbing, the cleaning, the clearing-up while Celie, who had, after all, the modest, well-mannered shyness, the instinctive taste and discernment to know when to keep her mouth shut and, when she opened it, what to say, attended to the customers. Although Kate had served tea to Mrs Latimer's guests, she had never been engaged in conversation by them and God alone knew what she might say in that bold way she had.

But Kate showed no resentment, whatever she was ordered to do, shouldering her bucket of hot water and scrubbing brush with every sign of good will and cheerfulness.

'Right, Cook, I'll get on with them bedroom floors, then,' she'd say, marching up the stairs and setting to with an enthusiasm which earned Cook's reluctant approval so perhaps . . . well . . . give the girl a chance, eh?

It took two months, which was what Cook, Celie and Dan had aimed for, timing it almost down to the minute. September 1st, they had advertised in several newspapers and on the beautifully illuminated sign in the window, and if it seemed they were not to achieve their target, Cook said, struggling on her trunk-like legs to get down the back steps to the garden which, as yet, Dan had not had time to touch, then they would have to get extra help in, but September 1st it would be, and September 1st it was.

At precisely eight o'clock Dan, in his dark green apron,

immaculate white shirt and black bow tie, well-pressed trousers and highly polished black boots, pulled up the blinds, drew back the bolts and opened the doors of Harper's on the Boulevard. All four were in the shop that day for they expected it to be busy, whilst in the refurbished, scrubbed, polished and spotlessly clean kitchen, Mrs Petty stood at the ready with the kettles boiling and several dainty trays set out with china teapots, cups and saucers and dozens of "fancies", biscuits of every sort, slices of Cook's almond cheesecake and neat square portions of Celie's pound cake. They did not of course, expect the ladies who would take tea to come into the shop at this hour but Cook wanted her staff to be on hand to see the right way of things and to be where she might need to call on them. Ivy's gentlemen had been left a cold breakfast for the first time since she had turned her little home into a boarding house but they could like it or lump it, she declared briskly, knowing full well that not one of them would desert the homely, well-fed comfort of her board. The last few days had been "bloody murder", she and Cook had privately told one another as they set out on the shelves the splendid bottled display of preserved greengages in syrup, morello cherries, nectarines and peaches in brandy and many others, each shining jar tied round its neck with a distinctive bottle-green ribbon edged in gold. There was plum jam, raspberry jam, rhubarb jam, strawberry, all the fruits of the summer, the small white labels on the jars edged in dark green and gold, describing in Celie's stylish copperplate what each one contained. There were jars of Everton toffee, wrapped individually and by hand, before being placed so many to a jar, in their shining and tempting glory, balanced in groups along the shelves. Small tables rented for the occasion stood about the shop, each one covered in a green-and-white check table-cloth with a small glass vase of mixed flowers in the centre and a couple of chairs to accommodate their customers. Glass-fronted cabinets sparkled and winked like diamonds. The oak floor was polished to a high gloss.

The big mahogany-encased clock ticked the minutes away and they waited, Dan at the door ready to spring forward and open it at the sign of the first customer, Cook and Celie behind the counter, Kate stationed by the door which led into the kitchen, in position for the first tray to be handed to her. The three women were not in bright green as Kate had hoped but in identical dark bottle-green cotton, crisp and well ironed with neat white collars and cuffs, sober but well-made, tasteful with dainty white caps and aprons so that all three looked as though they might be maidservants in a "good" family's home. In fact, just *how* the discriminating ladies of the "carriage trade" Jess Harper hoped to attract would like to see them in their own homes.

It was ten o'clock on the dot when the doorbell tinkled and the first customer put her nose hesitantly round the door. Several passing ladies, some with baby carriages and perhaps on their way to Sefton Park had stopped to study the display in the window but after squinting at this and that, standing back then pressing their noses to the glass, unaware that they were being watched, moving this way and that as though undecided on whether to come in or not whilst the four inside held their breath – each one moved on.

The woman who entered, though she was neatly dressed, was not of the carriage trade class. She was all in black, including her hat. She carried a shopping basket and when Cook stood up and gave her a courteous good morning, she seemed to shy nervously. She looked about her, almost in apprehension, Cook thought, eyeing the two pretty girls and the smart doorman with wary eyes. She came to a full stop just inside the doorway.

'Can I help you?' Cook asked in her Briar Lodge accent.
'Well . . .'
'Won't tha' come in, lass?' Cook had weighed the woman up and with a sure instinct, left over from her own days of shopping for the Latimer larder, knew exactly her position in life. The "lass" it seemed had reassured the woman. 'Sit thi' down,' Cook continued, 'and have a cup of tea whilst tha' decide what tha' wants. See, try one of our . . .'
'Oh, no.' The woman seemed quite alarmed. 'I only came in to see how much your custard tarts were.'
'A penny each or six for fivepence.' Celie's voice seemed to take everyone by surprise and they all turned to look at

her. They were indeed a penny each but where had the six for fivepence come from?

'Oh . . . right . . . well, in that case I'll take a dozen.' The woman was clearly relieved, reaching for her purse and turning to look around her to see what other bargains might be available. 'And what about them fruit scones?' she asked whilst Kate and Dan held their breath. Cook sat down heavily on her stool and, smiling pleasantly, Celie came slowly round from the back of the counter, somewhat in the manner of an animal trainer who has no wish to startle the animal he is about to take on.

'A farthing each or six for a penny.'

The woman began to walk round the shop then, clearly interested now she had an idea of the price of things, studying what was displayed on the shelves whilst behind her Cook hurriedly signalled to Kate and Dan to make themselves scarce for it had become clear to her, as it had to Celie, that this woman, obviously a cook in a lower-middle-class home, had been overawed by the sheer magnificence of "Harper's" and its numerous staff. A lesson to be learned, she thought, suit the circumstances to the customer. A grand personage such as a housekeeper to a lady of Mrs Latimer's calibre would be gratified to have shop assistants falling all over her, but not the plain, no-nonsense cook or housekeeper in a lower-class household. And, if a woman such as this ordinary but decent cook, or even cook general, could be catered to, *and* an upper-class housekeeper to the gentry, then Cook would not complain since neither one, should they find themselves in her shop together, could take exception to the other. This one, who had now purchased a dozen custard tarts, a dozen fruit scones, a raised plate pie of steak and kidney and a jar of plum jam, would perhaps have a tight budget to keep to and so, with a little good will on both sides, could be accommodated and having been accommodated would tell others in similar circumstances.

The customer was pressed to a refreshing cup of tea and a slice of almond cheesecake, served by a deferential Kate who even bobbed her a curtsey which clearly delighted her, and having spent a satisfying half-hour, satisfying to both sides of the counter, she made her departure promising to call again later in the week.

'Good morning to you, Mrs . . . er . . . ?' She nodded her head affably at Cook who nodded back.

'Mrs Harper, madam.' In Jess Harper's world all cooks were called *Mrs*, married or not.

'Nay, call me Mrs Turpin, do,' the customer replied, clearly feeling at ease now and among friends.

They had no more than a dozen customers, almost every one exactly like Mrs Turpin, decent women shopping for their mistresses who might be the wife of a doctor; a manager in a shipping office; a draper in Lord Street, men in a small way of business who could afford one or perhaps two servants. But each one went away satisfied, saying they would certainly be back. There were one or two who were evidently the mistress themselves, coming perhaps from one of the neat semis further along the Boulevard and, having no servants, doing their own shopping.

The last, at just gone seven o'clock when they were despairing of what they would do with the pies, the custards, the cheesecakes and shortcakes, the muffins, macaroons, honey cakes and which could certainly not be got out again tomorrow, stepped down from a carriage and swept through the hastily opened door of the shop as though she knew full well it would part before her like the Red Sea. She wasted no time on words. She was Mrs Richmond, housekeeper to Mrs Morgan of Heaton Crescent, she said tartly, dignified and aloof, and needed one or two things for a small informal soirée her mistress was to put on this evening, her manner implying to Cook who knew about such things, that Mrs Morgan had sprung this on her housekeeper no more than ten minutes ago.

'What do you have that would be suitable?' she asked distantly.

Cook knew just what would be suitable since it had been her job for the past thirty years to cater to such affairs and within half an hour every tart and cake and biscuit was packed away in the Morgan carriage by the aristocratic coachman and the jubilant Dan.

'That's most of the perishables gone,' Cook exulted, 'an' we can 'ave a steak an' kidney pie for us tea . . .' but no sooner were the words out of her mouth than a little sharp-featured woman in a shawl pushed open the door and peeped, bird-like, into the shop.

'Owt left?' she twinkled.

'I beg your pardon.' Cook drew herself up to her full height, which was not a lot at the best of times. She had sat for most of the day on the high counter stool but her feet had not been *up* and they were hot and throbbing on the end of her billowing legs. It made her testy.

'Nay, don't be like that, queen. I'm not askin' fer 'andouts. I've a stall down by docks an' if you've 'owt yer want ter get shut of, like stuff that'll not keep, then I'll tekk it off yer 'ands. If price is right, that is.'

'Well . . .'

'Come in, Mrs . . . ?' Celie moved forward, the singular sweetness of her smile as bright for this old stall woman as it had been for Mrs Richmond, 'and we'll have a look. You go and have a sit down, Cook,' she said, turning to Jess Harper, 'I can manage this.'

It was almost nine o'clock and they were sprawled about the kitchen table drinking tea when Celie came through. Ivy had gone to see to her gentlemen but before she had left, she had washed and dried the cups and saucers, plates and teapots, even those that had not been used, putting them away in the cupboard, and the kitchen glowed, clean and fragrant and tidy as the last of the low September sun crept through the open back door and laid its rays across the table. Dust motes rose in it, drifting lazily and Kate stirred a little, disturbing them further.

'D'you want a cuppa, Celie?' she asked, smooth-tongued, ready it appeared, to leap to her feet but Celie put a hand on her shoulder.

'No, not yet. I'm just going to do the till.'

'The till?'

'Yes, I know exactly what each item we have sold today cost to make and I'm going to work out how much profit we made. Of course we have to consider the rent and our wages, the overheads . . .'

'Overheads?'

'Mmm, unseen things like the gas, coal, things like that . . .'

'Bloody hell.'

'*Kate*, you know I will not have . . .'

'Sorry, Cook. An' how much d'you reckon then?' Kate hitched up to where Celie had put the day's takings on the table, beside the "accounting book" in which she meant to keep a record of daily transactions.

'Well, give me a minute. It takes a bit of reckoning.'

There was silence whilst Celie added up a column of figures, wrote down something at the bottom of it and then started on a second.

In the overgrown garden and about half-way down its length, Dan could be seen just standing, hands in his pockets, a cigarette between his lips. He seemed to be deep in contemplation of what he was to plant there when he had a minute, and his demeanour was one of deep, dreaming contentment.

'Well?' Kate prompted, and in her chair on the other side of the table, Cook eased her legs into a more comfortable position, if such a state existed. She'd a twinge just beneath her left breast an' all, which troubled her, but it'd go when she'd had a bite to eat, she was sure. Now what was that girl saying about profits, bless her?

'Two pounds fifteen shillings and elevenpence three farthings.'

'What, in one day?' Kate was clearly amazed.

'Yes, and considering we had no more than a dozen customers, I think it's a good start.'

'*A good start*! I think it's bloody marvellous.'

'Well, not quite that . . .'

'£2 – 15 – 11¾d six days a week, that's . . .' Kate's eyes became unfocused at the startling sum involved, doing her best with a task which was beyond her, that of multiplying the day's profit by six.

'That's £16 – 15s – 10½d,' Celie reckoned quickly.

'£16 – 15s – 10½d.' Kate's voice was filled with awe. She

didn't earn that in a year and the shop had, or would, earn it in a *week*! 'Bloody hell!'

'Kate Mossop, I won't tell you again.'

'Sorry, Cook, but . . .'

'Well, of course, if Mrs Richmond hadn't bought all that stuff,' Celie went on, 'we'd have been left with it and we would probably have only just broken even.'

'What does that mean?'

'We'd have earned nothing.'

'But we did, and you heard all them old women. They're coming back, they said. And I bet that old biddy will an' all.'

'Kate . . .'

'Sorry, Cook,' and neither Cook nor Celie noticed the proprietorial *we* which had figured in Kate's jubilation.

And so it continued, slowly at first, each day bringing curious ladies to have a look at what was being described, as it got about, as superb food at reasonable prices, not just the "fancy stuff", which was not always to the taste of the plain and decent folk who lived in the semis, along the Boulevard, but the wholesome, reasonably priced meat patties, scones, biscuits, tarts and home-baked bread which was. In a month, Cook and Celie were working so long and at such a killing pace at the kitchen range, turning out the fruit pies, cooked mousses, fancy pastries and dozens and dozens of varieties of creams, jellies, preserves and confectionery of all sorts, they became increasingly aware that they must have extra staff. Kate could not cook but under Celie and Cook's guidance, she had tried hard and done well in the shop, perfecting a quick and deferential manner towards the customers, whilst Cook and Celie cooked and baked for six, eight, ten hours a day in the kitchen to produce what she sold. Dan had a bicycle with two enormous baskets, one at the front and one at the back, with a neatly painted sign advertising HARPER'S ON THE BOULEVARD hanging from the crossbar. He spent the best part of the day delivering to the back doors of the substantial residences in Heaton Crescent, Williamson Square, Huskison Terrace, Gladstone Drive, Victoria Terrace and all the dozens of houses whose cooks and housekeepers made their purchases at "Harper's".

It went beyond even Cook's wildest dreams and as for Kate, she was clearly under the impression that they would be millionaires by the month-end. Her wages were now fifteen shillings a week and if she and the shop continued to do as well as they had, Cook told her, she might expect another rise soon.

Celie Marlow said nothing about rises or her hopes of being a millionaire but she and Cook exchanged understanding glances, for their hopes and ambitions ran on exactly the same lines and in the same direction.

Now, in the pale spring blooming which lasts for but a short time in the seasons of the year, Celie and Prudence strolled arm in arm along Bold Street through the frail warmth of the sunshine whilst Celie searched for the words with which she might convey to Pru her own feelings without upsetting her friend.

'I only wish,' she continued, 'that your . . . family could be . . . a part of your life. That your Mama and Papa might see how you and Jethro have . . . oh, forgive me, Pru. It's nothing to do with me but it seems so unfair that, though you have made a perfectly suitable, *loving* marriage, you are still judged . . . that . . . oh, damn it . . .'

'I know what you mean, Celie, but it would never do, you see, if the classes . . .' laughing harshly. '. . . were allowed to mix freely. No matter how mismatched a couple might be, if they are of the same class, a marriage between them is considered quite right and proper. And vice versa. Jethro and I . . . well . . . his father was a coal miner, a poor, hard-working man who did his best to give his children a decent life but failed because he was exploited by the mine owners who took the profit and paid him a pittance. Only Jethro managed to escape it and through his own endeavours, became what he is. But he is still not "good enough" for me, or so my Mama would have it, and naturally, she will allow no one from Briar Lodge to . . . call on me, not even Papa. Especially Papa. Of course Richard comes from time to time. His battalion is stationed at Warrington now and so he gets home quite regularly. To tell the truth he sometimes slips up here and stays with Jethro and me without Mama knowing. He says the company we keep is far jollier than Briar Lodge, though Mama would throw a fit if she knew. He is still the same, always up to some mischief. Do you remember him on that day . . . well, of course you do, how could you forget? How could you ever forget any of my family who were so cruel to you and Cook and the others . . . Celie . . . Celie . . . is anything wrong? . . .' for Celie had stumbled for a moment, leaning heavily on Prudence's arm and but for its support might have fallen. Several gentlemen had noticed and hesitated, ready to come forward with a steadying hand, for the young lady was very lovely.

Celie shook herself out of the dizzying greyness which had fallen over her like a thick dragging cloak at the mention of Richard Latimer's name. She smiled up at Pru, squaring her shoulders.

'No, really, I must have caught my heel. I'm fine. Now then, shall we have tea at the Adelphi? Though I make my own until I am sick of the sight of them, I can never get enough of their chocolate éclairs.'

Chapter Nineteen

Celie walked slowly along the narrow, neatly mown grass path which ran in a straight line down half the length of what was always called "Dan's garden" just as though it belonged exclusively to him. And so it did really since it was Dan who had laboured here in every hour of daylight which was not taken up with the business of the shop ever since they had moved to the Boulevard.

On either side of her were his flower-beds, the edges white and lacy with thrift and alyssum, and behind them, at varying heights until they reached the tall, moss-covered walls were the vivid colours of verbena, calceolarias, geraniums, petunias, of delphinium and hollyhock, the long spikes of gladioli and the pompons of dahlia, spilling against one another in the rich, well-fed soil Dan had created. Lining the walls were well-pruned apple trees, plum and pear trees, stretching from the back steps of the house to the end of what Dan called the "flower-garden". Here, half-way along the garden, were three steps edged by a wall of the same height leading up to an ornamental bird-bath on either side of which were two stone tubs erupting with the rich blue of plumbago. Beyond that and hidden by the growth of oak and elm and sycamore was the vegetable garden: peas and beans, cabbage and broccoli, young lettuce, carrots, turnips, onions and spinach, potatoes and radish, all growing happily cheek by jowl in the neat, well-planned, lovingly tended order which was the breath of life to Dan Smith's soul.

He had built a greenhouse at the furthest end, clearing a space where the sun might reach, and in it tomatoes ripened, grapes grew sweetly on the vine beside apricots and peaches, nectarines and early strawberries.

Beside the greenhouse was a small secluded area, hidden from the house and from the houses on either side. Dan had paved it, and growing up the wall was the beginning of clematis and honeysuckle and standing against the wall was a wrought-iron, white-painted garden bench.

Celie sat down on it in the shaft of sunlight which found its way there from noon onwards. She leaned her back tiredly against the bench and stretched out her legs, crossing them at the ankle, letting the high-pitched tension in which she and Cook worked from morning until night flow slowly out of her, a long, shuddering sigh going with it. Closing her eyes she tipped her face to the sun and became absolutely still, so still that a couple of whitethroats which had built a nest somewhere in the vicinity winged down to pick about the spade which Dan had left leaning against the wall, almost at her feet.

Against the sepia, sun-tinted canvas of her closed eyelids *his* face came. Slowly it drew into focus, not as she had seen him the last time, the last *appalling* time, but on that enchanted day almost eighteen months ago. A timeless day. A perfect day which she had never forgotten and though she told herself she must, she doubted she ever would. She had not allowed herself to brood over it, for what was the use? She had her life to get on with, as he had his but it had seemed to her on each occasion she had been alone with him that there had been a . . . what could she call it? . . . a . . . a HARMONY . . . was that it? A unity which she had known with no one before. She had not understood it. She had been young, smiling ruefully at herself as the thought whispered in her mind, and still was and she knew nothing of men, of love, of what took place between a man and a woman but if what she had experienced with Prudence Latimer's brother was any part of it then it was much to her liking. His kisses, the first she had known, had surprised her in their sweetness and she had responded eagerly, trusting him, waiting for him to show her what she should do next. It had been a new and, it seemed to her, a delightfully dangerous experience but she had gone with him on that first journey right willingly. He had been gentle with her but beneath his gentleness she had sensed something held tightly in check, a vigour and warmth she did not know but instantly recognised for it had begun to bud in her. In the hansom cab, as they raced back to Belle, he had bruised her lips for a moment and she had heard him groan, then he had cradled her head to his shoulder, murmuring something to himself she had not been able to hear.

Those moments, that day, had shone in her for weeks as she waited, waited for something, whatever it might be, but nothing had happened. He had gone. Made no effort to see her again. Nothing. Not a word, or a note, and sadly, for the day had contained, at least for her, a shimmering loveliness, she had let the memory blur and except for quiet moments such as this, slip away into the past where memories rested. It had been nothing. To him it had been no more than a masculine dalliance, forgotten, as she must forget it. Their last encounter on the day when he and Dan had fought, and when his eyes had told her that not only was the quality of magic they had seemed to share no longer there, it had never existed, was something which was mercifully softened, ill-defined as though the remembrance was too hurtful to be retained.

She opened her eyes and sighed and the birds flew off in panic. She shifted a little on the bench, putting both hands to the back of her neck, massaging the ache there with tired fingers. She rested her head against the back of the seat, staring up into the densely clustered leaves of the sycamore tree.

'I don't know what to do,' she said out loud, then looked about her hastily in case someone should have heard her though who that someone could be was not clear in her mind. Cook had her feet up in the kitchen, drained to the very limit of her capacity by the grinding industry of her day, declaring that she didn't know how she was to get through the next hour, never mind the rest of the day. Celie knew the old woman was at the end of her tether. Could you be *too* successful? Celie had wondered during the last nine months whilst the four of them – five when Ivy lent a hand – had worked every hour that God sent in the fear that this might not last and best make the most of it, but it had not only lasted, it had grown to such proportions that they could not cope much longer in the premises which had once seemed so enormous, nor with the staff which again had appeared to be all they would need. Cook and herself to do the cooking, Kate in the shop, Ivy to help wherever it was needed, a daily to do the heavy cleaning and Dan to be handyman, gardener and delivery man. But it was not enough and decisions must now be made, by herself and by Cook on how they were to tackle the dazzling growth of "Harper's on the Boulevard"?

If only Cook would allow her to sell some of the "specialities" offered by the numerous travelling salesmen who now called regularly at the shop, those whom Cook sent on their way with "a flea in their ear"! They did their best to persuade her to purchase beautifully wrapped boxes of chocolate-covered liqueurs, marshmallows of every flavour, boxes of Turkish delight, French bonbons, crystallised ginger, glazed fruits, dates and figs and many "novelties" which were imported from other countries. But no, every single thing sold at Harper's must be made on the premises, Cook insisted, including sweets, chocolates – each one decorated by hand – and toffee, and Celie was afraid the work would kill her if she didn't let up soon. Hours and hours she spent on her feet until the flesh of her ankles ballooned over the tops of her boots and her face would become a violent and dangerous-looking puce. Her breathing was ragged at times and she would press her hand to her left breast whilst begging Celie not to fuss and to get on with what she was doing. Celie did her best to take as much as possible on to her own slender but strong shoulders, beseeching Cook to sit down and put her feet up, finding her jobs she could do sitting at the kitchen table.

Christmas had been a nightmare, the pair of them, on the night before Christmas Eve, not getting to their beds at all as they worked through the hours of darkness to complete all the orders which streamed over the counter for days on end. Everyone wanted Harper's mince pies, from the smallest "tartlet" to the largest plate pies, each one decorated with coloured marzipan holly and berries. Delicious Christmas cakes, spread with marzipan and icing, with "Merry Christmas" piped in red and green, enormous plum puddings, rich with brandy, tied in immaculate white muslin, chocolate Yule logs, each one to be as perfectly embellished with rich, dark chocolate, white icing sugar and marzipan holly berries as its neighbour. If it was not *perfect* – and Cook's idea of perfect was vastly different from, say, Kate Mossop's – it would not do for Cook, for no matter what the circumstances, the time of night or who it was for, she would not lower her standards, those she had perfected in thirty years' service as a cook and which she had passed on to Celie. What did not pass muster was saved for Gladys, the old stallholder, and there was many a sailor or dockie, or a dockie's missus who was rendered speechless by the delicacy and beauty of some "imperfect" concoction which had not passed the test of Cook's exactitude.

Kate had proved to be worth her weight in gold, even Cook admitted, working staunchly beside them far into the night, doing what she could in the chopping, mixing and blending, washing up the endless dishes, scouring the endless pans, her poor hands back to the state they had suffered when she was a lowly skivvy, only going to her bed when Cook insisted for, as Cook said, the lass would be on her feet in the shop for twelve hours the next day, dealing with customers and must not only be strong, willing and of good appearance, but *polite*, which would be difficult if she didn't get a good night's sleep, wouldn't it?

Kate had also taken to hanging over Celie when she did her accounting, a simple form of book-keeping which Celie herself had devised and which showed at once the profit the business was making. Kate had begun to master the figures, proving sharp and quick and when Celie was busy had even managed the task herself. She showed a great interest in the ordering of the enormous amounts of sugar, butter, flour, eggs and all the fine ingredients Cook and Celie put in their recipes, how much it all cost to put together and how to do so without waste.

And of course, Dan was their mainstay and support, taking upon himself the work of three men, which, when you thought about it, Cook said, was exactly what he was. There should *be* a lad for the garden, another to do the deliveries, whilst Dan supervised them both and maintained the good working order of the kitchen range, the gas mantles, the erratic boiler in the cellar, the squeaking hinges on the doors and the hundred and one jobs which needed doing about the place.

Which brought Celie back to the problem of expansion. *Expansion*! It was a word which frightened Cook, though she would not admit it. What Cook had imagined, hoped for, dreamed of, grasped, had become real. It was here in her hands. Her own business which *she* had brought about. She had been wise, cunning even in her choice of the district in which to start it, in her choice of shop. Lucky in her staff who were devoted and hard-working but somehow it had all become a bit unwieldy, top-heavy, running away on a collision course which in her simplicity Cook had not perceived, nor made any arrangements for. She had imagined the kind of establishment in which the discriminating lady of Liverpool would be able to purchase the very best food at a fair price. Quality goods which Jess Harper and Celie Marlow would produce and sell with Dan at their backs to see to all the things a handyman sees to. She had not bargained for Kate Mossop but Kate had fitted in and proved her worth in the only way Cook recognised, but it was all getting away from her and she couldn't cope with it. She couldn't understand it when Celie told her they must "move forward" or they would "go backwards", for what on earth did *that* mean, for goodness sake? She was happy with this, just as it was and how could they possibly manage another shop, if that was what Celie was after? She couldn't go traipsing all over Liverpool looking for suitable premises and who'd do the cooking at this new place Celie had set her heart on? Becoming fractious, because if Celie thought that she, Cook, could manage here on her own whilst Celie waltzed off to . . . to wherever she had in mind, then she could think again. She was frightened, Celie could see it in her eyes, frightened of this success to which she herself had given birth. The autocrat of the Briar Lodge kitchen was gradually giving over her rulership into the increasingly capable hands of her protégée.

Celie sighed and stood up, moving slowly up the garden to the house.

'I'm off to town,' she told them as she entered the kitchen. 'You don't need me for an hour, do you, Cook? Everything's done and Mrs Petty said she'd give Kate a hand in the shop if it was needed. Monday's always a slow day . . .' – if such a thing existed in the swiftly moving routine of Harper's week – '. . . ah, here she is now . . .' as Ivy appeared from the direction of the shop, already removing the pins from her sensible black hat.

'Nay lass, tekk thissen off tot' shops an' if tha' sees a nice bit o' haddock fetch me a piece fer me tea, will tha'? I just fancy a nice bit o' haddock.'

'Where yer goin', Celie?' Kate hissed as Celie walked through the shop in which several ladies were "browsing" round the well-stocked shelves. Celie Marlow had astounded them all by becoming friendly with the daughter of their previous mistress, "popping round" to Croxteth Drive which was within walking distance of Harper's and where, it appeared, she was always welcome. And how had *that* friendship come about, Kate would have liked to know, but Celie was uncommunicative on that score, as indeed she was on many others. So, was she off there now, Kate would dearly have liked to ask but somehow, in the last few months Celie had changed from that rather reserved girl she had once been to being . . . well, "hoity-toity", Kate would have called her, "stuck-up" an' all. She had run to do Cook's bidding at Briar Lodge, not having a lot to say on anything much, nor joining in the "fun" Kate had loved to instigate and now would you look at her. Still quiet and hard-working but giving orders, to Kate Mossop, to Dan, and even to Cook who asked *her* what was to be done next! She it was who decided what to order and how much and when. What "lines" were to be popular and therefore to be continued and what would not be repeated, though there were not many of those. She handled the tradesmen who called, ordering what she needed and if it was not up to *her* standard, sending it back without a qualm. She handled the money, taking it to the bank where it was deposited in the account Cook had opened. Kate knew this because she had seen all the paperwork and a tidy sum it was, an' all. Apparently Celie had one as well, a bank account, putting part of her wages in it each week and when it had grown a bit she meant to "invest" it, whatever that meant and make it "work" for her, whatever *that* meant, and why didn't Kate do the same, she asked, but Kate didn't trust it. She liked to have her money where she could see it, what was left of it when she'd spent a bob or two.

No, Celie Marlow was a deep one and Kate would have to keep her eyes peeled and her senses sharp for she'd not let that little upstart put one over on her again.

Mr Pembroke was surprised to see Miss Marlow when his grim-visaged clerk showed her in, leaping to his feet and bowing her to the chair in front of his desk. It was a pleasant day, he remarked politely, wouldn't she agree, his shrewd but kindly eyes studying the young woman who sat quietly before him. A kitchen maid a year ago and yet he'd defy anyone to recognise her as such now. She wore a simple tailor-made outfit in a pale, dove-grey batiste, the bodice of which had a high collar and revers of rich cream. The ankle-length skirt was gored with pleats down the back. She had on a cream straw boater which was tipped saucily over the tumble of her short curls, and tied about the crown were broad taffeta ribbons in stripes of dove grey and cream, falling across the brim and down between her shoulder-blades. Her gloves were cream kid and her reticule was made of the same material as her outfit. She carried a dainty cream silk parasol. She looked every inch a lady, and acted like one too, he told himself, having a pleasant, gracious manner which still held that hint of shyness and innocence which he and, he was sure, other men found pleasing.

'What can I do for you, Miss Marlow?' he asked her. He had enquired after Mrs Harper's health and the state of business though he was fully aware that "Harper's on the Boulevard" had exceeded everyone's expectations in that direction, including his own. A little gold mine, he had been led to believe, so what was this young woman who, to all intents and purposes, ran the business doing here in his office?

'I wasn't sure what . . . well, . . . you are the only person I . . .' Drawing her back up straight and lifting her head as though to say she did not care *how* foolish he might think her, she said,

'We need another shop, Mr Pembroke, and more staff.'

Mr Pembroke showed no surprise. He nodded his head, leaning back in his chair. He placed his palms together, putting his fingertips to his lips as though in prayer. He studied her closely and she showed no unease, meeting his appraisal without looking away.

'I see,' he said at last.

'Do you, Mr Pembroke? We are making a lot of money, sir, putting it in the bank when it seems to me that . . .'

'Yes, Miss Marlow?'

'When it seems to me we should be using it . . . well . . .' For a moment she became confused, '. . . when I say *we*, I mean Mrs Harper, for it's not mine.'

'I know what you mean, Miss Marlow, do go on.'

'You know we are the middle shop in a row of three.'

'Indeed I do. My client owns all three and I collect the rents for him.'

'The . . . the gentleman's clothiers on our left . . . well, Mr Pembroke, he is an elderly gentleman and when I was chatting to him several weeks ago it seemed to me that . . .'

'Yes, Miss Marlow?' Mr Pembroke prompted.

'He is, he tells me, ready for retirement but unfortunately as yet, he cannot afford to give up. Now I thought that . . .'

'Yes, Miss Marlow?'

'If it was made worth his while. If someone *bought* his lease, perhaps . . .'

'He might be persuaded to . . . move on?'

'Exactly.'

'And have you plans for the newsagent, sweets and tobacconist shop on your other side?'

Celie smiled delightedly, revealing her fine white teeth, and the small indent at the corner of her mouth deepened. The colour flowed beneath her creamy skin and her eyes were brilliant between her long, silky lashes. She looked quite enchanting as the serious young business woman fled away and a warm and humorous, extremely lovely young girl took her place.

'I see you understand me exactly, Mr Pembroke.'

'Indeed I do, Miss Marlow, but I'm afraid the owner of the shops might not be so . . . far-seeing. I know what you have done in the past . . . nine months, is it?'

'Yes, sir.'

'But he will only see it from his own point of view which is that he has two perfectly good, well-proven tenants who have paid their rent for years without causing him a moment's trouble. You are a new venture and though you have done well who is to say that will continue . . .'

'It will, Mr Pembroke.'

'I know that, Miss Marlow, but my client does not.'

'Can't you persuade him? Already the lady next door has been heard to complain that we are taking her chocolate and toffee trade with our home-made assortments and that the constant smell of our baking, though it is not unpleasant . . . well . . . if she were to take it into her head to leave . . . you know what I am saying, Mr Pembroke? I can see no reason why a small financial . . .'

'*A bribe*, Miss Marlow?' but Mr Pembroke's twinkling smile told her that he admired her tenacity.

'Call it what you like, Mr Pembroke, but I *want* those shops. I know where I can get good staff and with . . . well, perhaps a loan from the bank, I could extend, refurbish, move into other lines so that . . .'

Her face glowed into his, its cool serenity gone in the high excitement her own plans, and the divulging of them to him had charged in her. There were pink roses at her cheekbone and she leaned towards him confidentially. She reminded him of a child who is to go on some exciting excursion the anticipation of which has quite gone to her head.

'I could knock the three shops into one and above them, on the first floor I would like to create a . . . well . . . a tea room. No, something more elegant than a tea room, though what to call it is not clear to me yet. Very comfortable, smart, where ladies and gentlemen might stop on their way to or from the park. Sefton Park, I mean, which is very popular. We are just a short walk away. And of course, with new kitchens which we badly need, and larger, we could cater to so many more people. The shop is in a prime situation, on that corner, and is begging to be converted into a . . . well . . . a . . . oh, Mr Pembroke . . .' Her enthusiasm was a lovely thing to see and Mr Pembroke found he was leaning forward in order to get the benefit of it. 'And then there is Princes Park directly opposite. Even the shape of Harper's would be enhanced by making the three shops into one, don't you agree? Like a small crescent, in a way, and with big windows overlooking the park, the restaurant would be very well placed. I would need good girls to serve in it, another cook I could train to my standards, a delivery boy and a gardener's lad since with three shops *and* three gardens our produce would treble and Dan couldn't do it all . . .' She smiled brilliantly. 'Oh, Lord, listen to me run on.' She put her hand to her mouth as though suddenly aware that her own rapture might not be shared by this busy and hard-headed businessman. Her eyelashes fluttered, not flirtatiously, Mr Pembroke was well aware, since that was not in her nature, but quite disarming nevertheless.

'And what does Mrs Harper think of all this, Miss Marlow?' he asked gently.

Her breath sighed out of her, taking her lovely excitement with it.

'Well . . .'

'You have not discussed it with her?'

'Yes, to a degree but she is . . .'

'Not quite so enthusiastic as you are?'

'Mr Pembroke, you must understand. Cook is elderly and is quite . . . content with what we have done already. She has not my . . . my . . .'

'Fervour?'

'She is . . . I am perhaps . . . the more ambitious now. Last year, when we opened, I had no idea that it would be such an enormous success, and so quickly. We *must* expand, Mr Pembroke, but we simply haven't the room nor the staff to accommodate our growth. Will you not help me . . . help *us*? I know I can persuade Cook . . .'

'It's not a question of *my* help, Miss Marlow. I can certainly talk to the owner for you and perhaps have a word with the bank manager where Mrs Harper has her account. If, and it's a big "if", they can be persuaded, there is still the question of the owner of the two shops.'

'So many "ifs", Mr Pembroke.'

'Indeed, Miss Marlow.' He stood up, ready to bow her from the room. 'But leave it with me, my dear. I will do my best for you.'

'I know you will, Mr Pembroke, and thank you.' They smiled at one another as he took her hand. Nodding pleasantly at the clerk, whose own eyes were seen to soften as she swept by him, she stepped out into the bustling, sunlit street. Her mind was still seething with excited, scattered thoughts but as she moved along Water Street she became aware that there was a great commotion coming from the direction of the docks, just beyond George's Dock gates.

"Sailor town", Liverpool was called, because of its huge population of seafarers in transit, and many of these, along with multitudes of the inhabitants of the great seaport, seemed to be pouring in an excited, voluble stream down towards the waterfront. Dock workers, stevedores, tally clerks and porters, men in cream straw boaters, similar to her own but without the ribbons, and check suits, men in round, felt "bowlers", with walking sticks of light whangee cane, men in caps and open, collarless shirts and in their midst women in shawls, women in light summer bonnets, some with frilly parasols. There were children and dogs; there were Shire horses, leaning into the strain of pulling enormous carts loaded with barrels, packages and bales, all to be unloaded into the vast transit sheds where cargoes were stored before being manhandled on to the great ships.

Quite dazed by it all but beginning to catch the fever of exhilaration with which the crowd seemed to be charged, Celie allowed herself to be drawn along with them, crossing through the traffic of Strand Street, beneath the massive and yet delicate fretwork of the Overhead Railway, through St Nicholas Place and down to the landing stage.

The crowds were enormous. A band was playing some-where, stirring martial music which set the foot tapping and encouraged small boys to march in step like soldiers off to war. There were flags flying and out on the river the shriek of ships' sirens rent the warm air of the June afternoon. The quayside was seething with hundreds of people and for the space of a few seconds Celie was taken back to that cold December day when she and Richard Latimer had stood together in their tiny, dream-like world containing just the two of them. Now, as then, the dock area was filled with a yelling, whistling mass of humanity, all doing their best to get as close as they could to the side of the enormous liner which was berthed there without actually being shoved into the narrow strip of water separating ship from shore.

But the dock on which she stood was not stationary today as it had been then. It was new, a brand new and enormous *floating* landing stage which could accommodate more than one ocean-going liner at a time. It rose and sank like a gently moving ship and directly behind it but at a height of about twenty feet in the air was the brand, spanking new Riverside Railway Station and railway line which had brought passengers directly on a special train from London. From the station, and discharging the travellers from train to ship in the most convenient manner, was a covered, mobile gangway, which, judging by the bustle which seethed at its end, was just about to be withdrawn from the liner's deck, severing its last link with the shore.

The newly opened station and the ship which was at the moment berthed there had been visited only yesterday by the Lord Mayor and Lady Mayoress of Liverpool accompanied by His Highness the Shahzada, son of the Ameer of Afghanistan. On June 12th, two days ago, the very first passenger train had been run here for those who were to sail on the Atlantic liner *Germanic*. The great ship had left the stage with a full complement of saloon, steerage passengers and cargo at two fifteen in the afternoon, Dan had read out to them from the *Liverpool Echo*, and on the same day, owing to the improved capacity of the berth, the Cunard steamer *Catalonia* and the White Star steamer *Teutonic* had both been berthed at the same time. Cook had been most impressed, she said, and would have liked to have seen it for it must have been a fine sight. She'd witnessed a few sailings and berthings in her time, both steam and sail, she'd told them wistfully, and once had almost married a . . . well, never mind that and Dan was to get on with what he was reading!

Today it was the turn of the *Campania* and by the look of it she might cast off late, Celie heard one official tell another. So densely packed with excited sightseers had the route between Waterloo station and the terminus become, the train had been forced to slow down. At Edge Hill a stop had been made whilst the crowds cheered the special engine before it drew the train through the Waterloo tunnel.

Celie enjoyed the spectacle as much as the rest of the crowd whilst passengers and their luggage were hastily transferred from the train to the straining ship and when at last the vessel was inched away from the stage, blowing her whistle to signal her departure, the tugs taking the strain as they pulled the liner sideways into the river, Celie found she had tears in her throat for it was truly a magnificent sight.

The moment was poignant, instilled with the strong emotion arrivals and departures evoke and when she turned and he was at her back she found she was not surprised. It was as though, eighteen months ago, she had bade him an emotional farewell in this very spot where so many partings had been enacted, and now the reverse was taking place as fate, chance, whatever caused these things, had brought him back to her.

They looked at one another, face to face, and yet with a great distance between them. Neither smiled, then slowly, so slowly it seemed to take for ever, he raised his hand, placing the palm of it against her cheek. His eyes which, moments ago, had been a clear tawny brown, became the colour of dark chocolate as the pupils widened and in them was a deep emotion which softened the bones of her. She swayed a little towards him and at once his arms rose to hold her.

'Christ Jesus,' he whispered, 'it is still the same.'

Chapter Twenty

He held her hand in the hansom cab, lifting it tenderly to his lips with both of his own in an attempt to soothe its trembling, smoothing her cheek with his fingertips and bending his head to look deep into her eyes.

'Hush now, hush, it'll be all right,' he whispered to her almost as if she was a tearful child who had taken a fall. But despite the uncontrollable quivering which ran through her inwardly, she was surprisingly calm. 'We're nearly there now,' he murmured, 'it'll be all right.'

They drew up on the broad gravel path at the front of Prudence and Jethro Garside's large detached house on Croxteth Drive and even before the cab driver got down from his seat, Prudence herself was at the door. She had never concerned herself with the niceties of polite society which said that the mistress of the house must never answer her own doorbell and her maidservants were used to her by now. Celie felt the quiver of laughter touch her. Laughter which she instinctively knew Richard shared, laughter which had been slowly bubbling up inside her ever since she had stepped into his arms. It was not the laughter which was caused by amusement, though Prudence had ever been the one to create that, but the laughter of happiness, of sheer radiant uncontained happiness which she realised, now that she had it, had been missing in her life, except on that one day, her heart reminded her. She had known deep contentment with Cook, a knowledge of comfort and shelter when she was with Dan, a fine sense of fun, enjoyment, rich pleasure with Prudence in what they had shared together during the past two years, but never this joyful longing-to-sing-and-dance happiness which was bursting in her now. She felt as light as a soap bubble, ready to drift up and up and if she never had another moment like this again, she thought, she would know how it was and never complain. Never. And yet she knew deep inside her that no matter how many times it was tested, this happiness would always endure as long as she was with Richard.

'Dear God, what on earth is the matter with the girl?' Prudence gasped, running down the wide steps, her skirts bunched up about her ankles in a way her Mama would have deplored. 'Is she intoxicated . . . ?' Then she came to an abrupt stop. She put a hand to her mouth which had opened soundlessly and her eyes widened. Perhaps it was her own knowledge of joy, of the luminous happiness she had found in her marriage to Jethro that gave Prudence the awareness of what was in Celia Marlow and her own brother. Neither spoke, merely smiled, first at her then at each other, just as though it was completely natural to be as they were, so completely right there was no need of explanations.

'I found her down by the docks,' Richard said foolishly.

'Really.' Prudence's voice had asperity in it, but there was a smile tacked about it. 'Well, you'd best bring her in. Tea, Nora,' she said over her shoulder to a hovering, deferential little maid, 'and thank the dear Lord I had no callers, not that there are many of those. The old sort, I mean.' She plucked Celie from Richard's sheltering protection, led her up the steps and into her large, square hallway.

'Take Miss Marlow's hat, Sally,' she ordered another smiling bobbing housemaid, 'and my brother's. We'll be in the drawing room. Now then, the pair of you, come in to the fire. Really, I know it's not cold but I do love a fire don't you? I cannot bear to see an empty grate . . .'

'Oh, do shut up, Pru. You sound like Mama rambling on about fires and grates. Aren't you going to ask us . . . ?'

'No I'm not, Richard Latimer. I'm not going to ask Celie *anything*. She looks quite stunned and yet I do believe I recognise that look in her eyes . . .'

'She was wandering . . .'

'I was not wandering, really I wasn't, Richard. I was watching the *Campania* making ready to sail from the new landing stage and when I turned round you were there . . .'

'I know, I'd been watching you for quite five minutes.' His eyes glowed into hers and Celie felt the impact of them strike her an exquisite blow. His long mouth curled upward in the most devastating way, making her heart move inside her with such joy she had great difficulty in stopping herself from placing her fingertips against it. There seemed to be a message in his expression, a kind of communication he knew she would understand, it said, and when she did it left her flushed and breathless.

'It seemed rude somehow,' he went on, 'to watch someone when they are not aware of it. Like a Peeping Tom, but I couldn't resist it. You were like a child, so excited . . .'

'Richard . . .' Celie glanced under her lashes at the open-mouthed Prudence, but Richard put out a hand and of its own volition, her own rose to cling to his.

'. . . your head turned from side to side as you watched everything that was happening, smiling, quite enthralled and every time you moved, your hat bobbed and the ribbons on it bounced on your neck. Other men were watching you too . . .'

'Oh, Richard, you exaggerate . . .'

'How can I exaggerate anything so . . .'

'*Richard*! You have not forgotten my presence, I hope. Really, I sound like some stern nanny reproving an unruly child, but wouldn't you like to . . . well, be *alone*, when you . . . say these things to Celie? She is quite embarrassed . . .'

'No, I am not, Prudence.'

'Well, I am, and I suggest we sit down . . . no, Celie, you sit over here next to me where Richard can look at you as he obviously wants to do . . .'

There was a small disturbance in the hall, then the drawing room door opened and the large frame of Jethro Garside filled the opening. He held open the door as no "gentleman" would, to allow the housemaid and her tea trolley to pass through, then followed her, his arms already rising to receive the rapturous welcome his wife seemed bent on bestowing upon him and under cover of their greeting which the housemaid, presumably accustomed to that as well, ignored, Richard leaned to touch Celie's hand.

'You see why I brought you here, don't you? I knew they would understand.'

She smiled down into her lap, overcome with the most delicious shyness, and when his fingers touched her chin, lifting it gently, she was devastated by the emotion working in his face.

They were completely oblivious to Prudence and Jethro who were watching them, spellbound, scarcely breathing, and it was not until the maid clattered the tea cups cheerfully in their saucers that Richard leaned back from Celie. He glanced round, saw his brother-in-law and at once leaped to his feet.

'Jethro, I didn't realise you were there,' holding out his hand.

'Mmm, I noticed you were . . . occupied,' smiling and taking Richard's outstretched hand. 'It's good to see you.'

'And you, Jethro. You're looking well.' It was evident that Richard Latimer and Jethro Garside had a great liking for one another.

'And Celie too,' Jethro continued. 'This is indeed a great pleasure. I was only saying to Prudence last night that we don't see enough of you, lass, and to remedy that, why don't you stay to dinner, both of you?'

As he spoke and with a lack of self-conciousness which was very engaging, he leaned down and placed an affectionate kiss on Celie's cheek. 'Unless either of you have other undertakings.'

'Well, I haven't and I'd be delighted.' Richard beamed and turned to Celie, perfectly sure that she would be too. 'Celie . . .'

'Cook will wonder . . .'

'The boy can take a message to Cook, Celie, and Jenkins will take you home . . .'

'Oh, there's no need. It's such a short distance, I can walk.'

'And I can walk with you, so that's settled.'

There was silence again as Richard's penetrating eyes

passed some message to Celie. Prudence slipped her hand into her husband's, turning to look up at him. She made a small grimace, shrugging her shoulders, as though to ask him what on earth he made of all this because she was quite bewildered at the suddenness of it all. It was very obvious, though Celie had made no mention of it in the last eighteen months, that there was something between her friend and her brother. Which was very strange. Richard had been home more than a few times since that day eighteen months ago when she and Jethro had slipped discreetly down to London to be married and Celie Marlow's name had never passed his lips. He had known of Prudence's friendship with Celie and of Celie's new venture with Mrs Harper for she was positive her Mama would have told him in detail about the mass betrayal of her servants. He had shown no more interest when Prudence had spoken of it than brotherly politeness demands and now here he was gazing at Celie Marlow as . . . well, as Jethro gazed at *her*, and Celie was returning it!

They drank tea and ate the small, rubber-like objects which Prudence's cook assured her were almond macaroons and which Jethro, when Prudence wasn't looking, threw into the fire. Celie bent her head, rosy and smiling, and Richard had to turn away spluttering and when Prudence turned to see what the merriment was all about, her face puzzled, he broke into roars of delighted laughter.

'Now what?' Prudence was clearly put out. Even Nora the bobbing little housemaid giggled into her hand and Celie felt herself relax in this lovely, love-filled atmosphere which, because of their feelings for one another, Prudence and Jethro had created about them. No one was excluded. The servants were very evidently aware of the way in which their master and mistress regarded one another but Prudence, despite her upbringing, was not domesticated and the standards in the house were not as high as her Mama would have had them, hence the cakes. But despite this her servants held her in high regard, taking no advantage, which servants will often do with a lax mistress.

The room in which they sat was luxuriously furnished, expensively so, rich with polished mahogany and satinwood, deep rose-coloured velvet chairs and sofas and carpets. There was heavy silk in cream and rose at the windows and a multitude of delicate ornaments, gilt-framed pictures and ticking clocks. There was a cheerful fire round which they sat, but though a lot of money had obviously been spent, the room was not grand. There was a profusion of flowering plants in pottery bowls, books lying about, some of them open as though the reader had just stepped out and would soon return to continue her enjoyment. There was even a large and beautiful golden retriever sprawled upon the rug before the fire, rolling her eye in welcome, her attitude saying that though they might do as they please, *this* was *her* place.

'I always wanted a dog,' Prudence said shortly when Celie had remarked on the arrival of the good-natured bitch soon after she had moved to the Boulevard. 'And Mama wouldn't allow it.' And that was that as far as Prudence was concerned. The dog's name was Bess.

The afternoon and evening continued in the same vein. There was no need to change for dinner, Prudence told Jethro, despite their guests, for Celie and Richard were family weren't they? They moved from the drawing room to take a turn round the extensive gardens which surrounded the house. The evening was as benign and perfect as only a June evening can be, clear and soft with the sky high and pale. The air was mild. The sun was moving down towards the stretch of trees which bordered the garden, the sky beginning to turn to a luminous lemon colour running into green. Jethro and Richard had strolled on, each holding a glass of sherry in one hand and in the other, a fragrant cigar, the smoke wreathing about their heads in the still air. Prudence cared not a jot for the custom of making the gentlemen smoke their cigars in the billiard room or the garden and Jethro might light his wherever he cared to, even in the bedroom. She *liked* the smell of cigar smoke, she said and once more, *that* was that, for Prudence Garside revelled in her new-found freedom to do as she pleased.

There was a dovecote in the middle of the slightly sloping lawn and the gentlemen stopped for a moment to admire the fine sight of the white doves in flight before they settled in fluted splendour on its roof. The sun caught the darkness of Richard's hair, putting a haze of chestnut about it and as Celie walked towards him, he turned, and beside her, even his sister was affected by the expression in his eyes as they fell on Celie.

'Dear God,' she whispered, 'oh, dear Lord . . .'

He held out his hand and Celie took it and without a word, leaving Jethro and Prudence again with their mouths foolishly open, they moved slowly down the garden, Richard's head bent to Celie's.

'This is . . . serious.' Prudence's voice was low as she slipped her arm in her husband's.

'Yes, does it matter? You married beneath you, my darling.'

'Of course I didn't.' Her voice was tart.

'Come now, Prudence. Don't pretend.'

'Oh, *that*. That's foolish and you know it. We *both* know it.'

'Of course we do, but are you saying that it would be different between Richard and Celie, if it came to that?'

'Mama cared nothing for me so it didn't really matter *who* I married in that respect, but Richard is the eldest son and is expected to make a decent marriage. His son will be the eldest son, and so on, d'you see?'

'Oh, yes, I do see, but surely things are not as strict as they once were.' He did not wish to hurt his beloved wife by saying what he actually thought which was "What and who are the Latimers anyway? It's not as if there was a title involved, only a great deal of money." 'Celie is a lovely girl,' he went on, 'beautifully mannered, quietly spoken. She dresses well and is intelligent. A fit wife . . .'

'Not for Richard, my love. She is . . . was . . . a kitchen maid. The daugher of the family gardener and as such . . .'

'*Prudence*, I'm amazed to hear you speak like that . . .'

'This is not *me* speaking, Jethro. This is *them*. *Society*. And have you forgotten Richard's career as a soldier? He is an officer in a good regiment and will do well, but not if his wife is a kitchen maid.'

'Christ Almighty, Prudence, must you be so . . . blunt?'

'I'm only telling you what *they* will say, Jethro.'

'But look at the pair of them.'

'I *am* doing, my dearest love, but really, can you tell me I am wrong? Dear God, I love Celie like a sister, but I love Richard too, and I can see nothing but adversity ahead for them. They are both strong, but are they strong enough?' Jethro shook his head in denial but the expression on his face told his wife that though he deplored it, he knew she was right.

Celie had to leave early, she said, since she rose at four in the morning to start the baking.

'*Four*!' Richard was aghast and Prudence was very definitely aware, even then, of his horror at the thought of the beautiful, fragile girl from whom, all the way through dinner, he could not tear his gaze, donning a workmanlike overall and setting herself to the task of baking. She could see the conflict begin in him, even then.

They walked in silence for a while. They did not touch though Celie was conscious of his hand ready at her elbow should she so much as stumble. She was conscious of his tall, upright figure, the figure of a soldier, his head erect, his stride, though he did his best to shorten it to hers, long and graceful. She kept her gaze ahead as they walked beside the railings which bordered Sefton Park. The leaves on the trees just inside the park trembled softly in an insubstantial eddy of wind, rustling above their heads.

A noisy commotion of sparrows inside an ivied tree disturbed the twilight then died away to a sleepy murmur as the brown owl which had come upon them flew off to another perch. It shrieked a time or two '*Ke – wik, ke – wik*', then it too settled. There was a half-moon rising above the monument across the park, silvering the silent frozen figures of Victoria and her Albert, turning the well-kept shrubs, the formal rows of summer flowers, the neatly trimmed lawns and the surface of the unruffled lake to a tranquil, frosted pearl. It was still mild and the sky was clear. The darkness settled about them alternating with circles of muted gold where the gas lamps cast their glow on the pavement. As they stepped into one, he put a hand on her arm and turned her gently to face him.

'Have you any idea how lovely you are?' he murmured

putting a finger to her chin. His face was vulnerable, made defenceless by the deep emotion which filled his heart and yet the question was seriously asked. She did not know how to answer it. She kept her eyes lowered, defenceless herself against the onslaught of feeling his words, his merely being there had induced in her. She hardly dare raise her eyes to his and when she did she felt her heart lurch in her chest. Like a blow it was, but a blow which struck her joyfully, for his love for her was laid bare, naked and exposed, hers at the moment to do with as she pleased. He was a soldier, a fighting man, a warrior well able to guard his back against attack, whilst he fought the foe before him, but to Celie Marlow he yielded his sword, his strength, his armour.

'I had forgotten,' he continued, his voice ready to tremble. 'No, that's a lie. I had *made* myself forget. I told myself I had to. I thought . . . on the day my sister was married, that you were . . . that you and the man who did his best to kill me . . .' He tried to laugh though the sound he made was harsh. '. . . that you and he were . . . more than friends.'

'Dan and I . . . ?' Her voice was incredulous.

'Dan . . . is that the one? Well, no matter, he gave the impression that you were . . . and so I went away and told myself that I would put you out of my mind, but when I saw you today . . .' His voice trailed away and his hand cupped her cheek. 'It goes back to that day . . . five years ago now when I came home and found you in the hallway. Do you remember?'

'Oh yes,' she breathed, for indeed she did. She was looking up into his face with the earnest consideration of a child and he felt himself draw even closer to her so that there was a bare six inches between them. The lamplight which was reflected in her pale grey eyes, a candle in each one, was for a second extinguished as she blinked slowly. Her eyelashes fanned her cheeks and her lips parted in a sigh of pure enchantment. The moment was so exquisite. He had not said the words but he had no need to for what was in his heart was in hers. There was a silence about them, a silence which held them both in a small protected world of their own. A hansom cab clipped smartly along the road, the horses' hooves rattling on the road. Couples strolled in the mild summer darkness, returning home after an evening in the park. A dog barked and another cab going in the opposite direction clattered merrily beside the kerb, the cabbie slapping the reins on the horses' rump, but the man and woman were scarcely aware of it. A great sense of peace surrounded them as they stood facing one another on the pavement. Several passers-by stared at them curiously but they were not aware of them. They stood quite, quite still in those precious moments of shared, acknowledged love, savouring them, their eyes seeking one another. It was enough for now, at least for her, grey eyes told brown, just to drift on the loveliness, to share the same small space, to breathe the same air, to feel the gentle mildness of it wrap them in the same impregnable haven. They knew that soon, when they were ready for it, perhaps in the next minute, perhaps not until tomorrow, or even the day after, they would take the next magic step, then the next and the next, until their hands would meet, their arms would reach out to cling, their lips would touch and fit together since they were made for just that. That they would both be safe and loved where they were meant and intended to be.

Celia felt her heart trip and begin to hammer. She could see the naked longing in his eyes, the wild need of something she knew he wanted of her and which, if he should put out his hand to take she would gladly give. His face was strained and suddenly the air about them tightened with a force, a power which alarmed her.

She said nothing. She stood quite still and looked up at him, not offering herself for she was too unworldly for that, but not turning away from the flame which was ready to consume him.

'Celie . . . ?' She did not answer.

'Celie . . . ?' Still she did not speak, but waited, *there*, the woman he desired, she realised that now, and would he take her?

'We had better . . . get you home.'

She nodded, obedient and submissive to his masculine strength and knowledge of how these things were done.

'Oh, my love . . .' he said, then, with a hurried movement

which told of his confusion, his yearning to possess her and at the same time to be the gentleman he was brought up to be, he led her out of the circle of light, through the park gates and into a small stand of full panoplied beech trees. Placing her against the trunk of one he began to kiss her.

Richard Latimer was twenty-six years old. In the years since he had first gone to school, he had grown from boy to man. An exceptional man with unmistakable assurance which those who first met him were quick to recognise. He was on the whole a kind man, kind and gentle with those weaker than himself as only a strong confident man can be, but he had in him a touch of arrogance as his hard jawline demonstrated, probably brought about by his upbringing as the first born, the eldest son of a socially prominent and wealthy Lancashire family. He was a complete man now, but at times he had the endearing look of a naughty schoolboy about him. This was not one of them. He was a soldier. He had seen action and had been wounded. His bravery and ability to command other men was beyond question and had earned him his captaincy. He was cool, well-disciplined, in control of his own destiny which was to climb as far and as fast as he could through the ranks of his chosen profession, but he was not in control now as he laid his tall, lean, urgent body along that of Celie Marlow.

He kissed her slowly, deeply. Then, as his kiss became more demanding, his lips began to hurt her, but it seemed she gloried in it, and the pain, twining her arms about his neck and pulling him closer to her. She knew the word sensuality for she had read of it in the books she had borrowed from his father, but she had no conception of what exactly it was or even, now, that she was experiencing it. She knew her skin was *alive* from the tips of her toes to the crown of her head, tingling with a joyous anticipation of what was to come, whatever that might be. She could not seem to get close enough to Richard, feeling the strangest desire to be inside his skin. She was sighing with the loveliness of it, her mouth lifting and opening beneath his, her trembling limbs blending with his, which trembled too. He stood away from her for a moment, his eyes unfocused in the dark, then swayed back again and his hands reached for her breasts, stroking delicately until her nipples peaked beneath his enquiring fingertips. She pressed forward into the caress, wanting it, wanting *something*, wanting him, and his hands burned her flesh through the fine summery fabric of her gown.

'Celie,' he gasped hoarsely, '*please* . . . Oh, dear God . . .'

'Richard . . . I love you . . .' and with all her young innocent heart, she offered him not only her love but anything else he might require of her.

It was perhaps this that brought him back to sanity and reason, to the knowledge of who they were and *where* they were and of the appalling consequences if he should lose his head and take what she plainly was offering. She was not aware that she offered anything, of course, since she was a child in such matters, but her body knew what it wanted, clinging to his, caring not a fig for consequences.

He strained away from her, breaking the power which held them together. He kept his hands lightly on her shoulders for she seemed in danger of falling. He shook his dazed head, watching her as she came slowly from the bewitchment in which their two bodies had spun her. Her face was pale as alabaster against the dark trunk of the tree and when she opened her eyes, they were deep, drugged, without light in them.

'Celie . . . Good God . . . Are you all right?' He shook her slightly to bring her back from wherever her female passion had sent her, then pulled her very gently, very carefully towards him, pressing her dazed face into the hollow of his shoulder. 'Celie . . . my love . . .' In his voice was such tenderness Celie felt it enter her soul, and she came to herself, relaxing against him, soothing, calming the quivering, clamouring, pulses of her body.

'Yes . . . I'm all right.'

'I . . . didn't hurt you?'

She smiled against his chest. No, he had not hurt her though it seemed to her that in places her body ached and ached with something she did not understand but which she knew she would need and *feel* for ever now.

'No, Richard.'

'I must get you home.'

'Yes, Cook will be waiting.'

'Of course.' The mention of the woman for whom Celie worked brought Richard Latimer fully back from the enchantment she had captured him in and taking her hand, he lifted it to his lips, not daring to do anything else. If he kissed her swollen mouth again he would not be able to stop this time.

'You are very beautiful,' he whispered into her hair and she lifted her face, smilingly to his, expecting his kiss, but instead he reached behind her for her boater which hung at her back. He did his best to return it to her head, tilting it this way and that and when she put up her hands to help him, laughing, he knew the danger was over.

She held his arm on the short walk home, shy again, her eyes modestly cast down. They did not speak. She was dizzy and bemused by her love for him, trusting, her belief in him not as yet put into words for it was all so new, but knowing that something had happened tonight and that her life would be different from now on because of it. He kissed her gently in the shop porch. His eyes searched her face and his finger touched her cheek with the lingering sweetness of a lover.

'Celie . . .'

'Yes?' She looked up at him, her heart in her eyes, good, loving, trusting.

'I must go.'

'Yes.' She smiled. 'Goodnight, Richard.'

He watched her as she put her key in the door, turning to cast a shining look of happiness at him, over her shoulder. There was a faint glow of light coming from a back room and it spilled into the shop, forming a golden silhouette about her, touching her smooth cheek to peach and putting a star in each eye. Again she turned to him, her smile enchanting in its loving, trusting simplicity.

'Goodnight, Richard,' she whispered again, putting the tips of her fingers to her lips, then turning them briefly in his direction.

He smiled. The door closed slowly, softly and when he turned away the smile was gone.

Chapter Twenty-one

It was a hot night, sultry with the promised threat of a thunderstorm pressing down on the roof-tops of Liverpool. Beyond the River Mersey, beyond Liverpool Bay and out in the Irish Channel, lightning danced, great jagged streaks which edged the ebony thunderclouds with gold, illuminating the heaving waters beneath into dashing, gilt-bordered waves. Vessels scurried towards the Rock Perch Lighthouse and the safety of the estuary before the storm broke, since one would, that was certain, but in the town of Liverpool it was still and airless, waiting.

Jess Harper shifted her aching legs beneath the one sheet which covered her, moving her feet in search of a cool place in the bed. She could feel the slick of perspiration beneath her white lawn nightdress and gradually, as she moved from one side of the bed to the other, groaning softly as the pain gripped her, the nightdress soaked through with sweat, sticking to her body as though she and it had been immersed in a bath of water.

She and Celie had been up as usual at four the previous morning baking dozens of almond puffs, custard tarts, apple cheesecakes, creamed apple tarts, bakewell tartlets, fresh strawberry vol-au-vents, since Dan's strawberries were at their most ripe and bountiful. Sausage rolls by the score, raised veal and ham pies, tarts of rhubarb and gooseberry, apple and damson, and all the summer fruits which grew so prolifically in Dan's garden, the garden which, if Celie had her way, would soon be three times as big! They had kneaded and rolled, whisked and stirred, chopped and mixed,

cut pastry with Cook's ornamental pastry-cutters, greased
dishes, keeping strictly all the while to Cook's insistence on
absolute cleanliness for only in such a way could the perfect
pies and cakes and tarts Cook and Celie prided themselves
on be produced.

There had been a special order to be got ready for Mrs
Richmond whose mistress, Mrs Morgan of Heaton Crescent,
had taken a great fancy to Cook's confectionery which *her*
cook, it seemed, had not the talent to turn out. She was a
great entertainer, was Mrs Morgan, her husband being in a
fair way of business in the City, and at least once a week
Cook was called upon to create some magnificent dessert.
Perhaps a buffet luncheon, or a supper buffet to grace Mrs
Morgan's table. So, a hectic day, as it always was, with each
one of them, even Ivy Petty who was called upon more and
more as business grew, on their feet with scarcely a break.

And now the lass wanted to *expand*, as she called it, and
how they were to cope with *three* shops when they could
barely manage one, was beyond Cook's imagining.

'Land sakes,' she said out loud, her voice revealing not only
her irritation but the extent of the exhaustion she felt. It was
hard to sleep at the best of times, what with her legs and the
indigestion she suffered more and more frequently, but in this
heat it was impossible. It was gone midnight, she knew that
because she'd heard the clock which stood in the downstairs
passage strike twelve, and in four hours it would all begin
again, but before that she'd have to get up and change her
nightdress because there was no way she could sleep in the
clinging dampness of it. Perhaps she'd slip to the kitchen and
make herself a cup of tea, better yet, a sip of brandy which
always put her to sleep, at least it did when she had a tot of
it in front of the fire after dinner on a Sunday.

Muttering to herself she began to heave her body from the
nest of her deep feather bed, throwing back the tumbled sheet
and placing her throbbing feet on the relative coolness of the
linoleum. Eeh, that felt good, and for two pins she'd sleep on
the damn floor like a dog, she thought, smiling to herself at
the very idea.

Fumbling her way across the dark room to the chest of

drawers behind the bedroom door, she took out a clean, freshly ironed nightdress. Her shoulders were stiff and creaky, like the rest of her, she thought grimly, and it took her a moment or two to get her damp nightdress over her head. When it was off she stood for another minute in her vest, savouring the coolness which, though it wasn't really cool, felt as though it was after the damp warmth of her nightgown.

She moved to the open window and drew back the heavy curtains, standing in the warm, night-scented air which drifted across the sill. She breathed deeply, firmly ignoring the jab of her indigestion, then sat down on the chair, the back of which was draped with her corsets, her bloomers, her stockings and all the paraphernalia she put on each morning under her working skirt and bodice.

Land sakes, that was lovely. It wasn't all that much cooler but the smell of Dan's flowers, honeysuckle and verbena, the fragrance of lavender and the roses he had tucked in amongst the other plants so that there would always be "cut" flowers for the shop, was pleasant in her nostrils.

As though her thoughts had conjured him up, the tall figure of Dan Smith strolled slowly down the path which divided the narrow garden. He stopped for a moment, turning to look back at the house and the cigarette between his lips glowed in the dark. And it was dark too, as the storm clouds began to mass in the west, and had it not been for the whiteness of Dan's shirt and the red tip of his cigarette, Cook doubted she would have seen him. The vague shapes of plants and trees could just be made out in the shadowy garden as they swayed ominously in a sudden gust of wind.

Cook sighed, watching as Dan moved slowly up the steps and beyond the bird-bath, vanishing among the trees which stood at the end of the garden. He couldn't sleep either apparently, and could you blame him? The air had an acrid taste to it, sulphurous and warm as she drew it into her lungs, and she wished the storm would break. Perhaps when it did, the air would clear and she might be able to get an hour's sleep before the dawn broke and another busy day began.

She was just about to stand up and put on her nightgown since it seemed hardly decent to sit before an open, uncurtained window in only her vest, when another blur of white floated, ghost-like from the back door which was directly beneath her bedroom window, and began to move hesitantly along the path, taking the direction Dan had gone.

'Dan,' she heard a voice whisper.

Dan! Well, would you credit it? The hussy! Trailing down the garden in pursuit of Dan *and* in her nightgown by the look of it, and give her a minute and Jess Harper would be down there an' all for she'd not have goings on such as these appeared to be, "going on" under *her* roof. Up to no good, the pair of them, with one thing only in their minds, no question of it, and she didn't care *what* it was, though she could guess, she'd not have it. The minx! She'd always known that Kate Mossop was trouble, aye, right from the first moment she'd put her cheeky face round Cook's back kitchen door at Briar Lodge. Larking about she'd been, from the word "go", ready for what she called a "bit of fun" but Jess Harper'd not stand for it, not *fun* of this sort, any road. She'd soon sort the pair of them out, so she would, though she had to admit she was surprised at Dan for he'd never struck her as a lad for a bit of hanky-panky. Mind you, weren't they all? Men? They'd not say no, even the best of them, to a kiss and a cuddle if it was offered. It didn't concern them what quarter it came from!

She was reaching for her stockings for no matter what the occasion, she'd never dream of appearing in front of anyone without them on her legs, when a jagged flash of lightning tore the sky into a dozen pieces, splitting it open with a noise which was hard to describe for immediately on its heels came a clap of thunder which stopped the white-gowned figure by the bird bath as though she had walked into a wire fence. In the white light created by the lightning she was clearly recognisable, the short darkness of her hair contrasting sharply with the unearthly whiteness of her long nightgown.

Cook stared in consternation and for a moment knew a sense of outraged shock, then slowly she lowered herself to the chair, resting her elbows on the window sill. She watched the figure of the young woman as she straightened from the huddled position the lightning and thunderclap had bent her into, then began to hurry towards the end of the garden as though she could not wait to get Dan Smith's strong, protective arms about her.

Cook stared at the Stygian garden which, a moment ago, had been lit as clearly as though it was noon. She blinked, scarcely able to believe her eyes, then slowly, her stiff and creaky shoulders relaxed, and she began to smile.

Celie! Celie and Dan! Well, it was what she wanted, wasn't it? What she'd always wanted and though she scarcely approved of what was obviously a love-tryst, she really didn't feel inclined to storm down the garden and put a stop to it. Celie wasn't a girl to allow liberties from a man, *any* man, unless her heart was involved and Dan Smith had loved Celie since they were children. He wouldn't harm her, or take advantage of her innocence unless he was serious. Oh, yes, Cook had seen it in him over the years and for the last two, since Celie became a woman, she'd wished more than once that he'd get a move on and ask her to marry him. It was about time and what could be more appropriate? With Celie's bright intelligence, her common sense and business skills which she'd developed recently; with Dan's loyal honesty, his capacity for hard work and his strength to protect what was his, they'd make a grand marriage and partnership. Aye, the time was right and if they . . . well, if they were anticipating their marriage vows by a month or two or even if . . . which was likely . . . Dan got Celie in the family way, it didn't matter, not really. In fact it would hurry things up a treat.

But the little minx, the sly puss! Her and Dan . . . the devil, the cheeky young devil!

She was smiling as she slipped on her clean nightdress and lay down on the bed. Within five minutes she was fast asleep, her heart quietly content, her snores gently rippling round the room and when the storm broke over her head, she was so deeply in her dreams of white wedding dresses and orange blossom, it didn't even wake her.

*　　*　　*

'What on earth are you doing out of your bed and what in hell's name have you got my cap on for?'

Dan's voice was vague, just as though the answer to his questions did not concern him over much. He continued to draw on his cigarette, his shoulders slumped against the back of the garden seat, his long legs stretched out before him and crossed at the ankle whilst he stared into the jetty darkness which enclosed the garden.

'It was hanging on the hook at back o' door. I thought it were going to rain and I didn't want to get me hair wet. You know how long it takes to dry. I'll take it off if yer want though.'

'Please yourself.'

With one quick movement, the black cap in which she had stuffed her hair was whipped from the wearer's head and a great silken cloak of silvery gold hair fell about her shoulders and down her back. It gleamed like wet silk in the smudged darkness, rippling and alive and at once, as Kate Mossop knew it would, Dan's interest was caught. She knelt down in front of him and with a child-like gesture, laid her head in his lap, feeling a small surge of gratitude, not to him, but to the fates which had given her this gift which affected him so. Once, in a rare burst of confidence, he had told her that his mother had hair like living silver and she supposed it was this which always had him reaching out to it, as he did now. That and her full, white-breasted, pink-tipped body with which she knew exactly how to subjugate him.

'Lord, it's hot,' she breathed and with another swift movement, she stood up and whisked off her nightgown, letting it fall from her hand to the flagged path. She was completely naked beneath it. Her hair settled about her, revealing only her face in which her green cat's eyes gleamed, and the pink tip of each breast. She leaned towards him where he sat, transfixed by her unearthly beauty and as he instinctively opened it, she placed a distended nipple in his mouth.

'There,' she whispered, 'isn't that lovely?'

Dan had seen Kate Mossop naked many times now, but never out of doors, never away from either his narrow bed and narrow room, or hers, and to take her here, on the garden bench, or in the dirt like an animal, filled him with excitement. He could smell the sharp tang of her sweat and the musky aroma of her aroused sexuality as she straightened and presented the full crest of her pudenda to his eager mouth and for an hour he played with her pantingly hot body, plunging his own into hers time and time again, groaning, desperate, unwilling in his mind, which did not love Kate Mossop, but unable to resist her body with his, which had a will of its own. The torrential rain which fell briefly slicked both their naked bodies to a slippery glistening sensuality which heightened their lust and Kate's hair wrapped around him, tying them together as though it was wet rope.

Dawn was breaking when they crept along the passage and past the door behind which Cook's snores still resounded. Beyond Cook's was Celie's door and for a second, no more, Dan hesitated outside it, and a great and despairing sadness settled in him, just below his still fast-beating heart, then he followed Kate. Neither of them heard the muffled weeping and when they reached Kate's door, to avoid a whispered argument, he kissed her goodnight before climbing the second flight of stairs to his own room.

It was a week later when Cook declared she was off to town. She'd a bit of business to attend to, she said, and could Kate and Celie manage without her? No, it was nowt to do with Kate Mossop, she added shortly, so would she kindly get on with what she was doing and stop minding everyone's business but her own. Cook had been a bit preoccupied these last few days, even Ivy Petty had remarked on it to Celie, asking if she knew what was up with her old friend, but Celie, who was herself a bit "liverish" in Ivy's opinion and in need of a good tonic such as Ivy's own which was beetroot, stout and brown sugar, all mixed up together, had nothing to say on the matter, in fact she was almost rude to Ivy as much as telling her, as Cook had told Kate, to keep her nose out of Cook's business. They had all been short-tempered, except Kate who was invariably good-humoured, Ivy was inclined to think, deciding it must be the weather which had continued airless and sultry despite the storm of a week ago. Dan was forever "up the garden", as he called his constant work on something

or other connected with the growing of his fruit trees, his
strawberry plants, his roses and the spreading beneath them
of the horse manure he collected from the streets, after the
carriages, drays and carts had gone by. His vegetable crop
must be watered, his autumn bulbs and his "pinks" planted
out, and his cabbages sown. A busy month was August, it
seemed, with no time to be sitting about indoors drinking tea
and gossiping!

The shop was busy as it always was and the three women,
neat and smart in their dark green dresses and snowy aprons,
were kept busy serving the dozens of ladies, most of them
regular customers, who did not really care to be kept waiting,
though of course they would, for where else but Harper's was
such delicious food sold? Besides it was pleasant, if rather a
tight fit to sit at one of the small tables on which fresh-cut
and sweet-smelling bowls of roses were displayed, drinking
fragrant China tea from thin china cups while they waited.

It was six o'clock when Cook returned stepping down
from the cab she had caught from town, as spritely as a
two-year-old, her face rosy, placid and smiling as though
she was well pleased with her efforts, whatever they might
be. The shop was still full, this time with a class of clientèle
lower than the afternoon trade. These were decent women
from further afield than the elegant tree-lined crescent and
squares which surrounded Sefton Park and Princes Park.
Semi-detached and even terraced houses off Harrington
Road and Smithdown Lane and Speke Road which backed
onto the railway lines and in which lived families who, if
they were to manage respectably, must make one penny
do the work of two. Harper's were in the habit, after five
o'clock, of selling many of their lines – should there be any
left – at half price since every item sold there, unless it
was preserved or wrapped in greaseproof toffee paper, was
freshly made each day.

At eight precisely, for though all the consumables had long
since gone, Celie would not close the doors early since their
customers liked to know where they were, she said, Dan
locked up and he, Ivy, Kate and Celie sank down at the
kitchen table. They declared they were too tired to eat,

really they were, but they tucked in nevertheless to the delicious meal Cook had 'knocked up' for them in the last two hours. Freshly poached salmon with a green salad and tomatoes and an enormous dish of buttered new potatoes. Apple and bilberry tart with thick whipped cream since she'd had no time to do anything "special" she said, with a few scones, Lancashire cheese and a freshly ground pot of coffee to finish.

'And was everything all right, Cook?' Kate said artlessly, 'I mean with your business an' that.'

'Yes, thank you, Kate, nice of tha' to ask.' Cook's voice was tart but she was ready to smile.

'All . . . fixed up like?'

'Oh, aye, indeed. All fixed up nice an' . . . well, that's for me to know and tha' to wonder at, Kate Mossop.'

'Oh, go on, Cook, what you been up to, then?' But Cook's patience was at an end and with a curt gesture she herself stood up and moved to her own chair, settling into it with a sudden drag of tiredness.

'Me stool, lass,' she said softly to Celie and when Celie knelt at her knee to help her off with her boots she placed an old liver-spotted hand beneath Celie's chin and lifted her face to look into it. 'Tha' looks done in, Celie,' she said just as though the others hadn't lifted a finger all day.

'I'm all right, Cook. It's the heat.'

'Aye, I know, but tha' . . . tha' looks peaky. Tha's not . . .' and then she stopped suddenly. Not that she had any intention of saying the dread words, dread to an unmarried woman that is. "In the family way" was how it was described and it had suddenly occurred to her that that might be what was wrong with Celie Marlow. If she and Dan were . . . well, not getting much sleep, then it was no wonder she looked a bit drawn. Round the eyes it was, which, it was said, was the first place pregnancy showed, though she herself had no knowledge of it first hand.

'Tha's not sleeping well, is that it?' she finished hurriedly.

'No, not really. I'll be better when the weather breaks.'

'Aye, we all will and 'appen I've a bit of news what'll perk thi' up a bit, though how he did it I'll never know.'

'What is it, Cook?' And in Celie's face which had looked strangely *plain* lately, a faint return of her usual fragile beauty stirred, heightening her colour.

'I bin ter see Mr Pembroke. A bit o' private business, which he sorted out fer me, but well, he sent thi' a message.'

'Me, a message, what about? Not . . . ?'

Celie's eyes shot open, widening until they were enormous pools of pewter grey in her pale face and into them a light began to glow, a candle flame at first, then growing until they snapped with excitement, brilliant as crystal, flashing about the others as though they too must share it. Her mouth opened and the colour flowed beneath her white skin.

'Aye, that's right, them next door on *both* sides is willing to sell their leases. The owner's not against it neither though he's put rents up.' Cook pulled a face, her eyes never leaving the fevered intoxication of Celie Marlow. Cook didn't want this but Celie did and that was enough for her. She knew better than most Celie's formidable resolution, her obstinate determination to succeed in the face of what looked like insurmountable obstacles and she knew that with these characteristics Celie could not fail to get on. Look at this place. Could anyone have foretold what heights it would rise to, certainly not her? But Celie had the . . . what was it? . . . a gift for knowing what people wanted and how to give it to them. This new thing was an enormous undertaking, a gamble with what they already had, a risk which, because Celie said it could be taken Cook was prepared to take, and really when you looked into the vivid exhilaration of Celie's face could you doubt it would succeed?

'A guinea each a week,' Cook went on wonderingly, the exorbitant rent being asked by the owner clearly alarming her.

'*A guinea*!' Kate echoed, not really knowing what was going on though she had heard talk of expansion for months now.

'Aye, that's three guineas a week. Can we manage that, my lass?' Cook spoke to Celie as if she was the only one present and in a way she was. The rest didn't count, not even Dan at that moment. Any man with a bit of muscle could do what Dan did, but not one girl in a thousand, a hundred thousand, had the talent and the brains to go with it that Celie had.

'Oh, yes. But we'll need capital.'

'Capital.'

'Yes, we'll have to borrow it.'

'Borrow?' Cook was not awfully sure she liked the sound of that. 'I've a bit put by.'

'How much?'

The others gasped. To ask Cook such a question was clearly overstepping the mark and would surely earn Celie a smart reprimand but Cook merely mentioned a sum that left them all dumbstruck.

'It's not enough, Cook. We'll have to go and see Mr Pembroke. He said he'd take us to see the bank manager to arrange a loan. If we show him our books for the past year I don't see how he can refuse, do you?'

'Eeh, lass, how do I know? I'm just a poor old working woman.'

'No, you're not, Cook. If it hadn't been for your cleverness and hard work none of this would have happened. I only know what I know because of you.'

Cook's face was soft and she lifted her hand to cup Celie's chin and in her chair by the table Kate Mossop's eyes narrowed in baleful speculation. Her mouth thinned and for a moment she allowed her thoughts to show. It seemed they were not pleasant. She might not have had much education, but Kate Mossop was in her way, as clever as Celie Marlow. She had a quick thinking, cunning brain and possessed the shrewdness and timing of a spider which watches the approach of an innocent fly to its web. She had plans, plans that would promote her own position in this household, in this venture which Cook and Celie had made so successful. Her teacher had been life itself and it had taught her many things not learned in the classroom. One was patience and another was the ability to recognise an advantage – to herself naturally – and to grasp it with both hands. But perhaps the greatest lesson of all was the knowledge of *when* to grab hold and when to be patient. She watched and waited and manipulated Dan Smith with her body which was young and glorious, but as old as the hills in its knowledge of men. She must not be too precipitate in her actions nor must she hesitate when the right time came or she would miss that one opportunity which would undoubtedly be hers. Was this it? her reflective expression seemed to be asking, or should she wait a while longer for that moment when she would not only land herself in the grand position she meant to have, but pay back Celie Marlow for the years of humiliation Kate had suffered at her hands. She'd always been a step behind Celie ever since Celie had grabbed Kate's job as assistant to Cook years ago and because of it was now Cook's favourite. Of course, in those years, Kate had learned a lot about what was known as the catering trade and when the time came . . .

'Nay, lass,' Cook was saying in that soppy voice she used whenever she spoke to Celie Marlow. 'Tha's not to say that. It's tha' own skill that's brought thi' to this. I only showed thi' t'way an' now look where it's led us. Who'd a' thought it.' Her voice was musing as her eyes became unfocused, looking back to something in the past. 'Who'd a thought it that day when Master Alfred an' Master Richard tangled with Dan 'ere,' turning to shake her head at the man whose actions in clouting the sons of the house had brought them to this. 'Look at us now wi' us own business an' set to see it grow even more. Eeh I hope it'll be all right, our Celie. I 'ope we're not tryin' ter run before we've got the proper hang o' walking.'

Celie's face, when Cook turned back to her, had lost its lovely rosy excitement and her eyes, for some reason, had gone quite flat. They had narrowed, staring, as Cook had done at some memory which, from the expression on her face, did not please her. Her young mouth thinned to a line which Jess Harper could only describe as "hard". She put out her hand to her, pushing back Celie's damp tangle of curls, through which it seemed Celie had pushed her own sweaty hand.

'What's up, lass? Tha' look as though tha's seen a ghost. Thinking about the past was tha?'

'No, Cook. Not the past. Never the past, only the future,' and in the narrowed charcoal grey of Celie's eyes was a look that startled Cook, for not only was it hard, but it seemed

to her to be hazardous. A trick of the light surely, for Celie
Marlow was the gentlest and least threatening young woman
Cook had ever had in her service.

'Tha's right, lass, of course thi' are. Now then, it's late and
there's a lot to be done in the next few days an' weeks an' all,
so let's be gettin' to us beds. Tha's stoppin' the night, Ivy?
Good, it's late to be traipsing about the streets. Tha' can share
wi' me and then . . . well, I think it's time thi' an' me and Celie
'ad a talk about what's to be done. Tomorrow, ay.'

'By the way, I shall be setting sail for the West Indies on the
seventh.'

The remark, doing its best to sound casual, as though the
speaker had declared his intention of taking a trip across
the Mersey, froze Prudence Garside into astonished and
temporary stillness. Then she whirled to face her brother,
the blood flowing hotly beneath her skin.

'*The West Indies*! You've kept that a bit quiet haven't you?
I thought the 2nd Battalion was to remain at Warrington?'

'It is, I've . . . I've applied for a transfer to the 1st.'

'*The 1st!* I was not aware that such things were possible.'
Her face showed her deep suspicion, just as though already
her sharp mind had considered the reason for this amazing
action on her brother's part and was surging to do battle in
defence of the vulnerable girl, who was, in her opinion, its
unwitting cause.

'It's not usually but in . . . mitigating, or unusual circumstances it has been known.'

'And what *are* these mitigating or *unusual* circumstances,
pray?' It was clear that Prudence was holding her outrage
barely in check and was waiting only to hear her brother's
answer before letting it loose on him.

Richard sighed, the breath running out of him in a ragged
tremor. He was sprawled deep in the chair beside Prudence's
drawing-room fire, his legs stretched out before him. He had
a glass of brandy in one hand and a cigar in the other and he
rested the brandy glass against his chest. His eyes narrowed
in contemplation of the dancing flames in the fireplace, the
bright glow putting a glint of gold in their brown depths. His

mouth was set in a line of grim single-mindedness, telling his sister that he would not argue with her over this, but as he had known all along, Prudence marched straight in with all guns blazing.

'Go on, Richard,' she challenged him. 'Do tell us why you are leaving a battalion which you love and in which you have served for eight years to go into another where . . .'

'Confound it, Prudence, must I answer to you for every action I take? I just wanted to travel again – *and that is that*, d'you hear me? Now if you don't mind I've things to attend to.'

Without another word, leaving his sister with her mouth hanging open, Richard Latimer stalked from the room.

The shop was closed for this one day only whilst the new and enormous plate glass windows were put in, the final link which made the three shops into one, and taking advantage of it, Cook had retired to her new bedroom. In fact she had not even got out of her bed that morning, declaring the night before that she meant to remain in it for thirty-six hours and they could bring her meals on a tray since she really did not know how she could possibly continue as she had been doing. Christmas in a few weeks and the roof rattling down about their ears as hordes of builders and plumbers and that new breed of tradesmen, electricians, swarmed in every room and how were she and Celie and Ivy to manage all the extra baking, she beseeched them to tell her? Them new gas ovens were a godsend, really they were, once you got the hang of them, she confided to Celie, but even so it would be a gargantuan task to prepare and display in the shattered shop front all the delicacies they had provided last Christmas.

'Don't worry, Cook. We'll do it. With Dorcas and Belle and Maudie and the other girls to help, it will run as smoothly as your Royal icing does on a Christmas cake. You just wait and see.'

Cook shook her head, her expression revealing the bewilderment she felt at Celie's unashamed "filching" – what other word could she use – of more of Mrs Latimer's servants. And Celie didn't seem to care a fig about it, neither, coaxing them three girls away from Briar Lodge with the promise of higher wages, and leaving Mrs Latimer without her parlourmaid, her kitchen maid and her scullery maid.

It had been like the mad-house, Dorcas had declared when she came to see them, on that day when Celie, Cook, Dan and Kate had walked out. With only herself to bring some sort of order to the leaderless kitchen, she thought she'd done right well, she added, but her resentment had been very evident when it seemed Mrs Latimer had not been in the least grateful, believing that Dorcas was quite capable of it, and worse still, had not even offered her a few more bob in her wages, which you'd have thought she would, wouldn't you? Dorcas certainly had expected it, for if it hadn't been for her, the family'd not have had a bite on their plates, not until the new cook, who wasn't a *patch* on Cook, she said wistfully, had been brought in hurriedly. But no, not a penny extra, and not even a word of thanks from *her*, though Mr Latimer, bless him, had come down to the kitchen to say a word.

And all the while, Celie had sat, a look on her face that would have froze hot custard, Jess Harper had thought, waiting until Dorcas had finished speaking about Mr Latimer and, when Dorcas seemed inclined to ramble on, cutting through her wordiness with the sharpness which had come on her just recently and which Cook was not sure she liked. She'd have to speak to her about it, she had told herself, but somehow, don't ask her why, she never had. It was as though, imperceptibly, their roles had been reversed and Celie was the one in charge and really, it was better that way for one day it would all be hers and she'd best get used to the feel of command, of giving orders and making decisions and, remembering the old days at Briar Lodge, hadn't she herself been sharp with the girls who were under her? You had to be if you wanted discipline.

'So you won't find it hard to hand in your notice, then, Dorcas?' Celie was saying crisply. 'It will be the three of you. Cook, Mrs Petty and I will do all the cooking of course, but you and Kate will serve in the shop. Will you be able to manage that d'you think?'

Dorcas was about to bridle for hadn't she been serving Mrs Latimer and her friends for years and didn't she know how to treat ladies, but something about Celie Marlow, her cool appraisal, the remote and authoritative look about her, the lift of her chin and the steady crystal-clearness of her eyes, stopped the words on her lips and to her own amazement, she heard herself answer as deferentially as she might to Mrs Latimer herself.

'Oh, yes, Celie. I'm looking forward to it.'

'Belle and Maudie will help in the kitchen for the time being and the two new girls, both good parlourmaids, will wait on in the tea room. There is a woman who will come in daily to scrub. We shall have to see if they'll be enough, but if not I'll take on a couple more. Now, can you start on Monday?'

'*Monday? Next* Monday?'

'Yes.'

'But that's not even a week's notice!'

'I appreciate that, Dorcas, so I suggest you leave on Saturday night. She will not pay you for this week, but I will, so tell the others they will not lose out. If you come straight from Briar Lodge – take a cab, by the way – that gives the three of you all day Sunday to get accustomed to the layout of the building and for me to tell you how I like things done. You, of course, will have your own room, and Belle and Maudie can share. You'll receive a guinea a week, all found, to start with . . .'

'A guinea.'

'Is that not enough, Dorcas?'

'Lord, it's more than me Dad earns, Celie. Eeh, thanks, that's grand . . .'

'Good, I'm glad you're satisfied. I want my staff to be happy, Dorcas.'

My staff! For a moment, Jess Harper had a dreadful feeling deep inside her. She could not really have said what it was, only that it was as though someone had placed a cold finger at the back of her neck, trickling it down her spine and causing an icy sensation to infiltrate her whole being. There was no doubt about it, there was a change in Celie which did not altogether please Cook, though she couldn't quite put a finger on what it was. It had nothing to do with the shop, with the air of businesslike authority Celie donned when she had dealings with the workmen who swarmed like monkeys about the scaffolding which climbed up every wall in the place. There was something about her, not just her determination which showed itself in the square set of her chin and the firmness of her lips, but a grim resolve, a positive confidence which Celie Marlow, the *old* Celie Marlow of Briar Lodge wouldn't have dreamed of assuming. It went deeper than that. It was something *inside* her, but there, Cook would think, shaking her head at her own foolishness, what could possibly alter the inherent sweetness of the young woman Cook had known since the day she was born? It was not altered, she told herself, it was merely *hidden* beneath the mountain of responsibility this new undertaking had heaped on her. Visits to Mr Pembroke, the bank manager, the building contractor, estimates and loans, collateral and leases and accounts to be paid, not to mention all the thousand and one items which must be ordered and when received, checked to ascertain their correctness for the new tea rooms. Colours and fabrics to be decided upon, uniforms and tablecloths and napkins, and all to be done *as well* as the normal running of the shop which could not be allowed to close.

And then there was the disappointment, known only to Cook, of course, of the lack of any advancement in the matter of Celie and Dan. Not since that night in August when Cook had seen them together in the garden . . . well, not together as such, but Celie *must* have been going up the garden to meet him, mustn't she, and since then, not a word, not a shared nor secret look, and certainly no sign of any . . . *baby*!

Well, Cook could only be patient, she decided as she lay, that cold day in late November in the lovely warm depth of her new bed in her newly refurbished bedroom which Celie had had done over for her from a sitting room on the ground floor of what had been the newsagent's next door. Save her legs, Celie had said, with the renewal of the loving kindness she had always shown to Cook. Those stairs were a devil to climb, she had smiled, and the back parlour would make a handy and comfortable bedroom and Cook had to agree with her, along with the small sitting room beside it which was for Cook's exclusive use. Celie had gone round to see Miss Prudence, she said. The last time before the grand opening of the new shop and the rush before Christmas, and when she got back, she'd bring Cook a little "tot" to help her to sleep. Despite the change in her she was still kind and lovely, was Celie, and Cook looked forward to a nice chat about Miss Prudence and that fine husband of hers, and even perhaps about the family. Just because she no longer worked for the Latimers didn't mean she had lost interest in their doings. Miss Anne and her new baby, Captain Richard, the engagement of Master Thomas to the daughter of a well-bred local family which had been announced in the newspaper, and all the others whom Cook had once served.

The strange thing was, though Cook distinctly heard Celie come into the brand new kitchens which lay next to Cook's bedroom, she went straight through and up the stairs without a word to anyone, not even answering when Kate called 'Goodnight' to her.

Cook sighed, then rang the little bell Celie had provided her with. Someone else would have to fetch her "tot".

Chapter Twenty-two

Celie glanced in the mirror which hung under the electric wall lamp just beside the door which led into the shop. It was put there, as was the light, so that the girls might check their appearance before entering the shop, for one of Celie's rules was that neatness, cleanliness and a pleasant smile must be employed at all times. She lifted both hands to smooth the shining wings of her dark hair away from her face, tucking a rebellious curl which sprang from the chenille net back into place. The net held the growing length of thick, springing curls which since she had cut it as a child, she had not even known she possessed. It was as though, now it was allowed to thrive again unhindered, it had gone quite berserk and only the severe confines of the chignon and the net she placed over it prevented it from rioting about her small head and down between her shoulder blades. It was twelve months since it had last known the scissors and already it was half-way down her back.

Lifting her head and arranging her face muscles into the automatic and pleasant smile she assumed with customers, she moved gracefully into the cresent-shaped shop.

The sight which met her eyes was one which never failed to gratify her. The three shops which had stood alone on the convergence of the Boulevard with Bentley Road, Devonshire Road and Croxteth Road formed the shape of a crescent, the outer curve of which faced the road, with a wide forecourt between them and it. Celie entered the remodelled shop from what had been the middle one in the row, in fact, the one which had originally been Harper's. Curving away on one side was what had been the gents' outfitter's and on the other, the newsagent's, the walls between the two shops demolished to make the new wide shop. The counter ran at the back of the shop from its centre to about ten feet from each outer wall. On the right-hand side, and at the back of the counter were row upon row of shelves climbing up to the ceiling, each one artistically arranged with all the merchandise, most home-made but some specialities brought from France, Germany, Italy and the Mediterranean which had been sold at Harper's for a year now. To the left of the counter was a wide doorway beyond which was a staircase leading up to the first floor, carpeted in a rich shade of dark red pile and above the door was a discreet sign which said "Tea Room". Cook had argued that Restaurant which it wasn't anyway, sounded too grand and what was wrong with Tea Room or Café and Celie finally concurred, knowing nevertheless that neither of the latter properly described the simple elegance and refinement of the room upstairs with its splendid view over the panorama of Princes Park.

As Celie entered it the shop was filled with ladies, some browsing from shelf to shelf or studying the contents of the glass-fronted counter and cabinets, others standing to admire the displays set out on round, lace-covered tables which dotted the shop floor. There was a constant ping of the doorbell as customers departed with their overflowing baskets on their arms whilst others arrived to fill theirs. There were several women, obviously cooks or housekeepers from the houses situated on the graceful crescents off the Boulevard and in the surrounding areas, sitting on chairs in front of the counter whilst they gave their orders which, being large, would be delivered by the Harper's horse-drawn van before the day was out. The van was dark green, inscribed in gold lettering with fancy scrollwork illuminating the name of the shop and beneath the name were the words "High class provisions and tea room". It stood at the front of the shop just now and giving orders to the driver was Dan Smith. He adjusted the horse's bridle to his own satisfaction, as he spoke to the man in the driver's seat then rubbed his hand on the animal's nose. He deftly reached into his pocket and on the flat of his hand offered some titbit to the animal's enquiring lips. The beast pushed his head against Dan's shoulder and Celie saw Dan smile, pulling its ear affectionately before turning to move in the direction of the shop's doorway. He called something over his shoulder to the driver who answered by pulling at the peak of his cap before slapping the reins on the horse's rump and moving off.

Celie's smile deepened, becoming warm with fondness as she watched Dan enter the shop. He wore a dark green overall coat with the name Harper's stitched on the pocket. His black peaked cap, which he removed as he opened the door, had the same name printed on the band across the front. His trousers, also black, were well-pressed and his boots highly polished. His shirt was freshly laundered, a clean one each day, and on his face was the good-natured and wide grin he reserved for Harper's customers. Good-natured, yes, but there was also something else which Celie knew the "ladies" liked, even those who were well past the age for such things. An audacious twinkle in his eye which told of his admiration for the female sex, a glint which Cook might have called "cheeky" but which had in it no impertinence or disrespect. He was well-liked by the ladies from whom he took orders and could, had he the inclination – and time – for it, have dallied with any number of young maidservants when, as he sometimes did, he took over the round.

'Good morning, ladies,' he said to those who were giving their orders or studying the delicacies on the shelves. He stood to one side, holding open the door for the comfortably plump figure of the black-garbed housekeeper who had been among their first customers two years ago.

'Good day to you, Mrs Turpin,' he smiled,' I trust I find you well.'

'Indeed you do, Dan, and yourself?'

'Fine an' dandy, thanks, Mrs Turpin.'

He was in his exact element in his job, Celie knew, doing what naturally suited him and what he was suited for. He liked people and they liked him. He greeted each customer by name and knew the family history, not only of the servants with whom he came into contact when he delivered their orders, but of the families for whom they worked, enquiring after them in a way which told of his genuine interest. He liked the freedom of being out and about, sitting high up above the horse's rump as he drove the van along the busy streets of Toxteth and Aigburth, Mossley Hill, Edge Hill and Knotty Ash.

But best of all he liked to be in the enormous and splendid garden which he had created at the back of the new shop. And he had a right to be proud of it too. He and the two gardening lads who worked under him, brothers, in fact twins, and so alike it caused no end of trouble, had knocked down the two dividing walls. They had done it with great care for growing against the walls, at least in Dan's original garden, there had been fruit trees and climbing plants which Dan treasured, having brought them back to glory in the first year they had moved to the Boulevard. The other two gardens, those at the rear of the gentlemen's clothier's and the newsagent's had been in a sorry state, and Dan's heart had sunk into his boots he admitted, when he first descended the broken-down steps which led into them. Talk about a rose between two thorns he had said ruefully. There had been rusting wheels and old bottles and tin cans by the hundreds, an ancient stone sink, discarded pipes and guttering, old gates and bricks and slates and the rubbish tipped over the walls of the houses which backed onto them. Amongst all this clutter and almost burying it were weeds and ancient decaying grasses as high as Dan's waist. The gentlemen's clothier had evidently had no use for a long back garden, nor for the cellars beneath the property he rented, and it seemed the newsagent had held the same view, but Dan, Frank and Fred, as the twins were called, set to one damp November Sunday morning and before dinner-time had half of one garden cleared. Working systematically through the winter days they and Dan, when he was not busy with deliveries, had cleared and prepared the gardens ready for spring planting. It had been strange at first, looking out of one of the many windows which overlooked the back gardens, to see the neat cultivation which ran down its centre, the jungle of neglect on either side. The ornamental pathways and steps and bird-bath Dan had put in, but gradually, as spring came, the whole had begun to take shape, the great trees which had stood at the back of each of the separate gardens running into one another and forming almost a tiny woodland at the far end. There were small lawned areas close to the back of the house, surrounded by the bright loveliness of spring and then summer flowers and between them and the trees, a wide stretch of tight, neat row upon row of every conceivable kind of vegetable Cook, Celie and Ivy might need in the dishes they created, not just for Harper's shop, but for Harper's Tea Room.

Fred and Frank who had come, recommended by Ivy who knew their mother, from a farm near the village of West Derby, lived in, sharing a room at the top of the house, putting on twenty pounds and ten inches apiece in the nine months they had worked at Harper's. Fifteen they were, big, agreeable, hard-working lads who relished Miss Marlow's good food and admired her good looks, though naturally they told no one of the latter except each other and they had been aware right from the start without being told, who was in charge of them, indeed of it *all*. They larked about a bit for they were only boys, bringing a sense of careless youthful fun to the house and the garden behind it, which, in the serious business of getting it all under way, had been sadly lacking. They called Dan "sir" which tickled him to death, and were respectful of all the females who worked about the place.

Percy Danson called nobody "sir" and had not done so since he had been wounded in Natal in the Boer War of 1881. The Battle of Majuba Hill it had been in, when all but a handful of the men ordered by the officer whom Private Danson had addressed as "sir" to climb the summit of Majuba Hill had been mown down and killed. Percy had been a survivor. He was a taciturn, lean-faced, stringy little man, who walked over from Borax Street every morning, constantly in pain from the abdominal wound which had nearly killed him, and though he was pathetically grateful for the job of driving the "delivery" van for Harper's, and indeed *anything* Dan asked of him, not by a lift of his grey and bushy eyebrows, or a curl of his lip, would he let anyone know it. He was his own man was Percy and woe betide anyone, even Dan or Miss Marlow, who forgot it.

Again it was Ivy who had found him, hefting a hundred-weight bag of coal off the coal wagon he drove for the local coal merchant and staggering with it to her "coal hole" which stood in the street before her front door and emptying it down the chute into her cellar. Even under the film of coal dust on his sunken cheeks she could see his pallor and when the question of a van driver arose she mentioned him diffidently to Celie, who, of course, did the hiring, and firing if necessary, at Harper's.

And Percy had a niece, a good girl who was the daughter of Percy's dead brother, and Percy's niece knew of another called Maggie who, wanting to better herself as Beth Danson did, and both being experienced parlourmaids, were delighted when approached to work in Harper's new Tea Room. Neat and pretty, deft and efficient, they had taken to their work with enthusiasm and panache just as though they had been trained for it, which in a way they had. Six tables each, almost always filled, for the attractive tea room, done in subtle colours of cream and peach and leaf green, was a popular rendezvous with the ladies who came to shop and stayed to partake of Miss Marlow's delicious tea and cakes. And on top of the girls' wages which were five shillings a week more than they had earned as parlourmaids, there were the tips! After the Tea Room closed at five they were expected to help in the shop if needed and with any task which had to be done in the kitchen, but at seven they were free to walk home to Portelet Road and Ionic Road, a full two or even three hours earlier than they were accustomed to finishing! And working among the fresh-cut flowers, the small, round, organdie-covered tables, the delicate gilt chairs, the discreet water colours and glowing lamps was scarcely different from the elegant drawing rooms where they had served tea and cakes to their previous mistresses. Then there was Fanny, Fanny who had been parlourmaid with Dorcas at Latimers', and who, now that her younger brothers and sisters were at school, or leaving home, had some free time on her hands and was only too willing to help out for a few extra bob a week;

and with Lily, once the donor of "dolly mixtures" to the young Celie, coming in each day to scrub; with Belle and Maudie in the kitchen, Celie's team was complete. Beth and Maggie, living close to one another, were walked home by Percy each night to their homes on the other side of the railway, but the remainder of the servants had rooms of their own, or shared, depending on their status, beneath Harper's roof.

Celie walked slowly about the shop, stopping to speak to several customers on what she called her "rounds". Most of the ladies knew Miss Marlow, of course, the manageress as they thought her to be, and the small courtesy she showed them, several times a day, pleased their sense of their own importance. They were not aware that she had been up since four o'clock with Cook and Ivy, preparing, baking and cooking the myriad delicacies they bought each day in the shop, for her straight back and swaying, graceful young figure, her lovely serene face, gave no intimation of weariness, nor indeed of her inner emotion.

It had been at the end of a particularly hectic day, when, having first discussed it with Cook, Celie first put it to Ivy, diffidently, that she might like to move permanently into one of the comfortable bedrooms above the shop.

'I know you're very fond of that little house of yours, Ivy, and you like the independence it gives you, but how would you feel about selling it and moving in here with us? That's if you want to, of course,' knowing how fiercely proud the old lady was. 'The money you got from the sale could be invested . . .'

'*Invested* . . .!' Ivy did not care for the sound of that and though she admitted to herself that trek back to Cable Street of a night was something she could well do without she was wary of change, of burning her bridges, so to speak.

'Yes, your money would be safe,' Celie continued, 'and not only that but you'd have a small income from it.'

'Nay, that's double Dutch to me, lass. I'd best stick to what I know.'

'But your house stands empty most of the time. When you are there you spend the day cleaning and polishing and get no rest, even on your day off.'

'I can't stand muck, Celie, you know that.'

'Indeed I do but you need a day of rest as we all do so won't you consider it? You know I'm only thinking of your own good and I wouldn't advise you to do anything which was not beneficial to you.'

'Well . . .' Ivy was very tempted.

'Think about it, Ivy. Talk to Cook. She has your welfare at heart and has a good head on her shoulders. I would feel so much better if I knew you were . . . comfortable.' She had been about to say "looked after" but knowing how savagely independent Ivy was she left it at that.

So Ivy had given up her small home in Cable Street six months ago to take up permanent residence with her old friend, and a permanent job as "plain" cook in the kitchen. She and Cook were at this very moment, draped, there was no other word for it, on opposite sides of the fire in Cook's small private sitting room, their early morning endeavours at the stove carving them both into speechless statuettes. Though they had Belle and Maudie to run hither and yon, to fetch and carry, and need hardly do more than sit on the high stools at the benches Celie had had built for them and at which they worked, they were both "jiggered", they told one another, sipping the hot, black, sweet tea their handmaidens had brought them. Celie could not help worrying, for neither of them were young and she, who had dozens of other jobs to perform, could not do all the cooking on her own. Mind you, she had noticed in Maudie a tendency to hang around at her back, as she had once done at Jess Harper's, so perhaps there might be another budding cook in the kitchen, who, with a bit of encouragement, as Cook had encouraged Celie, might in time step into Cook's or Ivy's hard-working boots.

'Good morning, Mrs Richmond, and how are you today?' she said pleasantly, 'And how is Mr Morgan? Has he recovered from his cold?'

'I'm well, thank you, Miss Marlow. And Mr Morgan is quite himself again now, though it seems the thing's going right through the house.'

'Oh dear, I'm sorry to hear it.'

'Indeed, Master Algie has gone down with it and Mrs

Morgan tells me Miss Rosemary was all flushed up this morning.'

'I am sorry, the poor things. Here, give them these with my good wishes.'

She took two small jars from a nearby shelf. They were bright with red ribbons about their tops and on the sides a label advertised them to be "Harper's home-made Peppermints". 'They're not too strong and as you know, only the best goes into Harper's produce. They might soothe their throats,' she added smiling.

'Why, that's very kind, Miss Marlow.' Mrs Richmond was clearly gratified as she moved over to the counter where a smiling Dorcas waited to take her order.

For half an hour Celie moved about the shop, her head turning constantly this way and that as her sharp eyes studied everything from the custard tarts she herself had baked, the gleaming brilliance of the glass in the cabinets, the polished perfection of the black-and- white tiled floor, the spotless purity of the tablecloths, the blinds, the girls' aprons – which must be changed the moment they were sullied – her eyes relentless in their search for a flaw in the flawlessness of her world. It was quite beautiful, not only to look at but in the fragrance which filled every corner. Fresh bread and scones, the aroma of fruit and herbs and spices, the sharp pungency of newly cut cheeses and the overall smell which is not a smell at all for it signifies the absence of anything which might be described as unclean.

'Is everything all right, Kate?' she asked, her eyes running automatically up and down the trim green immaculacy of Kate's dress, her white apron and collar, her cap and cuffs.

'Yes thank you, Miss Marlow.' Kate smiled sweetly in her direction before turning back deferentially to her customer who could not quite make up her mind between arrowroot or soda biscuits and to give Kate her due, her smile of infinite patience never wavered.

'I'm not sure whether Mr Lomax wouldn't prefer . . .' The customer's eyes roved over the rows of attractive jars at the back of the counter whilst Kate waited, paper bag in hand, for her to make her choice.

'Why not offer Mrs Lomax a selection, Kate?' Celie suggested, on seeing Mrs Lomax's dilemma.

'Well, Miss Marlow, that's kind of you but the . . . well, some are more expensive than others,' Mrs Lomax said sotto voce. Mrs Lomax was from one of the small terraced houses in Admiral Street on the other side of the park, one of those where Mr Lomax's wage must be stretched to its very limit. Kate's smile was still attached to her lips but, though neither Mrs Lomax nor Celie noticed it, her eyes were like pale green marbles.

'Mrs Lomax, I want you to try *all* our biscuits, but of course, I wouldn't dream of charging you more than the price of the arrowroot. Our lemon creams are delicious so please, won't you and Mr Lomax sample them? Give Mrs Lomax a pound of mixed, please, Kate. And in future, I think we will start a *new* line of mixed biscuits.' She turned to Mrs Lomax. 'Thank you for giving me the idea, Mrs Lomax,' watching as the woman who was not sure whether to be offended since she wanted no charity at once preened in pleasure.

Nodding and smiling, the hem of her dark green skirt whispering on the tiled floor, Celie moved towards the stairs which led up to the Tea Rooms, lifting her skirt to reveal her highly polished black boots as she moved up the stairs. Because she was not serving either in the shop or the tea room, she wore no apron or cap, though her white muslin collar and cuffs were spotless. As she entered the tea room, the muted sound of ladies chatting and their laughter, the small clatter of tea cups in saucers and the soft snap of the door closing at the back of the room, met her ears. The door led to another room at the back of the house in which the only pieces of furniture were an enormous set of shelves on one wall and a square table in the middle. On the shelves stood dozens of fine bone china tea cups, saucers and plates, tiered cake stands, tea pots and coffee pots, divided trays of cutlery and in drawers beneath the shelves were dainty lace-edged table-cloths and napkins to match, ready, should the slightest accident occur, to be changed. On the table were trays ready to be set with the orders as Beth and Maggie took them, and in the corner was what was called the "kitchen lift".

The dilemma of how to get piping hot pots of tea and coffee up to the Tea Room had been a difficult one for it was not practical to expect the two waitresses to run along the corridor, down the stairs and along the passage to the kitchen to collect their trays. Besides which the beverages would be cold by the time they returned so Dan had devised, with the help of the builder, a "lift" hauled up a specially built shaft by a pulley. Beth or Maggie would send down the tray with their neatly written orders – 'Tea and cakes for two', 'Coffee and biscuits for four', 'Tea, scones and cream for three' – and back it would come. A large plate with a selection of cakes, or scones and cream, or biscuits and the pots of tea, coffee, hot water, sugar, milk or cream. Beth and Maggie would then set on the tray the required number of cups, saucers, plates and cutlery and arrange the food attractively on the cake stands. All placed on a wisp of lace tray cloth and carried through the swinging doors from the "serving room" into the Tea Room for the ladies' appreciation.

'Good morning Mrs Featherstone, Mrs Hampshire.' Celie smiled pleasantly at two well-dressed ladies who sat by the large window and whose carriage, at this moment, stood at the front of Harper's. They nodded graciously. They had been shopping in town, she knew, for they were the wives of well-to-do gentlemen, with businesses in shipping, probably acquaintances of Mrs Latimer. They had nothing else to do with their time, or their husbands' money, than spend both in the smart shops in Bold Street. They both lived in large houses in Mossley Drive, or Aigburth Drive, overlooking Sefton Park, as the Garside house did, and on the way home, as it was becoming increasingly fashionable to do, they had stopped to take tea at Harper's on the Boulevard. They knew they might meet friends there, for Celie Marlow, wishing to serve only high-class customers in her tea room, had kept her prices high to ensure it. Mrs Featherstone and Mrs Hampshire would not care to mix with the likes of Mrs Lomax who could only really afford arrowroot biscuits, Mrs Richmond who might be *their* housekeeper, or Mrs Turpin who was even lower in the social scale than either.

The tables were all filled. The ladies who relaxed there

were quite young, none more than thirty or so since drinking tea in public was not quite to the taste of the older generation. Though this was 1896 and almost the start of the new century, they did not feel at ease with it and it was left to the younger, more modern lady to dare the quite new innovation. These were for the most part well dressed and confident, ready to discuss women's suffrage, though not to take part in it, of course, the latest concert at St George's Hall or exhibition at the Walker Art Gallery. Their young children would be in the care of Nanny and their lives would be spent much as their mothers' had been. They had been reared to be wives, mothers, the mistresses of comfortable homes, hostesses at the dinner table entertaining their husbands' business acquaintances. They were not quite upper-crust gentry but not far off it and their pedigreed background was very evident as they conversed in the cultured drawl of the upper classes just as they would before their own servants, about matters which said they were scarcely aware of Beth and Maggie hovering unobtrusively in the background.

Smiling pleasantly at them, Celie moved between the tables and through the swing door at the back of the tea room. There was plenty of space in the room and Beth and Maggie bustled competently about it, returning clean china to the shelves that they themselves washed in the brand new sink which stood beneath the window overlooking the back garden. There was a small window in the swinging door, and one or the other was on constant watch for any signs from "their" ladies, that something might be needed, or indeed, should any new ladies come in. They were both in a constant swirl of efficient activity, transferring clean china to the shelves and setting up trays and tray cloths, teapots and coffee pots ready to go down the lift with fresh orders.

They were dressed in the Harper uniform of bottle green, floor-length dresses, crisp, white frilled aprons tied about their waists, with streamers falling at their backs, almost to the hem of their skirts. Their frilled caps bobbed perkily on their neat heads, again with streamers falling between their shoulder-blades.

'Everything all right, girls?' Celie asked them, the incongruity of the "girls" not apparent to her even though both were five or six years older than she was.

'Yes, thanks, Miss Marlow,' they chorused cheerfully.

'Anything you need?'

'No thanks, Miss Marlow.'

'Well, I'll get down to the kitchen then.'

'Thanks, Miss Marlow.'

Belle and Maudie were on their knees when Celie walked into the kitchen. The ground floor was very different from the way it had been two years ago when she and Cook, Kate and Dan had first entered the shop. Gone were the dark passages, awkward stairs, ante-rooms, larders and pantries. Gone were the old ranges, the solid, four-square table, the endlessly high cupboards and shelves, replaced by streamlined, accessible cupboards and all manner of labour-saving devices. Chrome was everywhere, enamel sinks, three of them with bright taps from which running water came, HOT from the new boiler in the cellar. Celie had given a great deal of thought to the arrangement of the sinks, the high benches where she, Cook and Ivy might sit to work, the lower tables where they could stand if preferred, the brand new gas cookers. It had all been planned with a view to efficiency and the saving of Cook's legs! And the least distance any of them had to walk was surely beneficial in the endlessly wearying hours they worked six days a week.

The cookers had at first been viewed with suspicion for would they not blow them all to Kingdom Come, Ivy had asked fearfully? They were not at all popular with the buying public, Celie was aware, the anxiety that the servants might not understand how they worked, putting off many purchasers but these had proved to be worth their weight in gold, turning out time after time the perfect cakes, biscuits, pastry, toffee and all the delicacies which were produced in them, and on the dozen gas rings on their top.

The two swaying rear ends stopped for a moment as Celie entered the kitchen and two young faces peeped round from their buckets. As usual it was Maudie who piped up.

'We done the ovens and the pans, Miss Marlow, an' them

toffee trays so there's only the floors ter finish so I was wonderin' . . .'

'Yes, Maudie?'

'Could I 'ave a try at them curd tartlets you showed me the other day?'

'Well, I can't have food wasted, Maudie. Are you sure you're up to it?' Celie smiled.

The eager little face lit up joyously. Maudie squared her shoulders and tossed her be-capped head. Up to it, her expression seemed to ask? Just give her half the chance and again Celie was reminded of herself at the same age. Not that she had been as ebulliently confident as Maudie but she had been as eager to try. Maudie would be about fifteen or sixteen now, she supposed, and was it not time she took on the job of helper, serious helper and scholar under the tutelage of Cook and herself? Ivy was what Celie called a good plain cook whose roast beef and Yorkshire pudding, whose lamb cutlets and roast potatoes, whose pork and stuffing and apple sauce ranked up there beside Cook's own, but who, when confronted with it, had not the faintest conception of how to go about the "haute cuisine" which Cook had learned as a young woman and which she had passed on to Celie. Ivy was invaluable to Cook, working under her leadership, but someone with the gift for it, the light hand for it, the imagination and daring for it, must be trained to keep up the high standard Harper's had begun and which their customers now demanded.

'What about you, Belle?' Celie asked, and for an unexpected, delightful, *terrible* moment, the memory returned of that day when she and this girl had stood on the corner of Picton Road and Knowles Lane whilst the cab containing . . . containing . . . no . . .! *no* . . .! stop it! That way only led to pain, even now, and the vow she had made last November when . . . when Prudence had told her, told her that Richard was to go to . . ., the vow that no matter what happened from now on, she would stand no more . . . no more pain . . . never again . . .

'Not me, Miss Marlow,' Belle was saying adamantly. 'I'm no good with a bakin' spoon.' Her good-natured rosy face bore no resentment that Maudie, or so it seemed, *was*!

'Well then Maudie, go to Cook's sitting room and ask her if she will . . .'

Her words were interrupted, not rudely, for Maudie would never be rude to Miss Marlow who had once been Celie to them all, but sharply just the same.

'I can't do that, Miss Marlow. She's not there.'

'Not there!' Visions of Cook and Ivy dressed in their Sunday best, perhaps calling a cab to take them to town, flashed quickly and ridiculously through Celie's mind to be discarded at once, knowing the state of Cook's legs. Had they gone down the steps to take a turn about the garden then? Her eyes strayed beyond the two girls and through the open window to where Dan was hunkered down in the vegetable garden, Frank and Fred crouched on either side of him over some problem which seemed to be causing them a great deal of worry.

Her eyes returned to Maudie who was waiting with all the patience her quick brain would allow to impart the rest of her news.

'Where is she, then, Maudie?' and even before the girl answered, Celie's heart began to jerk anxiously in her breast.

'She's in bed, Miss Marlow. She was took badly . . .'

'Why didn't you tell me at once, you silly girl?' She whirled about and began to move jerkily towards the door. 'Has Mrs Petty telephoned for the doctor?'

'Eeh, I dunno, Miss Marlow.' Maudie fell back a little from Miss Marlow's wrath. As far as she knew *nobody* had telephoned the doctor, and certainly not Mrs Petty who was frightened to death of the blasted thing. Mrs Petty wouldn't even answer the new telephone when it rang in that insistent way it had, and she'd had to do it. *She* wasn't frightened of it, not her, not Maudie Evans. She turned to Belle, sighing hugely. It looked as though the curd tartlets were out.

Chapter Twenty-three

Jessica Harper died two days later and was buried in the churchyard of All Saints Church which stood on the corner of Bentley Road just across from the shop, with all the pomp and circumstance of a member of the Royal family, or so Kate Mossop privately thought. All that good money, all that hard-earned cash which Kate Mossop herself had laboured to put in the old biddy's bank account, chucked away on a coffin which even when empty, six men could hardly lift. Four black horses with plumes on their heads to pull the magnificent hearse, all shining wood and chrome and the blasted thing to go no more than a hundred yards down the road to the church. Bloody hell, Dan, Frank, Fred and Percy could have trundled the thing across the road on a pair of wheels but no, Miss High and Bloody Mighty Marlow had to do it in style, chucking away money as if it grew on trees.

'We must do it as Cook would like it, Dan,' Celie had wept on the day following Cook's sudden death, huddling close to him on the sofa in a way Kate did not like, her frailness, her absolute and devastating grief needing his arms about her, his shoulder to cry against, calling forth all the strength and protective love which even whilst Kate's body had bewitched him, had lain dormant in Dan Smith.

'We will, min liten älskling, won't we, Mrs Petty? You must tell us exactly what you think Cook would have wanted for someone *she* loved and we will do it for her.' He held her tenderly against him, his arms about her, his head bent to hers whilst his lips moved in her dark unrestrained hair. She had not slept. Cook had died just as the shop closed, going quietly, so quietly no one had known. Whilst Celie, with Cook's old recipe book before her, planned what they were to make for tomorrow Ivy had sat with her friend, dozing beside the bed, awakened only by the sudden awareness that she was alone.

'Her heart, Miss Marlow,' the doctor told her, somewhat taken aback by the force of the grief erupting from the young woman he had seen only as cool, unhurried, reserved. 'She was not strong, you know. Those legs of hers, well . . .' He had shrugged, lifting his hands in an eloquent gesture which showed exactly how her legs had been. And then there was the pain in her chest she had complained of, her shortage of breath, so really, could you expect anything else from an old woman who should have been sitting quietly by her own fireside at her age and not standing on those terrible legs for eight or ten hours each day as he heard she had, though naturally he did not say this last to the distraught young woman.

The shop was closed for a week from the day after Cook died which was a Friday until the following Thursday. In all that time Dan and Celie were scarcely apart, except for the few hours when Celie slept fitfully in her elegant new bedroom at the back of the house and even then, Dan crept in several times during the night to make sure she was all right. They went everywhere together, excluding everyone, even Ivy, for it seemed they had returned to the days when, as children of ten and twelve years old, they had forged that special bond which had been slackened in recent years. Cook had been a dragon then. The supreme authority who had ruled their lives, but the only woman in their motherless lives and her dictatorial command of them had been tempered by her fairness, her kindness, her fondness for them both.

Hand in hand they moved about the tasks which death calls for, arranging the funeral, ordering – to Kate's horror – black outfits for every one of the staff and enough flowers for a dozen funerals, calling on Mr Pembroke the solicitor who, after he had attended the interment, he told them, would return to the shop with them to read the Will.

They had not known of the presence of a Will, they told

him, like two children suddenly flung into an adult world, and that was how they both seemed to him, clinging to one another in their distress, giving credence to what the old lady had confided in him over a year ago. The man, Dan Smith, was starkly handsome in his mourning black, his thick corn gold hair brushed smoothly back from his sun-browned face. His piercingly blue eyes, or were they turquoise, it was hard to tell in the dim light of the office, turned constantly to the girl, his caring love, his protective tenderness towards her a lovely, throat-catching thing to see. He was nearly twenty-three now, Mr Pembroke reckoned, going back again to the day when Mrs Harper had talked about him, and the girl beside him, her grief making her seem even younger than she actually was, not quite twenty.

They walked behind the hearse the short distance from Harper's to the church. The blinds were drawn in the shop and in every house along the route. The shop door and the windows beside it were draped with wide black ribbons and every member of the staff, the women all in tears with black-edged handkerchiefs to their faces, moved slowly from it, across the wide pavement, falling in behind the hearse as it moved majestically away. Dan and Celie were at the front, followed by Kate and Ivy, the waitresses Beth and Maggie, Dorcas with Belle and Maudie on either side of her, Fanny and Lily and Mary who had scrubbed beside Lily at Latimers'. Percy strode alone, like a soldier on parade and at his back, their young faces quite excited since they had never seen such a grand turn-out, were Fred and Frank. Prudence was there with her hand in Jethro's. Reuben Ash and Mrs Ash, George Ellis and Mrs Ellis and dozens of decent folk from the market stalls who had in the past sold chickens and rabbits, pheasants and grouse, cheese and eggs and cream to the woman who had been Cook at Briar Lodge.

Strangely, Celie did not weep now. Her hand was in Dan's. It felt warm and strong, holding hers as they walked side by side behind Cook. She turned to smile at him, sharing something with him which he understood at once, smiling back to the amazement of the respectful men and women who lined the route, many of whom shopped at Harper's. They

were more accustomed to tears than smiles on occasions such
as this, they told one another, but they made a handsome
couple just the same and were obviously very attached to
one another.

It all passed by Celie in a merciful haze. She was aware at
a certain level of two things. One was Dan's hand in hers,
his arm ready to hold her upright, his shoulder strong for
her to lean on, his warmth, his love, his constancy and the
expectation that it would always be hers. It melted the harsh
pain which had encased her heart for almost a year now. It
pleased her, warmed her, gave her courage and steadiness
to go on, and it filled her with hope for the future. It told
her quite irrevocably that Dan would be in it with her, and
was that not how it should be? They were the same, she
and Dan. They had the same background and, for ten years,
the same upbringing. They had both loved Cook, and Cook's
dream of the shop they both worked in. They were matched.
They suited.

The second thing she was concious of were Kate Mossop's
eyes. Every time she glanced away from Dan, from the coffin,
the grave, the Minister, Kate's eyes were on her, green,
narrowed, the expression in them unreadable.

The shop, the tea room, the large sitting room where the
staff relaxed of an evening and on a Sunday, even Cook's
own private sitting room were packed from wall to wall with
people come for the cold collation which Ivy and she had
prepared the night before, many of the mourners straight
off the street to have a "nosey" at Harper's and a free plate
of the food they had heard so much about, or so Prudence
Garside suspected. There were persons of every standing in
life from old Gladys who kept a stall down at the docks and
bought "left-overs" from Harper's, to the likes of herself and
Jethro, Mr Pembroke, the solicitor and the minister who had
officiated at the service.

Prudence, who had known Cook for as long as Celie, if not
as well, hugged her friend speechlessly for several moments
when they returned from the church. She had been glad to see
the calmness in Celie though she was somewhat taken aback
by the overbearing protectiveness shown by the gardener –

what was his name? – towards her and the hostility which emanated from him when she and Jethro tried to draw Celie to one side. Prudence had only wanted to reiterate her long-standing invitation to Celie to come to Croxteth Drive whenever and as often as she liked. They had scarcely seen her in the past year, she said, which Celie explained was due to the shop and its expansion; but soon, Prudence begged. At the weekend? Next week? How about dinner one evening? Prudence would send the carriage for her but all the time the man was at Celie's back, his eyes narrowed, his mouth grim and Prudence could hardly press Celie, could she, not with her in such an emotional and vulnerable state.

They had all gone, Gladys willingly relieving them of the food which had not been eaten. It would sell well on her stall later that day she told them, for the seamen coming off the boats were only too glad to get a bit of English grub inside them after the foreign rubbish they had been forced to eat since they left home. Well, of course, the cooks on board the merchant vessels did their best, but there was nowt like Cook's raised veal and ham pies, was there? Oh, Lord, oh, dear God, she was that sorry. Just listen to her mouth, talking about Cook just as if . . . and her not cold in her . . . eeh, queen, she was that sorry . . .

Mr Pembroke took charge in his kindly but firm way, arranging those concerned about the sitting room for the reading of the Will whilst he himself sat at a table which stood in its centre. Ivy and Percy and, of course, Fred and Frank had been ready to wander off in pursuit of some job they were certain needed doing since Wills and things like that were nothing to do with them and they were quite thunderstruck when Mr Pembroke asked them to attend and to find themselves a seat.

'But . . .'

'Well . . .'

'Eeh . . .' they all said, bobbing and nodding, horribly embarrassed, giving rise to the thought which had not occurred to the rest of the servants that perhaps *they* should not be there but Mr Pembroke was adamant.

They didn't understand a word, naturally, for none of

them, or those who had gone before them to another life, had been fortunate enough to accumulate the wordly goods which necessitated such things. Wills were for the wealthy, those who had things to pass on, so what was Jess Harper up to, they asked one another, carrying on as though she was amongst that number.

'Now then,' Mr Pembroke said, looking over the top of his spectacles, his eyes moving from the stiff couple who sat side by side on the sofa, to the faces of the awkward members of Jess Harper's staff. 'I know legal documents are hard to understand so I will explain this to you again,' tapping the thick vellum paper in front of him. 'Mrs Harper was most insistent that you were all aware how much she appreciated the hard work you have all given to this venture of hers. Some of you have not been with her as long as others but nevertheless none of you have been overlooked so here's how it goes.' He paused for a moment, smiling kindly. 'To Lily Jones, Frances Armitage, Percival Danson, Frederick Johnson, Frank Johnson, Maude Evans, Isabel Hardcastle, Elizabeth Danson and Margaret Burke, the sum of five guineas each in recognition of the stalwart service they gave me.'

Even then they scarcely understood and the silence which followed went on and on.

Mr Pembroke glanced about him enquiringly, then cleared his throat.

'To Dorcas Benson, Katherine Mossop and Ivy Petty, the sum of ten guineas each and there is a stipulation that Mrs Petty,' Mr Pembroke nodded in Ivy's direction, 'that she is to have a home at Harper's for as long as she wants or needs it.'

Again there was a silence in which it seemed to Kate Mossop she could hear not only the beat of her own furious heart but the breath moving in and out of her lungs, even the sweat with which her body was slicked, pop from the very pores of her skin. She found she had her teeth clenched so tightly, her jaw ached, her teeth hurt and her eyes were opened wide and unblinking as she glared at the two motionless figures on the sofa. They were going to get it, of course. Dan and *her* and all the effort Kate had put in during the past two years and even before, all the bloody sweet smiles she had cracked her face into, all the words she had bitten her tongue over were to come to nothing. She had missed her chance. She had been too patient. The opportunity that she had been certain would come along, which she would recognise and grab with both hands, had whizzed past her without her ever noticing and if she didn't get out of this bloody room, out of this bloody building soon, she'd do Celie Marlow some mischief and it wouldn't be the sort you got a telling off for. She'd swing for her, the little bitch. Jesus Christ, why hadn't she *grabbed* him whilst he was hot for her? Why? Why? Why? It would have been . . . been chancy, bringing it out into the open when the old cow had been alive because as sure as the sun comes up in the east, she'd have done something to put a stop to it. She'd have got Dan out of it somehow which was why she, Kate, had kept hanging on, waiting for that one moment when fate would have been right. Right for her, for Kate Mossop, and now it had come and gone and it had all been for nothing. Ten guineas. Ten sodding guineas when she could have had *all this*. She could have been *mistress*, Mrs Dan Smith if she'd played her cards right and played them when it was right. Jesus . . . ! Oh Jesus . . . !

Mr Pembroke took off his spectacles and folded them before placing them carefully on the paper in front of him. He kept his eyes on them for several seconds, as though he was deep in thought, not quite sure how to tell them the rest, and was marshalling the words in his mind, until he had them right. A coal fell in the fire, sparks leaping up the chimney in a shower of gold and orange and the tension had become so great everyone jumped and Dorcas gave a little squeak. She smiled nervously, her hand to her breast, looking about her as though in apology. The clock on the mantelpiece ticked and tocked richly. Fred and Frank squirmed and Percy turned to glare at them.

'I'm not sure whether you know this.' Everyone in the room seemed to lean a little closer to Mr Pembroke when he at last spoke. 'When Mrs Harper came to see me about the making of the Will, she also had something else she wished to discuss with me.' He unfolded his spectacles and put them on again. Every eye was upon him.

'She was interested in the possibility of purchasing this building, you see, and she wanted me to . . . well, to cut a long story short, that is exactly what she did. Not only was she the owner of an expanding, thriving business but of the actual shop itself. There are debts, mortgages which the main beneficiary inherits with the property but . . .'

For some reason Mr Pembroke was not at ease and it showed, and deep inside Kate Mossop something stirred lazily. The solicitor sighed, shook himself and raising his head looked directly into Celie Marlow's clear honest eyes.

'After the bequests which I have already mentioned, the estate of Jessica Harper is bequeathed in whole to the man known as Daniel Smith.'

It took several long and painful seconds, at least thirty, in which every mind in the room, or most of them, struggled with the content of Mr Pembroke's words. Not only the content but the implication and when they had grasped it, those who were capable of it, the shock of it rendered them mute and paralysed. Dan . . . Daniel Smith. The man known as . . . and . . . Celie . . . nothing for Celie. Celie Marlow, who was as close to being Cook's daughter as if Cook had given birth to her. Thought the world of one another they had. Worked side by side for the last ten years. Cook passing on to Celie what she would have given to her own child if she'd had one and now, not even the five guineas the least of them had got, not even that.

There was a long sighing expulsion of air from a dozen throats. All eyes had gone to the couple on the sofa. Hand in hand they sat, just as they had done ever since Cook had died and slowly into the eyes of those who stared at them, began to creep a look of comprehension. It was obvious what had happened to Celie Marlow and Dan Smith in the last few days, at least it was *now*. Now that Jess Harper's strange Will had been read, and with understanding came a soft ripple of relief since it would be all right after all. You could see it in their faces. In Ivy Petty's who had known her friend for a woman of her own generation, one of those who believed, had been brought up to believe that a man was master in his own house. The *head* of the household, the holder of the purse-strings, and what did it matter anyway if they read Jess Harper's Will correctly, the Will which said as plain as the nose on your face that what belonged to Dan Smith would soon be in the hands of Celie Marlow. A bit of a funny way of going about it but then Cook had her own way of doing things and if she wanted to . . . well . . . *push* Celie along a bit, what better way to do it than to put what Celie wanted, *deserved*, into the hand of the man she would marry.

Celie was like stone, pale marble, the absolute black of her dress giving her skin the look of the translucent bone china out of which her customers drank their tea. You could see she was in a state of total shock but already Dan was turning to her, shocked himself, they could all tell, but ready to reassure her, lifting her hands, chafing them between his own, murmuring her name. Mr Pembroke had relaxed, a small smile – was it relief? – curving his mouth and when Kate Mossop stood up, everyone except Dan and Celie looked at her in surprise.

'Well,' she said softly. 'They do say as 'ow one door closes another opens and it's true, right enough, isn't it Danny?' She had begun to smile. It had not slipped by her after all, her chance. She had been right to wait, for *her* moment was here and she was ready to grasp it. The triumph in her was easily recognised by them all, even the two young boys, and Ivy Petty put her hand to her mouth and bent her head in anguish as though she knew full well what was coming.

Kate swayed gracefully across the room, sinking down on the sofa beside Dan. She suited black. The starkness of it gave her a strange beauty. It whitened her fine skin and put a deep green brilliance in her long cat's eyes. Her hair was severely drawn back from her pointed face, accentuating its bone structure. It looked almost white in the muted shadow of the fire-glowed room. She put a proprietorial hand through Dan's arm drawing it towards her full breast and when he turned to her, astonished, she placed a soft kiss on his cheek.

'Shall we tell 'em now, Danny? It seems only right.'

'Tell them . . . ?' Dan's face had lost every vestige of

the good colour it normally had, becoming a muddy grey beneath the brown the sun had put there. His cheeks seemed somehow to have fallen in, and his eyes had turned the flattest deadest blue as though the colour there had seeped away as well. Where was that briliant turquoise, Mr Pembroke remembered thinking as Kate Mossop sank her claws into the man beside her, and her sharp, vengeful knife into the girl on his other side.

'About us, Danny, you and me and the baby.'

'Sweet God . . .' Dorcas whispered and for some reason Belle began to cry.

'The . . .'

'Oh, yes, sweetheart. That's what happens when . . . well . . . you know . . .' hanging her head in what she pretended was modesty. 'It was bound to happen one day, wasn't it? And I'm sure Cook would only want what's best for the child. *Your* child, Danny, an' mine. A death and a birth like I said. One soul takin' the place of another, or so me Mam used to say. One door closin' an' another opening.'

Celie stood up with a sharp jerk, like a marionette suddenly pulled by its strings, her movements stiff, her head and hands palsied. Dan was ready to stand up with her, his limbs responding to the messages his heart gave, his heart which loved Celie Marlow and needed to reassure her that what Cook had left to him would be hers as well, as was only right. Show him a paper to sign and he would have the whole thing as it should be in the time it took him to scrawl his name. Tell him what to do, that's all he asked, and he would do it, but the girl on his other side, whose will was stronger than his, clung to his arm and short of grappling her violently away from him, flinging her aside, causing a *fuss* which he was reluctant to do on such a solemn occasion, he could not get free. He was dazed to the point where his punch-drunk brain could grapple with nothing, skittering frantically from one appalling disaster to another, since it seemed to his despairing mind that the inheritance which had just come to him *was* a disaster. A dreadful mistake on Cook's part. It was *Celie's*, all this. Her creation, brought about by her bright and courageous imagination, her dogged will, her hard back-breaking labour and yet Cook had left it in *his* care. Naturally Cook had known that what was Dan Smith's would be Celie Marlow's but now this second disaster had erupted, one that Cook had not foreseen, one *he* had not foreseen in the two years he had used, yes *used*, Kate Mossop's body and not only he, but Celie were to pay, for there was nothing more certain on God's green earth than the knowledge that Kate Mossop would not let Celie Marlow have one farthing of what was rightfully hers. Kate had staked her claim, the one *legitimate* claim a woman can make on a decent man, in front of a dozen people, telling them what had been going on between her and Dan, and the results of it, and he could do nothing about it because it was true. It had been nothing to him, an itch which must be scratched and he had thought, in his gullibility, that it had been the same for Kate. She had enjoyed it as much as he had, making no claims on him, going on month after month obliging him, saying nothing to alarm him, and he, like a fool, had accepted it all at face value. He had been unable to resist the allure and fire of her white body when it twined itself about his, each time telling himself that this would be the last. Her silver hair had drawn him, bound him and now . . . Oh sweet, sweet God . . . now, in one cruel and perfectly timed stroke, she had presented her account and he must pay what he owed.

'Celie . . .' His voice was strangled in his throat. He struggled feebly to get to his feet and from his side of the table Mr Pembroke looked at him with contempt. Contempt and bitter recrimination. He had argued forcibly with Mrs Harper on the wording of her will, pointing out to her how vulnerable she had left her protégée but the old lady had only smiled and tapped her nose.

'They'll be wed, those two, you mark my words, Mr Pembroke,' she had said, 'an' before the year's out,' and now look at them. Celie cut out of her rightful inheritance by the green-eyed hussy who was clinging to the beneficiary's arm and by the beneficiary himself. A weak man dominated by a strong woman which was the worst kind of combination and would spell doom on them all, for with the bad blood this would cause now, how were they to run the place as it had been run for the past two years?

Celie felt the kind carapace of shock settle tightly about her. She was conscious of Mr Pembroke's compassionate eyes as he stood up and began to shuffle his papers together. She could hear the sound the papers made whispering on the chenille cloth covering the table. She could hear the murmur of voices at her back where the confused servants whispered amongst themselves as they shuffled to their feet. Should they go or stay? they seemed to be asking, but none of it made much impression on her. Ske knew she had been struck some mortal blow but could not, thankfully, bring to mind what it was, and knowing it would hurt her she made no attempt for the moment. There was a kind of groaning going on beside her, where Dan and Kate sat, a man's groaning and Kate's voice, soothing, reassuring, quite kind really, as though she was doing her best to comfort, but again, Celie made no effort to unravel the meaning of it all.

She moved, smiling tightly, towards Mr Pembroke, her back as straight as a ruler, her head, heavy with the weight of the luxuriant coil of her hair, tipped slightly backwards, her chin high. Her lips trembled, though, despite the rigidity with which she held her mouth, and Mr Pembroke thought he had never seen anything quite so brave as Celie Marlow at that moment.

'Thank you, Mr Pembroke,' she said clearly, holding out her hand. He took it.

'Miss Marlow, I can't tell you how sorry . . .'

'No, no, Mr Pembroke . . . please . . . there's no need . . .'

'But this . . . your life's work to go to . . .'

'Mr Pembroke, Cook had her reasons, I'm sure, and a perfect right to . . .'

'No, *no* . . . not this . . .'

On the sofa the stricken man bowed his head and beside him the woman lifted hers. She smiled, turning to look about her, her eyes meeting those of Ivy Petty, of Maudie and Belle, of Dorcas and Fanny, and Lily, of Maggie and Beth. All those with whom she had worked for so many years. She continued to smile, her mouth lifting at the corners just as a cat's will, a female cat which has had a saucer of rich cream put before it and at which it is about to lap. They all looked back at her for several seconds and then one by one their eyes dropped before the triumphant gaze of the woman who was now, in all but name, their mistress, and that would soon be rectified. Frank and Fred stared awkwardly at the bowed figure of the man they had thought to be all-powerful, even they sensing that he no longer counted.

Three pairs of eyes would not be stared down. One pair was Percy Danson, the second was Ivy Petty. The last were the cold and steady blue of Maudie Evans.

Chapter Twenty-four

They were married a month later. The baby was due in March or April, Kate confided to Celie, just as though the pair of them were close confidantes and she could not wait to share the news with her, '. . . so we'd best get banns read right away, 'adn't we? Shall we 'ave it at All Saints, d'you reckon?' turning to the frozen-faced man beside her, and even Celie, still deep in the quagmire of wrenching grief and the senseless state into which Cook's death and Dan's perfidy had sucked her, was aware of the merciless pain he suffered.

'Whatever you say, Kate,' she answered politely. She was always faultlessly polite to Kate and to Dan. A passive aloof politeness which had very little to do with the fact that Dan and Kate were now her employers, though nothing had been said yet of wages, or indeed of any change in the way the shop and its staff were to proceed. Harper's had re-opened on the Thursday after the funeral, all of the women working under Celie and Ivy's supervision preparing the pies, the cakes and biscuits, the bread, scones and all the goods which Harper's had always provided for its customers. Maudie had been, as she confided later to Belle, 'chucked in at the deep end,' and she supposed it was due to the enthusiasm she had shown before . . . well, before Cook died, and which Miss Marlow was now prepared to take advantage of, though she did not, of course, word it exactly in that way. She was given many small, but important tasks to perform, tasks like whisking eggs and stirring custards, mixing the scone dough, at which she proved to have a fairy light hand, and weighing the dried fruit and spices which must be *exact*, to go into Miss Marlow's rich fruit cake.

Everything went on just as before and they all began to sigh hesitantly with relief. They had, they admitted to one another, especially when the wedding date was set for October 21st, expected Kate to throw her weight about, but no, she was as mim as a mouse, working cheerfully in the shop and doing exactly what she had always done, asking Celie for orders and guidance though it was noticed she no longer called her *Miss Marlow*. But if that was going to be the only changes in her despite her new status as fiancée of the owner of Harper's, then they could put up with that.

None of them knew of the conversation she and Dan Smith had had on the evening of the day the Will was read. The clock in the passage was striking a resonant fifteen minutes after the hour of twelve midnight when she slipped into Dan's bed. When the three shops had been made into one, the four-storey building had doors knocked through and in some places, partitions put up and in the newly designed arrangement, Kate had, without arousing suspicion, managed to fix it so that, apart from Belle and Maudie, who being young slept like the dead, she and Dan were the only ones to have bedrooms – there were six – on the top floor. Celie had one of the four big bedrooms on the second floor, at the back of the house. Because of the arranging of the staff and their sleeping quarters it had been easy for Kate and Dan to carry on their illicit relationship without the rest of the servants knowing, despite their growing numbers, and Kate saw no reason for it to discontinue. Besides which, the hold she had on Dan must be tightened, strengthened, re-confirmed, and she had only her body and her nimble brain with which to do it.

'Jesus Christ! Have you no shame? And have I . . . ?' For already his penis had quickened, eagerly. 'Aren't things bad enough without this?' he mumbled. 'We only buried her today . . . By God, neither of us are fit to . . .' He lay in the bed with his back to her. His utter self-contempt showed in the rigid length of his lean body, the way in which he stiffened away from her, recoiling as if he had come into contact with dead flesh and for a moment she was viciously offended, ready to rake her nails across his back, but she held on to her rage, just. The darkness could not hide his hopeless misery, the despair he had been plunged into that afternoon and Kate knew she would have to go very slowly, very carefully if she was to retain the advantage she had gained for herself that day. He would do the "right thing" by the woman he had "wronged" but until she had a wedding ring on her finger, nothing was certain and she must tread warily.

She began to weep soundlessly, amazing even herself by the naturalness of her crying. She was not a great one for tears and Dan had never seen her shed any and the force of them took him by surprise.

'Oh Danny, I'm sorry, I'm so sorry. I've put you in an awful position, haven't I? I didn't mean to, honest. I was goin' to this woman I 'eard tell of in Liverpool. She 'elps girls out, you know what I mean? Girls that fall like I did. She knows 'ow to . . . well, I didn't want to . . . but if you think I should get rid, I will. If it'd make it easier for you.' Her sobs shook the bed and her tears smeared against Dan's naked back and despite himself, he turned towards her.

'A woman, what woman?' She had his interest, if not as yet, his arms about her. 'What d'you mean . . . get rid . . . ?'

'The baby. Our baby. She uses a . . .'

'Christ Jesus! What're you saying!' He was appalled and of their own volition, his arms went round her, not round *her*, but round the body which held and nurtured his child.

'Don't talk like that, d'you hear? Don't even think of it. The baby is not to be harmed. Some woman in a back street . . . I have heard of it and what it . . . Oh, Jesus . . .'

'I know, Danny. I don't want it either but what am I to do? An unmarried woman with a baby and . . .'

'The child and you will not suffer.' His voice was flat and expressionless.

'I don't see how you can say that. You know what folk are like.'

'I know, I know all that and so . . .'

Her sobs became even wilder, her body moving in spasm against his. Her nightdress rode up about her body as her arms went round his neck. She buried her face beneath his chin, inconsolable in her grief for the child she was willing to murder for his sake and despite himself, he could not help but feel remorse and compassion.

'Don't, don't cry, Kate. It'll be all right.' He stroked her wildly tumbling hair, running his hand down her back to the taut and quivering nakedness of her buttocks. His fingers divided them, stroking, stroking, lifting her legs across his body then moving between them to the sweet moist kernel at the centre of her body. He had on a pair of long drawers but it took no more than a second to push them down, kick them off and plunge himself into her with the desperation of a man who had nothing to hold onto but this lusty bond she presented him with. But for a second he hesitated.

'The baby . . .' he gasped.

She almost said 'Bugger the baby,' smiling into his shoulder, but instead with a shy sweetness and a coarse thrust of her own body, she managed to convey to him that there was no need to hold back. He poured his seed into her with a relentless pounding which threatened to tear her apart.

'My word, Dan Smith,' she said, smirking into the dark. 'The way you carry on, it's about time we was wed.'

They lay for several minutes before Dan flung himself on his back away from her. He put his arm across his eyes as he spoke, as though even in the dark he could not face her nor look into her eyes.

'We must make Celie a partner, Kate. It's only right. Half to her and half . . . half for us. For you . . . and me.'

She had been expecting it, of course she had, but it took her a tense moment to drag herself back from the absolute need she had to spring up and shriek into the black night that she'd slit Celie Marlow's throat, aye an' her own, an' all, before she'd give her a bloody *farthing* of *their* inheritance. This was *hers* and she meant to enjoy it without that daft wishy-washy fool coming between her and what she had rightfully earned and as for having *half* of it – bugger that for a game of soldiers! She could stay on if she wanted and earn her bloody living like the rest of them would, doing what she was good at, which was cooking, but as soon as Kate Mossop became Mrs Daniel Smith, *she* would do all the ordering, the handling of the money, the accounts and the depositing of the enormous profits she meant to have, in the bank. That milksop'd get a wage like everyone else and bloody like it, but in the meanwhile there was Dan to soothe and put off until the wedding day.

'Dan, I've said it before an' I'll say it again. There's no one so generous as you, but you must do it right, you know that, don't you, you know you must.'

'What does that mean?'

'Come 'ere an' give us a kiss. Eeh, I've never told you this before but now, well, with us going to be wed . . . we are, aren't we Danny? You're going to do right by me, aren't you, sweetheart?'

'I said I was, Kate, and I won't go back on my word. We have made this baby and we have a duty to give it a proper name.'

'Oh, God,' she almost cried, ready to sigh in bored exasperation.

'I know, Danny. That's why I love you.'

'Kate . . .'

'You've no need to say it, Danny, not if you don't want to.'

He stirred uneasily, his man's discomfiture plain to see, to feel, but Kate was not offended now. She had what she had come for, she was prepared to wait for the rest.

'What about . . . Celie, Kate?'

'What about her, Danny?' Innocence in her voice.

'We must talk about . . . about what I just said.'

'What was that, chuck?'

'About sharing the . . .'

'We will, Danny, we will. Now I must get back to me bed. Goodnight sweetheart. Give us another kiss. Now you're sure you don't want to . . .' She squealed softly as her hand found the proud jut of his erection. '. . . You do, oh, Danny. What a man you are . . . see . . . put your hand . . .'

Though the wedding was hurried, it was as ostentatious as Kate and her love of the theatrical could make it. It took place on a pleasant Saturday afternoon, an autumn afternoon, on which the late sunshine filtered through the semi-leaved branches of the avenue of trees leading from the lych gate to the church porch. It was like walking under a delicate trellis work, the pale blue beauty of the October sky an arched background to the red, gold, tobacco and lemon of the dying foliage. The leaf fall under their feet, due to the dryness of the weather recently, was crisp, a rustling carpet which lifted in cheerful drifts as the party walked across them.

Celie had agreed to close the shop at noon, for which Kate said she was truly grateful for she did want them all to come to the ceremony. It wouldn't be the same without her friends about her, she said, and she was sure they would all agree with her that a girl's wedding day, which only came once in a lifetime, was very special. It was said without artifice and though most of them, at least among the women, would never forget the way Kate had blatantly announced her pregnancy, the minute she heard of Dan's inheritance, she had been so agreeable since, just as she *always* was, in fact, they were inclined to forgive her, to let her have the benefit of the doubt. It took two to make a baby so Dan must take his share of the blame for that, and though they had all been convinced in those few days between Cook's death and her funeral that Dan and Celie were . . . well . . . they had some sort of understanding, it seemed they were mistaken and that Dan had been no more than comforting Celie in her grief. Celie had been exactly as she had always been since. Hard-working, pleasant, soft-spoken, somewhat aloof and inward-looking, but then that was nothing new. The shop ran just as it always did, smoothly, profitably, with nothing to interrupt the seemingly effortless working of the machine Celie set in motion each day. She was talking of looking for another cook for she could not – nobody could really – take Jess Harper's place, not on her own and though Ivy was a great help, she wasn't getting any younger. Maudie was proving to be really talented with a great future ahead of her if she shaped, Mrs Petty told her and Celie agreed, but she had a long way to go yet.

Kate was in her favourite green, a vivid emerald which was too harsh for her, and certainly too vivid for a bride, but she thought it to be very elegant. The bodice was lined and boned in corset fashion, with a high collar. It fined Kate's waist to a mere nineteen inches, which would do that "babby" no good, Percy was heard to mutter as Kate climbed into the carriage which was to take her and Dan the hundred yards to the church. The gown was made of poult de soie, a pure corded silk of a rich quality since nothing was too good for Mrs Daniel Smith, it appeared. Enormous leg-o'-mutton sleeves ballooned from her shoulders to just below her elbow and her full gored skirt swept the top of her black kid boots. There were bows everywhere and scatters of black beading at the neckline, the cuffs and about the hem. Her black hat had emerald green silk ruching beneath the brim and a black-and-green bird perched, its mouth open as though about to sing, on the brim at the front.

When Ivy asked did Kate not think it bad luck to drive to church with the man not yet her husband, Kate laughed, throwing back her head and the bobbing bird, saying you made your own luck in this world, Ivy. The true reason, which was of course that Kate did not want Dan out of her sight, not for a minute, on that last day, was kept well hidden.

She began at once. An hour she had been Mrs Dan Smith, her left hand sporting the thick gold wedding ring tucked possessively in his arm and resting on the dark grey material of his new suit jacket to better display its winking newness. Only an hour. They were drinking what she called champagne, a cheap wine she thought good enough for HER servants, and nibbling the delicacies Celie and Ivy had made for the wedding breakfast, when she turned casually to Celie, as though in afterthought, as though she had quite forgotten to mention it in all the excitement.

'Oh, and by the way, Celie, that bedroom my 'usband seems to think is suitable for 'im an' me . . .' referring to Dan's room in which a double bed had been hastily shoved, 'Well . . . it's not.' She smiled and sipped her champagne. By God, her moment had come.

'I'm not sure I know quite . . .' Celie turned politely to the bride, smiling in that cool and irritating way which Kate had always detested, and inside her bubbled the delightful sensation she had looked forward to ever since the day Cook

had told her that fourteen-year-old Celie Marlow was to get
the job Kate had expected for herself. Five long years she
had waited for this moment and she was going to wring every
ounce of enjoyment out of it that she could. Out of this and
out of everything she meant to inflict on Celie Marlow. Every
indignity and injustice she could, even if she had to give Celie
Marlow Belle's job as kitchen maid to do it.

'It's not big enough, Dan's room, not for two people, and
o'course wi' me being in't family way and having to take a pee
every hour in't night . . .' She grinned maliciously as they all
gasped, even Frank and Fred, who had never heard that word
on a *man's* lips, let alone a woman's.

'. . . Well, I'll need to be near t'bathroom, an' then that
room ont' other side of the bathroom . . .' turning to smirk at
Dorcas, whose bedroom that was, and then at Ivy Petty '. . .
or the one at the front, will be needed for the nursery.'

'The . . . the nursery?'

'Yes, I don't mind which really, though I reckon two back
bedrooms wi't bathroom between . . .' which had been put in
when the renovations were made, 'would be best. Tomorrow,
I think. Dan an' me'll manage in his room tonight.'

She leaned back and smiled round at the stunned assembly.
She had done it, her expression said. She had nabbed him, the
owner of all this and she didn't give a damn now who knew
it. She had managed for the past few weeks since the reading
of the Will to this, her wedding day, to keep Dan from going
into Liverpool to see Mr Pembroke with a view to handing
over half of what Cook had left him to Celie. It had not
really been hard, for Dan was not at ease with things he did
not understand. He was bewildered by legal documents and
legal jargon, or indeed anything at all which smacked of legal
process, his uncomplicated and facile nature holding it in some
awe. He wanted her to go with him since she was quicker with
words than he was, he said, and she had promised she would,
and fool that he was, he believed her.

He tried to fight her.

'Oh, come on Kate, there's no need for that. You can't
expect Celie and Dorcas to move out of their rooms just
to . . .'

'Can't I, Danny?'

'No, you bloody well can't. They're both entitled to a decent bedroom . . .'

He was right when he said she was quick with words.

'An' I'm not? Your wife is not, is that what you're saying?'

'Of course not.' He began to shift uneasily, conscious of the others looking at him, knowing full well that they were waiting for him to put his foot down and to tell this new wife of his that he was the ruler of this particular household. If he didn't do it now, if he didn't let her know right from the start, he would be under her thumb for the rest of his life, and God help him if that was the case, for women like Kate Mossop, Kate *Smith* now, had no mercy on those they considered weaker than themselves.

'Then what?'

'Well, Celie and Dorcas have been in those rooms for . . . ever since the shops were knocked into one. They can't be expected to move upstairs to . . .' To where the lower servants slept, was what he almost said. To where Maudie and Belle, the kitchen maids slept. Where he himself had slept since he first came to Harper's and from where he had seen no reason to move. And which, had she not been so eager to get into his bed, Kate Mossop would have considered beneath her, since in her opinion she was an important and integral part of the structure of this business. She would have started a rumpus which would have been heard at the Pier Head in order to get herself one of the big bedrooms on the second floor, one of those occupied by Celie, Dorcas and Ivy.

'Danny, if you think the owner of Harper's and his wife should sleep in th' attic, then you're dafter than I give you credit for. We need space now, wi t' baby comin . . .'

'There's space enough in . . . where we are.' The words were desperate and written on every face amongst the embarrassed gathering were conflicting emotions. Contempt, irritation, dislike, pity, since it was very evident that Dan Smith was no match for Kate. He had proved it not only by his inability to withstand her mastery over his body in the past, hence the predicament he was now in, but by what looked like his awkward and ineffectual submission to her demand for the best bedroom in the house which was undoubtedly Celie Marlow's.

Percy growled softly in his throat, longing to give the new mistress a piece of his mind, his attitude saying quite clearly that no woman would treat him thus, but it was nothing to do with him who slept nowhere in this household. He had his own snug little billet in Borax Street where he lived alone and though it had been suggested vaguely that he might like to take over one of the empty attic rooms, the implication being that his occupancy on the premises would save his elderly strength and though he had been tempted, he was damn glad now he'd declined. There were going to be rare ructions at Harper's, before long, that was for sure.

'We could have Cook's old room.' Dan was saying, brightening suddenly. 'That way you'd have a sitting room as well. You know, for the . . . well, when the . . . baby comes.'

'I've no intention o' sleepin' next to't kitchen, me lad, an' besides, seein' as 'ow you an' me are married now and a married couple wi' a baby need a place of their own, I think best idea would be if we was to 'ave the whole of the second floor to ourselves. A bedroom, a parlour, a room for't baby an' a bathroom, then we could 'ave us a bit o' privacy, like. We want privacy, don't we Danny?' And to everyone's acute discomfort she placed her hand on her husband's inner thigh and trailed her fingers up towards his crotch. Worse still was Dan's instant response to it in the shape of the growing bulge between his legs.

To the relief of all those present, except perhaps Kate Smith, Celie rose quietly to her feet, moving towards the door, and at once they all did the same, covering their embarrassment and shame, not for themselves, but for the poor fool who was Kate's husband, with exclamations of things to do, and jobs to be seen to, for though it was Sunday tomorrow, the shop must be made ready for the following day. Celie stopped at the door, allowing Maudie and Belle and all the others except Ivy and Dorcas to pass through. When they had gone, she had closed it behind her, then turned to the two women her face quite expressionless.

'I for one have no objection to moving to one of the attic

rooms,' she said in her self-contained fashion. 'It makes no difference to me, where I sleep. But you, Ivy, and you, Dorcas,' her gaze moving to the open-mouthed maid, 'must take it up with Kate. I'll ask Frank and Fred to give me a hand in moving tomorrow morning, it that's all right with you, Kate.'

Dan sprang to his feet, still doing his best to cling to the authority which he had had thrust upon him by Cook's death.

'No, it's not all right, Celie. That's your bedroom and I'll not have you thrown out of it as though you were no more than a twelve-year-old kitchen skivvy. You run this place. Without you there'd *be* no Harper's. You're . . . you *should* be . . . *would* have been owner if . . .'

His distress was so great Ivy and Dorcas turned away, longing to slip through the door and back to the familiar and comforting warmth of the kitchen. But Celie had her hand on the door knob, barring their exit. The black undercurrents Kate had set to rippling appalled them. Dear God, scarcely more than an hour since she had married Dan and already she was getting everyone's back up with her high-handed demand to have, not only the bedroom which was Celie's, but theirs as well and the trouble was, if Dan didn't take a firm stand, she would have them. And what else might she take it into her head to fancy?

'But Celie isn't the owner, is she, Danny?' she was saying. 'You are and you're my 'usband, ant' father o' my kid, an' if a man can't stand by his wife an' kid, a decent man, that is . . .' She left the sentence unfinished as she calmly sipped her "champagne" and slowly, stiffly, Dan sat down beside her, the defeat washing from him in waves so that the three women by the door could almost feel it against their flesh. That was Dan's trouble, you see. He *was* a decent man and with his new wife reminding him of it and his obligation to his family which must naturally be put before all others, there was not much he could do about it. This was his place, and *hers* as his wife and so they were legitimately entitled to sleep in the best and biggest bedroom. And the baby, when it came, must have its own room. The bathroom which was still a source of wonder with its hot and cold running water, its large enamel bath, its lavatory which *emptied* itself when you pulled an overhead chain belonged to Dan – and so to her – and surely he was empowered to use the damn thing? Again, as a newly married young couple they would want to be on their own with their child when it came, so was it much to ask for their own parlour? No, it was not, so why did they all feel this surging resentment they asked themselves and would ask themselves a hundred times in the following months.

'Have you anything you would like to add, Mrs Petty?' Celie asked with scrupulous politeness, though there was something in her eyes when she turned them on Ivy that seemed to convey to her that Celie Marlow might not be the submissive and patient woman she appeared to be at this moment.

'No, I've not. Them lads can move me now. I might as well get mesen settled.'

'Dorcas?'

'I'll move when Mrs Petty does.'

'Very well. Will that be all, Kate?'

Kate smiled lazily, stretching her body for the approval of her new husband but he was not looking at her. His face was bleached of all colour and his lips were bloodless, his eyes staring into a future, at scenes which none of them could begin to imagine.

Chapter Twenty-five

She was at the far end of the garden, what she still called the "old" garden, when she heard soft footsteps on the flagged pathway between the neatly weeded, recently hoed rows of Dan's spring vegetables. At once she rubbed her handkerchief across her cheeks and knuckled her eyes, as a child would do, composing herself to the rigid, enduring restraint which she strove so hard to achieve at all times. No one must see her distress, not even Ivy who, though she said nothing, kept a watching brief on the slow downhill run towards despair which Celie was on. Slow now, but beginning to gather itself into that ever-increasing momentum which takes a toboggan as it glides from the top of the slope towards the bottom.

It was May. From where Celie crouched on the wrought-iron seat beneath the greening trees of the tiny enclosed woodland, she could see a dazzling lacework of blossom, pink and white, of apple and pear and plum trees, those which Dan had managed to salvage and cultivate from the old gardens, bringing them to the glory they now were. There were new trees, young and not yet ready for fruiting in amongst them, all lovingly tended by the owner of Harper's, as ethereally beautiful, as fragile as a froth of gossamer as they stirred in the slight evening breeze.

Beyond the small orchard were rows of vegetables. Asparagus and artichokes, the divided roots of rhubarb, French beans and runner beans, peas, celery sown in March, carrots and onions, leeks, parsnips and potatoes, and many many more put in over the months of winter and spring, for it seemed that only in his garden did Dan Smith find any kind of peace from the termagant who was his wife and Celie's mistress.

There were paths, three of them, where the old paths had been, leading from the house to the trees, all neatly flagged, and beside them, flower beds in which the golden trumpets of daffodils had recently triumphed and which now blazed with anemone and tulips and clarkia, ribbon borders of prince's feather, mignonette and antirrhinum. Beyond and close to the house were divided lawns, all surrounded by the growing shrubs and infant blooms which, Celie knew, were the only thing which kept Dan Smith attached to his sanity, for just before Christmas his wife had confessed to her silent staff, that sadly, there was to be no child, after all. She had hinted, with the greatest delicacy, at a miscarriage, turning to glare at Ivy when she snorted in disbelief. But the new Mrs Smith had said nothing for, of them all, Ivy, if she could stick it, was the most secure amongst the servants, thanks to Jess Harper's will. The codicil, which was quite explicit, stating that Ivy was to have a home at Harper's for as long as it suited her, could not be overturned, not even by the hard-eyed determination of Dan's wife and so Ivy felt no need to hide her true feelings as the others did.

'That were 'andy,' she sniffed, folding her arms across the bib of her apron, but her mistress chose to ignore it. What did *she* care what they thought, her expression had said, the pretence of sadness slipping away on a smile of pure malice.

'So back to work, everyone,' she had added, clapping her hands as though they were children in a classroom. '. . . there's a shop full of customers want servin', Dorcas, an' them pans won't scrub themselves, Belle Hardcastle, so back to that sink. An' what are you starin' at, Celie Marlow? 'Ave I got a spot on me nose or summat? Get a move on, there's three dozen almond squares to be put in that order o' Mrs Richmond's so you'd best look lively. Ten o'clock, I promised they'd be delivered.'

The footsteps hesitated at the top of the steps just where the bird-bath was set and an anxious voice spoke Celie's name.

'Are you there, Celie?' it said, and Celie breathed a sigh of relief. It was Maudie who had been just about to embark on her new and exciting career as a kitchen maid, assistant to herself and Ivy, until the death of Cook and the installation of Kate Mossop as their ruler had flung her back on her knees at the scrubbing pail, or up to her elbows in the caustic washing-up water she had thought to be behind her.

'I'm here, Maudie.' Her voice was low but Maudie heard her and her footsteps quickened as she slipped through the trees to the seat where Celie huddled. 'Is something wrong? Does she want me?'

Maudie flopped down beside her, her thin frame seeming to clatter the bones of her. None of them looked as glossy and well-cared for as they had done eight months ago, and was it any wonder, Celie thought wearily, with the thin rations their new mistress imposed on them in her obsession for profit. You'd think amongst all the good food which was abundantly available to them, the girls would thrive for there was nothing to stop them filching a meat pie or a fresh fruit scone, a thick slice of bread and best butter but as yet, probably due to their upbringing and training under the honest auspices of Jess Harper, it did not seem to occur to them. They ate the short commons, well cooked and seasoned, for how else would Celie and Ivy go about it, that *she* dictated, whilst in the shop the same superb produce poured in ever increasing amounts over the counter, for greedy as she was, Kate had the good sense to continue to use the very best ingredients for her customers. The shop continued to thrive and at Christmas, when all the specialities Cook and Celie had created and which now fell on Celie and Ivy, were on display, the clink of coins as Kate counted them into *her* box could be heard coming from the parlour she and Dan shared each evening.

'No, she's gone out.' Maudie's voice was as thin and weary as her body and Celie sighed, leaning to take the girl's hand affectionately in hers.

Maudie was only a few years younger than she was herself and yet it seemed to her that there was a decade, or perhaps even two between them. In years Celie Marlow was still only past girlhood. Was twenty-one *old*? It felt like it. Sometimes she caught sight of herself in the mirror. Not when she was arranging her hair, or checking to see that her appearance was neat and attractive as it should be for the shop, but unexpectedly as she happened to glance that way as she passed by it, and the utter sadness she saw there startled her. That, and though her skin was taut and young, a general look of maturity which disconcerted her. She was no longer youthful. Her girlhood had fled away nearly a year ago when the woman who had been the only "mother" she had known, had unwittingly tossed her to one side, giving Celie's life to Kate Mossop. Not only had she lost a friend whom she had loved and respected, but she had lost the exciting, fulfilling world she had made for herself out of the dead and painful ashes of her love for Richard Latimer. No, that was not quite true. Her love for Richard Latimer was not dead, nor consumed to ashes, but flickered wilfully in her bruised heart, and she knew she would never be free of it, never. She had tried, dear Lord, but she had tried, throwing herself fanatically into the building of Harper's and for eighteen hours out of twenty-four, the eighteen hours she spent labouring in the kitchens, supervising the running of the shop, the ordering of the provisions, the accounts and all the other tasks which were hers, she had succeeded in putting him from her mind. It was at night he came to her, smiling impudently in the dark of her new bedroom as soon as she laid her head on the pillow, coming to her in her dreams so that when she woke her face would be wet with tears. Why, oh dear God, why could she not pluck him from her heart? Why did her body still melt in that delicious way his hands and lips had shown her two years ago? Why did her *skin* remember his touch? Would she ever forget? Could she, especially now that the one consolation her wounded heart and mind had known had been ripped away from her, leaving another gaping affliction which could not seem to heal? How long could she manage it, this half-life she lived under Kate's despotic and petty tyranny? How long?

'Where's she gone to?' she asked Maudie.

'God knows, I certainly don't, nor bloody well care.'

'Maudie.'

'Sorry, Cook,' and they both smiled sadly at the small joke.

'Well, at least we can stop here for a few minutes until it gets dark.'

Celie stared up through the gently moving leaves towards the dusky sky. It was Saturday and the shop had just closed. There was still a lot to do in the way of clearing up but tomorrow was Sunday. Not that their new mistress would allow them to waste the day lolling about the place as she put it, even if it was Sunday, and the house and shop must be cleaned from attic to cellar in the absence of Lily and Mary who had been dismissed months ago. She could see no reason to employ "dailies" when she had six perfectly able housemaids to do the cleaning, Kate had declared, counting Celie Marlow in that number, and so from seven in the morning until noon everything that could be scrubbed was scrubbed. Everything that could be polished was polished, carpets cleaned with the tea leaves saved all week from the teapots, floors waxed and bed linen changed and laundered. It was a wonder that none of them gave in their notice, Celie often thought, at the same time realising guiltily, that the fault was probably hers. She and Dan had been dismissed from Briar Lodge, taking Cook and Kate with them, not purposely of course, but nevertheless, they had left under a cloud without the "character" a mistress would normally give to good servants and it had been Celie who had persuaded Dorcas and Belle and Maudie here beside her to do the same, unaware that within months, the successful world she and Cook had created was to fall about their ears in an avalanche of disaster. Naturally, if any one of them was to leave Harper's now, there would be no question of their employer allowing them to go with a good reference so they must stay, doing just what she told them, for if they left, no mistress would employ a servant without her "character" to vouch for her, or him.

Celie sighed into the growing darkness and the girl beside her leaned closer, so that their shoulders touched companionably.

'It's a bugger, ain't it,' she said.

Celie laughed. 'Oh Maudie, you really are incorrigible.'

'Am I? Is that good?'

'Sometimes. It depends.' She turned to look sadly at the girl beside her. Maudie was still small with the figure of a child, though she was nearly eighteen. Not quite pretty but given a less unattractive outfit than the scullery maid's balloon cap and sacking apron she wore, her little face had an impish and merry appeal. There was an endearing scatter of copper freckles across her upturned nose and a strand of curly hair to match falling across her white forehead. In a strange way she had taken Cook's place in Celie's affections. It was as though Celie was *Cook* and Maudie was herself all over again and a bond had grown between them, unspoken and apparently unnoticed by all but Ivy who had nothing to say on the matter. When they could, without attracting Kate's attention, they took their Sunday afternoons off together, walking in Sefton Park if the weather was fine, listening to the band which played with great verve and enthusiasm to the strolling crowds. Sometimes they would walk down to Upper Parliament Street and from there to the miles of dockland which lay along the busy, teeming highway of the River Mersey, breathing in the rich and redolent aroma of raw wood which assailed their nostrils. It came from Brunswick Dock which was devoted to the accommodation of shipping employed in the timber trade. There was Queen's Dock, built one hundred years ago, leading down to the Marine Parade where Celie and Maudie sauntered, past Wapping and King's Dock and the rippling multi-pointed roof of the Tobacco Warehouse, to Duke's Dock built by the Duke of Bridgewater to be used by boats in the canal trade. Albert Dock rising majestically on their right, one of the most costly and beautiful buildings of its kind with its lofty and gracious fireproof warehouses opened by Prince Albert in person. History surrounded them. The history which was in every building of the great seaport, where both young women had been born. Canning Dock beyond that, used chiefly by shipping employed in the coastal trade. George's landing stage where for centuries ferry boats of every kind

from sailing to steam had bumped their way across the river
and behind which, in George's Dock, a four-masted barque,
probably the last to be built on the Mersey, was berthed.
Bustling Princes landing stage where a young girl had put her
trusting hand in that of a handsome soldier, and on their right,
high above the dock, the clattering tumult of the overhead
railway.

Celie always hurried by at this point with her gaze averted,
unwilling to rake up memories of that day, only stopping
reluctantly at Maudie's insistence if some great ocean-going
liner, five days out from New York, was about to berth, or
another to plunge across the Atlantic to what had once been
called, the "New World". They would stand on the parade
beyond Victoria Dock with the smell of the sea from the
river's estuary slapping in their faces and study as though
they had not seen it before the fine view across the ever
moving waters of the river to the Cheshire Woods in the south
and the Irish Channel to the north. Bootle Bay stretched away
to the right, the Rock Perch Lighthouse and fort splitting the
shining, lapping water and the whole of the Cheshire coastline
from New Brighton to Eastham stretched like a living ribbon
before them.

Maudie was the eldest in a large family and with no money
to spare and the disinclination on her father's weary part to
get off his bum, as she put it, had been no further than
the outskirts of the parish of Childwall where she had been
born. Only three miles from this spectacular viewpoint where
the greatest stories of the world of shipping and adventure
might be found and until Celie took her, she had never in
her life seen a ship, nor the water on which it sailed. She
was bright and cheerful, her spirits rarely low and her vivid
interest in everything Celie showed her awoke some dozing
emotion in Celie which had not raised its head since Kate
Smith had taken over the running and absolute ownership of
Harper's.

Both girls sighed simultaneously, then shivered, for the
spring evening was chilly and as she did so Maudie clapped
her hand to her brow.

'Land's sakes,' she chirped in such a perfect imitation of

Cook, Celie could not help smiling. 'I'd forget me own head if it were loose.'

'What is it?'

'The reason I come out int' first place. You've got a visitor.'

'A . . . a visitor?'

'Aye, an' 'ere's me lollin' about, as our mistress'd say, when I should be . . .'

'Who is it, Maudie?' Celie's voice had such urgency in it Maudie turned to stare.

'Nay, I don't know. It were Dorcas who answered t'bell int' shop. All I know is that I was sent ter look for yer.'

She should have known, she thought dazedly, as Prudence Garside rose from the chair in Kate's sitting room where the flustered Dorcas had put her, not knowing where else to place the daughter of her previous mistress. And yet why should she not be surprised to see Prudence, Celie asked herself, since from the day of Cook's funeral, there had been no word, neither written nor on the telephone from the woman who had once been so dear to her.

'Prudence,' she nodded politely but made no attempt to sit, nor to invite Prudence to do so. But really, she thought later, was she so obsessed with her own damaged life, she had forgotten Prudence's outspoken disregard for anything which smacked of prevarication. Prudence had always liked things to be out in the open so why should she be any different now, and any move towards guile or pretence was over-ridden by her without a qualm.

'Don't Prudence me, Celie Marlow, particularly in that imperious manner you assume, just as though you think you are being hard done by. No, I will have my say and if you still insist on discarding me and our friendship, then I will leave at once. It is eight months since we last met under very sad circumstances, but it is at such times, at least I would have thought so, that one needs one's friends.'

She lifted her head regally, drawing in her breath for another onslaught but Celie suddenly sat down as though her legs had turned to jelly and with a gesture which was heartbreaking, put her face in her hands and began to weep.

At once Prudence ran to her, kneeling before her with an expression which was both horrified and bewildered.

'Celie, dearest, what . . . ? Oh, what have I said? Really I didn't mean to upset you so, you know I didn't. It's just that I . . . well, it's been so long and I couldn't bear your silence any longer. I realise how dearly you held Cook in your affections and I appreciate that grief is . . . but . . . well, Jethro said I must come and . . . "Put your anger and pride aside", he said, because I *was* angry, Celie, to be so ignored when we have been such good friends, and of course, being a Latimer I have my pride, but . . . Oh, Celie, do stop crying, please, see, take my handkerchief and blow your nose, and then you can explain why you have ignored my notes and my telephone calls and . . .'

Celie raised her head and stared at Prudence through the wash of tears which flooded her eyes and hung on her long, curling lashes. Her skin had turned to the pink which afflicts most women who weep but on her, Prudence could not help noticing, it looked quite enchanting. No blotches or streaks, just a rose-coloured flush across which fat teardrops slid and dripped from her chin to her bodice.

'Notes?' she answered.

'Yes, of course. The boy delivered one the very next day, no it was the day the shop opened. He promised me faithfully he had put it in the hands of the girl who serves in the shop, the fair one. When I didn't hear, giving you a couple of weeks because I knew how dear Cook was to you, I wrote again and again I had no reply. So I telephoned. A man answered, then a woman came to the machine and told me you were engaged at the moment and had told her to tell me that you would telephone me later and so . . .'

'Kate.'

'I beg your pardon.'

'Kate, it must have been Kate,' Celie's voice was so quiet Prudence could hardly hear her but she caught the name.

'And who is Kate?'

'She's the new owner of Harper's . . . This all belongs to her.'

'*What* . . . ?' Prudence sat back on her heels and after

that one appalled word, it seemed she had nothing further to say so great was her shock. It was so quiet in the room Celie could distinctly hear the clip-clop of horses' hooves as a carriage went by the front of the shop. Above their heads someone – Maudie? – clumped across the bedroom which had, until recently, been an attic and on whose floor the new Mrs Smith could see no reason to put down carpet. The whine of the lift bearing crockery down to the kitchen to have what Kate called a "good wash" carried from the corner of the room and down on the ground floor from the passage where it stood came the deep bass of the clock sounding half past the hour of seven. There was a shout, distance making it vague as Frank addressed his brother from somewhere above. They knew their mistress and presumably her husband were not on the premises, and though they also knew they had nothing to fear from Mr Smith, Mrs could be a right begger, if she thought her authority was being defied.

'You'd better tell me what's happened, Celie,' Prudence said at last. 'Come on, wipe your eyes. There, that's better, no, you keep the hankie, I have another. Now then.'

'Prudence, I don't know where to begin. It's such a long and dreary . . .'

'Well, before you start, why don't you fetch your coat and come back home with me? I have the carriage. You could have dinner with us. Just the three of us. We won't bother to change. Better yet, stay the night. It's Sunday tomorrow. You could have the day with us and then Jethro can bring you back . . .'

'Oh no, I can't do that. I have things to do.' Celie's voice trailed away indecisively.

'What things? The shop is closed tomorrow, isn't it?'

'Yes but . . .'

'Well then . . .'

'We . . . the girls . . . we have to . . .' She hung her head, as though in shame and Prudence stared at her, puzzled.

'Yes?'

'Kate has . . . got rid of the two dailies and . . .'

Prudence let the breath she had not been aware she had been holding sigh out of her softly.

'So you . . . and the other girls . . . clean the place? Is that it? Is that what you're saying? That you, an experienced and gifted cook on whom this . . . this upstart, whoever she is, relies for the very existence of this business allows herself to be treated as though she were no more than a scullery maid? I think you had better explain what has happened here, Celie.'

Prudence's eyes were flinty and the words hissed from her in outrage.

Celie sat, her head hanging down, beaten at last to the point where even Prudence's contempt, for surely it was that, failed to jerk her up from the deep and cloying pit of despair into which she had sunk. There was no escape from it – none. She had fought so hard and so long from that day over ten years ago when she had begun as skivvy in the kitchen of Briar Lodge, working herself and her fingers to the very bone to become the great cook she had so admired in Jess Harper. She had done it too. She had overcome heartache and injustice and together she and Cook had carved out the place that Cook intended them both to have, that Cook had meant her to carry on and now, not only had it been stripped from her, so had her self-respect, her pride, her ambition, her reason for living. She had nothing now.

'Stop that *at once*, Celie Marlow, d'you hear me? *At once*. I'm sorry you have had this setback . . .'

'*Setback!*'

'But I'm even more sorry to see the way you have taken it. Oh, yes, you may well stare, but I can only say I never thought to see the day when you would be so loaded down with self-pity, you would allow some little guttersnipe to treat you as though you were no more than the dirt beneath her feet. You are Cécilie Marlow, yes – that name has a grand ring to it, has it not, and can surely put to shame *Kate* . . . What's her name? *Smith* . . . why that sounds . . .'

Prudence became very still then, bending her head to peer into Celie's bleached face with sudden perception.

'*Smith* . . .?'

'Yes.' It was no more than a mumble.

'So he married *her* and not . . .'

'That is how . . .'

Prudence stood up, gathering her skirt and her bag which she still clutched about her. She pulled her bonnet more firmly over her ears, then, taking Celie's flaccid hand, dragged her to her feet.

'Come along, let's get home. Jethro will be wondering . . .'

'I can't, Prudence. I just can't leave like that. If she comes back and finds me gone, she might . . . sack me.'

'Fiddlesticks! Don't you think she knows that without you this business would come crashing down about her ears before the month was out? She knows nothing about . . .'

'She does, oh, yes, she does. She's clever. And if she got rid of me, she'd give me no character and then . . .'

'Dear God, girl, pull yourself together. I'm absolutely astounded. Don't you know what you've got in these hands of yours and in that thing in your head I once called a brain? Oh, what's the use, we can't talk here. Are you coming home with me or not?' Prudence dragged an impatient foot on the carpet.

'Prudence, I don't know whether I can . . .'

'Let me tell you right now that you can't, Celie Marlow, not if you want to keep your job.'

The voice from the doorway made them both jump guiltily, though what she had to be guilty about, Prudence said to her husband later, she couldn't think.

Kate was dressed in her "walking-out" costume. The one in which she liked to take a turn about Sefton Park on the arm of her husband. It was, like her, eye-catching, in a shade not far off scarlet, and she looked just what she really was – a kitchen maid on her afternoon off, despite her new status. Her hands were on her hips in an attitude which asked how dare this intruder *and* Celie Marlow use *her* private sitting room, even though she knew full well who the intruder was. She was not at all overwhelmed, for this was *her* place and her narrowing eyes told them so.

At once Prudence's head rose to that alarming and haughty level which her lineage and upbringing had taught her. This was her mother's kitchen maid who had once, respectfully unobtrusive, handed tea and cakes to her when Phyllis

Latimer had callers, and it made no difference that their roles had now altered.

'Ah, Kate,' putting her in her place at once. 'Good evening. Having had no reply to my notes or telephone calls, I came to call on my friend, Miss Marlow, but, finding her somewhat low in health, I have decided to take her home with me for the weekend . . .'

'Oh, you 'ave, 'ave you . . . ?' Kate Smith began, for she could be overbearing herself after eight months of total domination, not only of her husband, but a house full of nervous servants, but she was no match for Prudence Garside, who had had a lifetime's experience of it.

'Yes, I just said so. It seems to me that she is seriously overworked in this establishment and only a proper rest will put her back on her feet. Tomorrow being Sunday . . .'

'She's work to do tomorrow, as she well knows. As they all know. And won't be free until dinner-time. She has the afternoon off, so if you want to pick her up then, I'd have no objection.'

'Really, but I'm afraid that just won't do. In fact, I have a fancy to take her with me to Ambleside, where my husband and I have a small weekend cottage. It is very pleasant there at this time of the year and a week or two in the mountains would do her the world of good.'

'I don't care where . . .'

'That will do, Kate. Just step aside if you please. Miss Marlow and I are about to leave.' Prudence turned to the frozen figure of Celie. 'Have you a suitcase or bag for your things, my dear? I should pack for a week at least.'

'Now, look 'ere you, . . . you . . . You're taking Celie Marlow nowhere. She's a job to do . . .'

'Which she will return to when she's better, if she so wishes. Come along, Cécilie, show me your room and I'll help you to pack.'

It was perhaps CÉCILIE that did it. Her own full and splendid name that got Celie on the move, placing one stiff foot in front of the other beside Prudence.

Kate was elbowed aside, though in fact Prudence did not actually touch her. She had no need to. Despite the fury –

and fear – which had her in its grip, something at that last moment prevented Kate from laying hands on Prudence Garside. The generations of Mossops who had served the generations of Latimers, or families like them, had bred in them an automatic submission to authority and it took her voice from her and the strength from her limbs and, at the end, she stood silent and still as Miss Prudence drove away with Kate Smith's breadwinner.

Chapter Twenty-six

'I can't stay *for ever*, Prudence, so will you . . .'

'Why not? Jethro and I love having you here so will you sit down and stop jittering about as though you feel you should be serving tea instead of Nora.'

'That's just it. I do. Much as I love you and Jethro, and being your guest, I just can't get used to doing nothing.'

'Try.'

'I have tried. For a whole month I've tried but the habit of a lifetime, of almost fifteen years in a kitchen has instilled in me the need to be doing something and now that I am more myself, thanks to you . . .' her face soft '. . . I must decide what I am to do with the rest of my life. I've always worked, Pru, and I must again. You do see that, don't you? I must find something, a job of some sort at which I can earn my living. There must be someone who will employ me. I'm a damn good cook, the best . . .'

'So you would be content to take up a post in some household where your employers would overlook your lack of references, though of course that won't happen because Jethro and I would supply them . . .'

'But you and Jethro have not employed me. D'you mean you'd lie . . .'

'Dear God, Celie, you are the most scrupulous woman I've ever met . . .'

'No, I'm not, Prudence,' Celie interrupted sadly. 'I enticed all your Mama's servants from her with promises of better jobs and now they are stuck with Kate, earning less than your Papa paid them. Oh, yes, she reduced their wages as she did mine. They can't leave her . . .'

'Celie Marlow, I could shake you sometimes, really I could. Despite your head for business which you displayed so brilliantly at Harper's, you are a complete idiot when it comes to the *real* world. The world where *men* are employed and men, my dear, have no scruples when it comes to making a bob or two, as my Jethro says. How do you think he made his first million, my love? Not by telling the truth and being absolutely honest. You are a woman and you have a wonderful gift which you could use to get you all you ever dreamed of in this world. You have proved you have a flair in the business world. Look what a success you made of Harper's and yet you tamely talk of finding some post in another woman's kitchen and not only that but are shocked when I tell you that Jethro and I will give you a reference to enable you to do so. If that's what you want. But do you *really*? Do you really want to condemn yourself to apple dumplings and casseroles when you might be running your own concern as you did at Harper's? You took a hard knock, Celie. You had what you worked for stolen from you by a woman who was not squeamish and, my dear, if you want it back, you must be as she was.'

Prudence leaned forward and Celie found she was doing the same. There was a jut to Prudence's chin, a strange air of determination about her, so strange and so strong Celie found it difficult not to be affected by her magnetism.

'You mean . . . ?'

'I mean fight for what is rightfully yours. You know my family were not always wealthy. Oh, the Latimers had an ancient lineage going back into the faded time of the years when Liverpool had 334 ships instead of the twenty odd thousand the docks clear now, or so my husband tells me. They were not the owners of the best estates but they were astute men who accumulated blocks of property in Liverpool and the neighbourhood. Men like the Moores of Bank Hall, the Crosses of Crosse Hall and the Latimers of Briar Lodge, though why they chose to call their estate such a *pretty* name is a mystery. Anyway, they got their wealth from the rents they charged for the use of their property and then invested their surplus incomes in commercial ventures.'

'Why are you telling me this, Prudence?'

'Because I wish to point out to you that all wealth is not inherited. *Somebody* starts it. With a loan perhaps, or money worked for and saved, but mostly with daring.'

There was a long heavy silence whilst Celie did her best to assimilate, to form into a cohesive shape, the words Prudence had spoken. Pru was telling her, was she not, that she could become . . . become a businessman . . . woman . . . set up a business of her own, as she and Cook had done . . . *no* . . . as *she* had done, for Cook had, after she had found the premises in the Boulevard, allowed Celie her head. It had been Celie who had conferred with Mr Pembroke. It had been Celie who had dealt with the bank manager, who had studied the financial newspapers and nervously bought a share or two, here and there, when Mr Drake at the bank had advised it . . .

The shares! Her shares! The ones she had . . . the ones she had forgotten in the deep and abject misery and self-pity she had wallowed in ever since Cook died. They were still there in the small . . . what was the word? . . . portfolio the bank manager held for her, and the modest account she had opened when Harper's was born. She had added nothing to it since, merely shoving the ten shillings a week Kate had reduced her wage to, in an old tin box at the back of her chest of drawers. About sixteen pounds it now held, which was worth nothing, but who knew what her shares were worth and the answer, of course, was the bank manager, or Jethro.

She was unaware that Prudence was watching her with a sweet tide of triumph beginning to swell in her as she saw the colour flood excitedly to Celie's cheeks and the burning glow in her narrowed, speculative eyes. Her small chin lifted and her lips had firmed with unconscious resolve. The dappled shade of the leaves on the oak tree beneath which they sat cast dancing shadows across her tense face and though she sipped her tea with what seemed evident signs of enjoyment it was clear it might have been tap-water for all the notice she took of it.

It was June. The Queen's Diamond Jubilee day. Celie,
Prudence and Jethro were to drive down to the city to
watch the procession of Trade and Friendly Societies which
was to be composed, it was said, of some 15,000 people,
eighteen sections, each one led by a rousing band and carrying
banners. The Lord Mayor and Lady Mayoress were to give a
garden party at the Botanic Gardens and the guests, of whom
Prudence and Jethro were but two, were rumoured to be
2,000. At St George's Hall over 1,000 of the deserving poor
were to be entertained to a dinner, though what qualification
was needed to be among this group – beside being poor, of
course – was a puzzle none of them could solve. There were
to be medals struck to be presented to the thousands of school
children who would be lining the route before being marched
to the landing stage and embarked on steamers to witness
the grand marine display on the river. Over twenty-five ships
were to take part, representatives of the Lines of Steamships
trading to all parts of the world. After dark there would be a
brilliant display of electric lights and fireworks, on the river
and in all the principal parks of the city.

Celie drew in her breath, leaning back reflectively in the
white wickerwork chair which Prudence's servants had placed
beneath the trees for their mistress and her guest to recline
in. It was a warm day, the sky that vivid azure blue which
comes only at midsummer. There was a smell of lavender
heavy on the air and the sound of pollen-laden bees as they
browsed peacefully among the flowers. The flower beds
around them were brilliant with roses in every shade from
the palest pink to the deepest scarlet and in the far border
dahlias, ranunculus and carnation, polyanthus and pansies and
picotees danced in lively mixed abandon for Prudence did not
really care for *order*, even in her garden. The lawn, freshly
cut and watered that morning, shimmered a deep and velvet
green and on it Bess rolled on her back in an ecstasy of canine
joy. From the low privet hedge which divided the borders
from the gravel walks a young cat suddenly darted, flirting
with the startled bitch and in a second there was a flurry of
vigorous barking as she was chased by the dog round to the
back of the house.

Celie, if she saw them, which was doubtful, took no interest in their playing. She had placed her hands carefully in her lap to still their trembling, folding them about one another in the way she was to learn so that those with whom she did business would not be aware of her nervousness. A shaft of sunlight slipped through the leaves above her, illuminating her fine skin to pearl. Her dark hair, brushed to the hue and shine of a horse chestnut was pulled back from her forehead and gathered into a chenille net and although the style was severe several stray curls had escaped to drift about her ears and neck.

Her outfit, a two-piece, consisted of a bodice, and a skirt, the soft lines of which were deeply gored and skilfully cut with flounces, giving it a fluted effect. The bodice was of crisp white lawn, yoked, and the neck and wrists of the long sleeves were edged with broderie anglaise lace. The skirt was the palest caramel shade and when they drove to town she would put on over the blouse a sleeved bolero of the same colour, which had no collar, allowing the lace to show at the neck and cuffs. It had been made for her by Miss Edna Sykes of what had once been "Hawkins Dressmaker" of Bold Street and from where, years ago, Celie had bought her first dashing bonnet and dress material.

She was so tense, so held within herself to a state of high-charged excitement the only colour in her face was in her warm, coral pink lips. It was mid-summer and behind her on this great Jubilee Day was the life she had led for just over twenty-one years and before her, empty and unwritten upon was the rest of it and whatever she was to make of it. Surely she was not going to allow it to remain empty, colourless, drab, sterile? Prudence had dragged her from her apathy, her misery, and in the past month had returned her to the robust health she had always possessed, despite her delicate appearance. She had hardly been aware of how tired she was, how dragged down, so turgid had her mind been, and her spirit, but now, just as though Prudence had flicked the switch of the new electric lighting which was being installed in so many homes, her mind was filled with a shining brilliance, an illumination which was ready to reveal to her what she must do.

The deep black shadow of the house crept back across the lawn as the sun rose to its zenith. Bess, whose coat was the palely sheened colour of honey in the sunshine, had returned to the lawn and lay panting in the heat, her tongue drooling from her mouth, her eyes glazed and narrowed. From somewhere off to the side of the house where the stables lay someone was whistling and a voice took up the words of the old Liverpool street song:

> "There was a rich merchant in Liverpool did dwell,
> He had but one daughter, few could her excel,
> With her red rolling cheeks and her rolling black eye,
> She fell deep in love with her bonny sailor boy."

Cécilie Marlow heard it and smiled, then turned to Prudence. Gone was the pale, sad-eyed wisp of a girl who had, for the past nine months drifted from day to day with no purpose but to get through without further pain or even feeling and in her place had come a young woman of great vitality and purpose. Her expression said she was going somewhere and if at this moment she was not quite sure where that somewhere might be, she knew it was ahead of her and she had only to set herself to resolution and she would reach it. Her smile deepened and she leaned forward to take Prudence's hand.

'Celie?' There was a question in her friend's voice.

'Prudence, I must decide what I am to do. I am not a child. The child I was has gone. I'm alone now, but for you, my dear friend. I have no one to tell me what to do so I must make the decision myself. I know you and Jethro are here beside me but it is me, Cécilie Marlow, who must make up her mind what to do with herself.'

'And . . . ?'

'I shall . . .'

'Yes, oh yes, Celie, what will you do?'

Celie let out her breath on a long, soft sigh, then raised her head.

'I don't know yet, Pru. It's here in the depth of my mind but I shall have to think on it. Talk to Jethro. Go and see Mr

Pembroke and Mr Drake at the bank. I have a little money. Perhaps I can . . . oh, I don't know. I just don't know for sure but there must be . . . I must use the talents that were given to me, as you said, and I must learn to . . .' She turned to smile at Prudence, 'I must learn to use them, *all* of them.'

Her smile became brilliant and she straightened her already straight back, deliberately drawing Prudence's attention to her small peaked breasts and the narrowness of her waist.

'You know what I mean, Prudence, don't you? Men are such fools, aren't they? Most of them. Easily influenced by a woman's . . . charms.' Her silvery grey eyes hardened to the colour and darkness of cold pewter. 'I have seen it happen in my own life, Pru, with . . . with Dan . . . and *her*, so it seems I must make use of every advantage I have to get what I want. Now then . . .' At once she was lightness and shining delight, bringing a smile to Prudence's face which had begun to darken a little at her words. 'Let's go and see what is happening in town. If I'm not mistaken that's Jethro's carriage coming up the driveway.'

'So it is. Now while I go and greet him will you ring the bell and tell Nora to scoot up the stairs for our parasols? We'll certainly need them today. It must be over seventy degrees already. Poor Richard, standing to attention for hours on . . .'

They both became still, as still as two animals which have scented danger and to avoid attracting attention to themselves must make no movement. They stared at one another and from both young faces all colour fled away. Only their eyes had life in them, one the life of vivid guilt and the other of shock and dawning pain.

'Celie . . .' Prudence spoke in a voice that was barely above a whisper. 'I'm so sorry. I did not mean to . . . it just came out . . . this day . . . he is to . . . Oh God, I'm so sorry. He asked me not to . . .'

'Not to mention that he has perhaps returned to England, Prudence, is that it?' Celie's voice was harsh and unforgiving.

'No, not that, Celie.'

'What then?'

'That he never left.'

Celie reached behind her for the back of her chair, her hand fumbling for something on which to steady herself. When she found it she sank down, her face in which a moment ago the lovely bright glow of hope had bloomed, staring in ashen horror at Prudence.

'He never left . . . he never . . . you mean he has been here . . . ? You had better tell me, Prudence.'

Prudence sat down and drew up her chair so that she and Celie were knee to knee. She took her icy hands in hers, rubbing them gently, her own face drawn into lines of painful compassion. Neither of them saw Jethro emerge from the open doorway of the small conservatory at the back of the house. He stopped just beyond the shaded area of the oak tree, something in the two women's absorbed attitude telling him there was a matter here which he should not interrupt. The dog heaved herself to her feet and sauntered over to him, her tail pluming in welcome and he dropped a hand to her domed, silky head.

His wife's voice was soft as were her hands as she stroked Celie's between them.

'No, they would not allow him to transfer, you see. He longed to get to . . .'

'He longed to get away from me, Pru.'

'He . . .'

'Be truthful, please, you owe me that.'

'I'm so sorry. Yes, he did. I don't mean he *longed* to get away from you, but he *had* to. He was afraid of you.'

'I did not threaten him in any way.'

'He saw his . . . his love for you as a threat. To his . . .'

'To his career as an army officer, is that what you're saying? He could not associate with a girl who had been a maid in . . .'

'*No*! No, Celie . . .'

'The truth, Prudence.'

Prudence bowed her head in shame for her brother.

'Yes.'

'So, where has he been these two years in which his

name has not once crossed your lips?' Celie's voice was
hard and bitter.

'In . . . barracks . . .'

'In . . . *Liverpool* . . .'

'No, in Warrington.'

'Dear God, how could he be so . . . so heartless? It
seems he takes after his Mama after all. Oh . . . dear, dear
God . . .'

'I'm sorry, darling, but it was not my secret. I promised
him . . .'

'I thought you were my friend.'

'I am, Celie, I am . . . please . . .'

'And where is he today then, that he is to stand in the hot
sun? Surely you were not to take me into Liverpool where
he would . . . ?'

'Oh no . . . no, Celie. He is in London. The second battalion
is to line the streets of Cheapside for the Diamond Jubilee
procession and then they are to go to Aldershot. In September
they are to embark for Belfast and there is no . . .'

'No chance that he and I will . . . meet. None at all. He
has taken care of that, has he?'

'Yes . . .'

'Prudence, how could he be so . . . so cruel . . . and you?
Why didn't you tell me this? Did you and he imagine I would go
wailing up to Briar Lodge demanding . . . something of him?
Surely you . . . both of you, know me better than that?'

Prudence had begun to weep, bending her head in anguish
for her friend's pain, but the new Celie Marlow did not cry.
She was dry-eyed and stony-faced, allowing her hands to be
cradled by Prudence's as the tears dripped on them, then,
with a gesture of gentle rejection she withdrew them and
stood up.

'I know he . . . is your brother and so I cannot blame you
for your loyalty but I feel . . . I hope you will understand . . .
I feel I would like to get away from you, be on my own for a
while.' She looked about her desperately as though seeking
some safe place to hide and Jethro sprang to life, moving
swiftly to her, his wife, for the first time since he had met
her, taking second place. Prudence was huddled in the chair,

her knees drawn up, her hand across her face, but his arms went about Celie, not her.

'And so you shall, Celie, won't she, my darling?' speaking over his shoulder to Prudence. He had not approved of the deception Richard Latimer and his own wife had kept up, though he had understood that Prudence thought that she was protecting her friend from further hurt by not revealing Richard's true whereabouts. She had told Celie that Richard was to go to the Indies when she had believed it to be true and when he had not gone she had merely not told Celie of his changed plans. She had not lied, only by omission.

'Oh dear God, I am so sorry,' Prudence moaned. 'The Latimers have inflicted . . .'

'Stop it, lass. There is no need for that. Celie here is in need of . . . of seclusion, not histrionics. A place to find . . . peace and strength. That is what she needs, Prudence, and where better than the cottage near Ambleside. Come along, my lass, pull yourself together. This is not like you, giving in to tears and Celie here needs . . .'

'You're right.' Prudence blew her nose violently, then stood up, the storm over, her husband's practical and down-to-earth good sense bringing her, as it always had, back to reality.

Jethro smiled down into Celie's drawn face and he was rewarded by a tiny spark in her eyes. 'Then you and Celie shall be taken to . . .'

'No, I'm sorry, Jethro, and you too, Prudence, but if I may be allowed, I'll decide for myself.'

'Of course you may, so not a word, Prudence. We all know how you like to organise.'

'Thank you, Jethro.' Celie moved away from him. At once Prudence slid into the comforting circle of her husband's arms and they both watched Celie as she walked slowly down the garden. The dog went with her, sensing, as animals do, her need for sympathy of the kind only an undemanding creature such as herself could give. When she stopped, so did the bitch, standing patiently beside her, waiting.

She turned and began to walk back, the dog moving with her.

'Perhaps a few days at . . . where is it?'

'Ambleside.' They spoke together.

'When may I . . .'

'Now if you like, Celie. I can send the coachman to the station to enquire for train times. Prudence and I will take you . . .'

'No, I'll go alone.'

'Just as you like.'

'May I . . . ?'

'Anything.'

'May I take Bess?'

'Of course,' and as though in amiable agreement, perhaps knowing where she was most needed, the retriever wagged her tail lazily, leaning companionably against Celie's leg.

She went for three days and stayed for three months. They were gentle, slow-moving months, June passing into July, August and September, the calm acre of Yew Cottage on the shore of Lake Windermere soothing her torn and injured heart and mending the shattered trust of what she had thought of as Prudence's treachery. She had never been alone before and she found it luxurious, healing, a calm peace she had not thought possible. The cottage was old with low doorways and beamed ceilings from which the woman who looked after it for Prudence and Jethro had hung bunches of sweet-smelling dried herbs. There was a well-scoured stone floor, a crooked staircase and a small bedroom in which a large, lavender-scented bed lulled her to deep, dreamless sleep each night. There were kittens, who were not afraid of Bess, who stayed for the most part at her side. An old-fashioned kitchen range on which she cooked her solitary, tranquil meals. It was a restoring backwater in the mainstream of her life, a tick of the clock between her past and her future as she idled beside the silken, shimmering waters of the lake.

Sometimes it rained, a fine curling mist that drifted over her as she walked with the dog, cool, refreshing, reviving her spirit and curling her hair into a heavy cloak as it hung down her back. She dreamed for hours in contemplation of the mending beauty of the fells, watching the bracken begin to turn, the leaves to burnish, to gold, to copper as they drifted at her feet by the water's edge and when September came she was ready to go back. There was no need to hurry, for Celie Marlow had shed the habit of urgency with the anxieties and perplexities which had once beset her. She was her own woman now. She had no fears, no remorse, no blame nor reproach to heap on others. She no longer felt the need to defend herself, nor her heart for they were strong now, she and her heart.

Her plans were firm and so was her step as she and the dog boarded the train for Liverpool.

Chapter Twenty-seven

'The house is yours, Celie. I am doing you no favours. It is property I lease to anyone who has the rent I ask for, and it seems you have.'

'Jethro Garside, if I thought you were . . . well, offering me charity I would never forgive you.'

'Charity! Lass, when was it charity to give a helping hand to a friend? That is what friends do. They extend a hand to help those they are fond of over a rough patch. The house is in Great George Square. Many of the houses there are owned by the shipping lines. They lodge immigrants while they wait for a ship for the next part of their journey. When the opportunity came to acquire one that's what I did. I meant to rent it to a shipping company but it didn't quite work out as I had planned so I have been letting it to anyone who would pay my price. A solicitor, then a doctor who wanted rooms and also accommodation for his family. A week or two back he informed me that he had decided to move further away from the city and so you see, my dear girl, I am not evicting anyone, nor am I about to charge you some ridiculously low price, as my dear wife suggested that I do. In fact she would have been better pleased had I charged you none at all. The rent will be fair in relation to the property. I know how much this means to you. I know you wish to be "business-like", so that is what I am allowing you to be. I am doing *business* with you, lass. Now then, will you put on your bonnet and come with me to look the house over? If it is to your liking then we can discuss it further.'

It was exactly to her liking. The square was surrounded on

four sides by tall, narrow houses, terraced, simple, elegant, and each one exactly the same as its neighbour. It was four-storeyed, with two long windows on each floor except the top where those in the attics were set in the roof as gabled dormers. On the first floor each window had a neat, cast-iron balcony. The front door, flanked by pillars and reached by three worn steps, was glossy with new paint and above it was a graceful fan-light.

At this time of the year the square was quiet, devoid of all activity except for a horse-drawn cart on which sacks of coal were stacked. A burly chap wearing a cap to which a piece of sacking was attached and which hung down his back, grunted something to the horse. It stood patiently, evidently well used to the routine, as the man humped a sack of coal to the coal-hole before a house, tipped it expertly down the hole and returned to the cart for another. In the centre of the square and surrounded by iron railing was a garden. The trees in it were bare of all but a few tenacious leaves, those that had once danced merrily on their branches now a soggy wet carpet across the dejected flower-beds and worn grass. There were seats set about, empty now, and in the centre was a small statue on the top of a flight of steps, a boy clad in draped grecian type garments. There were trees not only in the garden but along the pavement which encompassed it, and outside each terraced house, and Celie's eyes were bright with anticipation as she pictured it in spring when they would be clothed in their full glory.

The house smelled dusty but dry except for a lingering overlay of something medicinal, perhaps friar's balsam she thought, which was tracked down to a small room at the back of the house where the doctor had evidently dispensed his own medicines.

The rest of the main rooms were large, the high, lath-and-plaster ceilings finished with ornate central roses from which depended old-fashioned gasoliers, and with moulded plaster cornices at the junctions of ceiling and wall. The floors were of polished wood. Heavy, cast-iron balustrades with lustrous mahogany handrails ran up the stairs.

The kitchen was situated in the semi-basement, lit only

by the area light. All the rooms were contained on one side of the entrance hall which led to the dog-leg staircase with a half-landing at the turn. The parlour was on the first floor, running from the front of the house where the balconies overlooked the square, to the back of it where there was a small enclosed garden. There was another staircase leading to bedrooms, two on the second floor and two in the roof space.

The ground floor, which was raised some few feet above the pavement level, had two rooms, one behind the other, the one at the back having french windows leading out and down several steps to the garden.

The kitchen, which was of particular interest to Celie, was a pleasant surprise. It ran from the front of the house, approached by the area steps, through to the back where there was a scullery containing sinks and draining boards and a wooden draining rack and off that, a small pantry. In the kitchen was a kitchen range known as a complete "kitchener". The fire when it was lit would be enclosed between two brick-lined ovens – both heated by the fire – with a water boiler on one side from which hot water might be drawn off by a tap. There were detachable trivets, grills and grids, and a hot plate where pans might be kept hot. Above the hob was a metal shelf on which plates and dishes could be warmed. There were many implements hung about it, kettle tilters, toasters, skewers and a chestnut roasting box to name but a few. There was a large well-scrubbed table, several simple wooden chairs, a dresser and, on a shelf, a splendid set of brightly polished copper pans.

Jethro had not spoken as he followed Celie from room to room up the stairs and then down again. He stood patiently to one side as, with an enquiring lift of her eyebrows, she moved down the steps from the back scullery and into the garden. He did not follow her this time. There was a dilapidated seat against the far wall sunk in old grass that had not been cut for a couple of summers, by the look of it. It stood beneath the bare and twisting branches of a black mulberry tree. The tree was not tall, no more than twenty feet or so in height but very broad with a rugged trunk which leaned slightly to one side. The bark on the trunk was of orange brown, dappled in pleasing patterns, decorated with lichen. Celie walked towards it. When she reached it she put out a bare hand and gently touched it with a questing finger, then, as though she was alone, and despite the coldness of the day, she sat down on the seat.

Jethro turned quietly and went back inside, leaving her to her thoughts.

She had many, all of them deep. One took her back to the Sunday five weeks ago now when she had excused herself to Prudence and Jethro, and, putting on the warm, high-collared three-quarter length cape Prudence had loaned her, walked briskly from Croxteth Drive to Sefton Park. It was six months since she had left Harper's and in all that time she had neither heard from nor seen any of the people with whom she had been so close over the years. It was as though what had been her world for all that time had simply slipped over the edge of somewhere and vanished without trace, indeed as though it had never existed. Cook had been at the centre of it, the hub, the lynchpin, the sphere around which they had all revolved, and now more than a year later Celie accepted that she had not functioned properly since. Her sojourn in Ambleside had made it clear to her. Her three months alone with no other company but the dog, the darting, capricious and ever multiplying kittens, the calm garden, the serenity of the lake and the fells, had cleared her mind, strengthened her heart and backbone, stilled her pain and pointed her towards the goal she must reach. There was much to do, but first she must talk to Maudie, before she bearded the lion, or should it be lioness, in her den at Harper's, and where else might Maudie be found on a Sunday afternoon but the park?

The park in November could be a bleak and empty place, but that day, towards the end of the month, had been unseasonably cold, the grass crisp and white, the trees, though black and bare, coated delicately along each branch and twig with a frieze of silvered hoarfrost. A weak and pearly sun cast shadows behind the trees and among them rosy-cheeked, bright-eyed children chased one another, their breath exploding from between parted lips. Little girls of the middle class in bonnets, calf-length coats, boots and warm mittens bowled hoops, more sedate than their brothers who raced along the edge of the lake in pursuit of toy sailing boats which had gone astray amidst the thin film of breaking ice which coated the water. Ladies and gentlemen, men and women stepped out smartly, taking advantage of the faint sunshine, arm in arm most of them, and when Celie saw Maudie coming towards her, though she was pleased, she was also disconcerted to see she was not alone and that *her* arm was through Belle's.

They both stopped and gaped, their eyes wide in their pink-cheeked faces then, absolutely in unison, their mouths split into huge grins of delight they began to gallop towards her, arms still linked, for all the world like two overgrown puppies on the same lead who had just spied a beloved friend.

'Celie . . . oh Celie . . . we 'oped we'd see yer, didn't we, Belle . . .'

'Aye, every Sunday since yer left except when I went to me mam's . . .'

'. . . I said to her, didn't I, Belle, I said one day she'll . . .'

'Aye . . . well . . . we didn't like ter call on Mrs Garside, her being the daughter of . . .'

'So we kept comin', didn't we, Belle . . .'

'Aye . . . an' when we saw yer . . .'

'Well, we thought yer was a ghost, didn't we, Belle . . .'

'We did an' all . . .'

'But it's right good to see yer, Celie.'

Celie was quite overwhelmed by the warmth of their gladness, their youthful delight in finding her at long last and for several rapturous moments the three of them, Maudie and Belle imbuing her with the same excitement they felt, hugged one another. Capering like the children about the park, laughing and all talking at the same time so that not one heard what the other two said, but did it matter? Bonnets were knocked askew and straightened only to be knocked sideways again, but at last they quietened, making a more searching scrutiny of one another, standing on the path which crossed what was known as Aigburth Vale and which led to the tree-encompassed Deer Park.

The two girls looked shabby and, Celie was inclined to think, thinner than the last time she had seen them, even Belle, whom she had once considered plump. They were young and healthy and in the twelve months of Kate's rigorous command had come to no great harm, but what of Ivy and Percy who were older, and of them all, those who, though they had always worked all the hours God sent, had been sustained by Cook's good and plentiful food and her fair rule?

'So,' she said, at last, 'how are things with you two then?' smiling.

They looked at one another, then down at their shuffling feet, even the ebullient Maudie silenced and Celie felt her heart go out to them. Well, not so much to Maudie for her hardship at Kate's hands was about to end, but to Belle. Belle was not exactly simple, just slow, slow to understand, slow to reason, but once she knew what was expected of her, what was needed of her, was as quick as the quickest of them all to give it. How would she manage without . . .? Oh dear, it was going to be hard. Why hadn't she thought about it? Why hadn't she realised that Maudie was not likely to come to the park alone, that someone was bound to be with her on her weekly walk, and of course the person most likely to accompany her would be Belle who was more or less her own age?

'Let's walk, shall we,' she said. 'It's too cold to hang about. It's a pity Harper's isn't open, we could have gone there for afternoon tea.'

They stared at her open-mouthed, and it was not until she winked that they realised she was joking. They laughed then, especially Maudie, who caught on a full twenty seconds before Belle, then the two girls fell into step one on either side of her, still inclined towards silence. She had been their . . . well, their *mistress* for nearly two years. Miss Marlow to them both, as Cook's health and authority declined and after that first joy-filled meeting, they walked beside her with the respect she was due. It seemed Maudie had had some of her impish good humour knocked from her and it was not hard to imagine why and by whom.

Celie talked. She told them all about Mr and Mrs Garside

with whom she had lived since she had walked out of
Harper's. She slipped for a moment or two back in time
to the tranquillity of the cottage by the lake and its healing
powers, painting them a picture of her days there, of the
dog and the sweetness of their walks together, but she
could see they barely understood what it was she described
to them since neither had even been across the waters of the
Mersey on the ferry, and the idea of a train which took you to
mountains and rivers and lakes was beyond their uneducated
comprehension.

Her step slowed and theirs slowed with her. It was as
though they were both aware, somehow, that she had come
to the park on this particular day for a special purpose
and that now, now they had got past the greetings and
the conversation, Miss Marlow was about to reach that
purpose.

She was.

'I . . . well . . .' Why was it she found it so hard to tell them,
she agonised, but of course she knew why and the reason for
it was standing before her, not exactly hoping because she had
not even *begun* to understand her own thrill of excitement but
knowing something was up.

'What's to do, Celie?' Maudie it was who spoke using the
Christian name she had called Miss Marlow in the brief time
they had been friends. She put her hand on Celie's arm
and Celie looked down at it sadly. It resembled a slice
of meat, pink- and red-blotched, scraped raw in places, the
cracks where the swollen fingers curled inwards, blood-red
and almost oozing. Chilblains flamed, the one on the thumb
infected. The fingernails were broken so low there were half
moons of scarlet flesh at the end of each finger. The thin wrist
was chapped and painful-looking. Celie put her own warmly
gloved hand on top of Maudie's and held it firmly as though
she would never let it go. She turned to Belle.

'Show me your hands, Belle,' she said quietly, and when,
mystified, Belle held them out to her, Celie took one, turning
it over to study the inflamed cracks in the palm, and held it
as she held Maudie's. They stood there, three young girls,
for Celie Marlow was not much older than Maudie and Belle,

their hands linked, and she began to walk, one on either side of her again, turning first to one and then to the other as she spoke.

'I'm coming to Harper's tomorrow,' she said, smiling as they both gasped. 'No, not to work. I'll never work there again I'm afraid, but to pick up my things. I presume they are still there?' She turned suddenly to Maudie who would know. 'They are still there aren't they, my clothes and personal belongings? I've been borrowing from Mrs Garside for the past six months, though she's taller than me, having nothing with which to buy new, though of course she wanted to lend me money to . . . well, enough of that. What of my things, Maudie?'

'Oh, they're all there, Celie. *She* wanted to chuck 'em in the street, or burn them she said, but he wouldn't let her. For once, he stood up to 'er. There was a hell of a row, sorry Celie . . . but he wouldn't budge. Put everything in a box he did, him and Mrs Petty and stored it in Mrs Petty's room . . .'

'Good. Then I shall be round tomorrow but there is something else.'

'What's that, Celie?' Maudie held her breath, not daring to hope, but hoping all the same.

'I'm starting my own business and I want you to come and work for me.'

The wonder of it flowered on Maudie's face, opening it up like a rosebud which turns towards the life-giving sun, the sustaining rain. Her mouth opened wide as though she was about to let out a roar of triumph or joy, then just as vigorously it clamped shut again and she turned her despairing gaze to Belle, who had not yet grasped the full implication of Miss Marlow's words.

'Eeeh, Celie . . . I've dreamed . . . of gettin' away . . . from her.' Maudie tossed her head in the general direction of Harper's. 'I never thought . . . not once . . . but you see . . .'

She turned an anguished expression from Belle to Celie then back to Belle again. Celie knew what Maudie was trying to say though Belle didn't. Belle was beginning to smile for *her*, for Maudie's good luck. Belle who was the victim of Kate's vicious temper and hard-handed clouts, the butt of her nasty jokes, the target of her wicked jibes. Innocent Belle who worked as hard as anybody in the place but who got no thanks for it and who, now that she understood what Miss Marlow had said, was *pleased* for Maudie.

'I can't, Celie, I wish I could . . .' still looking at Belle. You can see how it is, she was telling Celie. How *she* is, and I can't leave her.

'I know, Maudie.' Celie's voice was soft, ready to tremble a little at this girl's loyalty to her fellow servant, to the girl who would be lost without her own staunch friendship. 'But I meant both of you.'

She hadn't, of course, but the blinding joy, first on Maudie's face, then, ten seconds later, on Belle's was more than enough to make her realise that she had made the right decision.

Two wages to find instead of one and if the worst happened and the venture failed, two young girls out of work without a reference, for any *she* wrote, who was without one herself, would be worthless. Mind you, she'd be glad of Belle's strong and willing labour, for what she lacked in resourcefulness she more than made up for in brute force. A good team, Maudie and Belle and with herself to hold them together, like a careful driver leading two horses by the reins, they could be nothing but an enormous benefit to her business.

She watched them skip away, yes *skip*, as lightly as the little girls with the bowling hoops, turning time and time again to wave to her, their faces so openly alive with excitement she prayed Kate Smith would not be around to see them when they entered the shop for if she was she'd know at once that something was afoot. They had promised not to breathe a word of what had happened to them in the park. She would not need them for another few weeks, she had told them, and until then they were to continue to work just as they always did until she came for them and to tell no one they had seen her, let alone been offered a new position.

'Tell no one,' she repeated.

'Not even Mrs Petty?'

'No, it's not that I don't trust Ivy but if she and Kate had words, you know, like they used to . . .'

'Still do, an' all.'

'Well then, she mightn't mean to but . . . well. Off you go then.'

The shop was busy when she opened the door the next day. It was just on ten o' clock and the smell of freshly baked bread, of meat pies and fruit tarts met her as she closed it behind her. Dorcas was serving a customer, a decent woman, neatly dressed but not *quite* of the standard Harper's was used to, and when the bell rang Dorcas glanced from the woman's outstretched hand into which she was counting change, towards the door.

Her mouth popped open and the few pence she held clattered to the top of the glass counter. The woman tutted, then, caught by the amazed expression on Dorcas's face and in her eyes which were staring over her shoulder, she turned as well, looking at Celie in bewilderment, for what was there about her to cause such dismay in the shop assistant? 'Hello, Dorcas.' Celie nodded politely. She was again wearing the warm cape of rich plum-coloured box cloth belonging to Prudence. The collar was of Japanese fox with a pale grey squirrel lining and had cost Jethro Garside a considerable amount of money. Not that he or his wife cared about that, since she had jackets and full-length fur coats galore pressed on her by her doting husband. Celie's composed face was framed by the collar, like a lovely flower set in a bouquet, her pointed chin nestling in the luxuriant fur. Her eyes were brilliant like the silvery frosted stars which had shone the night before, and her cheeks were pink, the colour put there by the cold. She was quite, quite beautiful. A curious silence fell about the shop. All the ladies there who had come to purchase their bread and pies from the somewhat depleted stock now offered on sale at Harper's and which this woman had once run stared in wonderment. Her back was straight and unbowed though they had been told by the present owner that she had left in disgrace. She looked elegant and prosperous and they waited with bated breath to see what she would do next.

Perhaps warned by the sudden deathly silence in the shop

which normally hummed with voices, with the ringing of the till and the peel of the door bell, a figure appeared abruptly in the doorway which led to the kitchen and for the first time in six months Kate Smith and Cécilie Marlow came face to face.

Celie waited, smiling enigmatically, knowing quite well that when Kate opened her mouth something she would regret later would come out of it. It did.

'An' what the bloody 'ell d'yer think *you're* doin' in *my* shop, lady? You've got a soddin' nerve showin' yer face 'ere after all this time, an' after what you did an' all. Go on, eff off, yer bleedin' cow . . .'

She stopped then, the words bitten off as though her teeth had closed over the end of her tongue. Her temper was violent, longing to burst out of her like a swollen river held in check by the flimsiest of dams. For the past six months, though she had not been sorry to see Celie Marlow "bugger off" as she scathingly told her husband, since the sight of her long face was enough to curdle milk, the effect of the loss of what she now realised had been the best cook she was ever likely to find in Liverpool had been quite appalling. Ivy wasn't bad, give her her due. She made decent bread, pies and scones, good plain stuff, fresh and tasty and good sellers. Anything which could be knocked up by an experienced *plain* cook, and with Dan's fresh fruit and vegetables of which there was an abundance, the poultry, the good cuts of meat and fresh fish, the cheeses she herself purchased at the market, they did well enough. But the clientèle to whom once they had catered, those of the calibre of Mrs Morgan of Heaton Crescent and her wide circle of friends and who had given their well-bred custom to Jess Harper and Celie Marlow, had slowly drifted away to look for the *special* food which they sought. There seemed to be no shortage of ladies still willing to shop at Harper's from the villas in the Boulevard and the surrounding areas of terraced houses, for the food sold was still good and cheap but it was not these that Harper's or, more to the point, *Kate Smith* wanted. The kind of baking Ivy did brought in what Kate called "bread and butter" money and she wanted, though she could not have expressed it thus, "Champagne and caviar". She had seen what came in until the day Celie

left and she wanted more of it and without the superb artistry
which both Cook and Celie had brought to their work, her
hopes had been dashed on the hard stone of her own greed
and cunning. The stock of home-made toffee and chocolates,
the preserves, the fancy biscuits, the gateaux, pastries and
the many "specialities" devised by Cook, and then by Celie,
had gone within the first month, irreplaceable, and Harper's
had become no more than a plain "Confectionery". A bread
shop, a meat pie shop and from the depth of her vicious and
contriving heart Kate Smith blamed and hated Celie Marlow
for it, and it showed!

Celie's smile deepened. Her manner said she could not have
been more unconcerned if Kate had dropped dead at her feet.
But in her eyes was a glint which momentarily caused Kate
to falter. She didn't even know what it meant. She saw the
curl of scorn about Celie's lips as though Celie was not at all
surprised to hear Kate act and sound like a fishwife, but it was
the smile that chilled her, a smile which lit Celie's eyes and
yet reminded Kate of the ice on the grey waters of a pond.
Celie Marlow had always been a poor specimen, a simpleton
without the guts to make much of what she had. She'd let
Kate take Dan from her, hadn't she? *And* the business that
was to have been hers. She'd gone to pieces when Cook died,
only functioning in the kitchen, the rest of the time drooping
about the place like the spineless fish she was.

But now she seemed . . . different. There was something
about her Kate didn't quite care for. A look of *trouble*, a
narrow-eyed hardness, sharp and cutting, which was directed
unswervingly at Kate herself. And she appeared to be doing
well, by the look of her. You didn't buy a cape like that on the
bloody market but she supposed them "lah-de-dah" friends
of hers would see her right. Still, she'd need . . . well . . .
watching, she thought, though why Kate Smith should need
to keep her eye on Celie Marlow was a puzzle to her.

Suddenly aware that every person in the shop was avidly
watching and waiting for the next move in this quite amazing
event, Kate pulled herself together, thrust forward her
truculent chin and treated Celie to what she considered a
haughty stare.

'You've come for your things, I suppose,' she managed to say, 'cause there's nowt . . . nothing . . . no other reason for you to come 'ere where you're not wanted. Dorcas,' . . . turning imperiously to the open-mouthed assistant, 'kindly accompany this person to . . .' She had to think for a minute, the exact whereabouts of Celie's trunk momentarily escaping her, '. . . to Mrs Petty's room. Do not leave her side for a moment, if you please,' looking round at her customers, letting them know that Celie Marlow was not to be trusted. She tossed her head feeling she had had the last triumphant word.

'And that should be the end of it,' she finished cuttingly and was considerably startled when, as she passed by her towards the back of the shop, Celie said clearly,

'Not by a long chalk, Kate Smith.'

Chapter Twenty-eight

It was spring when the man was first noticed in Great George Square, though it was not the first time he had been there by any means. The Cook General at the emigrant house belonging to the Cunard Line just across the Square from Miss Marlow's place had her attention drawn to him by her scullery maid who had sharp eyes and a pert mind.

'That chap's there again, Mrs Wilson,' she said, as she heaved a bucket of coal across the threshold of the area door.

'What chap's that, Sarah?' Mrs Wilson lifted her head vigorously from her intent preoccupation with the accounts, which it was her job to prepare for the agent in charge of the house. Thousands of emigrants passed through Liverpool to be shipped abroad, many of them with as little comfort and compassion as cattle, but not those who rested at the Cunard emigrants' house in Great George Square and certainly not those who were placed temporarily in Flo Wilson's care, poor souls. Good nourishing meals she provided, but every penny must be accounted for, every column of figures correctly added up and each one to balance with another. Her staff, the scullery maid, Sarah, the kitchen maid, Doris, and the daily cleaner, Mrs Dudley, knew better than to interrupt her when she was occupied with this gargantuan task and it must be serious if Sarah chanced her arm with Mrs Wilson's formidable temper.

'I don't know 'im, Mrs Wilson, not personal like, only I saw 'im a couple o' times a week or two back sittin' int' gardens. I thought it were a bit queer, it bein' a chilly day. Not the sort of day you'd want to spend hangin' about on a park bench, like. I mentioned it to Doris but we thought no more of it, then last week he were there again. He were sorta . . . well, hidin' behind a tree, starin' across the square at t'other side, an' now he's there again. D'yer reckon he's up ter no good?'

'Nay, how do I know? But I'll soon find out.' Mrs Wilson heaved herself to her feet, her florid face beginning to show signs of the uncompromising resolution her staff knew so well. No one got on the wrong side of Flo Wilson, not if they wished to avoid the length of her tongue or the swiftness of her heavy hand.

'What you goin' to do, Mrs Wilson?' Sarah was thrilled, the vicarious thrill of the spectator, the one who has been at the receiving end of Mrs Wilson's sharp tongue and liked nothing better than to see someone else suffer it.

'Ask him what he's up to, that's what. An' if he shows the slightest sign of being abusive, I want you to run up to Grenville Street an' fetch a bobby. Not that *that'll* be needed,' she added grimly, the idea of anyone, man or woman defying Flo Wilson, absurd beyond measure. 'Now then, you show me where you saw him.'

The two women climbed the area steps, Mrs Wilson in front, Sarah who was a bit of a tartar herself, not far behind. They were dressed alike in the uniform of the kitchen servant. A serviceable floor-length dress in a drab grey, a spotless and capacious apron and a white cap which completely covered their hair. The only difference between them was the enormous sacking apron which Sarah donned for "dirty" work. At the moment it was filmed with the coal dust from the coal she had just carted up from the cellar, the entrance of which was at the bottom of the area steps, next to the basement door.

'There he is, Mrs Wilson.' Sarah who was inclined to screech at times of great excitement, pointed with dramatic hand at the figure of the man who hovered on *their* side of the garden. His back was towards them, his gaze directed to the other side of the square. He had his hand on the rough bark of the trunk of one of the horse-chestnut trees surrounding the garden just inside the railings. The tree was in full bloom, a dazzling cascade of brilliant white flowers and downy green leaves. An old tree in its full growth, and the man was almost hidden by its wide-spreading branches and luxuriant foliage. The May sun was bland and golden but the shadow beneath the tree was dense and it needed a good pair of eyes to spot the man, who was almost invisible against the grey-brown of its trunk.

The emigrant houses and the square in which they were set were no more than a stone's throw from the river. Across St James Street, down Blundell Street and there you were at King's Dock, with the quiet patient presence of the great ships berthed there. From the corner you could see the wrangling cranes perched on their high roofs and about the ships the long sheds from which came the ringing echoes of the voices of the men who worked there. Along Wapping Street which lay parallel with the docks, sandwichmen paraded advertising the wonders of *Odonto* for the cleaning of teeth, *Keating's Cough Lozenges*, *Dinnefords* and *Dr King's Dandelion and Quinine Liver Pills*. There were street musicians, fiddlers, a blind penny-whistler and an organ grinder and his grinning monkey vying with one another nearer to the Pier Head where returning seamen were known to be generous. A great bustle of activity which never ceased and which those who lived amongst it scarcely noticed, so familiar was it to them.

Mrs Wilson certainly didn't. She started across the road which separated the emigrant house from the gardens, Sarah in tow. There were a fair number of people about, groups of stunned-looking families from Scandinavia and Europe who were en route to North America and who had not yet cut that last tie with home. They hung about aimlessly, not at all sure why they had been put in the emigrant house instead of a ship, afraid to leave the square in case their transport went without them. From old men to infants in arms, they shuffled about the sunlit garden in bewildered step keeping a wary eye out for the shipping agent who was to direct them towards their new and frightening life. Many were still in the national costume of the beloved country from which they had come. A pleasing confusion of colour and style, but Mrs Wilson elbowed them aside, almost being run

down herself by a horse-drawn milk cart as she stalked across
the road.

The man was dressed in a decent suit of tweed and a
"wide-awake" hat of soft felt with a low crown and a wide
brim. He was young, tall and rangy with broad shoulders and
erect bearing, but beneath the shadowly canopy of the tree
Mrs Wilson got no more than an impression of a handsome,
unhappy face as he half turned and, seeing her and Sarah
bearing down on him, hurriedly moved away in the direction
of the far gate.

It took him no more than half a dozen long graceful strides
to reach it then he was off up Hardy Street towards St James
Street, disappearing at once into the Sunday crowds coming
from the Catholic church of St Vincent de Paul.

'We've lost him, Mrs Wilson,' Sarah said dolefully, the
brightness evidently gone from the heart-stirring moment.
She had really been looking forward to seeing Mrs Wilson
tackle that chap, whoever he was and whatever it was he was
up to, really she had, and now he'd given them the slip.

'Aye, an' he'd best not come back, neither,' Mrs Wilson
retorted with great satisfaction. 'Up to no good, I'll be bound,
skulkin' about where no decent folk should be . . .'

'What! In them gardens . . . ?'

'No, you simpleton. There's no 'arm in being in the gardens.
It's hangin' about *hiding*, I don't care for.'

''Appen he were watchin' out for a place to burgle, Mrs
Wilson, you know, seein' where there could be easy pickings
or . . .'

'Well he didn't look like no burglar to me. But you could be
right, girl. Then again, 'appen he's got his eye on one of them
flighty housemaids at Inman's. That'd be more like it. Anyway, if you see him again, you come an' tell me at once.'

'Yes, Mrs Wilson.'

They were almost at their own basement steps, still deep
in the mystery of the decently dressed young man when a
voice, a pleasant voice, interrupted their cogitation and they
both turned at once towards it.

'You look very puzzled, Mrs Wilson,' it said. 'Is there
something afoot?'

Mrs Wilson's stern, forbidding, nay, *imposing* countenance, softened ever so slightly and she smiled at the speaker. A young woman of impeccable appearance in a navy blue walking costume of short, fitted coat, and full-length "mermaid" skirt, so called because it hugged the hip and thigh and then flared at the back in a fishtail effect. The high ruched collar of her blouse was snowy white, her navy blue hat had a broad grosgrain ribbon of white about its crown and the brim turned up at the front to reveal the delicate loveliness of her face. A pale, flawless face with deep velvety grey eyes and a mouth which was a soft coral pink. A face to draw all eyes to it, even those of another woman, and a figure to match. She held her head gracefully, her back was straight and her small breasts were pert and taut above her tiny waist. From beneath her hat a shining tendril of dark hair drifted to touch her cheek and she lifted her gloved hand to push it back behind her ear. She was the sort of woman, the sort of beautiful young woman of whom Flo Wilson would have been immediately suspicious since she lived on her own at number 30, Great George Square – well, except for a couple of young girls – but in the past six months she had proved to be quiet, discreet, not *over* friendly, but pleasant and so hard-working, Flo had been heard to declare in amazement, that she didn't know why the woman wasn't worn to a pale shadow. All day she was on the go, and far into the night her lights were on and yet to look at her you'd think she did nothing all day but sit on her behind and sew a fine seam, which is what Flo had heard ladies did. She was *respectable*, was Miss Marlow. An unmarried woman *had* to earn a living and Miss Marlow did it unobtrusively and with decent modesty, conducting herself and the behaviour of those two girls who worked for her, with lady-like restraint. There were no gentlemen callers, the only males to cross her threshold the delivery men who brought her goods from the market.

She had invited Flo into her elegant parlour on more than one occasion, offering her tea in a fine, almost transparent bone china teacup, and cakes of such exquisite flavour and lightness it was no wonder she was doing well, or so rumour had it, with the business she had started. They had got on famously, her and Miss Marlow, each a hard-working and upright woman who admired those virtues in others.

'Good day to you, Miss Marlow. A fine day it is too.' Flo was polite though not gushing, despite her private regard for Miss Marlow. 'No, nothing wrong. We was just a mite concerned with some young chap Sarah here saw hanging about the square. Probably tryin' to do a bit o' sparking. There's some likely lookin' lasses work in them houses . . .' though not one could hold a candle to you was plainly written on her own stern face, and on that of the homely countenance of her scullery maid. Mrs Wilson did not pick her staff for their looks. Both Sarah and Doris were totally lacking in beauty but made up for it, in Mrs Wilson's opinion, with a capacity for the hard work and respectability she demanded.

'You're probably right, Mrs Wilson. You know what they say about spring.' Celie's eyes twinkled humorously and a small gleam of amusement showed in Flo Wilson's.

'Aye, you're right there, Miss Marlow. Well, we'd best be getting back to work . . .' whipping round smartly to Sarah who would have liked nothing better than to stand and gossip with the beautiful and mysterious Miss Marlow. 'Come on, Sarah, there's them coal buckets to fill.'

'Yes, I've a busy day ahead of me too. A dinner party for twenty-four to prepare and all to be ready for seven. Aah! there's my provisions now . . .' as a delivery van trundled round the corner from Nelson Street and the general direction of St John's Market. 'I do insist on fresh produce as I'm sure you do yourself, Mrs Wilson?'

She had a way of saying just the right thing, Mrs Wilson acknowledged. Of *pleasing* the person to whom she spoke. Of knowing exactly the nature and capacity of that person, so that, without guile, she drew a response which was warm and spontaneous. Miss Marlow was aware that Flo Wilson was, as far as her budget allowed, a good provider. That she prided herself on the spartan cleanliness and nourishing food the house she ran offered. That she liked quality at a fair price, a bargain in other words, which might be found at the market. And yet at the same time, Miss Marlow was clear-headed, capable and, in Flo Wilson's opinion, calculating, a description she did not mean in a derogatory way. What was the use of being in business if you did not calculate? Calculate to the last farthing how much a product would cost, how much you could sell it for and how much profit you could make from it. A shrewd young woman was Miss Marlow, who knew how to be what her customers needed of her, and yet at the same time, to do it with style and warmth. Flo liked her.

'I do indeed, Miss Marlow.' Flo smiled briefly, nodded her head and moved majestically down the area steps to her kitchen. Sarah did the same.

The moment Celie opened the door she experienced that lovely feeling of warmth and homecoming she had known ever since she had moved into 30 Great George Square, last November. She could not explain it, for how could a place in which she had spent only six months of her life have become so dear to her in such a short time? She had lived at Briar Lodge for eighteen years, making her home with her father in the atmosphere of the tiny cottage which had been created by her mother. A warm place of affection and trust and safety. For two years she and Cook had worked side by side at Harper's, making it *theirs*, building not only a business which they had both loved, but a home in which every item was chosen by them in the simple style they both admired and felt comfortable with. It was theirs and though Cook had not enjoyed it for very long, Celie had thrived in it, thrilled with its plain comfort on which was stamped her own preference. She found she liked the unpretentious and the furniture she and Cook had bought had satisfied something in her.

But neither of her past two homes had given her as much pleasure and contentment as the one she created at 30 Great George Square. It was not just her home though. It was her *sole* creation. Her venture into the world of business, *alone*. She it was who had planted the seed, watched over it as it took root in the minds of those who could help her make it happen, who had nurtured it and seen it grow, fragile at first and needing her constant attention, until under her loving, single-minded guidance it had come to delicate flowering. And her home had been the same.

The houses in the square had been built in the previous century by the merchants of the city who had made their money in shipping, but, as they had prospered, had moved away from the cheerful uproar of the docks area, to the more select districts of Everton and West Derby. The houses had been bought up by others climbing the ladder towards success and who in turn left the area for "nicer" environments until, as the emigrant trade doubled and trebled during the eighties and nineties, most had been taken over by the shipping lines. There were half a dozen or so which had been snapped up by speculators, men like Jethro Garside, split into rooms and let to young professional men working in the city. The houses were all bright with paint, the windows polished, door knockers buffed to a gleaming shine and steps scrubbed by neat housemaids to immaculate whiteness.

None so brilliantly as Celie Marlow's, though. And the inside was as lovingly tended as was the outside. The woodwork had been painted a glossy white and the walls, all except the enormous basement kitchen, papered a soft honey colour in what looked like silk.

Celie had scoured the second-hand shops until she found what she wanted, Hodgson's Rooms in Church Street, where auctions were held every Thursday and Friday and anything from a teaspoon to a drawing room suite might be bid for. In the parlour, just where she had pictured it, a dainty chiffonier stood on one wall opposite the fireplace. There was a deep sofa and a couple of armchairs, and beyond the arch which divided the long room, a simple rosewood table, oval in shape, glowing with polish, around which were six dining chairs. There was a sideboard, serviceable but with elegant lines to it and again polished to within an inch of its life. The curtains at each end of the room were of a heavy velvet in the same warm shade as the walls. Long and full and held back by thick braids of cream and honey. The carpets were patterned in honey and cream, even on the landing and the stairs, with a pale leaf green in the bedrooms at the top of the house, hers and Belle's and Maudie's, who each had their own, all three furnished simply. A slim-legged rosewood table beside a narrow, half-canopied bed, draped in white muslin, a dressing table in satinwood with a free-standing hinged mirror on its top, and a wardrobe. There was matching frilled muslin at the window, framed by curtains in the same colour as the carpets, a plain marble-topped washstand with a ewer and bowl decorated with rosebuds. Each one had a comfortable chair beside it's tiny fireplace where, during the winter, a fire was lit at the end of each day.

Belle and Maudie were overcome and rendered speechless by the splendour of it all, particularly their own bedrooms, not knowing how to thank Miss Marlow, as they called her once more, since she *was* their employer.

'Don't thank me, girls, for though I chose it, Mr Garside paid for it all.' And what they were to make of that they didn't know, nor care, really. Though they got little time to sit by their own fires in their own rooms, it was every lovely thing they had ever dreamed of all wrapped up into one when they retired each night – usually about midnight – to the unheard-of luxury of their fire-warmed, fire-glowed rooms, and Celie was repaid for it a hundredfold by the grinding and ungrudging labour and devotion they gave her in return.

The front door opened noiselessly as she unlocked it but before she had it half-way open and despite the quietness with which it slid inwards, she was almost knocked back into the square by the frantic and noisy welcome she received from the waiting dog. Not the one which had accompanied her to Ambleside, but one of her puppies and which, when she and Prudence counted the weeks, must have been conceived while she was in Cumberland.

'That dog of mine is pregnant,' Pru had said to her accusingly at the end of November, just as though it was Celie's fault, which it probably was since she had allowed the bitch to roam about as she pleased. The animal had never gone far, or stayed for long, just far enough and long enough to become friendly with a neighbouring Lakeland collie, it seemed, and the results of it, nine weeks later, had been a litter of mixed golden retriever and black and white collie pups causing a great deal of hilarity on Jethro's part since they were so comically endearing. Their shape was to prove, at five months, to be that of their mother, though smaller, but their coats, long and silky as it would be when they were full grown, was a mosaic of all three colours. They were, despite this, quite charming.

'You'll have to take one, Celie,' Pru told her as the four puppies, two of each sex, squeaked and wriggled and fought one another for one teat, though there were six available. The bitch raised her head, and treated Celie to a lazily knowing look. It was as though she was confirming their special relationship which had grown in Cumberland and almost as if she was choosing for her, she rose to her feet, dislodging her offspring into a snuffling heap. Picking up one pup with a gentle mouth, she dropped it at the front of the basket in which she had given birth, then licked it, like a mother giving a child a quick wipe round before presenting it to company.

'There you are, you see, she wants you to have that one.'

'For pity's sake, Pru, what do I want with a puppy? I have enough to do without running round all day cleaning up its mess,' but despite herself she began to smile in delight as she picked up the tiny wriggling creature.

And here it was five months later treating her to the rapturous welcome it always bestowed on her. The affection between them had been instant and had deepened and strengthened as the weeks went by. The pup slept at the foot of Celie's bed, padding after her wherever she went when Celie was at home. She was left for a good deal of the day and evening with Belle and Maudie whom she treated with casual tolerance, allowing them to ply her with titbits and fondle her silken coat, but her slavish devotion was reserved for Celie, the first human hand with which she had come into contact, only days after her birth. She had a lovely, kind temperament, like her mother, but she got up to as many tricks as a cageful of monkeys, or so Maudie said, and it was this which had given her her name.

'Hello, Trixie, hello my beauty, yes, I can see you . . . yes, give me a minute to get my hat off and then we'll . . . no, don't knock me over, you silly dog, I'm home now, I'm home now.'

And so she was and perhaps the animal had something to do with it, she thought, as it danced along beside her down the dimly shadowed, warmly carpeted hallway towards the stairs which led to the basement.

The kitchen was, or appeared to be, in a state of absolute pandemonium as Celie stepped through the door. The two delivery men were carrying in what she had bought at the market that morning. Boxes of freshly laid eggs, cheeses of many varieties, Cheshire and Stilton, Gloucestershire, Cheddar and Sage, and Dunlop, Gruyère and Brie. There were oysters and lobster and sole, quail and duck, hams and veal, fruit so fresh the dew of the morning was still on it, vegetables and baskets of flowers, for when Miss Marlow of "Marlow's Special Catering" did a dinner party, she attended to every detail, even the arrangement of the flowers which decorated the table.

Trixie barked furiously, not yet fully trained to accept what was a daily occurrence in her mistress's day and it was not until she was shut in the scullery, to her obvious disgust, that order was restored. With the deftness and serenity she had taught herself to maintain, no matter what the circumstances, Celie had the men and the provisions they carried flowing smoothly from the van to her kitchen and from there, under her quiet command, to their proper place in pantry or cupboard or scullery. The men, longing to be of assistance to this lovely creature who had become a part of their daily lives, tried to draw her into conversation, as they would any pretty housemaid, respectfully of course, for she was no servant to be winked at. They were inclined to stop, to stand and stare, mesmerised by her calm beauty, and her so *young* to be in charge of this business, but though she was pleasant, she did not encourage them to linger, and within ten minutes they were back on their van and clicking to the horse which pulled it, as they turned towards their next delivery.

'You can let her out now, Belle,' she said to the hovering maid, referring to the noisy young dog, 'and then, if you wouldn't mind, hand me down those mixing bowls before you start on the veg.'

If you wouldn't mind! That was typical of Miss Marlow, Maudie thought. She treated her and Belle as though they *were* somebody. Not just a couple of pairs of red, chapped hands and dumb, animal minds who must be ordered about with no concern for how *they* felt. They worked hard but not as hard as she did.

'You two get to bed,' she'd say. 'I'll finish the washing up,' but even if they were dead on their feet, which they often were, they wouldn't let her. 'I won't forget this, Maudie,' she'd say. 'I won't forget your loyalty. When . . . well, when we're more firmly established I shall take on more staff and you and Belle will be rewarded, but until then . . .', and honestly it was the only time Maudie had seen tears in Miss Marlow's eyes since old Cook died.

But there was no time for tears, Maudie was aware as she began *her* part in the herculean task of preparing and cooking a seven-course dinner for twenty-four people at Mrs Thomas Morgan's splendid mansion in Heaton Crescent. Not only must the three of them create the perfect meal, but they must get it from St George's Square in a hired hansom to Mrs Morgan's kitchen where her kitchen staff and parlourmaids would help and be under the supervision of Miss Marlow until the last course was served and eaten. Naturally, Mrs Morgan had her own cook, a woman who was perfectly adequate for the everyday needs of the Morgan family and even *family* dinner parties, but when it came to that *special* function, where food of French cuisine was required, to impress and please Mr Morgan's business acquaintances, or the local gentry of which the Morgans were members, then no other than the special talents of Miss Marlow herself would do.

Celie had called personally at every house in the smart upper-class district around Sefton Park, those where the mistresses could afford her services, handing in her beautifully inscribed business card to the parlour maid before being shown into the drawing rooms of the ladies who remembered her from her days at Harper's. They were curious, some of them, in particular Mrs Morgan who was anxious to see her husband get on, and knew the benefit to him of a splendidly planned, cooked and served dinner party. Her housekeeper had withdrawn her custom from Harper's, she told Celie, for the standard had fallen so dreadfully since Mrs Harper, and Miss Marlow herself, no longer ran it. Oh, yes, good plain foodstuffs, she had heard, but then that was not what she was after at *her* table. She was sure Miss Marlow would understand. Now then, *what* was it Miss Marlow was offering, peering at Celie's discreet card through her fashionable, silver-framed spectacles, which she wore on a chain pinned to the bodice of her gown. A *catering* service, dear me, what on earth was that? And really, as she already had her own cook . . . pardon . . . French cuisine . . . and what did *that* consist of, and when she was told courteously that it consisted of *anything* Mrs Morgan cared to name, and if Mrs Morgan was not completely satisfied *no charge* would be made, Mrs Morgan agreed to try her out.

Mrs Morgan *had* tried her out and was very gratified by the number of compliments her guests paid her; with the smoothness of the service which Miss Marlow seemed instinctively to know how to *get* from Mrs Morgan's own servants; by the magnificence of the food and the tasteful arrangement of the dinner table, and indeed the *very* next day, called on Miss Marlow at her establishment in Great George Square and offered her the post of Cook in her own kitchen at a wage which made Celie's breath quicken, though naturally her amazement did not show on her smooth face.

She had refused, of course, and to give her her due, Mrs Morgan had accepted it gracefully, extracting a promise from her that she would cater for every special function Mrs Morgan gave.

'Indeed, I will, Mrs Morgan, and if Mrs Richmond cannot find any of the commodities which she used to purchase at Harper's, I would be only too happy to oblige. Tell her to call on me and I will make special arrangements to see she has everything a lady such as yourself might require on her table.'

'Indeed, I will, Miss Marlow.'

Mrs Morgan was shown into her carriage, the likes of which had not been seen for a long, long time in Great George Square, and was driven away by her coachman whilst in the basement kitchen, Celie, Belle and Maudie danced round the table as though it was a maypole, their exhaustion from their labours of the night before forgotten in their jubilation.

Prudence had helped, there was no doubt of that, sending Celie the names of those of her friends, mostly business acquaintances of Jethro's, the newly rich like himself who were still not accustomed to the niceties of entertaining and who needed Celie's guidance. It grew slowly, by word of mouth and by discreet advertising in one of Liverpool's good newspapers, and the money she had borrowed from Jethro to get her started would very soon begin to be repaid. Every penny she had earned, apart from the small wage she paid the two girls, had been put back into "Marlow's Special Catering" but soon it would be making a clear profit and from there could only be even more successful, surely? She was beginning to sleep at nights now, those long hours of staring into the darkness of failure eased with each new triumph.

The two girls were absorbed in the tasks Celie had set them, their young faces intent, Belle's screwed up into what Celie called a "tight fist" since it did not come as easily to her as it did to Maudie. She was willing and conscientious though, taking on the simpler tasks about the kitchen and clearly pleased by Celie's trust in her.

'Is this right, Miss Marlow?' she asked, holding out the bowl of egg whites she was whisking.

'Just a bit more, Belle. It has to peak when you lift the fork.'

Her mind raced back for a moment to those very same

words which Cook had spoken to her years ago and as it did so, the doorbell rang.

'I'll go,' she said. 'You finish the whites, Belle, and I'll be back in a minute to show you what to do next.'

The egg whites were ruined and Belle in tears by the time Celie finally returned to the kitchen.

Chapter Twenty-nine

The man who stood on the doorstep smiled hesitantly, not at all sure of his welcome, it seemed, and Celie distinctly felt the blood drain from her head. She knew she had lost every vestige of colour from her face and had it not been for her hold on the door she might have fallen. The man must have thought so too, for he sprang forward, ready to offer his steadying arm, but she recoiled from him, the distaste she felt clearly written on her face.

'Oh, Celie,' he murmured sadly, 'for it to come to this.'

She could not speak. She could do nothing other than stand, her mind numbed, her limbs paralysed with shock. Trixie had followed her up the stairs from the kitchen and along the narrow hall to the front door, her body quivering with that anticipatory excitement which even the most mundane occurrence can trigger in a young dog. Now she pranced on to the step, jumping up against the visitor's leg, sure of her welcome, ecstatic in hers.

'Down, Trixie,' Celie heard the automatic words escape from between her own clenched teeth. She put out her hand to take the dog's collar, to drag her indoors and shut the door in Dan Smith's face. The need in her to get away from this man whose lack of will-power, whose weakness, whose irresponsibility had brought about her own downfall and put everything she and Cook had worked for in the hands of Kate Mossop, was so strong she was ready to slam the door to without a word. Her immediate response was to run away and hide from him. To avoid the confrontation he was evidently seeking. To shut him out of her house and her life, and forget him, forget the pain he had caused her. His friendship, his love, his caring had been a sweet and treasured part of her childhood and young girlhood, from the time she had been ten years old. She had trusted him absolutely and the simple truth was that if she allowed her feelings of betrayal to come to the surface, to be *spoken* of, the slender thread which she admitted still bound her to him would be broken completely. Broken and *never* mended. Which was strange really, her dazed mind agonised, for if that were to happen was that not what she wanted? To be wholly and irreconcilably disassociated from Kate Smith and her husband, the man who had once been Celie Marlow's friend. So why was she hesitating, dithering on her own doorstep, when all it needed was for the door to be shut firmly in his face? At this precise moment, she could not *bear* to speak to him, let alone invite him into her home. He had betrayed her. Not by marrying Kate Mossop which he was perfectly at liberty to do since Celie Marlow had no claim on him, but by the way in which he had allowed Kate to manipulate him. A coward's way, an unmanly way, and she could not forgive him for it. Kate had turned him into that joke, that laughing stock which all men and women despise, a doormat, a man under the thumb of a woman. And now he was here, smiling, hoping, expecting to be invited into her home, into the home of Celie Marlow who, but for his dishonest dealing, his philandering, his furtive and underhand affair with Kate, would have been if not the owner, then still running Harper's beside him. She would never, to the end of her days, understand why Cook had left it all to him, but remembering him as he was before Kate got her hooks into him, there was no doubt in her own mind that Dan would have shared it all with her, Celie.

And that was the sadness of it. She did remember him as he was. As he had been years ago at Briar Lodge when they had been young and carelessly happy under the guidance and rule of Jess Harper. The night her Pa died. The comfort he had given her. His defence of her on the day of Anne Latimer's wedding for which he was dismissed. A dozen moments, a hundred. He had been sweet-natured, generous, protective of the child Celie Marlow, watching out for her, making her laugh when she was sad with the sudden curious sadness which comes over young, growing girls. She had trusted him, understood him, right from the moment he had been brought into Cook's kitchen. A tall frightened boy whose defiance when he would not answer had infuriated Cook. He had always been there when she needed him. A boy, a young man, a *grown* man. But though his engaging ways had endeared him to all the servants, he had never been *tested*! From that first moment he had needed to do no more than take orders, work hard, drift through the days and years with no need of decisions, of plans for the future, of even making a home for a family for it had all been done for him. By Mr Latimer, by her own father, by Cook and herself. He had needed to show no initiative for she and Cook had done it for him. She and Cook *and Kate Mossop*.

The indecision must have shown in her face for he put out a hand to her pleadingly. He wanted to say something and he was anguished by his own inability to put into words what he so obviously felt and again that tender part of Celie's memory drove her back to their childhood and what they had meant to one another.

The dog was doing her best to get at Dan, choking herself on her collar but not caring in that daft way young animals have. All she wanted was to reach this fascinating new human and Celie was becoming overwhelmed by her need to keep the dog in and the man *out*. Dan's hand wavered as the foolish, infuriating tears flooded her eyes. She had grown a protective shell of hardness about her in the last year, the treachery done her by Dan, by Kate, by fate, if you like, giving her strength or perhaps bringing it up from within her where it had always been beneath the surface gentleness, the softness. A formidable quality of strength and indomitable determination not to allow what had happened to her to drag her under. She would recover, she told herself and she had. She would claw her way back and that was just what she was attempting to do. She was not absolutely sure *where* she was going, only that she must use her one talent to start her towards it. She knew nothing else but how to cook so surely that was the starting point? Gradually she had become aware in some silent, unseen, secret part of herself that she meant to get back what she had lost and even on that first day, the day she left Harper's, she had begun the process. The process of simply not being *there* in Harper's kitchen. Kate, clever as she had been, had not foreseen the effect Cook's and then Celie's departure would have on the successful business and though it was still a profit-making concern it had lost the carriage trade which was where the *real* money lay.

But her heart, her troubled woman's heart was ready to betray her at the sight of Dan Smith standing forlornly on her doorstep. He had removed his hat and the pale sunshine struck gold in his short cap of curls. His blue eyes, the blue of speedwell, looked at her so sadly, so desolately, so despairingly, that despite herself she felt the need to take his hand, to draw him inside, to comfort his pain as she had done as a girl. She could feel the weakness begin in her, that familiar softening he had always awoken in her, not like the softness Richard Latimer had reduced her to, but that of Celie Marlow for the boy, the youth she had regarded as her brother. Dear God . . . oh, dear God . . . don't let me weaken, she begged, not after all he has done to me, or at least, allowed to be done to me by the shrew he married.

She had not spoken out loud except to the dog, but now she did and her voice was hard.

'What do you want, Dan?' No more.

'Celie, please Celie, can't I come in? To stand here on the doorstep . . .' glancing round the busy square where already one or two inquisitive housemaids intent on their polishing of windows and door knockers were staring across at them.

'What for?'

'Please, Dear Christ . . . Celie . . . I could not let this go on . . . not without trying to . . .'

'To EXPLAIN? Is that what you have come for? There is no need of explanations, Dan, I am not such a fool as that.' Her voice was high and somewhat out of control as her old self fought with her new which was crumbling badly in the face of his pain.

'No, not to explain . . . well, yes, that I suppose, but . . .' He hung his head. How could he speak to this innocent woman of the torments and delights of the flesh, the temptation which had been thrust on him and which his strong masculine body had been too weak to resist. Kate it was who had initiated their first sexual encounter but it was Dan Smith who had been intoxicated with it, enslaved by it and had feebly let it run on for years. At first he had felt guilt and shame. He loved Celie, had always loved her and had been content to wait for the time to come when they would marry, but Kate Mossop's ripe body and knowing ways had distorted his vision, made him blind to the implications of the future and with that blindness had come the inevitable insensibility which dulls the mind because of habit, an acceptance. If he had thought about it at all, which was doubtful, he had assumed that when the day came for marriage with Celie he would simply tell Kate their relationship was at an end and whereupon she would obligingly slip away from his new life with his new wife. His own naivety never failed to astonish him and fill him with bitter self-recriminations.

'I don't know why I came, Celie. There is nothing to say that will make it better, it's just that . . . for so long we have . . . I have . . . loved you . . .'

'Stop it, Dan, I won't listen to this.' Dragging at the dog who had quietened now, sensing some tension which her young mind did not care for, Celie began to swing the door to but Dan put out his hand to stop her. There was a desperation in him which said he no longer cared what anyone thought, her, the housemaids who stared open-mouthed at the tussle on the doorstep of number thirty, even the stout woman, who it seemed had come from nowhere and was hesitating at his back.

'Let me come in, Celie, please. I've . . . it's taken me weeks . . . weeks of sneaking about in the garden there . . . seeing you . . . and now that I've found the courage to . . .'

Celie was beginning to weaken. She did her best to give him that forbidding, haughty expression she had perfected for the benefit of the dozens of men she met in her business day, those who longed, or so it seemed, to get to know her better. Stallholders, porters, delivery men, gentlemen who passed her on the street, those in the bank when she went there to consult with Mr Drake, men in all walks of life who were, apparently, captivated by something they saw in her which she was scarcely aware she possessed. Even Mr Pembroke bobbed and bowed and held her hand longer than was necessary when she greeted him. She was, of course, polite, but she made them all aware that she was not available for whatever they wanted of her, and she was doing her best to do the same with Dan but she really could not bear to see his tormented despair. He was tearing her apart, forcing her to suffer pity when all she wanted was to feel hatred, to despise him and his inadequacy, but love and compassion did not turn to hatred because the person one loved was flawed.

'Is this gentleman bothering you, Miss Marlow?' The voice startled them both and Dan turned swiftly, whilst in the doorway Celie leaned thankfully against the frame. The man presented a pleasant image to Flo Wilson, an image which was well-dressed and attractive, not a gentleman, but decent nevertheless with nothing about him to suggest violence but all the same Miss Marlow was cowering back from him, her grey eyes great pale and silvery pools of tears in a face that was white and strained. She was hanging onto the door frame, and to that dog of hers for dear life and though Flo was against interfering in what did not concern her, she could hardly walk by without a word when a neighbour was in trouble, could she? Particularly when that neighbour was the frail and vulnerable-looking Miss Marlow who had no one to protect her.

'Are you all right, lass?' she asked sternly.

'Oh, Mrs Wilson, it's you . . . please . . . oh, do come in . . .' Miss Marlow began to babble in a most uncharacteristic way, Flo was inclined to think, since she had never seen her other than cool, unhurried, controlled.

'Celie, I beg you . . .' the man said, so pitifully Mrs Wilson felt quite sorry for him but Miss Marlow, still dragging the dratted dog, had retreated into the shadowy hall, begging her to come and have a cup of tea with such fervour and evident relief, Flo brushed past the man unceremoniously and entered the house.

'Close the door, please, Mrs Wilson,' and Flo had no choice but to shut it in his distraught face.

They drank tea in Miss Marlow's pretty parlour, chatting about the price of fruit, the pleasantness of the day, the lightness of Miss Marlow's macaroons, the recipe for which Miss Marlow promised to give her, and for a full fifteen minutes, it was as though this was just an ordinary social call, one neighbour taking tea with another. Flo was just about to stand up and declare she must be off, indeed she was gathering her bag and straightening her hideously unflattering black hat when Miss Marlow returned her cup carefully to her saucer and asked baldly,

'Was that him?'

'Yes,' Flo answered knowing exactly what was meant. 'I never saw his face but he was dressed the same. Same build and height.'

'You'll be wondering . . .'

'Nay, Miss Marlow, it's nowt to do wi' me.'

'Call me Celie, please.'

'Well . . .'

'Please, Mrs Wilson.'

'Flo.'

'Oh dear, Flo, I swore I wouldn't cry again but . . .'

'Nay, lass, cry if you must,' though it was evident that such a pastime did not figure much in Flo Wilson's life.

'No, I've done enough, but the shock of seeing him there after all this time, and then . . . well . . . he looked so . . .'

'Pathetic?'

'Yes . . .' Celie leaned forward eagerly. 'That's it.'

'They're good at it, lass. 'Appen you know that, though.'

Celie subsided back into her chair, smiling a little at Flo's blunt assessment of the male sex. Happen *she* knew as well.

'He . . . cheated me, Flo. He and . . .'

'You've no need to say 'owt if you don't want, Celie.'

'No, I'd like to, perhaps I can get it straight in my mind then. Put it in its true perspective.'

Flo Wilson was not awfully sure what that meant but she

got the general idea. Problems shared, discussed, often were untangled, turning out to be not as catastrophic as was at first believed. Two minds instead of one, perhaps looking at it from different angles, studying the thing and bringing it down to its true size and proportion.

When it was told she admitted to herself that it was not what she had thought. It was indeed an injustice of gigantic dimensions and not the usual triangle she had imagined. She had thought, as one would, that either Celie, as she had been told to call her – funny name – had jilted, or been jilted by, the young man, with a third person involved somewhere, and she supposed in a way that was what had happened, and in her forthright fashion she got right down to the nub of the matter.

'Did Mrs Harper expect you and this chap to get married?' Celie looked astonished.

'Married? Good Heavens, what made you think that?'

Flo shrugged. 'Isn't it obvious, lass?'

'Obvious?'

'That's why she left it all to 'im. D'you think she'd a' done that if she'd had the slightest notion he was carryin' on with this other lass, and that he'd marry her? From what you tell me she was a fair woman an' she'd not be inclined to leave a decent business where a hussy such as that one might get her hands on it.'

'But neither Dan nor I ever indicated, to her or to each other, that we were more than . . . more than fond as brothers and sisters are fond. I . . . really . . . loved him, Flo, but not as . . .'

'A woman loves a man.' Flo's bluntness, though it took Celie by surprise, was pleasing. In a way she reminded her of Prudence. She was sharper than Prudence though, shrewd and far-sighted, seeing what Prudence and herself, and even Jethro had not seen, though she supposed that was because what the . . . what had happened . . . what had been between . . . the emotions Celie had harboured for . . . Prudence's brother . . . had got in the way. Prudence and Jethro, knowing how Celie had . . . felt about . . . Oh God, she could not even *think* his name, let alone say it . . . but knowing how it was, they had both completely overlooked the possibility of an alliance between herself and Dan. Of course, it was clear now, the reason for Cook's strange and unjustifiably cruel Will. If she had believed that Celie and Dan were to be married, had what was known as an understanding, in her old-fashioned way she would have thought it only correct to leave her property to Dan Smith who would, she must have been positive, soon be Celie's husband.

'He doesn't seem to . . .'

'What, lass?'

'Care a great deal for Kate.'

'No man likes to be trapped, Celie, no matter how much he deserves it an' she got 'im with the oldest trick in the world.'

'Poor Dan.'

'He's made 'is bed, lass, an' he mun lie on it.'

'Yes, but I can't help remembering . . .'

'Nay, none o' that. Remembering helps no one. Look tot' future, Celie Marlow, and from where I stand yours seems bright enough. Don't let that chap, *any* chap get in yer way. Now then, I'll be on me way. You've that dinner party you were telling me about earlier an' I've a meal to get started for fifty or so poor souls from God alone knows where. Off to t'other side of the world they are and frightened ter death at the prospect, most of 'em, so a bit of good grub heartens them. Now, you'll be all right, lass.' It was a statement rather than a question but kindly meant. 'If that lad comes back beggin' for yer to forgive him, don't be taken in.'

'No, I won't, Flo, and thank you. You've been very kind.'

'Nay, give over.'

That night, very late, she lay in her bed, her arms across her closed eyes as she tried to sleep. She was tired to the point of exhaustion after the frantically busy hours she had put in since Flo – what a *nice* woman she had turned out to be, despite her brusque manner – ever since Flo had left, preparing and cooking for Mrs Morgan's dinner party. The trek across town to Heaton Crescent, the hours in the kitchen, the supervision, the clearing and collecting of her own utensils which fortunately the Morgans' kitchen maids cleaned for her and then the ride back to Great George Square where Belle and Maudie waited up to help her unload them and put them away. She had spent the past week, apart from two functions for which she did the catering, making and bottling orange marmalade, since the Seville orange was, at this time of the year, at its peak of perfection. Pots of them she had stored down in her cool cellar, the tops covered with tissue paper brushed on both sides with the white of an egg. She had preserved and bottled pears in the latter part of last year, borrowing Pru's kitchen for the purpose, which had not been at all to the liking of Pru's cook. Plum jam and preserved plums. Rhubarb jam, quince jelly and raspberry jam, preserved strawberries in wine, again done in Pru's kitchen. Peaches in brandy, preserved morello cherries, nectarines, greengage jam, gooseberry, the fruits bought when they were cheap and plentiful and put up in readiness for the day she would sell them again. Over the winter months, before she had grown steadily busier, she had made the Everton toffee, the crystallised fruits, the bon-bons, sugared almonds and chocolates of every description, all tastefully wrapped and boxed ready for sale. She had sought out the firm of importers who had supplied Harper's with the novelties, the specialities from abroad which had been so popular with Harper's customers and, when they had been delivered to her, had let it be known that they were now available again at Cécilie Marlow's establishment of catering.

She heaved a sigh, twisting about in her bed and across the room where her blanket was, Trixie raised her muzzle from her paws, then stood up and padded over to her, putting her cold nose against Celie's warm cheek.

'Yes, I know, Trix,' Celie murmured, just as though the bitch had expressed her sympathy out loud. She sat up and sighed again. The face of Dan, sad and strained, thinner, older than she remembered it, forced itself into her mind and as though to elude it she sprang from her bed and moved to the window which looked out over the dark garden and square to the houses on the opposite side. Not a light could be seen anywhere, for those who worked in the houses were glad to get to their beds and their rest in preparation for the next day's labour, and those who were temporarily housed there needed that state of unconsciousness which allowed them to forget their fears for a few hours.

She put her flushed cheek against the cold window. She wished she too could find peace in sleep. Her body was exhausted but her mind darted backwards and forwards, moving from the aching remembrance of precious moments in the past to the contemplation of unknown pitfalls in the future. And there was not only Dan's face to bring it all rushing back to her but that of Richard Latimer whom she had not seen, nor heard of, in almost three years. Just that one slashing moment when, inadvertently, Pru had let it slip that he and his battalion were serving in England and then, last September, a brief report in the newspapers to say that the 2nd Battalion, the King's Liverpool Regiment, had sailed for Holywood, Belfast.

So he was gone. Gone from Liverpool and from her heart, finally, or so she had told herself, and would trouble her memory no more. They had both gone, the two men in her life, gone beyond her reaching and her own way stretched out, beckoning, promising, before her and she had no choice but to move along it. It was bright and hopeful so why did she feel so restless, so . . . dejected and it could could only be the encounter with Dan that day and the turmoil he had brought with him.

Everywhere was silence and beside her, Trixie stirred.

'Good girl, good little girl,' she murmured quietly, bending to fondle the animal's silken ears, glad of her company and her undemanding, enduring affection. 'What to do, girl? What to do to make me sleep? I've Mrs Linden's soirée to prepare for tomorrow evening and Mrs Broadbent's boy's birthday party on Saturday afternoon, and I've not even made his damn birthday cake, let alone iced it.'

The dog gazed up at her, her wide intelligent eyes bright and gleaming in the dark room. When Celie stood up, so did she, wagging her tail expectantly, ready for anything her mistress might care to name. She was at Celie's bare heels as she slipped through the bedroom door, pattering down the stairs so close behind her she was in danger of tripping her up. She hesitated for a moment at the hook by the basement door where her lead hung. Perhaps they were going for a walk, her cocked head asked, but when Celie continued on down the stairs to the kitchen, Trixie followed her equably.

Celie lit a lamp, placing it on the kitchen table and then, from a drawer in the dresser, took out a ledger, opening it at the first page at the top of which the date of November 1st 1898 was written. There was, on the left hand page, a long list of provisions, the cost of them, and the total at the bottom. The next date was November 8th, again with a list of goods purchased and their cost. Again on three more dates, the same thing and then, on December 12th on the right-hand page, another column of items, of which turbot soup, brill and shrimp sauce, roast pheasant and meringue à la Crème were but a few and their price to the customer. That had been the day of her first dinner party.

As though she had not done it a hundred times before, Celie ran her eye down the long column of figures on each left-hand page, then down the right, her lips moving soundlessly as she added and subtracted and when she arrived at the balance, the *profit*, she smiled in satisfaction. There were many blank *right*-hand pages at first, but as she moved into January, February, March, each side began to be written on and on every one there was a figure which spoke of gain. Not only did Celie Marlow know how to cook, she knew how to make one penny do the work of two, as Cook had shown her, and she used that talent, at the same time in no way detracting from the splendour of the dish she created.

She leaned back in the chair and the fire's gleam which was never allowed to go out polished the dark cloak of her hanging hair to chestnut and tinted her pale skin to honey. Her silver eyes narrowed in contemplation of the pages and she tapped her pencil against her pursed lips.

Again she reached into the drawer, bringing out a flat tin box. She opened it and inside were copies of documents which looked to be of a legal kind. Share certificates, one headed 'The Liverpool Overhead Railway Company' and the words 'Five per cent Perpetual Preference Shares' written on it, certifying that Cécilie Marlow of 30 Great George Square,

Liverpool, Spinster, was the proprietor of ten shares of £10 each. There were others. A sugar refinery. The Mersey Railway Tunnel. A salt mine in Cheshire. All small amounts but from Celie's gratified expression, all healthy.

She drew them out, one by one, studying them intently. The dates on them were for the most part almost three years old, some more recent. Again there were sheets of paper with figures on them, columns in which some of the figures had been crossed out and others marked with a tick.

For ten minutes she pored over them, absorbed, and when a small ember in the fireplace shifted, dropping down into the ashpan beneath, both she and the dog at her feet jumped a little.

Celie stretched then, rubbing the back of her neck. She yawned and through the yawn she spoke to the dog who obligingly thumped her tail against the stone floor at the sound of her voice.

'He's done very well for us, has Jethro, Trixie. That stock has gone up again. Remind me to get the *Financial Times* tomorrow, will you? I must check how those shares in that soap factory have held and Jethro said something about the Liverpool Electric Tramways, so that might be worth looking into. Well, girl, let's get to our beds. I think I'll sleep now.'

She did, and though the amber-skinned, brown-eyed face of the man who entered her dreams made her smile in her sleep, she had forgotten it by morning.

Chapter Thirty

'I think I'll walk up to Mrs Garside's, Maudie. She's very near her time and can't get about much so a visitor will be welcome. Besides which, it's such a pleasant day it seems a shame to sit indoors doing accounts. After the hard work we've put in this past week, I think we all deserve a break. Why don't you and Belle get out for a spell? This weather won't last for ever, neither will the chance to listen to the band in the park with winter coming on.'

'Right ho, Miss Marlow. We'll just finish doin' these pans an' we want ter knock up a few scones for us tea, but as soon as we've done, we'll put our bonnets on and take a stroll up tot' park, won't we, Belle?'

Maudie always spoke as though she and Belle were the two halves of one being. She spoke *for* Belle and Belle let her. Unless Miss Marlow directed a question or a remark particularly at *her*, Belle had got into the habit in the years she had worked in tandem with Maudie, of letting Maudie do all the talking, make all the decisions as to where they should go in their time off, how she should spend her wages and, Celie suspected, even how she should dress. Maudie took charge of her, and of Minnie who was the new scullery maid, a darting, eager thread of a woman, older than the pair of them by at least ten years. Minnie had come to their door last winter by way of Flo Wilson who had no need of casual staff as summer drew to a close and the emigrant trade fell off, and who had thought they might make use of her. She would work for a few bob a week and her keep, Flo had told Celie. She was cheerful, honest, clean and a good worker and Celie was to take no heed of her appearance, which looked as though a drifting feather would knock her for six. Flo employed her in the summer and was most reluctant to turn her out at the beginning of the winter but perhaps Celie could put her to some menial task, the harder the better since she seemed to thrive on work.

Maudie was proving to be all that Celie had hoped for in the kitchen. She was quick, bright, receptive and keen to learn and had become Celie's trusted right hand. She had not the imagination a natural cook needs but her hand was light, her instincts sharp and she could follow Celie's instructions down to the minutest detail without need of repetition. Her memory was astonishing and once she had the recipe in her head, she could turn out many of the complicated dishes Celie tutored her in. She could be left to prepare the basic particulars of any meal, allowing Celie's delicate and artistic gift to carry out what only real genius can effect. They made a splendid team and Maudie often went with Celie now when she travelled to many parts of Liverpool and the splendid homes where her services were increasingly in demand. Most evenings found them in some lady's kitchen. The cooks who worked there were used to her and her artistry by now. During the day their own kitchen in the basement of 30 Great George Square was a hushed bustle of disciplined activity, for Miss Marlow had taught them the benefit of order, routine, control, each pair of hands and the job it performed fitting like a well-oiled wheel or cog in the machinery she set in motion each day. There was none of the chaotic pandemonium which was evident in some of the kitchens they visited and the three servants had become used to her ways and her teaching; absorbing her calm and restrained manner of doing things until it became second nature to them. It might appear to be slow, but they found that in the long run they performed their allotted task in half the time. Even Minnie, who only scoured pans, scrubbed floors, shelves and working surfaces, cleaning up after those who were above her in the strata of servants, namely Maudie and Belle, imbibed this principle and found she was twice as efficient as once she had been, without that dragging, bone-crushing exhaustion she had known in kitchens where she had previously worked. She had a tiny boxroom all to herself, under the eaves at the back of the house. She was warm and well fed and in her eyes, Miss Marlow was to all intents and purposes nothing less than a divine being whom Minnie worshipped quite unreservedly.

'Why don't you pop out for an hour as well, Minnie?' the divine being said to her kindly now. 'It's Sunday and we've a quiet day tomorrow.'

Minnie bobbed her head and sketched a comical curtsey, pleased beyond measure to be included in the general good will which, until she took up employment with Miss Marlow, had been somewhat lacking in her hard life, though Mrs Wilson had never been cruel. She'd not take up the offer of an outing though since she'd nowhere to go and no one to go with. She accepted that Maudie and Belle were friends and wouldn't want her along, besides which she was only a skivvy and they were kitchen maids, a kitchen maid being a far superior servant to herself. Just to spend an hour or two on her own before the kitchen fire looking at the picture book Miss Marlow had given her, the one Miss Marlow called a "fashion magazine", was all Minnie aspired to.

'You'll stay in then?' Miss Marlow said to her questioningly and Minnie nodded shyly.

'Well, you get a rest, d'you hear? Don't let me hear you've been scrubbing a floor whilst I'm out or I shall be cross.'

Minnie sighed adoringly, watching as Miss Marlow adjusted her elegant hat then reached for the dog's lead, at which Trixie, who had been watching her expectantly, exploded into excited circles around the kitchen table.

'Daft beggar,' Maudie remonstrated good-naturedly, nodding to let Belle know she should go and fetch her own hat.

The September day was soft and warm with no hint of the autumn to come. More like June really, Celie thought as she strolled along Upper Parliament Street, turning right into the Boulevard. The leaves on the trees which had been planted in the central grassy reservation dividing the wide street were beginning to turn colour. Plane trees, handsome and tall, their dappled trunks smooth, with side branches sprouting from the arching main limbs. In the summer, the upper surface of their leaves were a rich shining green, but as autumn approached, they were already beginning to turn to many shades of yellow: a bright golden canopy under which Celie walked as she approached the corner where Harper's stood. In a perfectly straight line the trees were like soldiers on parade, their shadows a welcome protection from the sun.

Trixie, who was a year old now, walked sedately by her side, only now and again forgetting her manners when some particularly toothsome scent pricked her nose. She would dart after it, then, reminded by the lead which restrained her, look up apologetically at her mistress.

Celie wore a new dress in a shade of almond. Not white, nor cream, nor even the palest pink but somewhere in between, and its subtle colour touched her skin to a warmth which in itself was none of these. The dress had been made for her by Miss Edna Sykes, the clever seamstress from Hawkins', the very latest fashion as shown in the smart London store of Dickens and Jones. It was made of watered silk, the close-fitting bodice buttoned down the front with tiny pearl buttons. The neck was high, lifting her already tilted chin, the sleeves tight with tiny cuffs. There was a scatter of pearl embroidery on the front of the bodice and a six-inch lace-edged gauze frill inside the hem of the gathered skirt which just cleared the ground. Her shoes of white kid were high cut with Cuban heels of two and a half inches fastened across the arch of her foot with a bar and a pearl button. Her plain white hat had the fashionable wide brim with half a dozen white silk rosebuds pinned beneath it. She carried a small white kid bag on a silver chain and a long-handled white lace parasol lined with chiffon. She felt pleased with her appearance, knowing the pale and subtle shades of her outfit complemented the winged darkness of her hair and lit her shaded eyes to brilliant silvered diamonds.

She stepped out more briskly as she approached Harper's then slowed her step for she did not want to give the appearance of hurrying as though she was nervous. Trixie moved at her pace, slowing and quickening when she did.

The shop looked slightly neglected, she thought. Not dirty in any way, for the large plate-glass windows gleamed, the pavement was swept, the woodwork wiped free of dust, but it needed a coat of paint and she noticed that one of the blinds had a tear in it and another was coming free of its roller. Small things which required an outlay of cash to put right but were an indication of a lowering of standards. The tea room had been closed, Prudence had told her, the word from its owner, or so she had been informed, that with the increased success of the shop and the difficulty of obtaining good staff, she had been forced to let it go. What had happened, Celie wondered sadly, to Beth, to Maggie and Fanny, of whom no one could complain? They had been hard-working and keen to get on when *she* had been in charge so what had Kate done, or said, to make them leave, or had lack of trade been the reason? Was Percy still there, and those imps, Frank and Fred, and what of Ivy who had been such a tower of strength to her and Cook?

She averted her face and walked quickly on, not caring who saw her now, nor what they thought. She would find out soon enough. When her idea for her own expansion had come to fruition, when her plans were finalised, Ivy could come and . . .

She shook herself, and, with a small inward smile, touched the wood of the broad trunk of a tree with her gloved hand as she walked by it.

Nora opened the door to her, smiling and bobbing a respectful curtsey, stooping to give the dog a pat, rewarded by a wave of Trixie's plumed tail. Madam was resting in the conservatory, she told Miss Marlow, her bright eyes snapping with excitement, the anticipation of the coming event as pleasing to her as though she herself had arranged it all. After all these years, the expression in her eyes said, nearly six and at last there was to be a baby in the house and the servants were "made up" with it. They treated their mistress as though she was made of spun glass, to her intense annoyance, ready to take her arm if she should so much as step out into the garden, hanging about outside the door of whatever room she happened to be in, solicitous and protective. After all she was getting on a bit, and this was her first. Twenty-five, nearly, which was late starting when ladies of her age would have had four or five by now.

'Don't show me in, Nora, I can find my own way.' Celie smiled at the maid, handing her the parasol and Trixie's lead which she had unhooked from her collar. The dog at once pattered off across the shining hall floor and through the half-open door of the drawing room where the sound of her claws was lost on the carpet.

'She's a visitor, Miss.' The maid took the parasol and the lead, turning away to put them on the hallstand. 'Just this minute walked in he has, and no sooner through the door, when he's shoutin' for . . .'

She knew, even before the drawing room door was flung back. The sunlight was behind him, outlining the tall, lean shape of him in his immaculate uniform, the gleam of it burnishing his neatly brushed hair to polished chestnut. His amber-tinted face was in shadow but she caught the flash of his white teeth as he turned to Nora, ready to ask something of her and for a moment or two his words faltered on. The strange thing was, Celie thought in that dream-like drifting which followed, he had not yet looked directly at her and yet he knew her, as she had known him. Before either had seen the other, each was aware of the other's presence.

Slowly he turned his head until their eyes met.

She noticed every minute detail of him in that first thirty seconds of absolute silence. The narrowness of his waist beneath his scarlet jacket and the muscles which bunched in his strong thighs, the shapeliness of his calves, the breadth of his shoulders, the fine dark hairs upon his hand where it clung to the door handle. His deep brown eyes, though they were in shadow, glowed with that familiar warmth he had not yet had time to hide and it was as though the four years between had been no more than four short hours.

His beauty was still compelling. The beauty of a mature man, completely and absolutely male with a strength about him, a *wholeness* which had developed since she last saw him and which would be instantly appealing to women. Even Nora was gazing at him as though he was a god come down from Olympia, her mouth slightly open, her eyes wide and enchanted, a flush to her young cheek which made her pretty. That was the effect he had on the opposite sex, Celie remembered thinking, as she drank in the texture of his smooth, well-shaven face which had no softness in it, the fierce and sudden swoop of his dark eyebrows and the tightening of his mouth. His body was taut, hard, tough and durable, as though ready to spring into instant action for he was a soldier, but he was also a gentleman and with the automatic response his upbringing had taught him, he snapped almost to attention and bowed his head slightly.

He could not speak though. Even his training, at school and in the army, could not, at that moment, find the right words a gentleman uses to greet a lady and it was left to Nora to break the silence which she described to Cook a moment or two later as "creepy".

'Will you take tea, miss?' she asked politely, but Miss Marlow did not answer and as for Captain Latimer, he seemed as stupefied as her, she confided to Cook.

'Stupefied in what way, girl?' Cook had demanded to know, but the answer to that question was beyond Nora, who dealt with practicalities in her busy day and though a romantic at heart, could not have described the expression on the faces of either Captain Latimer or Miss Marlow had her life depended on it.

Richard Latimer's eyes clung to the fragile loveliness of Celie's ashen face. He wanted to say something, knowing that if somebody didn't, they would stand for ever frozen in the softness, the lightness, the quiet and contemplative dreaming state of simply looking at one another until someone broke the spell. He put out a hand, and her eyes followed it as though she was mesmerised.

His action shattered the moment and Celie knew she must get away. After those first moments of unbelieving, unbelievable joy, another feeling was beginning to take shape. A feeling of panic, of heart-stopping terror that asked was Richard Latimer yet again to inflict pain and grief on Celie Marlow? She simply could not bear to suffer once more what his . . . what was the word . . . desertion? . . . would that do? . . . it was as good a word as any to describe what

he had inflicted on her three times now. A day or two of
enchantment, of knowing without question that he loved her,
that they had discovered the strength of true and honest love,
a deep love which had no falseness in it and in which she had
believed implicitly. Then . . . then he had gone away without
a word. Without a word of explanation, of goodbye, of regret
or sadness, leaving her to flounder in the anguished puzzle
of it. False after all, that exquisite emotion he had seemed
to share with her.

Oh no . . . no, she must not let it happen again. She must
not let him see into her heart which was still bruised with the
wounds he had administered so cruelly. She must go, *now*
. . . now before . . .

She had turned away, reaching blindly for the handle of the
front door, her parasol ignored, Trixie forgotten, when Jethro
loomed at Richard's back, his face awkward and questioning,
ready to smile should everything be all right.

The dog scampering into the conservatory had warned
them of course, he and Prudence, as they waited the return
of Prudence's brother. He had thought Prudence would faint,
so shocked had she been, so alarmed for the state of her
friend's unsuspecting, barely mended heart at the sight of
Richard in the Garside hallway, and dear God, it looked as
though she was right, for Celie was fumbling like a child at
the door knob whilst Richard watched her in frozen, appalled
silence.

Jethro hesitated, his own keen brain itself trapped in the
quandary of what to do, for none knew better than he through
Prudence, what Celie Marlow had suffered at the light and
capricious hands of his charming brother-in-law. Should he
let her go, as she was evidently intent on doing, or move
towards her, bring her back, take her in to Prudence . . .
Jesus God . . . what a predicament . . . he was only a plain
uncomplicated man who had loved one woman in his life, a
woman who had returned his love, so what should he do . . .
what . . . ?

'Celie,' he said gently, instinct coming to his rescue.
'Come in, lass, Prudence is waiting . . . come . . . don't
leave without . . .' and all the while Captain Richard Latimer

stood rigidly to attention, just as he had on the day of Her Majesty's Jubilee celebration.

Celie turned mindlessly at the voice of authority, not knowing what else to do, moving jerkily towards him. Richard stepped back to allow her to pass, his own movements somewhat unco-ordinated, then followed her and Jethro through the drawing room and beyond to the sun-filled conservatory. There were flowers, plants, growing things, birds in cages, comfortable wicker chairs strewn with bright cushions and at the far end, just struggling to her feet, was Prudence Garside. She was in her eighth month of pregnancy, her slim figure distorted by the jut of her distended belly. At once, all other considerations of small concern to him when compared to the health of his wife and their unborn child, Jethro hurried towards her.

'No lass, don't get up. See, there's no need. Stay where you are and Celie shall come to you. How many times has the doctor told you you must rest and here you are leaping about like a frog in a pond. Sit down . . .'

If he had planned it with the careful consideration he brought to all his business transactions, Jethro could not have chosen a more successful strategy to ease the tension from the moment. All else was put aside as both Richard and Celie moved forward, willing to do anything to add to the comfort and take away the strain from the hugely pregnant woman and though normally Prudence would have been mortified by the fuss her condition engendered, this once she took full advantage of it, knowing it would serve the purpose of smoothing, however tenuously, the fraught moments of Celie and Richard's first meeting after so many years.

Celie had not spoken of him at all, not after that initial shock and grief at his speedy departure and of course, since mentioning the fact that he had taken part in the Jubilee celebration last year and had in fact not even left England, neither had Prudence. Perhaps Celie had forgotten him. Perhaps her new life had given her just that. A new life. She certainly appeared to be wrapped up in her own small business and was busy and apparently content. And Richard, from all Prudence had heard, was not short of romantic attachments. At this very moment it appeared he was making advances, with her Papa's approval, naturally, to the delightfully pretty and very young daughter of one of their Papa's own business friends. He was thirty years old and ready for marriage. A *good* marriage, so her sister Anne told her. Anne, married herself these six years and the mother of three small daughters, and who, surprisingly had called on her when she had learned Prudence was herself pregnant. She came once a week now to take tea, unknown to their mother, of course, who had never, and would never forgive her daughter for marrying so disgracefully beneath her.

It took quite five minutes to settle Prudence in her nest of cushions; to receive the laden tea trolley Nora wheeled in and which Celie took charge of; to calm the excited young dog who was nipping determinedly at her own mother's flanks in an effort to rouse her to play and with a task to set their trembling hands and stunned minds to, Celie the familiar tea things which calmed her at once, and Richard the lively dog which had them all smiling, the worst moment was over. It was still laden with a kind of abrasive tension but they had all got a hold of their appalled consternation and could manage, they told themselves, to get through the necessary polite half-hour, however tricky, which courtesy demanded.

Prudence and Jethro, who both declared weakly later that they wouldn't go through *that* again for a gold clock, kept it all together, asking questions of Richard which he answered shortly, his tea cup balanced precariously on his knee; of Celie to whom, though there was not much they didn't know about *her* life, something must be said; and all the while Celie and Richard carefully avoided one another's eyes and addressed not a word except to Prudence or Jethro. The dog helped, as the young do, showing off her tricks, sitting at Richard's knee with her ears pricked, not begging exactly but watching every morsel of biscuit he moved from his plate to his mouth.

'She's an appealing little beggar, isn't she?' he laughed, turning quite naturally to Celie and for an exquisite moment it was there, not only in his eyes but hers, an unsteady admission that it was still the same, a leap of something magical passing from one to the other, then he turned back to the animal and his hand shook as he put it to her head. He left it there for a moment or two, then stood up ready to take his leave and as though Trixie knew that the hope of a titbit was gone, she turned to look for other diversions.

The door to the garden was open. She darted through it, her delight at being able to run unchecked making her giddy. She raced about the lawn in a mad figure of eight, her tail and ears down then, attracted to something she had smelled or seen, skidded off into the shrubbery where she disappeared.

Celie sighed, 'Oh dear, now where's she gone? I'd better fetch her or she'll be digging up half the garden. She must have remembered that bone Nora gave her last week, Jethro, and has gone to make sure it's still there.'

'Would you like me to go?' Richard found he could not say her name, and when her eyes reluctantly met his, his heart began to thump and shake inside him as though it had come loose.

'That would . . . be kind.' Her answer was cool, polite.

'It's . . . no trouble. She's probably only . . .'

'Indeed.'

She watched his tall figure move energetically across the lawn, his stride long, his back arrow-straight with that bearing only a soldier has.

There was a long, painful silence in which none of them could speak. Prudence wanted to say something comforting to her friend. But what? There had been no confirmation – spoken or unspoken – that this was anything other than a social occasion. The normal everyday afternoon tea taken by Prudence, her husband, her brother and her friend, nothing out of the ordinary beyond the fact that her brother, who was stationed in Ireland, was home on a spot of leave. But of course, all three knew better, though none of them could voice it without dragging at old wounds, and might that not open them up again?

'He's taking his time,' Jethro said at last.

'She's a devil when she sets her mind to it.' Celie's eyes were haunted.

'Richard must be . . .'

'Yes, perhaps I'd better . . .'

'What . . . ?'

'Go and see . . .'

'She'd come for you, Celie. You have a knack with her.'

'Yes.' Celie got slowly to her feet, standing for a moment, clearly dismayed by the thought of walking across the lawn to fetch the dog with whom Richard was clearly having problems, of meeting Richard alone without the buffer of Prudence and Jethro to stand between them.

'Perhaps . . . ?' Jethro began, transparently eager to go in her place and save her pain but a slight movement of Prudence's head, unseen by Celie who was looking out towards the spot where Richard and the dog had vanished, stopped him and he sank back in his seat, reluctant to upset some plan his wife appeared to have devised.

Another couple of minutes passed.

'The weather is quite superb,' Prudence said lazily. 'At this rate those roses will be blooming until Christmas.'

Jethro looked at his wife in amazement for she abhorred "small talk" and never indulged in it.

'Don't you think so, darling?' turning towards him.

'I do indeed,' going along with whatever she had in mind.

'I hope that foolish dog is not digging amongst them because if she is I shall wring her neck.'

With a long, shuddering sigh as though at the inevitability of it all, Celie moved towards the garden door. 'I'd better go and see,' she said wearily.

He was sitting on the fallen trunk of a tree, one Prudence's gardener had cut down to allow light to reach a particularly fine bed of dahlias on the far side of the wide stretch of rolling lawn. He was hidden from the conservatory window, deep in the shade of several holly trees which had sprung up the moment there was space and light. He had his head bent to the dog, who sat between his legs looking up at him, his hands smoothing back the silky fur of her ears and about her eyes which gazed up sympathetically into his. His shoulders were slumped in a posture of absolute dejection. He was oblivious of time and place and it was not until the dog turned at Celie's approach that he looked up and saw her. He didn't move.

He made no attempt to conceal his evident despair, simply continuing to smooth Trixie's fur while he allowed Celie to look deep down into the heart of his love for her.

'I didn't bargain for this,' he said quietly, knowing she would understand. She did, and all the hardness, the bitterness, the sharp, hurting poison which he had left in her drained away, going with the swiftness and ease of ice in sunshine. Sharp corners became smooth and thorns vanished as her love softened, warmed, expanded to encompass this man who was as hurt as she was.

It would always be thus, she realised it at that moment. Each time they met it was like an echo of another time. An echo which came from that time to this, always the same, the echo of love, the sound of which would never end.

She sat down beside him in the space he made for her and when his arm lifted to pull her close to him she huddled against his side, drawing his warmth into her own cold body, her body which, even in the heat of this sun-filled day, had been frozen without his. Drawing his love, his amazingly tender love into her love-starved heart. He fed her and brought her back to life all in the space of a second, and she was whole again, undamaged, serene, ready to heal him who was also in need. They were not prepared to speak of it yet, the wasted years which had shrivelled away behind them, the years *he* had thrown away on the spikes of his ambition, his pride, but they would, for it must be dealt with, the detritus of it. Now there was only the awakening of their senses, the opening of their eyes to the beauty in each other which returned to life as love sprang like an underground stream and ran true and sweet-tasting from its source.

He bent his head with a great thankful groan and put his mouth on hers which was waiting, soft lips parted, moist, warm. Almost savagely then he stood up and pulled her to her feet, dragging her towards him and crushing her painfully against his straining body, his arms crossed at her back, one hand gripping the other wrist. His throat was warm beneath her lips and she could feel a frantic pulse beat there, thumping at the same pace as his heart against her breast.

'Dear sweet God,' he whispered into her hair, 'what have

I done to us? What damage . . . the waste . . . all this time
and just to satisfy . . .'

'Hush, hush my love . . .' Her hands gripped one another
in the small of his back, their strength formidable in their
resolution never to let him go again.

'My love, my sweetest love, can you ever forgive me . . . ?'

'Don't, Richard, don't . . . it's done with.'

'The years, and all I ever wanted was this . . .'

'I know . . . I know *now*.'

'I love you, Celie.' He looked down into her face, lifting a
tender hand to it and his touch was strange, unfamiliar after
so long, but sweet. He touched her again, her eyebrow this
time, wonderingly as though he had never touched her before.
He was shaking and so was she and he drew her to him with
a small sigh, just as though he had reached some blissful
and yearned-for heaven after travelling through unbelievable
adversity. There were no words really, nothing to say or do
but press against one another for comfort, as animals do,
overawed by the rich and incredible prize returned to them
and which neither had expected to know again.

He let her go for a second or two, both of them unsteady
and ready to fall with the joy of it. Golden brown eyes blazed
into silver grey. He cupped her face with trembling hands, his
body leaning to hers, already seeking to love her completely
as it had not yet done. His mouth covered hers, moving
to her cheeks, her eyes, her silken eyebrows, then back
to her lips which clung to his. Deep, deep kisses which
were never-ending, hot with passion which must soon be
satisfied.

'I couldn't bear it if you should leave me again,' she gasped,
falling against him in what was almost a faint.

'I'll never leave you again, my darling, never! I promise
you.'

Chapter Thirty-one

Prudence had sent a telephone message, knowing that if she didn't nobody else would, she said, shaking her head in exasperation at the bemused pair who clung together on her drawing room sofa. The message was to be relayed to the woman who looked after the cottage in Ambleside which must be cleaned and aired, food got in, fires lit and all the other household tasks performed, for no one had been near it since Celie had stayed there a year ago. She and Richard were to travel there this very evening. Prudence cared nought for convention, she cried, for had not she herself spent several nights with her husband before he became her husband, ignoring Jethro's pleas for some propriety and if Celie and Richard were to be married as soon as it could be arranged, which, if a special licence was obtained, would be very soon, what did it matter, for God's sake?

Celie came out of her rapturous, trance-like state every now and again to protest weakly, but not for long.

'Mrs McKenna's luncheon party . . .'

'Who is Mrs McKenna, my darling?' Richard kissed her fingers, his eyes almost black with sensual need and beneath her skirt, deep in her belly, Celie felt the heat glow and ripple to meet it.

'Never mind Mrs McKenna,' Prudence continued. 'I'll telephone Maudie . . .'

'Who is Maudie . . . ?' Richard's lips moved to her inner wrist, his eyes telling her he could barely wait.

'. . . to come and see me with a list of all your undertakings for the next fortnight, Celie . . .'

'*Fortnight*!' Celie echoed, touching Richard's cheek, not really listening, and Jethro turned away in some embarrassment for really it seemed *indelicate* to watch such joy . . . such, well . . . *need*!

'Leave it all to me. It will give me something to do until this dreadfully lively child of ours decides to make an appearance. They *can* be trusted to be left alone, your staff, I take it? Well, then, I shall telephone all the ladies concerned and convince them that you are prostrated on your sick bed and under no circumstances can you be expected to rise and attend their homes where you could possibly deposit some dreadful disease . . .'

'Prudence . . .'

'No arguments, Celie, and what about you, Richard?'

'I can go where I please and with whom I please for the next fortnight.'

There was a small pause in the enchantment as the lovers contemplated the temporary parting which loomed on the far and distant horizon which was the end of Richard's leave and his return to Ireland. By then, of course, she would be his wife and arrangements would be swiftly put in hand for them to spend the rest of their lives together, neither of them particularly concerned where that might be as they looked deep into one another's eyes.

'Well?' he whispered, his hand lifting to smooth back her dishevelled hair from the flush of her face.

'Well?' turning to press her lips to his hand, her eyes so filled with her love for him he felt a lump come to his throat.

His voice had a bubble of laughter in it. 'Ignoring Prudence's usual habit of arranging everyone's lives to suit herself, would you like to go to the cottage for a few days?'

Though the words were almost casual there was an intensity about them which told her he knew it was no light thing he was asking of her. His tone, his manner, his loving eyes assured her it would make no difference to them if she wanted to wait. They would be married as soon as possible, he had already told her so. If she would prefer to stay in Liverpool at her own home, as a bride-to-be did, perhaps modify her many commitments to an arrangement to suit herself, he would not blame her, but his eyes pleaded and his body called to hers. She wanted it as much as he did, he could see it in her enraptured expression. She trusted him now and knowing he needed it she could see no reason to hide it from him.

'I love you more than anything in the world, you know that, don't you?' he said, and Prudence and Jethro were frozen to silence by the truth and beauty of his words and the way in which he spoke them.

'Oh, yes, and I love you, Richard.'

'Well, then?'

'Well, then?' They smiled at one another, sighing, and it was done.

It was midnight when they reached the cottage. Borrowing Jethro's carriage, Richard had driven himself back to Briar Lodge, leaving a vague note for his Mama and collecting his things, then he and Celie had been taken by Jethro to Great George Square where Maudie, Belle and Minnie had stood in the narrow hallway where the splendidly handsome Captain Latimer, still in his magnificent uniform, had smilingly told them that their mistress was to be away "for a day or two" and Maudie was to take her orders from Mrs Garside who would be telephoning her shortly. Leaving aside the alarm of speaking into the telephone which none of them really cared for or were even asked to tackle since Miss Marlow was always available when it rang, the sheer enormity of not only being without her but of dealing with Miss Prudence of their Briar Lodge days threw Maudie and Belle into instant panic.

Celie had to speak to them very sternly, lining them up in the kitchen, explaining that all contracts were to be postponed or cancelled. That they were quite capable of "seeing to things" and that Mrs Garside was no more than a telephone call away, which was all well and good if there was only someone to *use* the dratted thing for *they* certainly couldn't, though they didn't say so. What if it should ring with someone *important* on the other end, went through their flustered minds whilst Miss Marlow, her hand in that of Captain Latimer, begged them to be good girls, to take great care of Trixie and, blushing, they were to tell no one where she had gone, or with whom. Did they understand?

Not a word, really, not even from Maudie, though they nodded obediently and promised to keep in touch with Mrs Garside. They were young women, used only to taking orders from others, and they needed a leader, someone of authority to tell them what they must do but Captain Latimer's hand was urgent, pulling Miss Marlow towards the front door and it was evident, even to the slack-faced Minnie, that she didn't need much persuading to go with him.

Their baggage was in the carriage. Jethro stood on the pavement, not because he was needed but to give an air of circumspection to the journey, at least while they were still in Great George Square. Bending, Celie kissed each worried cheek with a spontaneity she could not have shown two hours ago, waved a bemused hand and was gone!

The door to the cottage was unlocked, the woman not long gone, the pretty parlour filled with golden dancing shadows from the apple-wood fire in the grate. Lamps had been lit and placed, one on the window sill, another on the shelf above the fire, the third a welcoming glow in the upstairs bedroom window which stood open. There were flowers, a great jug of wild, red campion which grew on the edge of the surrounding woodland, mixed with the heads of the common poppy and the creamy white of fragrant meadowsweet. On a lace-covered table white water lilies from the lake floated on the surface of a wide water-filled bowl. There was food under an immaculately snowy cloth and the kettle simmered above the fire but, with a fierceness which called to some basic female need in her, Richard lifted Celie into his arms and carried her up the narrow, crooked staircase to the peach-glowed tranquillity of the bedroom. There was the fragrant smell of lavender, more flowers, this time mallow and the aromatic purple of wild marjoram, and a bed, wide, the covers turned back just as though the woman, whoever she was, had known how it would be with Celie Marlow and Richard Latimer.

Without drawing the curtains or turning down the light, he undressed her, his expression intent, not with haste or urgency but with a loving attention to every inch of her body his disrobing revealed. There was a spark of desire in his eyes which excited her. He was a man of some experience with women, of women's bodies, their physical appetite and emotional need which were not the same, though just as strong, as those of a man, but it was not this which concerned him now but his deep and abiding love, a love he now knew had never died and which he had shared with no other but the woman in his arms and beneath his ardent gaze. It was as much, in *that* sense, the first time for him as it was for her. She was virginal and his hands and his deeply glowing eyes were reverent.

'I love you, Celie,' he murmured, his mouth against the faint, childish hollow of her collar bone, his hand reaching to cup the tight, hard-nippled bud of her small breast. There was a delight in him which contained the wondering quality of a child, a slow enchanted wandering of his hands as they explored the fine bones beneath the skin of her shoulder, the long curving column of her spine, the soft melting curve of her waist. He pulled the pins from her hair, ruffling it until it fell in a midnight shower around her shoulders, down her back and across her bare breasts to reach almost to her buttocks as she knelt on the bed. She was not ashamed, nor even shy as his hands spanned the smooth nakedness of her waist and caressed her belly.

'You're beautiful,' he told her, his face working with an emotion which had what seemed to be agony in it, and as he caressed her her skin rippled and came alive under his searching hands. Hesitantly, wanting to please him and knowing somehow that it would, she raised her arms, displaying the rose-tipped whiteness of her flesh which glowed to honey in the lamplight.

'I love you, Celie.' He buried his face in her hair, inhaling the fragrance of it, and his hands lifted her, allowing the rest of her garments to fall from her so that she knelt before him, naked and beautiful, clothed only in the stunning fall of her hair.

He sighed, his content rich and satisfying, his masculine need very evident as he removed his own clothing, smiling as she watched him, for as he had examined and sighed over every detail of her body, it seemed she must do the same with his. She reached out a wondering hand, running her fingers down the length of his breastbone, his flat, lean belly, his thighs, his brown, male skin, returning to touch the strange, almost flower-like growth which sprouted from the bush of dark hair between his legs.

'You know this is right, don't you, my lovely Celie?' he asked her. He was not a man who loved a woman in silence and when she did not answer he lifted her chin to look into her eyes.

'Tell me how you feel,' he murmured. 'I must know that . . . it's . . . good for you. That you are . . . happy.'

'Oh, yes, Richard . . . yes . . .' reaching for his hand and putting it to her breast. Her nipple was hard and demanding in the palm of it. Slowly he moved it, rolling it against his flesh and she arched her back, like a cat does, pressing her breast against it. Her hand rose and fell, moving against his chest and, taking it in his, he guided it to the smooth, warm hardness of his penis. Her fingers closed about it and his breath came more quickly and she could hear him begin to pant, as she was panting, then a voice moaned and she knew it was hers.

'Richard . . .'

'I love you, Celie.' He leaned forward to take the nipple of her breast between his lips. He fastened his mouth on it, feeling the cushion of satin flesh peak to the pressure of his tongue, and her hands went to the back of his head, holding him there.

'I love you, Richard . . . and . . .'

'Yes . . . ?'

'I want you . . .'

'Aah . . . my dearest heart . . .'

'Richard . . . please . . . won't you . . . ?'

'Now . . . ?'

'Yes . . .'

He laid her back on the bed and parted her legs. Running his hand delicately down her flat belly he combed his fingers through the mound of dark hair at the base of it until they reached and parted the smooth, secret warmth of her, the part of her body which was so secret, so private it had no name, and the extraordinary melting, a melting pleasure so intense it dissolved the bones of her, overwhelmed her. She was moist, welcoming, and he in his turn was overcome by her innocent sensuality. Her body quivered in its need, then he moved, laying his length over hers, keeping his weight from her with his elbows. Her hand fluttered at the rigidity at the centre of him, then he entered her. There was a moment's burning pain which made her gasp then he bent his head and placed his mouth against hers, his tongue thrusting with the same rhythm as his body between her parted lips. Intense sensations of pleasure shook them both. It grew and grew, the pleasure they had aroused in each other. Her body lifted to his, demanding more. Movements became quicker, stronger, harder, until they were moving in unison.

'Is that good, my darling . . .'

'It's good . . . Richard . . .' Something was happening to her, something extraordinary and she wanted to shout out loud. Her hands gripped his buttocks, driving him deeper into her and then it exploded in the darkness of her body and she held on to him desperately in case she should be swept away on it.

'I love you, Celie,' he shouted triumphantly, his head arching back.

'Richard . . . Richard . . . Richard . . . oh, dear God . . . Richard . . .'

His name was torn from her as they reached that perfect moment together, that moment in loving pleasure, that moment which is the fulfilment of two bodies and minds which know not only intense sexual pleasure in one another but trust, tenderness, affection and the realisation that it will never end. Ever.

They slept then in the luxurious lassitude of after-love, curled together in the deep, lamp-glowed bed, then woke to love again, the fragrant mountain-scented, lake-scented air whispering through the window to cool their damp bodies. Their cries of rapture quietened the night creatures which rustled beneath the window, turning the heads and ruffling the silken fur of the cats who stalked the garden, those which had been kittens a year ago. The laughter of the man and woman was soft as were their kisses until passion came to claim them again.

When dawn broke and he examined her indolently stretching, rosy rumpled body he swore she had gained weight in the night since it was a well known fact that man feedeth woman with his loving.

'And, my sweetest darling, I would say you have had a sufficiency, wouldn't you?'

'Oh, I don't know about that, Richard Latimer. I'm sure I could manage another . . . shall we say . . . MOUTHFUL . . .' showing him exactly what she meant.

The days moved slowly at first, and the long, love-filled nights, as they do at the start of looking forward to the joys which stretch out into the future, but gaining momentum as time begins to turn its back and drift away. They did little but walk, pausing frequently to stand face to face, drinking in the simple marvel of just being together, of being given the gift of *gazing*, no more, for as long and as deeply as they cared to, into one another's eyes. Eyes which spoke for them of the endless continuity of their love with scarcely need of words though they spoke those too.

'I think I have always loved you ever since I first saw you, *really* saw you in the hall at Briar Lodge. You were so light and ethereal you might have been a ghost come to haunt me, which I suppose is exactly what you have done. Your hair was a dark halo round your head turning to gold where the sunlight fell on it. A halo of light and dark, glossy and rippling. It was like no other I had ever seen and I was mesmerised. You were in white, a gauzy, misted thing so that you seemed to be without substance and it was as though I could see through you. You were beautiful, even at that age. How long ago was it . . . ?'

'Years . . .' She was scarcely listening, bemused by the way his mouth curled up at each corner, one side slightly higher than the other so that his smile was endearingly lopsided.

'Do you know your smile is crooked?' she asked him dreamily.

He shouted in laughter. 'Crooked . . . ?'

'Mmm. When you smile it goes up and . . .'

'I was talking about you . . .'

'And I am talking about *you* . . .' stretching to place a slow butterfly kiss on the mouth in question.

For several long minutes they would consider the loveliness of his crooked mouth against hers before they returned to the intriguing question of how many years it was that they had loved one another.

'Does it really matter, my love?'

'Yes, I want to know how old you were then. In the hall at Briar Lodge I mean, though God knows you look no older now. God, I love you . . .'

Several more long minutes would pass as he showed her how much whilst the silken waters lapped in small waves at the edge of the lake, sucking and gurgling musically against the shore. Long shadows cast subtle-patterned colours on the surface of the lake and up on the hills the dying bracken waved and rippled, for the summer was almost at an end. Birds were blown helter-skelter across the clear blue of the sky and on the fells smoke spiralled lazily from the chimneys of remote cottages and farmhouses. From far off on the top of Loughrigg came the scream of a hawk. The mingled smells of the valley in which they wandered, fresh and damp after the previous night's rain, drifted about them. There was the sound of the breeze in the pines, the scent of bog-myrtle, the pungent aroma of wet fern and heather, the springy feel of moss beneath their feet, but the lovers were oblivious of it all. Of the beauty about them, for they were too deep in the enchanted beauty of each other. Later, much later, when they left it behind, when it was no more than a memory, treasured, protected from prying eyes, taken out when each was alone to study and dream over, then it would all come back, the sounds, the sights, the smells of which they were scarcely aware then, as sharp and clear as though they were experiencing it at the precise moment of remembrance.

The cart they had met at the top of Loughrigg Fell rattling and bumping along the rutted track and the carter's invitation to "hop up" as he took them across the "wilderness" where

visitors to the high peaks never went. 'They say you can 'ear
the shouts of men in battle over Moundale way,' he told them,
'and the tramp of marchin' men along the Roman Way.'

The day they walked the tops above Rydal Water, silent and
enthralled, engrossed in one another so that the breathtaking
wonder, the stillness and perfect peace, stretching away into
infinity, was not of their world until later, later when they
were apart and brought it back to dream over.

The moment of mirth when the oar in the boat Richard hired
drifted away as he kissed her and the wetting they got as they
tried to retrieve it.

On their last night, curled on the rug together before the
fire, they fell silent, the laughter gone, the merriment gone,
leaving a quietness which had a touch of sadness in it at the
prospect of leaving this place of miraculous enchantment.
They looked forward to that which was to come when they
returned to Liverpool, they told one another, but these days
they had spent at the lake had contained a magic which they
were reluctant to part with even though they knew it would
never be really lost. They would come again, they murmured
to one another, kissing tenderly, but the future lay ahead.

Jethro had it all in hand, Prudence had written to them, and
the marriage ceremony was to take place on October 14th at
the parish church of St Stephen's in the pretty village of Lee
Vale beyond Wavertree. The family had been informed, she
wrote, meaning her own and it would be up to the individual
members of it to choose whether they wished to see the
eldest son married. She and Jethro would be there, of course,
the "lively child" permitting!

'Will it . . . trouble you, not to have your mother and father
present, Richard?' Celie took his beloved face in her hands,
searching it intently for the signs she dreaded to see. The
signs which would tell her that he would regret marrying his
mother's erstwhile kitchen maid. 'They may come, of course,'
she added hastily though she knew in her heart that it was
unlikely. Mrs Latimer had not spoken to her daughter in the
six years since she had married Jethro, but perhaps, Celie
thought hopefully, remembering Mrs Latimer's fondness for
her son, she might accept *his* marriage with better grace.

His eyes were clear, honest, steady as they returned her gaze. He put his hands to hers where they cupped his face, looking down at her. They too were steady, warm and strong, as she was.

He and Celie had been standing in the doorway of the cottage before moving to the fire, their arms about one another, looking towards the western side of the lake where the sun had just slid down behind the high rise of Loughrigg Fell. The trees beyond the cottage were almost black, a lacy trelliswork against the sky which at that moment was without colour. A pale grey shading delicately to pewter where it met the earth. As they watched it turned slowly to silver, and then, above the mountain peaks, to the softest apricot, a blush at the back of a trail of pearl-grey clouds. There was a mist in the trees and the lights on the far side of the lake, coming from the cottages and farm which were dotted there, appeared to be hanging in the trees which hid the buildings. The apricot deepened imperceptibly to pink and rose and then to crimson, its glory indescribable and painful to the heart.

Now, as he spoke, it was as if the simple goodness of the splendour, the truth and majesty of the land, spoke through him, letting her know at last her true worth to him.

'You are my life now, my beloved girl. You and no one else. No one else matters to me, you see. No one. I need only you to be there for the ceremony. The church, the parson, you and I.' He smiled, a good smile, filled with the decent essence of Richard Latimer which had been truly revealed to her in the last few days. 'Of course I shall be glad to have Prudence and Jethro and . . . it would please me if my father were to come for I know he would like to but . . .' He bent to lay reverent lips to hers, a vow in the gesture, '. . . but only you really matter.'

She was satisfied. She knew he spoke the truth.

The three girls were whitewashing the washhouse in the back yard as she and Richard moved hand-in-hand through the kitchen to the back door and the steep steps which led down to it. She could hear Maudie's voice, the voice of authority in it sounding just like Cook's, which she knew Maudie unconsciously copied.

'That's it, Min, put plenty on yer brush an' slap it on thick
but mind yer don't gerrit all over yersen. Pull that cap down
over yer 'air, yer daft beggar. See, yer puttin' too *much*
on now. Well, it will run down yer arm if yer don't shake
proper. Watch Belle, she's got the 'ang of it. That's it, good
lass . . .'

They all three jumped guiltily when Celie spoke to them,
just as though they had been caught lolling about drinking tea
from her good china. Minnie even went so far as to hide
her dripping brush behind her back. Anything she happened
to like doing, and whitewashing the washhouse seemed to
be included in this, smacked of enjoyment and surely they
should not be *enjoying* themselves whilst Miss Marlow was
absent? Mind you, she enjoyed doing about everything at Miss
Marlow's and with Miss Marlow smiling that lovely lit-up smile
she seemed to have acquired recently she couldn't be mad at
them, could she?

'I might have known I'd find you hard at it,' Miss Marlow
said, turning to shine up into the face of the man whose hand
she amazingly held. At least it was amazing to Minnie who
had never seen a man and a woman holding hands. It wasn't
the sort of thing people she knew did a lot, especially for all
the world to see.

'I suppose that with nothing else to do while I've been
away you've spring-cleaned the house from attic to cellar,
even though it's not the time of the year for it,' Miss Marlow
went on.

They all looked crestfallen.

'Eeh, Miss, we 'asna done t'cellar. We thought that wi' coal
there, like, t'weren't no good puttin' whitewash on't walls but
we give it a good sweepin' an' . . .'

'Maudie, Maudie, I was only joking, really I was.'

Minnie watched Miss Marlow wonderingly. She had always
been beautiful. Like an angel, she was, though of course
Minnie had no personal contact with such beings but once
she had seen one in the window of the church in Agnew
Street. All in pretty colours it had been with the sun shining
round it and through it, just like Miss Marlow looked now.
Maudie and Belle could see it too, Minnie knew that by the

faces on them as they watched Miss Marlow smile at the man. She glowed, as steady as a candle flame which no draught touches, lovely and serene and yet . . . *merry* at the same time, as though the world was the most wonderful place to be in. It was deep inside her, the happiness, so that the smile shone out to touch the man and you could tell he was made up with it. Minnie had never seen anything like it before. She had not had a great deal to do with what went on between a man and a woman. Well, she wouldn't, would she, not with a face on her that was plainer than a blank piece of paper, but she could recognise it when she saw it, and without envy.

She smiled. They all did. That was the loveliness of it. It made you smile.

'And have you managed under Mrs Garside's leadership?' she was saying. 'Did you cope with the telephone, Maudie? I know you don't care for it . . .'

Maudie clapped her hand to her forehead, obviously exasperated by her own forgetfulness. Yes, she had mastered the telephone during her employer's absence and had even become quite pleased with her own performance on it. It had shrilled out this dinner time for the third time today and the message it had delivered was very important.

'It went just now, Miss Marlow, an' I were ter tell yer that it were most important, Mr Garside said an' you were ter call back because Mrs Garside 'as started. Last night it were, half past seven, he said an' would I ask yer to get in touch the minute yer got back. Askin' for yer, she were, he said, and . . .'

The three girls watched Miss Marlow sympathetically for though none of them had actually suffered the pangs of childbirth they had all witnessed it, coming from large families as they did. She was up the steps as quick as a flash, screeching to the Captain to call a cab whilst she telephoned Jethro and Maudie had to smile a bit for it was well known that the first took a while and Miss Marlow was acting as though, if she didn't get there in the next five minutes she might miss it.

'Right then,' Maudie said briskly to the others, 'we can't stand about like one o' Lewis's dummies, can we? 'an shut yer mouth, Belle. It's not first babby ter be born, nor the last.'

Chapter Thirty-two

Prudence's pains had begun just after seven last night, Jethro told Celie as she removed her hat and coat and handed them to an anxious-faced Nora in the hallway, a bit early, but the doctor had assured him that everything was all right.

There was the excited tension in the air which heralds an event of some importance, a strung-up, waiting tension which affected everyone in the household and even in the garden, it appeared, for the gardener and his two lads were fiddling about with something or other as close to the front door as they could possibly get.

Celie had allowed Richard to do no more than brush her straining cheek with his lips, scarcely hearing his assurance that he would be back at the Garside home as soon as he had taken his bags up to Briar Lodge, before leaping from the cab and flinging herself up the steps to the front door where Jethro waited for her.

'How is she?'

Jethro's face was a haggard mask.

'God knows. The doctor's with her and the nurse and there's a constant simmering of hot water on the stove though I don't know for what purpose.' Jethro, as a boy, had lived in a society where women had babies, one a year for the most part and being brought to bed with no one but a neighbour or perhaps a self-taught midwife in attendance. No fuss, no apparent difficulties, just another job of work to be done, like cleaning out the grate or doing the weekly wash, these tasks performed very often right up to the first labour pangs. A woman survived it, or she didn't, in his world, and the ways of the gently reared woman in childbirth were unknown to him. Delicate they would be, as they were in all things, having no need to be anything else, so how his Prudence was faring, whom he had always thought of as strong, in this drama of her life, he could scarcely comprehend. They would not let him in to her and again he let them bully him since, as a lady, Prudence must be allowed to give birth to their child as someone of her standing presumably chose to do.

'It's been twenty hours, Celie, and not a bloody sound from her. Why doesn't she scream . . . ?' because if she did he'd be in there so fast the doctor and nurse wouldn't know what hit them, his unfinished sentence said.

'It's her first child, Jethro, and if the doctor says she is fine then we must trust him.'

Celie moved quickly up the stairs with Prudence's husband so close behind her he was in danger of stepping on her heels. 'I can't speak from first-hand knowledge, of course, but the first often takes longer, they say.' She did her best to sound reassuring though twenty hours of the pain those in childbirth suffered, or so she had heard, sounded a long time to her.

'Now let me go in and see her,' she continued gently.

'Nora took some clean towels in and Pru was speaking your name. That blasted doctor wouldn't have told me and if Nora hadn't mentioned it . . .'

'I know, Jethro.' She did her best to soothe him as they moved, almost tied together so great was Jethro's anxiety, along the wide hallway towards the closed bedroom door. 'Now I'll just go and . . .'

'Promise me you'll come right out and let me know how she looks. The doctor keeps telling me that this is one little job a woman must carry out alone, the pompous fool, but if she says one word about me, about going in to her, I mean, no matter what *he* says, you'll come for me, won't you?' His face was agonised and his hands clutched at her. 'I'm trusting you, Celie. You know her as well as anybody and if it seems to you that she really wants me beside her . . .'

'Jethro, I promise I'll come for you. Now let go of my arm, there's a good chap.'

Celie tapped on the bedroom door which was opened by a trap-faced woman in a starched white cap and apron.

'Yes?' the woman asked, clearly determined to let in no one who was not needed, especially the husband.

'I have come to see Mrs Garside.' Celie's voice was calm.

'No visitors . . .'

'I think I am expected.'

'Oh . . . ?'

'Asked for by Mrs Garside. I am Cécilie Marlow.'

'Well, I don't . . .'

Celie brushed by her, no mean feat as Jethro, who still lurked at her back, knew to his cost.

Prudence lay on her back, no more than a slight mound beneath the neatly arranged bedcovers except for the enormous and seemingly immovable rise of her belly. Her eyes were closed and her face was in repose. Her hands were still, her arms lying one on either side of her body and for a moment Celie felt a surge of relief since it appeared her friend was, if not sleeping, then at rest. Her face was small and pinched-looking but that was only to be expected after twenty hours in childbirth.

The doctor, as though to justify his presence, and presumably his fee, took Prudence's wrist between his fingers, studying his watch as he did so with a look of intense and important scrutiny.

Celie approached the bed ready to kneel down and put a gentle hand to her friends pale face but with a violence which jerked her heart in her breast, Prudence arched her body, throwing her head back into the pillow until her chin pointed directly at the ceiling. Her jaw was rigid and the tendons in her neck stood out like strands of knotted rope. Her mouth grimaced in a rictus of agony in which her teeth showed as though she was smiling and her breath panted through them like that of a dog lying in a band of hot sunshine. Her hands reached out for something as the silent scream tore her lips back and hollowed out her cheeks and without hesitation Celie took them in hers. They gripped her like two vices, clamping on her soft and vulnerable flesh until she felt a scream ripping and tearing to get out of her own throat.

The sweat burst from Prudence's skin, from her face and neck and half-exposed breasts, from her arms and the hands which were nailed to Celie's, and Celie could feel the same thing happen to herself. It was as though they had become joined at that moment, sharing the labour which Prudence was hard pressed to continue, sharing the labour, the cruel pain, the sweat and tears and blood of birth.

She was in labour the whole of that night and the next day and it was not until half-way though the following night that Celie brought in Jethro Garside for despite the doctor's assurance that it was all quite normal with a first child, she could not stand what Prudence was suffering a moment longer. Jethro burst into the bedroom which he had shared for six years with the woman on the bed and who, it appeared to him, was dying; where their child had been conceived, the one which was killing her and his voice and manner declared that he would no longer be denied admittance.

'My dear sir,' cried the doctor, deeply offended, 'this is no place for a gentleman . . .'

'I'm no bloody gentleman and no bloody man neither to let my wife suffer as she has done for the past three days and nights, you bastard. Get out . . . get out . . . I've sent for another man. Let me get to my wife . . . Oh, dear sweet God . . . Oh, Jesus God . . . look at her . . . Dear God . . . Prudence, what have I done to you, my darling . . .'

'Perhaps if you would leave us alone,' the doctor said to Celie who had sunk once more to the floor beside the bed where she had been for the past thirty-six hours. 'Mr Garside and I . . .'

The woman on the bed tossed weakly, her pains so rapid and severe and so useless, it seemed, she could barely draw breath between them. It rasped harshly in her chest. Her cheeks had sunk into deep, black hollows and there were great bruises about her eyes. She was hardly conscious, unable to cling any longer to Celie's red, raw, chafed hands, her hair a wild, sweat-darkened tangle about her head, her lips bitten and flecked with blood. There was a smell about her of approaching death.

'Sir,' the doctor began, 'you are naturally worried by your wife's pain but she is young and strong . . .'

'Get out . . . get out . . . and you, too,' Jethro snarled at the doctor and the affronted nurse. 'Celie, go and tell Nora to wait for Dr Henry by the front door. She is to bring him up at once . . .'

His arms lifted his wife's weakly struggling body against his own strength, forcing it into her, willing her to hold on, and even then the doctor, self-important and not a little put out by the high-handed attitude of this . . . this man who was, despite his great wealth, a member of the working classes, did his best to assert his authority.

'Perhaps it is time for the use of forceps, my dear sir, though I cannot conceal from you the damage they can do to the skull of a child. Certainly if we continue as we are doing there is the danger of strain to mother's heart but . . .'

'Celie, I swear if you don't get this man from my sight I will do him an injury.'

The new doctor, a younger, more businesslike man altogether administered the slow, merciful drops of chloroform whilst Celie sprawled lifelessly on a chair by the window and Jethro held his wife in his arms until she lost consciousness. Then, with swiftness and dexterity the doctor and his nurse delivered the child. A tiny, wailing girl. There was some small but urgent emergency. The doctor was sharp and the nurse moved hurriedly, placing the weakly flailing bundle of new-born humanity into the only convenient arms available, those of Celie. There was the smell of blood and the deposits of violent birth clinging to the baby's flesh but the tiny dark head folded itself neatly against Celie's breast and the fingers of a minute hand came to rest, curling in perfect trust on hers. Long, fine eyelashes fluttered and shell-pink lips sucked hopefully. Dark eyes, unfocused and of no particular colour stared into hers. Latimer eyes, the same shape as Prudence's, and Richard's.

The baby was whisked away to the nursery by the smiling, efficient nurse where a woman waited to nourish the child with her own rich milk. Jethro would not be moved from his wife who lay sleeping and though still in a frail and critical condition was apparently to live and Celie – except for necessary bodily needs – moved from the bedroom for the first time in thirty-six hours.

There seemed to be servants everywhere. Pale faces staring up from the hall below and a feeling of movement in the shadows. Nora and Sally hung about at the head of the stairs, ready to break into tears, or smile through them if the news should be good. They were all eager to know how Mrs Garside was, they said, bobbing their curtseys, and not one of the servants was in their bed on account of being so anxious. They'd seen the little 'un going past on her way to the nursery and even had a peep at her, bless her little heart and that nurse had said Mrs Garside was as well as could be expected but they weren't awfully sure what that meant and if Miss Marlow could just give them a word, settle their minds like, they'd nip down and tell Cook and the others. Oh, and Captain Latimer was waiting to see her . . .

He rose from the chair in the hall as she moved wearily down the stairs and when he opened his arms she sank into them, ready to fall at his feet, and would have done had he not held her.

He was in full uniform.

The Boer War or the South African War was quite different from others the British soldier of recent times had fought in, for whereas before he had been pitted against ill-trained and ill-equipped "native" armies, this time the battles he fought in would be waged against troops of European descent.

How had it all come about? the ordinary man in the street wanted to know, taken by surprise at the rapidity of the onslaught of the hostilities. He was not, of course, privy to the factors and influences which had brought it to a head, knowing virtually nothing of the Boer republics of the Transvaal, though he was of the opinion that the Boer was acting recklessly if he thought he could get the better of the British.

He knew nothing of the resentment felt by the Boers at what they considered to be a threat, aimed at them by the British, to their independence and way of life. The Boers found intolerable the way in which the British had annexed

Zululand, Bechuanaland, Basutoland and other territories, effectively hemming them in and blocking their access to the sea.

The discovery of diamonds on the Orange River, and of gold in Southern Transvaal had attracted huge numbers of investors and foreign settlers, described as Uitlanders by the Boers, and it had caused great bitterness as they fought for control of what had become one of the world's richest countries. The Uitlanders complained that they were being harassed and denied equal voting rights by the Boers, which was most unfair since it was they who had developed the Rand goldfields in the first place.

For the better part of 1899 the crisis had been growing as Chamberlain, who was Colonial Secretary, did his best to unite all of South Africa under one flag, British naturally, which would be a crowning achievment for him. The independence of a Boer Republic, bursting with gold and bristling with imported rifles, threatened Britain's status as a paramount power and a decision must be made on whether to risk a war by sending troops to enforce it. President Kruger would not be mad enough to challenge Britain in a fight and would surely be prepared to do a deal giving Britain immediate political control of the country.

To prove the British government's determination in this matter the Cabinet made up its mind to send troops to show Kruger he could not easily confront the British. Among those to sail would be the 2nd King's Royal Rifles, the 1st Gloucesters and 1st Devonshires from India, the 1st Border Regiment from Malta, the 1st Royal Irish from Alexandra and the 2nd Battalion King's Liverpool Regiment from Ireland.

Celie was almost senseless with exhaustion and did not at first notice what he wore. Her cheek came to rest against the grey cloth of his greatcoat, the two rows of polished buttons which marched down his chest scarcely registering as they dug into the soft flesh of her face. She could feel the trembling begin somewhere inside her where the sick knot of acute physical fatigue had gathered. It seeped through her body moving down her legs which really felt as though they were about to buckle if she didn't lie down somewhere

soon. It ran along her arms which, though they did their
best to cling gratefully to Richard who was blessedly there
just when she most needed him, would keep flopping away
from his waist and falling to her sides. Her eyes drooped and
she was convinced she would fall asleep standing up just like
horses did. The wool of his greatcoat was soft on her skin
and the buttons would leave imprints, she was sure of it,
smiling at the thought but it didn't matter for he was *here*
to sustain her, which was all she cared about. Here waiting
for her in Prudence and Jethro's hall where, she supposed,
he had remained for the long hours of Prudence's labour.
Why had he sat just here, she wondered tiredly, and not in
the drawing room? Why by the front door as though he was
about to . . . and why? . . . her mind was so dazed . . . why
was he dressed in . . . in his uniform?

It was then that the chill of ice pricked the back of her
neck and she distinctly felt the hairs there tingle and rise
as though at the first intimation of danger. She had not seen
him since the afternoon of . . . when was it? . . . God, she
was so tired, so near to collapse she could not collect her
stunned thoughts into any sort of order . . . yesterday? . . .
no . . . the day BEFORE yesterday? Wednesday, the day
they had come back from Ambleside and now it was . . . *was*
it Friday? . . . Friday 13th and . . . yes . . . tomorrow would
be Saturday. Saturday, October 14th. Her wedding day. The
day she and Richard were to . . . Prudence would not be able
to be there . . . not now . . . not tomorrow which was Celie
Marlow's wedding day. Hers and Richard's . . .

She lifted her head. It took a great deal of effort for it felt
too heavy for her weak and wilting neck to bear but she did
it, dreading what she would see there, dreading what she
knew would be there, wanting to close her eyes and go to
sleep *now*, for what she could not see, what she did not *know*
about, had not happened and if it had not happened it could
not hurt her.

But it was true, the full horror of it. He *was* wearing his
uniform, the army greatcoat worn by an officer in the King's
Liverpool Regiment. His peaked cap rested on the hall table
and beside the table was a bag.

They stared speechlessly at one another. He was over-whelmed by the agony in her eyes and in himself for causing it. She was at the limits of her endurance and it showed in the waxy pallor of her skin, the great smudges beneath her eyes and the soft and vulnerable droop about her mouth, and yet her loveliness managed not only to transcend her utter exhaustion but to enhance it. Her hair had come loose from her chignon, falling wildly about her face and shoulders and as he watched she put up a hand and did something completely useless to it for it continued to tumble wilfully about her neck and ears. Her hand shook and he wanted to tell her not to trouble herself, knowing that she was not even aware that she did it. He wanted to tell her how beautiful she was and how much he loved her at this moment of parting. He wanted to draw her into his arms again and bury his face in the untidy, shining mass of her hair, to breathe in the smell of her which he knew so well now, but he remained silent and motionless.

'Richard . . . ?' There was a terrified question in her voice, one she was afraid to ask. She reached out and took his hand, holding it beseechingly in both of hers, those which had so recently given strength and hope and life to his labouring sister and which now needed the same reassurance and comfort from him.

'Jesus Christ . . .' he whispered. 'You know why I've come . . .' He turned his head away, his hands still clinging to hers, the distress in him so acute he did not think he could cope with it. She was so frail and delicate-looking, this beautiful woman of his. She had come directly from his sister where she had given of herself, emptying herself until she resembled a spent butterfly which has come to the end of its life.

But as he turned back to her he knew he had misjudged her. She was not empty, nor spent, only gathering her strength which had momentarily deserted her in her confusion. Before his eyes she seemed to gather something to her, something she had learned with each hard blow life had struck at her and he knew she was not frail, nor delicate but as steadfast and true, as deeply rooted in life as the oak trees in Prudence's garden. She was not asking for comfort but *giving* it, holding on to his hand to give *him* strength, refusing to be ground down and refusing him the right to falter. *She* was *his* strength, his joy, his life, his love.

'I don't know how long . . .' he faltered.

'I love you, Richard.' She did not even question him. She did not really know where he was going, or why, though she must have guessed since he had not known himself until he got back to Briar Lodge, though naturally, being a soldier he had been aware of the situation in the Transvaal, and yet she stood like a rock, holding *him* firm.

She leaned forward and delicately placed her lips on his. 'I'll love you always.' She put her arms about his neck and with a sigh he drew her to him again.

'Tell me . . . where?' she whispered into his neck.

'I am to sail for Cape Town tomorrow.'

Tomorrow! Their wedding day!

'It was decided at the end of last month apparently. I . . . we knew it could happen. There have been rumours but I hoped that the Boers would see sense and come to the conference table which is what the Cabinet wanted but . . . it seems Kruger is adamant. He invaded Cape Colony and Natal yesterday so we are to . . . to go . . .'

They could not speak then. They clung together desperately with so much to say, but they could not say it. Only a few words.

'I'll wait for you.'

'We'll be married the moment I get back.'

'How long . . . ?'

'This is the last time I shall ever leave you.'

'Take care, my beloved . . .'

'I love you more than life . . .'

'I love you . . .'

The words flowed almost soundlessly between them. They held one another so close each could feel the familiar, loved shape of the other, even through the heavy material of his greatcoat, and when she raised her face for his kiss it was wet with tears she did not even know she had shed.

'Don't cry, my darling, I can't bear it . . .' wanting to weep himself. He kissed her wet cheeks and smoothed back her tangled hair from her face, knowing he must leave her now. Now, this minute. He was already late. Another fifteen minutes and he would have had to leave without saying goodbye to her. He fumbled for a moment in his pocket then withdrew his hand. In it was a ring, of what sort she could not tell since her eyes were blind with tears. His hand trembled as he slid the ring on her finger, the one on which he would have placed the wedding ring the next day.

'With this ring I thee wed . . .' he whispered, then, turning, he reached for the door. Hesitating only to pick up his cap and bag he was gone.

She stood for what seemed hours, listening to the click of the door as it sounded again and again in her head and to the sharp tattoo of his soldier's footsteps as they echoed down the steps to the waiting cab. There was the sound of a voice encouraging the horse to "walk on" and then wheels crunching on gravel. She listened to it until all sound of it had died away, imagining she could still hear the whisper of the wheels as it turned out of the gate and into Croxteth Drive. The noise of it circled in her aching head, round and round and round on an endless treadmill of anguish. He had promised . . . he had promised . . . when? . . . only a few days ago that he would never leave her again, never go away and yet he had gone. How optimistic was human hope and how frail. He had meant what he had said and she had believed him but neither of them had foreseen this when the promise was truthfully given and trustingly received. He would take her with him, he had said, wherever he went, on whatever duty he was ordered to, India, Ireland, Egypt, she would accompany him as his wife. They would set up home in whatever far-flung outpost of the British Empire the army sent him and she had not been afraid.

At first the idea of Celie Marlow, the daughter of the man who had dug the Latimer garden, entering the society in which officers and their wives moved had filled her with misgivings. A close-knit society, hostile to those who were not as they were. She had little education. She knew nothing except how to cook but she had come to realise that none of it mattered. Richard had *made* her realise that none of it mattered. She was the woman Richard Latimer loved and because of that her worth was measureless. But it was not just Richard's love that had made her valuable, she knew that, too. She was a woman of strength, of character, of great endurance for she had, *all alone*, reached the position in life where her own efforts had put her. She was proud of that. She was the friend of Prudence Garside because Prudence held her in great esteem. She was proud of that, too. It did not matter where she had started from, it was where she had *got to* that counted and though she had come to realise that although the wives of other officers would know at once that Celie Marlow, Celie *Latimer*, was not one of them, she would not allow them, as she had not allowed life itself, to beat her.

And now . . . now what was she to do? Through no fault of his own Richard had been forced to abandon her again but she must not allow that first stirring of resentment at what her mind had seen as a broken promise to weaken her. He loved her. She knew that as she had never known anything else in her life and he would come back for her. *Through no fault of his own*, he had left her on the day before they were to be married and she must hold on to that truth as she waited for him to return. If Prudence had not been so desperately in need of her during her long and difficult labour, she and Richard might still have been married. But it did no good to think like that. They had been dealt this blow and they must accept it. Accept what you cannot change or it will break you. Life had taught her that.

But, dear God, it was hard, as hard as the labour Prudence had just suffered. This time tomorrow they should have been man and wife, sleeping together in their marriage bed after the wild sweetness of their lovemaking. Plans they had made, dreams in which they had lingered together as they walked the woods and fells of lakeland, the future, the home they would make wherever Richard was stationed, for she had been willing to give everything up, her growing and increasingly successful business, her hard-won independence, her individuality, the sweetness of knowing that when she was ready she would regain what she had lost to Kate Smith. Now it was all in her hands again, the hands which had been gladly ready to relinquish it. It had once been precious, something she had gloated over in the dark days and nights when Harper's had been taken from her, something she had thought to be the most important factor in her life.

Now it was dust and ashes in her mouth. Nothing. All she cared about, all she had *ever* cared about, she knew it now, had just gone through the door, climbed into a hansom and been driven off to war. He was gone. He would take ship and sail away to another part of the world, perhaps never to return, and her life was as empty and barren as her womb into which, for the past two weeks, he had poured his seed. The proof of her inadequacy had come only that morning.

Slowly she sank down into the chair where he had waited for her for thirty-six hours, her world in devastation about her. Her arms stretched straight out across the small table where his cap had rested. Her hands gripped the table's edge until her knuckles were white and when her head bowed and her face was pressed into her arms she began to weep again. Silently she wept but with a fierceness which shook the table.

When Jethro came down the stairs an hour later she was asleep, her face still wet with her tears. They put her to bed, Nora and Sally, under his supervision and when she awoke Captain Richard Latimer had been at sea for twenty-four hours.

Chapter Thirty-three

Though she did exactly what she had done before Richard came back into her life it seemed unreal to her now, just as though another person had lived it, then gone away, and left Celie Marlow to continue with it. *She* wasn't that woman any more. She was someone else and that someone else cared nothing for Mrs Morgan's Cheese Soufflé nor Mrs Gulliver's concern with the small soirée Mrs Gulliver planned for her daughter's engagement to the son of a prominent Liverpool worthy. She still carried on her duties, of course, and to the best of her ability. She was too professional to do anything else but her heart, her enthusiasm, her teeth-gritting determination to succeed was no longer fully committed. They saw nothing different in her, Mrs Morgan and Mrs Gulliver, Mrs Kenyon and all the other ladies who lived in Heaton Crescent and the tree-shaded, well-bred streets which surrounded it. Her work was just as superb and they could find no fault in her manner which was as gracious as ever, but it did not take them long to begin to wonder about the magnificent diamond-set gentleman's signet ring she wore on the third finger of her left hand. They were too well-mannered to question her, naturally, but it was one of those irritating puzzles which they longed to solve since it was very evident that the extremely expensive ring was too large for her small hand and was held in place only by a twist of cotton thread. Later the thread was replaced by a gold inset which made the inside of the ring smaller so that it did not slip up and down on her finger but it was still so obviously a *gentleman's* ring they could not but wonder.

Mrs Wilson had no such delicacy. Though she and Celie had not known one another long enough to be called "friends", they *were* on first-name terms and in the eighteen months since they had become acquainted over the appearance of the chap who had hung about Great George Square, Flo had taken a cup of tea on a regular basis with Celie, either in her own cosy sitting room off the kitchen of the Cunard emigrant house, or in Celie's pretty drawing room. Celie had confided in Flo at the time, and she felt it gave her the right, as someone who had Celie's welfare at heart, to find out what was going on. None of them, not one person who worked in the square had missed the arrival of Celie in a carriage, nor the tall and very handsome chap who had handed her out of it. Her disappearance for a fortnight had caused some speculation, a great deal of it suggestive which was really only to be expected in view of the fact that the pair of them had gone off in the carriage surrounded by enough luggage to sink the White Star liner *Oceanic* which was the largest transatlantic liner in the world!

Now she was home again, serene, fashionably dressed, lovely as ever, all alone but sporting the biggest ring Flo had ever seen and though she *looked* the same and acted the same, Flo knew she was *not* the same.

'Come an' have a cup o' tea wi' me, lass,' she ordered, her face set in that firmness her staff knew so well and which meant she would brook no argument. Celie made none. Though she had not fully acknowledged it even to herself in the lonely darkness of each night since Richard had gone, she knew she needed to tell *someone*, to confide in someone, to confide her terror, her desolation, her slashing worry for Richard's safety. All the fears his departure to fight the Boers had exposed in her. Prudence was recovering, but so slowly and painfully Celie knew she could not unburden herself to her even though she was Richard's sister. Pru was worried about him too, besides which she was guarded so zealously by her husband she might have been a wisp of swansdown which would blow away at the slightest current of air. He had almost lost her and if Celie mentioned one word which might upset her he would never forgive her. Her wedding had been postponed, she was to say, he told Celie fiercely, which was true, but by how long, her anguished heart demanded to know, skirting feverishly round the horror that it might be for ever.

General Sir Redvers Buller and the first instalment of the invasion force, Richard among them, she supposed, had been seen off at Southampton by a noisy, patriotic crowd, accompanied, so the newspapers reported, by such throat-catching songs as "For he's a jolly good fellow" meaning each one of *their* lads, and "God Save the Queen." The British people did not know a lot about Africa beyond the fact that Stanley had discovered Livingstone there but they did remember that their soldiers had been cut down by the Zulus at Isandlwana, by the Boers at Majuba and who could forget Gordon and *Khartoum*? Now it was our turn, they said. Their soldiers would be in Pretoria by Christmas. The Boers would be squashed flat by Buller. The British were not to be intimidated by what was known as "a war at tea-time" or "a war in a tea cup".

But it seemed the Boers and the British were evenly matched in numbers and by the third week in December – "Black Week", as it came to be called – the nightmare that the Boers might *win*, was actually becoming a reality. They had overrun the smooth veld of Cape Colony for a hundred miles south of the Orange River and the rugged hills of Natal down to the Tugela and beyond, cutting off the British garrisons at Mafeking, Kimberley and Ladysmith. Buller's troops, numbering 60,000 regular soldiers and 150 field guns, had marched as fast as they could to the three garrisons.

But the "bull-at-a-gate" tactics which had served the British soldier in the past made no impression on the Boers who were armed with the new smokeless, long-range, high-velocity rifle. Mounted Boers who snapped up columns of British soldiers, killing, wounding or capturing them and by the end of "Black Week" the British casualties numbered 7,000.

In Britain "Black Week" brought a dread to the heart of the British people, a shiver of fear which none had known before. Theatres and restaurants emptied and for the first time since she had started Celie began to have cancellations.

As Mrs Morgan told her tearfully one did not want to appear to be celebrating when so many of one's friends' sons, nephews, husbands were spilling their life's blood on the veld of South Africa. The élite of the British Army had been sent to conquer men who were no more than farmers and it seemed they could make no headway at all. And they were to send another 10,000 men, volunteers drawn from the hunting and shooting classes of Britain who could presumably out-ride and out-shoot the Boers, and among them was Mrs Morgan's sister's boy who was only just nineteen. No, one didn't feel one could entertain at such a moment, didn't Miss Marlow agree? And not only the gentlemen, it seemed, were eager to fight. Great numbers of volunteers from all levels of society were rushing to join the army and even from the new nations of the Queen's Empire they were rallying to the support of the Mother Country.

'Now then, my lass, what have you to tell me?' Flo began, after pressing a cup of tea into Celie's hand. 'What about that there ring, fer a start? An' don't pull a face at me, Celie Marlow fer I'll 'ave none of it. You've to share it wi' someone, girl, an' wi' that friend o' yours still low after the birth of her little 'un . . . what's she ter call it, by the way . . . ?' cutting in on Celie's polite protest in that clever, side-stepping way she knew so well.

'Grace.'

'Grace. That's right pretty. Me Mam were called Grace.' 'Was she . . . ?'

'Aye, so now then, where's that lad gone? The one you went off with?'

'Flo! I don't think . . .'

Flo leaned forward and put a compassionate hand on Celie's knee. It rested there for a moment before she leaned back in her chair.

'Are you an' me friends, Celie?'

'Of course we are.'

'Well then, you'll have need o' one o' those, I'm thinkin'. An' if yer can't confide in me then who *can* you confide in? Tell me that? You've a pain in you that needs seein' to, Celie lass, an' the first thing ter be done is ter fetch it out an' face it.'

'Oh, dear God, Flo . . .' Celie's face, though it was set in a mould of white, unmoving marble, was suddenly flooded with tears which, when they came, flowed across it in a torrent. Without moving a muscle they simply deluged her, dripping freely from her chin on to the fine blue wool of her bodice. 'Oh, Jesus God, Flo . . .'. She couldn't say anything except those few words in her desolation. The cup and saucer clattered in her hand and Flo hastily put her own down and reached to take Celie's. Celie was perched on the edge of Flo's maroon velvet sofa but with one swift movement Flo was beside her drawing her down to her own plump and comforting shoulder, murmuring and patting and soothing for minutes on end until the initial tide of Celie's grief was done with, then she sat up and briskly moved back to her own chair.

She picked up her cup and began to sip, waiting.

'He's in South Africa,' Celie began, the relief so great at just being able to say the words she was almost ready to burst into hysterical laughter. 'He's Prudence's . . . Mrs Garside's brother, Richard . . . his name is Richard. This is . . . his ring.'

'Richard, oh aye.' Flo sipped her tea but her face was soft.

Celie's eyes had become deep, unfocused, a dark pewter grey with a prick of light in them which was like the flame of a candle. 'Captain Richard Latimer of the 2nd Battalion, King's Liverpool Regiment. We were to have been married on October 14th when we came back from . . .' She stopped, looking warily at Flo for a second, aware that to most people and especially a woman, what she and Richard had done was one of the most wicked sins committed by two people, then she lifted her head with pride, straightening her back for did she care what people, even Flo, might think of her?

'I know about that, lass. Not where yer went, of course, but yer weren't exactly . . . discreet, Still, what's done is done so there's no use moanin' about it . . .'

'I'm *not* moaning,' Celie said indignantly.

'P'raps yer should be.'

'Look here, Flo, if I'm to confide in you then please remember that I'll have nothing said about Richard or . . .'

'Nay, I'll not condemn a brave soldier who's off fightin' fer 'is country, nor the woman who loves 'im. I just want yer ter know that if any of yer fine clients get ter know about it yer'll be finished.'

'It's been two months so I don't think there's any danger of that. Besides, business is falling off anyway. Nobody is having parties with things as they are. I've had one letter from Richard, only one, and he'd only just arrived in Cape Town. None since, but he's bound to have been on that march to Ladysmith or Mafeking or wherever it is and for all I know he could already be . . .' Her face spasmed in horror but at once Flo took umbrage.

'Now then, Celie Marlow, I don't want ter hear yer sayin' daft things like that. I know I told yer ter fetch out yer pain an' face it but that don't mean imaginin' things an' bringin' them ter life when they aren't there at all . . .'

'But all those men, Flo . . . killed . . . wounded . . . what if he should . . . ?'

'An' what if he *shouldn't*, lass? He won't want ter think of you broodin' when yer should be gettin' on wi' yer work . . .'

'What work, Flo? I've done one dinner party in a fortnight and one children's Christmas party. At this time of the year I should be run off my feet. I've a living to earn and I can't do it if no one wants me, can I? I've wages to find for the girls and . . .'

'There's other work for a woman wi' your talents, lass.'

'Such as what?'

'I could find you a job right this minute, well paid an' all. I'm friends wi't'housekeeper at The Grange up near Toxteth an' I know fer a fact their old cook is ready fer retiring.'

'A COOK! In a house?'

'An' what's wrong wi' that? 'Tis honest work an' wi' me ter give you a character you'd have no trouble landin' it.'

'But . . .'

'I know, lass. After what you've had in the past few years, bein' yer own mistress an' all it'd be a bit of a come-down but beggars can't be choosers. Now then . . .' shaking herself briskly, '. . . we're looking ont' black side. Remember what the Queen said, God bless 'er.'

'The Queen?'

'Aye, in't newspaper. "We will not be depressed in this 'ouse," she said. "We are not interested in the possibilities of defeat. They do not exist." So just you take heed, lass. If the Queen of England ses so, then it *is* so!'

Using the tactics taught them so tellingly by the Boers themselves, the bronzed veterans of the British Army marched triumphantly into Ladysmith at the end of February and the first victory was won. Three hundred miles to the west Kimberley was similarly relieved and two weeks later the Union Jack was raised on a flagpole in Bloemfontein. They went wild at home. Parties and balls and dances to celebrate the victories of their brave sons, and once again Celie worked herself and her girls to a standstill as she catered to the dozens of ladies who wished to share the jubilation of the nation, and for the time being it seemed Celie's fear that she might have to take up Flo's offer of work as a cook in a family household was averted.

Prudence had recovered from her ordeal and was her old self again. The baby, Grace Cécilie, was christened in the small country church where Celie was to have been married, held in the arms of her godmother, Cécilie Marlow. The infant thrived in the adoration of everyone in her small world, sunny-natured as her father, though she was a true Latimer in her looks. Celie would sit in the pretty nursery and hold her, gazing into the small face from which deep brown eyes looked steadily back at her, and her heart was pierced for so would a child of hers look, hers and Richard's. Of course she knew precisely what would have happened had she become pregnant in that rapturous fortnight they had spent in Ambleside and in her mind, where sense reigned, she was relieved that it had not happened but deep in her woman's heart, a heart in which maternal stirrings had been aroused by the clear gaze of Miss Grace Garside, she could not help feeling sad that their lovemaking had produced nothing but empty arms and a desolate premonition that she would never know what it was to bear Richard's child.

His letters came infrequently but when they did there were often three or four at a time, filled on every page with his love and hope and need. His positive belief that "this little lot" would soon be over and when it was he would be home on the first ship out of Cape Town. She was not to worry, he begged her, for was he not a seasoned campaigner and no "stick-in-the-mud" farmer could catch a smart British soldier such as himself, though of course, that was exactly what the "stick-in-the-mud" farmers had done to thousands upon thousands of his brothers-in-arms. He'd had a slight dose of the unpleasant but familiar infirmity which struck the British soldier in a hot climate, one he would not put a name to but apart from that he was as fit as a fiddle and she was not to worry. They were doing well, he and his battalion under the command now of "Little Bobs" as Lord Roberts was affectionately called by his troops and Richard had been proud to march behind him into Kimberley.

She treasured his letters, reading every one each night before she turned out her light no matter how late it was or how tired she felt. They were under her pillow as she slept and never far from her hand during the day, for they were like a talisman to her, a good luck charm which, whilst they were there in her apron pocket, meant that Richard was safe.

She had had a surprising visitor just before the end of January and when Maudie showed him in she felt for a moment that she had strayed back in time to the day, fourteen years ago now, when Reuben Ash had escorted into the kitchen a tall and lanky boy with his elbows out of his jacket and his toes out of his boots. He scarcely looked any different now with the width of the room between them, apart from his decent suit. Fair, tousled curls, a boyish face that wanted to smile but daren't, blue eyes as lovely as a summer sky but there the likeness ended for as he drew closer she could see the deep grooves slashed at the sides of his mouth, a mouth that curled down in misery, and frown lines between his eyebrows.

'Dan?' Her voice was soft and wondering, bitterness and

hurt gone, for what did all that matter beside the joy of her own love and the constant fear that she might lose it? She knew now of the trap the physical nature of love can set, for had she herself not fallen into it? Dan did not love Kate and never had, she also knew that, but his flesh had been snared by hers and it was a heady potion while it lasted.

'Celie.' His voice was hesitant. He was unsure of his welcome but in him she could see his determination to be heard at whatever cost to himself and she wondered what it was that had brought him to chance her scorn and anger once more.

He told her.

'I'm to be a soldier, Celie. I've come to say goodbye.'

Her heart lurched painfully and with a will of their own her arms rose to enfold him. He sighed thankfully as he stepped into them and she felt the rigid inflexibility with which he had held himself ever since he had married Kate, drain away.

They stood for several minutes with their arms about one another, both of them remembering the children they had been, remembering Cook and the life she had given them, the dreams which had been stolen from them, then he took her arms from about his neck and stood back a little to study her face. He cupped it with his big, hard hands, hands callous from fourteen years of digging. His thumbs caressed her cheeks and her eyes as she closed them to hold in the tears. His fingertips touched her lips softly then, for the first time as a man, he placed his mouth on hers. She did not stop him. His lips were gentle with no more exertion than a father might press on a beloved child but she knew he loved her, not as a brother, nor as a father but as a man.

'When?' she managed to whisper.

'This afternoon, min liten älskling.'

'Tell me please . . . what that means.'

'It means "my little darling" and so you have been ever since I first saw you but of course, it's too late now.'

'Yes.'

'Richard Latimer?'

'Yes,' wondering how he knew.

'He will be home, Celie. He has someone to come home *for*.'

'Dan . . .'

'No, don't say anything more. I'm happy that we are . . . friends again.'

'When you get back promise you'll come and visit me.'

'Well, we'll see.' He smiled engagingly and for a moment he was the Dan she had always known, and loved.

'Good luck, Dan.'

'Min liten älskling, take care.'

It was two weeks later when she received a note from Mr Pembroke whom she had not seen for many months asking her to call at her convenience at his offices in Water Street. There was a matter he wished to discuss with her and one which might be turned to her advantage.

She was looking her best and Mr Pembroke's elderly but male smile of approval told her so. It was March now and the day was mild, spring-like and everywhere a bit of soil was available, in window boxes and beneath the trees in the garden of Great George Square, daffodils lifted their eager golden heads. The air was as soft as velvet against her face and she felt a hopeful stir in her heart, for surely Richard would be home soon. The news that Kimberley had been relieved had raised the spirits of the nation, and her own, and it was being reported in all the newspapers that the Boers were done for at last. In a wave of gladness she had put on her new, figure-hugging costume in a rich shade of russet, the narrow skirt clinging to her hips and flaring into a dozen box pleats below the knee. The jacket was in a military style, double-breasted, and beneath it she wore a waistcoat of ivory silk with a high collar and stock to match. It was severe and yet its severity enhanced her soft loveliness. Her hat was wide, the brim turned down so that it resembled a large, inverted basin, the crown swathed with cream feathers, and beneath it her face glowed with excited hope.

She leaned back in the chair Mr Pembroke pulled out for her and smiled, and the solicitor was quite transfixed. By God, but she'd become a beautiful woman. Gone was the hesitant girlish sweetness she'd shown when they had met almost six years ago and in its place was a maturity, confident and relaxed. She was sure of her own strength, her weaknesses overcome. She had a head start on any business rival, that was for sure, man or woman, for she had only to arch a delicate eyebrow, lift her chin and smile that brilliant silvery smile of hers and she would achieve everything she set out to do. And yet it was not just her looks, he was well aware of that. There was about her a steely determination to succeed, a resolve so obstinate, so bright and positive it was quite irresistible and it showed in the lift of her small jaw and the firm set of her coral-pink lips. There was something different about her since they had last met, a completeness which, despite her years which he knew to be no more than twenty-four, gave her a sophistication, a womanliness which sat well on her slender shoulders.

'Now then, Mr Pembroke,' she said firmly, her manner implying, though it was by no means offensive, that she was a woman with no time to waste on trivialities. Her warm smile softened her firmness. 'What is it that you wish to discuss with me?'

Mr Pembroke leaned forward as he spoke. 'You know, of course, that Daniel Smith has volunteered to serve in the army and has, in fact, sailed already for South Africa. He told me that he intended calling on you when he was in here just after Christmas. I presume he did?'

'Yes, two weeks ago, but why . . . ?'

'He had some legal affairs to put in order before he went away but he also wanted you to know that during the last year Harper's has gradually . . . well, you will have heard that it is no longer the successful concern that it became when you and Mrs Harper were in charge. It needed . . . well, cash flow was a problem and . . . Mrs Smith had heard that to raise the money Harper's badly needed spending on it for various reasons, could be achieved by floating a company. Shareholders, you know what I mean. With a great deal of hard work and a certain amount of business acumen, I told her this was a viable proposition but that she must be prepared to . . .' Mr Pembroke cleared his throat and sighed deeply, '. . . well, Miss Marlow, to cut a long story short shares were offered and were snapped up. Harper's, though it had become run down, had a good reputation but unfortunately Mrs Smith has neither the shrewd business brain nor the capacity for hard work that you and Mrs Harper had. The shares have slumped and those who bought them would be glad to get rid of them. Mr Smith wanted you to know this I have just been reliably informed that . . . ahem . . . Mrs Smith has . . . well, I believe the phrase is "done a bunk" The property is heavily mortgaged and trading has finished Now this morning I received a letter from the lady in question asking me to dispose of the whole kit and caboodle in any way I can, sell it or rent the property and I thought that if you could raise the necessary capital you might be interested The shares will be relatively easy to purchase since they are at rock bottom. The property, which I inspected yesterday is still in good heart though in need of some minor repairs. All the equipment seems to be working and with the good will *and* your talents it might be possible to restore it to . . .'

Mr Pembroke's words had drifted off as Celie listened to them, dissipating like smoke into the high ceiling of the room as she did her best to grasp their meaning and when she had, what implication those words could have on her life. It seemed so . . . incredible she could barely think, but what she did know quite conclusively was that there was nothing she would like more than to restore Harper's to what it had been when she and Cook had been in charge of it. Nothing would give her more satisfaction than to have restored to her what Kate had taken from her and six months ago she would have seized the opportunity with both eager hands. But now? How could she? She was to be Richard's wife as soon as the war in South Africa was finished, which would be soon, please God, and it would be impossible to run a business as Mrs Richard Latimer. She would probably be off to Egypt or India or Africa or any one of the dozens of places where Queen Victoria's soldiers served, before the end of the year, so how could she start something it was extremely unlikely she could ever finish? She couldn't, that was obvious.

But oh, the challenge. Oh, how she would love to take it on, to get back to Harper's where it had all begun, where she and Cook and all the others, Ivy, Dorcas, Percy had worked so hard to make it the success it had been. And Dan? When he came home what . . . ?

Her mind sharpened again and her gaze returned to Mr Pembroke who was still talking.

'. . . to be in Brighton of all places, in the company of a man old enough to be her grandfather, or so the old lady who is still living there told me, so I cannot think . . .'

'Ivy, d'you mean Ivy?'

Mr Pembroke looked startled.

'Well, she did not tell me her Christian name . . .'

'Mrs Petty?'

'That's the one.'

'And she is living there alone?'

'I believe so, though there was an old gentleman doing something in the garden.'

'Percy, it would be Percy. Percy and Ivy! Oh, Mr Pembroke, they are still there and in all this time . . .'

She leaped to her feet, a young girl again, her great silvery eyes gleaming with excited anticipation. 'They'll know where Dorcas and Beth and Fanny and . . . I must go there at once and see. Oh, thank you, Mr Pembroke, thank you . . .'

Without a word of farewell, or indeed on any matter which concerned the future of Harper's, or even her own involvement in it, she dashed across his office, down the stairs and the last Mr Pembroke saw of her she was striding, head up, shoulders back, every male gaze turning to watch her, in the direction of Castle Street and, he presumed wryly, Harper's!

Chapter Thirty-four

During the next few months the war on the veld continued, not just a war of man fighting man but of man fighting shortages of provisions, cut rations, collapsed transport, pitifully few medical supplies, chaos and disease as a typhoid epidemic swathed its way through the ranks. A typhoid epidemic which struck down far more of Little Bobs' men in the safety of Bloemfontein than Boer bullets and shells had killed on the battlefield.

On May 3rd Lord Roberts launched his attack across the veld to relieve Mafeking. For eight months the British public had focused its breathless attention on this plucky, enduring garrison where, so they had been told, 1000 men with four cannons and a few machine and quick-firing guns had held out against 8000 Boers and ten guns, one a siege gun known as "Long Tom". Day in and day out Mafeking had been subjected to heavy bombardment. Stories from Mafeking had fired the imagination of the British public. Stories such as the one about the horse which, among others one supposed, had died. His mane and tail had been cut off to be used as stuffing for mattresses and pillows, his shoes for the use of shells. His skin, after being shaved was boiled with his head and feet and served as "brawn", his flesh minced and his insides made into skins in which the mince was stuffed making a form of sausage. His bones were boiled for soup. Not a scrap of that horse was wasted.

'Breakfast for today,' a young journalist called Winston Churchill had reported, 'is horse sausage and for lunch minced horse and curried locusts.'

On May 17th, Lord Roberts' men relieved the town after an uneventful ride across the veld. Back in Bloemfontein the annexation of the Free State was formally proclaimed and Johannesburg was captured at long last. The war, surely was practically over?

Harper's opened its doors for the second time just two weeks before Mafeking was relieved and it was as though the time between Cook's death and the shop's re-birth had never been. Then Mrs Richmond had swept in on that first morning, stepping down from Mrs Morgan's carriage as though she was related to the Royal Family itself and now she did it again six years later. She moved round the familiar but much restored and handsomely polished interior, scrutinising every commodity and its price whilst Dorcas and Fanny stood courteously awaiting her order behind the gleaming counter. When she had peered, high-nosed, through her glasses at everything she found of interest, she had moved majestically to seat herself on the chair before the counter, snapping out her orders as though it was only yesterday when she had given the last.

'How nice to see you, Mrs Richmond,' Celie told her. 'I trust you are well?' following the housekeeper's lead.

'Indeed I am, Miss Marlow.'

'I hope we have everything you need?' smiling graciously.

'Indeed you have, Miss Marlow, as always.' And that was all that Mrs Richmond was prepared to say on the matter of her renewed patronage of the newly refurbished Harper's on the Boulevard and the newly returned head of it, Miss Marlow herself. It was a long time since Mrs Richmond had bestowed her custom on Harper's, for she did not concern herself with establishments where the service was not deft, discreet, efficient and polite, nor did she purchase goods which were not as fresh as this morning's dew. Though it was not her way to praise, since her very presence in the shop was praise enough, she had thought highly of Miss Marlow and had admired the way in which she had picked herself up from the knockdown blow that other hussy had dealt her. She had seen the work she did at first hand in Mrs Morgan's own home and, being a fair woman, she would give

Harper's and Miss Marlow a second chance. She had seen the new sign, well, it was the old one with a fresh coat of paint.

Harper's on the Boulevard
Home Baked and Speciality Food
Home Catering Supplied.

and beside it the discreet 'Re-opening May 3rd'.

So it seemed had all the ladies who had once been so well served and well satisfied in the old days. Mrs Turpin still looking for a bargain to put on the spartan table of Doctor and Mrs Sharples since the good man was more likely to *give* his services away than to charge for them. Mrs Gulliver's housekeeper, Mrs Kenyon's housekeeper, both nodding politely to Mrs Richmond. The Cook general from the small detached villa belonging to the manager of a bank in Lauriston Avenue and all the ladies whose trade had been taken elsewhere as the rapidly declining standards of the food served and the increasingly high-handed attitude of the woman who had served it had made it impossible to rely on Harper's any more.

Even old Gladys who had the stall down by the Pier Head, as though informed by some magical means of communication, had put her head round the door at the end of the day and said the very same words she had uttered on that first day.

"Owt left, queen?"

She had her standards, she said, and she'd not take that muck *Madam* had offered to her, no, not even to sell to sailors who were known to be not over particular.

Ivy had been so pathetically relieved to see Celie she had wept the painful, jerking tears of the old and the weak. Celie would never forget it. She remembered Ivy as proud, hard-working, independent and sharp-tongued, willing to give a hand or a bob or two to anyone who genuinely needed it. A good friend who, if somewhat sparing of words, would be staunchly true to anyone of whom she was fond. Kate had stripped her, layer by layer, of everything that Ivy had held dear. Not material things, for Ivy still, as she put it laconically, had a few bob put away, but of her self-respect and self-determination, her initiative and trust, and had it not been for the sad fact that she had nowhere else to go she would have walked out long since, she told Celie. She had let go her little house in Cable Street years ago and her home was here now but how she had stuck it with that little madam queening it over them she'd never know. The others hadn't, of course. Dorcas had gone soon after Celie. Worked in a soap factory in Renshaw Street, she did.

'A *soap* factory! Dorcas . . . ?'

'Oh aye. Missus wouldn't give her no reference, see, so Dorcas couldn't get a job in domestic service . . .'

'Dear Lord . . . !'

'And the others the same, though Beth managed to get took on at a café in Lord Street, I forget the name, an' Fanny's scrubbin' for a Mrs Johnson over Tuebrook way . . .'

'*Scrubbing*!'

'Aye, an' Fred an' Frank, you remember them? well, they've took the Queen's shilling an' gone with Dan to South Africa, while that slut's earnin' her livin' on her back with that chap what were manager at Grimshaw's, an' good luck to 'er I say, for how any woman could stomach that fat-bellied bag of lard puttin' his hands on her is beyond me. He had his hand up her knicker leg even then. Even before Dan went. I saw 'em meself one day at back of pantry door, her wi' her skirt round her waist an' him wi' his pants round his . . . well . . . He retired at sixty-five. He used ter come in here, sellin' that fancy stuff from . . . eeh, I forget, them things in boxes . . . dates, that's it. His wife died, any road, an' Kate saw her chance ter get away from this place. Debts, yer never saw 'owt like it, an' then with Dan dead set on goin' ter fight the Boers, poor sod. He was glad of the excuse ter get away from her, if you ask me. She didn't care *who* saw her with that fat pig, even Dan. God, the rows, I thought he'd kill her, the way she taunted him an' flung it in his face. Poor Dan, poor, poor lad.' Ivy shook her head sorrowfully.

'Oh Ivy . . . I don't know what to say.'

'There's nowt to say, chuck. Any road, me an' Percy are still here . . .' nodding her head in the direction of the garden where Dan's spring flowers were bursting from their winter beds in a glorious hosanna. The blazing, golden glory of daffodils, the shy purple and gold and white of crocus, and patiently turning over a bit of earth, his cap slung to the back of his grizzled head, his pipe smoking between his teeth, was Percy.

Jethro and Mr Pembroke were introduced to one another and between them, explaining to Celie what they were doing every step of the way, they gradually unravelled the great financial tangle which Kate had carelessly knitted together over the past three years. When they had finished Celie owed a great deal of money to Jethro which she had calculated, working on the figures and accounts kept during the years she had managed Harper's, and her time in Great George Square, would be repaid in three years and despite his protests had insisted on having drawn up a document to that effect.

'I can well afford to . . .'

'You will give me nothing, Jethro Garside, if that's what you intend to say. Do you realise what it would cost me to borrow this money from the bank, or a money lender?'

'Yes, I . . .'

'You have already done enough. The house in Great George Square . . .'

'The rent of which you have paid regularly, not to mention the improvements you have made.'

'I did not lose by it? Jethro, I have money saved . . .'

'And neither did I, Celie, so won't you allow Prudence and me to . . .'

'Please, Miss Marlow, Mr Garside.' Mr Pembroke held up his hands in mock horror. 'Let us get back to the question of the mortgage and the shareholders of the company. Their holdings must be bought from them before they get wind of Harper's re-opening, or their price will rocket. Or worse still, they will refuse to sell for they are well aware of the prestige having Miss Marlow at the helm again will bring it.'

'Mr Pembroke . . . please . . .'

'It's true, Miss Marlow. If I held any, believe me, I would not part with them.'

And when it was all in hand she wrote to Richard and explained to him what she had done and what she meant to do with it all when they were married. She had discussed it at length with Jethro and Prudence for she felt if *they* understood, then so would he.

'It all goes back to when I was a child, Prudence, and living at Briar Lodge. My father was a good man but he loved my mother and when she died giving me life he lost something which I could not replace. I didn't understand it then, of course, but when I began to work in the kitchen with Mrs Harper I was given something I didn't even realise I had missed. It was a feeling of importance. Strange for a ten-year-old child but I think Cook saw it and she encouraged my interest in what *she* did, which was cooking. She did more than cook, of course. She *created*. As an artist creates a picture which everyone finds beautiful to look at, *she* created something which pleased, delighted another sense as well, in fact two other senses if you count the sense of smell. The sense of taste. She was a genius and had she been a man would have become a great chef. She gave that to me. Oh, I have some talent but not like hers and had she not nurtured it in me I doubt I would have become as proficient as I have. Now, Harper's was *hers*. Her creation and I helped her in it and I want to give it back to her. I don't know why she passed it on to Dan though I suspect she thought that he and I . . . well, that's in the past but now I have the chance to bring back what she and I lost. For her. *And* for me, I'll be honest. Until Richard comes home, or . . . or if . . .'

Her face worked painfully and she twisted her hands together in a knot of terror. 'If it should . . . happen that . . . well, it will be there to keep me busy. Dear God, Pru, you do see that I must keep busy or I shall go mad . . . but until the day when Richard . . . when that day comes I will hand it over to my successor. I am training her now.'

'And that, of course, is Maudie.' Prudence smiled, then leaned forward to wipe away the tears which slid down Celie's cheeks.

'Yes. She's a good and clever girl and works hard. She wants it, Pru, and I *need* it . . . for now. When Richard comes home . . .'

'I know, darling, I understand.'

'Do you? Do you think *he* will?'

'Celie, if you were to write and tell him you fancied becoming a labourer down on the docks he would ask you when you wanted to start. As long as you are waiting for him when he comes home he would not care how you filled your time, you know that.'

He did understand. He told her so in the letter he wrote to her from Mafeking and he told her other things too about what he would do to her when he had her alone in his arms and what he required she do to him and as long as she promised to give up all thoughts of Tipsy cakes and custard tarts and cinammon buns when she became Mrs Richard Latimer, then she had his blessing in this new venture. It wouldn't be long now, he promised her. Now that Ladysmith, Kimberley and Mafeking were theirs again the war was practically over.

It did keep her busy. It did keep her daytime thoughts occupied and her body so active she was positive she would fall at once into a deep and senseless sleep the moment she dropped like a stone into her bed at night, but even though she was on the go with Maudie and Dorcas clamped to her side from five in the morning until ten or eleven at night she still twisted and turned sleeplessly in her thoughts of Richard.

Though the war was over, they all said so, he still did not come home and she could not get it out of her mind which would not let her rest that there was some great and malevolent being waiting to take it all away from her. It had all been returned to her so easily. The shop, the staff, the money made available to her. Richard, who loved her, and whose wife she would soon be. The fates were too kind, the blackness of the night whispered to her and soon they would demand their payment. Richard, my darling, she agonised, *please* come home so that I can guard you, watch over you . . .

She had given up the house in Great George Square, continuing her catering to the ladies who required her services from Harper's on the Boulevard, bidding Flo a fond and sad farewell, though the woman who had befriended her had promised to visit her. Celie had moved once more into the bedroom which had been hers at the back of the shop overlooking the garden Dan had created. Ivy was at the front and beside Ivy's room was the living room they had used before Kate married Dan and where her staff now relaxed when their work was done.

Dorcas, like Ivy, had wept tears of desolate shame mixed with great rejoicing when Celie had come for her. Celie had scarcely recognised her for the pert and pretty young housemaid she had once been. The factory in Renshaw Street had stunk of the hides which had been rendered down into the fat which was one of the ingredients from which the cheap soap was made. The other was some kind of alkaline chemical and the mixture of the two caught at the throat and eyes and coated the hair and clothing with its obnoxious smell.

'Miss Benson, if you please,' she had said imperiously to the corpulent, slack-jawed man who had tried to stop her entering. A curious silence had fallen as she brushed past him, walking in her dainty, high-heeled boots across the factory floor, holding up the pretty, cornflower blue skirt of her outfit to keep it from the filth, at the same time doing her best not to breathe, or if she had to, in short panting breaths. Everyone in the place might have been hewn from stone as they watched her go by, all the rough, carelessly swearing men and women amongst whom the cheerful, well-trained, attractive parlourmaid who had once served tea into the particular hand of Mrs Latimer and her friends, had worked for almost three years. She was neither cheerful nor attractive when Celie found her. Her hair was about her face in greasy tatters, escaping from her grimy cap, and her skin colour had changed from the pink and white complexion of a bonny English rose to the tallow grey of a cheap candle.

Celie took her home in a cab though the cab-driver was ready to protest, wondering out loud, and fiercely, on the mystery of what a lady like her was doing dragging a drab about at her coat-tails. Thunderstruck he was, when the lady held the drab in her arms and told her to stop crying, murmuring "there, there, they'd soon be home and have her in a nice hot bath!" What they were to do with her then he couldn't imagine.

Fanny was found, and Beth and Maggie, brought back to the jobs they had performed so well under her guidance years ago. The tea room was re-opened and a couple of men were found to help Percy in the garden. The money she had borrowed from Jethro did not yet run to a horse and waggon for deliveries, she said, but a cheerful sparrow of a lad managed very well on a bicycle. Wages were paid at the end of each week. Jethro was given, with the interest which she insisted upon, a portion of the capital she had borrowed, bills were settled and tiny profits were made, each week growing less tiny!

And still Richard did not come home and all over the country women were asking the same question she asked. Why? What was stopping the men from returning to the women who awaited their return so anxiously? In August Little Bobs' division had joined those of General Buller's and their combined forces had finally crushed the last of the Boers and their army was dissolved but incredibly, though they were incontestably defeated, they would not give in and it was then that a new word, a new war, a guerrilla war, began to be spoken of by the newspapers and Richard Latimer took up his pen and wrote to his love saying that he might not be home for a while yet.

'I can't understand it, Jethro,' Celie told Prudence's husband in November. 'There *are* soldiers coming home now, so why doesn't he? Only last week there was a huge commotion down by the Pier Head. The crowds were going wild as a company of the 5th Irish Battalion of the King's Liverpool Regiment disembarked from South Africa. The war is over. He's been gone for more than a year and the war which took him out there is finished but still he doesn't come home. Why? What is happening?'

'It *isn't* over, lass, that's just the point. The Boers won't let it be over because they simply won't give in and a lot of people are beginning to sympathise with them. Even Richard in his letters . . . well, he must have said the same to you. They are engaged in a war in which the Boers are not strong enough to fight and yet they're too strong to surrender and so the army is burning the farms of combatant farmers and stripping them of their cattle and horses. It will never end like this, not for years, and the true soldier, like Richard, knows it is a crude and . . .'

'Jethro, I know this,' Celie interrupted. 'He has said the same to me and I have heard, as no doubt you have, that women and children are involved.'

Prudence, who had been sitting quietly by the fire, her child in her arms, taking no part in the discussion, lifted her head from her contemplation of the baby's sleeping face and spoke suddenly, cutting through her friend's words.

'I saw Anne yesterday,' she said harshly. They both turned to stare at her in astonishment for what had Anne to do with this conversation? The statement, spoken so strangely, so abruptly, cutting across their exchange, placed a cold finger of something strangely like dread down the length of Celie's spine though the words were innocuous enough.

She moved slowly across the warm, peaceful comfort of Prudence's drawing room until she stood before the seated woman and her child. Jethro followed her. His face was troubled and he placed a careful hand on his wife's shoulder.

'Oh, yes?' His voice was deliberately casual, just as though he was doing his best to make the moment no different to any other he and his wife and Celie Marlow had spent together in the years they had been friends. It was Sunday. They had walked in Sefton Park that afternoon, pushing the baby carriage, the little girl who could now sit up, pointing and babbling her own infant language of delight at all she saw. It was icily cold, more like January than November, they told one another. There had been a hoar frost the night before which had turned the world into a white, snapping, sparkling, breathtaking wonder. Skaters were on the frozen lake and Celie's and the child's faces had glowed with colour and excitement as they had shared the magic of it. Prudence had been quiet but then only she and Jethro knew she was carrying another child so could you wonder at it, he had agonised, remembering Grace's birth. Trixie had barked enthusiastically at boys sliding on home-made sledges. Beth had walked sedately by the side of the baby carriage, guarding what she obviously thought was *her* property, and the day had been a good one, despite the worry over South Africa and Richard's failure to return.

'Yes,' Prudence said now. 'She called yesterday afternoon.'

They both knew, he and Celie, that she was about to tell them something she was reluctant to inflict on them and in the back of her throat Jethro heard the tiny moan of denial that Celie did her best to retain.

'Is she . . . well?' Jethro heard himself ask. God, what was he saying? Babbling as his baby daughter did but the slowly blanching face of Celie Marlow was something he could hardly bear to watch and all of them knew it was only the beginning.

'Oh, dear sweet Christ,' she whispered. 'Please . . .'

'I'm so sorry, darling,' Prudence said helplessly.

'I cannot bear it if he's dead.'

'No . . . not dead, wounded.'

Celie threw back her head in an ecstasy of relief, then bent it forward to bury her face in her hands.

'Thank you, God . . . oh, thank you, dear God . . .'

Jethro thought she was about to go down on her knees and he moved to take her arm, guiding her to the chair opposite his wife and daughter. Trixie pushed her nose under Celie's arm, wagging her tail placatingly and when Celie raised her tear-stained face, did her best to reach it with her tongue.

'What . . . what are . . . his injuries . . . how . . . ?'

'I don't know. Anne had not seen him.'

'*Seen him?*' Celie got slowly to her feet. 'Seen him!' Her voice fell, hesitant and wondering and it was evident she was at pains to make sense of what Prudence was saying. 'Where . . . how could Anne . . . ?'

'Please Celie, won't you sit down . . .'

'Anne has heard . . . Dear God, what are you saying?' Her voice rose then, harsh and strident and the dog moved away to sit beside Jethro. 'Where in God's name is he?'

'He's at . . . Briar Lodge. He was brought home on . . .'

'At Briar Lodge! You mean he is back in England and has not . . . That *you* have known . . . all day today you have

known and have not told me? Oh, dear Christ, he must be
badly hurt. I must go . . .'

She whirled about and began to run towards the door and
the dog followed her questioningly. 'I had a letter only last
week,' she was muttering, 'and he . . . it must have happened
since he . . . but why? . . . why was I not told? . . . he said
that if anything . . . he promised I would be told . . .'

Jethro was at her back, compassionate hands reaching
for her and from her chair by the fire Prudence watched
them. She herself seemed to be only half sentient, her
eyes dulled, her mouth turned down in a sadness which
was for her friend more than her wounded brother. Of the
three of them in the room only she was really aware of the
power, the determination, the obstinacy of Phyllis Latimer.
She had escaped it and her mother had never forgiven her
and there was no doubt that Phyllis Latimer would have been
completely cognisant of her son's relationship with the girl
who had once worked in her kitchen. Had she not been
told only a year ago that her son and Celie Marlow were
to marry? But she would not have believed the true depth
of their devotion to one another. She would have seen it
as the usual alliance young gentlemen form with servant
girls, shop assistants and actresses, but there was nothing
more sure in this world than the certainty that Celie Marlow
would be forbidden access, not only to Phyllis Latimer's
wounded son but to her home and indeed anything else which
belonged to her.

'Lass . . . wait . . . sit down,' Jethro was saying, his strong
hands on Celie's shoulders. 'Let's not go off without . . .'

'I'm not asking you to "go off" anywhere, Jethro Garside,
so if you would take your hands from me I would be
obliged . . .'

'No, Celie, no! You can't expect just to knock on the door
at Briar Lodge and gain admittance, you must know that. Let
me find out first what the extent of Richard's injuries are, then
we . . .

'*Let go of me*, Jethro.' She turned, her face ferocious, her
eyes blazing. She struck at his hands, knocking them from
her shoulders and Trixie slunk back to lie down next to the

older bitch who was at Prudence's feet. 'I will go, I *will*, so if you will ask Nora to call me a cab . . .'

'Celie, I'll take you myself in the carriage, but think first, girl. You know Mrs Latimer. Good God, after what she imagines you did to her on the day of her daughter's wedding she would slam the door in your face. She lost half her staff because of you, not to mention the attachment Richard and you . . . God's teeth, do you honestly think she will allow . . .'

But Celie Marlow was beyond reason, beyond the power of judgement, beyond any mental process which might conceivably tell her that Jethro was right. She did not *think* at that moment. She *felt*. She experienced only an intense need, an unconscious instinct brought about by the knowledge that the man she loved was damaged. Nothing, *nothing* mattered to her in the basic primeval state into which she had been flung, but to get to him. To see him, touch him, put her arms about him, hold him, comfort him, tend his wounds, whatever they were, and make him whole again. She was the only one who could do that. He needed *her* and she must get to him. Nothing else mattered but that and anyone who got in her way would be battered aside with all the strength and desperation she could summon to her aid.

'Very well, I will walk to the end of Croxteth Drive and hail a cab from there. Stand aside, Jethro, if you please.' Her face crumpled pathetically for a moment as her mind conjured up images of the strong, laughing face of the man who was her whole life. A face now sweated in pain, blood perhaps, bandages, his virile body shattered, his limbs distorted, the elegantly graceful swing of his legs gone for ever. Then her eyes hardened to an implacability which made Jethro move back in defeat.

But not Prudence. Leaping to her feet, a fierce movement which woke the infant, she pushed her into her father's arms and sprang after Celie who had moved into the hall. Nora stood there, brought in some confusion from the kitchen where the sound of the raised voices in the drawing room had frozen all activity to a standstill. She bobbed a curtsey, a questioning smile ready to curve her lips but when Mrs

Garside took hold of Miss Marlow and swung her forcibly round to face her, Nora scuttled back the way she had come. God knows what was up but it was nothing to do with *her*.

'I won't let you go, Celie. Believe me, I *cannot* let you go. Richard is . . .'

'What? Tell me or I swear I'll hit you.'

'He is . . . not himself.'

'Not himself? What the devil does that mean? Not that it will make any difference. I shall still go . . .'

'He was . . . caught in an ambush. The Boers struck at a British convoy and Richard was . . . a shell landed . . .'

'Dear sweet God in Heaven . . .'

'He is very badly wounded, darling. A fragment . . . his head, and another in . . . well, his legs are . . .'

Celie began to scream then, tearing away from Prudence's grasp and in the kitchen the servants cowered against one another for surely murder was being done. The baby wailed in terror and both dogs leapt to their feet barking.

'I will go to him,' she shrieked, '*I will go to him*, Prudence. Please don't stop me . . . please . . . I cannot . . . *cannot* stay away. You must see that. Oh please . . . please . . .'

She turned violently to Jethro who put out a protective hand, fearing for his child. Celie was in a state of dementia which could lead to anything.

'Take me, Jethro, I beg you. I will be calm, I promise, but I *must* go, you see. You *do* see, don't you, Jethro?' She trembled so violently her teeth chattered in her head. She was in a state of deepening shock and she must be brought from it before it took a firm hold. He knew, as Prudence did, that Phyllis Latimer would not allow Celie Marlow access to her wounded son, even if Celie's presence proved to be beneficial to him. She would see him suffer, even die rather than accept the love he and Celie shared but Celie must be given her chance. She would go, with or without him.

He tried one more time.

'Let Pru telephone Anne. Perhaps there is news of . . .'

'No.'

'I will telephone Briar Lodge then. If I could speak to Richard's father . . .'

'*No!*'

'Very well, then.' He put the distressed child in her mother's arms and reached for the bell to summon Nora.

Chapter Thirty-five

The curtains were drawn across the two bay windows of the bedroom and the daylight which seeped round them did little but pick out the blurred outline of the handsome furniture which filled it. A mahogany wardrobe loomed against the rich stripe of the papered walls and beside it was a massive chest of drawers on which there were silver-backed hairbrushes and clothes-brushes, a cologne bottle, a silver match container and striker, a ring box, several silver and crystal pots, one for pomade, the other for a shaving brush, and other bottles with silver lids, each one embossed with the initial L. Shoe horns and boot pulls and a spirit flask still reposed in a large leather travelling case which lay on the white runner across the top.

An ornate, immaculately polished satinwood dressing table with a large oval mirror stood between the two bay windows and on the floor was a rich carpet in a shade of plum to match the stripe in the wallpaper. There were a couple of deep, comfortable-looking armchairs, several unlit electric lamps and half a dozen sporting prints on the wall.

A red and orange embered fire glowed in the grate and beside it a woman sat, her hands busy with the bandages she was rolling and which task, apparently, she could manage in the semi-dark.

In the centre of the room with its head against the wall opposite the windows was a large and imposing, old-fashioned four-poster bed. It was not exactly a "four-poster" since a tall, solid headboard did duty for two of the posts supporting the velvet canopy which hung about it, and the curtains which, though drawn back, fell at each side.

On the bed, silent and scarcely raising the covers lay a man. His head was heavily bandaged. The quilt was pulled up neatly beneath his chin but though he gave the appearance of being deeply asleep, his eyes were open. They were a flat and murky brown, staring blankly up at the canopy above him.

The woman by the fire stood up and with a brisk movement laid the rolled bandages on the table beside her. She was dressed in a floor-length grey cotton dress, an immaculate and capacious white bibbed apron tied at her back and a no-nonsense starched white cap which completely covered her iron-grey hair. She reached for the poker and gave the glowing fire a stir, watching for a moment as it leaped into life, then leaning across it she gave the bell at the side of the fireplace a vigorous pull.

Within one minute which she counted out on the watch at her bosom there was tap at the door and after waiting a moment, a be-capped head peeped round it.

'Come in, girl, come in,' the woman said tartly.

'Yes, Sister.' The maid bobbed an instinctive curtsey.

'See to the fire, if you please,' the nurse said imperiously, 'and I would be grateful for a cup of tea.'

'Yes, Sister.' Again the maid sketched a curtsey before tiptoeing across the deep carpet and with scarcely a sound replenished the fire from the coal scuttle beside it. From under her frilled cap she peeped furtively at the silent man on the bed, her young face soft with sympathy but he did not stir.

When she had finished she slipped quiely from the room. Before she closed the door she whispered, 'I'll not be a minute wi' yer tea, Sister.' Her tone was very respectful.

The nurse again consulted the watch on her bosom, then, in the stately, unhurried manner which was the mark of a proper nurse and which she had been trained in since she was a girl, she moved to her patient's bedside. She was very gentle as she turned back the quilt and reached for his hand which was folded on his chest. She held his wrist, her eyes on her watch for a minute or so, then, just as gently she replaced his hand

and the bedcover. She smiled kindly into his empty, staring eyes for it did not seem right to simply ignore him, despite his condition, then turning away she made a note on the chart beside his bed.

She was just about to return to her chair by the fire when there was another tap on the door and the maid slipped inside the room bearing a daintily set-out tray. She placed it carefully on the small table beside the bandages.

'Cook ses could yer manage a bite o' lemon cake, Sister?' she whispered 'She's put a slice out for yer, but if yer don't fancy it she ses ter leave it.'

The maid leaned forward, intent on straightening the china tea cup which was not quite central on its saucer. As she did so the starched white cuff of her sleeve caught the silver sugar tongs and with a clatter they fell out of the sugar bowl and struck the milk jug. For a moment she and the nurse froze, both their heads turning anxiously to the still figure on the bed, then, when he did not move, they let out their breath on a long sigh.

'Will that be all then, Sister?'

'Yes, thank you . . . er . . .'

'It's Ellen, Sister.'

'Thank you, Ellen.'

The voice from the bed startled them both and Ellen put her hand to her mouth as the sound floated thinly on the warm air.

'Is . . . that . . . Celie?' it asked.

'Oh, Lor',' Ellen whispered, her heart wrung with pity for the poor chap who, it was said by those who had access to his room, never stopped asking for "Celie". This was the first time she'd been up here and that was on account of Molly, who was head parlourmaid, being on her afternoon off and Mabel, who was second-in-command, having a bad attack of the cramps and taking to her bed.

The nurse hurried across to the bed and put a hand on the man's brow for he must not be allowed to thrash about.

'It's all right, old man,' she said softly. 'Just lie still. The doctor will be here soon,' which was the way she had been taught to speak to all wounded soldiers and she'd nursed a few, not all of them officers like this one but they were all the same. Reassure them. Tell them they'd be all right. Say the doctor was not far away and they soon quietened.

'Is . . . that . . . Celie?' he asked again, his voice fretful. His eyes still had that blank and unnerving stare about them though the nurse was not unnerved, naturally.

'No, but she'll be here soon,' she told him. She'd heard the gossip in the kitchen when she had reason to go there on occasion. The whispers about the girl who had once worked there though none of those who were actually employed in the house now had known her, and what she'd had to do with the man in the bed was anyone's guess. The outside men, some of the gardeners, it was said, those who had not gone off to fight the Boers, and an old chap pensioned off in a cottage at the back of the grounds, had known her, but Mrs King who was now cook, allowed none of *them* into *her* kitchen. There was a great deal of speculation, of course, about this *Celie*, some of the maidservants giving her the status of a ghost, as though she still haunted the place and by the look on Ellen's face she was of the same opinion.

'Off you go, Ellen,' the nurse said briskly, 'and thank Cook for the lemon cake. I'm sure it will be delicious,' reducing the whole incident to nothing, just an ordinary occurrence in the day of a nurse and her patient.

'Yes, Sister.'

'He's askin' for 'er again,' Ellen remarked importantly as she whisked into the kitchen, her participation as an actual onlooker in the event giving her some standing, at least in her own eyes, and it seemed, in theirs, a standing she had never before had in the kitchen.

'Never!' Even Mrs King stopped what she was doing to stare, open-mouthed.

'Aye, 'eard 'im with me own ears, I did.'

'Go on!'

'Is that Celie? he ses. Like a voice comin' from a grave, it were. 'Onestly, I felt me flesh creep but *she* never blinked an eye. She'll be 'ere soon, she ses, calm as yer please.'

'An' what did 'e do then?'

'Nay, don't ask me. She sent me off quick as a flash an' damn glad I were ter gerrout, I can tell yer. Poor sod, lyin' there all broke ter pieces an' no one fetchin' whoever it is 'e's askin' for. What d'yer reckon 'appened, Kitty . . . ?' to another open-mouthed, wide-eyed maidservant, 'between this Celie an' 'im? D'yer reckon they was . . . well, yer know,' winking and nudging Kitty's arm.

'Eeh, never! Mrs Latimer'd never put up wi' anythin' like that. Not under *'er* roof.'

'Who said 'owt about it "'appening" under her roof . . . ?'

'That's enough, you two. I'll have no talk like that in my kitchen,' said Mrs King sounding remarkably like her predecessor, '. . . and I'll thank you to keep your nose out of things what don't concern you, Ellen.' The cook, regretting her previous interest, was incensed. 'Now get into that scullery and help Molly with those pans.'

'Eeh, Cook, that's not fair . . .'

'I'll say what's fair in this kitchen, Ellen Connor, so get that clean apron off and put Agnes's old one on or I'll give you something to *really* make your head spin.'

It was full dark when the carriage drew up to the front door of Briar Lodge. Ellen had finished the pans, burnishing them to a state which satisfied Mrs King, vowing viciously that no matter what she overheard in the future she'd not share it with that frozen-faced martinet, not if she was put to the torture. She had replaced her white cuffs and apron and as Mabel was still in her bed, clutching a hot-water bottle to her stomach, she was to help Molly, who had not yet returned, to serve dinner to the family. She had got out the cutlery ready to set the table when the front door bell rang.

'Shall I see to that, Mrs King?' she asked respectfully.

'Well, there's no one else, girl. Where's that Molly got to? I'll give her what for when she gets back. Yes, go on. See who it is, though who'd call at this time I can't imagine. Kitty, take that cloth from Ellen and give them knifes and forks a polish.'

A tall, well-dressed gentleman stood on the doorstep. He wore a dark grey Homburg made of stiff felt with a dent in the crown and a turned-up, silk-bound brim. His Chesterfield overcoat was also dark grey, of the finest, softest wool and his black boots were cloth-topped. Standing beside him was a frail and delicately boned young woman, her face like death, hatless, her hair somewhat loosened about her face and swathed from chin to foot in a fur-lined tobacco brown cape, the hood of which had fallen back. She was trembling violently and her eyes pleaded with Ellen in the most moving way, though for what reason the flustered maid did not, at that moment, know.

'Is it . . . would it be . . . will you inform Mr Latimer that . . .' the gentleman stammered, which seemed quite incredible to Ellen since he was such an *important*-looking personage. Why was he so . . . so *nervous*, she wondered. After all, there was nothing strange – apart from the timing just before dinner – of one gentleman calling on another but before he could collect himself and his words, and Ellen her composure, the young lady started forward and would have brushed Ellen to one side had not the gentleman caught her arm.

They all three spoke together.

'How is he? Is he badly hurt? Please, won't you just tell me how he is? Are his wounds serious . . . ?'

'Celie, for God's sake, let's do this properly . . .'

'Just a moment, miss. You can't . . .'

Celie! That was the name which clutched at Ellen's staggering attention. Even while she struggled to keep a hold on the door which the woman was doing her best to push inwards, the name riveted her to the carpet for here, in person, was the subject of the debate which had raged in the kitchen ever since Captain Latimer had been brought home from South Africa only three days ago.

'Please, Jethro, let me go. I know which is his room. Just let me slip upstairs. *Get out of my way, girl*. Open this door or I shall be forced to knock you down, I swear it.'

'Miss . . . oh, miss, please, I can't let you . . .'

'Celie, you promised you would let *me* speak. Jesus Christ, girl, d'you think they're going to allow you, the state you're in now, to get into . . . *Celie* . . . !'

The door to the drawing room was flung open and standing in the doorway was the elder Richard Latimer and behind him was his wife. Their faces were apprehensive, for surely some intruder was making a forcible entrance into the Sunday evening peace of their home. At their mother's back were her two remaining daughters, Katherine and Margaret, nineteen and eighteen years of age, soon to be respectably married to gentlemen of their mother's choosing as her eldest daughter had been. Her two youngest sons, Charles and Edward were away at school and James was studying law at Oxford. Alfred, Robert and Thomas were all three married and her eldest and favourite child lay in his bed bearing the wounds he had so honourably received fighting for his Queen and country and for which it was rumoured he was to be decorated.

Her face, which was drawn into lines of deep fatigue and worry, became transformed and Jethro Garside, had he not been there to witness it, would not have believed that a human face, particularly that of a woman, for were they not known to be of a gentler nature than a man, could contain such loathing. It drained of almost every scrap of colour, becoming whiter than the snow-white apron of her parlourmaid except for two hectic red spots on her cheekbones no bigger than a penny piece. Her eyes gleamed with an incandescent brilliance, polished and glassy, opening so wide they seemed to fill her face, and her mouth thinned, white-edged, as a hiss of astonishment escaped them.

'Dear God, it's Celie,' Mr Latimer said in bewilderment. 'What on . . . ?'

'Of course it's Celie and should I be surprised to see her here for she was well known for her lack of manners, dignity and taste. The last time she stood on this same doorstep, on the day of our daughter's wedding she comported herself with as little decency as she is doing now. Dear God, will she never give this household some peace? She had my sons brawling in their own home when she incited that gardener's boy to attack them and when she was dismissed she took half of my servants with her, then, only months later came back for the rest. She is nothing but a trouble-maker and if she does not get out of my house I shall be forced to call the police to remove her.'

'Phyllis, my dear . . .'

Phyllis Latimer's mouth sprayed flecks of madness across her husband's shoulder and her two daughters shrank back from her in alarm, but for all the notice Celie took of her she might have been some puppy dog yapping excitedly about her feet. Ellen, whey-faced and wide-eyed, had let go of the door and taken several steps back towards the safety of the kitchen. Though she liked nothing better than a bit of gossip or a hint of scandal, or indeed anything to relieve the monotony of her hard-working day, this was none of these and it alarmed her. This was . . . was nasty and would you look at her, the woman called Celie, defying Madam and walking like some bloody mechanical doll across the hall towards the stairs.

'Richard . . . ?' she cried out, cocking her head for his answering call.

'Dear God, stop her, Mr Latimer.'

'Celie, Miss Marlow . . . please . . . you must leave. Richard is in no fit state for visitors, my dear. He is . . .'

Celie whirled towards him, moving back across the hallway, clutching at his lapels in anguish. Her face, no more than three inches from his, was as white as his wife's, her eyes dark and staring, the grey in them almost displaced by the black of her pupils. Her expression implored him to tell her the truth. Could he not see, it asked him, how deeply she loved his son? Did he not know how deeply his son loved her because if he didn't he had only to lead her to him and she would demonstrate it. She knew, as nobody else did, what she meant to Richard Latimer and she knew, for would she not feel the same if their situations were reversed, how healing the beloved presence of the man she loved would be to her. She could restore him to health. She did not know the extent of his wounds. Perhaps they were fatal but if they were, whilst he lived she would drag him back from the very jaws of death, or go with him.

'Please tell me . . . please, sir . . . at least tell me . . .'

Richard Latimer felt his heart move in his chest for how could anyone, man or woman, resist the poignant appeal, the truth and honesty, the passionate love this woman was revealing to him? He felt his shoulders sag tiredly. What did it matter? His son would die anyway, the doctor had as good as told him that and if he didn't he would no longer be the upright, long-limbed graceful young man who had marched blithely through life to the beat of the soldier's drum. What harm could it do to let this suffering woman go to him? They had been something to one another once, that was apparent, for the girl's name was constantly on his son's lips, which was one of the reasons why Phyllis was so venomously antagonistic towards her.

He opened his mouth to speak but his wife pushed him abruptly to one side and with the icy, well-bred disdain with which she dealt with her inferiors she lifted her head.

'Get out of my house, you slut. I shall not argue with you since you are not worthy of it. Katherine, pick up the telephone and ring the police station in Wavertree. Tell them we have intruders and I shall expect them here within five minutes.'

'Mother, I really . . .'

'Do as you're told.'

'Celie . . .' Jethro took her arm and began to draw her backwards towards the door but still she resisted.

'No! . . . no! Please, Jethro. In God's name let me go to him . . .'

'Katherine, do you have the police station?'

'Yes Mother, they are coming.'

'Celie, they will arrest you.'

'*I don't care, dammit.* I must know how he is, please . . . please . . . someone . . .'

Margaret Latimer began to weep, her young heart wrenched by the desolation in Celie's voice.

'Mother, won't you just allow her to . . . ?'

Phyllis Latimer turned on her daughter, hissing through clenched teeth as the girl cowered away.

'Please return to the drawing room, Margaret. This does not concern you.'

'But, Mother . . .'

'Do as I say.'

Jethro had both arms about Celie's struggling, weeping figure, dragging her forcibly across the hall towards the door. He was well aware that if he did not get her out of the Latimer house and into the carriage the police would have every right to arrest not only her, but himself.

'Please . . . for pity's sake . . .' she screamed. 'Tell me . . . Richard . . . tell me . . .'

'*He is dying . . . dying . . .*' Phyllis Latimer's younger daughter, driven beyond the point where her mother's anger meant anything to her, screamed back at her.

'*Richard . . .*'

In the quiet dimness of the bedroom at the side of the house the man in the bed spoke into the darkness.

'Where's . . . Celie . . . ?'

'She'll be here soon, old chap,' the nurse soothed him.

Dr Henry had gone and upstairs Celie Marlow lay drugged and sleeping in the deep comfort of Prudence's spare bedroom. She had given no trouble since Jethro had bundled her limp body into the carriage and hoarsely ordered his coachman to take them home. They had passed the police wagon on the Latimer drive.

'Best give her a draught,' the doctor told them for though she was quiet and amenable it was evident she was not right, as Mrs Garside had said when she called him. 'Perhaps a good night's sleep will steady her. She's had a bad shock, you say?'

'Yes, she has just heard her . . . fiancée has been seriously wounded. He was brought home from South Africa three days ago.'

'Poor chap. And what are the extent of his wounds?'

'I'm afraid . . . I don't know, Doctor.'

'I . . . see . . .' though it was obvious he didn't. 'Well, I'll call again tomorrow, first thing. Keep her warm and in bed and if she wakes persuade her to eat a little. Something light.'

They sat, one on either side of the fire, Prudence and Jethro, the two bewildered dogs at their feet. The baby was asleep in her nursery and all the servants were in their beds. They had telephoned young Maudie who had declared stoutly that she and Mrs Petty would manage fine and Miss Marlow was not to worry and if her chill was no better tomorrow she wasn't to dream of getting out of her bed. Privately she was aware that Miss Marlow's customers, only recently wooed back to the re-opened shop, might not take kindly to "making do" with the baking she and Mrs Petty could manage between them but there was not much to be done about it, was there, she and Mrs Petty told one another as they began to weigh out flour and best butter and all the other ingredients they used in the specialities for which Miss Marlow was justifiably famous.

'We've not heard the last of it, you do realise that, don't you?' Prudence asked wearily of her husband. He moved across to sit beside her. She leaned against him, glad of his arm about her, his steadiness, his strength, at the same time blessing the gods who had allowed her to be his wife.

'Oh, yes, my darling. As soon as she wakes up she will be doing her best to get to Briar Lodge and when she does she'll move heaven and earth to get in to him. Until they show her his dead body . . . Oh God, I'm sorry, Pru, I shouldn't have said that.' Jethro shook his head at his own lack of tact, then rested his cheek on his wife's dark hair. 'But she won't give up and can you blame her? Your mother is filled with . . . a poisonous hatred of her which goes beyond what happened all those years ago. It wasn't even Celie's fault in the first place. God, it seems so paltry now I can barely remember how it came about but in Phyllis Latimer's mind Celie was squarely to blame for it, and of course, the idea of any sort of relationship between her son, her *eldest* son and a kitchen maid is absolutely unthinkable. I suppose she had some suitable young girl picked out for him when he returned home from the war and now . . . well . . . Jesus . . . poor Richard. I can't believe it. I can't take it in, what Margaret said. D'you think it's true, or was she hysterical? Celie was enough to pull at the most callous heartstrings and a young girl is very impressionable.'

'You mean that Richard . . . could be . . . dying?'

'Yes, I'm sorry, my dearest, we won't speak of it if it distresses you.'

There was a sorrowful silence for several minutes. The clock on the mantelpiece ticked the minutes away. Trixie stood up and moved towards the french windows. She whined uneasily then returned to flop down beside the older bitch. The fire spat and she jumped, looking about her as though she did not really care for the tension which had invaded her calm and pleasant existence.

'What can we do then?' Prudence said at last.

'There's only one thing I can think of.'

'Dr Henry?'

'Mmm. These medical chaps would surely confide in one another.'

'He might not know Dr Maynard. That is if Dr Maynard is still the family doctor, and even if he is he might not be willing to tell Dr Henry, and *he* might not be willing to tell *us*!'

'I know, my love, but we have to do something for the lass. She'll lose her mind if . . .'

'Perhaps if I telephoned Anne. She might know something more.'

'You could try but it *is* past midnight.'

'Oh, God, what a . . .'

'I know, darling. Come let's go to bed.'

The clock in the hall was striking the hour of four when the dark and silent figure of a woman slipped down the stairs. There was not a sliver of light to be seen anywhere for it was almost December and the nights were long and black, but the woman stepped confidently and smoothly on each carpeted tread until she reached the bottom. On an old rug by the open drawing room door the two dogs who lay sprawled there lifted their heads in unison, ears swivelling, eyes gleaming bright in the pitchy gloom. One stood up and her tail began to twitch rapturously.

'Lie down, girl,' the woman whispered, but the young dog was too entranced by this unexpected visitation to remember her manners and she ran to the door, whining in the back of her throat.

'Lie down, Trixie, there's a good girl. Lie down, please.'

The dog cocked her head, one paw raised, the long plume of her tail moving faster and faster. Her eyes were on the door-knob expectantly and when the woman put her hand to it she crouched slightly, ready to spring through the moment the way was clear.

'Please, Trixie, please be a good girl.'

Trixie wagged her tail more fiercely.

'Oh, very well then, but I can't go at your pace, you must go at mine.'

The door was opened and closed again silently. The older dog grunted and put her head down again on her paws but Trixie flew across the nocturnal crispness of the frosted garden as though she had springs in her heels.

The woman ignored her. She began to walk strongly across the grass towards the gate, keeping away from the gravelled drive. When she reached the gate she pulled Prudence Garside's warm cape more closely round her, arranged the hood over her loosely tied hair, then turned right into Croxteth Gate and Ullet Road. She did not speak to the dog who was attending to a call of nature on the grass verge which edged the pavement but as soon as she had completed it, Trixie pattered silently after her.

Walking briskly in the shadowed darkness they moved side by side until they reached Smithdown Road and after that first snap of excitement the dog settled down with no need of even a word. It was as though she now realised the importance of this outing; its seriousness must not be treated in a puppy's way and her mistress was entitled to the companionship and protection it was Trixie's canine nature to give her.

It was still dark when they reached the gates of Briar Lodge. Not a light showed anywhere but with perfect confidence Celie Marlow, followed by the quiet dog, moved inside the gates, following lawns and paths that were just as they had been when her father had tended them. The cottages at the rear of the grounds were curtained and a wisp or two of smoke came from their chimneys but nobody stirred. The gate on the far side was bolted, rusted solidly into place.

'Oil,' she whispered and the dog moved her tail amiably then followed her mistress back through the gardens towards the front gate. When they reached it a thin line of oyster grey showed above the trees in the east.

'Here, Trixie,' Celie murmured, 'good girl, come to me,' then to the dog's surprise she sat down beside the gatepost and drawing Trixie close to her, leaned her back against it with every appearance of settling there.

Chapter Thirty-six

The horses shied and the coachman swore quite prolifically when the figure of the woman rose from nowhere at the corner of Picton Road and Knowles Lane, just before the first cottage in Wavertree Village.

'Bloody 'ell, woman. What d'yer think yer doin'?' he said hoarsely. 'D'yer want ter gerrus all killed and watch that bloody dog an' all. Get out a t'road, yer daft cow, an' take dog wi' yer. Steady, Blackie . . . steady, Ginger . . . whoa boy, whoa . . .' doing his best to calm the nervous horses but the woman seemed disinclined to move, standing quietly at the animals' heads, leaving the apprehensive dog to fend for itself.

The coachman was incensed and bewildered for why was a woman, a *lady* by the cut of the fur-lined cloak she wore, leaping about at nine thirty of a Monday morning on this bit of quiet country road, or indeed on any bit of country road, terrifying unsuspecting coachmen such as himself? Perhaps there had been an accident of some sort. He glared about him struggling with Blackie who was still inclined to toss his head fretfully, but there was nothing about that was different to any of the hundreds of other mornings he had driven Mr Latimer to his office in town so what the stupid bitch was up to he couldn't imagine. She just stood there between the tossing heads of the two horses, calm as you please, staring up at him with those great big smoky grey eyes of hers, the hood of her cloak pushed back to reveal a mass of dark springing hair which had been bundled any old way into the back of it. A slender woman, patient and silent, a bit . . . strange really, so strange he felt his flesh begin to prickle and the bluster in him, which after all he'd a right to, began to drain away.

Then . . . 'Jesus Christ . . . it's . . . aren't you . . . ?'

'Yes, Bertie, Celie Marlow.'

'Good Christ, girl, what in 'ell's name are you doing out 'ere? You'll get yourself run over doing tricks like that.'

Reuben Ash's son Bertie didn't know whether to slap his knee in amazed delight at the sight of the lovely-looking woman who had once been his playmate or continue in the state of high dudgeon her reckless appearance in front of Mr Latimer's carriage had caused in him. And of course like all the servants of Briar Lodge, he had heard the whispers about Captain Latimer and his strange calling for the girl who stood before him. It was difficult in any household, not just at Briar Lodge, to keep a secret or a rumour, or indeed any bit of gossip from those who lived under its roof, and the mystery of it and of Captain Latimer's sad condition had reached his Mum and Dad's cottage at the back of the estate.

'What is it, Albert?' Mr Latimer's head appeared at the window of the carriage, the newspaper he had been reading still in his hand, the warm breath of his lungs falling on the cold air and steaming about his head. 'Has there been an accident? Why have we stopped?'

From the right-hand window of the old-fashioned carriage Richard Latimer could not see the woman who stood between the heads of the horses, nor did he catch the quick movement of the cloaked figure as it slipped to the left. Before he could collect his thoughts which were, on this sad morning, not at their best, she had opened the left-hand door of the carriage, heaved herself up and was sitting beside him on the seat. He turned open-mouthed with astonishment and alarm, the newspaper crumpled in his hand, banging his head on the window as he drew it inside but Celie sat quietly, nodding a greeting as though he picked her up on this corner every day of the week.

'Good morning, Mr Latimer. I do apologise for intruding on your privacy like this but I could think of no other way of finding out how . . . What . . . ?'

For a second her calmness seemed ready to shiver away

into a dozen cracked pieces and Richard Latimer could see she was making a terrible effort to hang on to it. Underneath her quiet, patient exterior, assumed to show him she was in control of herself *this morning*, was a raw and painful anguish, a desperate, only just bearable, agony of spirit which was harrowing to witness. Last night had been grievous enough, that explosion of tormented demand to see his son, to be told of his condition, but this somehow was worse for the feeling of tension about her was one which threatened at any moment to run madly out of hand.

'I'm sorry, sir, forgive me, but I must know how Richard is. I ask for nothing more. I'm . . . I'm sure you and . . . that he is getting the very best care . . . medical care that there is but . . . not knowing . . .'

She gulped, clinging desperately with her fingernails to the last of her frail endurance. 'I was . . . not myself last night, Mr Latimer, and I'm sorry I caused such a . . . commotion. I had only just heard, you see, that Richard was home . . . wounded. I had received a letter from him only a few days before when Prudence told me . . .'

'You are a friend of Prudence's?' His voice was cold.

'Yes, sir.'

'And how do you come to know my son?'

'We met at . . . dear Lord . . . does it matter? I only want to know . . . oh God . . . I'm sorry . . .' She had begun to tremble violently. 'If someone doesn't tell me the truth soon, I shall go mad.' She spoke through gritted teeth, hanging her head low. Her hands were clenched, one on either side of her lap. She sat, broken, he thought, defeated, and his heart bled for her but Phyllis would never forgive him if he so much as spoke to the girl. It would get back to her, this incident, he knew that, for Albert could be relied on to have it round the kitchen the moment he returned from town. When she heard of it, he must convince his wife that it was none of his making and that he had discouraged the girl as she herself had done yesterday.

Richard Latimer was a kind man, generous to a fault with a nature which could not stand to see a tear on a woman's face, or hurt in a child's voice. A good man, but a weak man who had for the past thirty odd years been totally dominated by his iron-willed wife. He had not been unhappy. She was, beneath her well-mannered, well-controlled exterior, a surprisingly passionate woman. Their private life was extremely satisfying even now, and providing she was given her head and was in no way defied by him or her children, she could be very pleasant. To achieve this state he had got into the habit of allowing her to make all decisions to run his life, except in his business of course, those of their children and their servants, feeling that no harm could come to any of them since she was basically a decent woman. But she was possessed by her absolute conviction that the girl who sat beside him would do her son, indeed her whole family, no good. That Celie Marlow had, from pure spite and quite without reason, taken a grudge against the Latimers. That years ago, because of what Phyllis had believed to be a well-deserved dismissal, her kitchen maid had embarked on a course which had led her to entangle the Latimers' eldest son in her impure web. She was a hussy. A woman of low birth who earned a living by God knows what means and with whom . . . perhaps . . . for it was known women like her lied as easily as they breathed, formed some sort of low relationship with Richard before he went to South Africa, and was now determined to exploit it and Phyllis Latimer's son. Her son who was dreadfully wounded, perhaps dying, and Phyllis would guard him from anyone, *anyone*, not just this girl, who offered him a threat. If the good Lord saw fit to spare him then his mother would nurse him back to health and do her best, which was formidable, to marry him to some completely suitable young woman of their own sort, and Celie Marlow would interfere with that at her peril!

Dare he, *dare he*, after all these years of bending to his wife's will, defy it now? He didn't think so.

'Celie . . . Miss Marlow, will you not allow me to take you home . . . ?' wherever that might be, he thought distractedly. 'You are not well, that is plain to see and should not be about on such a bitter morning.'

'Mr Latimer . . . we won't be kept from each other,' Celie mumbled, her head still bent in despair. 'I won't give up . . .'

'No, of course you won't, but this is not the way . . .'

Her head shot up and her eyes blazed for a moment into his. 'Then what is the way, sir? How can I convince you that Richard and . . . look, look at this . . .' lifting her hand on which the heavy signet ring hung, '. . . don't you recognise this? Richard gave it to me before he went to South Africa.' Indeed, Mr Latimer did recognise it, for he and his wife had given it to their son on his eighteenth birthday. 'We were to be married, Mr Latimer, on October 14th . . . your daughter was . . . so ill bearing her child, your grandchild . . . aah, I see that touches you' . . . for Richard Latimer's face had spasmed in pain at the mention of his daughter and her child, the daughter he had not seen for almost seven years and the granddaughter it was unlikely he would ever see at all.

'I was there . . . helping her when the call came for Richard to return to his regiment. One day, only one more day, if it had been allowed us, and I would have been his wife. It would have been to me that the army would have returned him. I would have received notification that he had been wounded, not his mother . . . Oh, God help me . . . and if *He* can't, won't you? Sir . . . please . . . tell me . . . if he is dying . . .'

It was almost more than he could withstand. Outside his carriage the horses stamped their feet on the frozen surface of the country road, the harness jingling like bells on the crisp air and he could hear Albert blowing on his hands. A cart rattled by going in the opposite direction, loaded with a steaming pile of manure, pulled by a farm horse, the farmer plodding beside it. As he passed the carriage window he could be seen to be staring curiously at the equipage and those inside it wondering what the hell Mr Latimer's carriage was doing standing in the middle of the road so that folk on their daily business such as himself could barely get by. He touched his cap as he caught sight of Mr Latimer's pale face and was clearly astounded by the presence of the weeping girl beside him. By gum, he'd have summat to tell his old lady when he got home.

'Miss Marlow, my son's condition is . . . serious, that is all I can tell you, but I will say this. He is in the best hands and if it is at all possible he will be restored to full health. When, and if that happens, then he will do as he thinks fit, but until that day comes he is in his mother's care. That is all I have to say.'

'Mr Latimer, *how* is he wounded . . . ?

'That is *all* I have to say. Now may I drive you to your home?'

Trixie, barking her displeasure to Albert's annoyance and also that of Blackie and Ginger, sat on the grass verge. When instructed by his master to 'fetch that dog and put it inside' Albert did so, poker-faced.

Nora nearly fainted when she opened the door, shrieking for someone to come and help her as Miss Marlow swayed across the threshold, the dog at her heels.

'Don't disturb Miss Marlow,' Mrs Garside had told them only an hour since. 'Let her sleep, she is not at all well this morning. A chill, I think,' though of course they had all been made aware by Jackson, Mr Garside's coachman, that there had been some funny goings on last night and here she was, looking half-dead on the doorstep when they'd thought her to be in her bed.

They tried to put her back in it but she'd have none of it. Mr Garside had gone down to his office but Mrs Garside had poured almost a tumbler full of brandy down Miss Marlow's throat, which had brought a fevered flush to her cheeks and an icy brilliance to her dulled eyes, but she'd still been as sober as a judge. Enough to fell a man used to it, Nora thought awestruck, but it might have been a glass of milk for all the effect it had on Miss Marlow.

'I'll go home now, Prudence,' she said as grim as the weather outside the window. 'I must see to my business and then . . .'

'Then what will you do, darling?' Nora could see Mrs Garside was close to tears over something, though Miss Marlow was dry-eyed. She wondered if it was anything to do with last night's little drama.

'I shan't give up, Pru. I shall never give up,' Miss Marlow said and though she had no idea what it was about Nora could see she meant it.

It was three days later when Prudence's carriage drew up outside Harper's shop. The weather had turned milder. A day of drifting mist and drizzle. A day when it really never got light and lamps were lit from morning 'till night.

'Go through and have a cup of tea in the kitchen, Jackson. I may be some time,' she said to the coachman. Like that was Mrs Garside. Not one to let her servants hang about in the cold as some ladies would.

Nodding respectfully to Miss Marlow, who stood by the counter, looking as though she'd been struck to a pillar of stone and drained of every drop of blood in her body, Jackson moved gratefully through the crowded shop to the warmth of the kitchen where Maudie, second-in-command now to Miss Marlow herself, thrust a strong cup of tea in his hand.

Mrs Garside took Miss Marlow's arm, he noticed as he went through, whispering to her and guiding her towards the stairs which led up to the first floor.

'Sit down, darling,' she said gently, drawing off her gloves, 'whilst I ring for tea.' Prudence had been brought up in a household where tea was immediately available whenever it was required, with a smiling housemaid to fetch it.

'I don't want to sit down and damn the tea, Prudence. Tell me.' Celie stood by the crackling fire, tall, thinner, dressed in a simple dark grey dress with a touch of white lace at the neck and cuffs, a sombre dress to match her mood, her hands gripped tight before her.

'We didn't want to say anything before we . . . well, Jethro had this idea that Doctor Henry might be able to approach Doctor Maynard . . .'

Celie's voice was cracked. 'For Christ's sake tell me . . .'

'He was reluctant at first but . . .'

'I'll knock you to the floor if you don't tell me.'

'He was struck in the head by a splinter from a shell. It . . . he was . . . unconscious for many days . . . the army doctor, a good man they say, got it out, God knows how, but it has left him not himself.'

'What the hell does that mean?' Celie snarled.

'He is dazed. He knows who he is and where he is but he is almost insensible . . .'

'Oh, Jesus . . .' Celie put a trembling hand to her mouth.

'But that is not all, Celie.' Prudence's face was filled with compassion and she put out her hand resting it gently on Celie's quivering arm.

'Please . . .'

'Both his legs were . . . shattered . . .'

'Shattered . . . ?'

'Fractured . . . badly. Father is acquainted with men of influence at the War Office. They brought him home at once, on the first available ship, but it is a six-thousand-mile trip. There was a doctor and nurse with him at all times and since then the very best men have been brought in. They did not think he would last the journey but . . . he's strong, Celie, and he's still alive . . .'

'Oh, Richard . . . Richard . . .' Celie's face worked as she did her best to control her longing to weep.

'That is all we could find out and naturally both Dr Henry and Dr Maynard were defying all medical ethics in telling us. Of course as Richard is my brother, and having explained the circumstances . . . Dr Maynard knows me . . .'

'Thank you, oh thank you, Pru.' Tears ran unchecked down Celie's face and she dashed at them with the back of her hand. 'At least I know what . . . all I have to do now is to get to him somehow. I mean to do it, when they are all asleep perhaps. I know the layout of the house and if I could just see him I know I will be able to tell at once . . . how it is with him. In here . . .' She struck at her own chest with the flat of her hand, then turned away to stare distractedly from the window. She pushed her hand across her forehead and through her neatly drawn-back hair and Prudence could tell she had withdrawn from all the normal guidelines of life and was deeply entrenched in the false belief that she had only to get to Richard's bedside and all barriers would fall away. Even now she had still no conception of the invincibility of Richard's mother and never would, Prudence thought sadly.

'What are you talking about, Celie?' she said to Celie's back. 'You wouldn't try to? . . . you must accept . . .'

'There is the gate. Remember the gate, Prudence?' Celie whirled about, her face white and paper-thin but alive with resolve. 'You escaped through it and so could Richard . . .'

Prudence was appalled. 'He cannot be moved, even if

you could get to him . . . Dear God, Celie, you could kill him . . .'

Her friend was obsessed, out of her mind, her expression said. Usually so calm, so unhurried, so patient and clear-headed, this tragedy had turned Celie Marlow's brain to the point when she could no longer think coherently. Wild plans . . . gates . . . what gate . . . ?

'The gate, Prudence. The one in the wall at the back of the estate. It needs oiling, but if we had a carriage waiting . . . Jethro and . . . and Jackson could carry Richard . . .'

'Stop it, *stop it*, Celie. Get a hold of yourself. You cannot intend to try and carry Richard . . .'

'Why not? He should be with me. I am his wife, if not in name then in all else. I love him. He loves me. I don't care how badly he is wounded, I shall always love him. If he should never walk again or . . . or regain his . . . his complete senses I will look after him for the rest of his life. He is mine, Prudence, *mine*, and I am his and I mean to . . .'

'Celie, before I let you bring my brother from a place where he is being properly cared for by a good doctor, I would telephone my mother and warn her about what you mean to do.' Prudence's voice was flat and cold. 'He is seriously ill and only God knows what it would do to him if you carried out these wild and completely idiotic ideas. That's if you could get to him, which I seriously doubt. My brother will recover, or not! Yes, I mean what I say, so don't glare at me like that. If he recovers he will walk away from Briar Lodge and come for you, or he will die. I do not mean to be cruel but if he dies that is the end of it, for both of you.'

'*Prudence*,' Celie's cry of torment echoed about the cosy room.

'I love you, Celie. You have been dearer to me than a sister, but I love Richard too, and I wouldn't let you kill him with this . . . obsession.'

'Dear God, Pru . . . don't say that.'

'I must. Leave him alone for a while. I will try and keep up with his progress . . . or deterioration through Dr Henry, and perhaps Anne, but that is all I will do . . .'

'I need to see him, Prudence . . . Oh, please . . . how would you be if it was Jethro and they kept you from him . . .'

'I hope I would have the strength and the . . . the devotion to see where his best interests lay, Celie, even if it meant we were separated.' Prudence spoke with great dignity. She stood up and drew on her gloves. 'I must go now. Grace is a little fretful with her teeth and I promised Dr Henry I would . . .' She stopped speaking abruptly for she had no intention of heaping a further burden on Celie's already grievously burdened shoulders, with the news that she was expecting another child.

'I'll telephone you, darling, as soon as I have news. Now then give me a kiss and dry your eyes.' She softened, her plain face almost beautiful in her great affection for Celie Marlow. 'He's strong, Celie, and he knows you will be waiting for him. Let him recover . . .'

'Dear Christ, if he does, if he *does*!'

'He will. He loves you and you love him.'

'If only you knew how much.'

It was almost eight o'clock when the last customer finally left the shop. Old Gladys it was, from her stall by the Pier Head, who made the journey by foot each evening, though it was very seldom that anything was left at Harper's as there was at other shops she called on in her search for cheap leftovers.

'Ask Percy to call me a cab, will you, Dorcas? I am going out.' Celie returned the empty tea cup from which she had just drunk a welcome cup of tea to its saucer.

'At this time of night?' Dorcas did not mean to be impertinent for after all Celie was her employer. She had rescued Dorcas from a hell on earth, restoring her to her proper place in the order of things and Dorcas would be eternally grateful, but to go out at almost eight thirty of a night and in a hired hansom cab was quite unheard of. Whenever Celie went to Miss Prudence's home Mr Garside sent the carriage for her, so where the dickens was she off to? It was concern, not curiosity, which prompted Dorcas to question her.

Celie turned a cool stare on her and Dorcas wondered, as she had so many times in the past, where that little slip of a girl, all big eyes and innocence, who had played in the kitchen at Briar Lodge had gone.

'Yes, and I would be obliged if you would do as you are told without questioning my actions.'

'I'm sorry Celie, but it's . . . well it's half past eight and raining stair rods, I didn't mean to . . .'

Celie relented, putting out a hand to pat Dorcas's arm. 'Don't worry, Dorcas. I'm not up to mischief. I have an errand to run that's all.'

An errand to run! What a strange way to describe it, this journey she was taking, she mused dispassionately as the cab jolted on its way along Ullet Road. It would do no good, not to her nor to Richard, even if he was to hear of it, which was doubtful if what Prudence said was true. She bent her head and drew a deep ragged breath of pain. A small agonised sound murmured in the back of her throat but she held it in for it would not serve to fall apart now. She must keep strong. She must bear herself well for there was so much to be got through before she and Richard could be together again. The lights along the road flickered against her face and she turned to stare into the darkness beyond the railings which bordered Sefton Park. The trees round its edge clustered thickly together, shadowed and secret, and she was carried back to that moment when she had received her first kiss beneath their twisted branches. Richard, his brown laughing face softening with emotion, his deep brown eyes warmed with love. She could see his eyelashes droop along the length of his heavy lids, curling and glossy brown, and in her mind's eye where memory took her, she kissed his dark eyebrows where the tumble of his ruffled hair touched them. She reached up to push it back from his brow. Her hands cupped his lean brown cheeks and with trembling fingers she traced the outline of his curving lips. They parted and gently bit her finger, then drew it into his mouth . . .

Dear sweet Lord . . . Richard . . . I love you . . . it

was there . . . there just inside those gates you leaned
me against a tree . . . I can still feel the roughness of
the bark through my gown . . . it was summer . . . your
body fitted to mine, my breast to yours, my belly to yours,
thigh to thigh and your mouth . . . your hands at my breast
. . . Oh, my darling . . . my darling . . . how can I bear it
if we are never to know that loveliness again. She could
feel the warmth of him still, long and lean and hard just
as it had been then, his voice murmuring her name as it
had done a score of times in the nights they had shared
at Ambleside. Love, so much love it could not be lost, there
was too much of it, it was too strong simply to die away
and never be.

She pushed the knuckle of her bent finger into her mouth
and bit on it so that the agony of her loss would not
escape for the cab driver to hear, then when she had
controlled the trembling which in the past few days had
threatened to tear her to pieces, she lifted her head and
concentrated on the rippling back of the horse which pulled
the cab. The reins, coming from above her head, flapped
against its shining wet coat and the driver urged it to
"giddup" since it was a long way there and back to their
destination.

'Is this it, Miss?' he shouted twenty minutes later.

'Yes, driver, thank you. Turn in at the gates and drive up
to the front door, would you? I shall be but a minute then we
will go straight back.'

It was Molly who opened the door and though she was
patently bewildered at the sight of the neatly dressed figure
of the woman on the doorstep, and at *this time* of night
as well, she told the caller she would see if Mr Latimer
was at home. 'Could she say who was calling?' she asked,
repeating doubtfully, 'A friend of Captain Latimer's,' as the
caller instructed her.

'Who is it, Molly?' Celie heard him say from the chair in
the hallway where Molly had put her, but she could detect
the note of apprehension in his voice for who among Richard's
friends and acquaintances would call unannounced at past nine
o'clock? Behind him was his wife.

'This is outrageous. Call the police, Mr Latimer,' she spat out the moment she saw Celie, 'and have this creature put in gaol. She's quite mad and should be locked up, or better yet put away . . .'

'I merely called to enquire after Captain Latimer, ma'am,' Celie said politely, standing up. 'I don't mean him, nor you, any harm. Will you not tell me how he is and then I will leave immediately . . . ?'

'You'll leave *now*, you shameless hussy,' Mrs Latimer hissed, her well-bred composure beginning to ebb away in the face of the hussy's determined impertinence. 'Have you not realised yet that you are not welcome here, by me, and certainly not by my son? Are you determined to shatter our peace of mind completely? Accosting my husband in his carriage and coming here *again*.'

'How is your son, Mrs Latimer, please tell me?'

'Mr Latimer, will you please telephone the police constable at . . .'

'It will do no good, Mrs Latimer, I will not be stopped. I shall keep coming until you have told me Richard has either recovered or is dead . . .'

'Get out of my house. *Get out of my house*.'

Celie turned quietly to Mr Latimer, who hovered, grey-faced and trembling, with his hand on the ear-piece of the telephone which stood on a table at the back of the hall. Molly was behind him, her eyes enormous and glittering with excitement. Dear God, it was *her* again. The one Ellen had told them about on Sunday. The one whose name Captain Richard kept muttering. She'd heard him herself when she took up the tray with the light meals the doctor had ordered and which the nurse spooned into his obediently opening mouth, or so it was said. Would you look at the gall of her facing up to Madam and her once a kitchen maid, no, *scullery* maid in this very house.

'Mr Latimer,' she was saying, 'have you nothing to tell me that would set my heart and mind at rest? I love your son, you see, and I am . . . tormented . . . you are a good man, sir, can you not find it in your heart to ease mine?'

'Mr Latimer, put this . . . this whore from my house and see to it that she doesn't return. It seems she is impervious to the suffering of our family and to a mother's request to be left alone to nurse her son. Perhaps the police will make her see reason. You will go and consult your solicitor first thing in the morning.'

'Please . . . Miss Marlow, it would best . . .' Mr Latimer's voice was anguished.

'Very well, but I won't give up. I love your son, sir . . .'

'Get her from my house, Mr Latimer,' Phyllis Latimer's face had turned from the violent puce of hot temper to the icy white of menacing rage, 'or I shall call Albert and the other men to throw her out.'

Celie left quietly, climbing into the cab and speaking to the driver in a low voice which contained her will to succeed.

She made the journey to Briar Lodge twice more before she was arrested. She was taken to Wavertree Police Station where the dumbfounded police sergeant was forced to lock her in a small ante-room since there was no accommodation in the cells for female prisoners and certainly not for the quality of this one.

Mr Pembroke was called by a frantic Prudence whom Celie had been allowed to telephone and within the hour she was released on bail. The next day, at the Magistrates' Court in Liverpool she was bound over to keep the peace or be re-arrested, when she would be sent to gaol for thirty days.

On the following day, in the gloom the doctor thought suitable for a patient with a head injury, Richard Latimer opened his eyes, but instead of merely lying on his back and staring sightlessly at the canopy above his head, he turned slowly until his gaze fell on the figure of the nurse by the fire.

'Nanny?' he said wonderingly, his voice hoarse and very weak.

The nurse looked up, and smiled triumphantly. Good nursing had worked its cure again, her expression said. She rose from her chair and moved across to the bed.

'No, I'm not your nanny, sir, but I am a nurse.'

'I can see that, dammit,' he croaked. 'What in hell's name is happening here? I feel bloody queer . . .'

'Now then, Captain Latimer, no need for swearing . . .'

'I'll say something stronger than that, Nurse, if you don't tell me what's happened, and where the hell is Celie?'

Chapter Thirty-seven

'Now then, Sister, you understand exactly what I require of you. Good. You and your nurse here are to be the only persons, besides myself and Mr Latimer, who will have any contact with my son. At all times one of you must be in attendance. Nurse Atkinson, you will bring Captain Latimer's meals from the kitchen and . . . this is most important . . . you are to speak to no one. If I hear of either of you exchanging any word that is not to do with my son's diet, or his laundry and such, then you will be instantly dismissed and I shall make it my duty to ensure you will never again be employed in a decent household. Is that clear?'

'Yes, madam,' both the sister and the nurse chorused.

'Nothing he says, *nothing*, is to be repeated outside his bedroom. I will, of course, spend some part of the day with him and so will my husband naturally, when he comes home from his place of business, but I want neither of my daughters to see their brother. They are young, gently reared girls who know nothing of life, or young gentlemen, and I should not like it if either of them were to be distressed by his condition. Do you understand?'

'Yes, madam.'

'Very well. Now I believe two of my housemaids are waiting outside. Kindly ask them to come in and then go directly back to my son's room. He was asleep when I left him . . . if he should awake and find himself alone . . .'

She left the words hanging in mid-air as the two nurses backed deferentially from her small morning parlour. It was the room where Phyllis Latimer consulted with her cook on the day's menus; where she studied the accounts; where she shrivelled ill-advised housemaids who had erred, reducing them to tears; where she conducted all the behind-the-scenes household tasks which fell to her as the mistress of a large house such as Briar Lodge. She had given birth to and raised eleven children and it was here, when it was needed, that she had chastened them. This was her room, her working room and anyone summoned here approached the closed door in some trepidation.

The two housemaids bobbed deep curtseys, their eyes cast down, their hands clasped in front of them. Ellen and Molly had agonised together over what their mistress wanted to see them about since for the life of them they could think of nothing either of them had done wrong. Mrs Latimer had been most pleasant to them this morning, when they had served her, the master and their two daughters at breakfast. Pleasant for *her*, that is, for she was not one to smile or pass the time of day with her maids. They had broken no ornaments, nor been late, or found out in the most grievous of sins a housemaid could commit, that of keeping company with a young man.

'What I have to say to you is very important,' Mrs Latimer began, her eyes forbidding as they rested on the anxious faces of the two young women. 'Do you understand?'

'Yes, madam,' though they didn't of course.

'Very well. You have heard that Captain Richard has taken a turn for the better.'

'Oh, yes, madam,' both daring to look up and beam at their mistress.

'We are naturally delighted that my son is on the slow road to recovery but he still needs very special care, very special nursing and it goes without saying, complete rest and quiet. You understand.'

'Yes, madam.'

'Sister Andrews is a highly trained and competent nurse but now that Captain Richard is . . . well, not mobile, for he is still confined to his bed . . . but more active, Sister Andrews cannot manage him alone so a second nurse has been employed. She will come to the kitchen for all that the

Captain requires so there will be no need for either of you to go near the sick room. Do I make myself clear?'

'Yes, madam.'

'Good. Now I come to a matter of very grave importance which concerns you both.'

They raised their eyes fearfully to her face, then hurriedly dropped them again.

'You have both, I believe, been present at my son's bedside when he was . . . delirious.'

Delirious? What was she getting at, two young and innocent minds conjectured. They were not *awfully* sure what the word meant. It implied a hectic feverish excitable kind of activity, when Captain Richard had done nothing, at least when they'd been in his bedroom, but lie like a log and mutter a word or two here and there.

'Beg pardon, madam, but . . .' Molly, head parlourmaid and the elder of the two, managed a puzzled murmur.

'I have been told by Sister Andrews that my son has . . . spoken of . . . has spoken the name of a woman who was once a servant in this house. Is this true?' Her voice was icy and both girls cringed.

'Well . . . we didn't mean to . . .'

'I am not implying that any blame can be laid at your door, Molly, nor at Ellen's, I merely want to impress on you the seriousness of . . . gossip.'

She might have said *murder* and got no greater heart-sinking.

'You are, I can see, aware of my meaning,' she continued.

'Yes, madam.'

'I shall not repeat that name here nor refer again to the indecent behaviour which took place on several occasions in the hallway of my own house but the matter has been taken in hand by the police. A very serious matter. Is that clear to you both?'

'Yes, madam.' Ellen had begun to cry. She didn't know why. She only knew she was badly frightened.

'Now, I know neither of you are involved, at the moment, and if that person's name is not mentioned again, in this house, or out of it, I can see no reason why you should be. I never,

never want to hear that either of you have repeated it, in the kitchen of this house, to anyone who works in the garden, or indeed to any member of your own family. Do I make myself clear, both of you?'

'Oh yes, madam . . . yes, madam,' they both babbled.

'Very well, you may go but remember what I have said and abide by it or the seriousness of the consequences will not be pleasant for either of you. And do not repeat this conversation to any other member of the staff. If you should be asked, you may tell them that . . . I was praising your work.'

'Well, it beats me why Madam should have the pair of yer into 'er parlour just to tell you she was pleased with yer work,' Kitty said petulantly, for wasn't *her* work as good as theirs any day of the week? 'What about the rest of us, heh? We work as hard as what you do, isn't that right, girls?' looking about her at Mabel and Agnes and even at Cook who had her feet up to the fire, for confirmation of her words.

They all nodded, flabbergasted at this strange turn of events since, in living memory, it had never been known for Madam to praise *anyone*, servants or family, but, Ellen and Molly had said so and that was that. The matter was pondered over for an hour or so then, as such things are, forgotten, as was the strange young woman whose name had been bandied about for a day or two. No more was heard of her, or *from* her, apparently, and those who worked in the kitchen at Briar Lodge returned to their tasks, their days enlivened only by the periodic appearance of Nurse Atkinson who came down to fetch Captain Richard's trays and to deposit his bed linen which was picked up by the laundry maid. The nurse was sadly uncommunicative about the patient, though, saying only that he was coming along slowly. None of them saw him since, surprisingly, it seemed Nurse Atkinson was attending to the cleaning of his room, *and* to his fire, as well. Agnes, when rung for, was to fetch the coals, leaving them just outside Captain Richard's door, collecting yesterday's ashes when she did so.

'I wonder why he never 'as no visitors?' Agnes mused when the captain had been home for three weeks.

'There's plenty telephone to ask after 'im,' Kitty replied,

'but 'is Mama always takes the call. She don't want no one troublin' 'im, she ses, and if anyone asks after 'im, I've to fetch 'er to speak to them.'

'Is 'e . . . right in the 'ead, d'yer think?'

'I'm sure it's nothing to do with us,' Molly interposed, 'and Mrs Latimer'd 'ave a fit if she was to 'ear the pair o' you discussing him like that, Kitty Mason. O'course he's right in the 'ead but he were badly wounded and only complete rest'll cure 'im, Madam says. He can't be bothered with hordes of visitors, mornin', noon an' night so you just watch what yer saying. Isn't that right, Cook?'

'Well, excuse me for breathing, Molly Parkinson. An' who said you was to give orders round 'ere, I'd like ter know? Cook's above you and when *she* tells me to shut me gob, I will . . .'

'Shut yer gob, Kitty.'

'Yes, Cook.'

'And not another word do I want to hear about Captain Richard. He's no concern of ours except to provide him with decent, nourishing food to build him up, so get that old pinny on and whisk those eggs for me. Nurse'll be down in a minute for his eggnog. Fetch that fresh milk, Molly . . .'

'Yes, Cook.'

'. . . and *not another word*, d'you hear?'

The letter was handed in by the postman the following day. There were five deliveries each day and though the postman could quite easily have pushed the mail through the letter box, he had taken a shine to Ellen Connor who at eighteen, though not exactly pretty, had the rosy bloom of youth about her and not only that, a pert tongue in her head. They exchanged nothing more exciting than a smiling good morning, a remark or two about the weather and that certain vibrancy which a man and woman trade when each is aware of the other's charms. The postman had hopes, though, and one of these days, when the moment was right and the "missus" not about, he had made up his mind to enquire when Ellen's day off might be. She had called him a saucy devil when he had asked her her name, but she'd told him just the same.

The letters which came in the first delivery were placed

on a salver and presented to Mr Latimer at breakfast, but thereafter, they were taken in to Mrs Latimer, or, if she was out, or busy, left on the table in the hallway where she picked them up when she had a moment. She liked to study the envelopes of those not addressed to herself or Mr Latimer, and of course, should a letter arrive for either of her daughters, to demand to read it.

The one that came that day arrived in the second delivery, just after ten o'clock. It was addressed to Captain Richard Latimer and for some reason, Ellen felt her heart miss a beat. The postman was disappointed when the daring wink he directed at her was completely ignored. In fact she barely glanced at him, as, her eyes on the letter which was at the top of the pile, she shut the door in his astonished face.

Ellen stood for several indecisive minutes in the hall. She studied the letter with the intensity of someone who has just been handed a live bomb. She didn't know why she felt uneasy since the Captain had received many letters since he had been brought home, presumably to wish him well, but this one had a Liverpool postmark and was . . . well . . . it seemed different. It was very *thin* for a start, almost as though there was nothing in it, which was strange. All the ladies and gentlemen in the society of which the Latimers were a part, wrote to one another on thick, creamy notepaper, like velvet it was, but when it was folded, even one sheet made a bulky package. And this one *smelled* so lovely!

Ellen dithered in the hallway. Mrs Latimer was in her parlour and so was Cook who was going through the menus with her and Ellen had only to pop the letter in the pocket of her apron and no one would be the wiser. She supposed if she was to hand it to one of the nurses, they would then pass it on to Captain Richard. For nothing had ever been *said* about his *letters*, had it? . . . but . . . oh Lord . . . she could still see that poor young woman's desolate face . . . now why should she think of *her*? . . . her mind begged to know . . . but somehow . . . it seemed to Ellen that . . . this was from a woman and surely . . . but then, what if Madam found out . . . Ellen would be bound to get the sack . . . Mrs Latimer was the head of this household and if you got on her wrong side . . . and she *had* said that woman . . . what had her name been? *Celie* . . . was not to be mentioned and if this was from *her* . . .

Sighing, Ellen walked across the hall and down the passage to Mrs Latimer's parlour. She tapped on the door, entering when bidden to do so.

'Excuse me, madam, the post has just come.'

Mrs Latimer looked surprised.

'Well, couldn't you have left it on the hall table, Ellen. You know I don't like to be disturbed when Cook and I are doing the menus.'

'I'm sorry, madam, but there's a . . . well . . .'

She put the pile of letters in front of her mistress, bobbed an excruciating curtsey and fled. Mrs Latimer studied the letter on the top of the pile, then with an abrupt movement of her hand and a murmured word indicated to Cook that she should leave. With suddenly trembling fingers, she slit the envelope.

There was no letter inside, no notepaper of any sort, but when she tipped it up, a tiny sprig of dried rosemary fell onto the table top. Nothing else, just the lovely aroma of the flower. Rosemary, rosemary for remembrance! She stared at it in amazement, momentarily mystified, then slowly the red tide of anger flooded her face except for a thin white line about her compressed lips. She stood up and turned about, floundering to the window, crumpling the envelope which was still in her hand into a vicious ball. She pounded the fist which held it on the window sill, drawing her lips back in a rictus of frustration. That clever little bitch! That clever, clever little bitch! She had known full well that there was absolutely nothing Phyllis Latimer could complain of in a harmless sprig of rosemary which could have come from anybody and which presumably would mean something to Richard. She could no longer come to the house for fear of being arrested. She would know she could not reach Richard by means of the telephone so she had chosen this way in which to let him know that she was . . .

Phyllis Latimer's livid, clever brain slowed from its racing, circling explosion of rage and gradually cleared as she considered the implication of the girl's action. There were no words, no ramblings telling him how much she . . . she loved him – if she did, which seemed doubtful, for women of her sort were only out for what they could get. There was no message, no questions, no plans nor pleading, only this simple sprig of rosemary, just as though *that* was all that was necessary. As though Richard *needed* nothing else. As though whatever it was that was between them, did not require words. It implied a commitment, something other than the sexual alliance Phyllis Latimer had imagined. Something serious. A reminder of something. *Remember*, it said, remember.

Drawing in a deep breath she returned to the table. She brushed the rosemary contemptuously into the waste-paper basket, not looking at it, her eyes narrowed and contemplative as she stared from the window. She sat back, her hands folded in her lap, erect and regal as befitted the lady that she was and for fifteen minutes or so, she remained in the same position. At the end of those fifteen minutes she relaxed and about her lips a small smile played, then she rose to her feet and made her way from her parlour and up the stairs until she reached her son's room.

There was only the head nurse with him and she stood up at once, sketching a crude curtsey as Phyllis Latimer entered the room without knocking.

'Good morning, Sister.'

'Good morning, madam.'

'And how is my son today?'

'He is improving, madam. He has eaten a good breakfast and Nurse and I have just completed his bed bath.'

'Good, good, that's the ticket. The doctor will be pleased.'

'Yes, madam, and he had a good night. The wound in his head is healing nicely and I'm sure when the doctor comes, he will tell you so . . .'

'Good God, Mother, am I invisible, or an imbecile who cannot speak for himself?' The voice from the bed was sharp and irritable.

'Of course not, dear boy. How are you today?'

'You have just had a complete report from that old harridan over there so I can see no reason to repeat it all. Of course she did not mention my bodily functions which are becoming more normal and . . .'

'*Richard*! There is no need to be coarse.'

'Mother, coarse and nasty things happen in a sick-room. Did no one ever tell you? There are smells and sights which would turn the strongest stomach . . .'

'Richard. I will not have you talk to me like that . . .'

'Mother, for God's sake, let me get up, even if it's only to the bloody window. If I could just have something else to look at beyond this eternal canopy and those two eternal women I believe I would make a much faster recovery. And will you tell them to pull back the damned curtains . . .'

'Richard, I don't like to hear you swearing . . .'

'*Mother*, I have been in this bed for weeks now.' Richard Latimer spoke through clenched and furious teeth. The bandage had gone from his head which had been shaved when he was wounded and the half-healed slash of the scar where the splinter of shell had struck him, wended its way through the cap of short dark curls which now covered it. His face was drawn, the rich amber brown of his skin paled to a sickly yellow. His eyes were somewhat feverish, for the infection which had attacked his shattered legs as he lay in the burning sun and stinking remains of his dead horse, kept returning to drag him down. His long thin hands plucked fretfully at the tight smoothness of his bedcovers. A cage had been erected across the lower half of his body and his eyes constantly turned to it as though he dreaded, but was obsessed with what lay beneath it.

'Darling,' his mother interrupted him. 'I know that and I am sorry but if we are to achieve a complete recovery we must not hurry these things. You know what the doctor said, slow but sure . . .'

'I wouldn't mind going slowly, Mother, it's standing still, or rather lying flat on my back that's driving me mad. They won't even allow me to read . . .'

'Sister Andrews will read *to* you, Richard, or I will if you like . . .'

'And why cannot the girls come in and see me?' just as

though she had not spoken. 'Just a change of face . . . *anybody*
. . . for Christ's sake . . .'

'Richard, please . . .'

'You heard Dr Maynard yourself. He said I could have family
visitors . . .'

'And you will, darling, in time . . .'

'Mother, please . . . *please* send up a couple of the
gardener's lads to take me to the window. God knows there
is nothing to look at this time of the year but it would be a
change from those two.'

Sister Andrews, who agreed with him, stood quietly by the
fire, not at all offended by the names her patient called her.
She was herself mystified as to why this woman, who clearly
doted on her son, seemed to be doing her best to hold him
back. She was kindness itself, spending an hour or even two
each day with him, but she would allow no one to cross his
threshold besides the two nurses and her husband of course,
and only then when she was with him. The captain was a
virtual prisoner in this room, even the cheerful presence of
the two young maids was denied him and Nurse Atkinson was
none too pleased at having been asked to clean his room. A
bonus for both of them Mrs Latimer had promised at the end
of it, but still it was very strange. The captain had stopped
asking for the girl called Celie. Almost as soon as he was
himself again, he had given over mentioning her name but
you could see he was fretful about something and she'd a
good mind to speak to Dr Maynard about it. Then again if
Madam found out she'd not like it and Sister Andrews didn't
want to jeopardise her own job. The patient *was* recovering,
of course. He was young and strong. A healthy man whose
healthy bones would heal and whose body would naturally knit
together and be . . . well, *almost* as it had been. Perhaps a
suggestion of a limp – so could she, Sarah Andrews, rock the
boat, so to speak, by talking out of turn?

Mrs Latimer was at the door when Nurse Atkinson bustled
in with Captain Richard's luncheon tray and the sister took the
opportunity to draw her patient's mother to one side.

'A word, if I may, Mrs Latimer.'

'Of course, Sister. What is it?'

'The captain, madam.'

'Yes?'

'He has been asking about writing letters.'

'I see,' and Mrs Latimer's face hardened.

'May I ask what you want me to do about it, madam?'

'Why, oblige him, Sister, of course.'

'You . . . will allow it?'

'Why ever not, Sister?' Mrs Latimer appeared astonished.
'As long as he does not tire himself. A great many people have
written to him but if he dictates one or two at a time . . .'

'Dictate? To me?'

'Yes, I think that would be best and of course you will bring
them to me for posting.'

The two women exchanged glances of perfect understanding and Mrs Latimer smiled.

'Of course, madam.' Sister Andrews nodded her head
briefly.

'Anything else, Sister?'

'No, madam.'

'Oh, and remind Nurse will you, just in case my son should
. . . dictate one to her while you are absent.'

'I will, madam.'

'Good.'

The letter he wrote was cool, even stilted since Richard
Latimer was writing to his love with another woman's hand.
It said little beyond telling her he was recovering and hoped to
see her soon. It might have been that of a gentleman writing
to an acquaintance and Phyllis Latimer wondered why, since
Richard was not aware that anyone but the woman to whom
it was addressed and the woman who wrote it for him, would
read it. Perhaps that was why. He could hardly pour out his
. . . well, she hardly liked to call it *love* . . . whatever it
was . . . shuddering . . . into the ears of an employee. She
studied it thoughtfully for several minutes before consigning
it in pieces to her waste paper basket.

In January, eight weeks after Richard Latimer was returned
to Briar Lodge, the Queen for whom he had fought and been
wounded, died at her home on the Isle of Wight. Between
Her Majesty's death and her funeral on February 2nd, the

country and the Empire went into the deepest mourning. The weather was quite glorious, almost spring-like, the sun rising continuously on a world wrapped in sorrow and flags at half-mast in distress all over the globe, on nations shocked with grief. London, the capital of the Empire was a city of dreadful black, a city mute as were all the cities of the British Nation. Parliament was adjourned, all public and official engagements were cancelled, theatres and places of entertainment closed, functions suspended, windows were shuttered and businesses came to a standstill. Streets were draped in deep royal purple and church bells tolled the passing of the Queen, who had reigned for almost sixty-four years. There were indeed very few people who could remember, or even who had lived, in the reign of another monarch.

Ivy Petty begged Celie to accompany her to the Memorial Service in the cathedral church of St Peter. The procession which began at the Town Hall was probably the greatest and most impressive the City of Liverpool had ever known, its progress accompanied by pipers wailing out the mournful dirge of the Black Watch, "The Flowers of the Forest". Massed bands, muffled drums and the slow tread of members of the police, the fire brigade, the Royal navy and the army, including a detachment from the King's Liverpool Regiment amongst whom, Celie presumed, Richard would have marched. There were dignitaries of Liverpool, city officials and other influential citizens, one of whom was the senior Richard Latimer. In the cathedral his wife, shrouded in the deepest black of mourning, stood with the wives of other leading businessmen.

Ivy wept sharply, her usual self-containment deserting her. She could remember when the Prince died, she said, forty years ago and now the poor lady, who had grieved for him all this time, was resting beside him, happy and peaceful at last.

Unmoved by it all, and by Ivy's surprising grief, Celie stood beside her at the back of the packed cathedral as the Bishop of Liverpool pronounced the benediction. Forty years! Forty years the Queen had lived without the man it was said she had loved devotedly, and somehow she had built a life for herself without him. How had she done it? How had she done it knowing she would never see him again? It was only eight weeks since Richard had come home. Eight short weeks and already Celie was beginning to feel lost and frightened at the appalling prospect that she might suffer the same loss that Her Majesty had known. Richard was beginning to recover, that much she knew, the news given to Prudence by Dr Henry via Dr Maynard who considered that as the captain's sister, she had a right to know. In a way though, the knowledge that he was no longer insensible alarmed her even more, for if he was himself again, able to think again, why had he not written to her? Mrs Latimer guarded her home and her family with the ferocity of a she-cat, Celie was well aware of that, but there were servants surely who would be willing to post a letter for him? So why, why, had no letter come?

As she stood beside Ivy who was lifting her voice with the rest of the congregation in a hymn, the sound of which was no more than the humming of bees in Celie's stricken brain, her eyes were haunted and her face quite without expression. She could not face a future without Richard in it. Her heart hurt her sorely and constantly and the devastating truth of it was she did not know how to ease it. She didn't know what else to do. Her instinct was to drive up to Briar Lodge and hammer on the door until someone let her in. To battle past those who would bar her way and force herself up that splendidly wide staircase until she came to Richard's room, and Richard himself. To *see* him. To see the expression in his eyes which would tell her all she wanted to know. But if she so much as put a foot on the Latimer property, they would have her arrested for disturbing the peace. She had telephoned on more than one occasion, asking politely of the maid who answered if she might enquire after Captain Latimer's health and if a message might be passed on to him but each time she had done so, the voice at the other end had stated that she would fetch the mistress to the telephone, and who was she to say was calling?

In despair, Celie had replaced the mouthpiece on its hook. It seemed that whatever she did she came head on to some barrier which was insurmountable. She had expected that of course and had been prepared to wait patiently. No, *impatiently*, but wait nevertheless – until Richard had recovered sufficiently to get in touch with *her*, but now, eight weeks later, he had still not done so. The rosemary she had sent – how clever she had thought herself – had gone ignored, if he had received it, which was unlikely, she supposed. His letters to her during the past year, dozens of them, had been filled with his love, his longing to get home to her, his hopes and plans for the future, *their* future, even the last one which she had received the week before he returned home. Written, of course, several weeks earlier but, surely, his feelings for her would not change so drastically in such a short time? A shell splinter in his skull, Prudence had said, which had been removed and had healed. He was himself again, the doctor had told her, or would be when the bones in his legs had mended, so what possible explanation . . . Oh God . . . Oh, Lord God . . . if you are there . . . in this great place which is yours . . . please, oh, please . . . listen to my grieving heart . . .

She bowed her head, her eyes dry, no tears to shed now for it was long past the relief of those . . .

Richard . . .

Chapter Thirty-eight

The telegram was addressed to Miss C. Marlow and for a moment when it was held out to her by the telegraph boy who did his best to look suitably mournful, Celie could not for the life of her reach out to take it from him.

'It's a telegram, Ivy,' she said fearfully, staring down at the small neat envelope. She held it slightly away from her, her expression one of dread for she could stand no more, really she couldn't. It was almost the end of February and still she had not heard from Richard. He was progressing nicely, Dr Henry reported to her sister, and even Anne, Prudence's older sister, had been allowed in to see him for half an hour and had remarked to Prudence when she took afternoon tea with her, that he was looking more himself. Mother had been with her naturally, since, as Prudence was aware, she watched over her darling boy like a hawk, her devotion to him, her attention to his needs and the hours she spent each day fulfilling them, a constant source of wonder to her family. She had given up many of her social duties to be at his side, Anne informed Prudence, and had proved her devotion in a hundred ways. Richard was getting out a bit in a wheelchair, pushed by one of his nurses, trundled about the winter gardens well wrapped in the rugs his mother insisted upon, but he was very irritable, she reported, as was only natural for a man of his age and vigour. Longing to get back to his soldiering, she supposed, and the life he had known before he was wounded. A while yet before he could do that, of course, since he could not yet actually *walk*, but it was obvious that he was determined to resume his career as soon as possible.

Prudence had given an edited version of this conversation to Celie, watching the expressions which played across her friend's drawn face. Expressions ranging from hope and relief to the deepest despair.

'You'd best open it, lass,' Ivy said to her now, drawing her to the chair beside the fire in the kitchen. 'Pour us a cup of tea, Belle, there's a good girl,' for Celie gave the distinct impression that she might crash to the floor if Ivy didn't get her seated, and a nice cup of tea was a great steadier.

'You open it, Ivy, please. I can't imagine who it can be from,' since the only emergency which could affect Celie Marlow was up at Briar Lodge and they'd hardly be likely to let *her* know if one should occur.

Ivy put on her spectacles then peered at the envelope over the top of them which, in other circumstances, would have brought a smile to Celie's lips. Maudie was there, a crock of flour held to her chest, a spoon in her right hand as she prepared to measure out the ingredients for the pastry and the steak and kidney pie she meant to serve for their dinner. Belle was beside her in much the same way Celie had once hugged Jess Harper's side, ready, should she be asked, to fetch a bowl, another lump of lard, a smidgin more salt, or any of the requirements a budding cook such as Maudie might need. At the sink, a box beneath her feet to lift her to the necessary height, was Minnie, her arms up to the elbows in sudsy water, a pile of greasy pans on the draining board to the left, a pile of shining clean ones on her right. She peered anxiously over her shoulder, her hands still, her expression proclaiming that if there was anything, anything at all, she could do to ease the burden her beloved Miss Marlow was surely about to have laid on her, Miss Marlow had only to ask.

''Tis from War Office, lass.' The telegram rustled in Ivy's trembling hand.

'The War Office?'

'Aye . . . Oh, dear Lord . . .' Ivy put her hand to her mouth.

'What . . . for God's sake?'

'It's . . . Dan . . .'

'Dan . . . ?'

'Eeh, I'm that sorry, lovey . . .'

'Oh, God, Ivy . . . he's not . . . dead?'

'I'm that sorry, chuck,' Ivy said again, tears beginning to trickle across the pouched wrinkles beneath her eyes. She pulled off her spectacles, placed them slowly on the table and drew her handkerchief from her apron pocket. She blew her nose vigorously. From the doorway which led into the hall and through to the shop came the babble of voices that proclaimed that, as usual, business was brisk at Harper's. There was the constant tinkle of the bell above the shop door as customers came and went and the equally constant "ting" of the till as money poured into it. Dorcas's voice could be heard chatting to a customer, asking how their Freddie was.

Fanny, who had, until the death of her mother, worked in the kitchen at Briar Lodge and was now, with her brothers and sisters full grown, employed beside Dorcas in the shop, told someone she was looking a lot more herself today. The cheerful hubbub contrasted sharply with the frozen silence which reigned in the kitchen. No one dared move, afraid to smash the protective shield behind which Celie appeared to have withdrawn at Ivy's words. She just stared into Ivy's face, her own almost puzzled, her eyes enormous, the eyes of an animal which is already grievously wounded, the impact of this second blow more than she could bear.

'Drink your tea, lass,' Ivy commanded kindly and Celie obeyed like a well-brought-up child. Ivy studied her, knowing that soon, if this lass was not carefully watched, she would go under. She knew about the Captain, up at Briar Lodge, for how could such a thing, a thing which affected Celie so disastrously, be kept hidden? One man she loved tragically wounded, the other dead, and her expected to do no more than stand by and suffer it. Not a word from him in his fine uniform and his splendid background of wealth and privilege and it was tearing Celie Marlow into small, malevolently agonising pieces which, if not soon seen to, would destroy her. And now this. Ivy had not known Dan all that long, but a more likeable lad she'd never come across, and he'd thought the world of this blank-eyed, almost senseless girl . . . no, *woman* . . . who sat obediently sipping her tea. Why he'd married that strumpet had been a mystery to them all. No, that was not true, since she'd trapped him, him being an honourable chap, with the oldest trick in the world and he'd stood by her. Now she'd run off with that chap who'd had his hand up her skirt *long* before Dan had taken the Queen's shilling and poor Dan, likeable, warm-hearted Dan had gone and got himself killed and their Celie would take it hard. And why had he left Celie's name as next of kin she wondered, though come to think of it, with Madam gone off with her fancy man, who else's name could he have given?

'D'yer want ter go an' 'ave a lie down, lass?' she asked pityingly. 'You go up, we can manage, can't we?' looking round the circle of sympathetic faces.

'No . . . no, I'm all right, Ivy. I'd rather work . . .' which was all well and good, and quite understandable for Ivy had been the same when her Stanley had died, finding some consolation in working until she dropped. But what would them customers out there think when they saw the grey-faced, grey-eyed blankness of Celie's woebegone expression?

'Righto, my lass. Yer must do as yer think best but . . . well . . . I'd keep out o't' shop if I was you.'

Celie looked even more puzzled, then, just as though Ivy's words had triggered some mechanism in her brain which had allowed in the true measure of her loss, she put her face in her hands and began to weep. At once they all swarmed round her. Minnie leaped down from her perch and though she did not touch her beloved mistress, she hovered on the fringe of the compassionate group about her, her face distressed, her wet red hands wrung in the folds of her apron.

'There, there, lovey, have a good cry. He were a brave chap, were Dan, an' we'll all miss him, poor chap, won't we, Maudie?'

'Eeh, not half, Mrs Petty. He were always kind to me and Belle, weren't he, Belle?'

'He used to fetch me first strawberry . . .' Belle said tearfully and they all knew what she meant. She loved strawberries, did Belle.

Minnie hadn't known him so she could say nothing but if Miss Marlow wept for him, he must have been a good 'un, so she shed a tear or two for the brave young man who'd died fighting for his country.

The letter from Mr Pembroke came a week later. Daniel Smith had made a Will before he left Liverpool and he had named Cécilie Marlow as his sole beneficiary. It seemed that while Kate Smith had been spending her share of the profits made by Harper's, with all the abandonment of a careless child, her husband, without her knowledge, had been investing what he could, a little bit here and a little bit there, guided by Mr Pembroke and Mr Drake, mostly in shipping and businesses connected with it.

'Of course, if Mrs Smith was to know of it, there is no doubt she could contest this Will, Miss Marlow, but as her whereabouts are unknown and I for one, have no intention of looking for her, I can only follow the instructions of my client to the letter. There is enough here, if the shares are sold, to pay off all your debts and a little bit over besides . . . now, now, Miss Marlow . . . please don't cry. I cannot bear to see you so upset . . .'

'Dan . . .'

'. . . was a good and decent man . . .'

'. . . I know, Mr Pembroke. He was . . . like a brother to me. I loved him . . .'

'. . . and I think he loved you, Miss Marlow. That is why you must use what he has left you and not be troubled by thoughts of his wife.'

Celie raised her head sharply, her face awash with tears. Her eyes were a pale dove-grey, the tears she shed seeming to wash the colour from them. They hung on her long black lashes, great fat crystal droplets which she allowed to splash onto the charcoal-grey bodice of her three-quarter length cape. It was made of fine boxcloth, warm and smooth with a high, "Medici" collar of pale grey squirrel. Her skirt was the same colour as her cape, box-pleated at the back of the hem. The day was cold and blustery and her hair was tucked beneath a pale grey brimless toque, undecorated except for a band of grosgrain. She looked severe and in keeping with the general air of mourning for the old Queen, which many folk still assumed. And yet her beauty was ethereal, translucent, her skin as fine and pale as the petals of a white rose. Only in her mouth was there colour, a rich apricot ripeness which was startling in the pallor of her face.

'Oh, make no mistake, Mr Pembroke. I am not concerned with Kate Mossop, or I suppose I should call her Kate Smith, though even that was not her correct name. Dan was from Sweden and he was christened Anders Sigbjörn. It was Cook who gave him his English name. No, Kate Mossop can go to the devil for all I care, she had no right to Harper's and this money, this . . . that Dan left, came from Harper's. I shall sell the shares as you suggest and pay Mr Garside what I owe him, then . . .'

For a moment she wavered, her face beginning to crumple so tragically Mr Pembroke was ready to leap to his feet again, but she steadied, her hands clenched in her lap.

'Yes, Miss Marlow, then . . . ?' he asked delicately.

'I shall look for another shop. It's time Harper's expanded,' and besides, I have nothing else to occupy my time, her breaking heart whispered.

The little cavalcade moved slowly along the gravelled path, the wheels of the chair in which Richard slumped, crunching on the freshly raked stones. Nurse Atkinson pushed the wicker chair, naturally. On one side of it walked Mrs Latimer, warmly wrapped against the chill March wind in a full-length sac Inverness waterproof coat. It had a reversible tweed lining and a high collar, which met the small black hat she had pulled well down on her head. It was a sensible, no-nonsense outfit, which, along with her sensible no-nonsense black boots, was intended for the kind of outdoor pursuit one conducted in one's own garden. Her daughter, Margaret, who walked on the other side of the chair, was similarly dressed.

'Look, darling,' Mrs Latimer said to her son. 'The daffodil buds are just breaking into yellow. Aren't they delightful? And would you look at the primroses? I don't think I've ever seen them out so early. It's been so cold too.'

There was no answer from the man in the chair.

'The birds are busy as well,' Mrs Latimer continued, determinedly. 'What is that, there on that bush, Margaret?'

'A blackbird, Mother,' said her daughter dutifully.

'A blackbird, how splendid.'

'They are quite common, Mother.'

Mrs Latimer threw a disapproving look at her daughter, but did not allow her impertinence, nor her son's lack of interest, to deter her.

'And is that not a robin, just there, see, it's flown off into the trees.'

'I believe it was, Mother.'

'How nice it is that spring will soon be here. Really, it won't be long before we shall be having tea on the terrace. Another few weeks perhaps. And, I swear, if spring is as kind as it was last year we shall be giving garden parties before long. I saw Bennett rolling the tennis court only the other day. I know it will be a while before you can manage tennis, Richard, but Dr Maynard told me that if you continue to progress as you are doing, there is no reason why you should not be out of that wheelchair very soon.'

The nurse shot a startled look at her mistress, then on catching her eye, hastily looked away again. They walked along in silence for a while and though Nurse Atkinson actually pushed the wheelchair, Mrs Latimer kept a gloved, proprietorial hand on its handle. The path sloped gently down between the smooth lawns towards the pond. They had moved beyond the front of the house, beyond its clipped hedges and neat ornamental, geometrical flower-beds, its squared lawns and well-trimmed bushes sauntering down towards rougher ground and the stand of trees which surrounded the estate, just inside its high wall. To the left was a stretch of water where once Richard Latimer had escaped from Nanny Ella and romped with the sons of the odd-job man, the stableman and the coachman. Where once a tiny girl had stared in wonder at a tall, dark-haired boy whose brown eyes had flashed as he told them that *he* was to go for a soldier.

Just as they were about to turn back, for the path ended there and it was too much to expect Mrs Latimer to walk on rough grass, the gardener came out from among the trees, his lad at his heels. He had an axe over his shoulder and the lad carried a saw and they were deep in earnest conversation over some worrying thing which plainly showed on their open, country faces. They hesitated for a moment on seeing the small group, then, before Mrs Latimer could hurry her son away, for he was – in her opinion – not yet up to the rough presence of *workmen*, the gardener nodded respectfully and came straight on.

'Mornin', madam,' he said.' A grand day.'

'Indeed, Bennett,' doing her best to catch Nurse's attention, and when she failed, pulling at the wheelchair herself in an effort to turn it about.

''Ere, let me do that, madam,' Bennett said cheerfully, passing the axe to his lad. 'A bit awkward on this gravel, and can I say 'ow grand it is to see thi' out an' about, sir. Spring air'll do thi' a power o' good.'

'Thank . . . you . . .' Richard turned his head slowly, his eyes looking up into the concerned face of the man who had taken over Dan Smith's job seven years ago. Bennett had been Smith's "lad" himself then, and now he had a "lad" of his own. He was quite startled by the expression in the eyes of his employer's son. He could not even say what it was, he told his missus later. It reminded him of summat, he said to her, scratching his head, before tucking into the heaped plate of scouse she placed before him, but for the life of him he couldn't remember what it was. It was not until several days later that it came to him and then he never said nothing to his Betsy, since she'd think he was being a bit fanciful. Happen he was, but the eyes of the captain brought to mind those Jim Bennett had witnessed in the face of a leopard they'd seen on a day out at the Zoological Gardens. A leopard which paced backwards and forwards in a cage and stared unblinkingly into the faces which had stared back at *it*.

Well, it was a bit of a facer, but nothing to do with him, so he let go of the wheelchair and was just about to reach for his axe when he remembered the chrysanthemum bed. Mrs Latimer was most particular about her chrysanthemum bed and this was the month for sowing them. She liked certain colours and those she favoured must blend exactly with their neighbours, Alfred Salter which was pink with Adriane, a delicate cream. Cassy, orange and rose, with Bacchus, a rosy fawn and Defiance which was a fine white.

'Oh, madam,' he said politely, 'could I have a word?'

'What is it, Bennett? I am in rather a hurry.'

'It won't take but a minute, madam. It's about the chrystanths.'

'The chrystanths?' Mrs Latimer's head rose imperiously.

'The chrystanthemums, madam, I was wondering what colours you was wantin' . . .'

Mrs Latimer turned towards him, her tone icy. For several seconds her constant vigilance over her son was distracted. Nurse Atkinson, her own attention engaged by Mrs Latimer's haughty vexation at being accosted by her gardener when she was so obviously concerned with her son, watched her in fascination, for there was no doubt about it, when it came to being *regal*, there was none to touch Mrs Latimer.

'Really, Bennett, could you not have chosen a more convenient moment to discuss the garden? It is cold and my son has been out for the best part of half an hour.'

She was infuriated, not only by Bennett's inappropriate timing, but by his temerity and her own failure to avoid it, in approaching Richard, the first servant to do so – apart from the closely supervised men who carried him down the stairs since she had brought him home.

'Come and see me in an hour and bring the gardening record book with you. We will discuss it then.'

'Very well, madam.' Bennett touched his cap and stepped back, watching as the small cavalcade moved on. He muttered something under his breath but when his "lad" said 'Pardon, Mr Bennett,' he did not repeat it.

'I think I'll just go and . . . I thought I might . . .' Margaret Latimer stood in the hall at the top of the stairs whilst her mother, who had just supervised the carrying up of her son to his room by Bertie Ash and Tom Ellis, both of whom worked about the stables and workshed, unbuttoned her coat and prepared to move into her own room.

Margaret hovered hesitantly, her young face rosy, her eyes inclined to look anywhere but at her mother, and at once Phyllis Latimer turned from the door which she had just opened and looked at her daughter with a steady, all-seeing eye which she had directed at her children and husband for over thirty years.

'Yes, dear?' Her hands rose to remove the pins from her hat, then took the hat from her head. She smiled, moving away from the door and towards her daughter. Her manner was deceivingly benign.

'Well, that walk was . . . very short . . . I thought I might . . .' Margaret's voice stumbled on and all the while her face became rosier and rosier and for some reason, she plunged her right hand deep into the pocket of her full coat.

'What did you think, Margaret? That you might walk down to the nearest post box. Is that what you thought?'

Margaret's rosy face drained of every drop of colour and she sagged a little against the newel post at the top of the stairs. How did she *know*? How did her mother *always* know, her agonised mind asked, but despite her fear and despair for her brother, she gamely struggled on.

'I don't know what you mean, Mother. I thought I might take a turn about the lake and then . . .' *inspiration* '. . . have a look at old Mr Ash. He's not . . . well and . . . and Bennett was telling me . . .'

'When did you speak to Bennett, my dear?'

'Why . . . it was . . . just today . . .'

'But you have not been out today, Margaret. You and Katherine have been with me all morning. We lunched together and then took Richard out together. Why are you lying to me, Margaret?'

'Mother, please! How could you accuse me . . . ?'

'Do you think I don't know when one of my own children is telling lies, Margaret? Guilt is written all over your face. Now then, give me what you have in your pocket and no more will be said about it.'

Phyllis Latimer moved implacably closer to her daughter, who was in imminent danger of falling backwards down the stairs.

'There is nothing, Mother. Richard gave me nothing,' and she began to weep.

'I said nothing about Richard, Margaret. Nor did I suggest

he had given you anything. You did that, so give me the letter if you please . . .'

'Oh, Mother, won't you let me post it for him, please? He loves her so much . . . so much . . .'

'Don't be more stupid than you really are, girl. A stupid silly girl who knows nothing of life, nor what it means to do one's duty, as one has been brought up to it. Have you learned nothing in your eighteen years, Margaret? This woman will ruin your brother. His life, his career, his position in society . . .'

Phyllis could feel her control beginning to slip, as only the girl who had once been her scullery maid could make it slip and she straightened and raised her head.

'Richard is going through a phase that all young men go through, my dear. They like to . . .'

'He is thirty-two, Mother. Surely he can no longer be called a *young* man in that sense.'

'That will do, Margaret. Allow me to know what is best for my son, as your father and I know what is best for all of you. Four of my children have made splendid marriages, as will you and Katherine, and in time, Richard will meet some suitable young lady. A lady of his own class and all this will be forgotten.'

'But Mother, you have *seen* him. He is . . . he is not recovering . . .'

'*Not recovering*! How dare you say that to me, you wicked girl. He has had the best care that is available. The constant attention of two nurses and I myself have . . .'

'But he is fretting for her.'

'Don't be so ridiculous, Margaret. But then I suppose young girls like yourself are impressionable and easily . . .'

'I'm not *blind*, Mother.'

'*That is enough*, Margaret. Now give me that letter and go to your room. I will speak to your father and you will be dealt with as I think appropriate. In fact, it might be a good idea if you went to stay for a week or two with your Aunt Maud in Scarborough . . .'

A very good idea, her shrewd brain whispered, as her daughter, beaten at last, her brief defiance over, handed her the crumpled envelope in her pocket. The best thing would be for the girl to go away, and as soon as possible. It might look strange if Margaret was suddenly denied access to her brother, who would undeniably question her on the whereabouts of the letter, but if she were to go away, if those concerned were to be informed that she needed a breath of sea air, young girls were known to be peaky at times . . . Mr Latimer would back her up and then in a week or two, by April when Richard could no longer be held back . . .

For a moment, her strong will wavered, for how was she to convince not only her husband, the two nurses, and the doctor who was urging her to let Richard *stand up* . . . *walk* . . . *leave his room* . . . that he was not yet ready for it? But for the weakness left by his long inactivity, his legs were completely healed. She needed time, more time to make absolutely sure that Richard was completely and irrevocably separated from the madness of his relationship with that . . . that woman. It was only Richard's own deep and depressing fretting . . . yes, Margaret was right . . . he was fretting, a state caused by the apparent unconcern and desertion of Celie Marlow, that was holding him back, allowing him to be manipulated, but soon he would be up and about and capable of getting downstairs to the telephone. Of searching out the woman he professed to love and all her own efforts to keep them apart all these months would be for nothing. Worse, Richard would discover her own . . . well, Phyllis Latimer called it protective devotion, but he would probably see it as interference, and might not the discovery turn him against her for ever? Richard was not a weak man and in normal circumstances, she would have little control over him and the day would soon come when what control she had now would be ended. Before that day came she must ensure that Celie Marlow and her son were separated for ever.

Watching her daughter for a moment, as she listlessly trailed up the wide hallway to her own room, Phyllis Latimer tore off her coat, threw it hurriedly into her own bedroom, followed by her hat, caring not where they landed. She smoothed back her hair and then moved gracefully in the direction of her son's room. When she opened the door, he turned eagerly from the chair by the window in which he was sitting and she saw that for the first time since he had come home, he had a flush of colour beneath his skin. His dark eyes, such a lovely toffee brown, she had always thought, glowed for a moment, then, on seeing who it was in the doorway, he turned away abruptly, staring out again into the garden.

Sister Andrews, who had risen from her chair by the fire, as her employer entered, nodded her capped head respectfully. Phyllis Latimer smiled in her direction.

'Would you leave us alone, for a few moments, Sister,' she said sweetly. 'I would like to have a private word with my son.'

'Of course, madam.'

'Thank you. I'll call you when we're done.'

When the door closed on the nurse, Phyllis moved slowly across the room and sat down in the chair which faced her son, then, leaning forward she held out the crumpled letter she had taken from her daughter. It lay on the palm of her hand, Celie Marlow's name and address plainly in view. Her face was unutterably sad and when, after staring at it in shock, her son looked up into her face, she shook her head slowly as though in a state of deepest puzzlement.

'Oh, Richard, Richard.' Her voice was low and filled with compassion. 'Richard, how could you?'

Richard Latimer slowly sat up, abandoning the indifferent lounging posture in which he had been ever since they had got him out of bed. His face was thunderstruck and it seemed he could not speak.

'Richard, I am quite, quite, devastated. Have you the slightest idea how distressing it is for a mother to learn that her son does not trust her? That he cannot find it in his heart to confide in her? That he goes behind her back, makes his own sister a party to this . . . this deception, when all he had to do was tell the truth.'

'The truth . . . but . . . you cannot . . . you dislike the very idea of Celie . . .'

'My darling, I will be honest with you. This young woman on whom, it seems, you have bestowed your affection, is not the one I would have chosen for you, but do you really think that I would see my son . . . fade away before my eyes when the answer to his recovery is so close to hand?'

Richard Latimer came alive before her eyes. The transformation was quite incredible and for a moment, she was convinced he was about to leap up on his weak legs and make a dash for the door, presumably in search of that . . . that little madam who had him so cruelly in her clutches. His gaze was strong and vibrant, a vital glow in it she had not seen since before he went to Africa. He had begun to smile, his firm mouth curving in delight and some other emotions she could not recognise.

'Mother, do you really mean it? You would have no objection to . . . God in Heaven, I can't believe it. All these weeks I've been looking for some way to get in touch with her . . . I don't even know if she's aware that I'm home . . . I wrote, of course, before I was wounded, but since then I've been in a fog and then, when I came out of it, I knew you . . . you did not approve of her . . . she was . . . she worked in the house and then there was the incident of Anne's wedding . . . and . . . oh, all the rest of the damned nonsense . . .'

'Richard, Richard darling . . .' His mother laughed gaily. '. . . slow down, please, I am in a state of such confusion. You are making no sense. I only know it is worth . . . anything to see the change in you. We have been so worried that you were not picking up as you should. Now I know why I can do something about it. I don't like the idea of you and . . . Miss Marlow, you know that . . .' She had to stand up, turn away for a moment, in case her son should see the loathing in her face, but he was so overcome with joy, he was blind to it.

'. . . but if she is necessary to your complete recovery, then I have no alternative but to accept it.'

She turned back to him, touching his flushed cheek, disconcerted momentarily by the change in him, but her gaze did not falter.

'So, I shall post this for you at once, unless you want to write another, explaining . . .'

His expression became confused for a second or two.

'I have written . . . now you must not blame Sister

Andrews for it, Mother. I made her post them, but they were only very short and perhaps Celie did not understand, so if you will give me half an hour, I'll write another, or perhaps . . .' His face glowed up into hers '. . . perhaps you might telephone her, at Harper's. Invite her . . . beg her to come, please Mother . . . Dear God, why didn't I tell you before? . . . all these weeks . . .'

'Now Richard, don't let us trouble ourselves with what is done. The past is over and we must look forward to the future. You write your letter. I think that would be best, and then you can tell her how it has been in your own words. I will be back shortly and I will personally post it for you. Tell no one though, dearest. It will be *our* secret. Your father . . . well, I'm afraid I have had rather a lot to say against Miss Marlow, *no*,' she held up her hand imperiously. 'I felt I had a right to be aggrieved when my servants left to follow her . . .'

Richard shuffled uncomfortably in his chair, but he had no wish to antagonise his mother just when it seemed, amazingly, that she had mellowed.

'Mother, she did not intentionally . . .'

'I realise that now, darling, but just the same, until everything is settled, let us keep this between the two of us.'

Richard Latimer did not care if his mother demanded he swing from the electric light and gibber like a monkey, just as long as, finally, she was prepared to soften on the matter of his love for Celie Marlow.

He leaned back in his chair and began to daydream.

Chapter Thirty-nine

'Darling, you know I would send at once if there was any news. Anne saw him last week and said he was looking considerably better. In fact she was quite amazed at the change in him. Bright and cheerful, she said, and talking about getting downstairs on sticks, although apparently Mother pooh-poohed that. He can stand on his own and the doctor says he will soon be walking about the bedroom. Now that he is recovering so well, the doctor admitted to Mother and she told Anne, that in the beginning, there was some doubt that he would ever walk again. Both his legs were fractured, but in more than one place, and it's only thanks to the cleverness of the army doctor who attended to him immediately after the ambush, that they have healed so true. Two of the men carry him downstairs and he is pushed in a . . . oh, Celie . . . darling, don't . . . don't . . . I'm sorry . . . I shouldn't tell you all this when . . . but I thought you'd be glad he's doing so well . . .'

'I *am*, Pru . . . Dear God, d'you think I'd want him to remain an invalid all his life, just so that I can tell myself that, had he recovered, he would have come to me? But don't you see, *that* is what has kept me . . . steady during these dreadful months, the hope, the belief that, as soon as he was well enough, he would . . . send word, but now he is better, and still he does not write. Dammit, do you think I don't know how his mother would guard him, do her best to keep us apart? She proved that at the beginning when she had me arrested and thrown into prison. I have telephoned a score of times but I can't get past that maid. Oh, I know it's not her fault. She is only doing what she has been ordered and of course, my letters will have been intercepted, but there is nothing to stop *him* contacting me. Doesn't he know how *frantic* I am? Has he no heart, Prudence, that brother of yours? Does this . . .' twisting the heavy signet ring Richard had given her round and round on her finger,' does it mean nothing to him? The fortnight we had in Ambleside . . . Oh, God . . . he might have left me with a child but he sailed away without a backward glance and . . .'

'*Celie*, that's not fair and you know it. He had no choice but to go. He was a soldier and soldiers must obey orders. And as for going without a backward glance, that is nonsense. He has written to you the whole time he was away, loving letters, from what you tell me, speaking of your marriage and your future together. You talk as though you suspected him of deserting you, of being glad of the excuse to . . . to . . .'

Celie stood up and flung herself despairingly across Prudence's untidy drawing room, stepping over the two dogs, the crawling child, a dozen toys, a newspaper Prudence had been reading when she arrived and which she had crumpled carelessly beside her chair, all of them strewn in that haphazard casual homeliness that Prudence created in her life. Celie stared blindly from the window to the bright sunlit garden beyond. Daffodils, wild and dancing, were scattered about the broad stretch of lawn and green leaf buds hazed the branches of the trees which edged the perimeter of the garden. Primroses grew thickly between them and two wall butterflies fluttered crazily as though drunk with spring against the wall which separated this part of the garden from the vegetable plot. The old gardener plodded slowly through the gate which was let into the wall, pausing, a hand in the small of his back as though to ease an ache there. A sparrow darted low over the trees making towards its nest and Celie watched its flight.

Her voice was dull and lifeless.

'I'm sorry Pru, but I cannot but begin to have doubts. It's almost May, he has been home for five months and in all that time he has made no attempt to . . . Oh, God, wouldn't you begin to wonder if he was . . .'

'Dallying with you? Is that what you're trying to say?'

'He's done it before, Prudence.'

'No.'

'*Yes*! Kissed me and gone away and not come back.'

'But he was . . .'

'What? What excuse are you going to make for him this time?'

'Don't, darling. Don't do this to yourself. Have faith in him. Give him a little more time. Now that he is so much better he will come to you . . .'

'I wish I could believe that, Prudence. The thing is, even if he does, can I forgive him for these months he has made me . . . suffer? I know, at the beginning, he was not able to write, or even speak, but when his head healed and he could . . . when he was . . . Oh, God . . . we could go on like this forever, Prudence. Debating and wondering and never getting anywhere and I swear I'll go mad with it. So let's talk about something else. How are *you*? How is it with you and the baby? What does Dr Henry say?'

Celie swung back from the window, her face resolutely bright. As the day was warm she had put on a soft summer gown of ivory muslin, very pretty and feminine, as though in desperation at her own unhappiness she had thrown off the drab of mourning and the businesslike severity of the outfit she wore in the shop. The dress had yards of ruching round the full hem, edged with pale pink satin ribbon. The bodice was pin-tucked, the neck high, the sleeves tight to the wrist, except above the elbow where they were full. She wore a hat on her high piled hair, wide-brimmed and pretty, massed with silk roses of the palest pink and ivory on the crown. Though she was thin the ruching on the bodice hid the almost childlike bud of her breasts. She seated herself on the chair opposite Prudence and began to sip her cold tea with great determination.

'Let me get you some fresh tea.'

'No, I don't really want this. Now then answer my question.'

'Which one?'

'You know very well, which one.'

'I am fine. The baby is fine but I am to rest.'

'Then why aren't you?'

'I have only just this moment got out of my bed, Celie Marlow, so don't you start on me. I have enough with Jethro . . .'

'He loves you, Prudence,' and Celie bent her head over her teacup in a moment of deepest anguish, then raised it again, a smile as lovely and false as the flowers on her hat and Prudence watched her sadly.

'Now ask me about Harper's,' she demanded of her when she had regained her composure.

'Tell me about Harper's,' Prudence asked obediently.

'I think I have found a place.'

Prudence leaned forward eagerly. The child on the floor reached for the dog, sinking her baby hands into the retriever's soft fur, clinging on as she hauled herself up onto the animal's back and the dog, after lifting her head resignedly to watch her, lay down again with a deep sigh. Trixie stood up and wandered across to them, sniffing at the little girl, nudging her in the hope of a game and the child squealed, flinging a loving arm round the second animal's neck.

'Go on, then, where is it?' Prudence ignored her daughter's play, trusting the two dogs implicitly.

'Between Stanley Park and Newsham Park on the Parade, there's a small shopping area already there. The usual thing. A chemist, a greengrocer, butcher, et cetera and a confectioner who is ready to retire. There's also an empty shop next to the confectioner, and next to that on the corner of Prospect Drive, a large house. Well, not as large as this, of course, but big enough for my purpose.'

'Which is?'

'To open a proper restaurant.'

'Of course. A logical step but don't you think . . .' Prudence bit the words back, then sighed deeply.

'Don't I think . . . what?'

'Nothing really.'

'Say what you were going to say, Prudence.'

Prudence took a deep breath. 'Don't you think you had . . . it would be wise to . . . well . . .'

'Don't dither, Pru. For goodness sake spit it out.'

'If Richard . . . *when* Richard is completely recovered, and you and he are . . . Oh Celie, please darling, I really believe he will come for you, so won't you . . . ?'

'Wait? Is that what you would have me do? Hang around . . .'

'You *love* him, Celie. Is it too much to . . . ?'

Celie's voice was passionate. 'I must do *something*, Prudence. I have worked all my life. Ever since I was a small child. It's the only thing I know and . . . Prudence, it's . . . I'm good at what I do. It . . . makes me . . .' She hung her head in great pain, then put out her hand to stop Prudence who would have got up to her. 'It gives me . . . worth . . . value . . . when I most need it.'

'Celie, don't say that. Good God, woman, nobody values you more than I do. You are my dearest friend. Do you think I will ever forget what you did for me when Grace was born? I love you. After Jethro and my child, you are the dearest thing in the world to me, and your staff are devoted to you, you know that. Don't . . . please . . . because of what has happened . . . recently . . . Dan loved you too and if it had not been for that damned woman he married . . .'

'He would have married *me*, is that what you are saying . . . ?' but Celie had straightened her back and lifted her head, beginning to smile. 'Well, we shall never know, poor dear Dan. At least he has given me the means to get on with my life. Mr Pembroke is making an offer on the properties for me and I shall need another mortgage. Mr Drake says there will be no problems there. Harper's is doing well and I must say I seem to have no trouble getting staff.'

'I told you, they all love you, darling.'

'Well, I don't know about that, Pru, but when I last saw Mrs Wilson, you remember my friend from Great George Square? she begged me to consider her for manager of the restaurant. "Catering to folks' appetites is the same whatever the class of establishment," she told me and, of course, she is right. Maudie is rapidly becoming capable of running Harper's on the Boulevard and Dorcas can be put in charge of the second branch on the Parade whilst I cook at . . . now what am I to call it, Pru, this new venture of mine?'

'Well, there is only one name you can give it, surely.'

'Oh yes, and what is that?' Celie leaned forward.

'You have said it yourself, darling. You already have Harper's on the Boulevard, so what else can your second shop be called but "Harper's on the Parade"?'

Celie's face lit up joyfully and she smiled a smile which was for the moment as natural and lively as the sunshine falling on the garden.

'Of course, that's right. Harper's on the Parade. It sounds wonderful. Wait till I tell Ivy and the girls.'

She beamed at her friend, her mind, thankfully, absorbed with her new venture; on cash flow and mortgages, on alterations and colour schemes, on staff and menus and transport problems, on the marvel of the name for the restaurant and Prudence's cleverness in thinking of it, while up in his room at Briar Lodge Richard Latimer stared moodily, his chin in his hand, into the depth of the crackling fire.

'Is my mother at home, Sister?' he asked, turning abruptly to the nurse who sat opposite him.

Sister Andrews was darning a sock, and her face was placid and rosy in the fire's glow. The sun shone beyond the window and across the lawns bobbed the great golden trumpets of hundreds of daffodils, but the bedroom was as cosy as a hothouse. Sister Andrews had gained some weight in the months she had looked after the captain, particularly in the last few weeks, for in a sudden burst of something she could not name, her patient had simply *bounded* towards recovery and she now had little to do. He insisted on dressing himself, going to great lengths of acrobatic skill, flinging himself on the bed, whilst he struggled into his trousers, perching himself on a kitchen stool of all things, whilst he shaved.

'I'll employ a valet,' his mother had said, but he wouldn't hear of it, saying the more exercise he had, the quicker he would recover. Talk about a miracle, and he'd even stopped begging Sister to write to Miss Celie Marlow, so what was she to make of that, she asked herself. He and his mother got on like a house on fire now, which was another marvel and the only thing that bothered Sister Andrews was what *she* would do, for there was no doubt that very soon she would no longer be needed. Nurse Atkinson had already gone. A splendid job this had been, but still it was good to see the captain almost recovered.

'I don't know, sir,' in answer to his question. 'Would you like me to find out?'

'Please, Sister. Ring the bell and ask Ellen to fetch her if she is.'

Phyllis Latimer was in her son's room within five minutes, dismissing the nurse, telling her kindly to go and get herself a cup of tea. They had all seen her son now. Ellen and Mabel, Molly and Kitty, bringing his trays up, no doubt having innocent little conversations with him, pleased that he was himself again and ready to wink at them, in that audacious way he had once had. Cheerful he was now, with a smile for them all, shuffling about on his sticks, itching to get downstairs on them he told them all, not saying why, of course, since that was a secret between himself and his mother, who was doing everything in her power to fetch her son's love to him she told him. The only thing nagging him, and with increasing urgency, was the mystery of why she did not come.

'Mother,' he said without preamble, 'I want you to call two of the men to carry me down to the telephone. It's been a fortnight now and there is still no word from Celie. I don't know why I didn't think of it before. I have written five times and . . . well, I can stand it no longer . . .'

'Darling, don't upset yourself. You have been doing so well . . .'

'Now, Mother, if you don't mind.'

Suddenly the thought of speaking to her, of hearing Celie's voice, filled him with a terrible doubt. He had been home for nearly six months and in all that time she had not, as far as he knew, even enquired of him. He had written and written, begging her to come, telling her over and over again how much he loved and needed her. He was getting better. He would . . . he *could* . . . *longed* to . . . love her again, as he had loved her in the deep and richly lavender-scented bed in the cottage at Ambleside. The very idea of holding her in his arms, perhaps sitting her on his lap since he could not stand

for long, caused him to swell and throb in the dark area at
the pit of his belly. A joy to him, that was, for it meant that
in *that* department at least, he was a man again, and soon he
would walk properly, run, run to her and . . . Jesus . . . why
hadn't she answered his letters?

'Of course, Richard. I'll go at once. You're right, I don't
know why we didn't think of it before. Perhaps she'll be
more . . .'

'More what, Mother?' His face anxious enough to start
with took on an expression which could only be described
as "lost", like a child who had misplaced his mother's hand
and is terrified by it. Her son was a soldier, a brave soldier
mentioned in despatches, a gallant gentleman, a humorous,
strong-minded man, but the thought, the appalling thought
that the woman he loved might no longer love him, weakened
him until he was reduced to the state of a small boy still in the
nursery.

'Well, I have to say this, Richard, but . . . well she has
not answered your letters.' She did her utmost to appear
saddened.

He looked so wretched that for a moment Phyllis's fierce
heart was strangely troubled, then she pulled herself together,
telling herself it was for his own good. She already had her eye
on the twenty-year-old daughter of an acquaintance of hers,
a lady, of course, of impeccable breeding, a good dowry and
quite pretty too. As soon as Richard was downstairs, she
would have a small celebratory dinner party and . . .

'Mother . . . please . . . I must know.' Her son's harsh
voice interrupted her pleasant thoughts and she moved
forward to place a compassionate hand on his shoulder.

'I'll do it myself, darling. I'll telephone her at . . . where is
it . . . ?' A faint flicker of distaste crossed her face, but he
did not appear to notice it.

'It's called Harper's. Here is the telephone number,'
eagerly handing her a scrap of crumpled paper he had ready.
'Tell her . . . ask her . . .'

'I know exactly what to say, darling. I won't tell whoever
answers it who is calling. I don't want her to . . . well, when
she hears the name . . .'

'Why should the name of Latimer . . . ?'

'Oh, I am sure it won't, darling, after all she's not to know that . . .'

'What for God's sake? Are you saying that she would not come to the telephone if she thought it was me? Is that what you're saying?'

'Of course not, Richard, don't be silly, but . . .' She stood up, then with a last sorrowing look in her son's direction she moved towards the door.

'Be quick, Mother . . .'

'I will, darling.'

She was back in five minutes and his face when he turned to her was a confusion of hope and despair, of eagerness to hear what she was to tell him and a dreadful terror that he could not bear it when she did.

She smiled. 'The person who answered the telephone said Miss Marlow was not at home, darling, but she promised to give her your message – I particularly mentioned your name – and would make sure that Miss Marlow telephoned you the moment she got back. Shall I ask the men to carry you downstairs, so that you might be near to the machine when it rings?'

'Please Mother. Did the person say . . . how long . . . ?'

'No, darling, I'm afraid not, but you can sit in the drawing room. What a lovely surprise for your father when he comes home, to find you there, I mean. And then, if you are up to it, you might dine with us. Oh, Richard, how lovely after all these months to be getting back to normal at last. To have you back at the dinner table with your family, won't that be splendid?'

'Yes . . .'

'Now then, I'll ring for Ellen and tell her to fetch Bennett and Ash.'

'Thank you, Mother.'

'We won't bother to dress, not tonight. It will be enough for you without that. Aah, I think that's your father's carriage in the drive. I'll just go down and . . . will you be all right until the men come, darling?'

'Perfectly, thank you, Mother.' His face was wooden and

so was his voice and he wondered later, when he lay in
his bed, how he had known, even then, that she would
not ring back. It was not surprising really, he supposed.
She had known all these months . . . Oh Christ . . . spare
him . . . that he was home. She was friendly with Prudence,
who though she was ostracised by her family, would certainly
know of the seriousness of his wounds and his slow recovery
and would have told Celie. Even if his letter . . . *all* of them,
a jeering voice in his head said . . . had gone astray, there was
simply no way that Celie Marlow could have been unaware of
his situation and a woman in love, a woman who truly loves
a man, will let nothing deter her from getting to him. Hell
and high water she would brave in her need to be with him
knowing *his* need to *have* her with him and Celie, Cécilie
Marlow, whom he had loved, who had been the centre of
his heart, his very heartbeat, the most precious thing in the
world to him, had not come. He did not know why. He did not
want to know. Another man . . . No! Jesus . . . Sweet Christ
. . . not another man taking . . . what was his . . . *had* been
his . . . He could not stand it . . . he could not cope with the
images which crowded his mind. Sweet Jesus Christ, rather
he had died of his wounds than this . . . How was he to tear
her from his mind and his heart where she had rested for so
long . . . ?

The small flame which had kept him warm, kept him alive all
these months shrivelled in him then and though his body was
alive, his heart died and as it deadened, the pain in him was
searing. He sat in his chair, in the window, staring lifelessly
out into the blackness of the garden, in which, since he had
been home, he had come to know every blade of grass, every
leaf, every tiny piece of stone on the gravel pathways. The
nurse had gone, knowing of her patient's need to be alone,
knowing her work was done now. Knowing his *mother's* work
was done and Richard Latimer faced the future ahead of him
with the realisation and acceptance that Celie Marlow would
not share it with him.

For a moment, he allowed her back. That lovely laughing
innocent girl who, it seemed, no longer cared about Richard
Latimer. A girl she had been, a sweet untouched girl, their

first night together had proved that and it was his body which had turned hers into that of a woman. She had given herself to him unashamedly, gloriously, and taken him into herself with a passion of love he had found overwhelming in its beauty. A woman in love, he had been sure of it then, a woman with a space to fill and he, as the man who loved her, had filled it making their two bodies one. There had been no shyness. Shy she had been on that day he had first seen her in the shaft of sunlight which filled his parents' hall. A softness, a gentleness which had without his knowing it, appealed strongly to his own maleness, holding him fast with it, though he had done his best to escape. A softness, a delicacy, and yet there had been something strong, a deceptive strength which had not been immediately apparent in the petal-like fineness of her smooth skin, the grey velvet lustre of her wide eyes, the frailty of her slender bones. A firmness to her small jaw and a resolute curving of her mouth, the way she held her head and her shoulders, a mature woman's strength which had grown and developed in the years he had known her.

And now, it seemed, she had plans for her own life and they did not include . . . a cripple . . . No! . . . Jesus, no . . . the Celie he had known would not think that way, would not desert a man in his need . . . God in heaven . . . but she *had*, she *had*. She no longer wanted anything to do with him. Her indifference to his letters, the telephone call today. Celie . . . *Celie* . . .

He began to weep then, burying his face in his hands, the tears dripping through his fingers, and running down his wrists, his mind torn with the pain of his grief, rocking back and forth in his chair by the window.

'Celie . . . what am I to do without you, Celie?' he whispered and in her bedroom above the shop known as "Harper's on the Boulevard" where she sat before the mirror brushing her hair, Celie lifted her head, turning it slowly as she listened to something she thought she had heard then after a moment or so, when it was not repeated, she resumed the long strokes with her brush.

Two weeks later Prudence Garside gave birth to a fine boy. The delivery was short and easy and she laughed with her friend, Celie Marlow, who was cradling the child, saying she was getting the hang of it now and would Celie please give the boy to the nurse to be washed and fetch her one of those delicious custard tarts she was so clever at making.

'A bowl of nourishing broth first, I think, Mrs Garside,' the nurse said disapprovingly, doing her best to prevent Mr Garside from gathering his wife into his arms and indeed she said privately later to her friend who was also a nurse, from climbing into the bed with her! It had taken all her powers, and Dr Henry's, to keep the distraught gentleman from his wife's bedroom during the birth, which mercifully had been short, not like the last one, she had heard, and only the presence of Miss Marlow, who was a sensible sort of a woman despite her frail loveliness, and who promised to let him know how Mrs Garside was *every* five minutes, had quietened him. He sat on a chair directly outside the room and refused to be budged and now would you look at him, clutching at his wife and *her* not cleaned up yet, kissing her for all to see and scarcely glancing at his son who caterwauled in Miss Marlow's arms.

'Broth! *Broth*! I could eat a horse, and the man who rides him, Celie. Won't you go down to the kitchen and see what Cook has tucked away in the pantry and which she is bound to be saving for the servants' supper? Something succulent and *filling* . . .'

'*Mrs Garside*, please! You're in no fit state to eat . . .'

'Nonsense, Nurse, I have just worked hard and it has given me an appetite. Celie, darling, you know what I like. See what you can do for me, will you? And you, Jethro Garside, are you not going to have a look at the result of your endeavours of nine months ago? You have a son . . . Oh, Nurse, do forgive me, I have shocked you, and Dr Henry, but I feel so well after the last time, I was . . .'

For a moment Prudence's face became serious.

'I was afraid you see, but now . . .' She beamed round the room, her well-being encompassing them all, her beloved husband, the nurse, the good doctor, her good friend, her fine son and when he was put in her arms, and with her husband's arms about them both, nobody noticed the expression on

Celie's face when she slipped from the room, promising to bring Prudence a tray of something special.

She leaned against the wall outside the bedroom, doing her best to control the violent fit of trembling which shook her slight frame. Her arms gripped one another across her breast, her hands clutching at her forearms, her head bent in an excess of grief which threatened to have her over. She pressed her back against the wall, willing herself not to fall, not to slide down it until she crouched on the floor, her hands over her ears to prevent herself from hearing her world break into pieces. Fragments of words, sentences, slid through her anguished mind. Where has he gone? . . . my love . . . he was my whole life . . . what am I to do without him? . . . what? . . . I will never see him again . . . He has fallen out of my life, ripping a ragged hole in it which will never mend . . . Oh, God in Heaven . . . to see Pru's happiness . . .

The pain inside her was terrible and it was getting worse with every bitter moment of knowing he no longer loved her. Her life was draining away and there was nothing . . . nothing she cared about any more. She felt as though she was full of holes and her life was leaking out of her and yet she must . . . *must go on*. All she wanted to do was crawl away to some secret place where no one could find her, where no one could seek her out and force her to live on. You have your work, they would say. You have a business, people who are dependent on you. You have friends who love you, they would say. Bear up, it will become easier. You will find comfort . . . another man . . . babies, like Pru's . . . and it was not true, none of it. A man's rich brown eyes, his sun-darkened face kept getting between her and the hope she did her best to nourish. An arresting face, aggressive at times, vigorous, grave and serious, grave until the humour melted the gravity and the smile, the audacious grin broke through . . .

'Miss Marlow . . . Oh, dear, are you all right, miss?' an anxious voice asked her. There was a gentle touch on her arm and when she flinched, turning violently from it, Nora gasped beside her.

'Oh, Miss Marlow . . . don't tell me she's . . . Oh, please miss . . . Mrs Garside's not took bad is she?'

She thinks I'm sorrowing for Prudence. Her mind, clearing slowly began to function on a near-normal level and with a great effort she let go of herself though she kept her back to the wall. Lifting her head, dry-eyed for no matter how it was needed, she could not cry for Richard, she did her best to smile into Nora's appalled face.

'No. Oh, no, Nora, Mrs Garside has a son. A fine boy . . . both are well. I was . . . just so relieved after the last time.'

Nora's face beamed and she put her hands to her cheeks.

'Oh, Miss Marlow, that's grand, grand! They were so worried in the kitchen. Go an' see, they said, so I just slipped up . . . Oh, wait until I tell them . . .'

She hesitated. 'Is it all right, miss, if I was to run down . . .'

'Of course, Nora, I'll follow in a minute. Mrs Garside is asking for something to eat . . .'

And if I can do nothing else with my life I can provide people with something to eat!

Chapter Forty

The table looked splendid and Mrs Latimer praised the servants as she inspected it before her guests arrived. Well, Richard's guests really for this dinner party was in his honour. No expense, nor effort, had been spared and the formal table setting was a work of art. Of course, the employing of a butler, and not before time, in her opinion, had made all the difference to the entertaining the Latimers engaged in, for there was no doubt Williams had transformed the maidservants into positive wonders of self-effacing efficiency and he ran the household like a well-oiled clock, just as he would run this dinner party which was to mean so much to Phyllis Latimer.

The dining room was bathed in a subdued glow from the lamps which were spaced down the length of the table and from the cherry logs burning in the huge marble fireplace. A separate table had been set at the end of the room, just inside the door, for the service of dessert, and already the maids had placed there silver gilt compotes and tazzas piled into an elegant pyramid of the fruits grown in the Latimer hothouses, nectarines and peaches, figs and many more, all cascading with lustrous green and black grapes.

The main table, naturally, was set with the Latimer Crown Derby ware and silver cutlery, eighteen places, each flanked with an array of gleaming knives, forks and spoons, four delicate crystal wine glasses and pristine napery, each napkin folded and arranged in wings about a fresh rose in its centre. There were hothouse roses decorating the length of the table between each lamp and swathed at its four corners in trails of fern and ivy. There was no need of name places, of course, since Williams knew exactly where everyone was to sit, having had impressed on him that Miss Madeline Hammond would be placed on Mr Latimer's left hand and on her other side, the guest of honour, her son Captain Richard Latimer.

Phyllis Latimer sighed in satisfaction, gently touching with a careful fingertip, the exquisite finger bowls set on their own plates, each one containing water scented with orange and rose and carrying a tiny fleet of pink rose petals on its surface. The light from the dancing flames of the fire caught the shimmer of silver and glassware, the glossily polished sideboard and mirrors, and the warmth of it drew out the fragrance of the roses. She did hope the rosebuds would not open too soon, for they were looking at their best and didn't the artfully arranged napkins look just like doves about to take flight, she smiled. Really, it was all perfect, just as she had always imagined it during the difficult months which were now behind them, thank God. Richard was well again, though he could not yet walk without his stick, but when he did, he was to sail for Ireland to rejoin his battalion, which had moved to the Curragh.

There were rumours that two battalions would embark once more for South Africa, where it was reported over 20,000 Boers still fought in an increasingly foolhardy fashion. Such dreadful tales there were too, of women and children – Boer women and children – being herded into what were called "concentration camps" the families of men who were still out on commando, and the newspapers were filled with the enormity of the tragedy in which those women and children were suffering and dying in the most appalling fashion, and in their thousands. If only those foolish Boers would admit defeat, *give in*, make peace, for the last thing Phyllis Latimer wanted was for her son to go out there again. Surely, he had done enough, besides if he was 6,000 miles away how was she to conduct his courtship of Miss Madeline Hammond? Ireland was far enough away, but at least he could get home on leave more frequently from there. But she must not trouble herself with that now, she decided firmly, since he was still far from completely fit. This was the second time Richard and Madeline had met, for he had been present in the drawing room when the girl and her mother had called to take afternoon tea with Phyllis Latimer, and had been most attentive to Madeline, seeming to be very taken with the sweet vivacity the twenty-year-old Miss Hammond had displayed. The signs looked very propitious, she and Madeline's mother had signalled to one another with carefully raised eyebrows, smiling across the tea-trolley. They would do very well together, the agreeable, well-brought-up, socially acceptable and extremely well-trained young girl and the equally privileged and wealthy son of Richard and Phyllis Latimer. He was . . . well, he was more mature now, her son. Quiet, where once he had been inclined to flippancy, serious and often unsmiling, his disarming grin seldom seen, that engaging impudence with which he had viewed everything except his role as a soldier gone for ever.

'Is everything to your liking, madam?' Williams enquired, his long-jawed face solemn since he took his work very seriously.

'Splendid, Williams. It looks splendid. Is all going smoothly in the kitchen?'

'Indeed, madam,' his expression, though it did not alter, implying that under his direction how could it be otherwise.

'I shall go into the drawing room, then. I believe Captain Latimer is already there.'

'He is, madam, and Mr Latimer. I am told Miss Margaret and Miss Katherine will be down directly and Mr and Mrs Osborne have just drawn up to the front door. If you will excuse me, madam.'

He bowed, then with the deceptively slow, but stately step, which was his stock-in-trade, the butler made his way to the front door where Phyllis Latimer's eldest daughter and her husband were indeed just alighting from their carriage.

Eight of the gentlemen were resplendent in the full black and white of evening dress. A dress coat with knee-length tails, worn open, of course, with a white waistcoat, a white bow tie. Trousers to match the coat, which had a waist seam and silk-covered rolling lapels, completed the outfit. Captain Latimer, at his mother's insistence, let it be said, wore the magnificent full dress uniform of a captain of the King's Own Liverpool Regiment and was quite the most dashing and attractive gentleman in the room. He had always been a handsome man, but it had been a boyish, engaging handsomeness with an air about him of a man who had never known adversity or hardship, or indeed, anything more troublesome than how to get the most pleasure from life, and that had come to him easily. He had possessed that indescribable characteristic known as natural charm, though it had not been the deliberate sort for he had never used it knowingly. He had laughed and loved his way through life, even his sometimes dangerous career as a soldier affording him nothing but enjoyment. When he was twenty-five he had looked no more than twenty. At thirty, his unlined face, his wryly smiling mouth and narrow amused eyes gave him the appearance of a man in his early twenties, but now at almost thirty-three, he looked several years older. Of course, he had been ill, the ladies told one another as their eyes covertly studied his lean, indolently lounging frame, the length of his almost mended, but extremely well-shaped legs, the whipcord strength of his shoulders, wondering how it might feel to be clasped against his manly uniformed chest. And that long sad mouth, how they would like to kiss it back to smiles . . . to . . . to . . . shivering delightfully beneath the splendid elegance of their own expensive evening gowns. His face, which had once been burned to a deep amber by the sun, had a pallor to it, a drawn fineness which the ladies thought tragically attractive. Because of his incapacity, and the difficulty in getting about on his sticks in his mother's drawing room, they came to talk to him. He listened attentively to Mrs Palmer whose son Wilfred was engaged to Richard's sister, Katherine, and who was to marry her next month, as she discoursed on the splendour of the coming London Season where her niece the Honourable Alice Palmer, perhaps Captain Latimer knew her, was to be presented to their Majesties.

He was gravely considerate of Mrs Hammond, who, it transpired, had injured her ankle at Knowsley where she had attended a shoot last week. He smiled kindly at Miss Hammond, who gazed into his face as she sat beside him on his mama's sofa with the fascination of a child viewing a rare and magnificent species of exotic animal for the first time, until her mama coughed and, having caught her daughter's eye, shook her head warningly.

He took Miss Hammond in to dinner, or at least walked slowly beside her, sitting her next to his father, who was at the head of the table, balancing as he had taught himself to do on his sticks, waiting until all the ladies had removed their gloves before sitting down next to her. He helped her with her napkin, to dispose of her gloves and her fan, then conversed with her throughout the whole of the first course, as he was supposed to, each gentleman doing the same with the lady on his left. When the plates were changed, then he might turn to the lady on his right, who was Mrs Palmer, and who no doubt, would be longing to engage him further on the subject of the wedding arrangements she and his dear mama were conducting on behalf of Katherine and Wilfred.

Nothing of his thoughts or feelings showed beneath his smooth courteous exterior and his mother watched him proudly, congratulating herself on her own . . . well . . . she hated to call it *cunning*, rather *skill* and care in removing him from the appalling consequences which would have ensued had he continued his reckless alliance with that woman. She smiled as she caught his eye and perhaps it was then that the first prick of disquiet touched her.

The conversation flowed genteelly round the table. The talk was of nothing controversial, mostly dictated by their hostess and the gentlemen as etiquette demanded, making sure that what *was* discussed could not possibly disturb the fine sensibilities of the ladies. Correct social formulas to suit the occasion and the company.

'Do you play the piano, Miss Hammond?' Phyllis Latimer heard her son say.

'Oh, yes, indeed I do,' was the breathy answer.

'And what else do you like to do?' he asked patiently, his voice absolutely colourless and for some reason Phyllis found herself watching her son with more than careful attention, though she could not have said why.

'I paint in water colours and I love flowers and the garden.'

'How delightful. You are fond of flowers then?'

'Oh, yes, Mama has given me the task of arranging them, since she says I have an aptitude for it.'

'How splendid. And what is your favourite?'

'I think the rose. Yes, definitely the rose.'

'And why is that do you think?'

'It is so lovely' . . . batting her innocent eyelashes in his direction, waiting for the correct response to her small flirtatious remark. He did not make it.

'Do you like to ride?' he asked her instead.

If she was disappointed, her upbringing did not allow her to show it.

'Oh, yes . . .'

'And I'm sure you look quite splendid on a horse, Miss Hammond.'

'Well . . .'

'And do you have other accomplishments, besides those you have mentioned?'

'I'm not sure . . .' The girl was plainly puzzled and she looked across at her mama for guidance.

'Is that all you can do, Miss Hammond, arrange flowers and paint and ride a horse?' He smiled at her lazily, a smile which had nothing offensive in it, despite his words, a smile which contained some quality which nevertheless alarmed her and at once his face softened. She was only a child after all.

'I do apologise, Miss Hammond, I should not have said that to you. It was unforgivable.'

Everyone at the table, some later than others, had fallen silent as the possibility, surely not, of a dreadful breach of good manners, was apparently about to take place at their host's end of the table. Miss Hammond was staring round-eyed and trembling at the captain who, having thrown his napkin to the table, rose to his feet, reaching for his sticks which lay beside his chair.

'You must forgive me, Miss Hammond, I am being abominably rude, not only to you, but to my mother's guests, but you see I am come at last to the end of what I believe is known as one's tether, though how or why it should be called that is unknown to me.'

'*Richard*!' His mother's astonished voice rose from her end of the table and every head but his turned towards her, stunned to silence.

'I can't do it any more, you see,' he continued, pushing his chair away from the table. 'I thought I could when . . . well it will mean nothing to you, Miss Hammond, nor to any of you, but I suspect you know that you and I are being thrown together.'

'*Richard*! What are you saying? Darling, will you not sit down . . . ?' Phyllis looked beseechingly round the table at her guests, doing her best to imply that though it had been thought he was recovered, he very evidently was not.

'I don't think so, Mother. I have simply had enough of this play acting . . .'

'Richard . . . Dear God . . .' his mother pleaded with him.

'And I find as a man I have no taste for . . . children.'

'Richard.' The pleading note in his mother's voice became shrill and Mrs Hammond, who had turned a vivid painful scarlet at the last sentence, slumped sideways, prevented from slipping into her soup only by the presence of mind of her host.

'Mother, for God's sake, let's stop pretending, shall we? Surely you cannot seriously believe I would be content to marry this . . . Oh, Miss Hammond, I do beg your pardon. It seems I am to offend you again, but I do not mean it, really I don't. You are a charming young lady and will make some charming young gentleman a fine wife. But I am neither charming, young nor a gentleman I fear, so, as my presence is an embarrassment, at least it is *now*, I will leave you to enjoy your splendid dinner. I'm sorry, Mother, but you must surely see it would never work.'

He bowed to the open-mouthed, wide-eyed company. As he moved clumsily round the table towards the door, which the impassive butler smoothly opened for him, he caught his father's eye. His father, amazingly, was smiling. The silence was total, except for the crackle of the splendid fire, which seemed excessively loud.

Richard had been moving awkwardly around the house and

gardens for a week or so now, dragging one leg after the other as he methodically went about the business of strengthening their weakness as he had been instructed by his doctor. Hanging on to the banister, one foot at a time down the stairs as a small child does, he had managed the journey on his own but there had always been someone with him, someone to carry his sticks, to put them carefully in his hands when he had arrived at the bottom. Someone to guide him, to open doors, *be there* should he stumble. In the garden with the bright spring sunshine smiling cheerfully, gleefully, his grieving heart seemed to say, into his worn face, Bennett or his lad, or Bertie Ash, kept an eye on him as he limped slowly from one spot to another, an aimless progression, a slow careful progression in case he should fall.

Now he began to hurry, moving through the door Williams held open for him, struggling from the dining room and out into the hall as though the devil himself was after him. He could bear it no longer. He had waited for six whole months, waited and waited and she had not come and he had no idea why. But he was a man, wasn't he, not some bloody puppet whose strings were pulled by any careless hand which had a fancy to take them up. A man who had his own destiny to shape, a life to be led and if it crucified him, which it would, he MUST know. He must know why she had abandoned him. He had picked up the telephone a score of times since he had been able to get at it, but always he had replaced it, afraid of her cool voice at the other end. A polite indifferent voice asking him how he was, as any acquaintance would. He must see her, see her eyes, look into them as she told him – for he would ask her – that she no longer loved him. Jesus God, he would rather face an armed, screaming horde of fierce Dacoits, or a charge of grim-faced Boers than do this but he must. It must be done if he was to know any peace in the future. If he was to . . . Jesus . . . ! Jesus! . . . marry some pretty little thing like Madeline Hammond who would bear him his sons. Poor Madeline . . . poor little thing and his mother, her guests, but it must be done *now*.

The expression on his face was fierce, determined, his mouth clamped tight, his eyebrows dipping in a vigorous scowl. Ellen, who was on duty at the small serving table by the door, stepped back hastily, her young face thunderstruck though she was not awfully sure what was happening. Something *Madam* didn't like, that was for sure, something which had struck her dumb and senseless as they had all been struck dumb and senseless at the dinner table.

'Nip up to my room and fetch my overcoat, Ellen,' the captain said to her, 'there's a good girl, and be quick, will you? I have no time to waste.'

'Your . . . overcoat, sir?'

'Yes, and look lively, Ellen.'

'Which . . . which one . . . ?'

'Jesus God, I don't care which one . . . anything, and Williams . . .' turning awkwardly to the butler . . . 'Whistle me up a cab will you? Quick as you can . . .'

'A cab, sir . . . ?'

'Dear God, man! A *cab*, you know what a cab is and be quick about it, there's a good fellow . . .'

'But, sir . . .'

'*At once*, Williams . . .'

'Yes, sir.'

The rubber tip on the end of his sticks squeaked on the tiled floor as he stumbled towards the front door and before the butler or Ellen could get to him, so great was his eagerness to be away, he fell awkwardly, his left leg crumpled beneath him, and from the dinner table where she watched his painful scramble, his mother moaned and his father sprang to his feet. His chair crashed backwards to the carpet as Richard Latimer rushed to help his son.

'Oh, dear God, he has lost his mind.' Phyllis's voice was strangled in her throat and Madeline Hammond, to whom nothing more serious than a dropped stitch in her embroidery had ever happened, had begun to cry.

Richard Latimer put a compassionate hand beneath his son's arm.

'Let me help you, old man. See, lean on me.'

'I can manage, Father, really I can,' though he turned to smile into his father's face. 'I must learn to do these things for myself, you know. At least until I have my legs again.'

'Of course, and you will, old chap, but until then, let me give you a hand. It's about time I did.'

There was a flurry of brocade and lace in the dining room. Williams, who stood at his post as was his duty, was pushed unceremoniously to one side as Phyllis Latimer, under control again now and conscious of the open-mouthed horror of her guests, stood glaring, icy-faced, at her husband and son.

'Leave him, Mr Latimer, if you please and let us return to our guests. Send for Bennett and Ash, Williams, and tell them to come at once and then I would be obliged if you would telephone for Dr Maynard. My son is not well. There is no need for that, Mr Latimer. The men will do all that is . . .'

'I am helping my son to his feet, Phyllis. We can hardly leave him here . . .'

'The servants will care for him, Mr Latimer. He has obviously had a relapse and should be returned at once to his room. Come, Mr Latimer, we have guests waiting and there has already been . . .'

'I will not leave my son sprawled on the floor . . .'

'*Mr Latimer*! We have guests . . .'

'Really Father, I can manage, really I can . . .'

'Take my hand then,' and with a great heave father and son were both upright. For a moment, as though they were aware that this was an important milestone in their lives as *together* they defied the formidable will of Phyllis Latimer, their hands clung and they smiled, then Ellen flew down the stairs with the overcoat, his army greatcoat which she had thought appropriate to his present attire.

Phyllis Latimer spoke through clenched teeth. 'Richard, it would be advisable, I think, if you were to return to your room, dear. You are obviously not well . . .' clinging, even to the last, to the illusion that he would obey her, that they could somehow smooth this over, after all he *had* been very ill; that her guests would be mollified, even Miss Hammond, and that she, Phyllis Latimer, would keep her good name, her reputation as a clever hostess, and her eldest son by her side.

Richard shrugged into his greatcoat, his father's hands steadying him, passing him his sticks, ready to help with buttons, then, at the last minute, when the cab driver arrived, holding him for a moment in awkward arms as though he knew well his son's destination.

'Good luck, my boy.'

'Thank you, Father.'

'*Richard*! I must insist that you return to your room. You are not *well*, darling, really you're not. Mr Latimer, stop him, please . . .'

'He is able to make his own decisions, Mrs Latimer, don't you think? To decide where he is to go . . . and with whom.'

Nora nearly had a heart attack, she said tearfully later to Cook, when she opened the door and saw *him* there after all this time. And at that hour of the night, an' all. You didn't expect the doorbell to be rung at nearly ten o'clock did you? not in a nice neighbourhood like theirs and for a *soldier* who she did not at once recognise to be doing the ringing made it even more alarming.

'Is Mrs Garside at home, Nora?' he enquired, his voice inclined to be thready for the journey had been painful and tiring. It had taken a great deal of his father's and the cab driver's help to get him into the cab, which, having only one small step on which only one foot at a time could be rested had put enormous strain on his frail legs. The lane from Briar Lodge and through the village of Wavertree was not smoothly surfaced and he had felt every bump. He had told the cab driver to hurry and the horse which pulled the vehicle had been encouraged to go at a breakneck speed which threw him about even more and when he staggered to the gravel path outside his sister's front door, he had almost fallen into the sympathetic arms of the driver and his pale face had become even paler.

Nora put her hand to her bosom, her eyes wide with astonishment for they had not seen the captain since the night Miss Grace was born but she pulled herself together and answered his question.

'She's in bed, sir.'

'Off you go and fetch her then, there's a good girl, but before you go, fetch me a brandy, would you?'

'Yes sir, but I'll have to close the door,' for the captain was still swaying between its frame.

'Yes . . . of course. I'll just sit here.' He sank gratefully to the chair where, eighteen months ago, he had waited to say goodbye to Celie Marlow.

Nora's excited knocking on Mr and Mrs Garside's bedroom door got them all up. Sally and Cook and the scullery maid who had just been about to fall into their own beds. The dogs barked and Mrs Garside clung to Mr Garside's arm, having made no sense of the maid's garbled message and as they came down the stairs Mrs Garside's guest, who had been staying overnight, followed them down.

It was strange then, Nora said later, to the rest of the over-wrought servants, for it wasn't Mrs Garside or even Mr Garside who came forward but Miss Marlow. In her night attire, she was, a flimsy wisp of a thing the colour of the apricots in the hothouse, all lace and silken ribbons and nothing like Nora had ever seen in her life. Almost, but not quite *transparent*! Her dark hair was loose down her back, long and swinging and those grey eyes of hers were like saucers in her face, and as deep and dark as the Mersey on a winter's day. And she'd no shoes on her feet neither, not even a pair of slippers and her running down the stairs as though she had wings. But the strangest thing was that Mr and Mrs Garside had ordered Nora to take the dogs and get back to the kitchen, quite sharp they'd been as well, and the last she'd seen was Miss Marlow flying into the Captain's arms as he stumbled to his feet and the both of them weepin' as though their hearts were broken. What did Cook make of that then?

They didn't speak at first, nor even notice that they were in Celie's bedroom where Prudence and Jethro had gently led them before returning to their own room.

They did not speak because neither was capable of it. There were tears, a great overwhelming saturation of them, their bodies violent and shuddering against one another. A pulling away to stare wildly, blindly, unbelievingly into the lost, beloved face, the miraculously found beloved face, a frantic clutching again, arms straining, voices hoarse with an emotion too distressing to form actual words. It could be seen in their eyes, a great and terrible terror that this was not true, that this was a mirage, a fantasy, a dream which would shatter and they would be cruelly parted again. That they were both imagining the wonder of it, as they had imagined it a hundred, a thousand times before.

For a full ten minutes they stood, wordless, in the centre of the room, the door closed, holding one another with the strength of their clinging arms, the strength of their formidable love which had withstood so much in all the years that had gone before but which was as shining and vigorous as it had always been. Strong and more perfect, for does not steel go through fire to perfect it and had not what they suffered been more harrowing, more devastating than any fire?

'I love you, I have never stopped loving you,' laying a hand along her cheek.

'Yes . . . I have waited . . .' putting up her own hand to cover his.

'You love me . . . ?' bending to put his mouth on hers.

'Always. I will love you always . . .' opening her lips to him.

'We will speak of what happened . . . ?'

'Later . . .'

'Yes, I have waited so long for this. Later . . .'

'Come, let me help you.'

'We will help each other.'

'Always . . .'

'Christ, I love you . . .'

With no more words they undressed one another, Celie gentle with his tired, wounded body which was inclined to fall against hers in terrible exhaustion but when she slid between the sheets of her bed, drawing him down next to her, he sighed deeply and with great satisfaction.

She began the delicate and slow movements which were an adjustment between what he needed of her and his own ability to satisfy it; between the pain of his legs and the building pleasure of his body and hers. She held him lightly, letting him direct the strength of their movements, soothing him with the incomprehensible crooning women use to comfort and sustain for she knew of them both he had been hurt the most. When he entered her she moved her hips, pulling him deeper into the warm, healing depths of her, coaxing his tiring body to climax and when it did holding him against her breast with passionate tenderness. He lay, limp and heavy, along her body then lifted a weary hand to cup her breast where it lay beneath his cheek.

'It's good to be home,' he murmured before he slept.